LINDSAY BUROKER'S
REPUBLIC

FOREWORD

After I finished *Forged in Blood* I & II, I wasn't sure if I would revisit these characters, but I polled you guys, and you said you wanted to see more stories with the Emperor's Edge gang. Amaranthe and Sicarius were the most popular request, and I've taken note of that, but I decided the transition from empire to republic probably wouldn't go too smoothly and that we might have to have some adventures back in the city before sending our heroes globe-trotting. Thus... *Republic*. Amaranthe, Sicarius, Maldynado, Sespian, Tikaya, and her daughter Mahliki are all point-of-view characters in what turned out to be quite a big adventure. I hope you'll enjoy spending time with all of them.

I would like to thank Kendra Highley, Becca Andre, Cindy Wilkinson, and Sarah Engelke for giving the story an early read and offering feedback. I would also like to thank Shelley Holloway for editing what turned out to be the longest novel I've ever written, and Glendon Haddix and his team for the cover design. Lastly, thank *you* for picking up a new adventure with these characters. I hope you enjoy the ride.

CHAPTER 1

AMARANTHE SPRINTED DOWN THE NARROW, muddy trail, leaping past snarls of mossy roots and ducking leaves so large they felt like wrecking balls when they smashed against her face. The shouts behind her had dwindled, and she wondered if she might have outrun her pursuers.

A stone-tipped spear blurred past her ear, almost depriving her of a chunk of hair—and scalp. Ah, there was that pursuit.

The weapon slammed into the trail in front of her. It landed at an angle, and she almost impaled herself on the butt of it. Fortunately, a year of training with Sicarius hadn't been undone by a couple of months of vacation, and she twisted to evade the obstacle at the same time as she ducked under a branch thoughtlessly growing across the path at eye level. She did bump into a bush before finding her way back onto the trail, and thin branches shuddered, raining droplets of water onto her head. Monkeys howled in the treetops, either irritated by her disturbance or entertained by her plight.

Amaranthe eyed the foliage to either side of her. Getting off this main route and finding another way to the beach might be wise, but the lush jungle grew denser than soldiers in a Turgonian infantry unit. And some of those spiky vines were just as dangerous. If she had thought to bring her sword, she might have cut a path, but she had gone to that village to trade, not to start a war.

She plowed onward, sticking to her trail and hoping to reach the lagoon before her pursuers caught up. She thought about hollering for Sicarius, but it was his presence on the island that had gotten her into this predicament. If he started slitting throats...

As Amaranthe leaped over another mossy log, something snatched her about the waist, yanking her into the foliage. She kept from yelping in surprise, but barely. And only because she had a hunch as to her captor's identity.

Yes, the blond hairs on the muscular arm wrapped around her waist were familiar. As usual, Sicarius put action above words and hauled her several dozen meters into the jungle before pausing to discuss anything. *He* had a sword, of course, and used it to cut canes and vines, though he had a knack for weaving through the dense undergrowth as if he were simply pushing aside silk curtains. Having a woman—a woman who was more than ready to start using her own feet again—tucked against his side didn't slow him at all.

Finally, he stopped, crouching in the hollow of a giant red tree that was broader than some of the shopfronts in Ink Alley back home. Amaranthe wriggled free, noting for the first time that he was carrying his black dagger clenched in his teeth, because he was—

"You're naked," she whispered. As much as she usually appreciated the view of those lean powerful muscles, it seemed foolish to run through the jungle without protection. She already had numerous gashes from those razor ferns. And the spiky vines? She would hate to have anything important punctured by them.

Sicarius removed the dagger. "I was fishing." Despite the shouts of the male villagers racing past on the trail they had just left, his tone was as dry and unconcerned as ever. The dampness of his short blond hair attested to how recently he had left the water. "You assured me that you would find no trouble in the village." His eyebrow twitched.

"And I wouldn't have, but—"

Foliage rattled in the direction of the trail, and a clunk sounded, an axe shearing away a branch. Sicarius peered around the tree, lifting a hand for silence. The villagers must have realized Amaranthe had left the path.

She dug into her pocket and pulled out a crinkled piece of parchment, deciding it could do the talking for her. The yellowed sheet held a portrait of a face. The black ink had faded to dull gray over the years, but it was still possible to make out the familiar features. A younger and harder—at least to Amaranthe's eyes—version of Sicarius without the recently obtained knot of scar tissue at his temple. She didn't recognize the language of the lines written below the portrait, but she knew a wanted poster when she saw one.

Sicarius knew it too. What he thought of it, she couldn't tell. Even though they had been friends for over a year and lovers for the last couple of months, she still struggled to read his angular face, one he'd learned to craft into an emotionless mask from his earliest childhood. When he did show emotion, it seemed a conscious effort, as if he was trying to please her by doing so, but when other things were on his mind, he grew as hard to decipher as a granite slab.

"Is there a way we can get back to the beach?" Amaranthe whispered.

"Yes, but there are men on it."

"Men with spears?"

"Yes." Sicarius gazed into her eyes, waiting, she sensed, to see what she wanted to do. He had been an assassin all of his life and still tended to think in terms of eliminating people as answers to problems, though he'd gradually grown willing to accept less violent solutions if she could propose feasible ones. Or unfeasible ones that she could finesse—or manhandle—into working, regardless.

"Lead us as close as we can get without being seen," Amaranthe said, aware that the rustling of leaves and hacking of branches was drawing nearer. "Then we'll... think of something creative."

The other eyebrow twitched, his silent version of, "Oh, really? This should prove interesting, challenging, and crazy all at once."

She smiled.

Without a word, Sicarius led off toward... hm, was the beach in that direction? Amaranthe didn't think so, but he must want to throw off their trackers. This time, he let her walk, though he did glance back often to keep an eye on her, or maybe to ensure she wasn't leaving a riotous trail of footprints for their pursuers to follow. How he could walk over the same ground without leaving a trace, she would never know, but she did her best to emulate him, stepping on rocks and roots whenever possible, hard items that wouldn't hold a print. Nonetheless, he slipped behind her a few times to scatter dead palm or fern fronds over her inadvertent smudges in the mud. She kept from rolling her eyes at this overzealous tidying, especially since the sounds of their pursuers had grown more distant, though she did huff in exasperation when, without warning, he jumped several feet, caught a vine one-handed, and whisked himself into the canopy.

"I need a running start for that," Amaranthe whispered, waving behind her, "and that'll leave a long streak of footprints and broken branches."

She stood on a boulder, the same one from which he had launched himself, and eyed the distance to the vine. It hung three or four feet above her and out several more feet, with some of those spiky ferns waiting below if she jumped and missed.

Sicarius gazed down impassively from a branch. Deciding whether she was whining or if she spoke the truth? Amaranthe propped a fist on her hip. He knew her physical abilities better than anyone else, even herself.

Sicarius bent and pulled the vine to the side, as far from his position as he could, then let it go. What was *that* supposed to do to help?

A distinct call came from the jungle a hundred meters back. The language was gibberish to her ear, but she guessed it to be the villager equivalent of, "They went this way!" Either way, it reminded Amaranthe of her predicament—if she didn't follow Sicarius quickly, or if she allowed herself to be trapped, he would stop playing Hide and Sneak and start dispatching people.

"Amaranthe, now," Sicarius whispered and pointed to the vine.

It was swaying back and forth like a pendulum. Oh, so that was his idea of help. Now, if she timed it precisely, she only had to jump eight feet instead of ten. Lovely.

She crept to the edge of the rock and waited until...

"Now," he ordered.

Amaranthe jumped. The vine swung to its peak and started to fall backward. Cursed ancestors, she was going to miss it. She lunged out with one arm and caught it with the tips of her fingers. She closed those fingers like a vise. When gravity caught up with her, it jolted her shoulder, but she didn't let go. She swung her other hand to the vine and climbed the twenty feet to join him.

"Hm," Sicarius said, then rounded the trunk of the tree and headed out onto a thick limb on the far side.

Up here, the branches crisscrossed each other like a latticework—an agile squirrel might run for a mile without touching the ground. Oh, she realized. They were going to do that too.

"What do you mean, *hm*?" Amaranthe whispered, using her hands on the upper branches to help with her balance as she skipped along the narrow perches. "My performance didn't even rate an 'adequate'? Because you had to help with the vine?"

"Our lives have been indolent of late," Sicarius observed.

Amaranthe grimaced. That *hm* had been a rating, a dubious rating, of her performance. "We've been on *vacation*, remember? And how much exercise can one get in a tiny submarine? Aside from certain bedroom activities, which *I* thought were actually quite vigorous and challenging in a cardiovascular way, surely as good for training as jogging around the lake."

Sicarius kept skating through the treetops without so much as a backward glance. She thought she had gotten past trying to impress him at these physical challenges, but she found herself disappointed. Maybe she shouldn't have balked. Maybe she could have made it if she'd had her original momentum. Maybe she shouldn't have acted as if some sharp plants were the equivalent of phalanxes of upturned spears. Maybe—

Sicarius stopped to wait on a thick branch, with his sword arm wrapped around a moss-carpeted trunk. The canopy, thick and green above and below, hid them from the ground. As he watched her approach, his expression didn't *seem* disappointed. In fact, was that the faintest hint of a smile?

"You're teasing me." Amaranthe swatted him on the chest.

"Yes." He flipped his dagger so his forearm sheltered her from the blade, pulled her close, and kissed her. Not a long kiss, but there was certainly a promise of *later* in it before he drew back.

"Dear ancestors, Sicarius," Amaranthe said, breathless from more than the exercise, "has being chased through the treetops by aborigines always been the key to putting you in an amorous mood? Or was it my talk of cardiovascular challenges that roused your passion?"

His dark eyes glinted. "Yes."

She thought about kissing him again—surely they could spare another minute or two—but he pointed at something on the other side of the trunk. "We've arrived at the beach."

They had? Amazing how disoriented one could become while running across branches. She would think more highly of squirrels when next she visited a climate that had them.

Using Sicarius to brace herself against—his chiseled flesh made a more appealing handhold than a mossy tree—Amaranthe leaned around the trunk for a look. And barely kept herself from groaning. No less than ten bare-chested, brown-skinned men stood at the lagoon's edge with knives and spears in hand. Out in the water, two outrigger canoes carrying more spear wielders floated on either side of the oblong black hull of the submarine.

"You've formulated a plan?" Sicarius asked.

"Well, I would have, but you distracted me with that kiss. Now I'm going to need another minute."

She smiled at Sicarius, but his face had lost its humor. A distant shout drifted up from the jungle floor. Their pursuers might have fallen farther behind, but they were still coming.

Movement overhead distracted Amaranthe. She lurched backward and might have fallen off the branch if not for Sicarius's grip about her waist. A large green snake with black spots was slithering down the mossy trunk toward them.

"Uhm," she blurted, pointing.

"It's not poisonous," Sicarius said, though he hadn't looked up. Doubtlessly, he had noticed it when they first jumped into the tree. "It feeds on fish, birds, and small mammals."

"Yes, but it's *big*. And I..." Amaranthe tried to tell herself that there was no reason to worry if he wasn't worried, but she couldn't help but think of the last time she had dealt with a large snake. She had been naked and wounded, having escaped that awful alien ship and the more awful torture-loving Pike, and that cursed snake had wanted to eat her. She hated *anything* that reminded her of that time. "I'd prefer not to share a tree with it," she whispered. "Mind if I borrow your knife?"

Sicarius tilted his head back, considering the snake. It did, she admitted, look like it might slither past without bothering them. "I can see your reason for alarm. It is similar to the green marshal, a snake also indigenous to these islands and one that *is* poisonous."

Yeah. *That* was why she wanted it out of her tree.

Afraid the real reason would make her seem weak, Amaranthe braced herself to let the creature slither off the trunk and out onto one of the branches. She forced herself to return to the problem. Finding a way past those men without causing a massive throat-slitting. She needed a clever idea. Such as setting a fire in their village to draw them all back? The times she or her team had used arson before, it had never turned out well, usually causing far more damage than she had intended. How could she justify doing that to these people, especially when their interest in Sicarius seemed more about ridding their home of an assassin before he could hurt them, rather than collecting a bounty? What did these aborigines care about money, and to whom would they turn in a head, regardless?

"They are after you because they saw me," Sicarius said.

Amaranthe didn't know if it was a statement or a question, but she nodded slightly. "A scout ran in while I was trying to explain to the old medicine woman what it was I wanted to trade for. He raced into the chief's hut and came out waving that poster and pointing at me and at the beach. I'm not quite sure how all those chaps got here ahead of me..." she tilted her head toward the lagoon, "but they did."

"It is my responsibility then. I will distract them so you can swim to the submarine."

Amaranthe shook her head as he spoke, but he kept talking.

"You can take it out beyond the lagoon. If you come up again on the other side of those rocks—" he pointed to a promontory jutting into the ocean at the end of the beach, "—I will attempt to join you. After nightfall, I might—"

Amaranthe hushed him with a finger to his lips. All those months they'd worked together, trying to save his son, she had never dared such an intimacy. She was pleased to see it worked, though his eyebrow was in danger of twitching to express indignation.

"If you try to distract them without simply... dispatching them, you might get yourself killed," she said.

His chin rose. "We have not been *that* indolent."

"Forgive me, you might get yourself *injured*, and, as you know from first-hand experience, I'm not the most skilled medic. We're all alone out here, with a lot of days of travel to get to a civilized port. We're still in a bind from our last mishap." The pirates who had presumed to steal from them wouldn't do so again—Sicarius's justice remained harsher than she would prefer, but she'd had a hand in sending their ship to the bottom of the ocean, so who was she to judge? But either way, she and Sicarius had lost half of their provisions overboard.

"They are simple hunters. Those spears were designed for slaying boars, not men. I can deal with them without killing them or being injured."

11

"What are you going to do? Call out to them from the wilds and tie them up one at a time as they come to hunt for you?"

"Precisely. It will be dark in an hour as well. A better time to hunt."

"They know every inch of this island," Amaranthe said.

"They don't know me."

"Oh? I'm sure that poster had some choice words to say about you in whatever language that is."

Something disturbed a flock of birds in a tree twenty meters away. Colorful wings batted and a dozen tanagers flew inland.

"There isn't time for further debate." Sicarius pressed the sword into her hand, keeping his black dagger for himself. "I will distract them. You will take the sub out of the harbor."

"Fine, fine." Amaranthe stepped onto a neighboring branch for a better look at the rock promontory. "Where do you want me to wait while you're distracting people?"

She didn't receive an answer. He was gone.

"I liked it better when you were going along with my orders," she mumbled and started out along the branches, hoping she could get closer to those rocks before climbing down. She decided her last words hadn't been fair—she hadn't given any orders, after all—or particularly true. After being responsible, however inadvertently, for the deaths of so many during the upheaval in Stumps, she wasn't eager to deliver orders to anyone anymore. These last couple of months free of responsibility had helped her heal, but some scars would remain forever.

Amaranthe passed the snake as it continued along the branches on its way to sun itself on the beach, or whatever snakes did. She gave it a wide berth—fortunately, it didn't pause to contemplate her in the way one might an Emperor's Bun, a pastry that would need a new name now that an elected president ruled the nation—and found a likely spot to go down.

Using the palm trees for camouflage, she picked her way to the promontory without attracting attention from the men farther up the beach. Nothing grew from the volcanic rock itself, but its humps and craters offered numerous hiding places. Staying low, she jogged along the bottom of a crevice heading toward the water. Though she wasn't working as hard as she had been during the run, sweat slithered down her back and dripped into her eyes. The sun was dipping lower toward the horizon, but the air remained warm and humid.

When she reached a protrusion jutting up like a thumb, she peeked around it to study the lagoon. The aborigines on the beach were gone, and rowers were paddling one of the canoes toward the shore. Unfortunately, the other craft remained by the submarine with six natives sitting all-too-vigilantly inside. One man's eyes came close to settling on Amaranthe's spot, so she lowered her head.

The canoe floated near the submarine's hatch, but if she could sneak past the men somehow and slip inside, she could seal that hatch and keep them out while she started the engine. Once the craft dove, they would have no way to track her. Picking up Sicarius would be a simple matter.

Yes, but how could she reach it without being seen? Swim underwater? The pale blue lagoon was clearer than any lake back home. She had thought it beautiful when they had arrived. At the time, she hadn't been contemplating sneaking up on boats. It was a long swim from the rocks or from the beach. There was no way she could stroke the whole way underwater while holding her breath. She remembered old stories of clever soldiers sneaking up on riverside enemy camps by cutting reeds and using them to breathe through. Alas, this island had only coconut trees, spiky ferns, and at least seven types of foliage that made her skin itch every time she brushed against them. No reeds.

A splash came from below, and Amaranthe chanced lifting her head. An enormous turtle paddled away from the rocks. It was either done sunning itself for the day or...

Ah. Another one of those green snakes was slithering along near the waterline. She wouldn't think it big enough to swallow a turtle, but maybe the turtle knew something she didn't.

Amaranthe touched a finger to her lip. If the snake's approach had alarmed a turtle, might it alarm a canoe full of men? She had a sword. If she could distract those islanders for a moment, long enough to clamber into the craft, she might be able to get the best of them. Six on one wasn't ideal, but they would have a hard time attacking her all at once in the narrow canoe.

"So how do I get that snake from here to there?" she murmured.

Giving up on the turtle, it slithered inland and dipped into the shady

LINDSAY BUROKER

crevice. Amaranthe tapped the hilt of the sword thoughtfully. She could get to it without being seen now, but that didn't answer her question.

"Shouldn't have left that purse full of trade goods in the village." Not that she ever would have been able to stuff the big snake in a purse. She snorted at the image of herself trying. No, she would need something larger. Her hand strayed to the buttons of her shirt. "Well, that can be my second distraction for the men if the first doesn't work."

After removing her shirt, Amaranthe crept from her hiding spot, staying behind cover as she angled toward the snake. Out in the water, the big turtle had stopped to nosh on a straggly clump of seaweed bobbing with the tide. She wondered if turtles could be coerced to paddle in a desired direction.

In the canoe, the islanders maintained their vigilance, despite numerous shouts that had arisen in the jungle. One man pointed toward the dented green crown of the dormant volcano at the center of the island. A thin line of dark gray smoke wafted toward the blue sky.

Amaranthe grinned. "Sicarius, you're getting crafty now that you're not simply killing everyone in your way." The villagers probably believed the volcano dormant, too, but a wisp of smoke still wouldn't be taken lightly. "I hope that's his work anyway."

After a deep breath that wasn't as fortifying as she would have liked, Amaranthe descended into the crevice with the snake. Its tail was to her, though she didn't know if that mattered. It might sense her creeping up through vibrations in the rock. Her grip tightened around her sword. Lopping off its head wouldn't leave her with a very effective distraction, though she would reserve the tactic if necessary.

She tiptoed closer, trying to estimate the snake's size—and whether it would fit in a shirt. It lay stretched out rather than coiled up—taking a nap, she hoped. It didn't seem as big as the one in the tree... maybe only six feet long and with less girth. She passed the brown-spotted tail and approached the back of its head, suspecting it would be the most dangerous part. Though that was a guess; for all she knew, it was some species of constrictor.

The flat, arrow-shaped head reared up, its maw opening, fangs catching the fading sunlight...

Amaranthe lashed out with the flat of her blade. She aimed for the back of the head, but the snake had been spinning toward her and she

14

connected with the side instead. The maw smashed into the side of the crevice with a crunch. Doubting it would be stunned for long, if the tough creature was stunned at all, Amaranthe leaped in, thrusting her shirt over its head. She had buttoned it and done her best to turn it into a bag, but, even as she stuffed the long sinewy body into it, she feared her flimsy trap wouldn't be sufficient.

The fear spurred her to speed. With the sword in one hand and her "bag" in the other, she raced for the water, toward a spot that was out of the canoe's line of sight. They would see her if she swam toward them, but maybe...

She paused to poke her head over the ridge and check on the turtle. It was still floating beside the seaweed. Good.

Amaranthe immersed herself in the cool water, took a deep breath, dunked her head, and pushed off the rocks. Swimming with her hands full was a challenge. She would have thanked Sicarius for all the horrible sculling and treading-water drills he had inflicted on her if she weren't so busy. The sword didn't weigh much, but the snake was stirring, bulging and flexing against the confines of her bag. Snakes doubtlessly had the same concerns about drowning as humans.

The clearness of the lagoon allowed Amaranthe to navigate, and she spotted the dark shape above her. She came up a couple of feet behind the turtle and angled herself so its bulk would hide her from the canoe. She rapped the snake a few times with the flat of the blade, hoping to stun it again, though she was probably irritating it to a murderous state instead. Then she switched the sword to the same hand that held the bag and grabbed the back of the turtle's shell. She expected it to take off or turn around and snap at her, but the large thing didn't react. Maybe it was too busy eating to care that she had latched on.

Amaranthe kicked, trying to propel the turtle forward, away from the seaweed and toward the canoe. It snapped up a few more bites of its meal. She was about to give up, to swim over to the canoe on her own, hoping the men were too focused on the volcano to notice, but then the turtle started paddling. It nearly clobbered Amaranthe with one of its fins, or flippers, or whatever sea turtles had. She would have to ask Starcrest's biologist daughter Mahliki about them if she survived this craziness.

Whatever its limbs were called, the turtle swam away from the seaweed, not bothered, or at least not overly slowed, by its tagalong.

Amaranthe kicked as well, trying to guide the creature in the direction she wanted. It chose its own route though, one that headed toward the second rocky promontory that framed the other side of the lagoon. The path would take Amaranthe close to the submarine and allow her to remain hidden, so she judged it close enough.

A soft tearing sound reached her ears. Uh oh. The shirt.

The canoe was less than thirty meters away. That would have to be close enough. She took another big breath, submerged, then smacked the side of the blade against the shirt again. A foot of snake body stuck out through a tear. At least it wasn't the head. Amaranthe angled toward the canoe.

Her burdens made the swim slow, but the wooden bottom of the vessel came into view before her breath ran out—or her prisoner escaped. She didn't hesitate. She angled toward the bottom of the lagoon, so she could push off for momentum, then burst out of the water inches from the canoe's near side, thrusting the shirt into the craft. She dropped back down and swam under the hull to come up on the far side.

Pausing only long enough to ensure nobody waited with a spear aimed at her head, Amaranthe pulled herself over the side. The volume of the men's shouts made her wince, but at least nobody was facing her. The snake had shredded the shirt and escaped—she glimpsed its green body on the other end, with four men backpedaling from it. Four men. The other two... She glanced over her shoulder, making sure nobody was behind her. No. They were in the water swimming away. Good.

Amaranthe slammed the hilt of the sword into the back of the closest man's head. He didn't crumple into unconsciousness the way people did when Sicarius clobbered them, but he bent in half, his spear falling into the water. She shoved him over the side. Three left to go.

At that point, someone noticed her. Fortunately, it was the man farthest from her and on the other side of the snake. He would have a hard time throwing his spear or getting to her through his comrades. But his shouts made the other two men glance in her direction.

Though fighting in a wobbling, tilting canoe wasn't her forte, Amaranthe darted in quickly enough to catch the first before he could do more than gape. She sliced her sword through his spear, cutting it in half, then slammed the flat of the blade into his side. He grunted, but didn't tip into the water. He hurled the broken half of his spear at her. She could have simply ducked but thought it might worry him more if she displayed some unexpected weapons prowess, so she whipped her blade up and sliced the wood haft in two before it could strike her head. The ends veered away, splashing harmlessly in the water. Not as impressed as she'd hoped, the man launched himself at her. Amaranthe dropped to her knee and thrust up with her arms. With her help, his trajectory took him over her shoulder and into the water.

When she stood again, the man behind him had a spear raised to his shoulder, ready to throw. The obsidian point was aimed at her heart. She forced herself to relax, the sword ready before her. She had deflected the stick. She could do this too.

Before he could throw, the man flung his head back and screamed. The snake had plunged its fangs into his calf. He jabbed down at it with his spear. The last man, the one behind the snake, forgot about Amaranthe and also tried to stab the snake to death.

She thought about hurling them both in, but decided they were busy enough where they were. The natives she had flung overboard already weren't waiting around—they were headed toward shore.

"Always nice to have a little luck," Amaranthe said and dove out of the canoe.

She reached the submarine and unfastened the hatch, hoping none of the natives had been clambering about inside. As fine of an engineer as President Starcrest might be, she imagined a spear through the navigation controls—or maybe that glowing orb that powered the engine—would be trouble.

Fortunately, the floor was dry with no sign of wet footprints. She pulled the hatch shut, securing it behind her, then double-checked to make sure she was alone before starting the engine. Angry clangs reverberated through the hull—someone banging at the hatch with a spear. Though she doubted they could find a way in with their primitive tools, Amaranthe was glad when the power dial on the control panel hummed to life, showing the engine ready. For all that the glowing energy source in the back unnerved her—even after being around Akstyr for a year, she wasn't fully over her Turgonian superstition toward magic—she appreciated that it didn't take the twenty minutes to fire up that a steam engine would.

Beyond the viewport, the scenery shifted as the submarine descended.

Dials and gauges warned her of the shallow floor and other obstacles as she navigated toward the deeper ocean. She spotted a sea turtle chewing on waving grasses growing on the bottom of the lagoon. It might not be the same one, but she gave it a quiet salute anyway. She would owe Sicarius a salute too. She doubted she could have handled *two* canoes, though throwing the snake in had upset them more than she had dreamed it would. After seeing the bite it had inflicted on that fellow's calf, she could see why. She had a feeling only luck had kept her from a nasty bite of her own. And here she had been warning Sicarius to be careful because they were so far from civilization.

By the time she came up in deeper waters on the other side of the promontory, the sun was about to dip below the blue horizon, and reds and oranges filled the western sky. After scanning the shoreline with the periscope and not spotting anyone, Amaranthe risked opening the hatch. Figuring it would take Sicarius a few moments to reach the meeting point, she allowed herself to admire the view. They hadn't decided how much longer their vacation would last, but she would miss these tropical waters, inhospitable natives notwithstanding. Back in the capital, there was probably still three feet of snow on the ground.

An uncomfortable feeling disturbed her moment of sunset appreciation, the sensation that she was being watched. Sicarius? She checked the shoreline again and spotted a bare-chested man with a spear raised to throw. Not Sicarius.

The submarine had to be close to fifty meters from the shore, but she lowered herself anyway. No need to present a tempting target. Maybe she ought to simply shut the hatch and wait for Sicarius to swim out and knock.

She'd no more than had the thought when a naked man glided out of the foliage behind the islander. Mud and blood smeared Sicarius's flesh, though he didn't appear wounded, at least not significantly. Normally, he wouldn't make a sound sneaking up on someone, but he must have cleared his throat, for the native spun around. Sicarius held his dagger and could throw the weapon easily enough—probably faster than that fellow could throw his spear—but he hadn't lifted it from his side. It didn't matter. The islander threw down his spear and sprinted down the beach and into the brush.

Sicarius strode down the sandy swath as if he had expected no less.

He waded out, then stuck the dagger between his teeth and swam toward the submarine. Amaranthe wondered if he would chastise her for gaping at the sunset like some mawkish poet composing verse.

She dropped inside so he would have room to enter, which he soon did, clanging the hatch shut behind him. The water had cleaned him of grime and blood, leaving a sleek, powerful form that a panther would envy. It crossed her mind to help him dry off, but she waited for him to comment on the spear wielder she almost hadn't noticed. At least she had thought to change clothes—and dig out a clean shirt—before bringing the submarine up. His sardonic eyebrow would have even more reason to twitch if she'd been standing shirtless before him, trying to explain what happened to the garment.

But there was nothing sardonic about his gaze when it landed on her, nor did he open his mouth to deliver a lecture. Rather he used his mouth for something exceedingly rare... a pleased smile. "You did well."

"Hm?"

His smile always warmed her, but surely he didn't refer to her shirtless acquisition of the submarine. He would have been too busy in the jungle to watch that.

Sicarius stepped toward her, slipping an arm around her waist. "Bagging up a poisonous snake to hurl at one's enemies is dangerous, but it was effective, as so many of your schemes are."

Amaranthe would have liked to bask in this rare praise, but her mind hiccupped at one of his words. *Poisonous?* Dear ancestors, he *had* said the one in the tree looked similar to a poisonous breed, hadn't he? And she'd even noted that the one on the rocks was smaller. The markings had been the same, hadn't they? She decided not to ask *how* poisonous the snakes were—or how close she had danced to her death. Instead she offered an eloquent, "Uhm, yes."

"You handled the men on the canoes easily as well," he said, bringing the other arm around her waist. "However interestingly clothed."

Erg, he *had* seen that. He'd seen it all. Well, he was praising her instead of mocking her, so she couldn't complain. Unless it was to point out that he was getting her wet; but she wouldn't push him away for that. She had spent too many months dreaming of having a nude Sicarius pressed against her to have grown blasé about it yet. She wished she had managed to secure her trade before that scout had burst into the village...

She would have to tell him, especially since his eyes had softened and his mouth had drifted closer to hers...

"I, ah... I've seen you dispatching enemies while utterly nude before, so it could be said I'm only emulating my tutor."

"Hm."

"Remember that discussion we had as to whether or not you could be menacing without wearing black all the time? It's clear that those people were intimidated by you. That fellow with the spear nearly pitched backward into the ocean when you strode out of the jungle. Naked. That should prove that I was right."

"In that discussion, you argued that I could be menacing in a lemon yellow shirt and plaid shorts. *That* has not been proven yet."

"Yet? Does that mean you're willing to don such clothing for an experiment?"

"No."

"Only nudity, eh?" Amaranthe rested a hand on his shoulder, thumb brushing his collarbone, the defined muscle beside it.... "I suppose I wouldn't mind seeing you roam around menacingly in your... natural state. So long as you don't get cold."

Sicarius caught her hand, his gaze locking onto hers. "I am not feeling cold right now."

She wanted to ask him what he *was* feeling, but stopped, sighing. "My... shopping mission failed. I suppose we shouldn't contemplate further heat today." Or tomorrow, she thought glumly. Or the next day, or any other day until they returned to the empire or somewhere else that they could restock certain supplies. "Although I do wonder. I don't even know if I need egata tea, or whatever the islander equivalent is. I may not be able to..." She avoided Sicarius's eyes. He had never proclaimed that he wanted to have children with her, but he had hinted from time to time that a second chance at fatherhood might have its appeal.

"There is a way to find out," Sicarius said softly. His hand lifted, as if to stroke her cheek, though he hesitated. They had grown closer and more comfortable with each other in the past months, but he still didn't quite seem to know what to do in situations that involved her feelings.

Amaranthe caught his hand, kissed it, but ultimately released it. "That is true, but I don't want to find out by becoming pregnant. I mean, eventually I could see having children," she rushed to correct, lest he think she was eternally opposed to the idea, "but I don't think I'm ready yet. I'm still trying to figure out... I'm not sure who I am now that I'm not fighting to save the empire. A mother should know who she is, shouldn't she? And I'm not sure I'm ready to give up having adventures yet, either, though I'm terribly relieved not to be responsible for anything or anyone anymore. Out here... it's been quite delightful seeing and experiencing new places. Though I suppose one needn't stay locked in a tower once one has a baby. The Starcrests went all over the world, raising their children on a submarine, didn't they? And it worked out. Their kids are all bright. Though they'd have to be, you'd think. With, uhm." She realized she had been talking for a long time. The topic made her nervous and brought back her burbling tendency, as Sicarius called it. They had never discussed children other than obliquely. Just explaining that she had lost her special tea—yes, she had called it "special tea" like she'd been talking to a toddler rather than a grown man—to the pirates had been difficult.

"I meant you could see a doctor," Sicarius said.

"Oh." Amaranthe flushed. He hadn't been suggesting sexual abandon after all. "Yes, that makes sense. Though I'm not sure I trust imperial medicine in this manner. Er, republican medicine." She grimaced, not sure if that was the right term. It would take a long time to get used to thinking of Turgonia as anything except an empire.

"We could visit the Kyatt Islands," Sicarius said. "Their scientists are known for medicinal acumen."

"That's true. We could even visit Akstyr."

Sicarius's expression grew flat.

"I didn't mean visit him for medical advice," Amaranthe said, in case that hadn't been understood—Akstyr might have healed her before in an emergency, but she shuddered at the idea of asking a teenage boy for advice on her... womanly parts. "I meant we'd stop by and check on him as long as we're there."

Sicarius grunted. She supposed she couldn't expect more enthusiasm. Those two had never bonded.

"While I'm there," Amaranthe said, "you might be able to get in to see some of the other submarines Admi—President Starcrest built there. I understand there's a whole fleet of science vessels." There, that ought to stir his interest more than chatting with old comrades.

Before he could verify her supposition, an unfamiliar noise came from the sleeping cabin, a long beep that repeated three times. Amaranthe had grown used to the various glowing and blinking doodads—or Made devices, as the practitioners called them—around the sub, but she hadn't heard this before.

Sicarius headed for the compartment. The cabin didn't hold much more than a bed, but that bed had cabinets beneath it, and he delved into them. As soon as he opened the one on the left, a bright yellow glow washed over him.

"Er." Amaranthe hadn't realized she had been sleeping above some strange wizard device during the whole trip. "What would that be?"

Sicarius set it on the bed. "A communication artifact."

"Oh, right." She had seen a set of those before—her first nemesis Larocka Myll had communicated to her Forge allies with them. "Is someone trying to reach us? Or maybe someone's trying to reach Starcrest." Who from superstitious Turgonia would know how to use one of these devices? Maldynado would probably think it a lamp or a hand-warmer. She smiled at the thought, a twinge of homesickness touching her. Though she had enjoyed her time with Sicarius, she *did* miss her friends back home.

Sicarius placed a hand on top of the orb. This seemed to be the required gesture, for the yellow glow faded, and shadows stirred behind the opaque surface. President Starcrest's head and shoulders came into view. The short gray hair, dark eyes, and handsome if determined visage were as Amaranthe remembered, though the furrows along his forehead and the creases framing his eyes seemed deeper, his face more tired.

She would not want that man's job.

Starcrest turned his head toward something or someone out of sight—the orb showed only him and a few maps on a wall behind him.

"Ready," a faint voice said. Professor Komitopis?

Starcrest nodded and faced forward, giving the illusion he was gazing at them.

Sicarius straightened like a soldier coming to attention. Amaranthe found herself leaning forward with interest. Nobody had contacted them before. This might signify trouble.

"Sicarius and Ms. Lokdon," Starcrest said, his voice sounding tinny through the device, not quite the rich baritone she remembered. "I trust you are both there and well. I apologize for interrupting your vacation, but we have... a problem here."

"Just one?" came the faint voice from the side again. Yes, judging by the fondness in Starcrest's not-quite-squelching glower to the side, that was definitely his wife.

Starcrest faced forward again. "We have one problem in particular that's proving nettlesome, and I hate to ask, but..."

Amaranthe braced herself, anticipating some soul-devouring favor. A request to return to the capital to lead her men again. A request for Sicarius's assassin skills, skills she wanted him to be able to retire. Some mission that would thrust them both into the deadliest dangers again.

Starcrest cleared his throat. "We need the sub back."

"What?" Amaranthe blurted, but he was still talking. This wasn't a live conversation, she realized, but a message that had been saved to display when she and Sicarius noticed the flashing orb.

"Building a new one would take time," Starcrest said, "and if there are any Makers looking to open their shops in the new Turgonian Republic, I haven't heard of them yet. Again, I apologize for this inconvenience, but I would appreciate it if you would return as soon as possible. Thank you."

The orb went dark, though Sicarius continued to gaze at it for a time.

"What do you think's going on in the city?" Amaranthe asked. "Or in the lake?" Starcrest couldn't need the sub for any land-based purposes, surely.

"Unknown."

Amaranthe tried to decide if he looked pensive, or if she was, as usual, reading things into his bland features that weren't there.

"We've left a few, uhm, inconvenient relics on the lake bottom in the last year," she said, thinking of the underwater laboratory in particular. "Someone might have dug them out. Or started up a new underwater base from which to vex the city. Forge? No, we decimated them, and Starcrest's new economist is working hand-in-hand with that Curlev woman, right? Some other enemy then? The Nurians? They couldn't have been pleased with how things worked out."

Sicarius was watching her, his face unreadable.

"What?" she asked, wondering if the term burbling would come up.

"You sound intrigued."

Huh. Was she? A minute ago, she had been cringing at the idea of being called back for some mission. Was it possible she had missed the chaos of the previous year? The need to come up with harebrained schemes on the fly? The need to talk fast and promise faster in order to win allies to her cause? She *did* miss her friends, that much she had no trouble admitting. As to the rest... perhaps she would welcome new challenges into her life.

"Maybe I am," Amaranthe said. "Aren't you?"

"Perhaps. Though..." Sicarius let his fingers trail down the riveted steel bulkhead next to him.

"You don't want to give back the submarine?" Amaranthe grinned. "Because it's a sleek mechanical wonder, a Starcrest original, and a prototype among the fledgling new generation of underwater exploration conveyances? Or—" she wiggled her eyebrows, "—are you reluctant to let it go because we made so many unique memories in this little cabin?"

"Yes," Sicarius said, the familiar glint in his eyes.

CHAPTER 2

MAHLIKI STOOD OUTSIDE THE DOOR, tugging at her braids, first the left and then the right, for at least a minute before knocking. She only managed *that* bit of bravery because university students were roaming up and down the hall, a few giving her odd looks as they swerved to avoid bumping into her.

A bald man with a couple of extra chins answered the door. "Office hours are in the mornings, as my sign clearly states." He pointed to a brass plaque on the wall that read Professor Edgecrest and started to close the door.

Mahliki thrust her shoe into the crack. "Yes, Professor, but I'm not a student."

He scowled at this admission. Before he could call security, use her for defenestration practice, or employ whatever other savagery Turgonians applied to trespassers, she rushed to add, "I'm here to see Sespian. I was told he's assisting you this semester?"

Her addition didn't soften the man's scowl. "He's too busy to dally with girls right now. In addition to his regular studies, he's working on his contest entry. The deadline is tomorrow."

Mahliki had been nervous enough about seeking out a private conversation with Sespian; she hadn't thought she would have to conquer some militant Turgonian gatekeeper to simply *see* him. "I know. My father recommended he enter it." Relying on Father's name to get through this man made her feel weak and incapable, but she also didn't want to spend fifteen minutes trying to find clever methods to bypass his defenses. "It's his contest, you know."

The professor's scowl abated, and his lips formed a silent, "Oh."

"I know Sespian is busy, but I'm here on an errand for my father. An important errand." That much was true, but said errand had nothing to do with Sespian, and she was technically wasting time by detouring to the university district...

"Yes, of course." The gatekeeper stepped aside. "But for the sake of his post-imperial career, I hope you won't delay him for long. Or frivolously." He arched his eyebrows with meaning. Not quite believing her story? Probably because she kept twisting the tip of a braid around her fingers. That was a sign of nervous prevarication, wasn't it?

"Yes, sir." Mahliki passed a large desk full of mathematics tests and sketches of bridges with comments scribbled in the margins, and headed for a partially closed door to the side. She knocked and stuck her head into the tiny office—cubby, might be the word—reserved for use by the professor's assistants.

Sespian sat on a stool at a large raised desk, the top angled toward him so she couldn't see what he was working on. He was bent low over it, his handsome face utterly still with concentration, the tip of his tongue sticking out of the corner of his mouth, one pencil in his hand and another perched above his ear. He wore simple trousers and a sweater that fitted his form nicely and made her think of the first time she had seen him, when he had been jogging bare-chested with her father and another man, plotting the retaking of the city. He had cut a fine, athletic figure, though even then, a gentleness about his face had said artist rather than soldier. Or maybe she had simply revised her initial impression of him after seeing his work and learning more about him. Learning more about him from a *distance*, admittedly. The classes she had enrolled in that winter had kept her busy, as well as countless silly dinners and formal events it was apparently imperative that a president's daughter attend. More than once, she had wondered if she shouldn't have returned home to stay with Grandmother and finish her studies on the islands, as her younger siblings had done.

Except then she wouldn't be here, gazing at a handsome man who... hadn't noticed she was in the room.

Mahliki knocked again, this time on the inside of the door. She didn't mind having to try again. She was used to being ignored—or not noticed—by people absorbed in their work, as it ran in the family. At home, only Father always retained awareness of the outside world, usually knowing when someone had arrived at his study before they did.

"Uhm, Sespian?" she asked. "Do you have a moment?"

26

He lifted his head. "Oh, hullo, Mahliki."

She smiled, pleased at the personal greeting. They had spoken to each other so few times since they had met that she wouldn't have been surprised if he didn't know her name, thinking of her only as one of Starcrest's children.

"Hello." She ought to get straight to her request—he was clearly busy—but curiosity, and the fact that she couldn't see what he was working on, prompted her to step into the small office and ask, "Is that your entry for my father's contest? Is it going well?"

"It's going..." Sespian pushed a waste bin full of crumpled papers under the desk with his foot. "I can honestly say this iteration is better than some of the others."

Mahliki grinned. She didn't consider herself a perfectionist, but the family had many of those as well, and she understood the type. "You sound so enthusiastic."

Enough early spring sunlight made it through the window to highlight the pink that flushed his cheeks.

"May I see it? I'm self-taught when it comes to art, and not very well at that, but I can appreciate good work." Mahliki decided not to mention how much of his art she had sought out. Unfortunately, there wasn't much, as most of his belongings had burned in the explosion that had destroyed the Imperial Barracks. "I've seen you in the courtyard between classes, sketching those caricatures for students." More than once, she had been tempted to stroll up and have him do one of her, but she hadn't been sure how he would react.

His cheeks flushed to a darker shade of red. "You've, uh, seen that? With the tip jar? It's not..." Sespian bent his head and rubbed the back of his neck, hair in need of a cutting falling into his eyes. "I guess a smarter former emperor would have put some money aside for himself before his career was demolished, but I was busy with... well, I never had to worry about money before, so it didn't even occur to me. I was shocked to learn the price of a flat in the city. A very, very small flat with a window the size of an arrow slit—actually I think it *was* an arrow slit once. And Trog—that's my cat, you know—he prefers fine food, not alley scraps. He's very vocal if I give him substandard fare—to the neighbors' chagrin."

Mahliki stared at him in chagrin of her own. Dear Akahe, she hadn't meant to *embarrass* him. Nor had she realized he was scraping by. Did

27

Father know? Sespian probably hadn't said anything. Surely Father would house him for free at the big hotel that had been donated for presidential use. There were plenty of rooms. Should she offer? Or would that embarrass him further?

"But, uhm, anyway, that's all temporary," Sespian said. "Professor Edgecrest is now giving me a small stipend in exchange for helping him with his classes and a few other chores, and once I finish school and know more fully what I'm doing, I should be able to find people to hire me." He pressed a hand against the drawing pinned to the table. "This contest could help. I'm sure I won't win, but all the entries will be displayed, and maybe I'll get some notice from people thinking of hiring architects in the future. Oh, and to answer your original question, which I seem to have deviated from slightly, yes, you can look."

Mahliki didn't usually have trouble coming up with things to say—or, as her little brother called it, butting into people's conversations—but she didn't know how to respond to Sespian's rushed rambling. She wanted to let him know she didn't care how much money he had, but he had moved on so quickly, he clearly didn't want to discuss it.

Glad for the invitation to look at his project, Mahliki rounded the desk and stood at his shoulder. Front- and side-view sketches for a simple yet elegant building sprawled across the page. Though rectangular, it had an originality that one didn't expect, at least not after viewing the thousands of sturdy and stolid Turgonian buildings in the city. "That's lovely. I like the front. It's almost... whimsical."

Sespian grimaced. "Probably too much so. President Starcrest is so... well, he just seems so military to me, even when he's not in a uniform. It's hard to imagine him appreciating something so... well, it is functional. I've made sure of that much. If anyone knows what a ruler's residence and offices need, that should be me." He shrugged and waved a hand, as if to dismiss what might be construed as bragging about his former position. Mahliki hardly found it so. If anything, he seemed self-effacing to the extreme.

"Just because your first president is a military man doesn't mean future ones will be," she pointed out. "Besides..." She lowered her voice, aware that the professor had settled back into his desk and was grading papers a few feet away. "I shouldn't tell you this, but he foisted this off on my mother."

28

"This?" Sespian touched the page.

"He might nod or grunt at a couple of final choices, but she gets to narrow them down."

"Ah."

Mahliki expected him to ask for tips on appealing to her tastes, but he merely stood back and studied what he had down. "Do you want to know what Mother likes?" she finally asked.

"Inside information? That hardly seems fair. Besides, I have to be true to my vision rather than worrying about pleasing the world. Or Kyattese matrons."

Mahliki didn't know how practical that was, especially if one wanted to win, but she admired his integrity in the manner.

"I wouldn't mind hearing her preferences," came the professor's voice from the other room.

Mahliki started—she had known he was close enough to hear, but hadn't expected him to jump into their conversation.

"Professor Edgecrest is entering a design as well," Sespian said.

"Ah. Is that window open?" Mahliki pointed to the wall, and while Sespian was looking, stepped around the desk and kicked the door shut. "Oops, must be a draft."

Sespian snorted. If the professor had a response, it didn't float through the door.

"Let me at least give you one tip," Mahliki said.

Sespian's eyebrows rose.

"Don't call her a Kyattese matron to her face." Mahliki winked, though she feared her joke came out crippled, for Sespian's lips puckered in contemplation. Odd how flirting was easy with men one didn't care about, but when one actually hoped to impress another... "She doesn't see herself as very proper and dignified, and might construe the word as an insult."

"Oh, thank you." Sespian didn't smile.

And why would he? Were jokes supposed to get *better* when you had to explain them?

"I came on another matter actually." Mahliki had better get to the point before he asked her to leave so he could get back to work. "I was wondering if you have time to come to the waterfront with me and sketch a few examples of the plant. I can do rudimentary drawings myself, but I

29

want to send these back to some of my mother's colleagues at home. They should be as good as possible. I've seen your work. You're very talented."

When jokes fail, try flattery...

Except that Sespian didn't seem to notice the flattery. He had been scratching his jaw since she had mentioned the plant.

"You have seen it, haven't you?" Mahliki asked. "Down on the waterfront? You must have heard of it at least."

"Sorry, no. I've been assisting Professor Edgecrest with his classes, studying all the texts from my own classes, and trying to catch up in a business course—apparently I need to know how to ply my trade when I'm ready." A bemused expression touched his face. It must be strange to have to worry about paying the bills after being predestined since birth to being the emperor.

Something she could talk about with him later, but *truly*? He didn't know about the plant? Had he been living and sleeping in this tiny office?

"Yes, I can see where that'll be important, but the plant is getting to be a problem. Father has called Sicarius and Amaranthe back, so it can be studied from beneath in the *Explorer*. In the meantime, I volunteered to research it since the current methods the city workers are using to eradicate it are primitive and limited." Mahliki bit her lip, wishing she hadn't chosen those two adjectives. He might think she was insulting his people. She actually found the Turgonians intriguing in ways—they made up for their rudimentary arts and mundane sciences techniques with impressive engineering skills, not to mention all those delicious things they made with apples, a fruit that rarely made it to the Kyattese Islands.

"I shouldn't think I'd have any knowledge that would be anything less than primitive and limited when it comes to plants," Sespian said— cursed banyan sprites, he'd picked up on that unintentional insult, "but if I can be of assistance to your father or the city as a whole..." He shrugged. "It's silly I suppose, but I do still feel a responsibility toward the empire's subjects, or the republic's citizens, as I guess we all are now."

"It's not silly. If you could do these drawings for me, it would be very helpful." And if they spent a couple of hours chatting in the early spring sun, maybe he would come to find her company pleasant. Especially if she kept from insulting his people for the rest of the day.

"Let me gather a few items."

"Excellent." Mahliki kept the triumphant fist pump internal.

Sespian grabbed pencils, charcoal sticks, pens, erasers, and a sketchpad. He opened the door and walked into the larger room. "Good afternoon, Professor. I'll be back in a couple of hours."

"Don't get too close to that plant," the professor growled without looking up from his desk. The doors were thin here. "There's talk of people going missing from the waterfront at night. And don't get distracted by womanly wiles, either—the contest deadline is tomorrow, and you've work left to do in there."

Mahliki was torn between mortification and indignation. The latter won out, and she jammed a fist against her hips. "Womanly wiles?"

"I'm sure Lady Starcrest has nothing but professional matters on her mind," Sespian said, "but I will maintain a rigid shield of propriety around myself just in case."

Mahliki might have been even more mortified, but Sespian winked at her as he said the last.

The professor grunted and muttered, "Good. You've a career to pay attention to. You don't want to spend the rest of your life drawing for tips in the student square—that's disgraceful."

Sespian flushed and hustled for the door. The professor didn't detain them further.

Mahliki searched for things to say as they walked out of the university district and caught a trolley heading for the waterfront. Oh, she thought of *things*, but they were all stupid things. There were stories she could share, but he would find her self-absorbed if she started spinning tales of childhood adventures without the slightest prompting.

They drew a few curious looks from trolley passengers, more for Sespian than Mahliki. Father was trying to keep pictures and news of his wife and children out of the presses, and she hadn't been recognized often when she'd been out.

"I have a confession," Sespian said as the breeze riffled through his short brown hair. "The construction site for the new capital building has been changed from Arakan Hill to a spot a few blocks up from the waterfront—something about donated land and politics, I understand. I've been meaning to take a look and see if the surrounding buildings and terrain should affect my design."

"So you're not coming with me purely for altruistic reasons? To help the citizens?"

31

"Well..." Sespian cleared his throat and looked down, seemingly embarrassed by having an ever-so-slight self-serving streak. "I think a handsome new capital building for the Turgonian Republic will help the citizens. By making them feel that this new regime has a permanence to it." He gave her a quick smile.

She had been thinking of teasing him for his grandiose statements, but the smile stole her words. It wasn't flamboyant or flirtatious, but shy and self-effacing, acknowledging the pompousness of his words. It warmed her heart. Well, all right, that wasn't exactly her *heart* getting all tingly. She rummaged through her mind for something to say that would bring back the smile.

Someone climbing onto the trolley jostled Sespian, and he looked away—to her disappointment.

His mouth drooped open as he stared past the trolley driver, toward the waterfront, which had come into view... "That's... unexpected."

Mahliki had visited the plant a number of times already, but she frowned at the snarl of tangles growing up from the shallows, twining around the support posts on the docks, and stretching across the planks in places. The green blur stretched up and down the waterfront, like some overambitious algal bloom that had mated with a vining plant from the tropics. Here and there, boats at the docks had been caught in its clutches, and their owners were hacking with machetes, trying to free everything from dinghies to yachts. Commercial fishing ships out in the deeper waters were unaffected, but they had to be keeping an eye on the shore, wondering if they dared return to their berths.

"I was here yesterday, but I swear it's even larger today," Mahliki said. "Amazing growth, especially for this climate."

"I had no idea... That can't be natural. Where'd it come from?"

"I don't know. I wish your Amaranthe was around to talk to, as I understand your lake has been the hotbed for all sorts of unusual activity in the last year."

"My Amaranthe." Sespian snorted softly as the trolley came to a stop. "Hardly that."

Mahliki tried to decide if there was something wistful in his tone, or if she was imagining it. Amaranthe and the assassin—Sespian's father, she reminded herself, though that still wasn't common knowledge—had been together for a long time, or at least that was the impression she had gotten.

"I do have some knowledge of what transpired here with the underwater laboratory in the last year," Sespian said. "Now and then, my intelligence department actually told me things."

"I've already read everything in my father's records. The old chief of intelligence salvaged everything possible from those offices in the Imperial Barracks."

"Ah, of course. You'd have access to far more information than I these days." Sespian didn't sound regretful; he was merely making an observation. Though did his mouth turn down an iota? At the notion he couldn't be as useful as he once had?

Mahliki should have asked for his information instead of squelching him. She had wanted something to discuss, and that would have gotten him talking. Fool.

Sespian lifted a hand toward someone in the distance. Between the not-entirely-frigid spring air and the plant spectacle, the wide waterfront street was bustling with people, everyone from enforcers in their gray uniforms to vendors hawking "I saw it first" shirts with vines snaking around the sides and backs of the garments. It took Mahliki a moment to spot the recipient of Sespian's wave.

The man strolling toward them was one of the first Turgonians, aside from her father, Mahliki had met. He wore a tastefully cut—if flamboyantly colored—suit and great coat that accented his height, broad shoulders, and muscular build. His facial features were strong enough so as not to seem feminine but elegant enough to draw the eyes of those who appreciated the aesthetically pleasing. Although the green hat on his head might make the owner of that same eye curl a lip—it was sprouting vines, not dissimilar to those on the garish shirts being hawked.

A woman in a crisp gray enforcer uniform walked at his side, her long strides matching his, though she was a few inches shorter than he, her height equal to Mahliki's own six feet. No one would call the enforcer woman a beauty, but she had handsome features that bespoke strength and determination. Her broad utility belt housed a dagger, a short sword, and a pistol, and her hand rested on the latter as she scowled out at the invasive plant. Mahliki hadn't yet seen anyone trying to shoot the biological curiosity into submission yet, but, this being Turgonia, it was only a matter of time.

"Hello, Maldynado," Sespian said as they drew closer to the other couple. "Sergeant Yara."

Maldynado swept the hat from his head and bowed, a tumble of brown curls falling about his cheeks. "Good evening, Sespian, and Ms. Starcrest. It's delightful to see you both."

He gave Mahliki what she would consider a flirtatious smile, and Sergeant Yara—his... friend? Lover? Arresting officer?—rolled her eyes. When Maldynado turned the smile on Sespian it was almost as flirty. Maybe he simply didn't know another way to stretch his lips. He added a wink to Sespian along with an unsubtle nod toward Mahliki. At least she found it unsubtle. Sespian's return smile had a faintly baffled air about it.

A sheltered upbringing, Mahliki decided, though, for all her travels, her upbringing also hadn't been as ecumenical in the ways of lovers and suitors as she might have wished, not with her very tall and very imposing father looming in the background. Amazing how little a man with his reputation had to do to make boys trip over their own feet in hasty retreat...

"Are you working?" Sespian asked.

"*Some* of us are." Yara slanted an exasperated look at Maldynado, or perhaps his newly purchased hat, though a fondness seemed to underlie her glare.

The exasperation bounced off Maldynado, who simply smiled wider. "Some of us are offering emotional and physical support to those who are working." He slugged Sespian in the shoulder, a common male-to-male Turgonian greeting, Mahliki had noticed, though it would have knocked a slighter man over backward. "Where have you been? You missing your loving pa?"

"Er," Sespian said.

"Want to come to the baths one of these nights? We'll box and throw the sand bags around for a while, then get steamed up and rubbed down by the ladies." Maldynado winked.

Mahliki thought Yara might scowl at this mention of a rubdown, but perhaps not. Mahliki's one and only experience in a Turgonian bath had left her with bruises. She wasn't sure what had been worse, the pummeling by the rotund loincloth-clad masseur or the flaying of her skin by the scrub lady with tree trunks for arms. If anything sexual ever happened in those baths, she doubted it was with the employees.

"Er," Sespian said again. "I have to finish—"

"Please go with him," Yara said, a tinge of desperation to her voice. "He misses his friends."

"Oh," Sespian said. "I can understand that. You and Basilard were close, weren't you?"

"Despite the fact that he cheated ruthlessly at every dice, tile, or card game that you played with him, yes," Maldynado said.

Yara mouthed, "Never happened," to Mahliki.

Mahliki smiled but found her gaze drifting toward the plant. Her parents had sent her down to study it, but she would have come of her own accord anyway. She had seen nothing like it, not in any of her travels, nor in any of her books, and it fascinated her. It could be some practitioner's project that had gotten out of hand—or perhaps it was doing precisely what its creator had intended—but what if it were some natural mutation?

"It's hard to believe, but I miss Akstyr too," Maldynado said. "Even if he was appallingly uncouth, he was just getting interesting when he left. And Sicarius? Well, all right, I don't really miss him, but Amaranthe, for sure. And, ah..." His eyes grew distant as he gazed down the waterfront.

"Books," Sespian said quietly.

This remembrance of old comrades Mahliki barely knew made her feel like an outsider. It would be an opportune time to start work, though she was hesitant to leave Sespian, lest he walk off with them instead of with her.

She touched his arm. "I'll be on that dock over there. If you still have time, those drawings would help." She lifted a hand toward the others. "Good day."

Though she told herself not to, she glanced over her shoulder to see if Sespian would follow or if he looked aggrieved that he had to go off with her instead of staying with them. His face didn't suggest that, though he was probably politically minded enough to mask his thoughts. He shared a few more words with his comrades, received another solid thump on the shoulder from Maldynado, and strode after her.

Mahliki plucked a specimen collection kit out of the satchel she carried, though most of the tools were inadequate for such a large plant.

The wooden dock, though broad and of recent construction, creaked and groaned as she walked down it. Not due to her presence, but because the vines wrapping the pilings and boards were applying pressure as they grew at an alarming rate. She paused near a clump of tendrils sticking out of the water like grass—albeit grass with inch-thick stems. Their tips wavered in the breeze, and one had a bulbous tip. She had observed those bulbs on her last trip, but none of them had been near enough for collection. She had a hunch that bud might produce a flower eventually, and she would love a chance to dissect the pistil, stamen, and ovule, or whatever organs it ended up having in there.

"Be careful." Sespian eyed the bulb. "Sergeant Yara said people *have* gone missing down here the last two nights. She's not ready to blame the plant, but everyone on the force talks about the oddity of it. An, ah, magical oddity. I know you Kyattese think us primitive for calling it that, but—" He shrugged and opened his sketch pad.

"You're not primitive. It's just strange that the mental sciences aren't practiced here at all, and that so many people don't even believe people can do things with their minds."

Sespian had started sketching, but he stopped to point a pencil at the tendrils. "Can you tell if these were a result of ma— the Science?"

"I'm not the expert to ask. My brother and sister would be if they hadn't gone home. I can sometimes sense the presence of artifacts or of people tinkering with the elements, but this just feels like a plant to me. My mother said the same thing when I brought her down to see it, and she's more of a Sensitive than I am. Still, a practitioner could have created the seeds in a laboratory, then planted them, and what grew up wouldn't necessarily feel Made, if that makes sense."

"Hm." Sespian set the pad on top of a piling and dropped to his belly. He peered under the dock. "Do you think this started as seeds? As in a lot of seeds?"

"It could have started as one plant and spread laterally via rhizomes. I haven't dug around in the soil down there to see yet. Someone said the water is fifteen or twenty feet deep around the docks here, and, at the risk of sounding like a weak-blooded foreigner, the lake seems cold for swimming at this time of year. I checked on the beach to the south and north of the city, but there's nothing growing around there yet, so I couldn't simply wade in and pull up some roots. I tried to pull on one of these tendrils, but it didn't budge."

Sespian slithered halfway off the dock to dip a finger into the water. "Very cold," he agreed, "but I imagine I could survive a thirty-second immersion to pull up a root for you."

Mahliki hadn't expected such an offer and beamed at the back of his head. "Thank you, but there's more than water to be concerned about down there. I wouldn't want you to become entangled and not be able to get back up."

She was on the verge of explaining how the plant could wrap its vines around anything—or anyone—quite quickly in its bid to grow up into the sunlight, but Sespian lifted his head first, his face fixed in an expression between repugnance and horror. A tendril from under the dock had fastened to his arm, wrapping twice about his wrist. The tip wavered toward his sleeve, as if it meant to slither into his shirt and take over his body.

"I see what you mean," Sespian said. "I don't suppose I could use your knife? Now that nobody has any good reason to assassinate me, I've been wandering the city armed with little more than pencils and sketch pads."

"Of course." Mahliki slid a hand into her collection kit and pulled out a scalpel with a sharper blade than her utility knife. "I have all manner of tools and weapons. My father wouldn't let me out of the hotel if I didn't carry something sharp and pointy. He's not particularly trusting of young men, at least when it comes to his daughters."

Sespian tried to wedge the tip of the scalpel under the tendril, but it tightened before their eyes. His hand grew a few shades darker than the rest of his arm.

"Not that pencils can't be turned into weapons," Mahliki said, edging closer and thinking of taking a pencil to the vine herself. "Stab a boy in the eye a few times, and he'll stop trying to touch your backside. Or, uhm, other parts." She knelt beside Sespian—the tip of that vine had grown an inch as she had been watching; she was sure of it.

"I'll keep that advice in mind, should groping boys ever accost my nether regions." Sespian gave up on delicately removing the vine from his wrist and hacked at a lower section instead. The scalpel cut through the finger-thick tendril, but it did take several tries. Sespian's face remained calm, though he did tear the vine free and fling it to the deck with feeling.

"I ought to forgo steel in my design for the president's residence and have the walls constructed from that stuff."

"That would be a unique look. In the meantime..." Mahliki nudged the severed vine toward him. "Would you mind drawing that?"

Sespian's lip curled. "It's still twitching."

"Yes, from my prior observations, I believe that'll eventually start growing a new plant."

"How... practical." He looked up and down the waterfront, at the number of docks and boats being violated by the vines. Then his gaze drifted inland. "Is it strictly a water plant? Or can it grow out of plain dirt? Or... cobblestones?"

"I'm not sure yet. Thus far, it's keeping its roots under the water." Mahliki pulled out a ball of thick twine and made a lasso. "I should have a bud to dissect in a moment. That'll give you more interesting material to draw. Assuming those *are* buds and not pods or some such. I haven't seen a flower yet. Or cone. Or spore."

"I look forward to it." Sespian started to sit on the deck, but peered through the boards, at more tendrils wavering below, and decided to stand and draw with his pad laid in the crook of his arm. The snipped piece of vine kept wriggling about, so he used a sturdy pen to stab it, pinning it to the nearest piling. "If you still need those roots, I do recall Amaranthe and her men finding diving suits somewhere in the city. One of the naval vessels might even have some with... tools built in."

Mahliki had a feeling "weapons" was the first word that came to his mind, not tools. Maybe he had changed it out of concern that she would think Turgonians all warmongers. If so, that meant what she thought mattered to him. Oh, that was progress. She smiled cheerfully, refusing to believe she might have read too much into his slight pause. "These suits would allow us to go down there, properly insulated against the cold and armed against groping plants, so we could collect root samples?"

Sespian looked up from his drawing. "We?"

"You *did* volunteer to dive into the frigid water for me. This should be an improvement, no?"

"I, ah... Hm. If Amaranthe hadn't been out of town for the last couple of months, I'd suspect you'd been spending time with her."

Mahliki didn't know whether that was a compliment or not. Did he prefer timid girls to those who... took the initiative? Or maybe he felt she was wheedling to persuade him into doing something unappealing? No man liked a wheedling woman, she supposed.

"You don't have to come." She tossed her lasso, trying to land the loop around the vine holding the bud. It stretched up higher than their heads. She bumped it, but the twine fell into the water. "I just thought you might be as fascinated by this plant as I am, now that you've bonded with it." As she reeled her lasso back in, she nodded at the cut vine hanging from the piling.

"Bonded, huh?" Sespian rubbed a patch of hives that had arisen around his wrist. An allergic reaction? Drat. He would be even less interested in studying it further.

"It seemed to like you anyway." Mahliki tossed the lasso again, this time succeeding in looping it around the top of the vine. "I'll find a diving suit on my own and go down. This is my project."

Sespian's attention had turned to the fire brigade approaching the waterfront in a couple of steam lorries, both towing cylindrical tanks behind them. The sides read KEROSENE in large letters alongside stamps of danger, some textual and some pictorial. Only in Turgonia would an image of a man with flames spouting from his clothes be considered an appropriate way to warn someone away from a flammable liquid. The firemen started unloading blowlamps. If she had been keeping track as well as she thought, this represented Serious Attempt Number Three at destroying the invasive plant.

"No," Sespian sighed. "I think this is going to be *everyone's* project. I'll go with you to collect the samples, if you can wait until after tomorrow when I turn in my contest entry. It's doubtful that someone with so little experience and no formal training in architecture will have a chance, but... what a way to be remembered, by leaving a building that can stand for centuries hence. If nothing else, it could help my career."

Mahliki had reeled in her bud and was concentrating on sawing it from its vine, but she spared an amused thought for a man who'd been *emperor* worrying about being remembered. True, it had been a short reign, but he had been the last emperor, so surely he wouldn't be forgotten.

The vine drooped down and touched her shoulder. She flinched and flung it away. It was like some creature's live tentacle rather than a plant's appendage. "I'm sure you have a good chance at the contest, though my understanding is that Mother will be judging the entries without looking at the names of the architects. She's fond of fairness."

"Good. That's how it should be."

"Ugh, it's like these things are made from rubber." Mahliki finally sawed the bud free, but not without cutting her own hand in the process. It was as if the vine had known what she intended and kept getting in the way on purpose.

"Yes," Sespian said. "I can't help but think it was sent here to trouble our fledging republic."

"I've had that thought too."

"In the old days, people just tried to assassinate the fellow in charge. Or drug him." Sespian grimaced.

"That happened to you?" Mahliki knelt on the dock and prodded at the bud with her scalpel, trying to find a seam or weak spot.

"Drugging, manipulation, attempted assassinations. I'm relieved to be nobody special anymore."

"Truly?" Mahliki looked into his eyes. Though the Kyattese didn't have a government that ran on bloodlines, she was fortunate enough to have been born into a family with land and money, so that she never had to worry about feeding herself or having clothing to wear—or books to read. It would be difficult to give up even that much privilege, much less power over an entire nation.

"Truly," Sespian said, meeting her eyes.

His were brown with golden flecks, warm and friendly. Nothing in their conversation should have made her blush, but Mahliki suddenly felt the need to return her attention to her work. "Even though being nobody special means that you don't have the power to delegate underwater specimen collection to someone else?"

He smiled. "Even so."

"The day after tomorrow will be fine. I'll have to figure out how to get some of those suits."

Sespian tilted his head. "Can't you ask your father for a favor? *He* can delegate things to other people now."

"He's so busy, it's hard to find him. You'd be shocked if you heard about half of the uprisings he's put down, squabbles he's had to mediate, and—I'm not supposed to know about this, so don't say anything—assassination attempts he's dodged. Well, I guess you're perhaps the one person who *wouldn't* be shocked, but it's been difficult for the family to digest. Favors. I'm not sure *Mother* is even getting favors, right now."

"Ah." Sespian tapped his sketchpad. "I'm ready for the next subject."

"Yes, one moment." Mahliki gave up on finding a tidy way to slice the bud open and hacked it in half. She peeled back the exterior and frowned at the dark green rounded cube inside. "That doesn't look like any pistil I've ever seen. How odd." She was debating whether to try and slice it open to see if it housed reproductive organs, but the cube opened of its own accord, the top peeling back, and something black bulging from within. She froze, torn between wanting to see what happened and wanting to back away in case it was something unpleasant. "That's..."

The bulging thing—it vaguely reminded her of someone's tonsil—pulsed twice, and—

Sespian grabbed her shoulder, and yanked her away as a fine black mist sprang into the air. Her butt bounced across several planks before he hefted her to her feet, pulling her back against him. From several feet away, Mahliki watched the mist spread, then dissipate.

"I apologize," Sespian said, though he didn't yet release her. "I thought that looked... ominous."

Mahliki thought about joking that she didn't mind a handsome man wrapping her in his arms, but couldn't bring herself to flirt so brazenly with him. She had a feeling he would give her a shocked look if she tried. Besides, they had more important matters to deal with.

"Perfectly fine," she said. "I thought it looked ominous, too, but I had to see what happened. Scientific curiosity, you understand."

"Hm, do your people have any phrases about curiosity and cats?"

Your people? She almost told him that she was half Turgonian, but supposed she couldn't lay much claim to the nationality when she'd never set foot on the continent until this past winter. "Yes, but it's about monkeys and shiny objects in logs. We... uh. What is happening to that wood?"

Before their eyes, the dock faded, cracked, and splintered. The boards sagged and warped.

"I don't know," Sespian said, "but it's only happening to the five feet around that bud."

"Where the spores landed," Mahliki agreed. "Or whatever they were."

One of the boards snapped in half and fell through to the water below. Others grew thinner and frailer, as if they were aging a hundred years in a matter of seconds.

Mahliki wriggled free from Sespian's grip and darted back to the bud.

"What are you doing?" he blurted.

She stabbed her specimen with her dagger and turned, intending to sprint back before the weakened boards gave way. One collapsed beneath her heel, and her foot plunged through. She yanked it free, but another one groaned beneath her other leg. She flung herself to the dock to spread out her weight and crawled back to Sespian. He had dropped his sketchpad and had been about to lunge out after her. She was glad he hadn't; their combined weight would have sent them both plunging into the icy water.

"Getting my specimen," Mahliki answered his question. She opened her jacket to peek at the vials, bottles, and fine tools she kept strapped to the lining, but none of the collection cases was big enough. She dug into her satchel and pulled out a glass box. She stuffed her half dissected bud into it, grabbed a sturdy lid, and fastened it as if speed counted for everything. Maybe it did. "You don't mind drawing it through the glass, do you?"

"No," Sespian said. "Not at all."

In the handful of seconds since she had been back with him, the dock had continued to deteriorate. Disintegrate, almost. By the time it finally collapsed, only splinters remained to float on the water below. Mahliki shuddered, thinking about what might have happened to her if she had been caught by those spores.

"I think this may be important enough to warrant a favor from Father after all," she said lightly, though she would have preferred to stand in Sespian's arms again. She would have to find a way to thank him for using his quick reflexes to pull her to safety.

"I'd say so. We'd better warn the enforcers and the fire brigade too. If they blasted one of those buds with a gout of flame..."

"It could be ugly, yes." Mahliki peered down at her specimen. The tonsil had stopped pulsing, but it was still the strangest thing she had seen in her years studying biology. "What *are* you?" she whispered to it.

She didn't receive a response.

After checking the office, the library, the conference room, and all the other places people liked to waylay Rias, Tikaya headed to the basement of the old hotel. The four-story, three-hundred-year-old Emperor's Bulwark had been converted to presidential use in the aftermath of the election, the mostly destroyed Imperial Barracks being deemed inappropriate housing for a nation's new leader. Considering all the tents, huts, branches, and bare ground Rias had slept in and on during his life, he probably wouldn't have been bothered by living in a room with one wall missing and shrapnel and soot adorning the rest. Tikaya appreciated the comforts of the hotel, even if it had been donated by one of the remaining leaders of the disbanded business coalition responsible for so much of the trouble in the capital of late. The donation had been less about charity and more about ingratiating oneself to the new president. That seemed to be everyone's agenda when interacting with Rias.

In contrast with the crisp evening air outside, the basement had the humidity of a greenhouse. Pipes knocked and hissed, and raucous laughs and cheers came from down a hallway marked Gentlemen's Gymnasium. Tikaya had been in the smaller Women's Gymnasium a few times, though she hadn't found many women in it to exercise—or socialize—with. Even in this reformed Turgonian government, the majority of posts were filled by stodgy military men, with the exception of the treasury and economics branches, where more women had run for office. Rias had rejected her suggestion that he take on a female vice president, choosing instead the man who had been the runner up in the election. Dasal Serpitivich was pleasant enough, and Tikaya understood making choices to appease the populace, but thought Rias had missed an opportunity to initiate *real* change.

"Incremental changes, love," he had said. "We're already bending the blades of brittle old swords."

Tikaya walked down the dim hallway toward the laughs. Doors to either side had labels such as Steam, Heat, and Structure Manipulation, leaving one to wonder if the rooms were for bath-related activities or for repairing one's steam carriage.

A door opened, emitting a cloud of vapor and a man with a towel draped over his shoulder and nothing else. He turned toward her, but halted with an ungainly stumble.

"My lady," he blurted, sweeping the towel down to cover himself. "This is the men's gymnasium."

"Yes, I know. I'm looking for a man. My husband, specifically. Have you seen him?" The man—a military intelligence officer she vaguely remembered as a chief of somebody's affairs... Kendorian, maybe—shrugged. "Yes. No. I mean, you're not supposed to be *in* here, my lady."

"Half of the public baths in the city are mixed gender," Tikaya pointed out.

"Yes, but not the *lodges*."

Ah, she had scrambled up into his girls-not-allowed tree fort. Too bad. "My husband? Is he here, or not?"

The man stepped aside and pointed toward the end of the hall. "I believe he's meeting with the heads of our department in the Rings."

"Thank you."

Tikaya strode down the hall, passing a few other nude men, some who appeared scandalized by her presence, some who smirked and bowed, and others who merely gave her the same polite, professional, "Evening, my lady" that they would when fully dressed and passing in the halls upstairs.

The laughs, she soon learned, were coming from the Rings portion of the basement. Here, the space hadn't been divided into smaller rooms. The entire end of the building lay open, the cement walls bare with exposed pipes running along the ceiling. A handful of circles of various sizes had been painted on the floor, and a bunch of men, some in exercise togs and others in nothing, were gathered around the closest one. The sound of flesh smacking against flesh rang out more than once, and a bevy of jeers and catcalls erupted from the onlookers.

Tikaya had no more than started toward the ring when spectators leaped aside so a familiar bare-chested man could skid out of the boundaries on his back, a wince on his face.

She stopped at the gray-haired head and peered down. "Good evening, love."

President Sashka Federias Starcrest blinked a few times before focusing on her. "Why, good evening. Do you... need me?" From flat on his back, he gazed about at the manly decor, such as it was, as if he couldn't believe there might be another reason she would have stepped foot down here.

"Is it my imagination, or do you sound hopeful that I do?" Tikaya asked.

"Yes. This meeting is proving painful. In more ways than one." Rias propped himself up on his elbows and stared at the person who had sent him flying.

"You told me not to hold back," the man said. He, too, was bare-chested, though only a few flecks of gray marked his short black hair. His battered nose had been broken at least twice, and a thick, knotted scar occupied the hollow where his left eye should have been. Apparently the compromised vision didn't affect his boxing prowess overmuch.

"I tell everyone that," Rias said, waving away a couple of offers of help and climbing to his feet on his own. "You're the only one who listens."

The man bared his teeth in something that wasn't quite a smile. Given his pugilistic exterior, Tikaya expected half of those teeth to be missing, but they were straight, white, and all present.

"Is this... some old enemy of yours?" Tikaya asked. Her husband had a knack for turning enemies into allies, if not always friends, exactly.

"Close," Rias said. "My brother's son. Daksaron Starcrest."

"Oh?" Tikaya considered the man anew, wondering if any of the family intellect lurked beneath his brutish facade. Rias had quite a few scars as well, she reminded herself, though none of the blows to his face had stolen his ability to draw a lady's attention, even now in his sixties. It was hard to judge intelligence from peering into a man's eyes—*eye*—she supposed, but she did find a hint of humor there at least.

"Call me, Dak, my lady." Rias's nephew thumped his fist to his chest and bowed.

"Why don't *we* get to call him Dak?" a man in the crowd whispered.

"With your checkered record, you're lucky he lets you call him Colonel," his comrade whispered back.

Rias and Dak were grabbing towels and pretended not to hear the commentary.

"Continue without me, please, gentlemen," Rias said.

"Wait, My Lord," a middle-aged man implored, managing to appear quite earnest despite having nothing except a towel around his waist. "What about the Nurians? They're the last thing on the agenda, remember? Those two spies we caught..." He glanced at Tikaya, as if he worried she wasn't on the list of people allowed to hear state secrets.

Technically, she supposed she had never signed any paperwork promising loyalty to Turgonia, and she certainly hadn't given up her

LINDSAY BUROKER

Kyattese citizenship. As far as she knew, Rias didn't keep any secrets from her, though with as little as she saw him lately, he had scant time to divulge the details of what he had for breakfast, much less anything juicy about the new republic's enemies.

"Ah, yes," Rias acknowledged, then gave Tikaya an apologetic look. "Can you give me fifteen minutes? I'll meet you in my office. We can have a nice lunch delivered." He brightened so at the notion of a private meal, one that might even involve sitting down to eat, that she was reluctant to mention...

"It's after dark, love."

His smile faltered, but he recovered it. "Dinner?"

Tikaya had already eaten with Mahliki, but she would take any time she could steal with him. "Yes, I'd like that. And while you're being beaten up by more of your men, could you ask someone to scrounge up a couple of diving suits?"

Rias had been turning back to the ring, but he halted at this. "For... the plant?"

"Yes, Mahliki wants to get samples of the roots and take a good look at it from down below."

"She can't wait until Sicarius returns with the submarine?"

"It's growing at an alarming rate," Tikaya said.

"That will be dangerous," Dak said. He'd had his arms folded as he watched a pair of younger men square off in the ring, but he scowled at Rias now. "I have all the latest reports on that thing."

"Mahliki is capable of taking care of herself," Tikaya said.

"Yes, I have all the reports on her too." The hint of amusement had returned to his eye, but something about the way his eyebrow twitched made Tikaya wonder if her daughter had been up to some trouble this winter beyond her studies, trouble she hadn't mentioned to her parents.

"I called Dak back from his post at Fort Deadend to head the intelligence office here," Rias explained.

"Fort Deadend...?" Tikaya remembered the remote military installation well; it was the northernmost outpost in the empire and had its nickname because everyone knew no career advancement happened there.

"I didn't get along well with those Forge snails spying from within the intelligence office in the Imperial Barracks," Dak said. "Someone whispered in the right ear, and I was sent north two years ago."

46

"An extreme posting," Tikaya said. "What did you say to the, ah, snails?"

"I punched them."

"Multiple times, I hear," Rias said mildly.

Tikaya couldn't decide if there was censure in his statement or not. If so, it seemed odd. Yes, Rias usually came up with creative ways to solve problems, but he wasn't above fisticuffs. That seemed to breed true in Turgonian men, no matter what their intellect.

"They deserved it," Dak said. "Send a few men with your girl. Some of the rumors about that plant aren't as farfetched as they sound."

"Yes, Mahliki had an... experience with it this afternoon. She's aware of the danger. She also said Sespian would go down with her." Tikaya had found the dreamy-eyed look in Mahliki's eyes as she mentioned this amusing, though she had seen her daughter infatuated a few times before and didn't know what to think of this new selection yet. Tikaya hoped to return home after Rias finished his five years here, but what if Mahliki were to fall in love with a Turgonian? To *marry* one and want to stay?

"I could find a couple of big, burly types," Dak said.

"It wouldn't hurt," Rias said, "though Sespian might surprise you."

"As I recall, he mostly surprised his own weapons training instructor with all the creative ways he discovered to get out of practice."

"He's a decent fighter now," Rias said, "Quick, agile. Given who his father is, it would be surprising if he *weren't*."

Dak grunted. "Blood doesn't necessarily mean anything."

Tikaya tried to gauge if that was some comment about their own shared blood, but his craggy features didn't reveal much.

"My Lord?" the earnest man from before called. "The Nurians?"

"Yes, yes." Rias smiled at Tikaya. "See you shortly."

"I'll arrange for the suits and the men." Dak grabbed a shirt and pulled it over his head.

Rias gave him an acknowledging wave. Tikaya was surprised he had volunteered. If Dak was running the intelligence department, he had to be every bit as busy as Rias. This ought to be the sort of task that could be delegated to a lower-ranking man.

"My lady," Dak extended an arm toward the hallway. "I'll come with you. If your daughter's upstairs, she can give me some measurements and her opinions on whether she wants a couple of bright officers or a couple of dull muscle-heads that she can order around."

"I imagine she'll end up in charge of any young men you send her, rank regardless," Tikaya said as they walked toward the lift. "Her physical attributes are much better proportioned for that than mine ever were. I haven't decided yet whether that's a kindness or a handicap for her."

Dak's grunt rang neither of agreement nor disagreement. She hadn't been fishing for a compliment so didn't mind that he didn't prove a flatterer. When they stepped into the lift, she watched him out of the corner of her eye, still wondering if he had a motive for volunteering to come up with her. He didn't seem the type to curry favor with an uncle—or anyone—to improve his military career; indeed, the dark smudges under his eyes suggested he wasn't getting much sleep in his new position, so she wondered how much of a reward it was.

Dak cleared his throat. "My lady?"

"Yes?"

"You know him a lot better than I do. Aside from a few family Solstice Day gatherings when I was a boy, I've... barely known him outside of the legend. But does he seem... less sharp than usual of late?"

"How so?" Tikaya had seen so little of Rias that she feared she would make a poor judge. He was *tired*, she knew that.

"It's hard to say exactly. With a normal man, I wouldn't think anything of it, but... well, yesterday, he wrote down a math problem. It was complicated for sure, but I remember a similar moment when I first arrived two months ago, where he did one in his head, between one breath and the next, and gave the courier the answer right away."

The lift had stopped, but neither of them pulled the lever to open the door.

"I haven't tested his math skills of late," Tikaya said slowly, "but he has admitted to a lot of headaches. And perhaps I have noticed more absentmindedness than usual. He's like that from time to time when he's working on problems..." Tikaya was even more so, so she never judged. "But... I'm not sure. I attributed it to how busy he's been. He comes to bed after I do, and leaves before I wake up. There are times he doesn't come at all, and I find him at his desk, facedown on a stack of papers."

"It's a challenging job, no doubt," Dak said. "It would be under any circumstances, but to be the *first* president and know that every policy signed into existence might have ramifications for decades, if not centuries to come... Not to mention that everyone's watching him and has the expectation that he'll be just as brilliant at this as he was at his military career. That weighs on him, I think. And the assassination attempts—I don't think he worries that much about himself, but you and your daughter. I know he was glad the younger children went back to your mother's home to finish their studies."

Tikaya had stopped breathing before he stopped talking. "Assassination attempts?"

An appalled expression flashed across the formerly masked face, as he realized his faux pas. "He... didn't tell you?"

Tikaya shook her head mutely.

"There were three, men paid by Nurians we think, but none of them got close. My soldiers and I are working day and night to keep abreast of all the plots and politicking that's going on out there, and we were ready for them."

"I see," she managed. "Thank you."

She couldn't be surprised, but she could be... irked that Rias hadn't told her. He hadn't even introduced his new chief of intelligence to her in the two months Dak had apparently been here and on duty. Chief of intelligence—it sounded like Rias needed a chief of *security*.

He wouldn't want her to worry, she understood that, but if she had known, maybe she could have helped gather and analyze information. With most of her work back in Kyatt and no colleagues to interact with here, she wouldn't mind a job where she could put her mind to use. She had been so... lost here. Apparently warrior-caste women didn't need to work or contribute to the family; if they longed for purpose, they could organize social activities, something for which Tikaya had no aptitude or interest. Maybe she was just supposed to sit by the fire, lamenting that her children had grown up and didn't need her anymore, until the assassins showed up. Dear Akahe, she missed home. She would never whine to Rias, but she had been looking forward to his last day in office since the day he signed in.

"My lady?" Dak asked.

"Yes?" Tikaya realized they were still standing in the lift, but she didn't open the door, in case he had some other devastating news he wanted to share.

"I'd thought..."

He had all of Rias's height and brawn, and seeing such a big man shuffle his feet with uncertainty made her nervous all over again.

"Yes, please tell me," she said.

"This'll sound daft, I expect, but I thought there might be some magical reason for his... absentmindedness, as you called it. I've studied a lot of other cultures and know some of what's possible, but I wouldn't know where to start in looking for a conjurer or artifact that might account for this." Dak shrugged. "If there's anything to this at all, and it's not all in my mind. I would figure he's just getting older and more forgetful if he hadn't been as sharp as any legend-writer might expect two months ago."

"I'll look into it, Dak. Thank you for telling me."

He exhaled slowly, the exhale of a man relieved to have shared a burden he had carried alone for a long time. Tikaya wished she could feel relieved. She had more to worry about than ever.

CHAPTER 3

MALDYNADO HUMMED TO HIMSELF AND stirred the soup pot while perusing the cookbook for a flat bread recipe that could be made quickly and wouldn't burn the way his first attempt had. The tiny kitchen had poor ventilation, and his eyes still stung from the lingering smoke. He prodded a sore spot on his bare chest where a piece of grease had spattered him earlier. Evrial was probably right that naked cooking wasn't smart, but he wanted to surprise her with dinner, and this was the one outfit he had that she never mocked.

He prodded a pectoral muscle speculatively. With little else to do while she worked, he had been training all winter. Not quite to Sicarius's standards, but he had kept his form. When Amaranthe came back, he would be ready to partake in whatever scheme she had in mind for their next adventure. *If* she came back. He had been certain she would, but it *had* been more than three months now...

In the other room, the tiny flat's *only* other room, a key turned in the lock. Ah, well, no time for bread. The chicken soup would have to do. After a long day at work, Evrial would doubtlessly be looking forward more to *relaxing* than eating anyway. And his current attire was appropriate for all kinds of relaxation.

Grabbing the soup pot, Maldynado strolled into the other room where he had already set their small two-person table. He halted in the doorway though, for Evrial wasn't alone. Two large brawny men had entered with her, one her age and one gray-haired, though both quite muscular.

They saw him before he had a chance to duck back into the kitchen and grab something to cover his love apples. Evrial gaped. The men gaped. From the similar nature of those gapes—and a few other similarities such as height, build, and noses—Maldynado realized these were relatives.

"Maldynado," Evrial hissed in exasperation, her face flushing brighter than the carrots in his soup.

"Good evening." Maldynado strolled to the table, determined to make the best of the moment. "I made dinner."

"This is my brother, Sovric, and my *father*." Evrial jerked her head toward the side of the room that held their bed and a wardrobe. "Put some clothes on."

Maldynado set the soup in the middle of the table, bowed toward the three of them, and strolled to the wardrobe. The brother's glower followed him, as if he wanted to charge across the room and pound on Maldynado. Well, he could *try*, but some rural metalsmith would hardly prove a threat. Still, Maldynado returned the glower with a friendly smile. No need to pick a fight, not with the relatives of one's lady.

"This is... *unacceptable*," Evrial's father said, not bothering to whisper. "You said he was a warrior-caste gentleman, not some brutish free-loading *nudist*."

"*Brutish?*" Maldynado protested, his hand in the wardrobe. Why certainly he had picked up a few scars on his adventures with Amaranthe, but nothing that detracted from his aesthetically pleasing physique. Despite a grease spatter here and there, he was clean and groomed—trimmed in all the right places—not some hairy behemoth from the mountains.

Evrial gripped her father's arm. "Let's wait outside until he's dressed. We can—"

"And look at this hovel you're living in," her father went on. "My daughter would choose to live in poverty with that, that *buffoon* when you could be back on the force at home."

"It's the city, Father. Of course, everything is more expensive. We're fine here. We—"

"The captain offered you a promotion! Lieutenant! You'd make more money and could rent a nice house there if you don't want to live with the family."

Maldynado paused, halfway into his trousers. She had been offered a promotion out in her own district? When had that happened? Why hadn't she said anything?

"I know, Father, but—"

"You're not staying here because of that *fop*, are you?" He thrust a finger at Maldynado, who did feel a touch foppish standing on one leg with his trousers around his ankles. "Does he even work? Contribute money? Isn't his family disgraced? Or in prison?"

"I'd vote for prison," the brother grumbled, giving Maldynado another glower. Brothers were always so terribly insufferable when men slept with their sisters.

"Not the *entire* family," Maldynado said.

The father glared at him, the brother glowered at him—it was more of a continuation of the same ongoing glower—and the two stomped outside. Evrial headed after them, though she paused in the doorway to look back at Maldynado.

"Thank you for making dinner."

"You're welcome. Will you be back to enjoy it?"

"I... hope so. Do remember to use your apron. I've told you before, cooking naked is dangerous." Though a sadness—almost a defeat—lurked in her eyes, she smiled and added, "Oaf."

Alone in the flat, Maldynado thought about trying again to make flat bread without turning it into a singed charcoal cake, but he sat down to contemplate Evrial's father's words instead. The man didn't know him, didn't know all the work he had done in the last year—Maldynado *deserved* a vacation. But, then, he had grown restless of vacationing after a few weeks, and he'd started to think of future adventures with the team. Even if half of the team was gone. More than half. Akstyr was studying in the Kyatt Islands. Basilard had gone back to reconnect with his daughter. Amaranthe and Sicarius were doing who knew what on some tropical beach. And Books...

Maldynado swallowed. With all of them gone, the city was drab. Bland. He was not a man who appreciated blandness. He also didn't appreciate that he had no income. Before Evrial... he had barely cared. He'd made do, offering his services to ladies for room and board and the opportunity to attend all sorts of fashionable events—Evrial had disabused him of the notion of returning to that line of work. But if he couldn't act as an escort, and he couldn't trade his handsome face and charm for items from women—Evrial also forbade this—he didn't quite know how to go about earning a living. Aside from dueling and thumping people, what could he do? He didn't even know how plebeians went about acquiring jobs. Not that he could imagine himself laboring from dawn to dusk in some factory anyway. He wanted to be... to do...

Maldynado huffed and pushed a hand through his hair. He didn't know. He couldn't stomach the idea of being some random worker or bouncer. Maybe he could ask President Starcrest for a job, something on his staff. Wasn't Maldynado owed some favor for the role he had played in helping to put the man into office? Not that he should need a favor; he was eminently qualified for... er... whatever the boss might come up with. He sighed. Amaranthe really needed to come back to town.

The door opened. Maldynado looked up warily. Evrial walked in alone.

"Apple brandy?" he offered, raising one of the tumblers he had poured. Once a week, he spent an hour smiling and passing out cards to affluent women at the Greenscale Market to earn his free samples. The fine drink should have been served in an aperitif glass, but these were the beverage holders that had come with their "tastefully furnished flat."

"Do I look like I need it?" Evrial plopped down in the opposite chair.

"Your *father* looked like he needed it. But he left before I could offer him a glass."

Evrial picked up a spoon and stirred and prodded her soup.

"Where did he go?" Maldynado asked. "And your surly brother? Is that the same one who greeted Amaranthe with a crossbow once?"

"No, that was Mevlar. This was Sovric. He's actually my favorite brother." Her face had grown glummer than a rainstorm.

Maldynado searched for words that might cheer her up. "You should try your soup. It's good." He supposed he should take a sip before making such claims.

"I will." Evrial continued to prod. "They're going to stay with smithing friends of my father's, since we don't have room, and because..."

"I'm here?"

She grunted, not taking her eyes from the soup bowl.

"Did you tell them about me beforehand?" Maldynado asked. "Or was I... unexpected?"

"Your *dress* state was unexpected." A fleeting smile touched her lips. "But if they'd warned me they were coming, I could have warned you. Not that you necessarily would have changed anything about your introduction."

"I would *too* have. I would have set four places at the table instead of two. And donned my apron."

"*Just* the apron?" Evrial asked.

"You told me I looked good in it."

"I believe what I said was that only you could manage to look good in a red rooster apron with real chicken feather fringes."

"Exactly," Maldynado said.

The smile flashed by again, but she didn't lift her eyes from the soup. Though he had worked hard at the meal, he doubted it was *that* engrossing.

"Anything I can do to get your family to approve of me?" Maldynado asked. "Besides wearing clothes?"

"Don't worry about them. You are who you are. You don't have to change yourself for them."

"That's a no, eh? They've already got their minds made up?"

"They like... solid, working class men, not those who were born into a gilded lifestyle."

"If it helps, Starcrest and his progressives are doing their best to strip the warrior caste of its influence. Pretty soon, we'll be nothing more than pretty faces with pretty surnames."

Evrial squinted at something in her bowl, or maybe at something in her mind. "Nobody's taking your land or money, or even your right to vote or hold office. All that's changed is that everyone else has a right to vote and hold office now too."

"Yes, Books is probably gloating from the spirit world. Meanwhile, the entire warrior caste is aghast and quite certain the nation's doom is written in the stars."

"Maldynado?"

"Yes?"

"Why are there grass clippings in the soup?"

"That's lemongrass. It's an imported delicacy. I had to schmooze a lot of grocers to get a free sample."

Evrial considered her spoon dubiously. "Isn't this chicken soup?"

"Yes, a recipe straight from Lady Stoatcrest's *Gastronomy Guide for Finishing School Pupils*." Maldynado tapped his jaw. "Have you ever noticed that most cookbooks in the empire aren't designed with the male chef in mind?"

"Perhaps that lack could explain the poor rations soldiers are always complaining about." Evrial braced herself, then took a sip of the soup. "Out of curiosity, would you ever find life in the bucolic countryside appealing?"

"Is this about that promotion you were offered that you didn't mention to me?"

"Maybe."

Maldynado tried to imagine himself moving to that tiny, tiny village Evrial's family lived in. What did people *do* there? One could only have sex so many times a day; after that, there had to be eating houses, taverns, theaters, baths, and gymnasiums to visit. "I thought your association with us had... soured your superiors on you over there," he said, hoping she wouldn't notice that he had avoided answering her question.

"It had, but the captain and lieutenant have both been replaced. I heard that, with the change of government, a lot of old complaints about enforcer corruption, negligence, and cronyism came to light for the first time." Her jaw tightened. "I wish I could say none of that existed, but I wasn't surprised when Starcrest assigned some civilian specialists to run inquisitions and it turned up... much. In the last few weeks, numerous promotions have been offered to those with solid records. Apparently my association with Lokdon ended up being a bright point on mine." Her expression changed to one of bemusement.

"Guess she made an impression on the president."

"Yes. So... if I want a lieutenant's position back home... it's mine." Evrial lifted her gaze, meeting his eyes for the first time that night. Was she holding her breath? Cursed ancestors, was this what she wanted? A dream fulfilled? And she wanted him to come be a part of it. That was good, but, smashed and dented ore carts, the *country*?

"I must offer you my congratulations, certainly," Maldynado said, trying to buy time, "but... couldn't you get that promotion here? You've been working in the NoDoc District all winter. I'd thought... well, I guess I thought you wanted to stay in the city."

Evrial's earnest expression faltered, her gaze dropping to his chest. "There aren't any lieutenant's positions opening up here. I'd have to wait for someone to get promoted or to retire."

"Or to get eaten by that plant," Maldynado said cheerfully. "That might start happening soon. I hear that thing's getting bigger and bigger every day. It's bound to start chomping on enforcers soon, and then there'll be all sorts of positions available."

She met his eyes again, but this time with irritation. "Be serious, Maldynado. If you aren't willing to move for me, say so. I won't be happy about it, but I'll understand. You're not doing anything with your life, and this is a big opportunity for me, but... Never mind. It's not as if I expected this—us—to last."

"What's that supposed to mean? We've been having a nice time this winter."

"Yes, but you keep muttering, 'I wonder when the boss'll be back.' 'Have to stay in shape in case the boss comes back soon.' 'I bet the boss will have some great new adventures planned when she gets back.'"

"That doesn't mean I want us to... not be an us any more."

"How do you think it makes me feel when your tide rises and falls for another woman?" Evrial dropped her spoon and pushed her chair back with an audible scrape.

"It doesn't," Maldynado protested. "And Amaranthe is hardly a woman, not like *that*. It's just that... emperor's warts, I don't know what I'm supposed to do with myself right now, all right?" And that curse didn't work any more, blast it. The whole world was upside down and confusing as a hedge maze right now.

"Why don't you try getting a job like everyone else?" Evrial grabbed her jacket and headed for the door.

"I don't want to be like everyone else. I want a statue." Maldynado frowned at himself; he hadn't meant to say that. It sounded ludicrous. It always had. But it had always been a joke. Hadn't it? Why couldn't he let it go?

"Oh, grow up, Maldynado." Evrial stomped out and slammed the door.

He sat down hard in his chair and shoveled a spoonful of soup into his mouth. He curled his lip at a brown soggy thing he bit down on. "Guess Lady Stoatcrest was wrong. This recipe doesn't tantalize and delight the female palate at all."

The joke fell on a silent room. He pushed the bowl away. Evrial's words echoed in his head. *Grow up. You're not doing anything with your life.*

She wasn't wrong, was she? Hadn't he just been thinking that he needed to find meaningful employment? Maybe if he got... a job, a good job that required him to stay in the city, she would be willing to stay too. He didn't want to ignore her dream, but couldn't she eventually get that promotion here? There was more going on in the city than out in Rural District Number Seven or wherever it was her family lived. She would have more opportunity to stand out and for advancement here.

He would be doing her a favor. And... and... if her father thought she should have a nice house, well, he could figure out a way to get her that here too. He would ask Starcrest for a job, an *important* job. The only problem was that he wasn't sure he could get in to *see* the president in a timely matter. He'd admittedly made a pest of himself at that funeral. If he could talk to Starcrest, he might be able to convince the man to give him a chance, but...

"You just need to find someone you're sure can get in the door." Maldynado drummed his fingers on the table. "With the boss gone, that leaves one person you know as a sure thing."

Maldynado finished dressing and headed for the door. Time to go a-visiting.

Sespian dodged the jab, blocked the punch, and stepped in behind it to thrust a jab of his own at the bare ribs. His knuckles grazed them, but Maldynado moved quickly for a large man, and he leaped back, spinning to face Sespian again, his fists raised. A judge might have awarded a point, but the light tap hadn't even knocked the smile off Maldynado's face, so Sespian readied himself to try again. Maldynado tapped his ribs to acknowledge the hit.

"You'd be dangerous if you trained more than once a month," he said.

Sespian had scored more blows than he had in the past when sparring or wrestling with Maldynado, not that there had been time for much training on that whirlwind of chaos Amaranthe had swept him through last fall. Still, he had the sense that Maldynado was being easy on him.

"I'm studying to be an architect," Sespian said. "If I ever find myself boxing with my clients, it'll mean I failed dreadfully somewhere along the way."

"In which case, it would be useful to be able to defend yourself. What if the roof falls in on some house you designed, and the cranky retired soldier-owner unleashes his battering rams on you?" Maldynado tapped his fists together. Apparently, he considered those battering rams.

"I can defend myself against most people adequately," Sespian said a touch stiffly. He had let himself be talked into this evening at the gymnasium more because of Sergeant Yara's pleading tone than anything Maldynado had said. He didn't care to receive lectures during his recreational time. He had *thought* they would go straight to the baths and steam rooms.

"Hm." Maldynado smiled and waded in, leading with a barrage of punches.

The sudden frenzy surprised Sespian, and he almost took the first fist in the face. He danced back, though, giving himself time to recover. The ring marked the boundary, and he could only retreat so far, but he soon had his rhythm and blocked each blow without giving more ground. Maldynado had six inches on him and tried to press in, to intimidate him into backing out of the ring. Sespian waited for his moment, then, after deflecting a chain of blows so hard that jolts ran up his forearms, he threw extra weight into his last block, forcing Maldynado's arm across his chest. He swept his leg in at the same time as he grabbed Maldynado's shoulder from behind, pulling with his arm and thrusting with his hip, intending to throw him to the ground. But Maldynado writhed like a greased snake, and Sespian lost his grip. Before he knew what had happened, he found himself on the ground with a foot on his chest.

Sespian sighed. "I did say *most* people."

"Yes, you did." Maldynado winked, removed his foot, and offered a hand.

Sespian accepted it—he had received a lecture in the end after all, a physical one, but he had deserved it. Maldynado had spent a year training with Sicarius; Sespian should have treated him more warily.

"Let's get washed and prettied up for the ladies," Maldynado said.

"I haven't a lady to impress, but Trog might be pleased by a clean bedmate."

Maldynado stared at him. "That's... the cat?"

"Yes."

"Why are you sleeping with the cat?"

"He's the only one who tormented Ravido during his unsanctioned rule. I believe he deserves a lofty station."

"I, ah... yes." Maldynado started down the hall toward the baths and steam rooms. "But I'm perplexed. I thought you and Starcrest's daughter were... enjoying each other's company."

Sespian tripped over an invisible crack. "What? No, of course not. Not in any way that involves beds." Whatever had caused Maldynado to reach that conclusion? "The other day, when you saw us together, it was because she had asked for help with the plant."

"Sespian, that's... a very capable young lady. When a girl like that asks a man for help, it's because what she really wants is his company. And probably to make him feel good about himself. In her presence. *Because* of her presence."

Sespian snorted. "Does Sergeant Yara ask you for help?"

"I'm still waiting." Maldynado held the door open for Sespian, and they walked into the changing rooms. Already clad in sparring togs, they did not take long to undress and grab towels. "Does this mean you're not planning to visit the president's hotel anytime soon?" Maldynado asked.

"Not unless she asks me to."

Maldynado scratched his jaw thoughtfully as they passed into the baths, steam hazing the air, the walls dotted with moisture. "I suppose you could gain access of your own accord, based on your unique former status."

Sespian was about to ask what he meant, but he spotted a familiar face among the men sitting at one of the steaming pools. Professor Edgecrest. Despite sitting in a relaxing area, he looked grumpier than he did when grading the test papers of particularly challenged students. Several of the men around him shared equally dyspeptic expressions, to such an extent that Sespian wondered if something was wrong with the water.

"Good evening, Professor," Sespian said, slowing down. Maldynado was heading toward the larger, cooler pool to swim. "Is everything all right?"

Edgecrest and the three men on either side of him rotated toward Sespian as one. They were all middle-aged and older gentlemen who, judging by the slack muscles and potbellies, preferred academia to soldiering or other physical labor.

One sneered at him. "Look who strolled by to gloat."

Sespian glanced over his shoulder, expecting Maldynado or someone else to be the subject of this comment. There wasn't anyone behind him. "Pardon me?"

Edgecrest nudged the surly one with an elbow. "Don't be insolent, Klav."

"Insolent? To an eighteen-year-old boy? Who just happens to personally *know* the judge?"

Sespian would have corrected the man—he was twenty, thanks to a recent birthday—but he was too bewildered to bother.

Edgecrest's elbow thumped into his comrade's ribs again, this time with enough force to quiet him. "Congratulations, Sespian. It'll be a privilege to see your concept turned into reality." He lifted a finger and pointed it at Sespian's nose. "But don't think that means you'll get out of the work you promised me. Not to mention your studies. You still have a lot to learn."

Sespian's mouth had been dropping farther and farther open while the professor spoke. "I... Sir? I won? The design competition for the president's... I won?"

"I think I'm going to throw up," the surly man muttered.

"Be gracious," the fellow next to him said. "He'll probably be your boss someday. Again."

"Cursed nepotism."

Sespian frowned at the men and thought about confronting the surly one, but Professor Edgecrest sighed and explained first.

"You're looking at some of the contest losers. Some of them have been working in the business for three or four decades."

"Oh," Sespian said, feeling sheepish. No wonder they'd found his delighted wonder at the news irritating. "I'm sure they had brilliant entries, and it was just luck that favored me."

"Luck or knowing the judge," Surly muttered.

Sespian lifted his chin. "I was told the judging was done blind, without names on the designs."

"Sure it was."

Some of Sespian's sheepishness was fading. It would be childish, he supposed, to shove the sneering man into the pool, and even less acceptable to hold his head under.

"Sespian, you coming?" Maldynado called from the large pool. "I need to ask you something."

"Good evening, Professor. Gentlemen." Sespian was proud that he kept his tone cordial.

He was even more proud—and stunned—that he had won. He had only dared hope to make a good showing. Sure, he would have to finish his formal schooling, but maybe he could look forward to a successful career sooner rather than later. Clients might start offering him work before he finished his education. He had no delusions about becoming wealthy as an architect, but he could at least afford better scraps for Trog.

By the time he hopped into the water beside Maldynado, he had forgotten the surly architects.

"Listen, Sespian," Maldynado said. "I could use a favor. I need to get in to see President Starcrest, and I thought if you were visiting with his daughter, well, I could come with you and sort of slip in between his appointments."

Busy dwelling on the ramifications of his victory, Sespian almost missed Maldynado's words. "Slip in?" he asked after a moment. "Why can't you get an appointment on your own? He'd see you."

"I am... less confident of that than you are. I may have tried a little too hard at Books's funeral, going on about statues. And then there was that incident with Evrial and me barging into that office while there was a meeting going on..." Maldynado cleared his throat. "It's possible he thinks I'm a buffoon."

Sespian decided not to mention that he'd often thought that of Maldynado as well. "I'm not seeing Mahliki, at least not in any capacity that would cause me to call upon her at home. I, ah... might check on her though, as I'm surprised she hasn't contacted me yet for the diving suit mission. It's possible she's found another. I wasn't as... enthusiastic about helping as I might have been. At the time, I was still finishing up with—"

"Sespian, if you can help me get into see Starcrest, I'll help you get the girl."

"But I'm not trying to get the girl."

Maldynado rolled his eyes. "Why *not*? She's pretty and smart and *your age*." He emphasized this final fact with a pointed stare.

So, everyone on the team had learned of Sespian's past... infatuation with Amaranthe. How lovely. He was over that now, though. He had smiled at a few of the women he'd passed in the halls at the university, and some had even smiled back. Of course, every time he had chatted with someone, the conversations had ended up on such subjects as homework, tests, and overbearing parents—all trite topics after the life-and-death situations he had survived. Sespian had found himself more likely to converse with his professors, people who didn't intimidate him the way they did the other students, not after he had grown up around sword-spitting generals. But neither fifty-year-old professors nor sword-spitting generals tended to interest him on romantic levels, so his winter had been rather... chaste.

"Actually, she's two years younger than I am," Sespian said, "and I think you're mistaken that her interest lies this way. Given my... dubious heritage and current circumstances, her parents wouldn't consider me a suitable suitor for their daughter." Not to mention that the idea of approaching President Starcrest and asking if he could court Mahliki was terrifying. The man hadn't said a cross word to him, but Sespian couldn't help but feel inadequate around the war hero. He was someone who had deserved to rule a nation all along. Sespian had never been more than a pretender, a day-dreaming callow one at that.

Maldynado snorted. "First off, I don't know what century you think you're living in, but I highly doubt the Starcrests are going to arrange a marriage for her or have much say whatsoever in who she sees. Second, girls that age don't pay attention to the wishes of their fathers anyway. Lastly—" Maldynado turned his head, frowning at something behind them.

A draft of cold air gusted across Sespian's bare shoulders, and he sank lower into the pool. Maldynado's hand landed on his head, shoving him under. Water deluged his nostrils, his backside slipped off the seat, and he almost cracked his skull on the concrete.

Sespian swam out of Maldynado's reach before coming up, wondering what stray boulder had knocked his ore cart off its tracks. He swiped water from his eyes, clearing his vision in time to see Maldynado's backside as he sprinted through the steam toward the changing rooms.

Surprise gave way to wariness. Just because nobody had tried to assassinate him for a while didn't mean it couldn't ever happen. He peered around for clues and spotted one of the grumpy architects walking over to a potted banana tree. He plucked an arrow from the dirt, its fletching bright with green and blue. Even from a distance, Sespian knew it wasn't a Turgonian design. He peered back and forth from the pot to the changing room doors. Direct line, and his head would have been in it. He might owe Maldynado a bigger favor than getting him in to see the president.

Several other people grabbed towels and stomped in the direction Maldynado had gone, either to find the idiot shooting arrows into the baths or to get out of there before more trouble came. In Turgonia, it could go either way.

The architect tossed the arrow into the pool in front of Sespian. "I believe that was meant for you."

"I gathered that, thank you." Sespian squinted at the man, wondering if he was disappointed it hadn't taken his head off, or if he might have even had prior knowledge of the attack. There wasn't a monetary prize attached to winning the design competition, and it was hard to believe someone would kill over losing, but he had seen crazier things.

After delivering the arrow, the man merely shrugged and walked back to the other architects, grabbing a towel and pointing back and forth from the pot to the doorway, pantomiming what had happened for those who hadn't seen it. Surely a guilty man would charge out of there as quickly as possible—and wouldn't have drawn attention to himself by retrieving the arrow. An arrow, Sespian realized, that had paper tied around the shaft. He plucked it out, lest whatever message it contained be dissolved in the water.

Feeling vulnerable in the pool—alone now, for everyone else had retreated from the baths—Sespian climbed out. He wrapped a towel around himself and put his back to an alcove, one that would let him watch the rest of the chamber—and keep an eye on those doors—while examining the arrow more closely. More specifically, he untied the note.

In crisp, tidy penmanship, it read, *I did not have to miss. You owe me your life. I may wish to collect a favor.* It wasn't signed, but at the bottom of the small page, the language switched for the final two lines. It reminded him of Nurian, but he would have been able to read Nurian, most of it anyway. This… was gibberish to him. As was the notion that he ought to owe someone a favor for threatening his life, though it did seem in line with what he knew of Nurian logic. He examined the fletching again. The brightness of the feathers could have been Nurian, for that culture loved its colors, but it hadn't come off a traditional war bow—the texts said those always had crimson-feathered arrows. The arrowhead had been napped from obsidian, and when he brushed an edge with his thumb, it drew blood.

"Reinforced and sharpened with magic?" he wondered.

Akstyr would have known if he were around, but Professor Komitopis might know as well. Also, she should be able to translate the rest of the note.

The steam by the changing rooms stirred, and Sespian tensed, ready to use the arrow for a weapon if he had to. But it was Maldynado jogging back toward him, grimacing and grabbing at his foot every few steps. His hand came away bloody. He hadn't stopped to put on any clothes or even grab a towel.

"Didn't get him," Maldynado said, "sorry."

"Did you see who made the shot?" Sespian held up the arrow.

"Sort of. Not when he made it though. It was too steamy back there. But I heard the back door clang when I ran into the changing room, and I sprinted out into the alley. I wouldn't have seen a thing if I hadn't had a hunch and looked up. Someone lean and fast and dressed all in white with a bow on his back was climbing over the lip of the five-story building next door. I scrambled up the wall, but by the time I reached the roof, that white figure was five buildings away. He glanced back, saw me, then jumped down into the next alley. How he could have heard me following, I don't know, because I'm not an amateur at such things, even if I wasn't—ahem!—properly clothed. Anyway, he must have had a rope or something I couldn't see, because nobody jumps off a five-story building."

"All in white, you say?" Sespian asked. "I guess it wasn't Sicarius then."

Maldynado snorted. "I thought you'd gotten over the notion that he might try to kill you someday."

"I have, but your description... that just sounds like him."

Maldynado scraped wet hair out of his eyes. "Yes, I guess it does. Isn't that just what we need? Another Sicarius in the world."

Sespian stared at the arrow for another moment, but it didn't offer further enlightenment. Not to *his* eyes anyway. He hoped the weapon would tell a different tale to Professor Komitopis.

"That meeting with Starcrest you wanted," Sespian said, "are you available tonight?"

"I can go right now." Maldynado peered down at himself. "I might put on clothes first."

"Yes... I believe the president's office may have a dress code."

CHAPTER 4

THE NIGHT AIR SMELLED OF jungle foliage, a strange scent for a lake bordering a city of a million people, and in a climate zone more suitable for oak and maple trees. Sicarius crouched on the hull of the submarine, the raised hatch at his back. Down below, Amaranthe was piloting the craft toward the docks. A niggling feeling made him want to tell her to veer toward another port. Though spring had come and the lake ice had melted, meaning berths on the waterfront should be accessible, dozens of ships were anchored a quarter mile or more from the shoreline, their masts and steam stacks creating a noticeable skyline against the flat, barren remains of Fort Urgot to the north.

Clouds obscured the stars, and Sicarius had only the gas streetlights of the city to rely upon to make out the waterfront. Interestingly, lamps that should have been lit along its main street were dark. The shadows held... he wasn't sure, but more than pilings and docks rose up from the lake. Whatever lay over there, it might be the reason Starcrest had requested the return of the submarine.

"Amaranthe," he called down. "We may want to dock to the north of the city."

"Uhm, just a minute."

Sicarius ducked his head through the hatchway. Amaranthe wasn't at the controls.

"Are you cleaning again?" he asked.

"No." A cupboard door clanged shut, the cupboard in the back—his ears told him—that contained a mop, broom, and various scrubbing implements. "Tidying perhaps."

"The *Explorer* is sufficiently clean."

"I know. But I want to return it in good order." Amaranthe trotted past, heading for navigation. "Now what were you saying? Dock north? I thought you were eager to head straight into town, so we could do all the things we've missed out on for so long. Visit fine eating houses, see the latest plays, catch the spring wrestling matches, shop for a certain blend of tea..."

Sicarius snorted softly. On the way back, he *had* missed the intimate moments—intimate *hours*, he corrected with a measure of satisfaction—that they had enjoyed for most of the trip. But they must learn if the city was in danger before succumbing to somatic pleasures. As well, he felt compelled to promptly return the borrowed submarine. Admiral—*President*—Starcrest had been generous to loan it to them.

"If we dock in front of the old Fort Urgot grounds," Sicarius said, "it is only a five-mile jog to the city." He waited for her to make a comment in relation to his use of the word jog, something about his over eagerness to return to an exercise regimen so soon. Only she would say it in a humorous way.

Except she didn't. For a long moment, Amaranthe said nothing, and a twinge of disappointment filled him. He reviewed his words to see if he could have said something that disturbed her. Ah, yes. Fort Urgot represented an immense emotional burden for her.

"That's... not a part of the lake I want to visit again for some time. Or forever." Her words sounded strained. She had probably wished them to sound nonchalant, but she couldn't hide the feeling—the *pain*—behind them.

Sicarius considered alternatives that wouldn't require them to visit that destination. "I do not believe we'll be able to dock on the waterfront. There are piers on the other side of the lake by the ice mining camps, but that would require a much longer jog." One that would still take them past Fort Urgot unless they took the longer route around the south end of the lake. In regard to emotional burdens, he found he did not particularly wish to revisit those ice camps. An illogical feeling, but he knew they would remind him of the night he had fought the soul construct, thought he had lost Sespian and Amaranthe forever, and had allowed himself to be enslaved by that wizard. "We could pull into a cove to the south of the city and swim to shore."

Another long pause followed before Amaranthe responded. As they had conversed, the submarine had continued to sail closer to the city's waterfront, and Sicarius could make out shapes in between the docks. Elongated trees growing out of the lake? That couldn't be right. He wished he had his spyglass, but that had also been among the items the pirates stole.

"Here I wanted to head straight to a hotel for a nice evening with you, and all you can talk about is jogging and swimming," Amaranthe said, having recovered some of her humor.

"It is my understanding that the tea takes a couple of days before it is effective," Sicarius said. "It also seems unlikely that you could find someone to purchase it from this late at night."

"Have I ever said how charming I find your practicality?"

"No," Sicarius said, anticipating her next word, his own humor piqued.

"Good." A soft thrum vibrated through the hull, and he sensed their course turning before Amaranthe added, "I'm taking us toward that cove where we trained with the bricks last summer. You'll have to direct me though. It's darker than—gah!"

Sicarius had been focused on the waterfront, on trying to make out what exactly was growing between the docks, but he peered through the hatchway to check on Amaranthe. "What—"

Something thumped against the hull. A log?

"Cursed ancestors," Amaranthe said, "there's more than one." Her words came out fast and clipped.

Sicarius stood for a better look ahead but couldn't see into the dark waters. The submarine had a probe light that illuminated the area in front of the nose, but choppy waves broke up the white blur, making it impossible to see details beneath the surface from his viewpoint. Whatever they had hit, it wasn't some log floating on the top. He slipped inside to join Amaranthe at the controls.

She stood frozen, staring through the viewport. Several strands of green seaweed stretched across the Science-enhanced glass, as well as a human arm—what remained of it. Fish had been nibbling at it for several days. It drifted away, not to bother them further. Sicarius wondered if the seaweed could become entangled in the rudder and affect the submarine's steering ability.

"I do not recognize that species," he observed.

"Of seaweed or arm?"

"Seaweed," Sicarius said before the sarcasm in her tone registered.

"There are other body parts tangled up in there," Amaranthe said. "The first thing that hit us was a man's torso with the head... there were tendrils of that—whatever that is—growing out of the eye sockets." She released the controls and rubbed her face with both hands. "Talk about an abrupt end to your vacation."

Sicarius considered her, wondering if this was a time when she would appreciate a hug or other gesture of physical support. She shouldn't have an emotional attachment to the bodies, unless they later discovered the parts belonged to someone they knew, but she clearly found their appearance distressing. Before he had decided one way or another, she took a deep breath and returned to the controls.

"Let me see if I can steer out of this, or if this whole end of the lake is full of mutilated bodies wrapped in seaweed," Amaranthe said, her composure regained. "If the latter, then I think Starcrest should have ordered a whole *fleet* of submarines to help."

Sicarius waited to see if they would have further trouble steering through the mess, but they soon pushed into clear water again.

"Some random tangle," Amaranthe said.

"That may be what's growing out of the water by the waterfront," Sicarius said. "Though from what I could make out in the dark, some of it seemed quite tall, almost like small trees."

"Seaweed trees, wonderful." Amaranthe waved toward the hatchway. "I'm fine. Go direct me to that cove, please."

Sicarius inclined his head, but paused before heading up the ladder. "For my edification, when you chance across bodies or body parts, is that a time for physical contact of an emotionally bracing nature?"

A faint smile crept across her face. "You mean, should you have hugged me?"

"Yes."

"I've seen enough bodies at this point to get over it on my own, though if you're inclined, you could put a hand on my shoulder or stand close or something. When you're looking into the eyes of death, it's nice to be reminded that you're not alone."

"Hm." Sicarius could not recall ever experiencing that need, but much of his boyhood training had revolved around desensitizing him to death and human emotions. His mentors had considered that training a success; Amaranthe, he suspected, would have another opinion on the matter.

Sicarius climbed up, again crouching on the hull with the hatch at his back. They hadn't reached the other ships yet, and he doubted anyone out there on the water would be hurling an attack at him, but old habits dictated current actions. He scanned the dark shoreline to the south of the city, its trees, rocky shores, and cliffs. By night, it would be easy to miss that cove, but he had jogged around the lake so many times that he knew the location of every feature along its shore. He guided Amaranthe with confidence.

A hint of orange light appeared through the trees. A lantern? It was part way up a promontory, one that thrust into the lake, its tip a good quarter mile from the trail that circled the body of water. Someone caught out late and walking on the popular route shouldn't have a reason to detour up that steep, rocky slope, though he did recall that a path led up to the top. Had someone seen the submarine? And been curious enough to climb up for a look? Given the black non-reflective paint Starcrest had used on the hull, it seemed unlikely, but Sicarius had been riding with the hatch open. Faint light from inside might be visible on the shore. The fact that this lantern was waiting at the north end of the cove he was directing them toward... he found it unlikely that it was a coincidence.

"More strange seaweed," Amaranthe announced from inside.

"Body parts?" Sicarius asked softly, not wanting his voice to carry to shore.

"A buoy from a ship and a piece of the wooden hull of a fishing boat. I've never seen seaweed that likes to collect souvenirs from its travels."

Sicarius, focused on the cliff, did not answer. The lantern light disappeared. It hadn't moved out of sight—there shouldn't be anywhere to hide on that bare rock—so it had gone out. Been *put* out. In his black clothing, he shouldn't stand out, but someone knew he was watching.

Perhaps nothing. To a local unaware of the existence of Starcrest's submarine, he must appear a strange sight drifting across the lake. Someone might report them to the local garrison—wherever it had been moved to—believing them spies sneaking up on the city at night.

Sicarius called out a few more soft directions to Amaranthe, and they soon glided into the cove. The *Explorer* drifted to a stop twenty meters from the bank.

Amaranthe stuck her head through the hatchway. "That's as close as I can get us without risking grounding the sub." She peered past him. "The water looks cold. I don't suppose you'd like to practice your swimming skills by carrying me above your head? And the luggage as well."

He thought about pointing out that they would not need to swim if she hadn't chosen this cove over the dock in front of the Fort Urgot remains. But he understood her reasoning. Besides, he wanted to see who carried that lantern.

"I will go ahead and check for danger." Sicarius slipped off into the water.

"Danger? Is there more seaweed around?"

He did not respond. After the warm tropical waters of the southern climes, the icy temperature shocked his system, encouraging him to start moving immediately. He would have to resume training and reacclimatize his body as soon as possible.

He swam underwater, not wanting the sound of surface-level kicks and strokes to reach whatever ears might be waiting on land. His fingers soon brushed the pebbly bottom. He patted around until he found a boulder that would hide his approach from someone in the trees or on the promontory. Despite the cold, he lifted only his head at first, listening, looking, and smelling the air before leaving the camouflaging water. He didn't hear anything beyond the rustlings of the grasses in the breeze and an owl hooting in the distance. This close to the city, he could smell little more than coal smoke from stoves and that unfamiliar jungle vegetation.

Once in the trees, Sicarius paused again to listen and smell. For an instant, he detected the faint fumes of kerosene, though the scents from the city almost overpowered them. Trusting his nose, he glided into the woods, like a hound after his prey. He came out of the brush near the wide running trail and hunkered down, gazing up and down the route, a hand to the earth. The soft crushed-brick surface had been recently re-laid, but not so recently that he might pick out fresh prints from amongst the hundreds that trod the route every day. Still, the freshness was a clue that whatever might have occurred in the city in his absence, this routine maintenance had not been neglected. Again following his nose, he crossed the trail and weaved through maples and aspens, tiny leaves budding from their branches. The scent of a recently snuffed lamp grew stronger. There, he spotted a lump against a tree, one with the blocky dimensions of a man-made item rather than the contours of nature.

A quick touch confirmed that he had located the lamp, its metal hull still warm from use, but nothing else waited on the forest floor. He patted around in the fresh spring grass and found some of the blades bent. Something had been resting in the spot. A rucksack? Someone had come out here prepared. Prepared for what?

Sicarius leaned close to the grass, inhaling with soft sniffs. A faint odor lingered. Black powder? No, not exactly. It was more like...

He bolted to his feet. Blasting sticks.

He had handled them often enough to recognize the scent. Whoever was out here... they weren't simply strolling along the lake, watching for spies.

Sicarius ran through the trees, forcing himself not to sprint so quickly he made noise, though concern for Amaranthe made him want to charge with reckless abandon. The submarine was the only thing out here one might employ blasting sticks on, and she might still be gathering their gear inside it. He leaped a log and was about to sprint onto the beach, when a dot of light drew his eye. It was up on the promontory again.

Though he suspected he was too late, he veered in that direction. He could hope he was wrong about the blasting sticks or that the person missed, but—

The dot of light spun away from the top of the rocks, arcing toward the submarine. Sicarius almost changed direction again, to run out to check on Amaranthe, but he would be another target down there. That person might have a whole bundle of sticks.

A soft clang sounded—the stick hitting the sub? Boulders blocked his view. He hoped the explosive had struck the hull and bounced off.

He charged up the rocky slope like a panther, bounding meters with each step. Just as he crested the highest part and the ground flattened, a boom roared and orange light fired the sky from below. Though tempted to sprint to the edge to check on the submarine—*Amaranthe*—the figure crouching at the end of the cliff, preparing a second blasting stick consumed all of his attention. If he had hurt Amaranthe...

In his haste, Sicarius didn't watch every footfall, and he landed on gravel that crunched softly. After the explosion, the noise was almost insignificant, but the crouching figure turned its head. A white cloak and cowl hid the person's face and any distinguishing features; it almost hid the movements of the figure's hands as he jumped to his feet. The blasting stick that had been meant to descend into the cove was hurled at Sicarius. He ducked and kept running. The figure jumped off the end of the cliff. Sicarius would have jumped after him, but the stick exploded behind him.

The force of it pummeled him in the back. He rolled with the power, using it to propel himself forward, and he jumped to his feet at the edge of the cliff. The rocky shoals below came into view, but the cove did as well, and that sight made him freeze.

The hull hadn't been torn open—there was nothing to burn on the steel ship, and the light from the first explosion had faded—but a dense pillar of smoke roiled from the open hatch. And that hatch was all that remained above water. Most of the hull had disappeared. It was sinking. With Amaranthe within? He scanned the beach, but nothing stirred out in the open.

Sicarius stared down at the water beneath the cliff. Had their cloaked attacker come to the surface, he might have leaped down and given chase, but nothing moved down there, either. The waters were choppy in the aftermath of the explosion, but he should have been able to spot a head. Any sign that another person had been there had disappeared.

Sicarius turned his back on the water and ran down to the beach, searching and listening for Amaranthe. He was about to charge into the lake again, to swim out to the submarine, but he halted on the pebbles. The craft had disappeared beneath the waves. He would have waded out anyway, but a familiar scent drifted on the breeze. Amaranthe's shampoo, one she had picked up on one of the islands they had visited: hibiscus and coconut. The scent of the latter he found pungent and easy to identify, and his nose led him up the coast.

"Did you catch him?" Amaranthe asked from the trees as he approached.

"No."

"You probably should have, because your luggage was still on board. I grabbed mine and planned to go back for your collection of black shirts, trousers, and boots, until, ah... someone threw a blasting stick in the submarine."

Sicarius drew close enough to pick out her form—and that of the duffel bag at her feet—in a copse of trees. She had chosen a spot where her back was protected. Good. From her voice, she did not sound hurt, but she was jumping up and down and swinging her arms. In agitation? Irritation at him for not capturing the one who had attacked her? He shared that irritation—that person must have doubled back after dropping off the lantern, intentionally hoping to lose him perhaps. Or maybe it had been ill luck and the person hadn't realized he was out there; instead, he had hoped to catch Sicarius still in the submarine. Had the attack been meant for him? Or Amaranthe? Or the Science-powered contraption itself?

Sicarius stretched out a hand. "Are you injured?"

"No, but this would be a good time for that hug."

He stepped closer. "Because you were emotionally upset by the attack?"

"Because I'm *cold*." Amaranthe flung herself into him, like a cat burrowing into a pile of blankets. "The calendar might say it's spring here, but I bet it's still frosty in the mornings."

"Likely." Sicarius wrapped his arms around her, though physical exertion would be a more efficient way of generating body heat. They ought to jog into the city to report to Starcrest promptly, though the idea of explaining that the submarine he had loaned them was at the bottom of the lake... Sicarius felt a renewed sense of failure. Perhaps on this vacation, he had allowed himself to relax too much, to grow less attentive. To have been fooled by this other person was unacceptable.

"How many people were up there?" Amaranthe's teeth chattered.

"One." Sicarius nudged her duffel bag with his foot. "You should change into dry clothing."

"Yes, I know." She pulled away from him, reluctantly, he thought, and dug into the bag.

He should have dragged his own gear out before slipping into the water, but the attack on the submarine had been unforeseen.

"And how did this one person know where we were going to anchor?" Amaranthe pulled out a shirt and trousers that had remained perfectly folded despite being stuffed in a bag. "*We* didn't even know when we came out of the river. Nor did we know exactly when we'd return. Do you think Starcrest told people we were coming back? So someone could have been waiting? But why would he do that?"

"Someone sensitive to the Science could have detected the sub's approach."

"Oh, right, because of the magic power source. That thing's big too. Or it *was*." Amaranthe frowned toward the lake. No telltale glow illuminated the water. "It must put out a large... aura. Is that the right term?"

"Sufficient."

"But it takes longer to run along the lake than it does to sail across it in the sub. How did this person figure out where we were going *and* beat us here?"

"A bicycle perhaps. I did not smell the smoke from a nearby lorry." Sicarius wished he had answers for all of her questions. He had already been making a lot of unfounded guesses. That someone could sense the sub's power source was not inconceivable, but to have sensed it from miles away? Even with artifacts and constructs being rare here, that would take an incredibly strong practitioner. More likely the person had been watching the river and waiting for them to come in. But who would have known to lie in wait? How many people had Starcrest told of their return? And *why* would one of them have wanted the submarine destroyed? "It is imperative that we report to the president."

"I agree. And you were right about something else. Spending all that time cleaning the sub wasn't necessary." She waved to the cove, where all sign of the craft had disappeared from sight.

Sicarius, gazing out toward the water where the figure had jumped in—where he had *lost* his prey—did not answer.

Amaranthe finished changing and fastened the duffel bag. "I wonder if there's any chance someone on the president's staff could do my laundry." She hefted the bag. "Seeing as we don't have a place of our own to stay in yet. Or jobs to *pay* for a place."

Sicarius took the bag from her before she could sling it on her back. They had three or four miles to march, and they could go faster if he carried the extra burden. And since his failure with their attacker meant he had no bags of his own to carry...

"Thank you," Amaranthe said, sounding faintly surprised. "Is that because you're being a gentleman and wish to do kind things for me or because you know we'll go faster if you carry the heavy things?"

"Yes." Sicarius trotted into the trees, angling toward the trail.

Amaranthe jogged to catch up. "Just so you're aware, I *know* you'll give me that answer whenever I ask questions like that, and I do it anyway because the ambiguity lets me choose to apply your response to the option that most suits me."

That comment was almost twisty enough to challenge a reader of one of Starcrest's advanced tactics and strategies books. Sicarius had heard enough of them to catch the gist though. "If you wish to see me as a gentleman, Amaranthe, I will not object."

"Good." They came out on the jogging path and picked up their pace, running side-by-side. Amaranthe nudged him with her elbow. "Just so you know, a gentleman steps forward to take the blame when a president wants to know how his submarine came to be blown up."

Sicarius had already intended to accept the blame for that, though he dreaded making the confession to someone who doubtlessly would have been clever enough to outthink that saboteur. Still, he sensed Amaranthe was teasing him and sought an appropriate reply.

"You believe he will not lend you his laundress if he thinks you are responsible?"

Amaranthe chuckled softly. "I fear he'll instruct said laundress to throw me in the bucket and grate me over the wash board."

That she could find the humor in this situation wasn't surprising, and it pleased him, for during that first month after Books's funeral, he had worried her spirit would remain dampened. For now, though, Sicarius could not share her mirth. As they headed toward the outskirts of the city, he kept all of his senses alert to the night, to any other danger that might be lurking in it. Their vacation was over.

Mahliki strode down the carpeted hallway with as much determination as she could, given that she carried a fifty-pound brass diving helmet. She intended to thunk it down on her father's desk. For emphasis. She had tried one of the diving suits in a bathing pool in the basement, and she had been ready to launch her expedition for two days. But she hadn't been allowed out of the *hotel* for two days. She had tried multiple times to walk out, but kept bumping into security guards that referred her to Colonel Dak Starcrest, a cousin she vaguely remembered hearing about a time or two growing up, but not anyone she had met before this winter and certainly not someone she wanted to be restrained by. That plant was growing out of control all along the waterfront, doing thousands if not millions of ranmyas of damage, and she might as well be locked in the dungeon.

Mahliki staggered up a short stairway that led to a balcony overlooking the grand foyer three floors below. The door to her father's office was at the end of the hall, an end much farther away then she would have liked.

In reflection, a diving glove might have been a sufficient prop to throw down on the desk.

A side door opened, and she almost crashed into the gray-haired man who walked out, studying an open book almost as big and heavy as her diving helmet. She halted at the same time as he looked up, saw her burden, and stumbled back into the doorway. His thick brows rose, and his gray eyes widened behind his spectacles.

"Pardon me, Vice President Serpitivich," Mahliki said, relieved she hadn't dropped the helmet on his foot.

"No, pardon *me*, Lady Mahliki. I'm clearly in the way of an important... delivery?"

"Something like that." If her arms hadn't been quivering from fatigue, Mahliki would have chatted longer—despite early tensions between her father and his election-opponent-turned-vice-president—she liked the older man. He had a lot of the academic eccentricities that ran in her family. "Do you know if my father is in his office?" The last three times she had tried to hunt him down for this talk, he hadn't been around.

"I believe so. Although..." Serpitivich closed his book—the title promised it a history of the city's waterworks and sewer system. "You may wish to come back at another time. He has a... visitor."

The idea of carrying the helmet back to her room and then back up these stairs again later was *not* appealing. Mahliki was about to announce that Father was about to have two visitors, but Serpitivich spoke again first.

"Perhaps..." He shuffled his book under one arm and extended the other. "I could help you carry that somewhere in the meantime. Or you could leave it in my office and retrieve it later."

"Thank you, but I'll leave this on his floor if he kicks me out." Mahliki smiled. Yes, Father would deserve that if he had been the one giving instructions to confine her to the premises. "Besides, I wouldn't want to interrupt your scintillating reading. Sewers and waterworks, eh? Must be fascinating."

Serpitivich's eyebrows shifted upward again. "Oh, you saw the title? Yes, there's a portion of the old city, a very poor portion, that isn't on the sewer system. I have long wanted to run infrastructure to that area to improve the living conditions, in hopes of attracting a more affluent element to the neighborhoods or even inspiring the current residents to greater economic aspirations. Now that I have the means to effect such change, it's simply a matter of making the numbers work. I have a few ideas if you're interested in—" he adjusted his spectacles, almost dropping the book in the process.

"That sounds like a worthy project," Mahliki said, taking advantage of his fumble. She needed to escape the conversation before her arms gave out. "If you write up a treatise on it, I should enjoy reading the paper." She smiled at him, then made polite nods and returned to her mission.

"Why, I'll certainly let you know if I write such a paper," he called after her.

Mahliki had made such offers to more academic sorts than she could remember, including her own parents. It wasn't exactly a brush-off—especially since it had resulted in more than one paper landing on her desk, including one that an earnest Polytechnic professor had mailed across an ocean and a continent for her perusal—but it did buy time and help her avoid being mired down in long conversations on subject matters that weren't her passions. Even if the papers came, she was a fast reader and could skim the contents in less time than those prolonged conversations often took.

As Mahliki walked closer to Father's door, she noticed it stood ajar with lamplight flowing out. Good. Whoever his guest was, the meeting couldn't be so important as to require utter secrecy. It was, however, odd that the guard who usually stood outside the door was missing. Father hadn't stepped out, had he?

But, no, as she approached the threshold, she heard voices drifting out. Father's and... a woman's. One of those business people angling for some concession? Hadn't he been directing them to the new Chief of Domestic Economics?

Mahliki softened her steps—as much as her burden allowed—and stopped a few inches from the door.

"...look so tired, dear," a woman said—Mahliki didn't recognize the voice. "And your brow is all furrowed together. Do you have another headache?"

Mahliki's mouth fell open. Who was calling her father *dear*? Unless Grandmother Starcrest had decided to visit the capital, this couldn't have a promising explanation. Father wouldn't be... cheating on Mother. Surely, not. They were too loving and supportive of each other. It was almost gooey. Mahliki and her siblings had rolled many an eye as they were growing up. Father wouldn't... he *couldn't*.

Mahliki wished there were a table in the hall that she could set the helmet on. Her arms ached, and her palms had started sweating. She wouldn't walk away from this conversation for anything though.

"What you need," the woman went on, "is a true confidant here. Someone who was born and bred in the capital and understands the Turgonian culture. That... foreign woman, what use is she here? There are no ancient pots to study, or whatever it is she does."

Mahliki was torn between holding her breath and not moving an inch, lest one of the old floorboards beneath the runner creak, and wanting to barge in and punch whoever this woman was in the face. *Father* should be punching her in the face. Or at least shoving her out the door.

An inside door thumped shut. The lavatory? Or maybe that big closet Father had converted into a file room.

"Are you still here, Sauda?" Father sighed, and a chair creaked. "Lieutenant Pustvan, I thought I asked you to escort the lady to the foyer."

"Yes, My Lord, but she threatened me when I tried to take her arm." Ah, there was the door guard. "And I wasn't sure how much bodily force you wanted me to use given her... status."

"She threatened you? You weigh a hundred pounds more than she does."

"Well, she threatened parts of me. Parts I'm partial to."

The woman issued a haughty sniff, as if she had done no such thing. Mahliki could have disliked her from the tone of that sniff alone. She definitely sounded like someone who deserved a punch in the face. And, cursed sand sprites, the stupid helmet was getting heavy.

"You may bully me out of here if you wish, Rias, but that does not invalidate the truth."

Rias? Only family members and close friends called Father that. None of the staff here ever called him anything except "My Lord" or, when they were trying to be modern and progressive, "Lord President." The proper title was supposed to be Mister President, but everyone in the warrior caste seemed to find the notion of leaving lord out of the address positively insulting. A few of his old friends called him Lord Admiral, but very few other people here presumed first-name intimacy. So who in all the oceans was this woman?

Mahliki leaned closer to the door, trying to see through the three-inch opening.

"Yes, Sauda," Father said. "I acknowledge that. As I said, leave the paperwork on my desk, and I'll speak with an attorney."

"But Rias," the woman purred, "there's no need for that. I thought the gift I sent would make my feelings clear on the matter. I am willing to accept you back, despite your... dalliances in other countries. Our agreement goes back more than forty years and certainly predates anything that's transpired in the last twenty."

The chair squeaked. "*Dalliances?* Such as a marriage of twenty years and three children?"

"A marriage you had no legal right to pursue, Rias."

On tiptoes in the hallway, Mahliki couldn't make out more than Lieutenant Pustvan's arm and the right half of the woman's back—her long black hair was swept up in an elaborate coif, and she wore a mink fur coat. That hair had to be dyed, Mahliki decided, as the reality of who this was sank in. Father had never spoken of his former wife, but Mother mentioned it whenever she told her version of the story about how they had met and fallen in love—over frozen and mutilated bodies.

The woman backed up, and Father came into view. Mahliki skittered back—or tried to. Her heel caught a wrinkle in the carpet runner and the awkward helmet threw off her balance. She kept from pitching onto her backside, but her sweaty palms betrayed her. The solid brass helmet clunked to the floor like an elephant falling through a roof. At least it didn't crash *through* the floor and into someone's bedroom below.

The door swung all the way open. Father stood there, gripping the back of the woman's arm, ready to escort her out—or perhaps propel her out.

Mahliki flung an arm out and leaned against the railing, as if she wasn't guilty of a thing in the world. "Oh, hello, Father. How are you doing? I just got here, of course. I was needing your help with, ah..."

Father gazed blandly down at the diving helmet blocking the doorway. The woman... wore a lot of rouge, lipstick, and face powder, among other things. It and the dyed hair succeeded in making her look younger than what must have been sixty-odd years, and Mahliki grudgingly admitted that she must have been gorgeous in her youth. Her facial features had a refined elegance even now. The woman—Sauda—returned Mahliki's scrutiny, her expression somewhere between curiosity, exasperation, and contempt. Well, Mahliki had suffered similar looks before, usually from tutors. She wondered if Sauda had ever had children. Or ever wanted them. She also wondered if she could have held that diving helmet for three more seconds so it would have dropped on the woman's foot. Open-toed shoes. Poor armor.

"There's a problem with your diving helmet?" Father asked.

"Yes," Mahliki said, "it's empty. It would like to be full. I thought we could discuss this discrepancy."

He sighed. "Wait inside, please. I'll be back in a moment. Lieutenant, bring those papers, will you? I want them dropped off tonight."

"Yes, My Lord." Lieutenant Pustvan, a stout man with a ruddy-cheeked face, grabbed a folder on the desk, then scurried for the hallway. He gave Mahliki a quick smile and a shy wave wholly incongruous with his supposedly fierce stature as presidential bodyguard. She didn't smile back, not with Father watching on. The fellow had enough trouble without receiving a lecture from the president on the fact that his daughter should not be flirted with while on duty, or any other time. The lieutenant dropped his hands to cover his genitals as he hustled past Sauda. Father wore a long-suffering look as he trooped off, escorting the wo—his former *wife*, Mahliki corrected, and yes, that was almost too bizarre to comprehend. Even though she knew it meant nothing, it was strange and uncomfortable to see him walking side-by-side down the steps with a woman who wasn't Mother.

She wrestled the helmet into the office and thumped it down on the desk. Too bad the lieutenant had taken those papers. She would have been curious to see them. *More* than curious. It sounded like Father's old marriage might never have been dissolved. How could that be? Surely he couldn't have *forgotten* about something that important.

Mahliki poked around the office while she waited, aware that it was taking longer for Father to return than it should have if all he had done was walk downstairs to the front door and back. Was he talking to *her*? Or had someone else waylaid him in the hall?

The woman had mentioned a gift. What could that be? Something spiteful? No, it had sounded like she wanted to stand at Father's side again, as if he would brush away his family of twenty years like lint on a sweater. Delusional woman. But if she could bind things up with legal entanglements, what might it mean for Mother? The Turgonians had no love for the Kyattese, and Mahliki had read a few snide newspaper articles pointing out the inappropriateness of a foreign wife for the first president. No one would take a jab at *Father*, of course, not with his military record. But Mother?

Did Mother even know Sauda had been by? More than once, it sounded like. Mahliki wondered if she could locate the gift. And arrange for a diving helmet to fall upon it. A petty thought, but she found herself smiling at the idea and peering around the office, nonetheless. The idea dwindled when her gaze fell upon the hundred-odd gifts stacked on and around the bookcases to either side of the door, with even more rising in stacks in the corners. People must have been delivering welcome-to-the-office-and-please-don't-forget-to-think-kindly-of-my-establishment gifts since Election Day had made Father's job title official. He either hadn't had time to open them or hadn't cared to open them. Perhaps he wished to remain oblivious to bribe requests.

Mahliki wandered over to one of the piles and started poking around, looking at name cards, but there were too many to go through. *More than a hundred.* Given what she had seen of this Sauda, something wrapped in flamboyant paper—or furs—might be expected, but she didn't see anything that grandiose. She paused over a black scroll case tied with simple but tasteful silver string. Unlike most of the gifts, it had been opened.

Her heart rate increased at the thought that Father might have opened *her* gift. What would that mean, when he had touched so few of the others? No, he had been indifferent to her; she had heard it with her own ears. This had to be from someone else. Still, her hand trembled as she reached for the case. She thumbed open the name card, and blinked in surprise. Not Sauda...

May your years in the chair be less turbulent than mine were. ~ Sespian.

Mahliki opened the scroll case and tipped it toward her hand. A small slip fell out, followed by a larger sheet. The first was a receipt to Father for ordering a custom-made frame from a local woodworker. The second paper made her breath catch. It was an ink portrait of the family, Mother, Father, Agarik, Koanani, and her. And it was beautiful. The family had never stood and posed for Sespian—Mahliki hadn't even been positive he knew who her siblings were, but he must have met them at the funerals last winter—so he had done it all from memory. He had even captured... all the right emotions. Father and Mother weren't as grave as they appeared in public, and they were standing arm in arm, sharing smiles with each other. She and her siblings wore mischievous expressions, and she marveled at how well he had captured each person's mannerisms, including hers. She was fiddling with the end of her braid in the picture. Hah, she hadn't realized she did that so often that others noticed. Or maybe Sespian was just an observant man. Artists tended to be so, didn't they?

"Yeah, then how come he hasn't *observed* that you would like him to kiss you?" she muttered. Maybe he had and simply wasn't interested. Not a heartening notion.

"Snooping?" came a voice from the doorway.

Mahliki jumped, almost dropping the portrait. She flushed but had too much respect for it—and the artist—to stuff it back into the tube with haste. Colonel Dak stood in the doorway. She wasn't sure whether that was better or worse than being caught rummaging by Father. She *was* sure she should have shut the door before, er, snooping, yes.

Her first instinct was to decry this accusation, but she *had* been caught with her finger in the coconut pudding bowl. She shrugged nonchalantly instead. "Would you tell Father if I was? Or try to recruit me for the intelligence office?"

"Depends." Dak walked in and slumped into one of the chairs at the desk, not Father's.

"On?" Mahliki carefully returned the portrait to its home. She hadn't run across her cousin often in the time he had been here—or known he was on the premises until recently—so didn't know how to interact with him. Even thinking of a forty-year-old man as a cousin seemed odd, as all her cousins on her mother's side were closer to her own age.

"On whether you were snooping out of concern for your father and the welfare of Turgonia, or whether it was because of a boy."

Mahliki flushed. His one eye was either extra strong to make up for the lack of the other, or he had seen the portrait before and knew who it was from. But how could he know Mahliki had an... interest in Sespian? Sespian didn't even know.

Dak rapped the diving helmet with a knuckle. "Guess that explains why I was called up here. You're wondering why your trip has been delayed."

83

"Yes." Mahliki couldn't keep from sounding a touch huffy. "I should think that finding a way to eliminate that plant would be a priority. I don't know if Father has told you, but I'm a biologist, and, despite my age, I have a great deal of experience with exotic foliage."

"He's told me. He's proud of you."

Her huffiness deflated. "Oh. I mean, I know."

"The plant *is* a priority, and it's becoming more of one everyday. That's why we're letting you go out on a naval vessel in the morning. With a military escort, in addition to Sespian and whoever else you're taking down." He lifted a hand, clearly anticipating an objection, though Mahliki didn't care how many men he sent along to clean their fingernails while she was under the surface, so long as she got to go. "There's a new assassin in the city, a good one, and we have no idea where he is or what his target will be, but he's Nurian. Given how many Nurian deaths your father caused in the last war, we must assume that he's in danger, and that his family may be too."

"Including you?"

Dak snorted. "I doubt the Nurians know I exist."

"A benefit of working in intelligence?" In truth, Mahliki had no idea what Dak's career had involved, but she had notions of military intelligence people doing a lot of clandestine spy work.

"A benefit? I suppose, but most Turgonians don't know I exist, either." For a moment, a wistful expression softened his gruff face, but it disappeared so quickly she might have imagined it. Time for a topic change.

"Did you see... uhm, do you know anything about... that woman?"

The wolfish grin that flashed across his face surprised her. "You mean your father's not-so-ex-wife?"

She frowned at the grin—and the amusement in his voice. "I believe so, yes."

"Forgive me my inappropriate delight in his predicament, but my uncle has lived a golden life. He deserves a flea bite now and then."

"I don't understand how... *what* is she claiming, exactly?" Mahliki asked.

"That they're still married."

"Didn't Father... file some paperwork or something? Say... twenty years ago? Before he married Mother?"

"Twenty years ago, he was declared dead by the emperor. Something everyone here believed for a long time." Dak grimaced. "Death nullifies marriage vows. As it turns out, he was imprisoned and later exiled. The emperor never forgave him for what he considered crimes, and to him, Rias was ash on the wind. His wife was never informed that he was anything other than deceased. Over the years, Rias sent a few letters, informing the family as to the truth—and about his Kyattese nuptials—but only to a select few. It wasn't until Raumesys died a few years ago that he might have had a chance to come home, but even then, he knew nothing of Sespian or what *he* believed about him. For all Rias knew, the coastal garrisons might have orders to shoot him on sight if he wandered into port."

Mahliki caught herself twirling the tip of her braid and stopped. "But didn't that woman, Sauda, ever get remarried?"

Twenty years, that was longer than Mahliki had been alive. An eternity. How long could a woman mourn for her dead husband?

"Oh, yes." Dak held up three fingers. "But none of the marriages lasted long. And she's conveniently—or inconveniently for Rias—unattached now. Except to him." He started to grin again but seemed to remember her disapproval and squashed the gesture. "He said you're welcome to share this information with your mother, if she doesn't already know. He's been... absentminded of late and doesn't remember if he told her." Dak's humor disappeared and was replaced by concern. "I trust the bond they've forged over the years will withstand this trial. Though they can expect some awkward moments."

"Why do I have a feeling that's an understatement?" And what did he mean that Father had been absentminded?

"Perhaps." Dak settled back into the chair and opened the folder he had brought with him. Ugh, he must be waiting for Father to return for some meeting. That was going to make it hard to continue snooping.

Mahliki wandered toward the window, as if to consider the view, and a hint of leopard print wrapping paper peeked out at her from behind a stack in the corner. Ah ha. She glanced back to see if Dak was looking. At the same time, he lifted his head, brows rising in inquiry.

Mahliki parted her lips, on the verge of asking him to look the other way or to help her pry into the gift. Maybe she could make a secret ally of him. But she barely knew him, and nothing in his scarred face said he wanted to be the secret ally of a teenage girl. No, he looked every bit the grizzled veteran, a mature adult who would not think of unwrapping his famous uncle's gifts.

"So," Mahliki said instead, "you say a team will be ready to go in the morning? Where shall I meet them?"

"Yes, it will be ready," came her father's voice from behind her. "Let's go over the details. Dak, are you ready?"

"Yes, sir."

Mahliki forgot about the leopard-print wrapping for the moment, eager to discuss the details of what she had come to think of as *her* mission.

CHAPTER 5

MALDYNADO HOPPED OFF THE TROLLEY at Legion and Oak, clothed in an elegant gray vest and black jacket—the sedate style had been Sespian's recommendation; with a straight face, he had sworn they were Starcrest's favorite colors. He and Sespian strode through the Upper Waterfront neighborhood toward the Emperor's Bulwark. Despite the building's age, the marble facade, gold-gilded columns, gold-plated roof tiles, and leering grimbal down spouts had held up well over the years, though Maldynado hoped the structure Sespian had designed possessed more modern flair. Like most of the dwellings in the city, the hotel firmly said Empire. The president should reside in a building that bespoke this new age, something with creative lines. A few curlicues, perhaps. Cheerful colors. Nude female statuary.

A pair of fierce-looking guards with repeating rifles stood on either side of the door, next to a sign telling travelers that the hotel had been requisitioned for presidential use and that they might find rooms at the Palisade. Maldynado slowed as he and Sespian climbed the stairs. He hadn't attempted to see the president yet and didn't know if these men would present his first obstacle. Were random people allowed in, or were appointments required to enter the foyer?

"Evening, Tems, Ruvolk," Sespian said and headed straight for the door.

"Si—Sespian," one greeted. Both nodded. Some of the president's guards must have once been assigned to Sespian in the Imperial Barracks.

The speaker gave Maldynado a curious look and lifted a finger. "Aren't you one of the people who—"

"Stopped the dastardly Forge coalition, keeping them from slaying then-Emperor Sespian, and laying the groundwork for this new governmental regime?" Maldynado asked. "Yes, I am."

The two guards exchanged glances.

"I was going to say one of the people who was harassing President Starcrest at that funeral."

The other guard snapped his fingers. "Yes, he was the one going on and on about wanting a plaque or something, wasn't he?"

"It was a statue," Maldynado said, "and no. That wasn't me."

"He's fine," Sespian said. "He's with me. Someone who might have been a Nurian shot an arrow at my head tonight." Sespian held up the projectile for perusal. "We need to see the president."

"Er, yes, sir." One guard held the door open for him and for Maldynado as well, though a suspicious squint accompanied the polite gesture.

The hotel lobby appeared much the same as it had when Maldynado had visited some years before, meeting a lady acquaintance for drinks and... other activities. It featured more columns, more gold-gilded marble, and a spacious foyer that rose several stories with landings and balconies from various floors overlooking the entry area. In spite of the late hour, several men and women staffed the reception desk, or whatever it was called now. The turn-away-the-riff-raff-who-show-up-without-an-appointment desk.

Maldynado stopped in his survey of the place to gape at two unexpected figures waiting in front of one of the receptionists, one facing the desk, one facing the door with his arms crossed and daggers sheathed at his waist—and other places. Both had bedraggled hair—though that short blond hair was always scruffy—and the dust and debris of the road adorned their clothing. Or... was that *seaweed* on the sleeve of the black shirt?

"Amaranthe?" Sespian asked at the same time as Maldynado blurted, "Boss? Sicarius?"

Sicarius had obviously seen them come in, but Amaranthe must not have heard the door. She spun around, and a broad smile sprawled across her tanned face. "Maldynado, Sespian."

She raced across the room and threw her arms around Maldynado first. He might have lifted his chin and beamed with pleasure at this choice, but he was too busy returning the hug. That smile warmed his heart—it had even reached her eyes; it had been a while since he had seen one like that from her. The vacation must have helped her recover from all the tragedy of the autumn. Perplexing that being in Sicarius's company could help one relax, but... perhaps she'd had some time alone, reading on a beach, while Sicarius had wandered off into the jungle to do pull-ups from branches and one-handed climbs up vines.

"Boss, it's good to see you," Maldynado said, "though you do smell a tad... like a wet dog. What *have* you been doing?"

Amaranthe snorted and released him, her smile having gone lopsided. "It's been an eventful evening." She gave her next hug to Sespian. "Have you two been well? It's nice to see you spending time together."

She was still hugging Sespian so probably didn't see his mouth twist in an odd expression.

"Yes, we're good buddies now." Maldynado slapped Sespian on the shoulder. "We've been carousing the city together, hunting for girls, drinking the finest applejack, getting shot at by changing-room assassins..."

Amaranthe stepped back. "Really?"

"Possibly only the last thing is true," Maldynado said.

Sicarius had been standing back and, other than a solemn nod toward his son, ignoring these hearty welcome-home acknowledgments, but his eyes sharpened at these last words. "You were attacked? When?"

"Tonight." Sespian held up the arrow he had deftly avoiding pronging Amaranthe with during their hug. "Less than an hour ago."

"An hour ago." Amaranthe gave Sicarius a long look. "When was our incident? About two hours ago?"

"Yes," Sicarius said.

"*Your* incident?" Maldynado eyed their bedraggled appearances again.

"Someone threw explosives at the submarine as we were anchoring it to come ashore," Amaranthe said. "The hatch was unfortunately still open and a blasting stick that might have otherwise bounced off bounced in. We escaped, but the sub..."

Maldynado gaped. "You got Admir—I mean, President Starcrest's prize vessel blown up? The one he loaned to you for your vacation? Free of charge? Out of pure kindness?"

"That... surprises you?" Sespian asked, smiling gently to take any sting out of the question.

"Well, now that you ask, I suppose it doesn't. I'm just glad I can't possibly be blamed for that one." Maldynado lifted his eyebrows toward Sicarius, wondering if *he* would be the one to receive the blame. Amaranthe certainly never did in these situations. Sicarius gazed back at him blandly, which made Maldynado doubt the certainty of his statement. He whispered to Sespian, "I can't be blamed, right?"

"You were with me." Sespian waved the arrow.

"It wasn't anyone's fault," Amaranthe said, "except for the person hurling the blasting sticks. Given the way he or she leapt off that cliff to escape from you, I'm guessing he or she won't be stepping forward to offer financial reparations." Though her tone remained light, her smile had disappeared.

Sicarius walked up to Sespian. For a moment, Maldynado thought his cold assassinly heart might melt enough to give the kid a hug, but he took the arrow instead, rotating it to examine from all sides.

"I guessed Nurian, but wasn't positive," Sespian said, going straight to business. He must not mind not getting hugs from pa. Maybe he was relieved. Maldynado would be. "There was a note attached to the arrow as well." He fished in his pocket and produced the message.

Sicarius examined it while Amaranthe leaned against him to read over his arm.

"Interesting," she said.

"Arrogant was more the word that came to my mind," Sespian said. "Since I missed when I shot at you, you owe me a favor? I think not."

Amaranthe pointed at the bottom line. "What language is that? Nurian?"

"It seems similar to Nurian," Sespian said, "but I didn't recognize any of the words, and I am fairly familiar with the language."

Amaranthe lifted her gaze to Sicarius's face; he had been silent as he studied the arrow and note.

"Not Nurian?" she asked.

"It's Nurian," Sicarius said. "A rare dialect."

Sespian tilted his head. "From what region?"

"If I'm correct, it doesn't belong to a specific region, but to a group of people."

"What people?"

Sicarius returned the arrow and note. "My memory may be faulty. I have not seen it for a long time. Professor Komitopis will be a better resource."

Amaranthe was giving Sicarius one of those shrewd I-can-tell-you're-withholding-information looks, but Maldynado barely registered it. The man he had come to see was walking down the stairs, along with his daughter and someone wearing the uniform and insignia of a colonel from the intelligence branch of the army, though his jacket lacked the usual identification nametag.

Mahliki spotted the group—or spotted Sespian—and trotted ahead, arriving in the foyer with her braids bouncing on her back. "Sespian, we can go tomorrow morning if you're ready," she blurted. Belatedly, she noticed the rest of the people in the foyer. "Oh, welcome back, Ms. Lokdon. And Mister Sicarius."

Mister Sicarius. Maldynado almost giggled. But he reminded himself that he needed a job, a respectable job, and men employed in respectable jobs didn't giggle. Although now that the boss was back, maybe she would conjure up some mission that would require the skills of a handsome pugilist. Of course, working for Amaranthe wouldn't impress Yara's family—or keep her in the capital. Maybe he could work for Starcrest day to day and have some adventures with the old team on the weekends. These attacks ought to need investigating, at the least.

"Good evening, My Lord President," Maldynado greeted as Starcrest stepped off the stairs. The man looked tired and older than he had three months ago. No, he definitely wouldn't appreciate giggling or other shenanigans. Maldynado had to be serious in speaking with him.

"Good evening, Maldynado." Starcrest gave him a nod before moving to the others. "Ms. Lokdon, Sicarius." He clasped both of their hands. "Your vacation went well, I hope." He looked them up and down, his gaze lingering on the seaweed on the back of Sicarius's arm. "You're... damp."

Sicarius craned his neck, spotted the seaweed, and plucked it off his sleeve. His expression never changed, so it was only in Maldynado's head that he came across as mortified. Doubtlessly only the darkness of the night outside had kept the fastidious Amaranthe from noticing it and removing it for him.

"We've had... an incident, My Lord," Amaranthe said.

Maldynado nudged her and whispered, "Did your blasting stick come with a note wrapped around it?"

"I wouldn't know. Whatever remains of it is in the submarine. Which is... uhm." She met Sicarius's eyes.

Maldynado tried to decide if she sought moral support or was hoping he would step forward and take the blame. "Don't do it," Maldynado mouthed, but he doubted Sicarius was paying attention to him.

"The submarine was attacked upon our arrival, My Lord," Sicarius said. "It has been damaged and sunken. I apologize for my error of judgment that allowed this to happen."

He *apologized*? Maldynado gaped. He'd never heard Sicarius apologize. Words like please and sorry weren't in his vocabulary. Even Amaranthe looked a little stunned at Sicarius's last sentence.

Starcrest grimaced. "My fault. I should have been more explicit in my message and warned you about the plant. I had thought the submarine would be a match for it, though it's admittedly grown much larger in this last two weeks."

"Er," Amaranthe said, glancing at Sicarius yet again. They had seen the plant, hadn't they? They must have on their way into the city. It was getting impossible to miss. "We didn't try to dock in the harbor, My Lord. In fact, we saw the plant in the distance and were determinedly avoiding the waterfront. In reflection, we should have... docked in front of the Fort Urgot grounds." She winced. "We chose another route, deciding to anchor at a little cove a few miles south of the city and to swim to shore."

"Swim?" Starcrest asked. "Didn't you find the collapsible boat for shore excursions?"

"Oh, we found it. The pirates we ran into around the Cape of Fensgroot also found it. That's... another story."

Starcrest's mouth quirked into a half smile. Either he was blasé at the loss of his sub, or he'd had memorable run-ins with pirates too.

Amaranthe didn't seem to notice the smile, for she was kneading the hem of her jacket and staring at his collarbone instead of at his face. Interesting how someone who hadn't been intimidated by a single villain all year could grow nervous in the presence of a cordial old admiral. "How our arrival was anticipated, I don't know, but someone was waiting for us in that cove. With blasting sticks."

"I also have an incident to report." Sespian lifted his arrow and went over the details of the bathhouse sniper.

"All this happened tonight?" Starcrest asked.

"Less than an hour ago," Sespian said.

"Two hours for us," Amaranthe said. "Miles apart. I don't know if it could be the same person or not."

Starcrest turned to the thus-far silent colonel leaning against the railing at the base of the broad spiral stairs. He hadn't been watching the gathering, but Maldynado had a feeling he hadn't missed anything, either. "*How many* Nurian assassins did you say had been spotted in the city?" Starcrest asked.

"One," the colonel said. "So far."

"This doesn't change anything, right, Father?" Mahliki asked. "The mission is still on for tomorrow? The plant must be dealt with. And now—" she smiled at Sespian, "—my backup is here."

Maldynado shook his head. How could Sespian not see that this girl was aching to spend time with him in non-platonic ways?

Starcrest looked at the colonel again. "How many suits do we have?"

"Ten. I got the whole complement off the *Sawtooth*. In anticipation of trouble."

"Imagine that," Starcrest murmured.

"My Lord President," Maldynado said, seeing his chance—even if it meant crawling into one of those awful diving suits and tramping around on the bottom of the lake again. "I would be pleased to volunteer to assist Sespian and your daughter in this matter. Then if you find my work adequate, perhaps you would consider hiring me for more long-term employment."

Maldynado didn't think he had said anything startling, but the entire group fell silent and stared at him.

"You're looking for a job?" Amaranthe finally asked. "An actual job?"

"Is that so hard to believe?" Maldynado asked.

"It's just that you never have. When we first met..."

Maldynado held up a hand. "Yes, I know, but a man can't traipse around in a loincloth forever."

"Tell her what really happened to change your mind," Sespian said, a smile teasing his lips.

"Ah... it's possible Evrial... Sergeant Yara's father... visited and suggested I was a less than suitable suitor."

"Because..." Sespian promoted, his eyes twinkling.

"I have no proof, mind you, as I was cooking her supper and am the model doting lover, but I believe it was my nudity that upset him. And perhaps the fact of my unemployment came up. Though the nudity seemed to distress him most. I don't know why. I'm quite magnificent nude."

93

Amaranthe dropped her face into the palm of her hand. Mahliki rolled her eyes. Strange, women usually agreed with him. If not with words than with their appreciative gazes.

"What sort of job did you have in mind?" Starcrest asked, unfazed by the women's strange reactions.

"I'm an able fighter, though I imagine you have many of those. I get along well with the ladies, though so long as Evrial and I recover from our last tiff, I couldn't *perform* for the ladies, if you catch my meaning. Perhaps I could be some sort of spy. Infiltrating groups of women— or men, I get along well with some men, too—and playing the role of harmless and affable dandy whilst secretly obtaining information for the intelligence office."

The colonel made a sort of throat-strangling noise, which he covered with a cough. Odd man.

"It's a role?" Starcrest asked.

"He *is* brighter than he lets on," Amaranthe said.

"Very well. Go along with Mahliki's team and lend her your assistance," Starcrest said. "I'd also like a salvage team to try and get the sub off the bottom of the lake, so I can see if it can be repaired. The sub would be much preferable to the diving suits for underwater operations."

Amaranthe grimaced. Even Sicarius's emotionless face seemed to grow a touch paler.

"Dak, will you see if you can get a wrecker out there for that?" Starcrest finished.

The colonel pushed away from the railing. "I don't know if that's in my job description exactly—don't you have presidential aides wandering around somewhere?—but I'll do it if *you* promise you won't be out there tinkering with that sub when it gets pulled up. You have more important things to handle. Like the Nurians. And those diplomats. And don't forget my report on all those zealots in robes that are crawling out of the cracks in the mortar, trying to found some new religion, now that it's not expressly forbidden."

"My aides aren't military men," Starcrest said, "as we're trying to incorporate more civilians into the government. You're a better liaison for dealing with the marines."

"Lucky me."

Maldynado eyed the colonel more closely, wondering why he didn't

"My Lord" or "Mister President" Starcrest. Someone who had known him a long time? A relative? Even twenty years younger, he wasn't as handsome a man as Starcrest, of course the missing eye put a maggot in the apple of his looks too. But Maldynado supposed there might be a resemblance in the jawline and build.

Starcrest must have considered the matter settled, for he nodded at Sespian and asked, "May I see that arrow?"

"Do you recognize the style?" Sicarius asked.

Starcrest accepted the arrow. "A Nurian design, albeit not their typical military issue one. One of the smaller independent sects, perhaps?" He held it up for the colonel's perusal. "You don't know what part of the country the assassin your men spotted is from, do you?"

"Not yet. I will."

"You're not thinking of going hunting, are you?" Amaranthe murmured to Sicarius, who was listening intently to the talk of assassins.

Sicarius looked into her eyes. "If Sespian is the target, I am."

"Ah, but it seems I'm not." Sespian pointed to the note. "Remember?"

"You may become a target if you choose not to redeem her favor."

"That was in the note you mentioned?" Starcrest said. "May I see it?"

"Of course." Sespian handed it to him. "That's why I came. I thought to ask your wife for a translation."

Starcrest studied the message. "The language is familiar, isn't it? I might have seen it in the war, intercepting a message or two." He stared at it, then massaged his forehead, and handed the note back. "The memory eludes me now."

The colonel, standing behind Starcrest, frowned at this admission.

"Mahliki, take them up to see your mother, please," Starcrest said. "And then you'd best get some rest before pursuing your mission. That plant is dangerous."

"We saw the bodies," Amaranthe said. "Or what was left of them. How many has it killed? Is it some wizard's spawn? Or might this assassin have an aptitude for botany?"

"Bodies?" Starcrest glanced at the colonel again.

The man stroked his chin. "There have been several reports of missing persons, but we haven't found any bodies. If it's killing people, it's doing so when nobody's watching."

"So long as you don't mess with the buds," Mahliki said, sharing a significant look with Sespian.

Maldynado wondered what he had volunteered for. He had better do some research before returning to his flat.

"There were bodies—body parts—floating among beds of seaweed in the lake," Amaranthe said. "An unfamiliar version of seaweed. The clumps might have come off the plant."

"I see," Starcrest said. "Mahliki, take as many men and swords with you as you think you might need. More than you think... What are you doing?"

Mahliki had unbuttoned her jacket, lifted the flap, and had her nose to her armpit as she investigated some hidden pocket.

"Listening to you," she said brightly, lifting her head.

Starcrest's grunt sounded dubious.

"And finding a sample for Ms. Lokdon." Mahliki held out a vial with a dried green husk inside.

Before she let the flap of her jacket fall shut, Maldynado glimpsed several other vials and... were those scissors? And tweezers? A scalpel? Mahliki closed the jacket before he could identify other tools.

Amaranthe accepted the vial and walked over to a gas lamp with Sicarius a step behind. They examined the specimen under the light.

"You carry plant samples around with you?" Maldynado asked.

"You haven't noticed that she clinks when she walks?" Sespian asked.

Mahliki threw him a quick glance, perhaps wondering if this was a criticism or not, then shrugged. "I carry all manner of tools around with me. A lady must be prepared whenever she chances across an interesting specimen. I'm certain that's not that uncommon."

"I *have* heard other women make similar statements," Maldynado said, "but usually the *tools* they carry around are mint candies, perfumes, and makeup kits, and the specimens they're interested in are male."

"Plants have male and female parts." Mahliki withdrew a small pair of scissors. "I'll snip a sample of anything."

Maldynado shifted his pelvis away from her. He wondered what her father thought of her snipping male parts, but Starcrest and the colonel had moved away from the group to discuss something.

Amaranthe and Sicarius returned and handed the vial back to Mahliki.

"It is the same plant," Sicarius said.

Amaranthe shrugged. "You'll have to take his word for it. I was too busy being distressed by the severed limbs and the vines sticking out of the eye socket of the half-eaten skull." She shuddered.

"It was your choice to forego the hug," Sicarius murmured softly—Maldynado blinked because he wasn't certain he had heard correctly.

Amaranthe smiled up at him. "Those offers of physical comfort are so rare that I figure I should save them for when I really need them."

The look Sicarius gave her was only slightly less non-emotive than the rest of his looks, but she must have read something in it, for her smile broadened.

Maldynado could *not* imagine those two in bed. Frankly, he couldn't imagine any woman in Sicarius's bed—or Sicarius with a bed for that matter. During their year working together, he had seen Sicarius sleep on the ground, in tree branches, on rooftops, and on ceiling beams, but never in something so sybaritic as a bed. It took a unique woman to appreciate a man like that.

"All should be set for the morning," Starcrest said, returning to the group. "Sespian, I forgot to mention it—" a faint wince crossed his face again, "—but congratulations on the winning design for the presidential residence. I admit I was of a mind *not* to choose your entry, lest it be construed as nepotism of a sort, but Tikaya informed me that it would be just as unfair to ignore your entry because we know you. She insisted that a blind judging was called for and brought in three art and architecture professors from the university to aid in the selection process."

"I must give her my thanks then," Sespian said.

"Give her the arrow and the note," Starcrest suggested. "She'll consider a mystery to solve an even greater reward."

"Work over flattery?"

"Just so." Starcrest nodded to them all. "It is good to see you. I'll leave you to the receptionists who will find rooms for those without abodes elsewhere."

Maldynado wondered if he should accept a room in the hotel. Evrial wasn't treating him frostily, but she *had* accepted a number of double shifts, and he worried she was avoiding him. No, he would go home and offer love and support—and brilliant sex—thus to tempt her to remain in the city. Her rural hometown couldn't compete with that. He hoped.

"The diplomat?" the colonel prompted.

"Oh, yes." Starcrest had started to turn away, but he faced Amaranthe again. "Your Mangdorian friend has returned from his homeland."

"Basilard?" Maldynado nearly bounced—he hadn't known when he would see Basilard again, if ever.

"Yes. He'll want to see you all, I'm certain. He's in room... two thirty-eight." Starcrest glanced at the colonel. For... verification? His man nodded back.

"Thank you, My Lord," Amaranthe said. "It'll be good to see him again."

"Tikaya also has a letter for you from Akstyr."

Amaranthe beamed. Maldynado couldn't imagine anything particularly long or effusive flowing from Akstyr's pen. Professor Komitopis's mother—and Akstyr's landlord, the last Maldynado had heard—had probably insisted he send the missive.

With the news delivered, and the arrow mystery still waiting to be decoded, people said their goodnights. Starcrest hugged his daughter, murmured a few words—eliciting a promise to be careful—then departed with the colonel, saying, "Alas, more work to do before bed." Amaranthe and Sicarius went with Sespian and Mahliki to search for Professor Komitopis, promising they would stop by to see Basilard soon. Though Maldynado was curious about the assassin, he had missed Basilard, so he trotted up the stairs to the second level right away. If Evrial chose to leave the city without him... Maldynado might have more need of a comrade to drink and game with than ever.

Nodding to himself, he knocked on the door to 238.

Naturally, no one called out with a "just a minute." Nor did he hear footsteps, but Basilard moved about almost as silently as Sicarius, so that wasn't unexpected, either.

The door opened, and Maldynado grinned like a mindless dandy at the familiar face. "Hullo, Bas. I heard you were in town."

Basilard returned the grin and stepped forward for a hug. They parted, and Maldynado studied his friend. It had only been three months, but Basilard appeared... more stately than before. Maybe it was the clothing. Instead of the ill-fitting cotton and wool cast-offs he had often worn as an outlaw, he was dressed in supple suede trousers and fringed moccasins. A Mangdorian style, Maldynado assumed, though he hadn't met many of the people besides Basilard. His tunic was suede, too, dyed a simple off-white and resting beneath a vest made from shaggy dark fur. A heavy brass chain hung around his neck with a thick rectangular medallion engraved with a hunter holding a spear and crouching beneath a sunburst.

My badge of office, Basilard explained, his fingers flickering in the hand signs he had always used to talk to the group. His clothing might have improved, but the months had done nothing to fix the scar tissue at his throat, nor the briar patch of old gashes crisscrossing his shaven head. Those scars would always be there, and some on his heart as well.

"Yes," Maldynado said, "I hear you're a diplomat now. Assigned by your government, I presume? Someone high up in the rankings?"

Basilard nodded.

"How did you earn such an esteemed position?"

Nobody else wanted to deal with the Turgonians.

Maldynado grunted. There was probably a degree of truth in that, but... "There must be more than that. What about your daughter? Did you see her?"

Basilard's hand rocked side to side in a sort-of motion. *Come in. I will explain. This room came with enough liquor to stock a bar. You are welcome to indulge, if you like.*

"I shouldn't indulge too much," Maldynado said, ambling toward the cabinet Basilard had pointed out. "It looks like I'll be hopping into a diving suit tomorrow. It's been a few months since I was nearly killed by some carnivorous underwater monster, so I figured it was time again." True, this wasn't *quite* what he'd had in mind when he came to ask for a job... but if he helped out, something more appealing might come his way. And maybe someone would talk Sicarius and Amaranthe into coming along. That would make things safer. Or more interesting, anyway. Watching someone snip female and—he shuddered—male plant specimens all day might be tedious if nothing interesting happened.

Basilard signed, *Diving suits? To examine that plant in the harbor?*

"Yes. It's a beastly thing. I have the hat."

Basilard blinked. *The hat?*

"Yes, to prove that I survived its incursion. That's what the merchant said anyway. I simply found it intriguing. I was going to wear it here tonight, but Sespian suggested something more sedate for a meeting with the president." Maldynado poured two snifters of apple brandy. "I don't know. Starcrest looked tired and grim. A vine-covered hat might have amused him."

*I did not think I would ever say—*sign*—this, but I have missed the team's exploits.*

"I bet you could come with us. Starcrest seemed concerned about letting his daughter go down there without a lot of hulking men around to protect her. Though after seeing her twirl those specimen-collecting scissors, I'm not sure how much help she needs."

Basilard's blue eyes twinkled. *Little, I would guess. Remember the ship?* He waved in the direction of Fort Urgot, where the ancient craft had ultimately been destroyed in the sky.

"How could I forget it? But, Bas, confession time. How'd you *really* get this gig?" Maldynado handed him one of the glasses. "Look at this room. It's posh. Quite an upgrade from underground pumping stations and the like, eh? But how are you going to be diplomatic with anyone when so few people can understand your hand signs?"

I have an assistant. Basilard's smile turned smug. *She has her own room. Also posh.*

"No kidding? A Mangdorian? Someone who's learned your extra signs? And can translate? And did you say *she*? Is she sexy? Does she like you?" Maldynado faltered as a thought rushed into his mind. "Er, it's not your daughter, is it?"

Basilard's smile faded, and Maldynado regretted voicing the question.

She is somewhat of an important person in my country, but she's also a teacher. We met last month. She works with handicapped children and was intrigued by the modifications I made to the Mangdorian hunting code. Some of her students are deaf or mute.

"That's brilliant, Bas. I never would have thought of the less, er, tactical applications for your signs, but that makes perfect sense."

Actually sharing the hand language was Professor Komitopis's idea. She planted it in my brain last winter.

"Ah. Did she also suggest you seek out your head chief or whoever runs your country to ask for this job?" Maldynado should have learned more about Mangdoria at some point, but Basilard had never spoken of his family or his homeland often. It had always pained him too much. Since his people were religious pacifists, he had, after the killing he had done in the pit fights and later as a mercenary, worried he would never have a place among them again.

That came about because of... a certain awkwardness. With me.

"Because of your scars and... past?"

Basilard nodded. *I was determined to see my daughter and the friends and family I had grown up with, and I did, but I was... judged harshly by our priests and... many of my kin.* He shrugged, though it didn't come across as blasé as he probably intended. The humor had left his eyes. *I anticipated as much. I was allowed to see my daughter, but it was made clear that I wasn't welcome, not for the long term.*

"Oh. Sorry, Bas." Maldynado didn't know anything more useful to say, so he took a swig from his snifter and waved at Basilard's glass, suggesting he should do the same.

I wish I could have spent more time with my daughter, because she seemed... curious about me. She did remember me, at least.

"That's something. You'd been gone for several years, right?"

Yes. As to how I came to the chief's attention, I can thank the makarovi.

Maldynado curled a lip. He couldn't imagine thanking those horrible beasts for anything. "How so?"

At the time, I didn't know why I was doing it, but before I left the capital, I cured a pelt and made a necklace of teeth and claws.

"That passes for fashion in Mangdoria, does it?"

For all that we—they—are a peaceful people, Mangdorians value great hunters. The makarovi may be rare, but they have long hunted in the same mountains where we live. As a child, you're told not to wander into the woods, or the makarovi will get you. There have been only a few times when my people have succeeded in slaying one, so when I came in wearing the proof of the deed—

"Dear ancestors, Basilard, is *that* what this shaggy fur is?" Maldynado tugged at the coarse black stuff on his vest. "I just thought you were cold. Very cold."

Makarovi fur, yes.

Maldynado sniffed the air experimentally. "How did you manage to get rid of the smell?"

My people are also expert fur and leather workers.

"Trade secret, eh?"

Basilard nodded. *So, news that I had slain makarovi reached the chief, and he called me to his yurt.*

"His yurt? Your people live extravagantly, don't they?" Yurts. Please. No *wonder* Basilard had come back to the empire.

Basilard shrugged. *It's a big yurt. Regardless, I had a long discussion with him, much to the irritation of his spiritual advisor. The priest stood in the background, glowered at me, and kept making signs to ward off the wrath of God.*

Remembering that Basilard actually believed he was going to some Mangdorian hell for his sins, Maldynado kept himself from making a snide comment about the religion and the idiot priests who preached it. Anyone who couldn't see that Basilard was a good human being... ought to be gnawed on by wild animals. Makarovi, perhaps.

The chief was more reasonable. He listened to my story, all of it. He suggested that a position going back and forth between Mangdoria and Turgonia as a diplomat would allow me to see my daughter on occasion without... making the whole village—and myself—uncomfortable by trying to live there permanently. It is not ideal, but it is perhaps the best I could hope for. In time... Basilard finished with a shrug.

"That's smart of your chief, not to waste your talent and connections."

Talent? Do you believe sticking knives in people will be required to negotiate with the president?

"You have other talents, Bas. You're patient and you listen well, and you're easy to confide in. Those sound like diplomacy things to me. Although..." Maldynado tapped his chin. "A lot of important meetings *do* take place in the gymnasium here. If I were you, I wouldn't let those defensive skills of yours get rusty."

I see. Perhaps we shall have to spar while I'm here.

"I may have an even better idea for a spot of training." Maldynado thought his casual statement sly, but Basilard's eyes closed to suspicious slits immediately.

Does it involve diving suits?

"Whatever makes you think that?" Maldynado finished his brandy and set the snifter down. "Now, why don't you tell me more about this cute translator of yours? She *is* cute, isn't she?"

CHAPTER 6

TIKAYA HAD ALREADY SEARCHED THE library, so she didn't know why she was searching again, other than that Rias spent a lot of time in there. The attached conference rooms were more spacious than his office, so he met with groups there daily. Also, their own suite was on the floor directly above the library and in the same wing of the hotel. That might be close enough to affect him. A mind-altering artifact would need to be in close proximity to him for a few hours a day to have an impact, and she had already scoured the suite from within and found nothing.

On a whim, Tikaya climbed one of the sturdy bookcases so she could peer across the aisles from above. She hadn't looked up there last time. Alas, she found nothing except dust and cobwebs. She would check his office next. It had been locked the last time she had tried. The last destination on her list was the gymnasium, though she hoped to find something elsewhere, so she could avoid that. The men might think her odd—or lascivious—if she kept strolling through their sacred area of steam, wrestling, and nudity.

A throat cleared behind her. "Mother?"

"Yes?" Tikaya refused to feel embarrassed because she was standing three shelves up on a bookcase.

"Have you... read all the other tomes already, and you're looking for some choice gem that might have been hidden?"

"No." Tikaya climbed down, careful not to miss a step and tumble—Rias wasn't around to catch her. "I'm looking for..." As she turned to face her daughter, she saw Mahliki wasn't alone.

Sespian, Sicarius, and Amaranthe Lokdon stood beside her, all regarding Tikaya curiously.

"Never mind," Tikaya finished. Though she liked Sespian and had come to know Amaranthe somewhat before the woman left the city, she didn't feel comfortable admitting that some weakness might be plaguing Rias. She was even less comfortable admitting it—admitting *anything*—in front of the assassin. He had been civil to her in all of their encounters, but he wasn't much different in his cool mannerisms than he had been twenty years earlier, so she struggled to believe he was a better person now.

"If you're not too busy—" Mahliki's eyebrows rose in her you're-being-odd-mother look, "—we could use your help to translate a language."

"Oh?" Tikaya wiped her dusty hands on her skirt and stepped forward.

Amaranthe eyed the dust smears, and her fingers twitched toward the garment. She grimaced and clasped her hands behind her back instead.

"Some ancient puzzle that needs to be decrypted?" Tikaya asked.

Mahliki lifted her own hand. "Don't get too eager, Mother. It's nothing quite that obscure. Sespian?"

He strode forward, holding out the note. "It came attached to this." He waved the arrow.

Tikaya perused the Turgonian line first, snorted at the idea of a favor being required for such an act, then read the last passage. "The honorable hunter does not kill the kits to avenge the chickens stolen by the vixen."

"That's... what it says?" Sespian asked.

Sicarius and Amaranthe exchanged looks, having clearly read some meaning into the old proverb.

"Yes." Tikaya returned the note to him.

"In what language?" Amaranthe asked.

"It's a Nurian dialect used solely among a very old, very secretive society over there."

"Such as?"

"The mage hunters," Sicarius said, as if he had known all along. Maybe he had.

"Yes," Tikaya said.

"That sounds familiar," Sespian said. "Can someone remind me?"

Tikaya thought Sicarius might respond, since he was obviously familiar with them, but he waited with his hands clasped behind his back, his face toward her.

"Nuria has long been a place where magic reigns," Tikaya said. "As on Kyatt, the Nurians shun that term now, having refined the skills required to turn various mental feats into repeatable sciences, but in the old days, they referred to those we call practitioners as mages and wizards. The difference in the terms has been largely forgotten over the years. A powerful practitioner is still called a mage or a wizard, and one who studies at Stargrind, an academy that teaches a combination of fighting and Science skills, can aspire to the title of warrior mage."

Amaranthe stirred and met Sicarius's eyes again. That man who had possessed him the winter before had been a warrior mage, but Tikaya decided not to bring it up. She had never forgotten the violation of having her own memories stolen by a telepath back during her first encounter with the alien technology. To be a slave to another... That could not have been a pleasant experience.

"Practitioners of all types and ability levels are given an honored status in Nuria with privileges not unlike those your warrior caste has had over the centuries, but the separation is even more pronounced. Mundane individuals without the aptitude or interest in pursuing a Science-based career can never aspire to wealth, government sway, or land ownership. For those who have family members with power, that is enough, for the entire family receives the right to claim honored status. For the rest of the nation, they are forever second-class citizens. This hasn't always gone over well with the populace."

"Imagine that," Sespian murmured.

Mahliki stifled a yawn. The hour had grown late, and she might be genuinely tired, but, in case that was a hint, Tikaya trimmed her history lesson to get to the point.

"More than a millennium ago, someone founded a secret training academy to study methods for defeating practitioners without using the Science."

"Methods other than a sword in the belly?" Sespian asked.

"They *did* train as fighters, with that making up a large part of their studies, but they also learned many methods for breaking a practitioner's concentration so they might close in and slay him with mundane means. They learned to block or deflect mental attacks and battle through assaults that could cripple another man—or drive him insane. The idea behind this secret sect was to overthrow the government and rid the land of any practitioner who sought to use his skills and powers to punish or exploit the mundanes."

"They couldn't have been very successful," Sespian said.

Amaranthe nodded as if she had heard this story before. Sicarius remained stony and impassive; one never knew if he was listening or not.

"They weren't remotely successful," Tikaya said. "As it turned out, it took years—*decades*—of training to master the skills to combat mages, and this was no path toward reward except for those who believed they could actually pull off a usurpation. Some did believe that to be possible, mind you, but not enough trained to become mage hunters. The organization never grew large enough to threaten the government. Still, there's always been a mystique about them, and practitioners do indeed fear them. That's one reason bodyguards are so often employed. There have been many assassinations by mage hunters over the centuries, with some of the great chiefs themselves falling to their blades."

Mahliki raised a finger. "Dak said there's a Nurian assassin in the city, so can we assume this person is a mage hunter?"

Tikaya spread her hands. Dak hadn't shared much with her.

Sespian rotated the arrow in his hands. "Why would a mage hunter be sent after me then? I'm no practitioner. Although... that thing about kits and vixens..." He looked toward Sicarius.

Now *all* eyes turned toward Sicarius. His face remained neutral, though he considered Sespian, Mahliki, and Tikaya in turn. Then he met Amaranthe's eyes—she was gazing at him, an expectant expression on her face.

"The honorable hunter does not kill the kits to avenge the chickens stolen by the vixen," Tikaya murmured, repeating the translation. "Is Sespian... a kit?"

"Only if Sicarius is a vixen," Sespian said dryly.

Amaranthe touched the back of Sicarius's hand. "Any mage hunters on your trail that you would like to tell us about?"

"I am unaware of anyone seeking me specifically," he said.

"Anyone you dealt with long ago, who might have kin out for revenge?"

"I dealt with many people for Emperor Raumesys."

Tikaya shivered. The man still uttered such statements without any humanity, any hint of remorse. Amaranthe seemed a sane woman, but Tikaya had a hard time seeing why she would have chosen Sicarius for a mate.

"Mage hunter people?" Amaranthe asked.

"No."

"Never?"

Sicarius's eyes narrowed ever so slightly. Tikaya wouldn't think anything of it on anyone else, but had a feeling the expression might pass for a sign of emotion from him. He glanced at the others again... and said nothing.

"Mahliki," Tikaya said, "perhaps we should leave them to talk about assassins and mage hunters among themselves."

"Does that mean you're going to take me aside to tell me what you were doing on top of the library shelves?"

"Yes, actually. I'd like your opinion on—"

Something banged against the wall, and glass rattled. Tikaya spun toward a bank of windows. None of the curtains had been drawn, and night pressed against the panes. But not *all* of the panes. One window had been thrown open, the frame still shuddering.

Amaranthe ran over and looked out.

"What happened?" Tikaya considered the size of the open window. This was the second floor, but a human could fit through it. "Did someone come in?"

"No, someone went out," Sespian said. "Sicarius."

It took Tikaya a moment to realize the assassin was gone.

"We saw someone outside, climbing past," Amaranthe said. "He reacted much more quickly than I did." She stuck her head outside, twisting it to look up.

"Did you see a face?" Tikaya wasn't sure whether she should join her at the window or run off to find Rias.

"The person was wearing white and some kind of wrap that covered the face."

"All white?" Sespian asked. "That's the description Maldynado gave of the shooter in the baths."

"I'm going to grab a sword and go out there to help hunt." Amaranthe jogged for the door. "Sespian?"

"Do you think he'll *want* our help?" Sespian waved toward the window. "I didn't even see the climber."

"I don't care whether he wants help or not. If we're interpreting your note correctly, he may be the target. And this all may be a trap."

"Right." Sespian ran after her.

They disappeared into the hallway.

"Mother," Mahliki said, starting for the door, "I'm going to—"

"Stop right there," Tikaya commanded in her firmest you'll-be-in-trouble-if-you-don't-listen tone. Her daughter could take care of herself in any ordinary situation and many extraordinary ones, but she was *not* trained to hunt assassins.

Mahliki halted so quickly the vials inside her jacket rattled. "But they may need—"

"You're needed here. The plant, remember? You may very well be this city's best chance at getting rid of it." And so what if that was only an excuse for Tikaya to keep her daughter inside and safe?

Mahliki's mouth opened and closed a few times, then her shoulders slumped. Good to know that she would still listen to her mother once in a while. At seventeen, she was a lot more headstrong than Tikaya had ever been.

"Come with me, please, so we can find Rias or Dak and warn them that—"

An ear-splitting boom shattered the night. The windows shuddered in their frames, doors banged open, and the floor heaved. Bookcases wobbled and tilted. Tikaya struggled to find her balance, to keep from wobbling and tilting herself. One of the massive bookcases toppled not ten feet away, hurling thick tomes to the floor.

"Mahliki." She pointed toward the hallway. "Get to the doorway."

Tikaya tried to follow her own advice but stumbled and flailed as she navigated falling shelves and a carpet littered with books. Mahliki ran toward her, took her arm, and helped her toward the exit.

They staggered into the hall together, almost crashing into soldiers and in-house staff, some uniformed and others in their nightclothes, who were racing about.

"Where to?" Mahliki asked, still gripping Tikaya's arm.

"Upstairs. Your father's office. That sounded like... I can't tell, but we have to make sure he's all right." Tikaya was running as she talked, guiding Mahliki past soldiers who were all jogging toward the staircases. What did they know that she didn't? She didn't stop to ask.

"You don't think... would Father be the target?" Mahliki asked.

Tikaya didn't mention the previous assassination attempts, the ones she had only recently been made aware of. She had to appear strong for her daughter, unconcerned, though in her head, she couldn't help but think how much she missed home where it had been a long time since anyone even glared at Rias. And where she had her friends and family for support. What am I doing here, she asked silently at least once a day. Her work was a continent and an ocean away. If anything happened to Rias...

They reached the top floor and ran along the landing to his office. The door stood open, but it had not, thank Akahe, been blown ajar. Her relief faded as she ran inside and spotted the missing window and blackened wall around it. Rias was kneeling beside a man in military blacks who was crumpled to the floor beside him, his arm raised while Rias held makeshift bandages to... the place where the soldier's hand should have been. Rias was trying to stop the bleeding and—Tikaya gulped—reassure a man whose face had the pallor of a glacier.

"Lieutenant Pustvan," Mahliki blurted.

Rias's eyes swelled with emotion when he saw them run in. Tikaya would have dropped to her knees and thrown her arms around him, but she dared not interrupt his ministrations.

"You're all right, thank our ancestors," Rias said, his voice oddly loud in the quiet that had befallen after the explosion. "I wanted to run and find you, but—"

"No, that's..." Tikaya stopped herself from saying something as mediocre as understandable and waved bleakly at the injured officer.

After a stunned moment, Mahliki walked around them and knelt in front of the man. She hesitated, then took his other hand. He blinked a few times—poor man, he had lost so much blood, why couldn't he fall unconscious and save himself some pain?—and focused on her. Though Mahliki didn't say anything, the soldier seemed to find her face more encouraging than Rias's.

"What happened?" Tikaya whispered, eyeing the office more closely now that she had examined Rias and found him uninjured. The furniture wasn't damaged, but many of the gifts on his shelves had toppled to the floor, and papers had flown everywhere.

He shook his head. "What? My ears are still ringing."

"What happened?" she asked more loudly.

"I was doing some final work for the night when the window shattered. A homemade explosive device dropped onto the floor. Pustvan and I both lunged for it, to throw it back outside before it blew up, but I was behind my desk, and he got there first. He made it to the window, but... that's it."

Tikaya reached over and gripped his shoulder, though she was careful not to jostle his hands or the lieutenant. A moment later, soldiers charged inside with a doctor clutching a medicine kit and wearing bed slippers.

"Here, bring in that stretcher," the doctor ordered.

Tikaya backed away as he and the soldiers worked to transport the injured soldier out of the office. As soon as Rias let someone else take his spot holding the bandage, she wrapped her arms around him and buried her face against his shoulder. "This place is turning into a nightmare," she said, her voice muffled by his shirt.

"I'm sorry." He returned the embrace. "I'd like to think it will calm down in a few more months, but if you... want to take Mahliki and go back home—"

Tikaya's grip tightened. "You want me to lie awake in my bed every night wondering if you're all right way over here? No, I won't leave you." She swallowed. "But I can't lose you. Not to this. Haven't you... suffered enough for these people during your lifetime?"

Rias sighed and didn't respond.

"They're coming," Mahliki said from the window—from the place where the window had been. Cool night air gusted in through the gaping hole in the wall. "Sicarius and Dak, and they've got somebody."

"My would-be assassin?" Rias wondered.

"What's the punishment for trying to kill the president?" Tikaya asked numbly.

"It's been death thus far, I understand. Dak is... Turgonian through and through."

"Would you have it otherwise for someone who tried to take your life?" Tikaya had never condoned killing or wanted to be a part of it, but she couldn't feel remorse for the person who had tried to blow up Rias, whoever he was.

"I don't know. To order people killed for attacking me seems as much a failing on my part as on theirs. I—" Rias winced and touched a finger to his temple.

"Was the explosion ear-splitting?"

"I... perhaps. My head hurt before this started, but it's hardly worth complaining about. Compared to Pustvan..."

"Has Dak shared his theory with you?" Tikaya wondered if she should have mentioned his name; he had confided in her, and though he hadn't demanded a promise of silence, he clearly hadn't been comfortable suggesting a mental deficiency to Rias's face.

"That I was a lunatic to accept this position?"

"No, that..." Tikaya hesitated. Maybe she shouldn't say anything until she had proof. What if it had simply been the stress of the job that was getting to him? With her toe, she nudged a leather pouch wrapped with green silk twine that had fallen on the floor. "Have you opened all of these gifts?"

"Few. I suspect most are bribes rather than gifts."

"Well, one might be responsible for your... headaches." She left out the absentmindedness that others had noticed.

"Hm, you don't think having explosives hurled through my window might be causing that?"

"I'm sure that doesn't help, but you've been rubbing your temples all winter," Tikaya said.

"Oh," Mahliki said from the window, "I was wondering—I mean, there's one in the corner with leopard-print wrapping that I thought might be from his first wife. She seemed shifty."

Tikaya frowned. "From who?"

"She was here tonight and once last week," Rias said. "And she sent an inauguration gift. I never opened it. Most of them, I just had the secretary stack up in... well, that's not much of a stack any more." He nodded toward the scattered gifts, some as charred as the wall around the window.

After twenty years of marriage, Tikaya wasn't worried about Rias's relationship with his former wife, but she couldn't help but feel miffed at having not been informed—and at the woman's presence here in the first place. What could she want after all this time? "It could be something more inimical."

"I don't think she wishes me ill any more," Rias said.

Mahliki walked to a particular corner and pushed gifts off the pile, clearly hunting for one in particular.

Footsteps sounded in the hallway. A man with a soot-stained shirt and a face almost as dirty was thrust inside, his face twisted into a rictus of pain. Sicarius gripped him from behind, pinning his captive's arms behind his back. The prisoner wore flamboyant yellow and red robes that were shredded in spots and as soot-caked as his face. Wolf-head pins held a crimson cloak back from his shoulders. Those wolf heads... they were a symbol of Nuria. Odd, this man appeared all Turgonian in height and skin-coloring.

Dak and a couple of soldiers clomped in behind them.

"This is the man who threw the explosive," Sicarius said.

"Is he the person you saw climbing outside the library window?" Tikaya asked. There was nothing white about the man's clothing.

"No," Sicarius said. "I chased that person onto the roof, but saw two other men, dragging guards into the bushes along the inside of the courtyard walls. I ran to capture them."

Dak's face flushed with anger or disappointment at this lapse. He was in charge of gathering intelligence, wasn't he? Not running security. Still, he must take the failures of soldiers personally.

"This man was on the opposite side of the building," Sicarius said. "I didn't see him until after he had hurled the explosive and was running."

"I should take him to a separate room for questioning," Dak said, giving Tikaya and Mahliki a pointed looked.

Yes... no torturing people in front of the women. Tikaya trusted her pursed lips would express disapproval on all levels. But could she truly object to force being used on someone who had tried to kill her husband? And who had succeeded in blowing that young officer's hand off? She massaged the back of her neck. What had made her think Turgonia would be a better—more peaceful and less violent—place if Rias took charge?

Time. This would take time. Entire cultures were not changed over night. She had promised him five years of love and support here. She could make it through.

"Agreed," Rias said. "Take him to a room that hasn't been damaged. I'll follow shortly." As soon as Dak had led the prisoner out, Rias took Sicarius aside. "I know you're not under my employ, but would you go along and watch while Dak questions him? I don't want to start this new nation off by torturing people, but that man doesn't need to know about our new progressive policies, eh? Perhaps you could touch your knife from time to time and glare at him from the doorway and let your reputation do the rest."

Sicarius glanced at Tikaya. Wondering if she was the one responsible for Rias's un-Turgonian-like lenience? She lifted her chin and met his gaze.

"Menacingly," Sicarius said.

"Pardon?" Rias asked.

"Glaring menacingly. That's what Amaranthe calls it. She has similarly progressive policies."

Rias gave him a tired half-smile. "Ah, yes, that will do."

The exchange surprised Tikaya. It had almost been... a joke. She wouldn't have believed the assassin possessed a sense of humor beneath all his somber black and those, yes, *menacing* glares.

Rias shooed away a few security men who had meandered into the room, their faces distressed as they regarded the hole in the wall, until he and Tikaya were alone, save for Mahliki digging gifts out from beneath a bookcase that had fallen over in the corner. Rias hugged Tikaya again, the gesture less about reassuring her and more about reassuring himself, she sensed. He would never admit to fear or uncertainty before his men, but with her, he had grown more open over the years. She doubted he feared for his own life, though he might regret passing before he had effected the changes he hoped for, but he must worry about having her and Mahliki here in the same building as he.

After a long moment, Rias stepped back, though he did not yet let go of her arms. "When you and those architects were judging the entries, you didn't happen to notice if Sespian's design had fewer windows, did you? In particular, I believe I would like an interior office at this point."

"It actually seemed airy and open, though I did notice a few defensible additions, and there was a note about a new break-resistant glass being manufactured in the south end of the city." Tikaya touched his soot-stained cheek, the day's beard stubble rough against her fingers. "I also noticed that it had a dungeon. If nothing else, you could put your desk down there."

"*Sespian* included a dungeon? I wouldn't have expected that from him, though I suppose there's a practical side beneath his idealism."

"He called it the Holding and Questioning Station, but I've learned to decode those seemingly innocuous Turgonian terms."

Rias squeezed her arms gently. "You *were* the cryptomancer."

And what am I now? Tikaya thought bleakly. She kept the thought off her face and gave him the supportive smile he doubtlessly wanted.

Rias sighed and released her, heading for the door. Before leaving, he paused to say, "I gave the order a while ago to have the site for the new presidential building—someone will have to think up a name at some point—ready as soon as the contest winner was announced. I do believe I'll order construction to start first thing tomorrow."

"Already fantasizing about a dungeon office, Father?" Mahliki stood up, a dented box with leopard print wrapping paper in her hands.

"Something of that nature." Rias pointed at the box. "Be careful opening that. I don't think it's more than a gift—or bribe—but after twenty years, I couldn't claim to know the woman. I barely knew her when we were married."

"Aren't you, uhm..." Mahliki glanced at Tikaya.

"What?" Tikaya asked.

"Well, it sounded like they were *still* married, at least by Turgonian law."

"What?" Tikaya repeated, her mouth dropping open.

Rias grimaced. "The attorney will get that straightened out soon enough. There's nothing to worry about." He waved, issued another, "Be careful," and left them to their investigation.

Tikaya was still standing there, gaping at the door, when Mahliki set the box on the desk and started unwrapping it.

"How is he still married and how is it that I didn't know about this?" Tikaya asked.

"Because you've been spending too much time poking around in dusty libraries and not enough time eavesdropping from behind people's doors." Mahliki dumped the black-and-white ribbon onto the floor where the trash bin would have been if it weren't upended in a corner of the room. "Apparently things are a little murky because he was dead, as far as the empire was concerned, and now he's not."

Tikaya pulled a chair up to the desk, feeling the need to sit. "I hope there aren't any obscure Turgonian laws about husbands being required to perform connubial acts at a wife's behest." She meant it as a joke, but it didn't sound all that funny to her ear. As far as she knew, Turgonian law had been changed a couple hundred years ago to permit a man to have only one wife. What if some attorney decided Rias and Tikaya weren't legitimately married in Turgonia? What if she were no longer recognized as his wife? Or was considered a mistress? The papers had already written articles on Tikaya, revealing that she had been the one who decrypted the secret imperial missives during the last major war. Yes, that was twenty years in the past, but she hadn't felt as comfortable walking the streets alone since those articles came out. For all she knew, there were men like that awful Sergeant Ottotark from the expedition, men who had long memories and who would wish her ill for their past losses.

"Mother?"

Tikaya drew her focus back to the desk. "Yes, I'm ready."

"I asked if you sensed anything. I seem to feel... I think there may be an artifact in here." Mahliki had finished unwrapping the box, but hadn't opened it yet. "Were you busy worrying about the first wife?"

"No, of course not. There's nothing to worry about."

Mahliki lifted her eyebrows.

"Though it would comfort me a little to hear that she's bald, obese, wart-covered, and has a reputation for slaying puppies."

Mahliki smirked. "Sorry, she's pretty. For an old lady."

Tikaya snorted. Anyone over thirty was "old" in her daughter's eyes.

"I haven't checked on puppies though. You can always hope. Did you want to see the note?" Mahliki held out a small card decorated with spots that matched the wrapping paper.

To my dearest Rias with love. I've missed you. ~Sauda

Tikaya couldn't keep her lip from curling with displeasure.

"It makes me want to gag too," Mahliki announced.

"Yes, well... Let's see what she sent him. And to answer your earlier question..." Tikaya rested a hand on the top of the box. The faintest tingle of sensation ruffled the hairs on her arm. "I think you're right. It's nothing strong, but it might be Made." Tikaya eyed the pile of gifts, wondering if there were other less-than-mundane items. "When Dak told me something might be affecting Rias, I should have checked in here first. Unfortunately, the door was locked when I came by this morning." And she hadn't wanted to come in when Rias had been working, for she would have had to admit to him that she was searching for a mind-altering artifact, thus implying something had been wrong with his mind of late...

"You wouldn't think someone would be so obvious as to send a gift if he or she wanted to harm the president." Mahliki held the box at arm's length, turned the lid toward the destroyed window, and eased it open. Nothing happened.

"People here didn't grow up around the Science," Tikaya said, "so they're not sensitive to being in its presence. This gift may appear innocent on the outside, yet have hidden power."

"Innocent?" Mahliki prodded whatever lay inside the box with her finger. "How about odd?" When it didn't zap her, she took it out and sat it on the table.

The six-inch-high jade figure crouched on four canine-like legs while two sets of insect-like arms were folded across a fat, round belly. Two vaguely lupine heads topped it off. The back of the statuette was flat, as if it had been designed to hang on a wall, though old runes were etched in the jade. Time had worn them down, and Tikaya would need to find good lighting and a magnifying glass to read them.

"Paperweight?" Mahliki rotated it. "Bookend?"

"A prayer statue, or maybe a luck statue," Tikaya said. "From the Kitaven Empire—they were here long before the Turgonians and are responsible for that pyramid in the middle of the city. Although..." She rotated the statue a couple of times. "This is either a very early or very late version of the Magu, one of the gods. I haven't seen it represented before with only two sets of arms."

"*Only* two?"

"It usually has six. The parents of this god supposedly slept with animals, hoping to create offspring with the power and agility of the greatest predators in the kingdom."

"The Kitaven—that was a few thousand years ago, wasn't it? Did they have practitioners then?" Mahliki prodded the bulbous belly.

It didn't glow or show any outward sign of being imbued with power, but Tikaya's arm hairs hadn't lain down yet. "I believe they had a few witchdoctors, but nothing sophisticated, nothing like we have today."

"Something sophisticated enough to give Father headaches?" Mahliki toyed with the end of her braid. "Though *I'm* not feeling any mind-altering effects, are you? And we're right next to it."

"No, but maybe prolonged exposure is required," Tikaya said. "Or maybe we just don't *know* our minds are being affected right now. It was news to Rias."

"True."

"It could also be keyed to him," Tikaya added.

Mahliki looked up. "You think it's a plain old relic and that someone

116

put a... *taenuowa* on it?" she asked, switching to Kyattese for the term. Turgonian was limited for discussing the Science.

"Well, it's not plain. It's quite old and quite valuable, but I don't believe those ancient people knew how to create artifacts. They mostly specialized in controlling the elements."

"So, maybe this Sauda had it sitting on a shelf and decided to find a shaman to give it some interesting new traits."

"Or," Tikaya said, "maybe someone approached her, knowing she used to be Rias's wife and that she might be able to get this... gift past security and into his presence."

"You think the wife is innocent then? And is being blackmailed? Or is someone's dupe?"

"I'm not sure I'm ready to declare her innocent," Tikaya said dryly. "But she may not be the mastermind behind this."

"Too bad Agarik isn't here. He could examine it more thoroughly. All I can tell is it does... something."

"Me too." Tikaya tapped on the figure's bald head. "This will require old-fashioned investigating, using nothing but clues and logic to solve the mystery."

"You sound excited at the prospect."

"I *have* been looking for something to do around here."

"Where will you start?"

"With the person who gave him the gift," Tikaya said.

"Uh, don't get yourself in trouble, Mother."

"Of course not," Tikaya said, though she was already debating the most likely place to research for Sauda's address.

Sicarius stood beside the door, glaring at the prisoner, who knelt in the center of the bare basement room, his wrists handcuffed behind his back. Colonel Dak Starcrest leaned against a wall watching him, his arms folded across his chest. A sergeant walked the perimeter of the room, swords, daggers, and more handcuffs jangling on his utility belt. He slapped a baton against his palm and eyed the prisoner.

Sweat bathed the captive's sooty face, and his labored breathing filled the room, rough and raspy. No one had struck him yet, nor had he received substantial injuries when throwing the explosive, but his eyes were bloodshot, his skin pale, and his black hair matted to his head from dampness.

"Nice outfit." The colonel considered his fingernails. "A Nurian style, isn't it? Are you a sympathizer?"

The prisoner's rapid breathing suggested fear, but he didn't answer.

"On someone's payroll, perhaps?" Colonel Starcrest added. He sounded bored, as if he didn't care whether the prisoner answered or not. "Or are you trying to fool us? Secret agents don't usually bomb capital buildings while wearing their employer's colors."

It pleased Sicarius that President Starcrest had asked him to assist in this matter, but he felt he ought to be contributing more. He gave the prisoner his usual cold stare, but the man didn't seem to notice. Sicarius wondered if the colonel would take a more physical approach to the questioning. Turgonian regulations approved the application of force.

"I will apply pressure on the prisoner if you wish it," Sicarius said. The president may have specified glaring, but the glaring was proving ineffective. There were a number of ways to apply pain without permanently damaging a man.

The sergeant thumped his baton into his palm a few more times, standing a couple feet away from the prisoner's ear as he did so. Perhaps he wished to perform the applying of pressure. Sicarius did not care either way, but in addition to finding out who was behind the assassination attempt, he wished to know if this man had something to do with the white-clad figure. It seemed unlikely that they would both be on the grounds at the same time without being connected in some manner.

Soft footsteps sounded in the basement corridor. Sicarius leaned out to see who approached. Amaranthe. He had left her and Sespian to detain the intruders in the bushes while he chased after the man who had thrown the explosives. He wondered if she would object to the application of force.

Gasps came from the center of the room. The prisoner pitched forward, his shoulders curling downward.

"I didn't touch him yet," the sergeant said.

"What's going on?" Amaranthe murmured, stepping inside to join Sicarius. "This is the one who threw the bomb?"

"Yes," Sicarius said. "He may be injured. Or..." He studied the man anew as a fresh thought came to him.

"Or?" the colonel asked.

The sweat... the labored breathing... Of course. "He may have been poisoned."

"You captured him right after he threw the bomb, didn't you?" the colonel asked.

"Approximately forty-two seconds passed between the time I heard the explosion and the time I raced around the building, spotted him, gave chase, and brought him down. It is possible that he was under orders to commit suicide if he failed or suspected he would be caught."

The colonel cursed.

Sicarius did not react outwardly, though he wondered if the curses signified displeasure with his performance or displeasure with the situation as a whole. Though he had only met the colonel that day, his relation to President Starcrest elevated his stature in Sicarius's eyes. He hoped to perform adequately for the man, especially since it might be reported.

"Should I get him some water?" Amaranthe was watching the prisoner with concern—odd how even criminals aroused that emotion in her. "Maybe we should lay him down, get him comfortable."

"Lay him *down*?" the sergeant asked. "We were about to interrogate him."

"That'll be hard if he's dead." Amaranthe pointed at the captive's face; it had grown noticeably redder, almost a purple, in the last minute or two. "Is there any chance of identifying the poison and finding an antidote?"

"A postmortem examination may reveal that information," Sicarius said.

"Oh, good. An antidote will be really helpful then." Amaranthe flung a hand toward him, or maybe everyone in the room, and said, "I'm going to find a doctor."

She need not have bothered. The man died less than two minutes later.

The colonel sighed. "Search the body, Sergeant."

Upon capturing the man, Sicarius had patted him down for weapons. He had removed a kit for making crude incendiary devices, but he hadn't been thorough at the time. Perhaps further evidence would be revealed, including a link to the white-clad figure...

When Amaranthe returned with a doctor in a rumpled sleeping gown and slippers, the gray-haired man stared at the body the sergeant was poking and prodding. "Is that the patient you mentioned?" he asked Amaranthe.

"Yes," she said. "I guess it won't matter that I forgot the water."

"I believe my services would have had to be rendered at an earlier stage."

"A postmortem investigation is required," Sicarius said. "To determine the type of poison employed. It may offer clues as to the origins and who he worked for."

"That's good," the sergeant said, kneeling back, "because he's not carrying any identification or so much as a business card or tin of mints."

"Doc," Colonel Starcrest said. "You didn't have anything else planned for the night, did you?"

The doctor sighed down at his sleeping gown. "No, of course not."

CHAPTER 7

THE EARLY MORNING BREEZE PULLED at Amaranthe's bun as the salvage tug rounded the rocky promontory, entering the cove where she and Sicarius had lost the *Explorer.*

"Not lost," she murmured. "We know exactly where it is."

"Just not its precise depth?" Sicarius asked from behind her.

His silent approach no longer made her jump—most of the time—but she always felt unobservant for failing to see, hear, or otherwise sense him coming. With all that gear on, he ought to have clanked or clinked at least once.

"Precisely." Amaranthe ticked her nail against the brass helmet balanced on the railing beside her. "Remind me again why we're dressed like this—" she waved to the canvas diving suits enshrouding their bodies, "—and the marines who run this ship, a ship specialized for aquatic retrieval, are dressed like that?" She pointed to the man at the helm, who wore a simple black military uniform and jacket.

"I volunteered to direct the marines to the place where the submarine sank. You volunteered to help them find it and hook it with their winch."

"All I remember saying is, 'I've used a diving suit before.'"

"Yes. The captain construed that as volunteering." Sicarius gripped her shoulder, though his eyes were toward the promontory and the woods as he spoke. Remembering their assailant? Lamenting that he had failed to catch him? Or was it a her? "It will not take long," he added. "I don't believe the sub was in water more than fifteen feet in depth when it sank."

"No, and if the water were as clear and pristine as those tropical lagoons, we wouldn't need diving suits to find it at all."

"Perhaps you can suggest to the president that a more comprehensive sewage processing program would be advantageous for our team's further aquatic adventures."

Amaranthe smiled. Their team? With Akstyr in the west and Books gone, did they even have a team any more? It had been good to see Basilard last night, however late it had been by the time she had been able to visit, but he had a new job and wouldn't likely be signing up for further missions as a mercenary. Maldynado was the only one who had asked her what their future plans might be, though even he had been looking for employment with Starcrest. Amaranthe hadn't seen Yara yet, but had heard she was back on the force, protecting the city. She wouldn't likely be interested in mercenary work, either.

"About here?" the helmsman called out.

"Proceed to the east another eighth of a mile," Sicarius responded.

The engines thrummed as the tug pushed against the current, navigating into the cove.

"Might as well get ready." Amaranthe hefted the helmet from the railing and headed toward the flat back end of the boat. The textured decking was cleared, ready to take on the submarine—what remained of it.

A crane, winch, and other machinery for heavy lifting waited with men prepared to operate them. Amaranthe stopped by the air tanks. A fellow who barely appeared old enough to enlist saluted her and stepped forward to attach her hose. Metal scraped as he fumbled with the attachment. No wonder. He was watching Sicarius, who stood impassively, the big helmet under one arm, his eyes scanning the shoreline. The wind ruffled his hair, which always managed to be unkempt, despite Amaranthe's regular haircuts. She didn't find his stance threatening, but the private might be intimidated by his reputation. Or was he nervous for some other reason?

Amaranthe checked the gauges on the air tank and her own hose connections after he moved on. Nothing appeared amiss.

"Sir?" The private held up the hose meant for Sicarius's helmet, though Amaranthe didn't know how the kid expected to attach it from five feet away.

Sicarius stepped closer. The private looked like he wanted to scamper back, but he licked his lips and closed in. His fingers shook as he fastened the hose. Sicarius observed this through hooded eyes, but said nothing.

Amaranthe hadn't yet donned the diving gloves, so she used Basilard's hand signs to ask, *You didn't maul any of his relatives when you were cutting down marines, did you?*

With the private facing him, Sicarius did not sign back. "Unknown."

The kid glanced at him, then skittered back. "All done, sir. You can double-check the connections if you like."

Amaranthe looked around the tug at the marines, most of who were busy at some task or another, rather than watching them. Starcrest had ordered this tug out, and Sicarius and Amaranthe had volunteered to go along, since they knew the location of the wreck. Starcrest surely had no reason to plot mayhem against them—unless he was secretly more irked about the loss of his craft than he let on—but would some marine captain or other officer on board risk his career for a chance at revenge? If Sicarius had wronged one of these men in the past...

"Private," Amaranthe said, "go get the captain, please. I'd like to talk to him before we go down."

"Erp?"

"You heard me."

For a long moment, the kid didn't move. Either he was intimated at the idea of going up to the captain and making demands, or he didn't think Amaranthe was someone he needed to take orders from, or... he was scared for some reason, something beyond Sicarius's reputation.

"If you don't get him," Amaranthe said, "Sicarius and I will simply sit here and play Tiles until he comes down." She patted her bulky suit and nodded to Sicarius. "You didn't happen to bring a set, did you?"

"I only brought my knives." He leveled a cool stare at the private.

"I'll be right back," the kid blurted and sprinted for stairs leading up to the navigation deck.

"What do you suspect?" Sicarius asked.

"Maybe nothing. Maybe something. We'll see."

He didn't question her further. By the time the captain walked down the stairs, the private trailing at his heels, Sicarius had a steel knife out and was making a point of noisily sharpening the blade.

"Good morning, Captain," Amaranthe said cheerfully.

The captain glowered darkly at Sicarius and glowered slightly less darkly at her. The honesty of the emotion reassured her though—one didn't openly show hatred for a person one was plotting against.

"What's the delay?" he asked gruffly. If he was intimidated by Sicarius, he didn't show it.

"I caught a whiff of an unpleasant odor," Amaranthe said.

His lips moved, as if he were trying to figure out what to say. Not surprising since she was making up her reason for delay as she went along...

"Near the tank here." Amaranthe tapped it with a fingernail.

The captain frowned at his private, who was standing by the tank. "Attendance to personal hygiene is recommended in the service, but not mandatory unless it interferes with the duties of others."

It took Amaranthe a moment to find a suitable response—she hadn't expected humor from the gruff officer. Nor was she a hundred percent certain this *was* humor.

"Do you have spare air tanks below decks?" she asked.

"Yes."

"I'd like this one replaced, please." She smiled, knowing she was asking for an irritating amount of extra work from someone.

Not surprisingly, the captain's glower deepened. He looked at Sicarius, as if this might be his fault. Sicarius had stopped sharpening his knife, but he resumed now. He watched the private rather than the captain as he made his long, raspy strokes.

"Ghomes," the captain growled to the private, "do it. They're the president's special friends."

"No." Amaranthe lifted a hand, stopping the young man from scurrying away. "I want someone else to do it. And I want you to watch, Captain."

"Listen, woman—"

The private—Ghomes—didn't stop. He started running, but instead of heading for the ship's stairs, he lunged for the railing, jumping onto it, then dove overboard. His arms were moving in swimming strokes before he hit the water.

"Should I go after him?" Sicarius asked.

"I'd rather you didn't," Amaranthe said, imagining an interrogation at knifepoint. "He's not going to try anything else today."

The captain's glower had turned into a look of stunned disbelief as his private paddled away, heading for the nearest stretch of shore. He recovered and called to a man in an engineer's uniform. "Tudolivc, come check this slagging tank."

"Yes, sir!"

The lieutenant who jogged over went straight to work without more than a glance at Amaranthe and Sicarius. He pulled off a panel and frowned at a couple of readings.

"Well?" the captain asked.

"The mix is off, sir. It probably wouldn't have been noticeable to the divers, but if they had stayed down there long enough without being attentive to their bodies..."

This time, the captain's glower went overboard, in the direction of the private who had clambered out of the water and was charging across a rocky beach. "I'll deal with him later. I know where his parents live, and the boy's too stupid to know he better not show his face in town again after this." The captain jerked a hand at the tank. "Change it out, Tudolive."

"Yes, sir."

The captain left without apologizing for his man. If anything, the over-the-shoulder frown he gave Sicarius implied he was more annoyed that having him on board meant he was going to have to court-martial the kid.

Amaranthe sighed and leaned against Sicarius. "I'd say that you know you're home when people start trying to kill you again, but it happened when we weren't in Turgonia too. Not very charitable of him to meddle with *my* air supply too." Unless she had been the target. If the relatives of those who had died at Fort Urgot ever found out she was responsible for the crash... But no, that couldn't be the case. For good or ill, everything that had happened aboard that monster ship had been locked down tighter than a safe.

"I am always attentive to my body," Sicarius said.

It took Amaranthe a moment to remember the lieutenant's words and figure out what he meant. "You're saying you would have noticed the dubious air?"

"Yes."

"That fails to reassure me. People are trying to kill you." Amaranthe gazed up at him. "I wonder how long it will take the world to forget about you."

"Twenty-three years."

"That's... a random guess? Or some knowledge based on a mathematical model?"

Sicarius rested a hand on her shoulder. "Yes."

The lieutenant lumbered out with a new tank. He replaced the old one and checked all of Amaranthe's and Sicarius's hoses and connections, then opened a lid on a storage bin built into the deck beneath the railing. He pulled out another bulky helmet.

"I get to come down with you," he said dryly. "Going first, even."

"Your suggestion or the captain's?" Amaranthe wondered.

"The captain's. He's a lot of spit and piss, but he's loyal as a hound. He won't risk any of Admir—President Starcrest's allies."

"I understand," Amaranthe said, though she found it odd to have herself considered an ally of Starcrest's. She might have helped change the empire into the republic so he could become the first president, but she wasn't sure how much of a reward that was. Further, she had only meant to end Forge and save Sespian. The rest had fallen into place by chance. And by Sicarius's hand. Amaranthe doubted anyone who didn't know him could tell, but he looked pleased at being called one of Starcrest's allies.

After the three had secured each other's helmets, they headed for a ladder off the stern of the tug. A private unpinned the access gate, making it easy to climb off the ship in the cumbersome suit. True to his word, the lieutenant led the way, descending into the dark water. Amaranthe followed, and Sicarius went last, carrying one of the large winch hooks with him.

They did not descend far before reaching the ground. Amaranthe found reassurance in the fact that they didn't need to go any deeper this time. With luck, there wouldn't be any giant krakens roaming about, either.

A wavering bit of green on the lake floor made her pause. Knee-high seaweed grew up all around them, but this was different, a long dark vine almost like a tentacle...

She gulped. So much for reassurance.

Amaranthe grabbed Sicarius's arm before he could head off, and she pointed to it.

The same plant, she signed, *right?*

Yes, though this doesn't appear to be floating free like the clumps we encountered. Sicarius gazed to the north, though the murky water didn't offer much visibility. *It's possible it's grown down from the core plant in the harbor.*

It can't be. That's three miles away.

The newspapers report that its growth has been exponential.

126

When had he had time to catch up with the papers? They'd barely been in the city for twelve hours, most of those night hours. *Busy* night hours.

Maybe, Amaranthe signed, *but three miles? Plants aren't three miles long. They just aren't.* Great argument there. Very reasoned and logical. She snorted at herself.

Our priority is the sub. Sicarius pointed toward the shoreline, or where it ought to be. As she had noted earlier, the visibility was poor compared to the sparkling waters they had visited in the tropics. At least the dark hull of the tug floated above them, providing a marker.

Yes, I know. Be careful. Amaranthe eyed the vine, the image of the body parts floating in that tangle coming to mind again.

Always.

The lieutenant had already disappeared, though the air tube leading back to the tug showed where he had gone. Sicarius headed off at a different angle, the knee-high vegetation stirring and wavering as he passed through it. Normal vegetation, Amaranthe told herself and followed him. Even though Sicarius had been busy chasing a blasting-stick-hurling assailant, she trusted him to have a good idea of where they had anchored the *Explorer.*

There weren't any fish flitting through the water. Odd. Maybe they knew this plant was something to be avoided.

The submarine came into sight sooner than she expected, and she exhaled a long breath, the sound echoing in her helmet. The oblong hull appeared to be intact, its body resting on the lake floor. Maybe the damage had been internal only and Starcrest would be able to recommission it with minimal repairs.

Amaranthe's relief and optimism didn't last long. Sicarius halted before he reached the hull, his body growing still, his head unmoving. Her stomach shivered with uneasiness. What now?

She moved up beside him. Oh.

Several of those vines rose up from the lakebed and curled around the sub's hull, grasping it like a lover. The carpet of seaweed had been hiding the plant's tendrils as they stretched across the ground, she realized. Vines might be anywhere down here. Grimacing, she peered down at her own feet, the diving boots barely visible amongst the wavering seaweed. She lifted one and then the other to make sure nothing was grasping *her* like a lover. Nothing green anyway.

She touched Sicarius's hand to draw his attention. *Think we can cut those off?*

He drew his knife, not the one he had been sharpening, but the black dagger from the alien civilization, a blade that had never needed sharpening for as long as she had known him. *I will cut the tendrils. You find a place to fasten the winch hook.*

Amaranthe nodded and took the big metal prong from him. While he waded in, she walked around the exterior, the winch's thick cable trailing behind her. For all that she had spent many weeks living in the *Explorer*, she had never examined the craft from the outside—ninety percent of the hull had always been underwater. Its smooth surface did not offer many spots for hooks.

"Maybe the hatch," she murmured, imagining it in her mind. Yes, there was a wheel on top of it for unfastening the lock and lifting the hatch.

The weights on Amaranthe's diving belt did not make it easy to swim. She had to release a few of them so she could scramble up the side of the hull. That was the plan anyway. But when she tried to jump, her right boot didn't lift off. A twinge of pain ran from her ankle to her knee at the failed attempt.

With that uneasy feeling returning to her stomach in full force, she bent and parted some of the seaweed. A green tendril two fingers thick had wrapped around her ankle.

"Sicarius?" she called, though her voice would not travel underwater. He was on the other side of the submarine somewhere, so she couldn't wave for his help, either. "Well, your suit came equipped with a knife too, didn't it?"

Yes, but she would have brought a machete if she had known this plant would be down here.

Switching the hook to her left hand, she pulled out her blade. At first, she tried to calmly slice through the vine. The knife cut its flesh, but barely. The thing proved harder to slice through than a branch of the same thickness.

"Stay calm," she muttered and looked for someplace to put the hook, so she could use both hands. She shrugged and attached it to the vine. Then she laid into the vine with the vigor of a logger with a saw.

Her progress was slow, but not futile. The blade gradually cut in until she reached the halfway point. After this, she would have to make sure she didn't stand still long enough for another one to grab onto her. At this thought, she lifted her other leg to make sure she could. Yes, good.

Motion behind her caught the corner of her eye. Sicarius?

No, another tendril, this one having risen several feet from the floor, its tip waving ominously, almost beckoning. It drifted closer. Dear ancestors, could it actually know she was a living being and could it be after her? No, that was preposterous. It had tangled up the sub after all. It probably had some inborn instinct to wrap itself all over everything.

Keeping an eye on the tendril, Amaranthe reapplied herself to cutting off the first one. The second one kept drifting closer.

The one wrapped around her boot snapped off. She yanked her leg away and ran several paces as quickly as the awkward suit would let her. But she had forgotten about the hook. With the vine no longer attached to her foot, it had slipped off and grown entangled in seaweed several meters away.

Amaranthe waved her knife at the upright vine and angled around it so she could grab the hook. As she bent to pick it up, the first vine reared into the air, its stump pointing toward her, the cross-section revealing a dark viscous green interior. Amaranthe stumbled back as that stump seemed to stare accusingly at her. Whatever this thing was, it wasn't natural. Not a chance.

As soon as she snatched the hook, she raced for the sub and tried to clamber up the side. Starcrest should have incorporated more handholds on the hull. The stupid rivets might have been serviceable if she weren't wearing the gloves and oversized boots, but—

"Oh, right," she grumbled and grabbed one of the vines attached to the hull. So long as it didn't try to grab her back...

She hauled herself up to the hatch, which hung at an odd angle, one of the sturdy hinges warped. Well, if that was all the damage the exterior had taken, Starcrest shouldn't be too distressed. She pulled the hatch shut—it squealed like a dying pig but complied. She secured it and attached the hook to the handle and hoped it would hold up against the stress of being used for lifting the sub.

A hand gripped her shoulder. Amaranthe turned, expecting Sicarius, but it wasn't a hand at all.

She shrieked and lashed out with her knife. It didn't bother the thick green vine at all. It simply curled closer to her helmet, a tendril threatening to wrap around her neck.

A flash of black came down from above.

Sicarius's dagger sliced through the vine as if it were a blade of grass. He grabbed the severed end—which was still gripping Amaranthe's shoulder with alarming vigor—and tore it free. He cut it again. The severed vine floated away. Sicarius landed in a crouch on top of the hull.

Thank you, Amaranthe signed. *I did battle with one over there, and my knife wasn't nearly as effective.* She hoped her shriek hadn't carried through the water for Sicarius to hear.

Nor was the lieutenant's, Sicarius signed. *I regret my delay. I saw him in trouble and moved away to help him.* He nodded toward the other side of the submarine. The lieutenant stood on the lakebed, eyeing the seaweed at his feet. He noticed them looking, though, and pointed at the hook and cable.

Amaranthe gave him a ready sign, then smiled at Sicarius through her faceplate. *Saving a stranger's life? That was very heroic of you. We'll turn you into a noble man yet.*

Would a noble man tease a woman for screaming at the touch of enemy foliage?

Absolutely not, Amaranthe signed. So much for shrieks not carrying underwater...

Then I shall pass on your label.

She might have kissed him, but with a pair of faceplates between them, it didn't seem very feasible. She swatted him instead, and Sicarius returned to cutting the sub free of the vines. A necessary task. Amaranthe wagered the evil things would prove stronger than the winch if they were still attached. Fortunately, with that knife, he finished shortly.

The lieutenant must have signaled someone above, because the cable attached to the hook tightened. Amaranthe reluctantly dropped off her perch and back into the seaweed. She hoped they did not chance across any more hidden vines on the way back to the tug, though having Sicarius beside her, his knife in hand, made that prospect less alarming.

She signed, *We should be done before afternoon, don't you think?*

Yes.

I made an appointment. With a doctor. To check on... things. Amaranthe rolled her eyes at herself. Someday she would learn to speak bluntly with him, to say exactly what she meant. But this wasn't that day.

Good, Sicarius signed. *I will go with you.*

That's not necessary. I don't think any doctor is going to feel comfortable examining a woman when her assassin lover is looming in the corner, fondling his knives.

Sicarius slanted her a sidelong look. *I can wait outside.*

Fondling your knives in the front room? That might upset the desk clerk.

They had reached the tugboat, but Sicarius lifted a hand, keeping her from dumping the rest of her weights and swimming up to the ladder. *You seem certain that I am the target of this assassin, but it's possible* you *may be the target.*

The bit about the vixen and the kit sounded more like you and Sespian than me and... I don't have any kits.

Yet. Her visit to the doctor would hopefully give her more information on that, though between the assassin and the twitchy marine who had fled, Amaranthe wondered at the wisdom of having a child with Sicarius, at least having one soon.

I will go with you to the appointment, Sicarius repeated.

It seemed she would have a bodyguard whether she wanted one or not.

Having double-checked that the sub was ready to move, the lieutenant joined them. Amaranthe kept her response to a quick, *As you like*, then swam up to the ladder.

Up on deck, she was tempted to toss the helmet aside with an unceremonious clunk. How she kept ending up back in these awful diving suits, she wasn't quite sure. Before this feeling of anarchy could take root, she spotted a stack of towels. She selected one and wiped the helmet clean of water instead, then started to wind her air hose neatly back around its reel.

A private jogged up. "I can handle that, ma'am."

"I'm glad you had that knife," the lieutenant told Sicarius as the men removed their own gear. "What's it made of?"

"An unknown material."

"Unknown?" The officer's brow furrowed. "Who made it?"

Sicarius gave him a quelling stare.

"Don't mind him," Amaranthe said, adjusting the hose on the reel—

the private was letting it wind in crookedly. "It's not at all uncommon for him to save your life and then utterly ignore you."

"Oh." The lieutenant lifted a hand and whispered to her behind it, "Technically, he's not ignoring me. He's glaring at me."

"That too."

"I hope the team going down in the harbor has something similar," the lieutenant said. "Those vines were definitely... grabby. My diving knife barely made a dent."

Amaranthe had been in the process of removing her boots, but she froze at his words. "The other team."

Sespian, Maldynado, and Basilard had gone with Mahliki that morning to get root samples. Sicarius met her eyes, his face unreadable, but he had to be thinking the same thing. If the vines had been difficult to deal with here, they would be a nightmare in their originating location. And the other team didn't have a special knife.

"Lieutenant," Amaranthe said, hose reels forgotten, "if you could urge your men to get that boat off the bottom as quickly as possible, I'd appreciate it. I'm going to talk to the captain."

Sicarius was on her heels as she jogged up the steps.

Sespian buckled the weights onto the belt of his already-heavy canvas diving suit and tried not to think claustrophobic thoughts as he eyed the brass helmet waiting for him. Hyperventilating at the bottom of the lake wouldn't be good. Hyperventilating on the deck of the ship wouldn't be good, either, not with all these burly marines strutting around, making preparations for his team. Mahliki's team, he reminded himself. He wasn't an emperor any more, and he certainly wasn't in charge of this mission. He wasn't even sure how he had gotten himself invited along. The construction workers were breaking ground over on the build site. *His* build site. He ought to be there, watching with a critical eye as the foundation was poured for the president's new residence.

Next to him, Mahliki didn't appear at all intimidated by the prospect of this mission as she tugged on the oversized boots.

"Have you done this before?" he asked.

"Gone out in diving suits? Oh, yes. I grew up in a submarine and for a time thought I would specialize in marine biology. I even took some classes on marine pharmacology when I was home last planting season. It's fascinating, and being down in the ocean, it's amazing."

In other words, she wasn't nervous at all. Sicarius wouldn't be, either. Sespian wondered why he hadn't inherited some of his father's fearlessness. Probably because he had spent most of his life indoors. If he were more experienced with adventuring, he might feel less daunted. After all, Maldynado and Basilard were tossing jokes and reminiscing as they donned their gear.

"I do admit to being the teensiest bit nervous about this setup though." Mahliki lifted one of the tubes attached to her suit. "Everything is self-contained on our suits back home. There's a tank and a device that provides air, and you simply wear them on your back when you go down."

"A... magical device?" Sespian wasn't an expert on diving technology, but he didn't think they could make self-contained units in Turgonia yet.

"Essentially. I'm not all that comfortable having to depend on strangers, but that's what we'll be doing with this surface-supplied air." Mahliki shrugged and released the tube. "At least we're not going that deep. The fellow who put out the anchor said we're at forty-five feet."

"I'm sure the marines can be counted on to keep you safe. In fact, if it came between choosing who to save..." Sespian pointed at Mahliki, himself, then Basilard and Maldynado, "you would be their first choice. None of them would want to answer to your father."

"I wouldn't want to answer to my father if *I* lost anyone on my team, either." Mahliki scooted closer and whispered, "Don't tell the others, but this is my first command. Unless you count ordering relatives around."

She grinned, but Sespian sensed a hint of anxiousness beneath her facade. She might not be worried about her own safety, but it seemed she did have some fears.

"That's tougher than it sounds," Sespian said. "I've never succeeded in ordering a relative around."

"Where is he today?" Mahliki asked. "Your relative?"

"He and Amaranthe are out with another marine vessel, a tug, to try and salvage the submarine. They volunteered. I gather they both feel responsible—and a little sheepish—at having lost it, especially this close to home."

"Sheepish?" Mahliki asked. "Sicarius? I have a hard time associating that word with him."

"His sheep is buried deep down. You have to hunt for it."

"I'd be afraid to try."

Maldynado and Basilard shuffled up, their helmets in hand. Both men had more weapons than the standard-issue diving knife attached to their suits. Basilard bore a number of daggers and a long serrated blade. Maldynado wore a cutlass in a scabbard across his back. Sespian would be afraid he would cut his own air supply tube if he tried to draw a sword underwater, but he supposed Maldynado had practice.

"We've been discussing this mission," Maldynado said, "and there's something we need to know before we get started."

"Oh?" Mahliki asked.

Basilard set down his helmet and signed a few words.

"Yes, yes, I'm asking," Maldynado said. "We used to call Amaranthe 'boss.' Or I did anyway. What should we call you? I'm suggesting a proper, 'my lady,' since your father is warrior caste, but Bas here thinks that since you grew up on the Kyatt Islands, you wouldn't expect a Turgonian title. You'd be a Miss Starcrest or something, but that doesn't seem proper to my ear."

"Uh, can you call me Mahliki?"

Basilard signed, *That sounds presumptuous. Won't the president think us overly familiar?*

Sespian hadn't seen his hand signs for a few months but found he remembered a number of them.

"What?" Mahliki asked. She would doubtlessly have a quick ear—or in this case eye—for languages, but Sespian didn't think she had spent much time with Basilard.

"He says that's a lovely name, and it would be a pleasure to use it," Maldynado said.

Basilard thumped him on the arm with the back of his hand.

"You should have brought your new interpreter if you wanted strict translations," Maldynado told him.

"We're ready to descend, my lady," a new voice said. It belonged to one of two marines walking up behind Sespian, neither looking much older than he.

"My lady," Maldynado whispered to Basilard. "I told you."

"Let's get down there then." Mahliki waved toward the harbor. "That plant spreads every day. It's going to be having dinner at Father's table before long."

Indeed, the green vines had smothered the docks and now stretched across Waterfront Street, some curving up the sides of buildings. From this far out, it looked like a green carpet. Soldiers were working with the fire brigade to hack at and try to burn the vines, but the appendages were growing back as quickly as they were destroyed.

Sespian and the five others in diving suits dragged their gear to the back of the vessel.

"Remember," Mahliki said. "Don't touch the pods. Don't touch anything actually. Just let me get close enough to take my samples of the root system. I appreciate you all volunteering to come along, but I hope I won't need you and that you'll merely be..."

"Decorative?" Maldynado suggested.

Maldynado is good at being decorative, Basilard signed.

"Extraneous," Mahliki said.

"I think I'd rather be decorative," Maldynado muttered.

Sespian followed Mahliki to the departure dock at the back of the ship. The team secured each other's helmets, and a marine in uniform came around to double-check everyone's gear. Sespian eyed all of the hoses coming out of the air tanks sitting on the deck and hoped people wouldn't get tangled up down there. The self-contained units Mahliki had mentioned sounded much more appealing.

"Everyone ready?" Mahliki asked.

"My lady, you need weights or you won't be able to sink down to the bottom," a marine said, stopping her with a raised hand. "The suits are heavy, but they're buoyant in the water."

"Oh, I know that." Mahliki grabbed a bag slouched against the side of the deck, using both hands to lift it. Dozens of zippers provided access to interior pouches that bulged with pokey objects.

"A... purse?" the marine asked. "That won't be sufficient."

"How much weight were you going to give me?" Mahliki asked.

"Fifty pounds."

She hefted her bag a couple of times. "Yes, that's about right. And it's a sample collection bag, not a purse. The tools and vials will weigh me down."

Maldynado leaned close to Basilard and whispered, "I'll bet she keeps the same weird collection of doodads in her purse."

Diplomatically, Basilard said nothing. But his blue eyes glinted with good humor.

Sespian saw the joke for what it was, but he felt compelled to defend Mahliki, in case *she* didn't recognize—or appreciate—the teasing. "I find it admirable that a girl—a woman—would carry useful items along on a mission. If Maldynado had a purse, it would be full of useless toys for wooing the ladies."

The group fell silent and stared at him.

Dear ancestors, he was as awkward as Sicarius at times. What a trait to inherit.

Basilard was the first to comment, his eyes still gleaming with humor. *Maldynado* does *have a purse.*

Maldynado propped a fist on his hip. "I do *not*. That's a man bag. Full of manly things."

Last I saw, it had cedar candles and perfumes in it.

"*Cologne*, not perfume. Goodness, Bas, don't your yurt-dwelling people have any sense of the fineries of civilization? And cedar... is a masculine scent."

Sespian shrugged at Mahliki. He didn't know if he had made her feel better about being teased, but he had at least deflected the attention away from her. These two looked like they had a lot of practice at flinging insults and were ramping up for a long bout, no doubt to make up for the months they had been separated.

Mahliki was... gazing back at him with an enigmatic smile. When Sespian raised his eyebrows in inquiry, she merely shook her head and clapped her hands to get the group's attention.

"Time to go, everyone. That plant's getting bigger every minute."

After a last check of everyone's gear, the team headed in, the marines leading despite Mahliki's protest that she should go first. Sespian would back her up on anything related to biology and plant research, but silently agreed that the strong fighters should lead the way. He waved for Maldynado and Basilard to take the rear and slipped in ahead of Mahliki himself, giving the excuse that their hoses would tangle if she went ahead. He thought she might protest—it *was* a feeble excuse—but she smiled again.

Sespian descended the ship's ladder into the dark water, expecting it to freeze him to the core. The suit insulated him, however, and he found the chill manageable. From the bottom of the ladder, the weights pulled him down ten, twenty, then forty feet before his boots stirred the seaweed and silt on the lake bottom. He worked his jaw to pop his ears. The hose trailed up above him, a beacon that would lead him back to the ship if he lost his sense of direction. Fortunately, enough light filtered down through the water to brighten the murky surroundings. Already, Sespian could make out the green horizon to the east, the forest of thick stems sprouting from the lakebed.

The marines had already fanned out to take the lead. Sespian waited until Mahliki landed so he could walk at her side. She clanked softly as she touched down. Sespian clanked a bit, too, when they headed toward the forest of green—after his encounter with the vine on the dock, he had not believed a standard-issue diving knife would prove sufficient. A sturdy one-handed axe hung from one side of his belt and a machete the other. He had a serrated dagger strapped to his calf as well. Maldynado and Basilard dropped down behind them, their weapons also clanking.

Sespian's boots squished in mud and silt as they walked. The greenery took up more and more of the horizon, and the water seemed to grow darker. His imagination, no doubt.

The team slowed as it drew closer to the edge of the jungle, the stalks rising up toward the surface, the vines sprawling in all directions, waving and twitching in the current. The density of the wall of green was daunting, more like reeds crammed together in a marsh than trees in a forest or jungle. Even if the plant didn't have appendages that liked to grasp a person, Sespian would be loath to push into the thick foliage. One might become entangled even without the plant doing anything.

The stalwart marines glanced back at Mahliki several times, perhaps wondering how close they would have to get. She kept striding forward, her faceplate pointed toward the wall of green.

One of the marines waved and pointed downward. A warning. Several of the vines or stolons—or whatever this thing had—snaked away from the forest core. They were branching out, the runners heading into the lake depths and also to the north and south, parallel to the shoreline. Here and there, vines rose from those runners, waving in the current as the group approached.

The marines were doing their best to avoid the green appendages. Mahliki strode straight up to the first one. She crouched, using pliers to try and lift the vine, but fine roots had grown from the bottom of it. She glanced at Sespian and pointed.

He took that to mean she wanted a sample. He stepped up to her side, his axe in hand. The way a nearby tendril—more like a tentacle—was leaning toward her made him nervous. He wasn't displeased to see Maldynado and Basilard close in behind them, their weapons out as well. A few meters ahead, the marines were gesturing and pointing. Arguing? Sespian doubted they could hear each other's words down here, but he followed their gazes... then swallowed.

Just inside the forest line, a swollen, waterlogged body dangled a few feet from the lake bottom. The remains of a body anyway. Green tendrils were wrapped about it, and the skin had been flayed away in places. From fish? Sespian hadn't seen any fish since they had dropped into the water. Dear ancestors, the plant wasn't eating that person, was it?

Mahliki jerked back, almost falling onto her backside. Sespian reacted before his mind caught up to his instincts—he lashed out with the axe and knocked away a tendril that had been darting toward her head. Less than a heartbeat later, Maldynado and Basilard had leaped over Mahliki and pinned the offending vine. Their daggers hacked through it in three places. The vine went limp and collapsed in the mud. The severed pieces drifted away. Sespian kept an eye on them, remembering the one he had cut on the dock and how it had continued to wiggle and writhe.

"I wasn't expecting any of the vines to move that fast," Sespian said, then, realizing nobody would be able to understand him, did his best to sign the same message with Basilard's hand gestures.

Is this plant... sentient? Basilard signed.

Maldynado tapped him on the shoulder. He had noticed what the marines were staring at. *Whatever it is... I'm thinking you should find a recipe and cook it. All of it.*

Mahliki had recovered from her surprise at having the vine dart toward her face, and she stood, a sample vial in hand. She tucked it into her bag.

I hope it doesn't start growing in your vial, Sespian signed before realizing she wouldn't be able to understand.

I hope not too, she signed. *I have some... uh... chemicals?* She looked at

Basilard, eyes questioning. *I don't know the sign. Maybe there isn't one. It should preserve the plants—and halt growth—but obviously I can't pour it into the vials until we get back out of the water.*

Sespian, Basilard, and Maldynado all stared at her for a moment before someone responded.

When did you learn my language? Basilard looked pleased.

We spent that day on the ship together, remember?

Sespian realized her earlier question about Basilard's signs must have been a result of her not seeing all of them rather than not understanding them.

One day? Maldynado moved to scratch his head, but his knuckles clunked against the hard helmet. He settled for massaging a rivet. *It took me months to see through Basilard's silent mystique.*

Mahliki shrugged. *He was at the funeral too. I need a sample of the core root system. I believe that was akin to an ancillary taproot, more for securing the vine than providing sustenance.* She pointed toward the dense forest ahead—the marines were still up there and seemed to be debating whether they could cut the corpse down. The idea of leaving someone's body down here without a proper funeral pyre bothered Sespian, but he wasn't sure how close they should risk getting. *He* didn't want to be left down here without a proper funeral pyre, either.

I think it's getting its sustenance right there. Maldynado pointed at the body, a disgusted sneer visible through his faceplate.

Perhaps, Mahliki signed as she walked closer, *but like the Seruvian Insect Trap, it should still draw nourishment from the soil and...* she groped for a sign again before shrugging and choosing, *the sun.*

Photosynthesis was the word she wanted, Sespian guessed.

Looks like the shaman who made it gave it some terrifying traits, Maldynado signed.

Shaman? Basilard asked. *Is that who we believe is responsible?*

Shaman, wizard, somebody. Maldynado shrugged.

Sespian didn't catch Basilard's response. He had spotted another dark form farther into the tangle of stalks and vines. Another body? There were smaller figures too. Animals? He shuddered. All of those tales of missing people... they had not been unfounded. Odd that nobody had actually seen someone get abducted, at least not the last he had heard.

139

Could the plant have the self-preservation instinct—the *intelligence*—to choose its targets carefully, when there were no witnesses around?

"But it's going after us with witnesses around," he murmured. "Unless it's sure it can keep all of us from escaping... Or maybe it's protecting itself since we're encroaching."

Neither were comforting thoughts.

Mahliki was drawing closer to the dense wall of stalks, so Sespian hurried to remain at her side. Seeing the forest of green stretch up thirty feet and more was intimidating, not to mention that some of those vines near the top spread out, like branches on a tree, forming a canopy of sorts. It *wasn't* his imagination; it was growing darker as they walked closer.

A commotion arose to Sespian's left. A vine had snaked out, wrapping around one of the marines' legs. His comrade was attacking it. Sespian clenched his axe tighter, tempted to jog over and help, but he was loath to leave Mahliki.

I'm fine, she signed and pointed toward Basilard and Maldynado behind her. *Go help*.

Sespian thought to send one of them instead, but the vine had pulled the marine off his feet. Did it intend to yank him into the forest and string him up like the bodies? Sespian ran toward the pair as fast as the cumbersome suit would allow.

The vine had a grip on the man's leg and... yes, the slagging thing was pulling him. Sespian could hardly believe it. Both marines were hacking at it with their diving knives. Somebody should have warned them to bring heavier weaponry.

Sespian arrived as the standing marine was finally able to cut through the vine. Released, his comrade scrambled away, though the tendril had not released his leg. He hopped, poking at it with his knife. Given the pained expression on his face, it must be tightening around the limb like a boa constrictor. Sespian lunged in, intending to help, but a startled squawk pierced their watery surroundings. The vine the other marine had cut, its dark green stump open to the water, a viscous ichor on the tip, rammed into the man, knocking him down. A second vine shot out of the forest, aiming for his leg.

Sespian hacked at it with the axe. He smashed it against the lake floor. The blade cut in, but not as far as he would have wished—the soft mud cushioned the blow. He slammed the axe down again, then whipped the machete out so he could attack with his left hand too.

"Get back," he shouted to the marines, not knowing if they would hear him.

Sespian severed the vine on the ground, then hacked more tendrils drifting toward him from different angles. He felt inept as the things swirled all about him. The water's denseness slowed his own blades, but did not perturb the plant at all. He stumbled backward as he continued to dodge and parry the whip-like attacks, hoping the marines had already escaped. He dared not take time to glance around.

Something grabbed him from behind.

Sespian hollered and launched an axe under his arm, hoping to catch the cursed vine. At the last second, he glimpsed the canvas of a diving suit instead of the green of the plant. He halted his attack, the blade inches from slamming into Basilard's faceplate.

Basilard and Maldynado were both there. They gripped him under the armpits and pulled him back, five, ten meters before stopping. The vines continued to wave in the air around the space he had left. Cursed ancestors, there were at least eight of them, anyone of which could have wrapped around his neck...

Sespian told himself to calm down. The diving suit would have protected him somewhat. Maybe.

"The marines?" he asked, keeping an eye on the vines. They weren't encroaching farther, not with Maldynado and Basilard standing there. He spotted the marines recovering a few feet away, but... Sespian's stomach sank into his boots. If Maldynado and Basilard were with him, then where...?

"Mahliki?" he asked, his voice cracking. He looked up and down the plant line. Mahliki's smaller diving suit was nowhere to be seen. No, wait. There was her air tube... He felt sick. It disappeared into the snarl of green where he had last seen her.

Maldynado shook his head grimly. Basilard held up a glass jar with a gnarly root bulb in it, its side slit open.

"What the blast does that mean?" Sespian demanded, then repeated the words as signs, his hands jerking so angrily he didn't know if the others would understand him.

She was cutting at some roots, and all these vines shot out to distract us,

141

Maldynado signed. *Only I didn't know they were the distraction then. We had to fight like you were doing to keep from being overwhelmed. I pushed through to her, intending to pull her back, so we could all get out of there, but just as she put this in the jar, a vine wrapped around her waist and yanked her into the forest. She had time to throw the jar at us and shout...* He hitched a shoulder. *I think it was something like, "Get this to my mother."*

Basilard nodded. *We tried to charge in after her, but the stalks pressed together. It turned into a wall, and we couldn't get past it.*

And then the vines started coming for us again. Maldynado made a rude gesture at the forest of green. *We barely made it out of there.*

Sespian snarled in frustration and stamped his boot.

I would have kept trying if there was a way, Maldynado added. *But we figured this sample must be something important and that we had to get it back for someone to look at.*

"Great," Sespian said, tired of the signs and not caring if they understood or not. "I'll let you hand that to Starcrest and explain where his daughter went."

Maldynado's face grew pale.

Sespian stalked back to the ship.

CHAPTER 8

T HE SUBMARINE LAY ON ITS side on the tug's aft deck, a black oblong shape, elegant even in this unnatural state. No obvious holes breached the hull, but once the hatch had been opened, countless gallons of water had poured out.

Sicarius climbed inside, wondering if the power source remained intact and also if there might be any clues inside as to the assailant. He doubted he would find more than the burned shell of a blasting stick—if that—but it wouldn't hurt to look. He had already glared—menacingly, Amaranthe had assured him—at the captain to urge him to depart as quickly as possible to join Sespian's ship in the harbor. The captain had promised this would happen as soon as they had the submarine tied down. Even now, privates were tossing cables across its body under the direction of the engineering lieutenant. This seemed wasteful for a short trip across a placid lake, but perhaps the captain anticipated trouble entering into the area where the plant dominated the waters.

The inside of the *Explorer* smelled much like the lake: wet, musty, and overpowered with the primordial jungle lushness that the plant emitted. The smell of black powder had been washed away during the submarine's overnight bath.

A couple of the vines Sicarius had severed had extended through the hatch, and he checked around before entering far, not positive cutting them had killed them. Like an earthworm, this plant had an amazing capacity for regeneration.

He spotted the two severed vines, both lying on the side—which was currently the bottom—of the sub. Both wriggling. One seemed to be inching for the hatch. Sicarius flicked it out onto the deck with his knife and the other one as well. He didn't know how to utterly destroy the pieces, but he didn't want them infesting the president's submarine when he delivered it.

Sicarius swung through the upturned boat, taking in the black scorch marks on the interior on his way to the compact engine room. Had that inside hatch been open when Amaranthe had left? She would have grabbed their luggage from the sleeping cabin, but might have left the rear compartment sealed. If so...

He halted and stared. The hatch leading to the engine room had been blown off its hinges. Shrapnel had gouged the walls on either side, and soot stained the floor. Odd that the damage should be more extreme back here, farther away from the entry hatch. He imagined their attacker up on the promontory and the trajectory the blasting stick would have taken. It must have flown inside, bounced off the wall, and through sheer luck rolled back here before exploding.

Luck? Dangerous to assume that. He reasoned that *he* might have made such a throw, calculating the precise angle to cause the stick to skid to the back. It would be wisest not to assume this stranger lacked skills he possessed. After all, the person had eluded him in the woods.

No hint of the power source's customary glow seeped from the engine room. And he soon saw why. The round orb still sat on its steel pedestal, but the side had been smashed in. Sicarius would have sensed it if any power remained; this was nothing but a useless husk now. Unless Starcrest could come up with a viable mundane fuel source, the *Explorer* would not run again, not until someone could hire another Kyattese Maker to craft a new energy source. *He* should be that someone, since he had been borrowing the submarine when this had happened. He would consider how such an artifact might be acquired after he dealt with the assassin.

He was about to back out of the sub when a scrap wedged under the corner of the pedestal caught his eye. He plucked up the wrapper—the shredded remains of the blasting stick. Though he doubted it would tell him much, he took it outside to examine in the daylight.

Sicarius found Amaranthe crouching beside the hatch, peering inside. Behind her, the rocky cliff of the promontory was drifting past. Good. They were en route to the harbor.

"It's going to take a lot of scrubbing to make those bulkheads seem new again," Amaranthe observed.

"The energy source has been destroyed," Sicarius said.

"I was afraid of that. I don't suppose scrubbing will make *that* seem new again."

"No." He opened his palm to study the thick scrap of paper. "Huh."

"Huh?" Amaranthe echoed.

"This wasn't a standard military-issue blasting stick." Little of the original color remained, but he could tell it wasn't the black and red model that the army and marines employed.

"I imagine an assassin would have a hard time walking in and buying military ordnance."

Sicarius thought about pointing out that assassins could get into most places without buying anything, but she spoke again.

"Something out of a mining camp? No, wait." Amaranthe plucked it out of his hand and looked at the end. It was in better shape than the other couple inches of tubular scrap, and she poked at a black mark, a tiny compass. "I recognize this craftsman's mark. I think." She squinted at the shape, less than a centimeter in diameter.

Sicarius tilted his head, waiting.

"Yes, I've ordered blasting sticks from this person before. Remember Ms. Sarevic's Custom Works on Molten Street?"

"You went there with Books last fall to purchase blasting sticks for Sespian's kidnapping."

A flash of pain crossed her eyes at the mention of Books's name, but she nodded. "Yes. Her explosives are known to be of a good quality, often better and more... creative than what the military and the mines use."

"She should be questioned then."

"Yes. If—"

A shout from the other end of the tug made Amaranthe turn her head. Sicarius had already been aware of the approach of the harbor and of the plant coming into view, but he jogged to the railing to see what had drawn some marine's attention. It was the vessel that had been assigned to take Sespian and the others into the harbor. A warship called the *Interceptor*.

"Why are they so close to the plant?" Amaranthe asked. "Given how effectively it's destroyed the docks and pilings with its vines..."

Sicarius could make out the people on the deck, the racing about and the agitation in the gestures. "They've already found trouble."

Mahliki hung halfway up one of the plant's tree-like stalks and judged that ten feet of water lay between her and the surface. And freedom.

"Technically not," she muttered, as the plant extended farther into the air and who knew how far in each direction. But if she popped up, the ship might be able to throw her a life preserver. Or a steam-powered jackhammer with which to trample all this wayward foliage. Not that she could operate either at the moment.

Three thick vines were wrapped around her torso and legs, pinning her to the stalk. One of her arms remained free, and she still had her bag, but she hadn't figured out how to put either to useful effect.

"You can collect all the samples you want now..." The plant flesh loomed close, with only the faceplate of the helmet separating Mahliki from it. She hoped the diving suit would armor her against... whatever these vines were using to break down people's bodies. There was something wrong with her, she decided, because she found herself more curious about how that was being done than terrified that it would be done to her.

"Terror comes later. When an uncertain fate becomes certain."

They were her father's words. Maybe she would get a chance to find out how true they were.

"Not yet," she whispered.

For the moment, she could fight and deny certainty. Air still flowed into her helmet, granting her life—and options. As far as she could tell, her hose was still attached to the ship—though she had to crane her neck to see it, and it disappeared from sight amongst the thick stalks.

"Hope the plant doesn't figure out that's important to me." Mahliki imagined one of the vines wrapping around her hose, tightening until it cut off her air. "No, it's not that smart." Though she had to grant that it had an animal-like intelligence. She wondered if there was a brain or something that functioned as a botanical equivalent. If so, where could she find a sample of it?

"Later. Time to plot a daring escape. Or at least an effective one." Mahliki wriggled her free hand under the flap of her bag and prodded around. Vial, vial, test tube, no. Scalpel? Probably too small to be effective. Pliers? Maybe, but again, she feared they would prove useless on such a large plant. A spade? Enh. She patted a jar in the bottom. Oh, that was her snail slime, a lubricant she made that had been inspired by the little gastropods. Usually she used it to lubricate her articulating tools, but maybe...

Mahliki tugged it out at the same time as the vine around her waist tightened. She almost dropped the jar.

"Maybe it's not going to eat me, it's just going to squeeze me to death."

With her other arm still pinned, opening the jar was a challenge. She forgot about her faceplate momentarily and clunked the lid against the glass in an attempt to use her teeth. Her mother wouldn't have approved anyway. She always said tools were far superior to teeth for purposes unrelated to digestion. When Mahliki finally pried the lid free, it slipped from her hand, spiraling down into the dark depths.

"Hope this works," she muttered and did her best to grease the vines—and herself. Canvas wasn't the slickest material, but whatever sealant they put on the outside of the suit helped. She slathered gobs of the slime on every part of her body she could reach, armpits and helmet included—more because she could reach them than out of a certainty that they would be tactically important against the plant.

Once she had used up all the snail slime in the jar, she stuffed it back into her pouch and prepared herself to make a big shove, one that would involve sucking everything in and pushing off the stalk as best as she could. The plant, alas, had not been kind enough to provide a launch platform for her.

Before she made her attempt, something caught her attention. The vines wrapped around her body had started to ooze fine dark blue droplets from their pores. Some sort of reaction to the slime? A sign of irritation? Or—she managed to feel unease and enlightenment at the same time—maybe this was some sort of enzyme to aid digestion.

"Interesting, but you are *not* digesting me, you sprites-cursed son of a three-legged goat." Despite her determined words, she didn't push off right away. She dug in her bag again and pulled out a vial so she could scrape some of the viscous droplets inside. "It would be a shame to waste this opportunity."

Once she had secured her latest sample, Mahliki took a deep breath... then exhaled every molecule of air. At the same time, she pushed with her legs and shoved down with her free arm. To her relief, it worked. Sort of. She moved an inch or two, before the vines readjusted their grip farther down.

"So we do it again..."

By pushing and straining—not to mention copious thrashing—Mahliki inched higher and higher. Once she got her other arm free, she thought freedom was a certainty. But shadows stirred at the edge of her vision. Other vines veering toward her.

She redoubled her efforts, twisting toward the massive stalk at her back and grabbing it with both hands. She pulled herself up it as if it were a rope dangling into a pit full of crocodiles. One of the vines she had escaped snaked up, trying to reestablish its grip at the same time as a new one darted toward her helmet. Mahliki kicked the first away, having no delusions that such an attack would thwart it for long, at the same time as she continued climbing. Wishing she hadn't dropped her diving knife, she batted at the new intruder with a fist. The blow did nothing to stop it. It snaked past her arm and tried to wrap itself around her helmet.

Mahliki whipped her head to the side. Fortunately the slime worked well on the smooth brass. The vine slipped away, and she practically ran up the stalk, the sunlight bouncing on the surface of the water so close she could almost—

A jerk at the back of her head yanked on her neck. She gasped in pain, but not so loudly that she missed the *clunk-snap* reverberating in her helmet. Her air hose—it had been torn off. A vision of water streaming into her helmet and drowning her flashed before her eyes, but she kept climbing. If she could reach the surface...

Then what? She would still have to swim across this cursed forest of plants if she were to escape. They would keep grabbing her and simply pull her down again, this time without an air supply...

No. They would try, but they wouldn't get her. She was slick. She was—

Her head breached the surface. Despite her pessimistic thoughts, she roared with triumph—and immediately spun in a circle, searching for the ship or for the closest beach.

The warship loomed much closer than she had expected. They had come into the forest, looking for her. She didn't know whether to thank them or call them idiots—what if the whole cursed ship became trapped?—but she swam toward them. Vines and stalks created an obstacle course, but she was inspired to greater effort by the men at the railing, pointing and waving at her. Twenty-five meters away. If she could get through these plants without being grabbed again...

She had no sooner had the thought than her suit caught. No, that was her bag. She dunked her head below again, trying to see—yes, a cursed tendril had wrapped around the strap. She tore into the bag, almost dumping the contents in her haste, and dug out the first tool she found. The pliers. She attacked the tendril in a frenzy of stabs, then grabbed it and twisted, trying to tear it away from the strap. This tendril wasn't as thick and strong as the vines, so it worked, but not before a new vine snaked around her leg. The plant was determined to keep her from escaping, and she had started to feel light-headed.

The air. She was out. The seal must have remained intact, for no water was flowing in, but she was sucking on the last of her oxygen. She had to escape and get the helmet off, or she would asphyxiate on the surface of the water.

Mahliki yanked her leg, and once again the snail slime saved her. A grip that would have otherwise held fell away. She turned around to sprint the last meters to the boat.

She almost crashed into the huge black hull, for it had sneaked up on her. Before she could do more than lift her head, hands descended from above, grabbing her arms... and slipping free. Erg, the slime. She looked up, hoping for a ladder or hook she could grasp, but someone caught her by the scruff of her suit. She was pulled out of the water and hauled onto the deck. She scrambled several meters—to make sure she was a long ways from those vines should they try for her again—before collapsing and rolling onto her back.

Having something hard and dry under her had never felt so good... not to mention the sun blasting through the water droplets on her faceplate. Those black dots probably didn't have anything to do with the sun. Air. Right. With shaking hands, she fumbled at the clasps of her helmet. Thankfully, someone knelt beside her and helped her get it off.

Mahliki had never inhaled so quickly in her life. She was lucky she didn't suck her tongue down her throat.

With all of her energy spent, and then some, she flopped back to the deck. Sespian leaned in, peering into her eyes. "Are you all right?"

She meant to say yes, but it came out as a raspy wheeze.

Sespian rested a hand on the top of her head. "Relax. Your job is done. The captain will figure out how to get the ship out of here."

In other words, they were trapped in the plant forest? Great. As much as she appreciated his solicitude, she wouldn't have minded a few more minutes of lying on the deck and breathing refreshing air before being alerted to their continuing danger.

A couple of other concerned faces leaned in, Maldynado and Basilard, both with their helmets removed, though they still wore their diving suits.

"Did you know your armpits are slippery?" Maldynado asked.

"Yes." Mahliki pushed herself into a sitting position. "Piece of advice for dealing with these plants. Don't go in without sufficient lubricant."

Maldynado's eyebrows waggled. "I never go anywhere without sufficient lubricant."

Basilard signed, *He keeps it in his purse.*

"It's *not* a purse."

Mahliki would have liked to show off the specimens she had collected, but a throaty thrum reverberated through the deck. "It sounds like we're taxing the engines."

"Yup," Maldynado said. "And we're not moving much."

"We're going to have to figure out a way to cut the vines free." Sespian waved toward the railings where marines were swinging machetes.

Stalks rose all around the ship, vines and leaves swaying in the breeze. The deck remained open and clear, but green tendrils had latched onto the railing. Mahliki had a feeling the belly of the vessel had far more vines attached to it.

"Unfortunately, I used all the snail slime," she murmured.

A squad of marines jogged past carrying barrels of black powder and boxes of blasting sticks.

"This is about to get interesting," Maldynado said.

"Or dangerous," Sespian said.

Basilard nodded solemnly.

"I better find the captain and see if there's a way I can help." Mahliki stood up. "I assume this trouble we're in is because of me." The ship had been anchored farther out, beyond the plant forest. It never would have ventured this close if not for her.

Sespian fell in at her side as she headed for the stairs. She supposed it wasn't the proper time to be pleased that he was sticking close—and she hadn't forgotten that he had defended her when his comrades teased her, either. All sorts of progress there. Something she would contemplate in full when she had the luxury to do so.

"Neither the captain nor any of his officers wanted to explain to your father that we'd lost you," Sespian said.

"But they're going to be fine explaining that they lost the *ship*?"

"That was deemed a better option."

They reached the navigation deck, but paused when someone called out. "Ship coming! The tug *Boar Tusk*."

"What?" Mahliki asked. "What's another ship doing coming in here? Can't they see we're mired?"

Sespian leaned over the railing and pointed. They were high enough up to see over the tops of the plant stalks. "Look, that's your father's sub on its deck. That must be the vessel Amaranthe and Sicarius went out in this morning. Maybe they're going to toss a line and add their engine power to ours."

"They better not get close to do it." Mahliki tried to gauge the distance to the edge of the forest. Forty meters? Fifty?

Sespian strode toward the navigation cabin. Nobody noticed when he and Mahliki entered. The captain stood inside, a lean, wiry man who jittered in place as he stood to one side, staring out the window at the approaching tug. He gripped a cider or tea mug in his hand, less because he was relaxed enough to drink, Mahliki guessed from his white-knuckled grip, and more out of habit.

"Get on the horn," the captain barked. "Warn them away."

A private spoke normally into a mouthpiece by a map-filled console in the corner, and his amplified voice shot out of a brass horn outside. "Do not approach, *Boar Tusk*. The plant is attacking. Efforts are ongoing to free this ship."

"The plant is attacking," Sespian murmured. "Words I never thought I would hear."

"No?" Mahliki asked. "Must be this sedate latitude you Turgonians live at. I've encountered all sorts of inhospitable and sometimes deadly plants in the equatorial regions."

"Is this some... magically-enhanced relative?" He waved toward the jungle.

"No. This is... a problem. A big problem that has nothing to do with the Science. Not *our* Science anyway. Did your friends get that root sample I threw at them?"

"Yes."

"Good. I'll explain later, once we've all had a closer look at that."

A response was drifting across the waters from the tug's own horn. The vessel had crept up to the edge of the forest and stopped there. "...pull you out," the speaker was saying. "Stand ready to receive our hooks."

A boom sounded off to the stern. The marines with the blasting sticks.

"Better pray to Akahe they don't sink their own ship," Mahliki said.

The captain frowned in her direction, noticing her for the first time. Mahliki shrugged and smiled. It did nothing to soften the intensity of his face. He might not be as big and burly as so many of the marines, but he did look like he could chew that mug into dust with a few irritated snaps of his jaw.

"Is there anything we can do to help, sir?" Mahliki asked.

"No."

"I've studied the plant up close now." Very close. "Might I suggest that it has trouble gripping things that are slippery? If you have some lubricant on board, it wouldn't hurt to grease the hull, at least those sections we can reach."

"Something that would be next to impossible if we're not in dry dock," the captain said. "Unless you want to volunteer to go back in the water and handle that."

"Uh, not at this time. But perhaps we could put your explosives team to good use and create some little grease-filled casks that could be detonated to spatter over the hull in spots."

"Corporal," the captain said, "how many square feet of exterior hull does the *Interceptor* claim?"

"Almost thirty thousand, sir."

"That would take a lot of spatters."

"Yes, sir."

Mahliki shrugged. She had tried. In truth, her studies had revealed precious little about what might harm the plant or encourage it to shy away. And now that she knew where it had come from, she was even less certain about what tactics to use.

"Hooks incoming," the private at the horn said.

"I see them. Send a team down to fasten them. Let's hope that tug's engine can add the power we need to snap those vines free. Lieutenant, are we still making progress?"

"We've slowed to... no, we're dead in the water, sir."

The captain glared at Mahliki. She couldn't manage the indignation to glare back. All of this—whatever damage this ship took and whatever men might be injured or lost—was because of her. Yes, she was doing this research to help the city, but what good had she done so far? None. And besides, she would have taken these risks to do this research even if it had nothing to do with the city. How often did one get a chance to study a—

A gentle hand settled on her shoulder. Sespian's. "Perhaps we should see what we can do to help outside."

"A good idea," the captain said. It wasn't quite a growl.

Mahliki wondered what words she would be getting if her father weren't the former Fleet Admiral Starcrest. She probably wouldn't have gotten words at all; she would have been thrown overboard. Or would they have even risked themselves to retrieve her? Coming from the Kyatt Islands, where there wasn't royalty or an aristocracy, it was hard to fathom the idea of one life being worth so much more than another. She wasn't sure what to feel about the fact that hers was apparently invaluable here, even to a bunch of marines she had never met. Especially to a bunch of marines she had never met.

"So, machetes or explosives?" Sespian asked as they stepped outside. "Which shall we volunteer to help with?"

Mahliki grimaced. The area to the stern where the first explosion had occurred was impressively clear of clinging vines, but there were more than ever clutching to the railings at other points around the ship. She pointed at two familiar figures working with axes below.

"Let's join them. I'd rather hear purse jokes than..." She left off the rest, the part about not wanting accusatory looks from all the marines who knew they were in trouble because of her.

"Probably the safest spot to be." Sespian smiled and led the way down the stairs. "They're good fighters. Though I am irked at them for letting you get taken in the first place."

"That was my fault, not theirs. I, uh, got myself into a situation from which extrication was not easy."

"I noticed."

"They're hard workers though and didn't give up until I'd completely disappeared."

When they reached the lower deck, Mahliki nodded toward Maldynado and Basilard. Sweat dripped from their faces. Given

Maldynado's flippancy, she wouldn't have expected it, but he seemed as ready to throw himself into danger and to lift an axe as these marines. Sespian strode forward, pulling out his own axe.

"You're a hard worker too," she added to him.

His grunt didn't seem to hold a lot of agreement. She would have to work on his self-deprecation. It bordered on self-disgust at times, and she couldn't see any reason for either. She preferred a man with a small ego to a big one, but he had no reason not to feel confident and self-assured.

"That's seventeen for me," Maldynado proclaimed. Speaking of egos... "And what? Three for you, Bas? Maybe four if you count that baby one."

Basilard leaned back long enough to wipe sweat from his forehead and glower at his friend. He might have signed something, but was too busy wielding the axe. He ran to the next spot along the tendril-infested railing and smashed down with the weapons.

"Good thing those are metal rails," Sespian said as he advanced with his own axe and machete.

Mahliki still had her collection kit and was poking through the contents, looking for a suitable weapon, when a hook clunked down a few meters away, startling her.

A marine scurried forward and grabbed it, hauling it and the long cable behind it to a sturdy eyelet in the bow. After securing it, he waved up to the navigation cabin. Two other such hooks were attached now, each with cables stretching back to the tug, which was barely visible through the towering stalks, but floated at the edge of the forest, still forty meters away.

"How did they..." Mahliki leaned to the side and squinted. "Is that a harpoon launcher?"

"Most likely," Sespian said, hanging over the railing, hacking at a vine.

"Only on a Turgonian tugboat," she said.

Before Mahliki could return her attention to her bag, a dark figure running toward them made her pause and gape. It—*he*—was running along one of the cables, cables that were less than an inch thick.

"Here comes the backup." Maldynado grinned and thumped Basilard on the shoulder, nodding toward the running man.

A fast-moving vine stretched into his path, as if to intercept him. He leaped over it and landed on the cable again without slowing down. Without so much as a wobble or flailing of arms along the way, he hopped over the railing and jogged toward Maldynado and Basilard. No, not them, Mahliki realized when he cruised past with nothing but a curt nod. Sespian.

"Father," Sespian said, standing back from the railing and flicking a severed vine off his sleeve.

Sicarius studied his son from head to toe, then nodded. "Sespian. You are uninjured?"

With some amusement, Mahliki realized that dead sprint across the cable had been borne of parental concern. Somewhere behind that stoic mask, he must have been agonizing over Sespian's fate.

"I am," Sespian said.

"Good." Such a fount of relief and emotion he was... Sicarius's expression never changed.

Sespian pointed at her. "Mahliki is the one who almost ended up as plant food."

She grimaced, not needing another reminder that the ship was in trouble because of her. And she wasn't sure she appreciated Sicarius's scrutiny, however brief. He gave her a much quicker head-to-toe perusal than Sespian had received, though he did deign to say, "It is good you, too, are well." Before she could decide if this warranted a thank-you, he held up a black dagger and continued on. "My blade cuts through the plant easily. I will assist with freeing the ship."

"Good," Sespian said, "because—" Another boom from the rear drowned out the rest of his words.

From her spot, Mahliki couldn't see where the explosives had detonated, but bits of plants rained down around them. Only the vines, she noticed, not the thicker stalks. It would take more than black powder to bring those down.

"Understood," Sicarius said. "It will be most important to free the screw for propulsion." He jogged off toward the stern without another word.

"You must have great in-depth chats on politics, religion, and the arts," Mahliki glanced toward Sespian.

His smile was dry. "I'm not sure he's figured out what chatting is yet. I know he opens up more with Amaranthe, but I don't think she would call him garrulous, either. I admit... I'd probably be horrified if he tried to chat with me."

"Horrified?" Mahliki asked.

"Well, not horrified, but... it's just awkward. I don't know what to say to him, and he doesn't know what to say to me."

Maldynado ambled over and propped an elbow on Sespian's shoulder. "You just described the father-son relationships of half of the men in Turgonia. You should be tickled that he cares. Not all parents do." Maldynado lifted his fingers, grimaced at a broken nail, and sighed. "This work is hard on the physique. Not at all what I had in mind when I asked the president for a job."

Mahliki watched him thoughtfully. For all his feigned indifference to... just about anything significant, she had caught a quick wince when he mentioned parents that didn't care.

Basilard tapped him on the shoulder and pointed toward the stern. *Sicarius just dove overboard.*

Mahliki blinked. "On purpose?"

"You should have told him to lubricate himself first," Maldynado said. "If nothing else, it would be amusing to imagine him explaining his slimy armpits to Amaranthe."

Sespian merely shook his head. "I'll go tell the captain that the engine is about to work a lot better." He waved and headed for the stairs.

Ah, yes, the black knives. Her father had one, too, though she didn't know if he had brought it with him to Turgonia. It made sense that the blades could damage the plant, a fact that did not bode well for the city, not when they had blown up the alien ship and the only source of that technology within thousands of miles.

Maldynado nudged her. "Why so glum? Things are looking up."

"Only for the moment," Mahliki warned him. "Only for the moment."

CHAPTER 9

AMARANTHE TRIED NOT TO FEEL out of place sitting in the plushy conference chair. Given the number of generals also sitting in the room, that was difficult. Colonel Dak Starcrest, the only officer present *not* ranked general, sat to her left. She folded her hands on the table and tried to appear undaunted. When Mahliki and Professor Komitopis came in, she relaxed an iota, though the president's wife and daughter weren't exactly low ranking when it came to social hierarchies. Basilard and Maldynado ambled in next, though with Basilard dressed in his country's clothing and wearing that chain of office, he had a new status—and a reason to be here. The Mangdorian woman who followed him in, her leather and cotton dress elegantly stitched and her red hair in an attractive coif, gave even more authority to him, especially when she took a spot on the opposite side of the table, where she could see and translate his signs. Maldynado, who plopped down and immediately flung one leg over the armrest of his cushy chair, had no obvious reason for being there, much like Amaranthe, though that didn't faze him.

Lots of friends here, no reason to feel out of place, she told herself. Why had she so easily spoken to people of all stations when she had been an outlaw? Because it didn't matter, she supposed. When she had already broken so many rules, who cared what people thought? But now, she wasn't sure where she stood anymore. After being gone for months, she certainly didn't feel a part of the president's inner circle. Indeed, she scarcely knew the man outside of his reputation. Sicarius had a closer relationship and link to him than Amaranthe did.

He was in the room, too, remaining by the door, his back to the wall, something that made at least a few of those generals cast nervous glances over their shoulders. Amaranthe had a hard time imagining a situation in which Sicarius would feel daunted. Supervising a room full of toddlers, perhaps. Not that he would likely be in that situation soon. Despite the morning's chaos, the tug had delivered her to shore in time for her to wash up and make her doctor's appointment. The news... hadn't been encouraging, aside from the fact that she wouldn't need to worry about stocking tea in the future.

The president came in last, trailed by a couple of security men. They attempted to take up positions to either side of the door, though Sicarius did not accommodate the flustered fellow on the left by moving. The guard had to stand by a potted tree in the corner.

As President Starcrest sat down at the head of the table, a couple of hotel staff came in, one to light candles and turn up the wall lamps—this interior room lacked windows, which was probably why it had been chosen, given recent bombings—and the other to take drink orders. Starcrest and several of the officers watched with some bemusement as the young man went around, explaining beverage options. Not a luxury they had typically experienced in their tents out in the field, Amaranthe supposed. Something to be said for having staff meetings in a hotel.

"Thank you all for coming this evening," Starcrest said when the wait staff had departed. "You're all here because you already have knowledge about the ancient alien ship that exploded in the sky a few months ago."

Several men exchanged nervous glances. Amaranthe almost groaned. *That* was why she had been invited? She wanted nothing to do with that ship or whatever legacy it had—

She froze. Legacy. If there had been a window she could have looked out, she would have stared at the harbor.

"The plant?" she whispered.

"Hm?" Starcrest, at the other end of the table, asked.

"I, ah, well, we just got here, but I had assumed that plant was the work of a practitioner. Is that... not the case?"

"It's not. And that is why it must now become our number one priority, rather than an inconvenience to be delegated to the municipal workers." He frowned slightly at the bespectacled man next to him, one of the few people in the room not wearing a uniform. Amaranthe had never been introduced to Vice President Serpitivich but remembered him from the elections.

The slight man adjusted his spectacles and closed a book that he had been perusing. "I merely suggested the assassins at your door were more of a priority, Lord President."

Colonel Dak Starcrest made a noise somewhere between a growl and a grumble.

"Let's put the focus on the plant now," the president said and extended a hand toward his daughter. "Mahliki?"

She had been fiddling with one of her braids, but she pushed it over her shoulder and opened a large satchel. A damp satchel that smelled of seaweed. She plucked out a jar with a bulbous brownish red object suspended in a pale fluid. It had been sliced open before being tucked into its glass home.

"This is one of the root samples I got today." Mahliki ticked the glass. "I cut it open, and—well, here. Pass it around, and you can see for yourself."

Amaranthe noted that the lid had been screwed on, glued, and then taped to the glass. "Is it... likely to try and escape?"

"I hope not." Mahliki handed the jar to the general beside her, whose face grew pale as he took a closer look. "I don't want anybody accidentally taking it out though. Who knows what it can do? Those pods... Sespian can tell you. Trying to dissect one almost got me... prematurely aged."

Professor Komitopis flinched.

"I was lucky I had him there to pull me out of the way." Mahliki probably would have beamed a smile at Sespian if he were in the room, but he had gone to the construction site to oversee the laying of the foundation for his building—the future residence for the president. She settled for throwing a quick smile at Sicarius. Sicarius, of course, gazed back with uniform blandness.

The jar passed through a few sets of hands before landing on the table in front of Amaranthe. She peered into the part that had been slashed open, expecting more of the same brownish-red, but a black disk lay embedded inside the root ball. It looked more like metal, rather than something natural. She slumped in her chair. Not metal, the same black material Sicarius's dagger was made from, that the entire ship had been made from. The lighting wasn't good, but she made out a single rune etched in the disk.

"What's it say?" Amaranthe looked to Tikaya, assuming she had already examined it.

The professor's lips thinned. "Roughly... Experimental Plant Number Three."

Amaranthe passed the jar on to Colonel Starcrest. "Meaning it's even more potent than numbers one and two?"

Tikaya spread an open palm. "I couldn't say. I'm not certain this plant is meant as a weapon. Though... given what I have learned about that... species over the last twenty years, it does seem likely."

"We're guessing some seeds or pods or something otherwise encapsulated in those disks—or produced by those disks—survived the explosion," Mahliki said, "and fell to earth. To the lake more specifically. While the water was cold and eventually frozen over, it would have laid dormant, but once the thaw came..."

"It spread faster than gossip about a C.O.," the colonel said.

"Essentially, yes," Tikaya said.

"Are your troops gossiping about you, Dak?" the president asked gently, a faint humor in his brown eyes.

"Always," the colonel grumbled. "I'm scintillating material."

He didn't seem to share his uncle's humor. There was a glumness to him that reminded Amaranthe of Basilard, although Basilard seemed less glum since he had returned to Turgonia. Even now, he kept smiling over at his translator, who was watching him attentively to see if he would contribute. Amaranthe needed to find time to talk to him and see how his meeting with the family had gone. When the jar got to him, he scrutinized it. Like the others, he passed it on without comment other than a displeased lip curl. It must not have the culinary merit that so much of the bizarre foliage he picked did.

"Mother and I are going to keep studying it." Mahliki set another jar on the table, this one with a snippet of a vine lying on the bottom with water around it. It twitched a few times. "Although keeping a live specimen is perhaps not that wise—"

"No," Tikaya said, "it's not." Her tone and the look she slanted her daughter suggested they had argued over this earlier.

Mahliki lifted a shoulder and continued with, "—it's the only way to see what affects it and what doesn't. We're going to have to find *something* to eradicate it, or your capital city won't be habitable for long."

"The way that thing's growing, all of *Turgonia* won't be habitable for long," Colonel Starcrest grumbled.

"It doesn't grow *that* fast," one of the generals said.

160

Most of the other heads around the room nodded in agreement with snorts for the idea.

President Starcrest wasn't nodding. "I've been down to the waterfront the last couple of days," he said. "Based on its current growth rate, if there are no other limiting factors, it would take less than a year to spread across the entire continent."

"What?" the general blurted. "That's impossible. We're talking about thousands of miles to cover."

Starcrest's smile was bleak. "For all the marvels that humanity can grasp, it fails again and again to comprehend the significance of the exponential function."

The general leaned back in his chair, his expression somewhere between thoughtful and befuddled.

"It's like the compounding copper coin, right?" Amaranthe asked. "If you're offered a million ranmyas or the sum of a copper coin that doubles every day for a month, you're supposed to take the coin."

"Yes," Starcrest said.

Amaranthe recalled from that particular math problem that the one million ranmyas looked pretty good right up until the last couple of days of the month, where the doubling copper turned into millions of ranmyas on its own. "So if we delay now, most people won't realize exactly how much trouble we're in until it's far too late to do anything about it?"

"Put her on the list," the colonel said. He was studying the jar with the live specimen in it and didn't meet Amaranthe's gaze when she gave him a confused look.

"The list?" she asked.

"I'm being pressured to add more civilians to government positions," Starcrest said. "The warrior caste is already grouching about being stripped of power, or so it perceives, but there are many scholars, entrepreneurs, and common citizens who now aspire to political careers."

"They can have our jobs when we die," one of the generals said. "None of the up-and-coming officers are worth their weight in spit anyway."

"Weak generation," another grumbled.

Amaranthe resisted the urge to roll her eyes at these geriatric opinions of youth—where had *they* been when Emperor Sespian was being poisoned and plotted against?—though she caught Mahliki doing just that. She waved for the return of her sample jars and stood. "Father, if your people are finished setting up that lab in the basement, I'll start on my experiments right away. Mother's already translated the runes and given me what information she has on the ancient race's horticulture methods, but if there are any experienced botanists or even limnologists in the city who could be talked into helping, I wouldn't mind some company."

Or expert opinions, Amaranthe wagered. The young woman appeared daunted at the task she had taken on—or, by default, been given. Amaranthe knew all about taking on impossible tasks and wished she could offer help. Well, maybe...

"Basilard may be able to offer some valuable insight," Amaranthe suggested. "His people are quite knowledgeable when it comes to plant life."

Basilard glanced between Amaranthe, Mahliki, and the president. *I am not knowledgeable about* alien *plant life*, he signed. The woman standing across from him translated it for the room.

"Who is?" Starcrest murmured. "Basilard, why don't you come see me in the morning, and we'll discuss the Mangdorian concerns you're here about? And with the rest of your time, if you're willing..." He extended a hand toward Mahliki. "Unlike any botanists we may scrape up off the streets, you already have the clearance necessary to hear about the sensitive origins of the plant."

Amaranthe wondered exactly how top secret any knowledge of the ancient aliens could be at this point. After all, the ship had crashed five miles from the city and been there for everyone to see for more than twenty-four hours last winter. But perhaps, in her absence, some sort of logical cover-up story had been concocted. She would have to visit Deret Mancrest at some point and get caught up with the news. Or she could stroll up and ask the president. The notion struck her as too familiar. She wasn't even sure why she had been invited to this meeting. How could she or Sicarius help with this situation? Other than by hewing at individual plant stalks with a certain black knife.

"That's it for now, gentlemen," Starcrest said, and Amaranthe blushed, realizing she hadn't been paying attention to the last minutes of the meeting. "Tikaya, Amaranthe, and Sicarius. Stay a moment, please."

The officers filed out, along with Mahliki, Basilard, and his translator. They were already signing and talking over the clinking of Mahliki's bag full of samples. At a hand-shooing from the president, the door guards also filtered out. The one who had ceded his position to Sicarius gave him a faintly peeved expression in passing. Not someone else who would hold a grudge against him, Amaranthe hoped. She wondered if that private would be found and questioned. Had he been some lone operator, seeing a chance to avenge some past wrong Sicarius had done him or his family? Or had he been suborned by the assassins already lurking in the city?

Maldynado lingered at the head of the table. "Ah, My Lord President? Shall I... report for work tomorrow?"

Starcrest managed to keep from looking exasperated at Maldynado, an impressive feat for many people. "Come to my office in the morning. I'll see if anyone can use you for anything."

"Thank you, My Lord." Maldynado looked pleased as he waved farewell to Amaranthe. Considering he had the status of errand boy so far, she wasn't sure why, but this employment seemed to matter to him.

When Amaranthe, Sicarius, Tikaya, and Starcrest were alone, the president waved for them to join him at the head of the table. This time, Sicarius deigned to sit, taking a seat that allowed him to observe the door. Amaranthe slid in next to Tikaya. She wanted to ask the professor a question regarding Kyattese obstetricians and what they could and could not do, though only if she could find a private moment. The president probably didn't care about her female problems.

"My friends," Starcrest said, spreading his hands, palms up, "I have a feeling the *Explorer* can be a great asset to us in defeating this plant—even if we find a way to eradicate it on land, we don't want the roots to remain at the bottom of the lake, waiting for an opportune time to repopulate. Thus I need it repaired. I can grab a couple of engineers and handle the mechanical aspects, but I can't do anything about the power source."

"Finding a Maker in the city—in all of *Turgonia*—may be impossible," Tikaya said. "Is there no way a mundane solution could be offered?"

Starcrest stroked his chin. "I've done a little reading since returning home, and I see progress *has* been made in regard to refining useful fuels from petroleum, but given our time frame, a coal-fired steam engine would be the most likely possibility, and that's not particularly feasible for a submarine. Especially that compact submarine, which, again given our time frame, is what we have available."

"We've encountered practitioners in the city before," Amaranthe said. "Aside from the ones who have traveled over just for the purpose of assassinating someone. Sicarius once found one to heal me of a disease with no mundane cure."

"They come as refugees or to hide," Sicarius said. "It may be possible to find a Maker."

"Excellent. Tikaya—" Starcrest gave her an apologetic smile, "— would you mind going with them if they find someone and relaying the specifications? You know the woman who Made the *Explorer's* power source intimately."

"Because she's my ex-fiancé's mother," Tikaya explained to Amaranthe dryly. "Though she's continued to Make models over the years because of *Rias* and not because of our relationship."

"Pardon?" Amaranthe had always found the professor's Turgonian flawless, but she didn't catch the nuances here.

"It's not important," Starcrest said.

"The woman is one of his admirers," Tikaya said. "She's read every Admiral Starcrest in the Such-and-Such novel out there. She's almost eighty now and has been retired for ages, but she continues to make submarine power sources for her special client."

"A fanatic, eh?" Amaranthe smiled at Sicarius, knowing he had read a number of those books as well.

He said nothing, though his eyes narrowed ever so slightly. Yes, he had been a boy at the time, but Amaranthe hadn't noticed that adulation wearing off much. Still, he could have far worse role models.

"Yes," Tikaya said. "It's a shame we can't simply arrange for her to be sent here to Make a new device. Or to send her a message, have her Make it, and then ship it. We do have that communication device to contact my mother if necessary."

"Even if Iweue began working right away, it would take three weeks to ship the item here," Starcrest said. "Unless you know someone who could teleport it to the capital?"

"Teleporting somewhere you haven't been before is difficult, and to travel across oceans and continents... I've not heard of that being done. If it's feasible, it's beyond the skills of my kith and kin."

"If someone can figure out how to ship packages from continent to continent overnight, there's an entrepreneur waiting to make that person rich," Amaranthe said.

"Indeed," Starcrest said. "In the meantime, let's see if you can find a local Maker. Some fool has given me access to Turgonia's tax funds, so I expect I can pay the person well for his or her time."

"Don't you have to get withdrawals approved by your treasurer?" Tikaya asked. "That nervous little woman with the tic?"

"Yes, but Dak intimidates her. I can simply send him to get the check."

"Intimidates her? I thought he was making moon eyes at her."

"Yes, but *she* didn't realize that."

Amaranthe pushed back her chair. "If there's nothing further, we'll head out, My Lord."

Tikaya stood as well. "I'll go with you."

"Er, we were going to check on a business in town first. The owner might be linked to the original attack on the sub."

"Tikaya, you needn't join them until they find a practitioner," Starcrest said. "I know Mahliki—"

"Has everything I can give her for now," Tikaya said. "I don't mind tagging along with them. I may be of assistance in locating a Maker."

Amaranthe had a feeling Tikaya wanted to go with them for more reasons than had been stated, but it would give her an opportunity to ask her personal questions, so she did not object. She glanced at Sicarius, wondering if he would mind company, but he was doing his impassive-as-a-statue routine, as he had for much of the meeting. He was probably thinking about the assassin hunt he planned for the night, rather than worrying about running errands in the city.

"You're gazing at me in speculation," Tikaya said to her husband.

Starcrest's thumb was hooked under his chin, fingers to his lips, as he did indeed gaze at his wife like a man contemplating a puzzle. If Amaranthe knew Tikaya had some ulterior motive here, he had probably sensed it too.

"Are those his bedroom eyes?" Amaranthe asked; maybe she ought to help Tikaya by distracting him.

"Not exactly," Tikaya said.

"I am contemplating whether you're stir-crazy and eager to escape the confines of the hotel or if you have something else in mind, something I should be disgruntled over because you're not telling me about it."

"Dak and I are working on a little intelligence mission," Tikaya said.

"He asked you to go out into the city?"

"No, I'm taking initiative." Tikaya smiled.

"In that case, I had better send guards with you."

Tikaya's smile turned sour. "To babysit me?"

"To protect you. As you'll recall, someone tried to blow up my office last night. I don't know who among my family might be targeted. Today has already been... worrisome, due to an overly aggressive plant that can't keep its vines to itself."

Amaranthe grimaced. The president and an entourage of men had been waiting when the tug and warship had come in at the old Fort Urgot docks. He must have been watching some of the trouble—that involving his daughter, for instance—from the roof of the hotel. With a spyglass, one ought to have a good view of the harbor. He had listened in stony-faced silence as the warship's captain had relayed the events to him.

"If your... friend Sicarius comes along, won't that obviate the need for a detachment of guards?" Tikaya smiled again.

"Now I *know* you're up to something," Starcrest said. "I could believe you wanted to spend time with Ms. Lokdon here, as she seems bright and resourceful, but you've shown no interest in getting to know our ex-assassin comrade here, am I right, Sicarius?"

Sicarius never gave Starcrest anything but respectful looks, maybe even looks of adulation—for those who knew how to read him well—but this time, he offered one of his why-are-you-involving-me-in-this eyebrow twitches. His, "Yes, My Lord," was a tad flat.

Starcrest must have read it, too, for he lifted an apologetic hand.

"She simply hasn't learned about his cuddly side yet," Amaranthe said.

"I'll wager not many have."

"I have only your safety in mind, Rias," Tikaya said. "I've done precious little since I've been here, except read and send letters home. Now that there's something that I can help with, I won't stand back and ignore it."

"I appreciate your help, but can't it be done with a contingent of armed and armored guards surrounding you?"

"No. In fact, such a contingent might scare off any practitioners, especially if they have been illegal refugees and hunted people here."

Starcrest sighed. "Sicarius, can I trust you to keep Tikaya safe tonight, as well as Amaranthe?"

If Sicarius felt irked to be saddled with this extra burden, he did not show it. "I will bring them back to the hotel before going on my own hunt."

"Very well." Starcrest came around the table and hugged his wife, murmuring something in her ear.

Amaranthe met Sicarius's eyes and nodded to the door. They ought to give these two a private moment. Something about that hug seemed to say they hadn't gotten many private moments lately.

The crisp evening air felt good against Tikaya's cheeks, even if it smelled of burning coal. Being out of the hotel without a guard felt good as well. She missed the days of simply being able to wander along a beach in her sandals, with nothing except the sound of the surf to keep her company. The capital claimed a million citizens, and she believed it. As she walked down a wide boulevard with Amaranthe, they had to weave around crowds lingering before eating houses, rushes of people disembarking from trolleys, and a pack of people in dark green robes with hoods pulled over their heads. She hadn't seen Sicarius since they left the hotel, though Amaranthe assured her that he wasn't far.

"Amaranthe, I have a question for you," Tikaya said at the same time as Amaranthe turned toward her with a finger up and started to speak.

"Oh," she said. "You go first."

"No, you can go first. I..." Tikaya had been summoning the courage to confide in Amaranthe as to where she wanted to go. Getting out without a guard contingent had been a blessing, but she still had to explain the departure she wanted to make to these two.

"Mine's silly," Amaranthe admitted, scuffing a crack in the sidewalk with her boot. "Well, not silly, but not related to our mission or anything... that matters. At least not right now."

This of course made Tikaya curious, but she wouldn't push the woman to share. How interesting that Amaranthe, too, had been searching for the courage to say something.

Tikaya withdrew a folded paper from her wool dress. "Do you know how we can most easily get to this address? I looked at a map, but I confess I haven't ridden on the trolleys yet, and the system doesn't at first glance seem... scientific. Or logical. Or entirely safe, if the muggings mentioned in the paper are to be believed."

"Right on all counts." Amaranthe opened the paper and headed for a street lamp. "It grew up over time, with more routes being added as needed. As you wander around, you'll see that we have some new boulevards like this one, suitable for steam vehicles and pedestrians, and then you'll see that there are a lot of older streets that are narrow, crooked, and were basically designed for a couple of people to walk through at a time. The trolleys are too big to run through these old streets, so they take some creative routes to get from point one to point two. There's a somewhat infamous one that detours four miles to take riders from one end of a bridge to the other, since the bridge is for pedestrians only, and the canal system offers further barriers." Amaranthe passed the sheet of paper back. "This is up on Mokath Ridge. It's a neighborhood full of expensive homes. New wealth and old."

"That's not surprising then. Do we... have time to detour up there?"

"Well, Ms. Sarevic's Custom Works is in a sketchier neighborhood, but her shop hours—the ones we're interested in—don't start until a couple of hours before midnight, so we can go to your destination first. Assuming you want us to come? Or were you hoping to explore on your own? Though, even if you were, I doubt Sicarius would let you wander off unaccompanied after he told the president he would watch you."

"If he watches from a distance, I don't mind." Tikaya decided she wouldn't mind Amaranthe's company, either. She had been an enforcer at one point; she might know a few tricks for talking a haughty warrior-caste woman into opening her doors and allowing a search of her home. "And, ah, if *you* don't mind coming along, it could be helpful."

"You mentioned intelligence. Are we doing something interesting?" Amaranthe sounded like she hoped so.

"Visiting someone who sent a tainted gift for the president's inauguration."

Amaranthe's nose crinkled. "A tainted gift? Something more inimical than stale tarts?"

"I should say so." Tikaya noticed someone watching them from a vendor's booth and pulled Amaranthe into an alcove. With the nights still bringing frost, she didn't feel out of place wearing a cloak with a hood, but she imagined her blonde hair still made her noticeable. In addition, there were her spectacles and her height, though here, in vertically endowed Turgonia, the height alone wouldn't have been a giveaway. "It's an old artifact that a practitioner tinkered with. We believe it's keyed to Rias and has been giving him headaches and perhaps interfering with his mental faculties. I've locked it in a metal box down in Mahliki's new laboratory, and I thought I noticed the new furrows between Rias's brow were less deep today."

"A practitioner? A Maker?" Amaranthe asked. "Does that mean if we find the person, Sicarius and I might have the answer to our power supply problem?"

Tikaya stared at the younger woman. This didn't sound like a particularly bright assumption, and she felt a touch miffed that Amaranthe had ignored the rest of the revelation.

"A Maker who wishes Rias ill," Tikaya explained slowly. "Perhaps all of us."

Now Amaranthe stared at Tikaya as if *she* were slow. "I convince people who wish me ill to aid in my cause all the time."

"With... your assassin's help?" Dear Akahe, had Tikaya made a mistake in coming out with these two?

"Well, he looms and glares, and that can help sway people, but I prefer less violent methods." Amaranthe smiled. "I like a challenge."

"Hm." If Amaranthe truly was good at swaying people, maybe Tikaya could send *her* in to chat with Starcrest's first wife. She didn't find the idea of the task appealing herself. "It is possible we may find out who Made the device by visiting this address. If—"

A shadow appeared in the alcove with them, startling Tikaya. It had seemed to come up from out of the ground or to have dropped down from some roof.

"It is unwise to remain in the open," Sicarius said without preamble. "Three separate persons are following you. More may have observed your departure from the hotel."

"Following *me*?" Tikaya asked.

"I'm not the president's wife," Amaranthe said.

"No, but I shouldn't think that makes me terribly fascinating."

"They may simply be following because they believe information on your whereabouts may be important to someone somewhere." Amaranthe met Sicarius's eyes—his sudden appearance at her elbow hadn't startled *her* at all. "Were they youths? Or more pernicious stalkers?"

"Adults. Armed. One in a green robe, one wearing civilian clothing but who moves like a soldier, and one I haven't gotten a good look at yet." Sicarius watched the street as the conversation continued, his gaze occasionally flitting toward the rooftops and the sewer grates.

The soldier wasn't that surprising. Someone had probably been instructed to keep an eye on her and make sure she remained safe. The robed person... "I just saw some of those people in robes. They represent a new religion that's forming, don't they? Why would they care about me?"

Amaranthe looked at Sicarius, but he only shook his head once. "I've seen a couple of those robes since we arrived," she said, "but we don't know anything about them yet. It's not an organization that was around—at least obviously so—before we left the city. I'd be more concerned about someone following us who's talented enough that Sicarius wasn't able to get a good look."

"The person is discreet," Sicarius said.

"Is it possible to elude these followers?" Tikaya asked.

"Likely."

"We're heading to Mokath Ridge," Amaranthe told Sicarius. "Professor? Care to follow me? I know routes that probably won't be observed."

"Lead on, Amaranthe."

Perhaps Tikaya should have inquired about those "routes that probably won't be observed" before agreeing to follow the woman. Amaranthe led her through urine-drenched alleys, boarded-up buildings, old underground streets, and finally a sewage pumping station that made the alleys seem like honeymoon destinations.

"I'm not sure how I'm going to explain my new stench to Rias," Tikaya murmured as they came up through a manhole in a park.

"I suggest spending some time in the hotel's baths before heading up to the bedroom," Amaranthe said, veering for a street.

Tikaya had lost all sense of direction. They might be in the next satrapy for all she knew. Though probably not. She could still smell that alien vegetation, the scent wafting up from the lake and mingling with the pervasive coal odor.

Amaranthe paused in the shadows of a hedge to wait for a pair of private steam carriages to roll past. Their presence, along with the lack of trash or graffiti along the streets, made Tikaya assume they had reached the upscale neighborhood they sought.

"We're close?" she asked.

"Two blocks," Amaranthe said.

Tikaya didn't see Sicarius, but that didn't mean he wasn't nearby.

After the carriages disappeared around corners, Amaranthe jogged across the street, heading for an intersection. Before they reached it, she turned up a narrow alley with trash bins posted at wide intervals—the house lots were big up here. Nothing compared to what Tikaya's family enjoyed on her plantation, but these people certainly weren't crammed in on top of each other, a rare finding in a city so populous.

Before they had gone far, Amaranthe paused. "I didn't ask. I just assumed this was a clandestine operation. Did you *want* to knock on the front door?"

Did she? Good question. Tikaya removed her spectacles to wipe sewer grime from one of the lenses. "Mind if we see if anyone is home first?"

"Presumably *not* by knocking?" It was hard to tell in the dark alley, but Amaranthe might have grinned.

"If she's home, there would be lamps lit. It's not that late."

"Yes, and we can check for those lamps from the alley behind the house." Amaranthe waved her arm. "This way."

Tikaya wondered if they had lost those who had been following them. She also wondered if it was odd that she would have preferred assassins to journalists, hoping for a story. *President's Wife Spies on President's Wife.* Not a title she wanted to see in the *Gazette* in the morning. Granted, the *Gazette* had printed more tasteful articles than the other newspapers that had featured her, usually focusing on politics rather than gossip.

"I think this is it." Amaranthe stopped before a brick wall dressed in ivy and a wrought iron gate, its bars shaped as branches and leaves. Beyond it, a park-like yard stretched, flagstone paths winding between manicured bushes and trees, with fountains and statues dotting the grounds. Some of them had glass baubles—or maybe those were gems—that gleamed, reflecting the moonlight. Granite benches rested beside the path for those who grew weary during the long walk to take out the trash.

"That's the *back* yard?" Tikaya whispered. "What's the *front* look like?"

"I don't know. This is your contact. I don't even know why we're here exactly." Amaranthe's tone suggested she wouldn't have minded the details.

Tikaya tried the gate, but found it locked. "I guess we have to climb over the wall." A wall that was over her head, even at six feet. Perhaps she should have been doing some exercise over the winter, something more vigorous than turning pages.

Amaranthe reached between the bars, and something clinked softly. She pulled the gate open. "I imagine the house doors will be more challenging, but there's no need to test our athleticism right away."

Tikaya decided not to mention that simply walking down a path in the dark was a test for her athleticism. No need to have the young woman think her some doddering old professor. She did gesture for Amaranthe to lead. Younger eyes might prove more apt at picking routes through the darkness.

The house loomed ahead, a blocky shadow rising out of the garden setting. None of the shuttered windows had lights burning behind them, at least not on this side of the three-story dwelling. It had left and right wings as well as a large central section. Numerous chimneys rose from the rooftop, making Tikaya wonder how many people lived there. Her family's entire plantation house could have fit in one of the wings.

"Wait here," Amaranthe said, then trotted down a side path.

Tikaya leaned against a fountain, the water gurgling softly in the darkness. She couldn't make out the details of the statue that loomed down at her, but found it threatening, nonetheless, as if some ancient gargoyle had been placed on guard to warn trespassers away.

A couple of minutes later, Amaranthe returned, coming in from the opposite direction. She must have checked around the entire house. "Shadowcrest, eh?"

"Pardon?"

"That's the name on the mailbox. It's one of the old and prestigious warrior-caste families." Amaranthe tilted her head. "You didn't know the name of the person we're here to spy upon?"

"Not her surname, no. I had assumed..." Tikaya had thought the woman might still be claiming Starcrest as a surname, since her husband had supposedly died at war, and there hadn't been an official parting of ways. Maybe this was her ancestral home though. "Nothing. Is anyone home? Can we sneak in?"

"There are servants living in that north wing, a small cadre of them if the number of lit rooms is an indication. They're playing Tiles, talking, and drinking. Must be done working for the day. If we go in the back, stay to the south, and don't make much noise, chances are good we can avoid them."

"I may need to search the house," Tikaya said, "but nothing I'm searching for would be in the servants' quarters."

"What *are* we going to search for? Made items?"

"I'm not sure. I'll know it when I see it."

Amaranthe snorted. "Sounds like one of my breaking-and-entering plans."

"Did you break and enter often?"

"No," came a male voice from behind Tikaya.

She jumped and almost fell into the fountain. She had forgotten Sicarius was about.

"She usually sent me for those tasks," he said.

"You're better at sneaking around than I am," Amaranthe said. "Did we lose our curious shadows?"

"All except one," Sicarius said. "I've been trying to find that person, but he or she is good. I am questioning my certainty that someone is there."

"Really? There aren't many people who can elude you. Is it possible this is the same person who threw the blasting stick?"

"Possible. But I would be basing this solely on the person's skill at remaining hidden."

Amaranthe shifted uneasily, not used to anyone being able to hide from Sicarius.

"The person is just watching for now?" Tikaya asked.

"Watching at the least," Sicarius said. "Possibly waiting for an opportune moment to act."

"I haven't sensed the Science being used."

"Nor have I," Sicarius said.

"Oh. Er, would you? I wouldn't expect most Turgonians to, ah... well, you all aren't raised around practitioners. Even to this day, Rias is oblivious when women on the beach are conjuring gusts of wind to whip his towel out of his grasp when he's coming out of the water."

"Is that... truly a problem on Kyatt?" Amaranthe asked.

"Well, not as much as when we were first married and he was younger," Tikaya admitted. "Though some of the naughty old ladies still try to sneak a peek."

Amaranthe swatted Sicarius on the chest. "We should have visited Kyatt to see if any maidens tried to play chase-the-ball with *your* towel."

"As I stated," Sicarius said, seemingly oblivious to her swat and teasing tone. "I am able to sense when the Science is being used."

"You didn't mention why," Tikaya said, curious as to the answer. She supposed he might have traveled extensively in his role as court assassin. The idea of him appearing in different countries as easily as he had appeared behind her, and then dragging a knife across the throat of some politically important person... She grimaced, wondering if she would ever stop feeling uneasy in his presence.

"No," Sicarius agreed. And said nothing further on the matter.

"I think we're going to pop into this house for a look around," Amaranthe said. "Do you want to join us or hunt for our shadow?"

Sicarius regarded the large brick mansion. "Why are you sneaking into the house of President Starcrest's first wife?"

Tikaya flushed. Of all the people she might have expected would know about Starcrest's background—and where his old wife lived— Sicarius hadn't been one of them. He sounded faintly disapproving too. Maybe that was her imagination; she usually couldn't read any hint of feeling or emotion in his voice at all.

"Are we?" Amaranthe's tone held none of that disapproval. She sounded... excited at the prospect. "Now I *really* want to know what we're looking for." She chuckled. "Or are we simply going to wrap washout paper around the entire place as a prank?"

"Of course not," Tikaya said stiffly. "This woman sent a gift to Rias that has been affecting his health. I intend to find out why and where she got it. As I said, a Maker modified what was an ancient statuette of minor historical interest. I assume Sauda is not a practitioner herself, so who supplied it to her? Did she hire the person? Or is someone more sinister using her without her knowledge? The someone stalking the shadows, perhaps?"

"Ah, a worthy question then," Amaranthe said. "Though I think Sicarius would have been more amused to have put his assassinly skills to use with the washout paper. With the way he can walk up walls and dangle one-handed from ceiling gutters, just think about what an artistic job he could do."

Tikaya... couldn't picture this image at all. Nor did Sicarius snicker,

174

grunt, or otherwise acknowledge Amaranthe's foolish notion. In the silence that followed, Tikaya could have sworn she heard crickets chirping in the corner of the garden.

"Assassinly?" she asked, thinking to save Amaranthe from this self-inflicted awkward moment. "That is not truly a Turgonian word, is it? I've not run across it with that particular ending."

"It may be a creative interpretation of a Turgonian word," Amaranthe said.

Sicarius snorted softly. "I will watch the exterior of the building and attempt to locate the last spy while you go inside. I will not leave the area to hunt solo until the professor is back at the hotel. President Starcrest would be displeased if I left her unguarded."

Maybe Tikaya should have opted for the squadron of guards after all. They, at least, probably wouldn't have known whose house she was sneaking into, though it would have proven conspicuous to leave them loitering in the street by the mailbox.

"He's fine about leaving *me* unguarded," Amaranthe whispered to Tikaya.

"Your creativity will protect you," Sicarius said and disappeared into the shadows before Amaranthe could respond.

"He has a way of getting the last word," Amaranthe said, "though I've learned he's listening even when he's skulking about out there."

"How... comforting," Tikaya murmured.

Amaranthe rounded the fountain and headed up the path to a broad cement porch framed by more statues, nudes of muscular young men this time—as Tikaya discovered when she stumbled over an uneven flagstone and reached for the nearest... handhold. A representation of Sauda's tastes? Or some long-dead matriarch in her family? Hers, Tikaya imagined. After all, something must have drawn her to marry Rias all those years ago. He had never said anything that implied they had been intellectual soul mates. Rias *did* have nice... handholds.

"Door's locked," Amaranthe whispered. "Give me a moment."

Tikaya had picked a lock or two in her day under Rias's tutelage, but not without any light. And not in the engineer-filled Turgonia, where the locks were probably as advanced as their firearms and steam engines. It was good to have Amaranthe along.

Soft scrapes reached her ears as the younger woman probed the

175

lock. She must have come prepared with a picking kit. She couldn't have anticipated this side trip, which made Tikaya wonder about her other destination.

"Professor?" Amaranthe asked softly as she worked.

"You can call me Tikaya." She thought she remembered saying that before, months ago, on that ancient vessel. These Turgonians put a lot of stock in addressing people by proper titles, even those who were no longer strangers. Tikaya supposed she could get used to it. There was a lack of charm to the Polytechnic students who wandered past with surfboards underarm and greeted her with, "Yo, Prof!"

"Tikaya, may I ask a question?"

"Of course." Tikaya recalled that Amaranthe had seemed on the brink of asking something earlier.

"On the Kyatt Islands... I've heard that there are practitioners that are the equivalent of our doctors. More than the equivalent because they use the Science."

And because we study topics beyond metallurgy, engineering, and making war, Tikaya thought. "That's right," was all she said.

"Are there skilled... female doctors?" Amaranthe didn't look up from the lock as she spoke, though in the darkness, she must have been working by touch alone.

"Those who specialize in the female reproductive system and diseases thereof, you mean?"

"Uhm. Yes."

Tikaya had not heard the woman sound so uncomfortable before. Turgonians had a cultural aversion to many topics the Kyattese found commonplace. "Yes, we have them," she said.

"Are there any who specialize in healing injuries? To those, ah, areas?"

"There are some, yes, though disease is more common than injury. Are you—"

"Almost done with the lock, yes. One more tumbler." The words came out in a rush. Relieved to change the topic, was she? But didn't she want an answer to her question?

"Have you been injured?" Tikaya asked.

"Yes. Makarovi claws last year. I almost died."

Tikaya blinked. "This was before the ones were brought into the city last winter? Why would you have... sought them out? Or gone to their native habitat?" Makarovi were rare from everything she had read, at least these days. They had been more common once, and some speculated that they and their northern counterparts, the grimbals, were the reason this continent had remained sparsely populated long after the Nurians had spread all over theirs. One scholar had posited that the reason the Turgonians had developed such a warrior culture had been because of the creatures they had been forced to kill to claim this land.

"We didn't," Amaranthe said. "These were brought in by a shaman too. We were just trying to find out why people in the city were getting sick, which involved a trip to a dam up in the mountains. Long story, but it messed me all up, and even though a shaman healed me, he was essentially an enemy and wasn't too worried about putting the puzzle pieces together exactly as he found them."

Amaranthe stood up and pushed the door partially open. She peeked around the edge, then held up a finger and disappeared inside.

Tikaya waited, deciding this was an odd place and an odd time for this conversation. Maybe Amaranthe hadn't wanted to discuss it in front of others. Perhaps Sicarius did not know of her issues?

Amaranthe stuck her head out. "There's nobody around, but I can hear laughter and raised voices from the other side of the house. I have a lantern, but I think we may want to go by touch until we get to a room you want to search, one where we can lock the door."

"I would actually prefer to risk a lantern," Tikaya said. "I am... not the most adroit under any circumstances, and I would be fully capable of knocking down a pot rack with my head as we pass through."

"Oh, all right. Come in then, and I'll light it."

Tikaya eased inside, closing the door behind her. Soft rummaging sounds drifted to her ear. Judging Amaranthe would need a moment to light the lantern, Tikaya went back to their conversation. "How do you know the shaman failed at... your puzzle?"

"I was examined by a Turgonian doctor today. An obstetrician."

Tikaya wagered it would make her sound like a foreign snob to admit she hadn't thought Turgonians had that degree of specialization amongst their doctors. She was glad to learn that not every one of them was a field surgeon, practiced in the art of amputating limbs and other garish practices that a Kyattese doctor would consider barbaric. Still, she shuddered inwardly to imagine what tools an obstetrician might use if he didn't have the mental sciences to call upon.

"Is that what all this is about?" Tikaya asked. "You seek to have a child?" With Sicarius? Her mind shied away from the thought.

A soft flame winked into existence.

"Not... right now, necessarily. I'd like to know it's an option though." Amaranthe rose to her feet with the lantern. "Where to first?"

"Let's see if we can find her bedroom."

Tikaya followed Amaranthe through a storage room and into a kitchen that could have serviced a restaurant—thanks to the lantern, dim though it might be, Tikaya managed to keep from crashing into the pot rack. From there, they headed into a wide hallway, and the voices and laughter Amaranthe had mentioned grew audible. The jubilant sounds of men and women drinking and enjoying a good time while their master— or mistress—was away.

In the hallway, doors alternated with statuary, with the nudity theme being prevalent. *Male* nudity. Sauda didn't seem to be quite the appreciator of the female form. Paintings lined the walls as well, a mix of simple—all Turgonian artwork seemed to favor a simple style—landscapes and more adult topics. Tikaya tripped over the edge of a carpet runner when she stared too long at creatures with male and female torsos and the lower halves of lizards. Well-endowed lizards. Fortunately, she kept herself from stumbling into Amaranthe or making too much noise, though Amaranthe must have heard her grunt anyway, for she glanced back, then wrinkled her nose at the painting.

"Granted I don't know him well," Amaranthe said, "but it's strange to imagine the president being married to someone with such, uhm, ecumenical tastes."

"It was an arranged marriage," Tikaya said. "Though I gather in his youth he was smitten by her beauty. After he graduated from the academy, he was at sea so much that they didn't see much of each other."

"Leaving her here to find methods of entertaining herself, eh?"

"Yes."

Amaranthe pointed to a set of wide travertine steps. "Bedrooms upstairs?"

Tikaya shrugged. She had no better guess than Amaranthe. On the second floor, they passed a lavatory the size of most people's bedrooms, along with several studies, guest rooms, a library, and more than one room dedicated to displaying taxidermy. All manner of predators rose from pedestals or had heads mounted on the walls, including giant lizards, lions and panthers, and a shaggy white grimbal that reared up, its broad head nearly touching the ceiling.

"I wonder if the president brought down any of those," Amaranthe said.

"His hobbies, when he has time for them, run in other directions, although he did perform admirably well on the postnuptial boar hunt."

Amaranthe pointed to a double door at the end of the hall. It was engraved with a mythological scene that also involved nudity. The woman was certainly consistent in her tastes.

"Bedroom," Amaranthe guessed and tried the knob. It didn't turn. "Huh. Maybe she's here after all and went to bed early."

A chill went through Tikaya at the thought of stumbling across the house's owner and having to explain her presence. Explaining it to Rias would be even worse.

"No, never mind," Amaranthe said. "The servants wouldn't be making so much noise. Nor be quite as jubilant, I'd guess. Maybe she locked it on the way out because she has something to hide." She smiled conspiratorially, then handed Tikaya the lantern and slipped out her lock-picking kit again. After a moment, Amaranthe said, "You haven't mentioned if you know of any doctors that might help me. Is it because we were distracted, or... something else?" Her voice had already been quiet, but it dropped even lower when she added, "Or is it unlikely any of them could help?"

"I don't know enough on the topic or about your injuries to say what is and isn't possible. As for the rest..." Tikaya had thought of two names as soon as it had become clear what Amaranthe wanted, but the idea of that assassin as a father, as a progenitor even... should she truly help that come to pass? On the other hand, who was she to deny a woman the right to have children? How would she have felt if some doctor had refused to help her all those years ago when she had married the Black Scourge of the Seas? "Having children is rewarding once you're ready and have found the right mate. Are you sure you want to have children with... I mean, from what little I know of you, you're a smart and talented woman, and you're attractive certainly. Perhaps you may wish to entertain other propositions and explore the world more before settling down with any one person."

Hypocrite. Exactly how many lovers had *she* had before flinging herself into Rias's arms? Of course, she had always been awkward and bookish; Amaranthe was comely enough and, judging by the men she had talked into joining her team, the assassin included, had a knack for winning people over to her side. If she applied herself, she could find some more appropriate suitor.

"Great, I've found a new Books to advise me on my love life," Amaranthe muttered.

"Pardon?" Tikaya wasn't sure she had heard all the words; maybe she should drop the subject.

"In the last year, Sicarius has done more and risked more for Sespian than any father could do for his son. He'd make a fine parent, and we work well together. In all possible ways. He was raised to be a cold-hearted assassin, true, but he didn't have a choice in the matter. They took him from his mother at birth and trained him to be a killer from his earliest days. That he's *not* a monster, and simply an utterly practical and logical soul, says much about his blood, I should think. And can you complain about the man Sespian is becoming?"

"No," Tikaya admitted, "but it was my understanding that Sicarius had nothing to do with the raising of Sespian. I assumed his mother must have been the primary influence."

"His mother died when he was young. He had Emperor Raumesys and Commander of the Armies Hollowcrest for his influences. I believe those are the two stalwart people who were responsible for declaring then-Admiral Starcrest dead and sending him into exile on that prison island."

"Yes."

A floorboard creaked on the level below, reminding Tikaya that this wasn't the best time for in-depth conversations on the worthiness of fathers.

Amaranthe torqued her wrist, and the lock clicked. She tucked away her tools and opened the door. They slipped into a dark room, pausing near the entrance for a moment to listen. Cool drafts came from the bank of windows on the far side and no fire had been laid in the hearth. Maybe Sauda wasn't returning home tonight. Or maybe this was simply an ornate guest room. But portraits occupied the walls, including one of a handsome couple, both of who shared a resemblance to Sauda. Tikaya had seen a tintype of the woman when she had been digging around in the intelligence office for this address. This would be her mother and father, she guessed. Painted ceramic eggs, vases, and suggestive bookends adorned built-in shelves to either side of a bed large enough for a whole family to share. Several rows of books were on those shelves, and they weren't covered with even a speck of dust.

"So, she likes to read after all," Tikaya whispered. "I wouldn't have thought her the type."

"Did you look at the titles?" Amaranthe asked dryly. "When Lady Dourcrest is the most innocuous author on the shelf, you know it's an... educational collection." She pointed upward, drawing Tikaya's attention to a mirror on the ceiling.

"Oh, I begin to see. I'm not that familiar with Turgonian authors, other than the handful that are considered classics out in the world."

"I don't think we ship these kinds of books overseas." Amaranthe waved a dismissive hand and headed for a desk with drawers.

Tikaya leaned her fingers against a wall and closed her eyes, trying to sense the telltale tickle of a Made device. If Sauda had one booby-trapped artifact, might she not have more about the house? The room appeared perfectly mundane though, to all of her senses.

"Not much here." Amaranthe was flipping through a journal. "She's going to the symphony tomorrow night, the theater the night after, and wrestling matches the day after that. There are quite a few cider and lunch social get-togethers penciled onto her calendar here, but nothing that suggests she's planning world domination with her friends. None of these names are familiar to me, though she's only mentioned a couple of surnames. Saltcrest. Edgecrest. Anyone you've run into?"

"I don't believe so, although there was a Professor Edgecrest who entered the building design competition."

"Ploris Edgecrest?" Amaranthe asked.

"No, I think it was Oddak."

"She had breakfast at Edgecrest Orchards with Ploris this morning. Conversation scintillating, her notes say. Enh, it's probably nothing." Amaranthe put the journal away and poked into dresser drawers.

Tikaya wouldn't have minded taking that calendar for further study, but she couldn't justify stealing from the woman—she could barely justify this snooping mission—and Sauda would be certain to miss such an up-to-date item. Instead, Tikaya peeked in the closet, under the bed, and in a wardrobe, hoping to find more condemning evidence. What exactly, she wasn't sure. She glanced at the dresser, about to suggest they try a different room, and found Amaranthe folding undergarments. "Uhm. What are you doing?"

"Nothing." Amaranthe hastily closed the drawer.

"I'm not an expert on sneaking into people's homes, but aren't they likely to know someone was there if they come back and find the bedroom tidier than when they left it?"

"She can blame the servants," Amaranthe said casually, though the lantern light revealed a blush to her cheeks. Maybe that had been some sort of habitual tic rather than a burglary tactic. "Besides, no one should object to returning to a tidier home. Really, what kind of person considers wrinkled undergarments stuffed into a drawer to be an acceptable organizational paradigm?"

"A disturbed one, doubtlessly." Tikaya decided not to invite Amaranthe over to the plantation back home. When Rias was out of town, the laundry rarely made it *into* a drawer. The military had hammered tidiness into him, at least insofar as storing clothing went, but either of their offices would cause Amaranthe to clutch at her heart in dismay. One couldn't walk to his desk without weaving around chalkboards and stacks of engine, vehicle, and submarine models. In her office... well, visitors tended to be hard-pressed to *find* the desk.

"Anyway, I was thinking while I was folding," Amaranthe said. "These old houses often have secret passages. Maybe she has a laboratory somewhere. All of this—" she waved toward the mirror and books, "—could be meant to disguise the fact that she's truly a mad genius who works in her lab, studying the Science and turning ancient knickknacks into evil artifacts capable of shriveling up a man's...er—" she glanced at Tikaya, "—mental processes."

"If this woman had anything resembling a laboratory, Rias probably would have missed her a lot more."

"Yes... he does seem to be one who appreciates brainy types." Amaranthe nudged an andiron with her foot.

"I'll take that as a compliment. I think."

Amaranthe prodded the matching andiron, and a soft click sounded. "Ah. A secret door."

"Good." Tikaya looked around the room. "Where is it?"

"Hm. I thought the click came from over here... behind one of these tapestries, maybe?"

Gravel crunched outside the window, along with the *chug-clank* of a steam carriage pulling into the driveway. Tikaya nudged a curtain aside. "What happens when you're sneakily rearranging someone's undergarment drawer in the middle of the night, and the lady of the house arrives home?"

"You duck into a hiding place."

"Have you found that hiding place yet?"

"No."

CHAPTER 10

Sespian stood before a steel door without so much as a fingerprint blemishing the sleek gray surface. Clearly a new addition, it was out of place among the centuries-old oak doors in the brick hallway. Not ten feet away, the arched wooden entrances to the cider and wine cellars were marked by intricate engravings of vineyards, orchards, and harvest scenes. The two guards in their crisp black uniforms also seemed an oddity in this half of the old hotel's basement. Unlike with the gymnasium and steam rooms on the other side, these hallways were empty of life, aside from Sespian and the guards, guards he didn't recognize and who might not be inclined to let him pass.

"Good evening," he said. "Are you here to keep visitors out or samples of plants in?"

"Yes," one guard said, no hint of humor on his face—or suggestion that he possessed a sense of humor at all.

Sespian hadn't seen Mahliki since their battle with the plant on the warship, and he wanted to make sure she hadn't suffered any injuries, physical or otherwise, from her brief internment beneath the surface. He also had to admit he was worried about all those samples she had taken. Given that the severed vines he'd seen had continued to live on after being cut, he worried those snippets she had taken might grow into mature plants if given time. Studying them here in the city sounded dangerous—the last thing Stumps needed was for this botanical beast to start spreading from another location.

"May I go in?" Sespian asked.

"Are you on the list?"

List? Uhm. "Yes?" he tried, though it didn't sound convincing.

The guard took a clipboard off the wall behind him. There were only four names on it—who needed a list for four names?—so Sespian didn't have trouble reading them: Lady and President Starcrest, Mahliki

Starcrest and Diplomat Basilard. Basilard's name surprised him, but then Sespian had been busy at the ground-breaking for his building all day and hadn't been to that meeting the president had held.

"Young Ms. Starcrest and Diplomat Basilard are inside," the guard said. "You're not the president."

"Must be his wife." The other guard smirked. Well, that one had a sense of humor. Somewhat.

His comrade gave him a cool stare and the smirk vanished.

"Listen," Sespian said, "I helped Mahliki collect the samples. I'm sure she'll want to see me." Well, he wasn't, though Maldynado seemed to think so. "Will you ask her if I can come in?"

"She's busy. She's not to be disturbed."

"But—"

"She hasn't even been eating her meals."

"I'm more helpful than a meal," Sespian said, though he wasn't sure it was a statement of fact. What did he think he could do in there?

"This work cannot be interrupted for frivolity." The guard made a shooing motion.

Sespian supposed the president wouldn't be pleased if he tried to subdue the door guards or otherwise bypass them. He wasn't armed and they were, so it probably wasn't a wise option anyway. He wasn't his father, thank their ancestors. How would Amaranthe get past these shrubs?

"How do you know she's doing well in there?" Sespian tried one last time. "When was the last time you checked in?"

"What do you mean?" the less humorless man asked.

"I mean that plant is deadly and grows fast. If it were to get out of hand... Mahliki and Basilard could already be in trouble. Before you know it, vines could be slithering out from under that door crack there and wrapping around your leg. A normal knife won't cut you free." Not entirely the truth, but it *was* a difficult chore with a normal knife. "I know. I've tried."

Both guards stared down at the crack beneath the door.

"I would check every hour if I were you," Sespian said. "The plant feeds on people, you know, and after Mahliki, you're the closest potential meals."

"Mr. Savarsin," the guard said. "With all respect for your former and current positions... please go away."

185

Sespian shrugged and backed up a few steps, then paused to admire the artwork of the cider engraving. It wasn't bad, though the shapes were blockier and less realistic than one might see in such examples in other nations. He touched an apple stem. At least someone had worked hard to include details.

While he studied the artwork, the guards kept glancing toward that crack under the door. Sespian wondered if either of them had lost colleagues down by the waterfront. Or perhaps they had simply heard the stories from the enforcers...

Grumbling under his breath, the humorless guard pulled out a key. He nodded for his comrade to keep an eye on Sespian, then unlocked the door. He opened it wide enough to peek inside and no wider.

As Sespian opened his mouth to shout a greeting to Mahliki—and suggest that she might like to see him—an explosion went off inside the room. A *loud* explosion. In the hallway, the floor trembled and crumbling mortar sifted out of the cracks between the bricks. The dust this caused was nothing compared to the cloud of smoke that rushed out of the open door. The guard stumbled back, coughing.

"Mahliki!" Sespian charged toward the door.

The second guard tried to stop him. Sespian blocked the grab and threw an elbow into the man's ribcage, then pushed the heavy door open wider and lunged inside. Black smoke filled the air. He couldn't see more than three feet in front of him. He stumbled forward, flapping his arms, trying to clear the haze, then bumped into a table or counter, and glasses rattled. He stopped.

"Mahliki? Are you in here? Are you... all right?"

"Yes," came Mahliki's voice from the back of the room. It was calm with a hint of of-course-I'm-all-right-and-what-are-you-blathering-about in it.

A rumble started up overhead somewhere. A ceiling fan? The smoke was gradually drawn upward, revealing a laboratory full of workbenches and counters, all covered with alchemical apparatuses. Liquids of different colors boiled above burners and tiny specimens floated in concoctions. The beakers and tubes were all secured with clamps, and as far as Sespian could tell, nothing had broken during the explosion. From the way Mahliki and Basilard stood calmly in front of a waist-high glass box—a vivarium?—wearing padded garments and protective goggles, Sespian realized that the explosion may have been intentional. The burning brand in Mahliki's hand was another clue.

She dumped it into an ash urn and lifted the goggles to her forehead. "Is it nighttime again? Look, you can tell my father I apologize if I woke anyone up, but we have to try everything. Some of these reagents are a little loud when they mix, I admit, but they're very potent. If anything is going to work on the plant..."

Sespian was patting the air with his hands. "He didn't send me. I—"

"*Nobody* sent him," one of guards snarled from behind Sespian. "He snuck past us when I was checking on you."

"We didn't want to grab him and rough him up, on account of him being the former emperor," the other rushed to add. Afraid he would get in trouble? Mahliki hardly seemed the sort to berate guards for not keeping people out. Or berate anyone. At least insofar as Sespian had seen.

Mahliki shrugged. "He can stay. Why are you grabbing your ribs, Balfus?"

The guard Sespian had elbowed glowered at him. "No reason, my lady."

"Let us get back to work, then, please. And if anyone comes down about the explosion, tell them there won't be any more tonight." She turned toward the vivarium, the "probably" she added not audible to anyone standing more than a few feet away. She picked up a pen and wrote something on a pad of paper resting atop the glass box. A three-foot length of vine lay pinned inside of it.

Sespian gulped. She hadn't collected any samples more than a couple of inches long.

Despite the clamps pinning it down, the end of the vine wavered back and forth like a pendulum. The fatter end had been sliced away, but blackened. Cauterized, maybe. Did that work to retard growth or was it simply something they had tried, hoping for the best?

"Basilard, check that gauge, will you?" Mahliki asked, alternately writing notes and nibbling on the tip of her pencil.

Basilard walked around the end of the vivarium, giving Sespian a nod as he passed by, and peered at one of three gauges set into the glass next to a control panel. *Still no oxygen inside.*

"I can't believe this thing is still alive," Mahliki muttered. "What did they do? Engineer it to survive in outer space?"

The guards exchanged dubious looks and shuffled back outside, shutting the door behind them. Sespian wondered how much they had been told about the plant's origins.

Good evening, Sespian, Basilard signed. He too had lifted his goggles. Soot smeared his face, save for the pale skin around his eyes; he looked like some sort of reverse raccoon.

"Good evening, Basilard. How did you get volunteered for the role of assistant?"

Basilard's expression turned wry. *Amaranthe. I believe I was signed up under the role of advisor, not assistant.*

"Ah, good. So you don't have to fetch her tea as well as reading her gauges?"

No, she hasn't had anything to eat or drink in the hours I've been in here.

"Perhaps she's gaining sustenance from the tip of that pencil." Sespian watched Mahliki to see if his teasing would draw a reaction, but she was so intent on her notes that he might as well have not been in the room.

It has *gotten shorter since I arrived this morning.*

"As an advisor, what advice might you offer, if she were to accept your input?" Perhaps Sespian could act as his translator. Though Mahliki could read Basilard's signs, if she was so intent on her own ideas, she might not see them. But a voice could cut through her focus more easily, surely. Sespian didn't see the Mangdorian translator around, perhaps because the president had been unwilling to give access to this room to someone who wasn't already familiar with the history of the plant.

I have already offered it. I do not know if anything would come of it, but I believe we should search for a natural predator. In the wilderness, plants rarely grow out of control because of predation and competition from other species.

"Any hungry herbivores we can bring in to nosh on that thing, Mahliki?" Sespian asked, this time prodding her in the shoulder at the same time to make sure she was paying attention.

She put down her pencil, propped her elbow on the glass, and faced them. "Basilard has already given me his theory, and I've invited him to find me such a herbivore, one with teeth like your father's dagger and the appetite of a tiger. Actually a blue whale. If memory serves, they eat four tons of krill a day."

"Would one fit in the lake?" Sespian joked.

Mahliki snorted. "Even if it would, this plant doesn't look like a krill to me."

"Maybe it tastes like one."

Mahliki gave him a flat look, the sort Sicarius was so good at.

Sespian found himself disappointed that she didn't appreciate his attempts at humor. Another time perhaps. She had probably been up all day and maybe the night before working on this. He lifted a hand. "I apologize. I can leave if I'm bothering you. I simply came to make sure you were well and had everything under control." He eyed the vine. The tip that had been waving back and forth earlier had either straightened or grown another inch in the short minutes he had been there. It was pressed against the glass now.

"I'm sorry for being a grouch," Mahliki said. "To both of you. I'm just..." She swallowed and faced the vivarium. "My father is counting on me. He believes I can solve this problem. If I can't..."

"Mahliki, I know you're very intelligent and have studied biology, but I'm sure he doesn't expect you to do this alone. Won't he let any experts in? He has to be willing to grant some people access and blast security concerns. This is more important than worrying about what the general public knows."

"Oh, several people have been by. The problem is they weren't helpful. At all."

She knows more than the biologists and botanists in the city, Basilard signed. *Your people are behind when it comes to the natural sciences.*

"Tell me about it." Sespian sighed. "I was the one to arrange the import of microscopes to the university when I was a boy, mostly because I wanted one for myself. We're making progress now, though. I've heard that one of our manufacturing companies is making some of the finest microscopes out there."

"Yes, and exporting them to real scientists in Kyatt and Alsorshia," Mahliki said dryly. "The last so-called professor who came in to help didn't know what a *cell* is. A cell, Sespian. That's kind of a basic thing."

"Perhaps we can arrange to have one of those microscopes sent to him," he said, though he wasn't sure why he kept trying humor on her. It wasn't working well today.

She dropped her face into the palm of her hand and exhaled abruptly. He didn't think it was a laugh. A cry of frustration? He stepped forward, thinking to comfort her with a pat on the back, but she rubbed her face and stood up, composing herself.

"I'm sorry," she said again. "I don't mean to insult your people. I know that neither the natural or mental sciences have been fostered here. I'm just frustrated."

"No, no, I understand. I find my people frustrating from time to time too." Sespian almost mentioned the idiot foreman in charge of his construction project. The work had barely started, and already there had been more accidents and injuries on the job site than most projects suffered in a month. Putting up a building was hardly a priority though, not compared to this.

Basilard tapped the vivarium. *The vine is applying pressure to the glass.*

Sespian eyed that tip again. More of it touched the glass now

Mahliki sighed. "I know. It keeps growing, even without oxygen." She waved to a suction apparatus at the far end, apparently the device that had removed the air. "That slowed it down, but—this plant is utterly odd."

"Excuse my ignorance," Sespian said, "but I thought plants created oxygen from carbon dioxide. Do they actually need it themselves?"

"Yes," Mahliki said. "They produce more oxygen than they require, but plant cells perform cellular respiration, the same as animal cells do. Granted many wetlands plants have developed a tolerance for low-oxygen conditions, but they shouldn't be able to survive without *any.*" She glowered at the vine. "Unless our gauge is lying to us, and we weren't effective at removing all the air, but Father designed that pump, so I'm inclined to trust it."

"Did he also design the case?" Sespian asked.

"Yes, though it was cobbled together from what could be scrounged on short notice."

That extra tidbit did not comfort Sespian. "Can you kill this particular piece before it breaks the glass and escapes?"

"I can't kill any of them, Sespian. That's the problem. We can hack them into pieces, but each piece has the potential to grow into a full plant."

When it grows too large for the experimentation case, we call the guards in, Basilard signed. *They lubricate themselves and run the plant down and toss it into the lake. It's the best we can do.*

Ah, so they had dealt with one outgrowing the case before. That might explain why those guards had been so leery at the thought of having a leg grabbed from below. If they had already dealt with the vines, they knew how difficult it was to remove them from human flesh.

Still, if they had successfully extricated all of the plant starts from the basement, perhaps Sespian's notions of one taking over the hotel had been premature. "You're able to keep it from taking root then?"

"Yes, it does seem to need a soil medium for that. Held suspended in air, the vines only grow longer vines." Mahliki walked to a different table and lifted a cover from a cloche. The root bulb she had cut into lay within. "This has remained dormant, though I don't believe it's dead necessarily."

"Like a seed lying fallow for years, waiting for the perfect circumstances for unfurling?" Sespian asked.

"Yes, but I don't think it'll wait for years."

I would like to fetch animals and experiment, Basilard signed. *If we find something that likes to eat it, our problem may be solved.*

"You're welcome to look for something," Mahliki said, "but I'm still skeptical that a terrestrial animal is going to be able to chew on that thing and digest it. Even if some rabbit with steel molars got it down, if stomach acid won't break it down—and we've experimented with acid already, remember?—then it might start growing in the animal's stomach. That would be a horrible death."

Beneath the soot, Basilard's face grew pale. *I hadn't thought of that.*

"Nor I," Sespian said, "but how disturbing."

I wouldn't wish to inflict that fate on any animal.

"If it has a natural predator, I doubt it lives on our world," Mahliki said.

"Your mother has a library on that ancient people, doesn't she?" Sespian asked. "Is there any mention of this in there?"

"Nothing, save one that says the Orenki—that's the name of the ancient people—were skilled horticulturists." Her mouth twisted. "Good to know you're going up against the best, isn't it? If I thought the fellow who didn't know what a cell is had primitive knowledge, I can only imagine what these people would have thought of me."

Basilard tapped the glass again. *This must be removed before the cage is damaged. I will fetch the guards.*

"Don't forget to tell them to grease up," Mahliki said. "We—"

A crack sounded, and Sespian jumped. His first thought was that the vivarium had shattered, but the sound had come from the other side of the laboratory, and the noise had been deeper than that of breaking glass. And muffled.

"What was that?" Sespian jogged toward the wall. Shelves filled with jars of bases and acids rose from the cement floor to the wood ceiling, but nothing appeared damaged.

"I'm not sure," Mahliki said.

Basilard tapped the glass for their attention. *It did not come from inside this room.*

"You're right," Sespian said, reconsidering the direction and type of sound he had heard. "But we're on the end of the building, aren't we? Is anything over there?"

"There's a side yard and the street, eventually. But we're ten feet below ground here."

Sewer? Basilard asked. *Could someone be trying to burrow a way into the hotel?*

"Through my *lab?*" Mahliki sounded more offended at this than at the notion of a security breach.

"Maybe," Sespian said. "I'll go see if there's a manhole cover or other access from the yard."

"Do you want us to go with you?"

"You'd better focus on your friends in here." Sespian waved at the vivarium. "I'll let you know if anyone is about to break down your wall and kidnap you."

"I'd be more alarmed at the idea of having my samples kidnapped."

Sespian smiled at her as he jogged for the door. "Yes, I imagine you would."

She returned his smile, and he decided it was quite a pleasant smile, even if it soon disappeared as she bent over her notes again. Sespian passed the guards in the hallway, nearly stumbling because they had their shirts off and were slathering themselves with grimbal grease. They glowered at him, glowers that clearly said, former emperor or not, they would have no trouble punching him if he commented on their state of undress and... slickness.

Sespian kept his comments to himself and ran up the stairs, through the corridors to the foyer, and past a yawning receptionist. Outside, numerous gas lamps kept the yard free of deep shadows. A spy or assassin would have been hard-pressed to hop the fence and approach a door or window without being spotted by the perimeter guards. Assuming that spy or assassin approached from *above* the ground...

Someone else must have heard the crack, for Colonel Starcrest and two young soldiers were already in the side yard. As a security precaution, the area had been cleared of shrubbery, so only clipped grass ran from the hotel walls to the fence at the street. There was a manhole, one Sespian might have had trouble finding, except that the two soldiers were standing on either side of it. One had a crowbar in hand.

"I don't care how rusty it is," Colonel Starcrest said. "Get it open. I want to know what's down there."

"Yes, Colonel."

Starcrest nodded to Sespian when he ran up. "You heard the noise?"

"Yes. I was in the basement lab. We thought someone might be trying to tunnel in."

"Hm." Colonel Starcrest didn't offer his own hypothesis, merely motioned for the men to try again to open it. Given the dirt scraped away from it and the pile of nearby sod, the grass had been growing over it for a long time.

After much heaving of muscles, the iron lid finally popped free. The first soldier held out a lantern and leaned over the hole to peer inside. He froze.

Colonel Starcrest strode over to join him. When he looked inside, he froze too. Then he swore. For a long time. In multiple languages.

Another time, Sespian might have been impressed by the colonel's ecumenical vocabulary, but now... he let his shoulders slump in defeat. Before he walked over, he had a notion of what he would see. He wasn't wrong.

The three-inch-thick greenish brown rhizome wasn't quite the same as the aerial vines that the plant sprouted, but there was no mistaking its identity. The long growth stretched across the sludge of the old sewer channel, its length disappearing into darkness in both directions.

Sicarius was crouching in the shadows on the rooftop, his back to one of the chimneys, when the steam carriage drove up. He thought of slipping inside to warn Amaranthe but trusted she would have heard the vehicle's approach. Besides, there was too much going on outside; he would be better served staying and watching. The person who had been following them since they left the president's hotel remained—Sicarius had tried twice to catch up with their stalker, only to find him gone when he arrived. He had no sense of the Science being used, and believed this might be their mage hunter. What had brought the person to Turgonia, he did not know, but he was well trained. Sicarius had yet to find so much as a footprint or hear a snapped twig. It was more instinct than evidence that kept telling him their follower was out there.

The man spying on the house from behind a shrub in the front yard had been easier to spot. Though also discreet, and clad in featureless gray clothing, Sicarius judged him a soldier. His way of moving stealthily—sweeping steps that were more circular than straightforward, designed to find objects in the dark and test the earth ahead before committing one's weight—was the method taught to scouts in the Turgonian army. This might be a veteran who had switched to mercenary work, but it seemed more likely that he was one of Colonel Dak Starcrest's intelligence officers.

Sicarius recognized the woman who stepped out of the sleek black steam carriage as President Starcrest's first wife. The well-dressed, gray-haired man who followed her out... Interesting. That was Deret Mancrest's father. Sicarius had not been back in town long enough to learn of the state of the *Gazette* or who was running it, though he recalled that Amaranthe had rescued Deret from imprisonment by this man the winter before. An unnecessary act on her part, since the journalist had done little to prove his worth to the team.

"Are you sure you should be seen so openly with another man," Lord Mancrest was saying, "now that you seem to be married again?"

"Now, now." Sauda patted his cheek. "You're just here to discuss that business proposition with me. Nobody could possibly think anything of that." She waved toward the illuminated wing of the house—the raucous laughs of the servants had been silenced with the arrival of the carriage.

"Unless they know I've already made my feelings clear on that proposition." Lord Mancrest caught her hand and kissed it. "And that we've moved onto discussing... other matters."

"Such as the story you're considering running to highlight the inappropriateness of that Kyattese woman as a president's consort?"

While Sicarius watched the interplay in the driveway, he habitually scanned the roof, and the front and the back yards, a task made challenging by the park-like setting, with all of its possible hiding places. Movement in the street fifty meters away halted his roving gaze. With the intersections so far apart and the lots so large, streetlights were sparse up on Mokath

Ridge, but his dark-adjusted eyes picked out the short, slight figure easily. A boy of ten or twelve approached wrapped in a ragged cloak two sizes too big for his body. Someone's messenger. Perhaps one sent to deliver or receive a report from the intelligence officer.

But the boy didn't venture onto the lawn. He crept around the influence of a single gas lamp burning at the head of the driveway and tiptoed to the mailbox, a stonework rectangle perched unobtrusively next to a shrub.

"I believe I got all the details of that story over dinner," Lord Mancrest went on, linking his arm through Sauda's.

"Did you?" she said, leaning against him. "Then you must be here to gather more details on *me*. The beleaguered and abandoned wife, naturally."

"Naturally."

Out in the street, the boy slipped a large envelope out of his cloak. He opened the mailbox and eased it inside, his eyes darting about as he did so, watching both ends of the street as well as the cozy couple pressed against each other in the driveway. The intelligence officer had crept around one of the statues so he could more fully watch the couple as well. He had not noticed the boy. The shrub might block his view, or he was simply too focused on other matters.

The boy closed the large brass mailbox door, then tapped something on the back of it. A red flag snapped into place, the cloth shivering in the night air. The boy raced down the street, his oversized cloak flapping.

Sauda and Lord Mancrest had been heading for the large flagstone front porch when the chauffeur cleared his throat. He didn't say a word, but Sauda gazed toward the street, squinting into the darkness—at the mailbox. Expectantly.

"Get that, will you, Pevat? And leave it in my office."

"Yes, my lady."

Sicarius thought about waiting for the servant to collect the item and deliver it to the office, then sneaking inside to take a look, but he should be able to beat the man to the box without being seen. Why not intercept the mail, and find out what midnight messages this woman was receiving? True, this side trip had been Professor Komitopis's idea, and it had nothing to do with Sicarius and Amaranthe's plans—or what President Starcrest had asked of them—but this might be a part of some scheme. Something that could threaten Starcrest. The first wife seemed about as trustworthy as black ice on a bridge.

After another quick scan of the grounds, Sicarius darted away from the chimney in a low crouch, using the apex of the roof to hide himself from those in the front yard. An urgent pluck at his senses warned him that, despite his dark clothing and the shadows, he might be visible to someone in the backyard, someone keeping an eye on him as closely as he was keeping an eye on everything else.

Instincts dropped him to his belly before something clinked into the slate roof tiles above him. His ear calculated the trajectory in an instant, and he hurled a throwing knife at a shrub behind the third fountain from the fence.

Knowing he was vulnerable on the roof, he didn't wait to see if anything came of the attack. He crawled for the edge and forewent the drainpipe he had climbed to reach the perch, simply dropping to the grass below, landing softly on his feet. No more attacks came from the backyard as he jogged for the fence running up the side of the property. He glanced toward the fountain to ensure nobody was sprinting after him. Utter stillness wreathed that half of the property, with not even a breeze stirring the leaves. He was tempted to pursue his attacker, but he had a limited amount of time to intercept the message in the mailbox.

Sicarius ran along the fence, using its bulk and deep shadows to his advantage. The crunch of footsteps on the gravel drive announced the chauffeur ambling toward the street on his errand before the man came into sight. Sicarius, racing along at a much quicker pace, soon passed him. But getting to the mailbox without being seen would be difficult with the servant looking in that direction. As he ran, he picked up a small rock. When he reached the street, he tossed it behind the servant. Frowning, the man craned his neck to look behind him. Mancrest and Sauda had gone inside. Sicarius didn't spot the intelligence officer.

He glided through the shadows, staying low and using the shrubbery along the street to avoid the street lamp and arrive at the mailbox. He plucked out the envelope as the servant was turning back around. Too much open space lay on either side for him to make it back to the fence and the side yard without being seen. He melted into the closest shrub, not stirring a leaf. Once wrapped in its embrace, he froze.

The chauffeur continued to the mailbox, opened the door, and peered inside. He stood there for a long moment, outlined by the street lamp at the corner of the drive, and finally scratched his head and straightened. Sicarius remained frozen, not three steps away, branches prodding the back of his neck. He could hear the man's breathing, smell the smoke and oil on his clothing, see the coal dust in the creases of his knuckles.

"Kid's prank," the servant muttered and pushed down the flag.

Sicarius waited for him to head back down the driveway to attend to the vehicle, then eased out of the bush. Aware of the other spy in the yard—two spies if the person in the back had moved to follow him—Sicarius crossed the street where shrubs on the other side could effectively camouflage him, then jogged to the next property before circling around. He climbed over the brick wall and dropped into the backyard of Sauda's house again, where a copse provided cover for him. He waited, listening, smelling, and touching the ground and the wall, in case vibrations betrayed someone approaching from close at hand. When he detected nothing, he followed the shadows until he reached that third fountain on the other side of the yard. He checked the area, but didn't find anyone there. At this point, he wasn't surprised. He did, however, catch the faintest scent of blood. After a patient search, probing with his fingers rather than relying on his eyes in this dark nook, he located his knife lying in the dirt beneath a rhododendron. From its impact angle, he knew it had struck, or at least glanced off something else, before coming to rest in the spot. He plucked it from the ground, held it up to his nose, and inhaled.

Damp earth and warm blood.

CHAPTER 11

THE SOUNDS OF MALE AND female voices drifted down the hallway punctuated by laughter. Amaranthe glowered at the tapestries on the wall. She had checked behind each one and pushed that andiron three more times, and she still hadn't found the secret door.

"We're going to have to hide somewhere in the room," she whispered.

Tikaya was on the other side of the bed, also poking and prodding sections of wall.

Amaranthe was certain the unlocking noise had come from somewhere near the fireplace though.

"While they have *sex*?" Tikaya whispered back, her lip curled.

"What? Voyeurism isn't an acceptable hobby on Kyatt?" Amaranthe prodded a rug with her foot. Could that secret room be beneath them rather than through a wall?

"Not when one of the subjects used to have sex with your husband!"

Something thumped against the door, and a woman giggled.

Amaranthe lifted the rug and would have snorted at herself in disgust, but there wasn't time—nor did she want to make any extra sounds. She grabbed her lantern and waved Tikaya over. She pulled on the circular iron handle set into the floor. The trapdoor creaked as it rose, and she grimaced, hoping the sounds of someone fumbling for the knob out there drowned out the poorly oiled hinges.

Stairs led into darkness. Tikaya was rushing for the trapdoor, and her knee caught on the corner of the bed. She tumbled forward and would have crashed, but Amaranthe thrust the lantern handle into her mouth and caught Tikaya before she could fall. Gripping the older woman's arm, Amaranthe guided her onto the stairs, trying not to jump up and down with impatience as she let Tikaya go first. But after the stumble, Tikaya moved quickly, disappearing into the utter blackness below.

The door opened amidst more giggles. Amaranthe blew out her

lantern and rushed down the stairs as quickly as she dared, pulling the trapdoor and the rug down behind her. She feared that rug wouldn't be as perfectly placed as it had been before and hoped the lovers were too engaged to notice. She also hoped whatever room they entered offered another way out. She didn't particularly want to wait for the couple to finish and pass out before sneaking out of the house.

Amaranthe had descended perhaps fifteen steps when heavy boots trod across the floor above, then the bed creaked. At the bottom, she bumped into something softer and warmer than the cold stone walls on either side of the stairs.

"Sorry," she whispered. "Is that your arm?"

"Not... exactly." Tikaya sounded amused—or relieved, more likely.

"So, just to be clear, voyeurism *is* acceptable when neither of the subjects has been your husband's lover?"

"I don't know, but it would be less uncomfortable. At least we're safe for the moment."

So long as the homeowner didn't realize that the door she had locked when she left had been unlocked when she had returned. Fortunately, her attention seemed to have been elsewhere.

Amaranthe and Tikaya felt their way through a corridor, the rough cement walls cool to the touch. At the end, a door made of the same material stopped them. Amaranthe would have assumed it another wall, but her groping fingers chanced across a latch. Though she expected it to be locked, she gave it a tug. It glided open with surprising ease. She doubted anyone lurked inside, but she paused to listen, knowing Sicarius would glower with disapproval if she barged in anywhere without checking. Amazing how the man could glower without moving his mouth or furrowing his brow. The stare simply hardened.

Amaranthe relit the lantern. The tiny flame revealed a windowless room with a low ceiling and another door on the wall to their right. With a coatrack, console table, and bench, the space looked more like a foyer than some secret hidey hole.

"Definitely not a genius's lab." Tikaya wandered over to the table.

"No." Amaranthe walked to a corner where a ladder led up through a dark hole. Probably nothing more than another entrance to the hidden chamber, but her curiosity sent her climbing up the rungs. She came to another small room, this one with two padded chairs and strange little windows. She peered through one into a bedroom, lit only by the wan moonlight drifting in through a window. Shadows of strange apparatuses filled the room, and Amaranthe was glad she couldn't quite make out the items hanging on the walls. "Speaking of voyeurism," she murmured and headed back down the ladder.

Tikaya was staring into a box sitting on the table, but she glanced over when Amaranthe landed on the floor again. "Anything interesting?"

"No. Also... I think it's good that President Starcrest found you."

Tikaya's brow wrinkled, but whatever rested inside the box distracted her from an inquiry. "This may be what the jade statuette originally came in."

"Because it carries the stench of foul magic?"

"No... because there's a note." Tikaya lifted a scrap of paper from the bottom. "Insert a lock of Starcrest's hair into the secret niche underneath the doll. It will make him more amenable to your suggestions." She lowered the note, scoffing. "Amenable. It's more that it degraded his faculties." Growling, she lifted it to finish reading. "Once you are at his side again, you can find an opportunity to repay me." Tikaya threw the note in the box. "At his side. I don't think so. It would take more than a piece of hair for that." She propped a fist against her hip. "I didn't notice a secret niche in that statuette. I should have poked around more."

"Any indication of who sent the note?" Amaranthe asked.

"There's no signature or seal."

"Ah, so inconvenient when the mysterious criminals don't sign their secret missives with their full names."

"Do you think it would be missed if I took the note back to the intelligence department?" Tikaya asked. "A young man in there does handwriting analysis. Maybe he's seen this style before."

"If we don't stumble into security on our way out—" Amaranthe hoped the door she had not yet checked led outside, "—then the note might be deemed misplaced. Another possibility is simply to confront the woman and ask her from whom she got the box. It sounds like she was fooled and wasn't aware of its true purpose. Maybe she would feel irked at the person who did the fooling. Irked enough to betray him or her."

"Perhaps not," a quiet voice came from behind them.

Tikaya leaped a foot, clunking her head on the ceiling.

"Sicarius," Amaranthe said, facing the door they had yet to check.

"Some people find your sudden appearances alarming, you know. You could knock before entering."

He stepped out of a dark tunnel, a cobweb draped across one shoulder. Tikaya, hand clutching her chest again, gripped the table for support. Amaranthe brushed the cobweb off his shoulder.

"Trapdoors disguised as brick walls do not lend themselves to knocking." Sicarius held up an envelope. "I intercepted a mail delivery."

"Late night mail deliveries? I had no idea the postal system had grown so efficient under this new government regime." Amaranthe peered down the tunnel Sicarius had stepped out of, but only darkness waited in that direction. "Where does this lead?"

"The carriage house."

"Which you were in because...?"

"The other spy inadvertently intercepted my path to the back door," Sicarius said. "I noticed an oddly placed splinter of wood as I passed through the carriage house, found another door, and decided to check on you."

"The *other* spy?" Tikaya asked.

"This is someone besides the person who was following us?" Amaranthe asked.

"Yes," Sicarius said.

"I had no idea the former Lady Starcrest was drawing so much attention," Amaranthe said, then admitted, "Actually, I had no idea there *was* a former Lady Starcrest until today." She slid out a knife and pried open the wax seal on the envelope, being careful not to break it in case they wanted to reseal it. Unfortunately, as with the note in the box, the brown blob didn't hold an emblem stamp or any identifying characteristic.

"I believe it's one of your husband's men," Sicarius told Tikaya.

"*Rias* is spying on his first wife?"

"Someone out of the intelligence office may have issued the order."

"Oh, Dak maybe. He seems the suspicious sort." Tikaya took a wide berth around Sicarius to join Amaranthe in examining the two pieces of paper that had slid out of the envelope.

"This one's for you." Amaranthe handed a page full of gobbledygook letters to her.

"A different language?" Tikaya adjusted her spectacles and held the paper close to the lamplight. "Or an encoded message. Interesting. I haven't had a chance to decrypt a message in some time. This should be fun."

"Fun might not be the precise word." Amaranthe tilted the second page toward Tikaya, this one a detailed blueprint of the president's hotel, including information on security guard positions and change-of-shift times.

The enthusiasm faded from Tikaya's face. "Someone inside is working for the other side?"

Amaranthe wasn't sure who exactly the other side *was*, but she nodded bleakly. "The blueprint may have been found in some old public archive—" she felt a twinge of loss, remembering how Books would have known exactly where to research such things, "—but the rest of the information shouldn't be available outside of the hotel and those working there. And we don't even know what's on that sheet yet." Amaranthe pointed at the one in Tikaya's hand. "Unless you can read that."

"Not yet. I'll have to spend some time working with it."

"You may not want to ask for advice from anyone working in the intelligence office," Amaranthe said.

Tikaya stared at the hotel map with the tidy notes in the margin. "No, I should think not."

"Unless we can use the information at some point to build a trap for the snitch."

"Let me find out what it says first, then talk to Rias," Tikaya said. "No one's better at designing traps than he is."

Amaranthe nodded, though with assassins about, it would be better to know sooner than later whom they could trust. She wagered that the person who was leaking information on the security rotation had also told that would-be assassin about the *Explorer's* arrival. Maybe the submarine had been targeted specifically because of the plant. Maybe someone didn't want Turgonia to fix that problem and return normalcy to the city. And the continent, she added, remembering Rias's calculation that the plant might eventually take over the whole republic if it wasn't stopped.

"You are scheming," Sicarius said. He had moved close enough that she could feel the warmth of his body in the chilly room.

She would have leaned against him if Tikaya hadn't been there, but the professor's unspoken disapproval at the notion of Amaranthe having children with Sicarius made her a little shy about showing affection. Not that either of them usually did so with others looking on, anyway, but she occasionally engaged in supportive leaning in public.

"I'm just thinking right now," Amaranthe said. "The scheming comes later."

"In two minutes? Or three?"

She snorted softly, wishing Tikaya would notice his attempts at humor—surely he had changed from the sinister employee of the emperor she had met all those years ago—but she was engrossed in the encrypted page.

Amaranthe touched her arm. "You've been living in the hotel all winter. Is there anyone who comes to mind as a suspicious sort? If we could narrow things down..." If she had a short list, she could ask Sicarius to wander the halls and spy on the various parties.

"I'm not certain," Tikaya said. "I haven't gotten to know many of the soldiers, and there aren't many educated women around to speak with who don't have... an agenda. Without employment of my own or colleagues here in town, I've admittedly been a tad reclusive this winter. I have noticed all the people, military and civilian, jump to obey any orders Rias issues, even the crusty old generals. He inspires such loyalty in them that it's hard to imagine one of them betraying him."

"What about that colonel?" Amaranthe asked.

"Dak? He's Rias's nephew."

"I know, and I've only seen him a couple of times, but he seems... grouchy. Maybe bitter. He sort of grumps around, not all that eager to jump at the president's orders."

"I'm sure Rias wouldn't have called him down if he wasn't trustworthy," Tikaya said.

Sicarius, still standing at Amaranthe's back, stiffened.

"What is it?" she asked.

His head was tilted toward the door leading back to the bedroom, his face intent. "A window opening."

"What?" Tikaya looked at Amaranthe. Former cryptomancer or not, even she needed Sicarius's oblique messages decoded.

Amaranthe grabbed the lantern and headed for the door that led back to the bedroom trap door. "Is it possible Sauda would be a target?"

Jogging around her, Sicarius reached the door first, but he had only taken two steps into the hallway when an ear-splitting scream erupted from the floor above. His jog turned into a sprint. Amaranthe and Tikaya charged after him. The screams continued, though they were moving. Had Sauda fled the room? Was that her screaming? Maybe a servant had walked in on the pair, but that didn't make sense. The servants would leave their mistress her privacy.

The trapdoor clunked open before Amaranthe had even reached the bottom of the stairs. By the time she raced up and into the bedroom, Sicarius was already gone. Out the door? Or the window with the lacy curtains blowing in the breeze? Sauda wasn't anywhere to be seen, but the bed... it wasn't unoccupied.

"Dear ancestors," she murmured.

Lord Mancrest lay tangled in the sheets, the hilt of a slender dagger thrusting from his bare chest. From his heart. Even in the poor lantern light, Amaranthe could tell there was no possibility that he remained alive.

"I didn't..." Tikaya whispered, coming up behind her.

"Expect that," Amaranthe finished.

The screams hadn't stopped, though they were on the other side of the house now.

"She must be getting the servants," Amaranthe said. "We... might not want to be caught in here."

Tikaya's eyes widened. "No, we shouldn't be here. We have to..."

"Back down." Amaranthe nudged her toward the stairs, trusting Sicarius would find his own way out without being caught. She did worry, however, that he had gone after the killer. A while back, he had admitted to knowing of a few other assassins in the world of his caliber. Amaranthe was beginning to worry that they were dealing with one of them.

Tikaya scampered down the stairs. Once again, Amaranthe closed the trapdoor behind them, being even more careful to drag the rug across this time, so it wouldn't be rumpled for the first people who walked in. And for the enforcers who would come after. Unless Sauda squelched the story—she might be blamed for this if she couldn't explain who *had* done it.

In grim silence, Amaranthe and Tikaya ran down the secret passage, heading through the little room and straight for the tunnel Sicarius had used. Amaranthe grabbed the empty envelope on the way by. No need to leave evidence that someone had been in there tonight. Tikaya still had the papers with her, clutched to her chest. She wasn't going to let them go until she reached the hotel, Amaranthe wagered.

They came out of the tunnel and into the dark carriage house, then headed for the backyard. Lamps were being lit all over the house, but nobody seemed to be searching the grounds yet. Aware that there was an assassin out there somewhere and that she was responsible for the president's wife tonight, Amaranthe chose the most direct route to the alley. She watched every shrub and every shadow for movement as they ran. She strained her ears to listen as well, but the screams from the house hadn't abated, and other voices had joined in, barking orders and yelling for someone to get a doctor. Too late for that.

Tikaya yawned so hard that tears sprang to her eyes. A couple of gas lamps remained lit in the library, but the room had been quiet for hours, save for someone else a few aisles away who turned a page now and then. The candles on her own table burned low—they had been fresh when she started. She should have gone to bed hours ago, especially given her nocturnal adventures with Amaranthe, but she had hoped to decrypt the message first. It would be nice to be able to hand Rias something more than lines of gibberish when she explained that she had been snooping around his first wife's house. What would he think about that trip? That she was some insecure virago who had rushed out to confront the other woman? Or to dig up evidence to sully her name? No, he would listen to her, but it would still be an awkward conversation, maybe because Tikaya truly did wish to sully the other woman's name.

"How petty," she acknowledged with a sigh.

After another jaw-cracking yawn, Tikaya pushed herself away from the table. She felt she was close to breaking the code, but it wasn't going to happen tonight. She was too tired to see the obvious. Maybe if she slept with her notes under the pillow, her brain would solve the problem overnight.

"Wishful notion."

A chair creaked, then footsteps headed for the door. Tikaya didn't know whom she had been sharing the library with and decided to wait for the person to leave first, but the footsteps paused, and someone poked a head around the corner of her bookcase-lined aisle. Gray hair in need of a cutting hung over eyebrows not quite hidden by his large round spectacles.

"Vice President Serpitivich," Tikaya said. "I didn't know that was you over there."

He opened his mouth to speak but a yawn caught him, and he lifted an apologetic hand—his other hand clutched two books, a folder stuffed with papers, and a long scroll that looked like a blueprint or map. "Yes, working late. I'm on my way out, but I heard you... mutter thoughtfully and just wanted to make sure you didn't need help with anything."

Mutter   thoughtfully.   A   polite   euphemism for talking-to-yourself-like-an-unhinged-person.

"Just working through a problem to solve." One she had best not share with anyone else before Rias. Fortunately, Serpitivich didn't ask. He merely nodded as if he understood. "And you?" Tikaya pointed toward the scroll. "Anything you need help with?"

His mouth twisted wryly. "Yes, but I won't attempt to foist this burden on you." At her raised eyebrows, he explained. "It seems subterranean plant incursions are a new concern. I've been tasked with studying the sewers and pipes around the hotel, to see if there's a way to divert that plant from the building."

"You have? I would have thought that would be a task for some young private in security."

"I may have made the mistake of mentioning that I'd been studying the city's sewer system for another project of mine." He blew out a breath, ruffling his shaggy bangs.

"Ah." Tikaya's single syllable turned into another yawn. "If there's nothing else, I'll wish you the best of luck with it and take my leave."

"Of course." Serpitivich bowed his head and started to back away, but stopped, lifted a finger, then lowered it, and shook his head.

"Something else?"

"No." He started to leave, but paused again. "Yes. Oh, I don't know. I shouldn't bother you with... government business."

"No? Quite a few other people have used me as a conduit to Rias." Or they had tried. Tikaya was doing her best to avoid finding herself in that position.

Serpitivich's expression turned glum. "That's what I was afraid of. I won't bother you. I... can handle him on my own."

He turned, but Tikaya, her curiosity piqued despite her weariness, asked, "Him?"

Serpitivich hesitated again, clearly torn on whether he should bother her or not. "It's Colonel Starcrest. I'm loath to approach President Starcrest about him, since they're related..."

Tikaya stood very still, remembering Amaranthe's question about Dak's loyalty and remembering also that they now knew there was a snitch somewhere in the building. "What is it?"

"I just... caught him looking through my office this morning, uninvited. And he's said a few things that have made me wonder..." Serpitivich spread his free hand, palm up. "Maybe it's nothing, but it's hard to bring concerns about him to the president when—" he huffed, stirring his hair again. "I was against his appointment from the beginning, so maybe he simply doesn't like me. His record is not... well, I don't know if you've read it, but he certainly doesn't seem qualified for such an important station. I respect your husband very much, but assigning a relative is nepotism, plain and clear, and that's the sort of thing for which the warrior caste has been known for so long. Cronyism and nepotism. I wanted a fresh start with this new government, for people who had *earned* being appointed to offices, and... oh, I'm sorry, my lady. I never should have said anything."

Tikaya's heart was pumping in her ears. No, she had never seen Dak's record, nor did she know much about him at all. Had Rias made a mistake in recruiting him? Serpitivich was staring at her, his face twisted with concern, almost anguish, doubtlessly fearing he had made a faux pas she wouldn't forgive. "It's... all right," Tikaya managed. "Appointing a relative to a government position would be frowned upon on Kyatt too."

Relief spread across Serpitivich's face. "I knew—well, I'd hoped—you might understand. Anyway, I don't want anything of you, my lady. I just had to tell someone, and I didn't want to make accusations to the man's uncle."

"I understand, though I believe Rias would hear such accusations with an open mind."

Serpitivich lifted his narrow shoulders. "Perhaps so, my lady, but even after these months of working under him, he still intimidates me." He lifted his hand. "But I'll leave you to your rest. Be well."

Tikaya let him go without stopping him again. His shoulders seemed more relaxed as he walked away, a burden unleashed. Too bad he had given her another one.

Shaking her head, she gathered her own material, blew out the candles, and left the library. Upstairs, she climbed the final stairs to their rooms, then turned left and walked past them. Since the bombing of Rias's office, they had been sharing a more modest suite at the other end of the hall.

A guard came to attention and gave her a professional, "Evening, my lady."

She returned the greeting, though having people stationed outside her door hadn't stopped seeming strange yet. Strange and not particularly welcome. She knew they were there to protect Rias—and her—but she couldn't help but wonder what these young pups thought of the bedroom noises of two older folks. The walls in the old hotel weren't particularly thick. Of course, since he had become president, Rias rarely came to bed early enough—or stayed in bed late enough—for noises more exuberant than snores.

When Tikaya slipped inside, she found a lamp burning low near the dressing table. Bumps of the appropriate size lay stretched under the covers on Rias's side of the bed. Assuming him asleep, she started to undress and reached for the flannel sleeping gown that she would probably be wearing halfway into summer if the nights didn't start getting warmer soon.

"So," Rias's voice came from the bed, "Sauda's house is where you went to take initiative?"

His tone was carefully neutral, and Tikaya couldn't tell if disapproval, concern, or disappointment lay behind it. Maybe none of them. Maybe she was feeling guilty and reading in emotions that weren't there.

"She was the one who sent you the gift that was making you sick," Tikaya said.

"I... wasn't aware that I'd been sick."

"All those headaches you've been getting?"

"I thought it was the job."

"The sudden need to use pen and paper to perform math problems you formerly did in your head?"

"I... thought... feared I was getting older. That the brain was getting a little soft along the borders."

208

"Love, you're not senile; you've been under the influence of a Made device."

A long moment passed, and Tikaya wondered if he might not believe her. Would he think she was making something up to justify her visit to his first wife's house?

Rias sat up in bed and leaned against the headboard. "I'm trying to decide if that's a relief or not."

"Let me tell you the rest while you ponder that." Tikaya shared the story of the night's adventures as she finished changing and performing her evening ablutions, explaining the gift and everything that had gone on in Sauda's house. "Sicarius knew you had a man in the yard, by the way. It seems he wasn't being as stealthy as he thought."

"*Dak* had a man in the yard."

Dak. Should Tikaya relay the vice president's concerns?

"Nobody else would be brazen enough to send a spy to any of my relatives' houses," Rias continued dryly. "Even former relatives. Although she's not as former as I had thought. Did anyone fill you in on that?"

"Mahliki did. I believe I'm all caught up." Tikaya brought the lamp to the bedside table along with the papers.

"I'm glad someone is." Rias pushed a hand through his tousled hair— if that "bed head" was any indication, he must have gotten some sleep before she had come in. Good. He needed it. "Shall I confess that I spent the evening hiding in a warehouse on the waterfront, tinkering with the sub? I needed a break from—" he waved vaguely to encompass the hotel, or maybe the entire city, "—everything."

Tikaya decided not to mention that Sicarius had been missing since he took off after that assassin, so his and Amaranthe's mission to find a Maker had been delayed. She wasn't even sure if she should mention the encoded message they had intercepted. Maybe it could wait for morning. She slid the pages under the lamp.

"And that is...?" he asked.

"Some of that everything you need a break from."

"Ah."

"It can wait until morning. I haven't broken the encryption yet anyway." Tikaya leaned over to cut out the lamp, but an arm wrapped around her, fingers clamping gently onto the back of her hand.

"Really, love, you can't toss a word like encryption into the bed, and then expect me to lay my head on the pillows and nod off into slumber."

"I thought you might have had enough work-related talk for the night." Tikaya rubbed his hand with her thumb and leaned back against him. He smelled of soap but also of engine oil and machine lubricant from the submarine. The familiar scent stirred nostalgia in her, of all those years when he had been working on some engineering project or another beneath the warm Kyattese sun, when they had little more to worry about than raising children and pursuing their passions.

"Oh, I've had enough for the year," Rias sighed, "but assuage my curiosity, regardless, please."

Tikaya handed him the blueprint of the hotel. "We have a snitch."

He accepted it and dropped his chin onto her shoulder as he stared at the other page by the lamplight.

"Sicarius intercepted this as it was delivered to Sauda's mailbox. We'd originally thought she was being duped—the instructions we found in the box that held your gift promised it would make you more amenable to her wishes, not that it would give you blinding headaches—but if she's acting as some sort of delivery point, she may be more entrenched in this plot than I had imagined."

"It seems I was wise to send along Sicarius to keep an eye on you instead of a squad of guards."

"Actually, I requested that. I believe that makes me the wise one."

"Yes, but I considered countermanding that request, since you were clearly up to something shifty." Rias lifted his eyes toward her face and offered a half-smile with these words.

"You know," Tikaya said, "your nose is close enough that I could insert a pencil in your nostril. Don't think I'm too mature for such antics."

"Oh, I know you're not, but I don't see a pencil, so I feel moderately safe."

Tikaya plucked a stub from behind the ear he couldn't see and waved it in the air.

"Ah. My feeling of safety is a delusion, it seems." His gaze fell to the blueprint. "In all senses." He nodded toward the other sheet and her stack of notes beneath it. "I would offer to dump that on the intelligence department, but given all that I've learned of you over the years, you're probably delighted to have a project."

"Yes, this is more appealing than taking up... what is that thing your brother's wife does? With the strings of sheep fur?"

Rias chuckled. "Knitting. With wool. Sheep have wool."

"Right, that's it." Tikaya waved away any embarrassment at her mistake—as far as she knew, the Kyatt Islands had never seen a sheep, and her encounters with them had all been in books. "It doesn't sound stimulating enough for my tastes. Besides," she said as she picked up the coded message, "since we apparently have a snitch in the building, the fewer eyes on this, the better, right?"

Rias lay back down on his side of the bed. "Please let me know as soon as you crack the code. I'll have Dak change the security shifts and patrol routes, but I'd like to know what other information has been leaked."

"I will." Tikaya fiddled with the hem of the blanket. "About Dak..."

"Yes?"

"Seeing as we don't know who this snitch is, should you be... reserved with what you tell him?"

That prompted a long moment of silence. "Do you have a reason to suspect him?"

"The vice president mentioned that Dak had been snooping in his office," Tikaya said.

"Hm, that's not appropriate, but not that surprising, either. I know Dak doesn't trust Serpitivich."

"Also... Amaranthe pointed out that he's your least eager admirer, if he's an admirer at all. When I met him, he was knocking you on your backside and enjoying it."

"It's true that I don't know him that well—I've been out of the empire for his entire twenty-year career—but I believe I understand him. He's grown up in my shadow and has a reason to resent me. But at the same time, I read his record carefully before bringing him down here. He's the sort to punch a commanding officer in the face rather than gossip about him behind his back."

"In most nations, that would earn a man a court-martial," Tikaya said. "I suppose that's grounds for respect here."

"It depends on the officer being punched. Some men admire that sort of forthrightness, and some don't. I, of course, prefer straightforward honesty, even if I've learned to deal with deceit and trickery."

"Yes, I remember you didn't care for the Kyattese government officials at first because they wouldn't attack you openly."

"At first?" Rias asked lightly.

"Just promise me you'll keep an eye on him. If he's a Starcrest, I'm sure there's a brain beneath that crusty exterior."

"Oh, there is. I wouldn't have brought him into the office if there weren't. Although he has made it clear that he's a field man and doesn't particularly care for desk jobs, especially one that involves supervising a lot of other people doing their desk jobs."

Tikaya fluffed up her pillow and cut out the lamp. "I'll let you know what I find as soon as I find it."

"Good. You should also prepare a suitcase in the morning," Rias said, "though I'm loath to give up ground and admit defeat."

"What? Why? And admit defeat to whom?"

"To that plant. I received word this evening that it's in the sewer system not five feet from the basement of this hotel."

That explained Serpitivich's research.

"I sent Dak on a reconnaissance," Rias went on, "and it's breaking through buildings' foundations and destroying their plumbing up to Fourth Street so far. This is all in addition to the surface damage. I've ordered all of the factories, warehouses, and canneries on the first two blocks abandoned. The owners are not pleased. I expect we'll have riots outside the gates soon, and those religious zealots are using this to their advantage to cow people into joining their cause."

"I suppose when you say pack a suitcase, you mean so that we can move your headquarters farther up the hill, not so we can hop onto the first steamer heading out to sea and back home." Tikaya thought he might laugh or at least chuckle wryly, but he was utterly serious when he responded.

"That remains an option for you. For me to leave would be the greatest cowardice."

"Maybe you could simply invite the vice president to replace you—he ran against you, so he must want the job. Then it would be more like a stately resignation rather than a fleeing of a battlefield with one's tail between one's legs."

"He seems... rather bookish for the job. The other day, I caught him reading up on the new religious cult, which is apparently a very old religious cult, when he was supposed to be perusing papers distributed by the chief of financial affairs. He didn't see this as inappropriate in the least; rather he launched into a lecture."

"I'd choose a history book over finance reports too," Tikaya said.

"In the middle of a staff meeting covering those finance reports?"

"Perhaps not, but I've found his knowledge interesting when he's shared it. Did you let him talk?"

"I asked him to have a paper sent to my desk."

Tikaya snorted. "Learned that trick from Mahliki, did you?"

"Perhaps so. Regardless, I can't leave. There's too much... *much*." He yawned, and Tikaya resolved to let him go back to sleep.

She patted in the darkness, finding his arm atop the blankets. "I was teasing, love. I know you can't leave. And I won't leave you here to face these madmen alone, either."

"The madmen don't concern me greatly. I've been dealing with such men for a long time and understand their ways. That plant is another matter."

CHAPTER 12

"H ERE." A BRUTISH MAN IN wrinkled clothes and with missing teeth thrust a shovel into Maldynado's hands.

"I... have familiarity operating heavy machinery. Do you need anyone for the steam shovel or dozer?" Maldynado waved toward the equipment on the edge of the construction site. Yawning firemen were loading the furnaces and heating up the boilers for the day's work. The sun hadn't come up yet—and thick black clouds that smelled of rain suggested it might never make it—but fire barrels brightened the sprawling lot.

"No. Your job is to shovel that into that." The man pointed at all the debris left from the razing of the doddering building that had formerly stood on the site, then pointed at the nearby dumpsters. Wheelbarrows leaned against them, waiting for the morning's workers.

That means you, old boy, Maldynado thought. When he had asked the president for a job, this wasn't quite what he'd had in mind. He eyed the shovel and thought about going back to the flat, to the warm covers he had left. Considering it was spring, there was an awful lot of frosty air forming in front of his face after each breath. Too bad Evrial had already left for the day, or they could have stayed in bed together. Maybe. She had been awfully busy of late, since their tiff the night her father showed up, and they hadn't spoken a lot of words since then. He kept catching her gazing off into the distance, contemplating deep thoughts. Well, if she was going to leave him, it wasn't because he was some jobless mooch. Maldynado clenched his jaw, tightened his grip on the shovel, and strode toward the debris pile.

He spent the next two hours, laboring amongst the commoners—and trying not to think of them as commoners. After all, who was he now anyway? Those Marblecrests who hadn't been tried for crimes against the government—and some of those who had—had fled the city. Those who remained were changing their stationery to read from the desks of Such-and-such Márblé in vain attempts to hide affiliation with the warrior-caste family name. Even if he hadn't been disowned, he would have had a hard time thinking of himself as aristocratic these days.

"Just one of the boys now," he said.

A worker in baggy clothing walked past pushing a wheelbarrow, his trousers sagging down in the back to reveal full moons no astronomer ever wanted to see.

"One of the more impeccably dressed boys." Maldynado patted his backside to make sure his suede button-down shirt was still tucked in suitably, then checked the sleeves to ensure they were rolled up the perfect amount: not so much that he grew chilled but enough to display the corded muscles of his forearms. Ladies had started to walk by the construction site on their way to work. If nothing else, he intended to be the most handsome fellow at this dubious place of employment.

A crash and the screeching of metal came from the back of the lot. Strange. Vehicles didn't tend to crash themselves when Amaranthe wasn't around.

"It's going to blow," someone hollered. "Everyone out of the way."

That was usually good advice, but Maldynado jogged in the direction of the commotion, curious as to what was happening.

Great plumes of black smoke arose from a vehicle behind a steam dozer. The cement mixer? Maybe it wasn't too late to solve the problem and keep damage from occurring. A notion of being seen as some hero who saved lives teased his thoughts, though as he passed a dozen men running in the opposite direction, most waving and shouting for him to turn around, he slowed down. Maybe running up into all that smoke wasn't such a good—

A great boom blasted the construction site. Three times as much smoke poured into the sky, and shrapnel flew in every direction. Maldynado flattened himself to the ground, throwing his arms over his head and lamenting that he had rejected the hard safety hat a supervisor had tried to foist onto him.

Shards of metal struck the ground all around him, and more than a few pieces pelted his back. Nothing large, thank the ancestors, but he cursed as some of the sharp projectiles sliced through his shirt and into flesh. When the pattering of shrapnel stopped, he lifted his head. The steam dozer had been knocked on its side. Behind it, the cement mixer remained intact, but it was now on the ground ten feet from the rest of the lorry. The cab was gone altogether. The engine too. The boiler had been peeled open like a flower, warped steel still smoking.

None of the other lorries were on fire, nor did anything else seem in danger of exploding, so Maldynado climbed to his feet and headed toward the smoldering mess. He was the first on the scene and poked around, careful not to touch any of the hot metal. Heat shimmered in the air above the wrecked boiler.

"No bodies," he said. "That's good."

The lorry would cost someone a fortune to replace, but that wasn't for a menial shovel-wielder to worry about.

"What the blast happened over here?" the foreman asked, running up.

Maldynado stifled the urge to say that it had blown up, that being rather obvious. "Don't know. I just got here."

"Find the fireman and the operator who were setting this up," the foreman yelled toward a crowd of workers that was edging closer. Nobody else had come forward to investigate. Maybe they didn't want to be blamed.

Metal squealed and a blackened panel tipped over, almost flattening Maldynado. He darted out of the way before it smacked onto the ground.

Or, maybe those workers were just smart enough to stay out of a disaster area.

Maldynado wandered over to look at the cab—at what was left of it. The doors had been blown off, and all of the controls inside were warped, melted, or missing completely. Shrapnel crunched under his feet as he drew closer. He almost stepped on a bent gauge with the glass blown off. It was the one that measured the steam levels, letting the operator know if more coal needed to be added to the furnace or if steam needed to be vented because too much pressure had built up.

"Interesting," Maldynado murmured, picking it up. The needle was stuck in the middle. If an explosion had been impending, shouldn't it have been pushed up into the red zone?

"Out of the way, big man." The foreman tried to push Maldynado aside.

Maldynado hadn't meant to be contrary, but he was focused on the gauge and didn't move. The smaller man almost bounced off.

"Yo, Shovel Head. This isn't your area. Get out of here."

"I thought you might find this gauge interesting," Maldynado said, holding it up.

An engineer with soot-smudged overalls stood behind the foreman, along with a rat-faced man who looked twitchier than the target in front of a firing squad. The cement lorry operator, Maldynado guessed.

"A broken gauge? I have a broken forty-thousand-ranmya lorry here." The foreman didn't try to push Maldynado aside again, but he did pointedly put his back to him. He grabbed the operator. "Come show me what happened. Your job is already forfeit. It's time to find out if there will be charges of negligence pressed."

"Boss, please." The rat-faced man winced as the foreman grabbed him by the scruff of the neck and pushed him toward the destroyed cab. "I can't afford no charges. Nothing was wrong, I'm telling you. Until the smoke started billowing out, and the lorry started shuddering, I didn't know nothing. The gauges all read fine, I swear. Ask Donok." He pointed at the fireman who was doing his best to look as inconspicuous as a post in the shadows of the dozer.

Maldynado walked over to the engineer, thinking he might be more interested in the gauge.

The engineer glanced at it and grunted. "Doesn't mean much. The needle might have been reset when it was blown out of the cab."

"Or maybe it's sabotage," Maldynado said. He wondered if he had been so quick to speculate about nefarious activities *before* his year with Amaranthe. He thought not.

"Over here, Nossev," the foreman said.

The engineer shrugged at Maldynado and obeyed his boss.

"Such a cheery group of people I'm working with," Maldynado said.

"You, Shovel Head," the foreman hollered. "Get back to work. And get all those other dirt-flingers back to work too. This is the most important job of the decade. There's *not* going to be a delay."

"Shovel Head, how witty and original." Maldynado stuck the gauge in his pocket and tapped his chin thoughtfully, wondering where he had left his shovel. Oh, well. He would find another.

"Maldynado?" a quiet voice called. "What's going on?"

He turned to find Sespian walking off the street, a sketchpad in hand and a tube for holding maps—or in this case, maybe blueprints—in a sling across his back. Though he had grown up some since Maldynado had

217

come to know him, he was still young enough to look more like a bicycle messenger delivering plans than a former emperor and current architect.

"Mysterious explosion of a cement lorry," Maldynado said, pleased that Sespian stopped next to him instead of going over to the foreman. Said foreman was still snarling and casting blame about; he hadn't noticed his prestigious visitor yet.

"*Another* accident?" Sespian lifted his eyes toward the cloudy sky. "Why couldn't this go well? My first professional gig and probably the most important building I'll design in my life."

"Nah." Maldynado thumped him on the shoulder. "Once you get known for serving presidents, the Kyattese government will want you to come design something snazzy for them. Maybe even the Nurian Great Chief. Oh, or Basilard's Mangdorian chief. How are you with yurts?"

Sespian smiled, but barely.

"What do you mean another accident?" Maldynado asked more seriously.

"Yesterday, the steam brakes on one of the lorries went out, and it and its operators plunged into the hole excavated for the basement."

"Did the operators survive?"

"Yes," Sespian said, "but with broken bones."

"And the foreman called me a dolt—actually a Shovel Head—for suspecting sabotage... One broken lorry might be bad luck, but two in two days? Sounds suspicious to me."

"To me as well," Sespian said.

"Did you tell the president?" Maldynado snapped his fingers as a new idea came to him. "Is that why I was sent here? Old Starcrest knew something was going on, and he wanted me to pretend to be a common laborer all the while mounting a private investigation to find the culprit?"

"Uhm," Sespian said.

Maldynado thrust a finger into that air. "That's brilliant. I knew he couldn't mean for me to simply wither and rot here at the lowest form of menial labor in the city." A couple of men glowered as they walked past with shovels on their shoulders. "Sorry, blokes. I didn't mean that. Everyone knows factory work is *twice* as menial."

They managed to simultaneously glare at Maldynado and thump their fists to their chests and bow toward Sespian.

Maldynado ignored them. "Now, what were you saying, Sespian?"

"That I didn't tell Starcrest. About the accident."

"Oh." Maldynado slumped. So much for having been strategically placed here. Did the president truly think him able of doing no more than shoveling dirt? "Why not?"

"He's running back and forth between trying to salvage that submarine, trying to help his daughter with the plant research, and trying to appease the thousand and one people who want to meet with him at every hour of the day. I'm sure construction mishaps aren't a priority for him."

"This is going to be *his* house," Maldynado said. "For the next five years at least. I'm sure he cares."

"I'll figure out what's going on and ensure nothing more goes wrong," Sespian said. "There's no need to bother him."

"Well, then I can help *you*." Yes, that could work. And Sespian would let Starcrest know how useful Maldynado had been. "You're a conspicuous sight around here. I, on the other hand, am—"

"Shovel Head, you're not bothering Lord Sespian, are you?" The foreman rushed up, walking, bowing, and apologizing at the same time.

Sespian faced the man, though he looked like he would have preferred to talk with Maldynado instead. Maldynado decided to take that as a promising sign.

"Foreman Bakost, as I've told you, I'm not a lord anything. You can simply call me Sespian. Or Mister Savarsin if you prefer formality. And no, Maldynado is not bothering me."

"We've had a little trouble this morning," the foreman said, "but nothing that will delay the building. Are those the updates to the rear elevation? Come to my office, and we'll take a look." He extended his arm toward the shack on the corner of the lot. Office. Right. Maldynado had seen it. A tiny room with a desk made from used apple crates hardly qualified.

Sespian headed off with the man, but he met Maldynado's eyes over his shoulder and nodded.

Maldynado perked up. Sespian's words might not be tantamount to imperial orders anymore, but he had Starcrest's ear, so doing good work for him might be noticed by the president himself. And if the boy ever opened his eyes and start paying attention to that fine young woman who was mooning after him, he could even become the president's son-in-law.

Shortly after dawn, Amaranthe grew tired of pacing. She packed a bag, strapped her sword-and-pistol belt to her waist, and left her room in the hotel. Ominous black clouds marked the sky, and it scarcely seemed that daylight had come, but she could stare at the ceiling and wait no longer. Sicarius hadn't returned to their room at any point last night. She had slept fitfully and had finally given up on trying. In most cases, she would trust that he could take care of himself, but this new assassin had her worried.

Amaranthe grabbed the first trolley and headed into town, intending to visit Ms. Sarevic's Custom Works. She didn't know if she could get into the fortress of a workshop uninvited, but she didn't know where else to go. She was supposed to be looking for a Maker, but surely figuring out who had attacked the submarine in the first place was just as important. What if they got the *Explorer* fixed, only to have it be targeted again? Besides, Sicarius would have more of a clue than she as to where to find a practitioner in the city. At the moment, Sarevic was Amaranthe's only lead for anything.

The trolley stopped at the corner of Fountain and Fifth, the construction site of the building Sespian had designed, and she spotted a familiar form strolling about amongst some debris. She jumped off on a whim. Though she had no reason to believe Sicarius would have stopped to talk to Maldynado, it would only take a few minutes to check, and another trolley would roll through soon.

By the time she picked her way past piles of earth, dumpsters, and the pieces of a cement lorry—how odd that it was spread all over in pieces, and, dear ancestors, what had happened to that boiler?—Maldynado was down on his hands and knees, his butt thrust into the air as he peered under a steam dozer.

"This is the work President Starcrest found for you, eh?" Amaranthe asked.

A clunk sounded—Maldynado's head hitting the frame. Grumbling and grabbing his skull, he wiggled backward and sat up. "Amaranthe?"

"Sorry, I didn't mean to startle you. Though... I have noticed that all the other workers here are wearing those hard metal hats, perhaps designed to protect one's head from bumps."

"Hideous, aren't they?" Maldynado stood up. He had something in the hand that wasn't busy holding his head.

"But effective, I'd wager. I don't suppose you've seen Sicarius today?"

"No, and if we limited ourselves to wearing headgear simply because it served some purpose, how tedious would that be? I've been thinking of designing these fellows something more stylish to wear on the job." While Maldynado rambled, he squinted at the blackened metal disk in his hand, something with what might have been a switch sticking out of one side. It looked like it had survived a fire. "Does this look suspicious to you?" he asked.

"In what way?"

"Like it could have caused a boiler gauge to misread or for a boiler to heat up too quickly or... something? I don't know. Considering how many boilers our team has blown up, you'd think I would be an expert on the topic, but I haven't *intentionally* sabotaged that many."

"It doesn't look like much to me." Amaranthe took it from Maldynado's hand. She withdrew her kerchief, spit on the disk, and rubbed it.

"When I gave that to you, I thought you would use your enforcer investigation skills to deduce where it had come from. I didn't expect you to *clean* it."

"Really? You gave me something dirty and didn't expect me to clean it?"

"Er, yes, I suppose I should have known better."

"Maybe you did some damage when you hit your head." Amaranthe held up the disk. Rain had started spitting from the dark sky, and there was no sun to gleam against the metal, but she believed it *would* gleam now if given the opportunity. She squinted at a tiny mark on the side opposite from the broken switch. "*That's* interesting. And not a coincidence, I'll wager."

"What?" Maldynado leaned in. "Oh, I remember that little mark. Isn't that from the shop that supplied us those blasting sticks last fall? The shop you later cleaned and organized as some form of payment—or because you simply like doing such things?"

"Ms. Sarevic's Custom Works. I am more convinced than ever that I need to pay the place a visit. What sabotage did you say had been done? That cement lorry?"

"Yes, and another lorry yesterday, Sespian said. He's around somewhere, talking to the foreman."

"Is he? Maybe he's seen Sicarius."

"Are you going to visit that shop now?" Maldynado pointed at her short sword and pistol. "You're dressed for war."

"I'm not sure why Ms. Sarevic's mark is all over the city right now—" All right, finding it in *two* places might not count as "all over the city," but it was starting to feel like the woman was providing the other side with all too much help, "—nor am I certain why she would be putting her mark on devices being used for sabotage, but I'm guessing she won't want to sit down and tell me about it without persuasion."

"Then you'll need me along. My fists can be impressively persuasive, in case our collective charms don't work."

In truth, Amaranthe wouldn't mind company, especially with Sicarius missing, but she didn't want to get Maldynado in trouble. "You're volunteering to walk away from your new job? Have you even been working here a full day?"

"No."

"A full morning?"

"That depends on what time it is," Maldynado said. "I shoveled a lot of dirt in the first two hours I was here. But then that lorry blew up, and Sespian came by, and it was clear he wanted me to be his special on-the-ground investigator."

"I see. That's what he called it?"

"No, he didn't call it anything."

"What did he say, then?"

"He didn't really say anything. He, ah, looked back at me and nodded."

"No room for misinterpretation there, eh?" Amaranthe asked. "Why don't we find him and make sure he won't mind you abandoning his construction site for a shinier mission?" And she wanted to ask him about Sicarius—if there was one person in the world Sicarius would delay returning to Amaranthe for, it was Sespian, especially if someone was mucking around, sabotaging his son's construction site. Might Sespian be a target as well? Or maybe this was meant to discredit him somehow.

"I'm sure he'll corroborate my interpretation of the nod," Maldynado said.

They walked across the site, with more than one shovel-toting worker glowering at Maldynado.

"Did you offend all of these people somehow," Amaranthe asked, "or are they simply upset that they're working hard and you're not?"

"They're upset that they're wearing those ridiculous hats and I'm not," Maldynado said.

"Ah, of course. I should have reached that conclusion."

The rain picked up in intensity, and Amaranthe wondered how much longer anyone would be working. From the black clouds hanging over the mountains in the east, it looked like it could storm all day. Maldynado lifted a hand to knock on the door of a wooden shack. It opened first, and a man with a gray mustache and beard strode out, almost crashing into his chest.

"Shovel Head," the man snarled. "Didn't I tell you to get back to work?"

"Uhm," Maldynado said.

"Explain the nod," Amaranthe whispered.

The man—foreman?—faced her, and she braced herself for another snarl, but he tipped his hard hat instead and asked, "Help you, ma'am?"

"They're here to see me, I believe," Sespian said from inside the shack. He stood before a desk propped up on crates, with unrolled blueprints stretched across the surface.

"Oh?" The fellow sighed sadly, gave Amaranthe a friendly smile, tipped his hat again, and said, "I'll leave you, then."

"Thank you for the use of your office," Sespian said. "We'll be out in a moment."

"No hurry, boss. You're the architect. You can use anything you wish." The foreman had taken no more than three steps before his snarls returned, along with bellows and orders for his men to get back to work and not let cloud spittle slow them down.

As Amaranthe stepped inside, Maldynado said, "Now I understand. He's one of those sexually frustrated types. Nice to the ladies, in hopes that one of them will take a liking to him, but grumpier than a dunked cat to those who are clearly competition." Maldynado artfully tossed his wavy brown curls around to shed water from them.

"You're sure he's not bitter because he's stuck wearing one of those hats too?" Amaranthe asked.

Maldynado snapped his fingers and pointed at her. "Another valid possibility."

Sespian watched this exchange with a bemused expression.

Amaranthe decided not to try to explain. "Good morning, Sespian. I'm looking for Sicarius. Also, Maldynado believes he should accompany me on an investigation. Can you help me on either count?"

"I haven't seen Sicarius," Sespian said. "As for Maldynado, I believe he's free to do as he wishes. He volunteered to work for the president, but I don't believe any contract was signed."

"But I'm working for you," Maldynado said, thrusting out the shard of metal. "Investigating, remember?"

As Amaranthe had suspected, that nod must have meant more to Maldynado than to Sespian.

"What is that?" Sespian touched the broken switch on the metal husk. "Something that fell off a lorry?"

"It's from the same place as the blasting stick that damaged the submarine," Amaranthe said. "Maldynado thought you'd like to send him with me to investigate."

"The lorry explosion may be related to the submarine explosion," Maldynado said.

"That seems... an unlikely stretch," Sespian said, "but I have no objection to you going with Amaranthe. You may want to check with the foreman though. He seems fond of you."

"Oh sure," Maldynado said. "We're closer than brothers."

"Given your relationship with your brothers, that might actually be true," Amaranthe murmured.

"I could come with you to the shop, too," Sespian said. "I'm done here. I wouldn't mind asking your opinion on something," he told Amaranthe. "Maybe both of your opinions."

Maldynado gave him a sly grin. "This is about the girl, isn't it?"

"No. Definitely not." Sespian shuffled through the papers on the desk, found a pencil, and tucked it in his satchel. "Maybe slightly."

"Girl?" Amaranthe raised her eyebrows.

"Mah-leeee-keee," Maldynado drawled with a wink.

"Let's start on this errand, shall we?" Sespian sounded brisk and professional, but his cheeks were as bright as hot embers. He bumped his hip on the table, knocking it off the crate it balanced on and dumping the blueprints on the floor. Cursing under his breath, he fumbled about, trying to set everything right. Interesting, considering Sespian had previously demonstrated that he had inherited some of his father's agility.

"Mahliki?" Amaranthe mouthed to Maldynado while Sespian pushed the table back onto its less-than-staunch legs.

Maldynado nodded once, his chin dropping all the way to his chest.

That could be a good match, Amaranthe signed.

She thinks so, Maldynado signed. *He's still trying to figure it out.*

Boys can be obtuse at times. Amaranthe smiled, thinking of Sicarius, though he hadn't been obtuse exactly. More like reticent.

"Young ones especially," Maldynado said.

"Hm?" Sespian asked. He had finished arranging his blueprints on the desk and turned to face them.

"Nothing," Amaranthe said. "We're ready to go whenever you are."

They left the construction site, taking a side street back toward the trolley thoroughfare. Lightning flashed in the northern sky, and thunder rumbled shortly after. The intermittent rain might turn into a downpour soon. Amaranthe hoped they wouldn't have to wait long for the trolley, a hope that faded when she spotted a crowd at the street corner. There had to be nearly fifty of them, standing, gesturing, and spilling into the street.

"Another inland appearance of the plant?" Amaranthe wondered.

"I hope not," Sespian said.

"Those are those religious blokes." Maldynado pointed. "Look at the cloaks."

Many of the people in the crowd were simple onlookers, but she spotted at least thirty of those dark robes. Some of the men carried signs.

"Are they protesting your building site?" Amaranthe asked. She couldn't read the signs yet.

"Not that I know of," Sespian said, "but I'm beginning to think winning this contest wasn't quite the honor I first thought."

"If this is about the building, it's likely to do with the presidency and not with you personally."

"And that's... comforting?" Sespian asked.

"Well," Amaranthe said, "it probably means they won't start throwing stones at you. Or rotten fruit."

Maldynado patted Sespian on the shoulder. "I would take that as comforting if I were you."

A trolley chugged down the street, but people were standing on the tracks. A whistle squealed. The crowd parted, but not to let the trolley past—the people were backing away from a man wearing a golden medallion in addition to his dark robe. He knelt in the street and pried open a manhole cover. A green vine that must have been coiled right beneath it burst forth, the top three feet wavering in the gloomy morning light.

Amaranthe grimaced. She had heard about the plant's incursion into the sewers—and that it was winding about the president's hotel at that very moment—but hadn't realized one could pluck up any manhole cover and find it. Maybe this person had scouted ahead of time and knew what to expect.

"There it is." The cloaked speaker pointed downward. "As if the monstrosity in the harbor were not enough, it's spreading, because of our sins, because we have turned our backs on the gods for so many centuries, because we have created yet another blasphemous government that denies the existence of greater powers."

"I didn't know President Starcrest was denying anyone's existence," Sespian murmured.

"I thought he had signed laws allowing people to believe and practice however they wish," Amaranthe said.

"He did, though he also refused to give any special rights and privileges to any particular religious group, though some were lobbying for that." Sespian scratched his jaw. "These people look like they might want to be privileged."

At the least, they wanted attention.

"Our president and his atheist soldiers have been unable to stop the encroachment of this verdurous evil into the city," the speaker said, his voice loud enough to be heard over the murmurs of the crowd.

"Verdurous evil?" Maldynado said. "What a blowhard."

"It is a sign that the gods do not favor them," the speaker—the priest, Amaranthe amended, for what else could he be but some leader of this religion?—went on. "Our order is the only one who has their favor, who has the right to rule in Turgonia. We were here millennia ago, and we have never truly left, even though we have been persecuted and forced to live underground, to deny the gods, and to carve the heads off our holy statues. But the gods live on, and so do we. We have the power to—"

"Shut your slagging yap," someone from the trolley yelled. "And get off the tracks."

The steam whistle screeched again. The operator frowned at a pocket watch and nudged the trolley forward, probably thinking that, at a slow speed, he could simply push these people out of the way without running them over.

Amaranthe, Maldynado, and Sespian had drawn close enough to read the signs now, though Amaranthe could have guessed at their messages based on the speech.

Pray to Dagu and Magu and be saved!

Keep the heretics out of office.

Let those with divine right rule!

"I see you need a demonstration of my power, my ability to save the city," the speaker said, lifting his arms, fingers spread to the sky. He tilted his face toward the dark clouds. Thunder rumbled again, louder and closer than before.

"You know," Maldynado said, "it would be hilarious if the trolley started up right now and smacked that shrub in the backside, so he flew headfirst into the manhole."

"Heretic," Amaranthe murmured.

The steam whistle screeched again. "Someone get that dumb slag pile out of the street," the operator hollered.

A few trolley passengers disembarked, pushing up their sleeves as they strode toward the would-be priest. The crowd of robed men seemed to thicken in that spot, providing a barrier.

"Should we do something?" Maldynado asked.

"Given our relationship to the president, it might not be wise to draw attention or be perceived as attacking people in his name," Sespian said.

"Why don't we see if we can find some enforcers to handle this?" Even though Amaranthe had been off the force for more than a year, it still seemed strange to say something like that instead of taking action herself. "If that man is going to stand there with his face getting rained on until the gods fill him with power, he might be there all day."

Another peel of thunder rolled across the sky. Maybe the storm was supposed to be a sign of some deity's power. Amaranthe wondered if the zealots had been waiting in their hideout for weeks with someone on watch for gloomy weather so they could race out and take advantage of it.

"Looks like we won't have to run and fetch anyone." Maldynado pointed down the street.

An armored enforcer lorry was rolling around a corner, the smoke billowing from its stack, matching the clouds in color.

"Maybe Evrial will be in there," Maldynado said. "This is her district, for now anyway. I do enjoy seeing her pummel brutes."

Under normal circumstances, a crowd would have dissipated at the approach of enforcers, but the robed figures didn't seem to notice. They had started swaying in synch with each other and chanting under their breaths—too low for Amaranthe to make out the words, or maybe it was simply that they weren't Turgonian words.

The enforcer vehicle stopped, and four men and two women leaped out with short swords hanging from their waists and shields and cudgels in their hands. Sergeant Yara was among them, jaw hard, eyes cool. Amaranthe wondered if she had dealt with this group before.

Though she was clearly on duty and busy, Maldynado grinned and waved at her. A flicker of the eye was the only indication that she saw and acknowledged him, at least insofar as Amaranthe noticed.

Maldynado, however, said, "She's ecstatic to see me."

"Clearly," Amaranthe said.

"Get out the handcuffs, boys," Yara ordered. "We're going to make some arrests this time."

The crowd continued to sway, ignoring everything going on around it. The priest continued to gaze up at the sky, rain spattering onto his face and dripping off his chin. The vine seemed to have grown another six inches, and it leaned toward him. Maybe it would grab him and pull him down into the hole. That would startle the crowd into breaking up.

The enforcers grabbed those in the rear. The people didn't resist, but they didn't show any sign that they would disperse without being forced to do so.

Thunder pealed again, and lightning branched across the sky. A second trolley came around the corner, and brakes squealed. It barely stopped in time to avoid crunching into the one ahead of it.

"What's going on up there?" its operator yelled.

Lightning flashed again. Thunder roared, and the sky dumped a waterfall. Amaranthe grimaced as cold water slithered past her collar and down her back. She should have brought a cloak and an umbrella, not that she had planned to spend much of the morning outside...

"We may want to find some cover," Sespian said. "We're not doing anything useful."

Amaranthe touched her short sword. "Actually, I'm going to go over and see if the enforcers need any help. At some point, the crowd might resist, and there are only six of them."

"Good idea," Maldynado said. "I'm sure Evrial will—"

Thunder boomed, and lightning streaked out of the clouds and hit the street in the center of the crowd. The sky lit up like a sun, and Amaranthe threw an arm up, jumping back.

Some of the people in the crowd jumped back, too, but others merely stared, transfixed.

"That, my friends, is the power of the twin gods," the priest cried, his arms stretched toward the heavens.

From the rear, Amaranthe couldn't see what had happened—nobody had screamed in pain, so she had assumed the lightning had struck the metal manhole cover—but judging by the wide eyes of those in front, their faces all tilted downward, something more profound had occurred.

She climbed the nearest street lamp and found herself staring with wide eyes as well.

The vine lay limp in the street, a charred and desiccated husk. Only the speaker's boot on the tip kept it from slumping back into the sewer.

CHAPTER 13

MAHLIKI WAS BEGINNING TO HATE the dark, underground laboratory, and the sprites-licked plant was turning her dreams to nightmares. The night before, she had been collecting specimens growing from the fragile eco systems on the sunny side of a volcano back home, when a vine had burst out of the hardened lava and grabbed her. She had woken with a scream on her lips and the memory of the prehensile thing wrapping about her neck.

Upon entering the laboratory, she first checked on the new piece of plant in the vivarium, hoping to see that it had not grown during the night. She had left it in utter darkness and with cubes of ice mounted around it, figuring that cold or dark ought to signal winter and tell it to enter a dormant stage. After all, it hadn't come up through the lake until the ice had thawed.

But her three-inch sample had grown a foot and a half overnight. Shoulders slumping, Mahliki sneered at the vine and walked around the lab, using her lantern to light others.

"If it's any consolation, I'm stuck with my problem as well," came her mother's voice from the doorway.

They had eaten breakfast together. Mother had mentioned that she planned to watch Mahliki like a hawk to ensure she actually ate, having heard of meals being ignored during the previous two days. Of course, Mother's resolution had lasted only until she grew distracted by her own project, the decoding of some intercepted message that she had uncovered the night before.

"I know," Mahliki said, "and I appreciate you coming down to take another look in that encyclopedia." Mother called the black sphere she had uncovered from the ancient tunnels twenty years earlier a "repository of knowledge," but Mahliki had always found that title cumbersome. Nor could she pronounce the name for it in the ancient language. "I thought there might be something on the world where they came from, specifically what the night and day and seasonal cycles are like, if they had those things at all. If we can't kill this plant, maybe we can at least figure out what makes it go dormant and buy ourselves some time."

"I will look." Mother slid onto a stool near a counter and pushed back a set of scalpels—little good they had done so far—to make room for her notes and the sphere. "Though I do wonder at the plausibility of creating an eighteen-hour-long night if we find out that is what's required. With the plant now occupying numerous square miles, we can't simply lock it in a dark closet."

"I know, but if that's what it takes, we can figure out a way to make it work." Mahliki believed her words, though she doubted darkness alone would solve the problem, especially not when her sample had continued to grow overnight. At the moment, it was snuggled up to the half-melted ice block in the vivarium with it. Cold obviously didn't damage its tissues either, at least not any degree of cold she could manufacture.

A knock came at the steel door a moment before it opened. Father strode in past the two guards who were busy bowing and thumping their fists to their chests for him. He had taken to wearing a pistol and a long dagger, even around the hotel, but at least he had been looking better in the last couple of days, less tired and headachy.

"Good morning, ladies," Father said, walking over to kiss them on the cheeks. He lingered beside Mother, clasping her hand in one of his—not the one she was using to tinker with the sphere. "I had meant to catch up with you at breakfast, but your dining was not a leisurely one, I hear."

"Mysteries to decrypt, and plants to kill," Mahliki said. "One can't tarry."

She made light of their morning's work, but in truth, she was disappointed in herself for not having a solution yet. Father might have come to visit to be supportive, but he probably also wanted to know what he could do to speed the process along.

"Indeed not," Father said, pointing to the vivarium. "Find anything that harms it yet?" He asked it casually, his elbow leaning on the table behind Mother, but the intensity in his eyes belied that calm. He had to be dealing with thousands of complaints, fielding thousands of idiotic suggestions, and worrying that the entire city would be devoured by the plant in the first few months of his presidency.

Mahliki hated that all she could say was, "Not yet. Sorry."

"I'm only taking an hour or so away from decrypting the note to look up a few things for her," Mother said. She didn't sound defensive exactly, but as if she wanted to let him know she hadn't given up on her task for him. "It's proving more difficult to crack than I thought, but I'll get it."

"I know you will," Father said. "And the plant should be the priority, so any insight you can provide..." He extended a hand toward Mahliki.

"I know. I'm trying." Mother's eyes seemed tight. Maybe she hated not having a solution for Father too.

"I mistakenly put out two versions of a report on our likely headquarters relocation," he said, winking at Mother. "If one reaches enemy hands and the other doesn't, I'll be able to narrow down the possibilities as to who our snitch might be."

"Good idea," Mother said.

"I wish Sicarius would return. I had Dak send out a few more men to keep an eye on possible suspects, but with Sauda compromised as it were, I doubt her house will be used as a mail drop any longer."

"Compromised? Was she arrested?" Mother asked.

"She's being held for her own safety—and for questioning. Apparently, enforcers aren't yet comfortable going right out and saying they're arresting warrior-caste people."

"Will you go see her?" Mother asked. Mahliki doubted she approved of the idea, but she was being careful not to let her feelings bleed through.

"I probably should, if only to get her side of the story, though I've already been informed by my new lawyer that this shouldn't be a public event. I'll have to figure out a way to sneak out in private."

An image came to mind of Father making a blanket rope and climbing down from his window in the middle of the night. Silly. He would more likely make some mechanical contraption that would launch him from the roof with a parachute on his back.

Mother either didn't have an opinion on this potential visit or had been distracted by something intriguing in her notes. Mahliki picked up a pencil and fetched a new chemical concoction to try on the plant. Time to get back to work.

Father looked back and forth between them. "Is there anything I can do to help? For either of you? I would gladly delay the fourteen meetings scheduled for me this morning if I could be of assistance." He sounded hopeful. Mahliki wouldn't want to go to all those boring meetings, either.

"Sorry, Father," she said. "If it turns out that we need to figure out a way to make it dark in the city for seventy-two hours straight or some other impossible task, I'll come to you first."

"I used to appreciate the challenge of an impossible task, but there have been far too many of them of late." He looked like he wanted to linger, but seemed to realize his presence, however benign he sought to be, applied pressure rather than offering support.

Mother sighed softly when the door closed.

"Do you feel it too?" Mahliki asked. Stopping a snitch might not be as important as stopping that plant, but she would like it more if someone else felt as beleaguered as she did. Mother always seemed so serene and unflappable in the face of catastrophe. Not this time.

"I am worried about him and sense that... the longer it takes me to figure this out, the more danger he is in."

"Oh. Do you ever feel like...?" Mahliki chewed on the end of her pencil. "Never mind. I better get this test going."

"You're not good enough?" Mother suggested.

Mahliki shrugged. "Maybe. It's not that I've never failed before—as you know—but there's never been so much at stake. It's frustrating and terrifying that I seem to be the person with the most expertise around— I'm not used to that, either—and Mother? I don't have a clue as to what I'm doing. I'm just shooting arrows into the jungle and hoping one will land in the turkey dinner the family needs to keep from starving."

"That is how many of us, even experts, must resort to solving problems at times."

"What if I don't figure this out? What if the only time it really matters, I fail?"

"He will still love you."

"I don't doubt that," Mahliki said, "but... it's his disappointment I guess I fear. And knowing that in failing, I don't just fail myself, but I fail him and this entire city. Maybe this entire nation."

"I understand," Mother said. "I'm the one who decided to destroy that ship from within, remember? I don't know how I could have foreseen this consequence, but perhaps I should have. If you fail, it's only because I set the stage for you to do so."

"Well, we're a happy pair, aren't we?"

Mother snorted.

Footsteps rang on the cement floor in the hallway, rapid footsteps. Raised voices, orders to, "Halt" echoed through the door.

Mahliki tilted her head, wondering who had charged down here so urgently to see her. Not someone reporting that the plant had breached the basement, she hoped. Men with machetes had been keeping the sewers near the foundation clear of the vines.

"...have to get in," a male voice yelled. "No time for..."

"I think that's Sespian." Mahliki ran to the door and opened it before her guards could bowl him to the ground—or vice versa.

"Mahliki," Sespian blurted as soon as she stuck her head out. "Lightning kills the plant!"

"What?"

"We were out on the streets, and a crazy priest stood in front of one of the vines coming up out of a manhole and—I'm not quite sure how he managed this yet—called down lightning from the storm to strike the plant. It fried it. Just that arm that was sticking up out of the manhole—we went in and checked how far the damage extended—but it's not growing back. It's charred and dried up. You could kick the dead limb into pieces."

"Lightning," Mahliki mused. "High voltage electricity."

"Was it a priest in a green robe, by chance?" Mother asked.

"Yes, there was a whole crowd of them gathered for the event," Sespian said. "And they had protest signs with them that mentioned a couple of gods. Twin gods."

Mahliki couldn't care less about a crazy priest or his religion. She was gazing around the laboratory and finding it depressingly absent in items that could produce electricity. She couldn't imagine simply driving lightning rods into the lake around the plant and hoping for another storm. They would have to find a way to duplicate the energy in the sky. And she didn't know how to do that. She knew people had ways of storing electricity—Father had some weird jar sitting on his desk back home, along with his quirky nautical instruments from times past—but creating it? An image of shuffling along one of the thick carpets upstairs and zapping an innocent guard with a static charge came to mind. Somehow she doubted that would incinerate the plant.

Mother stood up. "What were the names of the gods?"

"Oh, they were..." Sespian drummed his fingers on his thighs, then looked up, snapping them. "He called for us to worship Magu and Dagu."

Mother stared at Mahliki. Mahliki tore her thoughts away from speculation on lightning. "What?"

"Magu is the god featured in that statuette that Rias's first wife gave him."

"So Sauda is working with those zealots?"

"A lot of people may be. This gives me an idea about that encrypted message," Mother said.

"Good, but I'm more concerned about how to use this knowledge to kill the plant right now."

"The priest implied he could get rid of it if he were given the presidency and his people were put into positions of power," Sespian said.

"Right," Mahliki said. "Let's put that high on the list of things that *aren't* going to happen today."

"After that demonstration, he's going to get a lot of popular support," Sespian said. "I don't know what mental sciences—or did they simply call it magic back then?—priests from that religion might have practiced, or if all that was hokum and we simply need to figure out how he attracted the lightning strike. Professor Komitopis? Do you know if that cult would have had that kind of power? Ah, Professor Komitopis?"

Mother wasn't paying attention. She was bent over her notes again, with the sphere pushed off to the side.

Mahliki grabbed Sespian's arm. "Let's go tell my father. I don't know about magic, but if anyone can make lightning naturally, it'll be him."

"No argument there," Sespian said, letting her guide him out, though he did give a long glance back toward Mother as they left the room.

She was good. Very good.

Sicarius had known that from their first meeting at the cove on the lake, and a night trying to track the woman hadn't changed his opinion of the fact; he had only come to respect her ability more, especially when she had murdered Lord Mancrest scant meters from Sicarius's position. She had nearly murdered him as well. That tiny crossbow bolt... He hadn't consciously heard its twang as it left the miniature bow, nor had he sensed her moving about in the brush, aiming at him. Only instincts had kept him from being struck.

He crouched now on another rooftop in the old, decrepit part of the city, only the rain and the early hour keeping the gang members off the streets. Their numbers were diminished in the aftermath of Amaranthe's molasses flood the winter before, but it was still a dangerous area. Bold of a Nurian woman to acquire lodgings in a neighborhood surrounded by drug dealers and gang thugs, most of whom would shoot her on sight simply for being a stranger, never caring that she was a Nurian, but Sicarius doubted anyone here had seen her. Even the landlady had probably only received an envelope under the door to pay for the room. That is how he would have done it were he on a mission in a foreign land.

What her mission was exactly, he didn't yet know. He was a target, he felt certain, and wasn't surprised—not only had he assassinated important persons on the Nurian continent, but it was possible the mage hunters themselves had a reason to loathe him, if someone over there had a long memory. But why kill Lord Mancrest? Something to discredit the president? By causing his first wife to be thrown in prison? If so, why the wife he hadn't spoken to in twenty years? It would make far more sense to discredit Professor Komitopis.

Should he question her once he captured her? It seemed logical, but if she proved as dangerous as he thought she might, it would be wisest to simply kill her. To leave her alive to plot and counterattack... he might live to regret it. Or die to regret it.

It was only perseverance that had brought him to this rooftop from which he could observe a second-story window at the back of a tenement building, the shutters torn free long ago. Now and then, the grimy cotton curtain shuddered, but the cold breeze accounted for the movement, not anyone stirring inside. It remained drawn, as it had since she had dumped a chamber pot into the alley an hour earlier. When she had first arrived, she had climbed the old masonry wall, its mortar gray and crumbling with age, and shimmied inside, barely stirring that curtain as she entered. At first, he had assumed she was there for another mission, but one did not bother to toss out the piss when one was there to kill someone. That one action told him that he had found her lodgings—and that she wasn't aware that he had followed her.

After the senior Lord Mancrest's assassination, Sicarius had been swift enough in racing out of the house to glimpse the woman sprinting through the garden and into the alley—before that, he hadn't been positive the Nurian *was* a woman. There hadn't been time to let Amaranthe know where he was going; he had simply followed.

In the beginning, she had been aware of his pursuit, and she had taken to the sewers, much as Amaranthe had done earlier. He had grown up in this city though and held a map of those tangled passages, some modern and some centuries old, in his head. He had taken a risk in splitting off to choose a shortcut, but it had paid off in the end. He had come out ahead of her in the subterranean maze, running in the shadows to her front instead of to her rear, and she, listening for pursuit from behind, had gradually slowed down, believing she had lost him. She had varied her path impressively and come up several miles from her final destination, choosing alleys and cutting through basements and across rooftops and once through a brothel. He almost *had* lost her once, but as night had faded and a storm rolled in, she had finally needed rest and had returned to this place.

Water dripped from Sicarius's eyebrows and he wiped it away, lest it disturb his vision. When he was on the hunt, he was like a hound on the trail of prey and didn't notice the weather, ignoring the way it plastered his hair to his head and soaked his clothing. All that mattered was catching what he hunted.

Enough time had passed. She would have eaten and, after being up all night working, she would have lain down to rest. Now was his opportunity to catch her unprepared. To subdue her and ask questions... or simply to destroy a threat to him... forever. Were Amaranthe here, she might have had an opinion on the matter, a recommendation to spare the woman's life or even try to turn her away from her nation, but Amaranthe should be back in the hotel, sleeping or perhaps rising by now. And worrying about him. Once he could have hunted for days without informing anyone of his whereabouts, but now... he regretted that she would grow concerned with his absence.

Sicarius went down the back side of the building, on the off chance that his foe was watching from behind those curtains. She wouldn't have been able to pierce the deep shadows beside a chimney, where he had hidden for the last hour, but sliding down the drainpipe in front of her window wouldn't have been wise. The route along the back of the opposite building took the window—and the tenement's front door—from his sight for a moment, but it couldn't be helped. He hurried into the alley, using the shadows to hide his approach. He stepped lightly past broken brandy barrels, piles of excrement, and men sleeping in alcoves, none of whom stirred at his passing, then climbed up the corner of the building and across to her window.

For a moment, he hung outside like a spider on the wall, his toes wedged in cracks in the mortar, his fingers finding equally shallow handholds. His ear to the cool, damp brick, he listened for sounds within. Nothing stirred. He inhaled in quick sniffs, checking with his other senses before proceeding. The aromatic alley almost overrode any subtler scents, but he detected a hint of bacon and freshly baked rice bread. An ambitious meal for an assassin who must be eager to get some rest. He had usually lived on dried meat bars on his trips. Perhaps the scents came from another window.

Sicarius eased closer until he could step on the window ledge. The rusty screws remained from the shutters that had long since been ripped free—or perhaps rotted free—and he used them for a last handhold, as he parted the curtain with his free fingers. He spotted the dilapidated wood stove that had been used to cook breakfast, a greasy pan still on top, and other signs of recent habitation: a familiar cloak, a leather satchel, a heavy crossbow—that wouldn't have been the one she had used to shoot him—and what might have been a tool case, though this one probably contained weapons. Throwing knives or other blades.

The kitchen and living area had two doors, one that should lead to the hallway, and the other to a bedroom. A two-room flat: extravagant for the neighborhood. A rumpled blanket lay on a couch. He made a note to proceed with extra care. Someone else might be sleeping here, and if the other opponent was half as skilled as the first, he could have a difficult encounter ahead.

Soundlessly, he slipped into the room. He glided across the knotty pine floor, avoiding old boards that might creak, and headed for the bedroom door. He tested the knob. Locked. Not surprised, he slid out his picking tools. He listened at the door before starting, aware that an alert assassin would detect the faint scrapes of those tools being used. Through the thin boards, he heard the soft regular breathing of someone sleeping. Or pretending to be asleep. If there was a second person, might this be a trap? With one person acting as bait and the other behind the door, ready to pounce?

He resolved to remain aware of the possibility but set to picking the lock, regardless. The simple mechanism did not take long to thwart. After listening again, he opened the door slowly, ensuring it didn't creak. He slid inside, putting his back to the wall. He found himself gazing at a blanket-shrouded figure in a small bed. The room lacked a window, and the lamp on the table was out, though a book lay on the pillow, where it had apparently fallen from the sleeper's fingers. If she had fallen asleep reading, then who had turned out the lamp?

Sicarius eyed the rest of the room, but didn't catch any figures crouched in the shadows behind the faded wardrobe or old dresser, its paint peeling in great curls. He did spot two different sized sets of shoes next to the wardrobe, and two empty clothing bags hung on pegs by the door. His gaze drifted from the shoes—that set on the left was oddly small—to the figure in the bed. Unless his Nurian assassin was slighter than he had realized, this wasn't she.

He took a few steps inside, so he could see the sleeper's face and confirm his suspicion. Yes, a child of six or seven perhaps. The bundle of blankets had made it hard to tell at first, but it was definitely a girl.

His first thought was to leave in disgust, realizing that he had been fooled somehow, that the assassin had come and gone—impressive considering he had been watching both that window and the front door of the building. But the gears started clicking into place. Two people were living here, the child and the woman, as evinced by the clothing. He padded over to the wardrobe, picked up one of the larger pairs of shoes, and sniffed. Yes, those shoes had visited a sewer recently. He considered the girl's face again. The wan light seeping through the crack he had left in the door did not show much, but he could make out dark hair and thought the skin more yellow-brown than olive-bronze, more Nurian than Turgonian. If she were to open her eyes, they would probably have the same almond shape as a Nurian's. As... her mother's?

Sicarius couldn't fathom why an assassin would bring a child on an assignment, especially one that involved crossing oceans and continents, and he didn't know what to do about it. The logical move would be to kidnap the girl and use her as a bargaining piece to stop her mother's work in Turgonia, but he had fought too long and too hard to protect

Sespian to use a child that way. Besides, if this was the same person who had shot an arrow at Sespian's head, intentionally missing, then she had already set the ground rules for leaving children out of this.

Interesting. Had that been her intent all along? To set this up so Sicarius would feel compelled to leave her daughter alone if he stumbled across the child? Perhaps not, since she had claimed Sespian owed her some favor.

But what was he to do now? Leave an arrow sticking out of the headboard with a note attached? To send a chill of terror down her spine when she realized he had been here, in her home? He decided to search the room while the child slept, to see if he could find some clue as to the woman's mission here. Perhaps she would return home while he worked and solve a problem for him. Kidnapping her child might be off limits, but he would have no trouble kidnapping her.

You had more than *kidnapping* in mind earlier, he reminded himself. Hadn't he been considering her too dangerous to attempt to subdue? He had been planning to kill her, to make sure the president wouldn't fall to her hand, if he was indeed her target. And now that he knew she was a mother?

That didn't change that she had killed Deret Mancrest's father and might be the one who had tried to kill Amaranthe and Sicarius. Or did it? What would he do with the child if he killed her mother? Turn her over to an orphanage? He wished Amaranthe were here. She would know... the right choice.

While he pondered the questions, he searched the bags and the pockets of the clothing. He kept his ears open as well, doubting a mother would have left her child for long, especially when she must know she was being hunted. By scent, he found the clothing she had worn the night before. As with the shoes, it smelled of the sewers, and he found a few spots of blood on the cuff of her sleeve. If there had been any doubt that she had committed the murder, it was gone now. He delved into the pockets and was rewarded with an envelope that had been folded into quarters. Fingers light, he checked it for signs of a booby trap, though such devices were rare on paper. With this woman, he felt he couldn't be too careful.

The bedroom was too dark for reading, so he slipped back out into the kitchen. He pulled out a single sheet of paper to find a page full of gibberish. An encrypted message? Orders for the senior Mancrest's death? Or for her next mission? If so, she ought to have a key somewhere in the room as well.

Sicarius started to hunt for it, but his instincts went off like a bell. He couldn't have said that he heard a noise or smelled something or sensed a change in the atmosphere, but he darted for the window, certain someone would walk in the front door in a few seconds. He slipped past the curtains, steadying them with his hand to keep them from swaying, and checked the alley before climbing onto the wall. The slumbering drunks remained inert, and nothing moved except for a stray cat sniffing at trash. Inside the flat, a dark figure walked inside without making a sound. Though she had changed clothes, he recognized the form of the woman he had followed through the night.

He could leap in and attack, perhaps catching her by surprise, but to what end? To kill her? He had not decided if that was a suitable course, given the child's presence. To capture her, that would be ideal. She and the child could be brought to the president or a magistrate for judgment.

A rare thrum of nervous energy charged his limbs. This fight, he suspected, would not be easy, especially if she was fighting to kill while he simply wanted to render her insensate, but he accepted the challenge. He was ready.

Sicarius prepared to spring inside.

A door creaked open, and he paused.

"*Matera?*" a young voice asked softly. The girl.

Sicarius recognized the Nurian word for mother. The woman responded in the same language, common everyday Nurian, not the special mage hunter dialect. That might only be used for writing. Sicarius had never heard it spoken by the man Hollowcrest had brought in to train him many years ago.

"Yes, I'm back," the mother said. "Are you ready to take a trip? We need to leave this place and find another spot to hide."

"Do we have to hide again? Can't we go home? I miss Teelu and Morlanie."

"I know, but we're not welcome at home any more. Not unless..." The woman sighed. "Maybe not even then."

"I don't understand."

"I know, and I pray you never do, Mu Lin. But Mother has to finish her mission here and then... we may be able to stay. I've been promised... well, we shall see what a Turgonian promise means."

It crossed Sicarius's mind to attack now, while the woman was distracted, but violently subduing the mother in front of the daughter would not please Amaranthe. And, he admitted, it did not please him, either. Once, he might have done it anyway, choosing logic and efficiency over any sense of feeling or morality—indeed, he had killed some of the Forge leaders the year before, not caring what witnesses were about, but he had been filled with cold rage then and the need to protect Sespian. Now... he regarded this fellow assassin with dispassion but not vehemence. If she tried to kill President Starcrest, that might change, but thus far, the assassination attempts on Starcrest had all been thwarted—that bombing had been particularly clumsy and inept—and he doubted a Nurian mage hunter had been involved. Whatever she had been there for that night, it hadn't been to slay Starcrest.

"I don't want to stay here, *Matera*. It's cold and I miss my friends. This place is scary at night, and you're always gone, and I'm alone, and..." Something muffled the voice—the child leaning into her mother for an embrace perhaps.

The woman murmured some nonsensical reassurance.

Sicarius fought the urge to shift his weight and flex his muscles. Even the slightest movement could make noise, a rustle of clothing, a piece of mortar falling free from the bricks. If he could not remain stationary, clinging to the wall for at least two hours, he had not been training enough of late.

Voices came from the street behind the alley. All of the sounds inside the flat halted.

The speakers were more than a block away, but he made out several snippets of conversation and detected the soft clanks of gear—weapons.

"This building?"

"That's the one?"

"...said the second floor."

Sicarius struggled for dispassion, but right away he had a feeling whose voices these were—and that they would thwart his attempt to capture this woman. Six men walked past the front of the alley, heading toward the front door of the tenement building. They wore rags and had grime smeared on their faces, but the short haircuts, shaven faces, and bulges of sword hilts beneath their cloaks gave them away: soldiers pretending to fit into the neighborhood. They managed to keep from walking in step with each other, but barely. Were these more of the intelligence office's troops? He supposed he should be impressed that someone was doing a good job tracking down threats to the president, but he was mostly irked that they were interfering with his plans—even if his plans had been nebulous at that moment.

He eased an eye around the edge of the window, wondering if he might yet salvage the situation. If the girl had gone back into her room, Sicarius could attack the woman. Or maybe he would even catch her standing next to the curtain, peering out at the disguised soldiers. She must have heard their approach too. Someone higher up in the intelligence command might be bright and capable of locating threats, but these goons were even less discreet than the spy from the night before.

The woman wasn't by the window; she wasn't in sight. Sicarius guessed she had gone into the bedroom to pack, but then a hint of smoke reached his nose. Not the burning of wood or coal from a stove, but something less common. Cloth? Canvas? Clothing or furnishings?

"Fire!" someone cried from the first floor.

The soldiers had disappeared from Sicarius's view, and the building's front door banged open. Footsteps pounded old wooden floorboards. A window was thrown open below Sicarius. Smoke roiled out.

Familiar with the use of fire as a distraction, Sicarius waited calmly in his spot on the wall, thinking the woman might grab the girl and try to come out this way. Aside from the flat's front door, there weren't any other ways out.

Shouts sounded inside the building, the soldiers' voices mingled with the surprised cries of tenants learning their abode was catching flame. Sicarius wondered how the woman had managed to start a fire on another floor so quickly. It couldn't be a coincidence. If she was indeed a mage hunter, she wouldn't have studied the Science, though she could have Made artifacts with her. Or she could have prepared mundane traps all over the building, anticipating this circumstance.

Minutes dragged past, and more windows leaked smoke. It filled the alley and rose in plumes toward the gray sky, the soft rain doing little to squash it. Flames soon poured from the first floor window alongside the smoke. The air grew thick with soot and charry air that now smelled of wood as well as cloth and other materials. The core of the building was on fire, and even the brick wall was growing warm beneath his fingers. And yet the woman did not come out of the bedroom.

A crack sounded inside the flat. The front door flew open, and two soldiers burst inside, rags pulled over their noses and mouths. Sicarius didn't move, knowing they would be unlikely to see him through his spy hole, the quarter inch gap between curtain and wall. They charged inside, swords drawn, and ran straight for the bedroom. Sicarius might have anticipated the clash of steel as they met the assassin, but by now he had a feeling she wasn't inside any more. How she had slipped out without him hearing—especially with the girl in tow—he didn't know, but he was forced to admit that she might simply be that good. He hadn't detected the telltale gooseflesh-stirring prickle of the mental sciences being used, so she had escaped by mundane methods.

Crashes and thumps sounded—furniture being shoved around and searched in and behind.

"Blast it," someone growled. "There's a trapdoor behind here."

Sicarius pulled away from the window and climbed down to the alley, then up to the roof of the building next door. He jumped from tenement to tenement, watching the alleys, streets, and roofline as he went, thinking he might yet chance across the fleeing woman. With her daughter in tow, she wouldn't be as fast as usual. But he didn't see anyone except for the people milling in the street, some fleeing the burning building and others coming out to see if the flames took it to the ground. He avoided them, and they never noticed him.

With little other recourse, Sicarius set a route back to the hotel. He accepted that he had wasted his time—he had spent countless thousands of hours stalking some prey or another, and sometimes it paid off and sometimes it didn't—but he did chastise himself for not finding the trapdoor himself. Granted, moving furniture around without waking up the girl would have been difficult, and he hadn't had much time, but there might have been signs on the floor. A telltale draft, a few particles of sawdust left from the creating of the exit, uneven dust from a piece of furniture being moved after holding the same spot for countless months or years...

You were busy searching pockets, Sicarius reminded himself. He had failed to capture the assassin, but he would not return to the president empty-handed.

CHAPTER 14

AMARANTHE SAID LITTLE AS SHE, Maldynado, and Sergeant Yara headed into the quirky metal-crafting neighborhood where Ms. Sarevic's Custom Works was found. Yara's shift had been nearing an end, and Maldynado had convinced her to join them for this excursion, filling her in on the suspicious goings on at the construction site. Yara commented occasionally, though she seemed more thoughtful than talkative as well. Not surly and silent, the way she often was, but thoughtful. Was she, too, contemplating the religious zealots and what that demonstration might mean for the new government and the people in Stumps?

Amaranthe wished she had been back in town for longer and had more of a feel as to what was going on in the capital. To her eyes, these religious people had popped up out of nowhere, but maybe they had been here all winter. Or all... of forever. That priest had implied they had existed all along and had been in hiding. With religion having been forbidden since the reign of Mad Emperor Motash and magic for centuries longer, it was hard to imagine some underground cult surviving, but she couldn't think it impossible.

"Which street is it on?" Yara asked, ignoring Maldynado who had trotted over to take part in a common custom—rubbing the metal breasts of a female sculpture mounted in front of one of the shops. The gesture brought luck, supposedly. The old bronze statue had darkened to a smoky hue with time, save for certain areas that were rather bright and shiny. A copper top hat lay upturned at the statue's feet, inviting "tips for the lady" to further the likelihood of receiving good fortune.

"Molten Street." Amaranthe pointed to the intersection ahead where the brass street sign was attached to a stout gas lamp.

"And this woman makes illegal wares?" Yara rested her hand on the hilt of her short sword, as if she meant to enforce the law, whether this district was hers or not.

"I'm not sure the wares are technically illegal, though many of the people who order them are the nefarious sorts who don't always pay their taxes."

"*You* ordered some," Maldynado pointed out.

"Yes, and when I was a homeless outlaw, I found it difficult to pay my taxes as well. I tended to get shot at whenever I showed up in public buildings."

"And the nefarious part?"

"I'm sure there are some who would have classified us that way," Amaranthe said, thinking of all the Forge people she had vexed. At some point, she would have to check in with Deret Mancrest and see if he was still getting on with Suan Curlev. At the least, she would have to give him her condolences about his father, even if the two hadn't been close.

"Are you paying taxes *now*?" Yara asked.

"Er."

"Yes, Amaranthe, why don't you tell us about that?" Maldynado smiled as they turned the corner onto Molten Street. "Now that you're no longer an outlaw and staying at the same now-private hotel as the president, you must be an upright citizen again."

"I haven't been in the country for months. Or earned any income unless you count trading fish and octopus for supplies on remote tropical islands."

"The government taxes barter," Yara said.

"And as a Turgonian citizen, you're responsible for paying taxes on income earned even when you're across the borders," Maldynado said. "Really, Amaranthe, how do you expect to enjoy the benefits of being a citizen, such as enjoying the protection of the enforcers—" he waved at Yara, "—when you're not contributing?"

"I had no idea she wasn't paying her taxes," Yara said. "Should I be walking by her side, agreeing to help her with this investigation?"

Amaranthe gave them both the squinty eye. "I suppose you're saying you two have both kept up with your taxes, despite all the craziness that was keeping us busy last fall and winter?"

"I did," Yara said.

"And she filed mine for me too." Maldynado smiled. "You're the only criminal here." He nudged Yara. "I think you're right. You shouldn't be walking beside her, looking so enforcerly. At the very least, don't raise a hand to protect her until she's left a suitable deposit on the president's desk."

"Are you two enjoying this conversation?" Amaranthe asked, coming to a stop in front of the shop.

"I am," Maldynado said. "I've missed having you around, boss." He patted her on the shoulder.

Amaranthe eyed the spot then looked at Yara. "Should I accept that pat with good humor or feel offended because it's the same hand he was using to rub that statue?"

"I always make him wash before he touches me," Yara said.

"Sounds... hygienic." Amaranthe turned her attention to the brick shopfront with the metal shutters securing the windows. The patchwork copper-and-steel door appeared equally impregnable. Amaranthe tried the latch. It didn't open, though numerous scratches marred the frame.

"Does this look like it's seen the attention of a crowbar lately?" she asked.

Yara touched the scratches. "Yes."

"Perhaps a few customers were feeling irate due to the fact that the shop isn't open yet, and it's four hours past dawn," Maldynado said.

"Or perhaps someone wanted badly to get in," Yara said.

"She does have quality wares," Amaranthe said. "And a meticulously organized shop appealing to both customers and employees."

Maldynado snorted. "Assuming she's continued to use the system you installed. Some people simply fling their cogs and wrenches into the corners of the room when they're done with them."

"Yes," Yara said, "*some* people do the same things with their undergarments."

"You say this as if it's not normal. Strange would be stopping to fold them in the middle of amorous beginnings."

"I just don't see why the hats get carefully tucked into a glass display case when other garments are treated so cavalierly. Don't you think that's odd, Lokdon?"

"Uh." Amaranthe couldn't decide if being included in their not-quite-married-life conversation was entertaining or horrifying. She resolved never to discuss Sicarius's undergarments in public.

Maldynado nudged Yara with an elbow. "Don't ask *her*. Who do you think I was talking about with the folding?"

"Ah."

Amaranthe knocked on the door. As Maldynado had pointed out, it was well into Ms. Sarevic's first set of office hours, the ones publicly posted on one of the metal shutters. The perpetual-motion clock above the door confirmed that it was less than an hour until noon. Even a store proprietor who had overslept should have wandered out by now.

"Store hasn't been open for three days," a bald fellow with a beard down to his belt said from a vendor's cart a dozen meters up the street. Numerous automata toys stood, rolled, or teeter-tottered on the cobblestones around him. "Might be I can help you though. I can make all sorts of precision instruments, not simply children's toys."

"Thank you," Amaranthe said. "If we can't find her, maybe we'll come back to see you."

She headed around the corner of the building and into an alley she had been invited to use before. Without the invitation—and the key that came with it—she didn't know how she would get in, as Ms. Sarevic had designed the shop to withstand invasions by enforcers if need be.

"There's an entrance back here?" Yara asked.

"Yes, though we won't be getting into it unless my lock-picking skills are sufficient to tackle a steel door with what is likely one of the more advanced locks in the city." Not to mention that it might be booby-trapped.

Amaranthe slowed as she neared the side door. The formerly gleaming steel was distinctly soot-colored now. The entire wall around had a blackened hue, with broken bricks and disintegrated mortar littering the rough stones of the alley.

Maldynado ambled up to the door and pulled it open with a finger. It wobbled on its hinges. "Doesn't look that advanced to me."

"It's... changed," Amaranthe said.

Yara picked up a piece of iron. "This looks like the plunger from one of the old-style military hand grenades."

Amaranthe pictured the ordnance in her mind—when working correctly, the little ovals detonated on impact, the plunger being pushed in to ignite the black powder when it struck its target. "Too crude to be one of Sarevic's weapons, I think. But I guess it proved effective."

"Shall we invite ourselves in?" Maldynado peered into the dark stairway behind the door.

"Trespassing?" Yara frowned.

"It's not trespassing," Amaranthe said, "when you're simply concerned about the proprietor of a business and you're going inside to try and ascertain why she hasn't been here to open her shop in three days."

"Actually it is. I'm beginning to see why your enforcer captain hasn't hunted you down to offer you your job back now that you're no longer an outlaw."

"I'm sure he would have if I hadn't been out of the country." Amaranthe ducked beneath Maldynado's arm—he had been nodding knowingly through this discussion and holding the door open—and headed down the stairs. Broken glass crunched beneath her boots. The door at the bottom had been forced open too. Before they stepped inside, Amaranthe was already worrying that they wouldn't find Ms. Sarevic or anything useful left intact.

"Anyone bring a lamp?" she asked. What little light filtered down from the alley did nothing to illuminate the subterranean workshop. She crinkled her nose at the mix of leather, grease, and something that was either mildew or a crafting ingredient that smelled a lot like mildew. She took a step into the room, patting in the air to her right, remembering that there had been a tool-filled credenza there, and thinking there might be a lamp on it. Her toe clunked against something. She bent and identified it by touch. "Never mind, I found a lamp. Anyone have a match?"

A flame flared to life near her head. "Were you this unprepared when you were an enforcer?" Yara asked. "I always had this image of you being the model officer, before you started lurking about with an assassin."

"I got used to having Akstyr around to light things for me." Amaranthe held out the dented lantern toward the match.

"That lamp looks like an elephant stepped on it," Maldynado said.

"The whole room looks that way," Yara said.

With the lamp pushing back the darkness, Amaranthe gaped at the mess before them. The shelves and racks she had installed, labeled, and alphabetized had all been torn from the walls or had their contents flung onto the floor. Broken tools and machine parts lay everywhere. Pieces of leather and fabric dangled from the pipes running along the walls. A cog hung from a light fixture near the ceiling, as if it had been tossed there in a disc-hurling competition at the Imperial Games. Sticky substances competed with oily substances for space on the cement floor. The wooden stairs leading up to the street-level shop had been broken, the treads snapped in half as if Maldynado's elephant had been guided up them.

"I'm not sure the proprietor is employing your organizational system to its highest potential," Maldynado observed, prodding a manikin in an armored vest—its stuffed head had been knocked off to land who knew where.

"You worked for Sarevic at some point?" Yara asked.

"Don't answer that," Maldynado said, "or she'll have to stand witness before the magistrate when you're called in to answer about those taxes."

"I did some cleaning and organizing for her since we didn't have the cash to pay for an order in full." Amaranthe was torn between cursing over the fact that all her work had been destroyed and grabbing the nearest broom to set things aright. "Was this a robbery or a war zone?"

"Are any valuables missing?" Yara asked.

"Who could tell?" Maldynado asked.

"Actually..." Amaranthe wandered into the room and pushed an upturned case into an upright position. "I did an inventory when I was designing the system, so I could probably tell you that in a few minutes. Although the best items are supposed to be stored in the safe. Sarevic didn't let me in there. That's where all her prototypes and bars of precious metals were."

"Where is the safe?" Yara asked.

"This way." Though it made her fingers itch to step over a mess instead of straightening it, Amaranthe picked a route over, around, and between the toppled shelves and cases. It would take days to clean up, and they had more pressing matters to deal with. Admittedly, she did put a few items back on shelves if they happened to be on the way. "It's behind that bookcase in the corner."

"The bookcase that's clearly been shoved away from the wall?" Maldynado asked.

"Yes, someone may have already broken into the safe," Amaranthe said, though the wall lacked soot, and neither those shelves nor anything nearby had the utterly destroyed appearance of something that had endured a blasting stick discharge. "If this happened three days ago, our assassin and whoever else has been shopping here—" she waved toward the pocket where Maldynado was keeping the stamped scrap of metal, "—could have walked in anytime and taken what they wanted."

"The assassin probably *did* this," Yara said. "After killing the woman to ensure there wouldn't be witnesses."

"That's a possibility."

"A likely possibility," Yara said.

"The question is whether this assassin is also responsible for the sabotaged lorries at Sespian's construction site," Maldynado said. "And if so, why? You wouldn't think that would be related to someone trying to kill Sicarius and the boss. Or was it the submarine they were after?"

That thought had crossed Amaranthe's mind. Maybe someone hadn't wanted the submarine returning home, since it might be used against the plant. Those priests couldn't save the city if the president figured out how to do it on his own.

Yara, in the midst of climbing over a pile of scrap metal, paused to look at Maldynado.

"What?" he asked.

"Every now and then, you surprise me by actually seeming to care about something other than hats and sex. What is that construction site to you? And why are you bothering to research sabotage there?"

Maldynado lifted a shoulder. "Starcrest sent me there to do a job."

"Yes, one that involved shoveling dirt, at least that's what you were complaining about last night."

"I decided to take some initiative in hopes of earning a promotion."

"To what? Foreman over the dirt shovelers?"

"Nah, that would be too much responsibility. I want to drive the cement mixer. That would be fun."

Yara shook her head. Amaranthe couldn't tell if she had yet figured out that Maldynado cared about quite a few things beyond hats and sex. He might have to actually reveal that, and to be serious from time to time, to keep someone as strict, honorable, and work-loving as Yara.

"Starcrest might be afraid you would pour the cement into a Maldynado statue mold if he were to give you that job," Amaranthe said.

She had reached the wall and was patting around, trying to remember where the secret switch was to push aside the veneer and reveal the safe. She had never been allowed to touch it herself, but she had seen Sarevic do it a couple of times. As far as the combination of the safe went, she had no idea about that.

"I hadn't thought of that," Maldynado said. "I could leave a little present in the basement. Or on the front lawn."

"Ugh," Yara said.

A click sounded, and Amaranthe stepped back. "There we go."

The wall slid aside an inch. She pulled it open the rest of the way, like a door on a freight train, the rollers hidden inside. As she had suspected, the steel vault was closed.

"Emperor's warts," Yara said, "that's a big safe. Was she running a bank on the side?"

"Don't you mean president's warts?" Maldynado asked.

"Enh, I haven't gotten used to that yet. I'm not even sure that works. Wasn't that saying born in the fourth century, because of an emperor who truly was covered in warts?"

"Emperor Grigothferduvk the Crusty," Amaranthe said. Books had given her the story once; she wished he were here to expound on the details—and provide a history on safes and safecracking as well. She tried turning the wheel and pulling it open, but met resistance promptly.

"So we'll have to wait for a warty president to be elected before we can use that phrase?" Maldynado asked. "Starcrest does have that scar. Maybe we could design a curse around that. President's blighted eyebrows."

Yara stared at him.

"What?" he asked again.

"I'm surprised you were even able to talk him into giving you a shoveling job."

"I charmed him with my golden tongue."

"You know," Yara said, "if you're willing to shovel or wield other tools for a living, we could find you a job in my town. There are lots of farms around the countryside."

Amaranthe had her ear to the safe door and was spinning the dial slowly, hoping some click or tick might give her a hint. This new comment from Yara distracted her though.

"You're thinking of moving back to your rural home?"

"I was offered a promotion there. Lieutenant. I would be the first female lieutenant and one of the youngest overall in the satrap." Yara smiled. "I looked it up."

"Congratulations. When was this?"

"A few weeks ago," Yara said.

"When do you start?"

Yara glanced at Maldynado. "I haven't taken the job yet."

"Oh." Amaranthe wanted to ask more, but Maldynado was studying his feet, and Yara had stuck her hands into her pockets, the smile gone, her face masked.

Change the topic, those expressions said. "Anyone have any guesses as to the combination?" Amaranthe asked.

"One, two, three, four," Maldynado said.

"Anyone have any *good* guesses?"

"No," Yara said.

"Do you know what we should do?" Maldynado asked in an inspired tone, the sort that said he was indeed eager to switch to a different subject. "Plan a dinner party for Sespian and Mahliki."

"What?" Yara asked, her own tone flatter than the cement floor.

"The girl likes him. He likes the girl. Between all this craziness going on and their own painful shyness—Sespian's especially—they don't seem to be making much progress toward developing a relationship. Left to their own devices, they could be too arthritic and feeble to make the bed rock by the time they finally admit that they have feelings for each other."

"I'm sure they can figure it out without your help," Yara said.

Hm. Amaranthe wasn't usually the type to play matchmaker, but she had always felt bad that Sespian had developed feelings for her that she didn't reciprocate. It had been even more of a blow to him to have her fall in love with his *father*. To see him happy with someone else would be a pleasure. And, all right, it would assuage some of the guilt that she shouldn't feel but always did anyway. "I'll help with that dinner party," she said.

"You can't be serious," Yara said.

"Do you think we should let Maldynado plan such an event by himself?" Amaranthe asked, though she confessed that he probably had more of a clue as to what should go into a dinner party than she did. "Did he ever tell you about the birthday party he organized for me last year?"

"The one at the brothel?" Yara asked.

"Yes, need I say more?"

"I'm sure the sex-addicted oaf has more tact than to invite the president's daughter to a dinner party at a brothel."

"You are?" Amaranthe raised her eyebrows.

"Mostly."

"Come now, ladies," Maldynado said. "You can trust me to plan something suitable. I'm quite aware of how innocent Sespian is."

"You don't think Mahliki is innocent?" Amaranthe asked.

"I... wouldn't think so to look at her—surely, she's received ample attention from the young males of the species. And the not-so-young ones too. But then again, given that she's been traveling the world with her rather towering and intimidating father, I suppose it's possible she's been sheltered. Perhaps the dinner gathering should involve some educational activities? The better for both of their futures. What do you think?"

Yara's jaw dropped.

"We *definitely* need to help with the planning of this party," Amaranthe said.

Jaw still dangling open, Yara shook her head. "We need to stop this party from ever happening. And we also need to focus on what we're doing, before some *on*-duty enforcer comes by and arrests us as suspects in this dishevelment."

"Agreed."

Maldynado didn't say whether he agreed or not. He was busy stroking his chin and wearing a thoughtful expression. Maybe they would get lucky and the plant would eat all of the dining furniture in the city.

Amaranthe ticked the vault with a fingernail. She considered hunting for something that could be used to amplify the sounds of the dial clicking through the numbers. She had heard of criminals using such methods to thwart safes, but had never tried it herself and would probably be wasting their time. What did she hope to find inside anyway? Proof that the place had been robbed and not simply destroyed? A note signed by the assassin that read, "Thanks for the blasting sticks, and here's my address if you want to send the bill?"

What she wasn't expecting, as she stood there with her ear to the door, fiddling with the dial, was a resounding thump from the other side.

Amaranthe jumped back, almost tripping on a crate of oilcans.

"What is it?" Yara asked.

"Did you hear that?" Amaranthe pointed at the safe.

"No..."

Maldynado shook his head as well.

Amaranthe returned to the door, hesitated, then pressed her ear to the cool steel. The thumps came again, lots of them, reminding her of the frustrated fury of someone stamping her feet.

"Someone's in there," she whispered.

"What?" Yara jumped forward, putting her own ear to the door. "We have to get them out. A safe would be airtight, wouldn't it? How long could someone even stay alive inside?"

"No idea." Amaranthe grabbed a hammer and clanged a rhythm on the outside of the door.

The thumps inside stopped.

"Can you hear us?" Yara shouted. "Hello?"

"I saw how thick the door was when Sarevic opened it," Amaranthe said. "I doubt our voices would carry through." She did a few more clangs with the hammer.

The thumps returned, this time evenly spaced. By now, Amaranthe had a hunch who might be inside and she started counting right away.

"Seventeen," she said when they stopped.

"What is—"

"Sh." Amaranthe held up a finger. Another series of thumps had started. "Seven... Twelve."

"The combination?" Maldynado asked.

"I'm guessing so." Amaranthe spun the dial, hoping it worked the way other safes she had seen did.

On her first try, the lock clicked, and she was able to pull the door open. The safe was completely empty of explosives, precious metals, money, and any other typical valuables, but it did contain one red-faced, gray-haired woman lying on her side with her ankles tied together and her hands bound behind her back. She must have used her feet to bang on the vault door. Her bun was in utter disarray, her green-and-brown calico dress wrinkled and stained, and her red-rimmed spectacles dangled from a chain around her neck. The safe smelled of sweat, urine, and feces.

Amaranthe's nose crinkled, but she rushed forward, pulling out her knife to deal with the ropes. "Ms. Sarevic, how long have you been in here?"

The plump, older woman tried to speak, but her voice rasped, and little more than air came out.

"Long enough to have yelled herself hoarse." Maldynado stepped around Amaranthe, and as soon as the ropes were cut away, he picked up the woman and carried her out into the main room. "She needs a doctor. Evrial, can you find some water?"

"I need—" Sarevic's voice broke, but she cleared her throat and forced the words out. "I need to see the president. Those buffoons can't be allowed to wander the street, terrorizing businesswomen and wreaking havoc. And with my inventions!" Sarevic's wrists were raw and bleeding from the ropes, and she had to be thirstier than a slug in the desert, but she flailed about, almost lunging out of Maldynado's arms. She grabbed a pair of scissors off a shelf, taking them in her fist as if she gripped a dagger. "I'll kill them! Let me kill them!"

"Uhm." Maldynado didn't drop the angry woman—though he leaned his head back as if he were thinking about it. "What do we do with her?"

"You heard the lady," Amaranthe said. "She wants to see the president."

"Right now?" Maldynado sniffed gingerly. "Sespian informs me that there's a dress code over there."

Yara, returning with a dented metal urn filled with water, managed to punch him in the shoulder without spilling a drop.

CHAPTER 15

TIKAYA STRODE THROUGH THE FIRST-FLOOR hallway of the
hotel, passing a window and noting the soldiers charging around
in the side yard with weapons and blow lamps—since Rias hadn't
yet given the order to move his headquarters, the young men were doing
everything they could to keep the plant in check, though several vines
had popped open manhole covers around the building and were growing
up toward the sun.

"We need to resolve this soon," she muttered to herself, drawing
a glance from a passing butler. Apparently the hotel employees hadn't
grown as accustomed to her wandering around, muttering and lost in
thought, as the workers on her family's plantation back home.

She climbed the stairs to the second floor, her heavy Turgonian
footwear clomping on the carpeted treads. She missed her sandals,
though her toes would freeze off if she tried to wear them here. The
Turgonian calendar promised spring had come—and certain plants were
obviously coming up—but frost still smothered the ground most nights,
and the morning's rainstorm had turned to snow at some point. Still,
with her note decrypted, she was in a better mood than she had been in
recent weeks.

After knocking on the windowless conference room where Rias had
set up, she bounced from foot to foot, tempted to barge in with the news.
The guard stationed outside didn't regard her with the cool wariness of a
man who planned to thwart her if she should do so. But the door opened
before she had to test that notion, with Rias himself answering it.

"I thought it might be you." He stepped aside, holding out an arm to
invite her in.

She blew past him, forgetting their customary kiss, and laid her notes
on the table. Sespian and Mahliki already sat there, gesturing with each

other and debating—or maybe arguing; it was hard to tell with Sespian. He never lost his temper or grew noticeably irritated with people.

"Is that our hijacked note, now nicely decoded?" Rias closed the door and stood beside Tikaya, gazing down at the papers.

She noted with relief that no guards had been invited to stand *inside* the conference room this time, nor were any members of the hotel staff wandering around, taking drink orders. The note had done nothing to identify the snitch, but it had made her doubly certain someone on the inside was divulging information.

"It is," Tikaya said. "I'm sorry it took so long. I had assumed it was Old Turgonian, but the base language actually predates that. I've done so little work related to this continent that I forgot Turgonian started out as an amalgamation between Middle Nurian and Kriskrus, one of the languages of the people who lived here before your ancestors showed up. They're the ones who worshiped gods that were part animal and part their imaginations—the remains of a statue is on top of your big pyramid in that park."

Rias nodded. "I've seen it. Though the pyramid predates that civilization, doesn't it?"

"Yes, but the Kriskrusians thought it a lovely monument that would be perfect for their religious ceremonies, many of which involved animal and human sacrifice, and they made the pyramid theirs for a time."

Sespian held up a finger to pause the conversation he and Mahliki were having. "Those sacrifices weren't made to honor or appease a certain Magu or Dagu, were they?"

"Not those gods specifically," Tikaya said. "Those were actually two of the more benign ones from the religion, neither being portrayed as bloodthirsty, but they were a part of the mythology, yes. They were twins and represented fertility and power."

"What kind of power?" Sespian glanced toward the ceiling; he must be thinking of that lightning storm.

"Elemental power," Tikaya said. "Earth, wind, fire, and water."

"Electricity?"

"Lightning would fall into those realms. I'll have to refresh my memory with a textbook or two, but I believe there were some priests who had rudimentary command of the mental sciences in that old religion. Part of the reason the Turgonians were so eager to stamp them out is that the Kriskrusians were using their somewhat limited skills as a weapon against their sword-wielding invaders."

"While I believe this information will be important," Rias said, "and I'm always eager to listen to anything you have to say, I'd be obliged if you could explain this message for me first, love." He tapped the top sheet, a page of her notes, his finger touching something she had underlined: "Want to kill Rias!"

"Yes, of course." Tikaya patted the back of his hand. She shuffled the pages and found the one where she had written out the final translation. "When I learned that the Kriskrusian religion was experiencing a revival, and then remembered that Turgonian was based in part on that old language... figuring out the encryption key became much easier." She lifted the page to read.

Before she uttered the first word, the door opened behind her. Dak strode in, his black uniform clean and pressed, his face shaven, and his boots polished, despite the fact that the creases on his forehead and at the corners of his eyes were deeper than ever. He yawned as soon as he entered, started to cover his mouth, but turned the gesture into an apologetic wave to Rias.

"Sorry I'm late. We were so close to catching that Nurian assassin, but she saw my men coming somehow and escaped, lighting a block of the old city on fire in the process. I'm expecting a full report soon." He slid into a seat near the head of the table.

"Uhm," Tikaya said, the page still in her hands. She met Rias's eyes, widening hers slightly, hoping he would understand that she didn't want to read this in front of Dak. He was still on her list of possible snitches.

Rias's lips flattened. He caught her meaning, but he wasn't happy about questioning Dak. Or maybe he didn't want to alert a possible snitch that someone was questioning him. Either way, Rias shook his head minutely.

"What's that?" Dak nodded toward the paper in Tikaya's hands. "Something written in code?"

At least Rias hadn't mentioned Sicarius's find to Dak previously. She had wanted to keep it between direct family and those few people she knew they could trust. Sespian had played a role in having the presidency established and Rias elected, so she didn't mind him staying in the room.

"Yes," Rias said. "We intercepted a message being delivered to our enemies. Though we don't yet know which enemies." His tone grew dry. "There being so many."

"*You* intercepted?" Dak asked. "Do you have people working the underground for you that I don't know about?"

"Not officially," Rias said. "I believe it was more..."

"Accidental," Tikaya said.

"Yes. But the real reason I asked you to join us is that I'll need your help with... have you heard about the incident with the priest? We need to figure out how to build a high-voltage electricity generator that can fry a city full of plants without frying a city full of people at the same time."

Dak's brows had drawn down at the admission that someone else was out gathering intelligence for Rias, and he had given Tikaya—or maybe the papers she held—a look that managed to be curious, hurt, and sullen all at the same time. But as Rias continued, he leaned back in the chair and recovered his composure and a neutral expression, insomuch as a man with a missing eye could ever appear neutral. The scar *did* lend him a sinister cast.

"We?" Dak asked. "That sounds more like a *you* activity. In fact, I distinctly remember a story from Father about how you were trying to replicate a scientist's experiment as a boy, one that involved flying a kite in a thunder storm, and using a metal spoon from Grandmother's kitchen to invite a lightning strike. She called you into the house, and you left my father holding the kite, with the promise that if the storm gusted hard enough it would make him fly. You failed to mention why the spoon was there. He was, if not hurt, rather shocked by the experience."

"That's not quite the whole story," Rias said. "It sounds like he neglected to mention the part where he and Bresh had been repeatedly dunking me in the lake earlier in the day. Also... Mother didn't call me." Rias smiled blandly.

"I don't care what all your followers think," Dak said. "You're an evil man, Mister President."

"Yes, regardless... I need your help to figure out the logistics of troop and citizen movement. Whether we find a successful way to destroy this plant or not, we may have to evacuate the city. Temporarily." Rias said the last word firmly.

"I've already planned for that," Dak said. "What's the note say? If there's a further threat to you or your family, I'll need to alert my team."

"Your team may be part of the problem," Rias said, "or someone on it anyway."

Dak frowned at him. "What does that mean?"

Tikaya grimaced, wishing Rias hadn't said anything.

Rias waved two fingers at the note. "This was recovered from Sauda's mailbox. We don't know who sent it." He turned to Tikaya. "If you please, my lady."

Though she continued to have misgivings, Tikaya read the message aloud. "The Nurian assassin believes she's working for us, and that we'll offer her a home in the city and long-term employment. However—"

"Wait," Dak said. "*She?*"

"You didn't know?" Rias asked mildly.

"I'm going to have to have a talk with a certain operative about his observational skills."

Rias waved for Tikaya to continue.

"—we are setting everything up to place the president's death upon her blade and cast the blame on the Nurians. The public may think of us as saviors for figuring out how to kill the plant, but they'll never forgive us for slaying the great hero Starcrest. This way, the blame will be cast elsewhere, and we can step into power unopposed, and as heroes. We'll use the assassin to get rid of Sicarius as well. It's unclear whether he's truly Starcrest's right-hand man in this or not, but he's dangerous, nonetheless, and the Nurian loathes him, so pitting them against each other is perfect. Maybe they'll even kill each other at the same time. For your part, make sure that submarine doesn't get fixed. We can't have the president saving the city before we do."

Tikaya set down the paper. For a long moment, nobody spoke, then Dak dropped a disgusted hand on the table.

"They think *Sicarius* is your right-hand man? He's been out of the country for months."

Rias smiled at him. "Jealous?"

"No," Dak scoffed. "Intelligence officers are supposed to work in the shadows. If nobody knows *I'm* the one slaving day and night to gather information and keep you alive, then I'm doing my job right."

"Is that why your jaw is grinding back and forth so loudly it sounds like there's an army doing battle in there?"

Dak glowered at him. "You're not just an evil man, you're an evil,

261

evil man." He flicked a dismissive hand. "I would rather have your enemies—and I can give you a list if you've truly not kept up with all of them—focusing their enmity on Sicarius, anyway. It would interfere with my work if people started trying to assassinate me."

"It does get tedious," Rias sighed.

"I'll station troops around the submarine, though I've heard the plant has grown down the waterfront to that warehouse of yours, so that may prove a deterrent in itself."

"Not if these people have figured out how to kill the plant," Sespian said. "From those notes, it sounds like they know how it can be done, lightning storms notwithstanding."

"A practitioner trained in working with the elements would be able to create electricity," Mahliki said. "I think Agarik can do it on a small scale. Who would have thought we would regret sending those two twerps home?"

"Twerps?" Sespian murmured to her. "You don't care for your younger siblings?"

"Oh, they're all right," Mahliki said, glancing at Tikaya and Rias. "But little brothers and sisters are always... twerpy. You know how it is."

"Actually, I don't," Sespian said wryly.

"I believe Mahliki enjoyed being the older sister," Tikaya said, "aside from occasional babysitting duties, until Agarik and Koanani grew adept at... outmaneuvering her."

"They're *not* smarter than me," Mahliki told Sespian, as if she feared he would judge her poorly if he found out anything to the contrary. "But they outnumber me. It's not fair."

If there hadn't been so much else going on, Tikaya would have enjoyed watching her eldest attempt this courtship of Sespian. Even if he seemed a tad oblivious so far, he *was* sitting in the chair next to her and *had* been around more of late. Mahliki might yet charm him. Or maybe not. She was scowling at him now, perhaps because he was grinning.

"Stop smiling," she whispered. "You'll find out for yourself if Amaranthe and your father have children. Then *you'll* have to watch over them, and they'll probably be sneaking around as toddlers, climbing chimneys and drainpipes, hurling throwing knives at innocent babysitters..."

Tikaya had never seen Sespian look quite so alarmed and distressed, though she didn't know if it was from the idea of knife-hurling toddlers or the suggestion of his father having children with Amaranthe. Tikaya hadn't yet come to terms with that notion herself. She gave her daughter a warning headshake. If Mahliki meant to win Sespian's affection, she should leave mentions of Sicarius out of their conversations.

"Are you going to need any special materials for this electricity generator of yours?" Dak asked Rias, apparently not interested in discussing toddlers at the moment. "I don't want you wandering around the city, scrounging in junkyards when there are assassins after you."

"I should hope as president that I can requisition higher-end materials," Rias said. "I'll need to think about this for a couple of hours. I'll see if I can find Major Rydoth—he's one of the best engineers stationed in the area. And I'll make a parts list."

"Give it to me, and don't talk to your vice president about this project," Dak said. "You want to talk about people who might make a snitch. He wanders into my office to borrow books and maps of the city far too often."

"Serpitivich?" Tikaya stared at him. After hearing the vice president accuse Dak of snooping in *his* office, this was an odd turn. Who was telling the truth?

Mahliki and Sespian also looked surprised at Dak's suggestion. Serpitivich was a likable, if occasionally absent-minded fellow.

"He *is* working on a project to improve the city infrastructure," Rias said. "Research would be required."

"He *lingers*," Dak said. "Asking questions and looking over people's shoulders."

"Maybe he simply wants to keep apprised of events," Tikaya said. "Or maybe he likes your company."

"Nobody comes to visit because they like my company." Dak thrust a finger toward Rias's nose. "Don't forget he ran against you in the election. And came in second."

"I haven't forgotten," Rias said. "He's been nothing but helpful thus far."

"I know he seems inoffensive, but I don't care what you show on the outside: you're not going to be happy to come in second place in a contest like that. To be the first president of a new republic? That's a prize that will be remembered for all of history."

Sespian tapped his chin thoughtfully, though he didn't say anything.

"I'll keep your words in mind," Rias said.

"Do that," Dak said. "And don't show him that note, either. No need to let out that you're aware someone's looking at both players' tiles here."

"No," Rias murmured in agreement, glancing at Tikaya.

Was he thinking the same thing as she was? That Dak might be foisting the suspicion on someone else to take the attention off himself? Or was Serpitivich truly the shifty one, and Dak the person they could trust? Tikaya grimaced. Decoding ancient languages was so much easier than decoding people.

A knock sounded at the door. "Mister President?" a young man called. "You have visitors. Should I ask them to come back la—"

The door was thrust open and a smiling Maldynado strolled in, brushing past the security guards as if they were children with toy swords. One tried to grab him in an arm lock, but he melted out of the grip without losing the smile.

"Good afternoon, everyone. Pardon the intrusion, but we've uncovered some information we're certain you'll want to hear about."

Dak had risen, touching the pistol at his belt, but Rias stopped him with a raised hand. Amaranthe entered after Maldynado, along with an enforcer sergeant Tikaya hadn't seen since Professor Mugdildor's funeral early that winter—Yara, that was her name. After them came a plump, gray-haired woman in spectacles with old bruises yellowing her cheekbones. She had a wholesome, matronly look, and Tikaya would have guessed her a schoolteacher or librarian, but grease and oil stains smeared her calico dress. Several of the pockets in that dress bulged with items that clinked when she walked. Not weapons—security wouldn't have let her come up here armed—so maybe tools? Mahliki sat up straighter, regarding the woman with interest.

"We apologize for interrupting your meeting," Amaranthe said, meeting everyone's eyes and offering each person a solemn nod, "and we would have waited, but Ms. Sarevic here has been tied up in her own vault for the last three days, and she's eager to tell her story before finding a peaceful place to rest and recoup."

"The Kyatt Islands are nice," Mahliki suggested. "Warm, sunny, beach-filled. A variety of interesting flora and fauna."

The woman—Ms. Sarevic—scowled. "I don't take to those who spin magic. Real science is crafted with tools." She pulled a screwdriver out of her pocket and held it up for emphasis.

"Ah." Mahliki leaned back in her chair, some of her interest in the woman fading.

Maldynado nudged Ms. Sarevic. "Tell them who locked you up."

"Men in dark green robes," she said. "They wore hoods to hide their faces. They blew their way into my shop with grenades and magic and didn't even care that two of their people went down to my booby traps. They forced their way, demanding blasting sticks and whatever other explosives I could make. One was looking for tools to use against machines, to make boilers explode or otherwise be rendered inoperable. I told them to rip up their ugly robes, make rope with them, and hang themselves. They hurled me about my shop as if I were a rag doll. Then one stepped forward—he hadn't said a word, but I sensed that he was older—and he raised his hand. Lightning danced between his fingertips. He zapped me with it, the lizard-licking miscreant. It hurt like nothing I'd felt before. They forced me to tell them my secrets and somehow one of them found my vault. They made me open it. I was in enough pain to have lost my fight at that point. I told them to take what they wanted and leave me alone. They did, indeed, take what they wanted. Then they tied me up and locked me in there to die. I would have died, too, if I hadn't rigged that thing to have some airflow because I occasionally house valuable spiders and lizards for their... venom sacs."

Tikaya arched her brows. Explosives must not be the only things this woman crafted.

Amaranthe must have heard the story before—she wasn't paying much attention. She walked around the table to sit beside Sespian and whisper a question to him. Ah, she must be asking about Sicarius. Had he returned to the hotel yet? Sespian shook his head. Tikaya hadn't seen him, either, though she had been focused on deciphering the message.

"Devices for making boilers explode," Maldynado mused. "Sespian, your work site..."

Sespian nodded. "Yes, I thought of that too. Someone doesn't want the president's new building to be constructed. Or maybe someone objects to *my* design having been chosen." He chewed thoughtfully on that.

"Ms. Sarevic," Amaranthe said. "I know you didn't have time to take an inventory of everything missing, but do you know if blasting sticks were among the items taken?"

"Oh, yes, those were among the first things those robed hooligans grabbed."

"We found her craftsman's mark on the remains of the blasting stick that landed in the submarine," Amaranthe told Rias. "The one that so effectively destroyed the power source."

"Oh?" Rias leveled a cool stare at the woman. Odd how the man could brush away news of assassins stalking him but grew ever so protective over his engineering projects.

Ms. Sarevic shrank back. "There's... nothing illegal about civilians manufacturing those items. I checked. They're bought by the crate for mining operations."

"I see," Rias said. "If I were to send someone to fetch your sales records and contacts for the last month, we would find that *miners* were the clients who most often frequented your shop."

"Of course. Though... those records were likely destroyed along with so many other items during this abhorrent burglary." Ms. Sarevic smiled weakly.

"What *else* is missing from your shop?" Dak asked.

Rias nodded at him. "Yes, good question. What do we need to worry about next?"

"I..." The woman eyed the president, then Sergeant Yara's uniform. "I don't know. I will need time to take a thorough inventory after I recuperate."

"You mentioned venom sacs," Amaranthe said. "Do you make poisons that could kill a man?"

Interesting. She must be thinking of the bomber who had died of poison. Nurian outfit or not, maybe he was tied in with the religious fanatics. As the assassin apparently was.

"I don't make poisons," Sarevic said. "I simply make delivery mechanisms."

"And house the raw materials for making the poisons?" Dak asked.

"There's nothing illegal about gathering items from animals." Sarevic glanced at Yara again. The enforcer woman hadn't said a word, but between her height, her crisp uniform, and all the weapons she carried, she did make an intimidating representation of law enforcement.

Tikaya caught Amaranthe's eye. Since she was no longer an enforcer—indeed, might Ms. Sarevic know her from her days as an outlaw?—and was neither on the president's payroll nor a member of his family, she might be the ideal person to entice further information out of the sketchy craftswoman.

Can you talk to her later? Tikaya signed in Basilard's hand code.

Amaranthe hesitated. She probably wanted to search for Sicarius instead of taking on more tasks, but she nodded.

"Maldynado," Rias said, "why don't you take your charge down to reception and have someone check her into a room here? After this ordeal, I'm sure she'll find our secured hotel safer and more comfortable than her home."

Sarevic's ruddy face grew pale at this, and her red-rimmed spectacles slipped down her nose. She either had a good understanding of what a target the president—and his domicile—was at the moment, or she realized she was going to be held until she spoke more openly.

"Enh, I don't know about that." Maldynado rubbed his head. "I bet her home doesn't have vines growing out of the nearby sewers and trying to find an open window to get in."

Rias's expression hardened. He had made his request a question, but clearly meant it as an order. Ms. Sarevic wasn't to be allowed to roam free.

"Oh," Maldynado said. "Sure, My Lord. I understand." He and Yara guided the woman out.

"Should I go too?" Amaranthe glanced around at the family gathering plus Sespian.

Before anyone could answer, voices in the hallway distracted everyone.

"Uh," Maldynado said from outside the room. "Go right in with that, why don't you? No, no, I don't need a closer look. I'm sure that Mahliki will want to see that, Bas. Yes, impress *her* with it." His voice lowered into disgusted mumbles that didn't drift in clearly enough to hear.

"Basilard," Amaranthe said to Rias's and Dak's raised eyebrows. "Wasn't he working with Mahliki?"

"Yes." Rias waved to a guard standing in the door, the young man not certain whether he should block this newcomer or let him in, or—judging by the way his top lip was wrinkled halfway up his nose—run in the other direction.

Basilard nodded as he passed the guard and walked in with his translator behind him, though the red-haired woman wore a similar lip-wrinkled expression. Basilard carried a large jar in his hands, the lid firmly affixed, Tikaya was relieved to see, for the creatures inside were a mixture of antennae, slime, and green-gray squishiness. Trails of slick goo coated the inside bottom half of the jar, and one was in the midst of trying to scale the wall to the lid.

"Oh," Mahliki said, standing for a better look. "Are those Mangdorian Tree Snails?"

Basilard nodded, smiled, and placed the jar on the table. Tikaya managed not to push her chair back, but only because her nephew and Mahliki had been bringing unappealing insect specimens home for years. It was only alarming when they escaped their jars. Fortunately, Basilard had not drilled air holes that were overly large...

"This is... related to the plant?" Rias asked.

Basilard pointed to a green stub on the bottom of the jar. Due to the trails of slime all over the glass, Tikaya had to stand up and peer in from above to make it out. Mahliki rushed over to join her.

"They're eating the plant," Mahliki said. "Did you, ah... how long has it been, Basilard? Remember my theory about the indigestibility of the vine, due to its tendency to keep growing, no matter what the environment?"

It's been twenty-four hours, Basilard signed. The Mangdorian woman translated his gestures for Rias and Dak.

"And no snail stomachs have exploded?" Mahliki.

"*Exploded?*" Amaranthe blurted. She *had* pushed her chair back from the table, even though she was on the other side from the jar.

The snails have been fine, Basilard signed. *They seem to be thriving on the plant, and have even chosen it above other foods that I've placed into the jar.*

"How fast do they consume the plant?" Rias asked.

I put a three-inch-long piece of vine in there last night, and these four have almost consumed it.

"Uh," Mahliki said.

"Unless you have a few billion of those snails," Rias said, "I believe we'll have to go ahead with our plan to create an electricity generator."

Billion? No, but I thought we could start breeding them here in the city. Their reproduction cycles are relatively short... Basilard shrugged, looking daunted at the prospect of trying to breed a billion slugs.

"What then eats the slugs when we've let them loose on the city with an unlimited food supply?" Tikaya asked.

Snow lizards are their natural predators, Basilard signed.

"Is anyone else having a vision of us trying to bring a million snow lizards into the city to eat the billion slugs running—or sliding—around?" Amaranthe asked.

"Yes," Rias said, "and we'd then have to find a predator for the lizards. Basilard, I'm glad you've found something that enjoys that plant, but let's put that down as Plan B for the moment."

I understand, Basilard said.

"Dak, prepare to have the city evacuated, or to at least have people moved to high ground. Mahliki, would you help me with the generator? We need to make sure to create something that can indeed slay the plant. Amaranthe, if you would talk to that craftswoman and find out what else we may face, I would appreciate it."

Tikaya glanced at Rias, not realizing he had caught that exchange. She shouldn't be surprised though.

"Sespian, we may have to put your building's construction on hold for the time being, though it *is* interesting that the same party seems to be behind all of this chaos. Dak, find out who's leading those people, will you?"

"Already working on it," Dak said.

"Sespian," Rias continued, "Would you like to lend your design skills to the generator project?"

"Er," Sespian said, "I don't have any engineering experience. All I could do is make it aesthetically pleasing. Is that... important?"

"I was thinking more about compact and portable enough to be moved about by teams of soldiers."

"Ah, I can try to help. Do you already have ideas as to how to do this?"

"I have a head full of ideas," Rias said, "but if this were easy, my submarines would already be running on generators instead of magic balls. We'll be designing a prototype. Speaking of submarines, whoever wrote that note seems to believe we'll need ours to defeat the plant. Perhaps the underwater roots are the most vulnerable to electrical currents?"

"It's possible," Mahliki said. "If you can provide me a tool, I can do some experiments."

"All right. In the meantime, it would still be nice to find someone who could simply replace the power source so we don't have to worry about rewiring everything in there from scratch. Amaranthe, did you—"

Amaranthe was shaking her head, but another knock at the door came before Rias finished asking his question.

A guard stuck his head in. "My Lord President, Sicarius is here to see you."

Amaranthe jumped to her feet.

"Let him in, thank you," Rias said.

Amaranthe raced around the table, bumping her hip on a corner, and met Sicarius at the door. She wrapped her arms around him in a fierce hug. He wore the same black clothing as he had the night they had parted, his hair perhaps more wind-tossed than usual, though otherwise he was unchanged. He carried a small envelope in one hand and looked like he wanted to deliver it straight to Rias's hands, but he returned the embrace first. If not as enthusiastically as Amaranthe—his gaze flicked toward those watching—he did at least lower his head and murmur something in her ear. An apology for being missing so long without sending word, Tikaya hoped.

Amaranthe released the hug, though she kept hold of his free hand, and they walked to the table together.

"Sicarius," Rias said by way of greeting.

"My Lord," Sicarius said.

Tikaya expected him to hand the note to Rias, but he laid it in front of her instead. "It is encrypted. It was in the belongings of the Nurian mage hunter."

Dak's head came up. "You found him—*her*? Is she still alive?"

"She lives, yes. Several soldiers disguised as poor citizens charged into her tenement building, interrupting me before I could capture her." Sicarius stared at Dak as he spoke.

"Mage hunter?" Rias asked. "Is this the Nurian assassin you spoke of, Dak?"

Dak rubbed his jaw. "I'm not that familiar with that profession, but it might explain the assassin's aptitude. I can do more research on the matter."

"And on evacuations," Rias said. "The assassination threat must be secondary to the safety of the city right now."

Dak grunted and headed for the door. "If you say so."

Rias touched Tikaya's shoulder. "Is that note important?"

"One moment." She had been deciphering it while the others spoke and only had one line to go. "I'm almost done. Er..." She swallowed and blinked a few times. It couldn't be right. Maybe it was a bluff.

"Tikaya?" Rias murmured.

She frowned up at him. "How are you feeling today?"

"No worse than any other day. Better of late, since Sauda's *gift* was removed from my presence." His brows rose. "Why do you ask?"

Tikaya lifted the translated note and read. "Ji Nah, focus on ridding us of Sicarius. Do not concern yourself with the president. The poison has been delivered. He won't be a problem much longer."

The room grew silent, with all sets of eyes swiveling toward Rias.

"I don't feel poisoned," he said.

"Something slow-acting?" Sespian looked at his father.

"Many such poisons exist," Sicarius said.

"Any of them developed via lizard or spider venom?" Amaranthe asked.

"Not slow-acting ones," Sicarius said. "Not that I know of."

Amaranthe sighed. "Of course it couldn't have been that easy."

"You found this note today?" Tikaya asked Sicarius. "So it might have been delivered this morning? Or yesterday?"

"The assassin was busy last night and this morning," Sicarius said. "It is likely she received it yesterday at the latest."

Tikaya stared at Rias, her vision blurry. "So something might have been in your system for two days now."

"Just because someone told a Nurian assassin that I've been poisoned doesn't make it the truth," Rias said. "Remember the first note. These people are using her. This may simply be what they're telling her to make her focus on Sicarius."

"I don't think anyone would need to make her focus on me," Sicarius said. "I may be why she's here."

Amaranthe, still holding his hand, frowned up at him. "I knew you knew more about this Nurian and the mage hunters than you were letting on. What is it?"

Sicarius shook his head once. "Until you translated that name—Ji Nah—I had only a suspicion, but she has similar features to someone I once knew."

"Someone you... hunted over there?" Amaranthe asked.

"No. The first mage hunter I ever met, the man who taught me about practitioners and withstanding their attacks when I was a boy. Hollowcrest brought him in as one of my tutors. Soo Jhin Nah." Sicarius gazed down, meeting Amaranthe's eyes. "He did not make it back to his homeland."

"Because his pupil was commanded to make sure he did not?" Amaranthe asked so quietly Tikaya almost missed it. Her stomach grew chill at the implications of the question.

"He was," Sicarius said.

Amaranthe sighed but didn't step away from him. By now, she must know all about his past and those he had killed, or she must at least suspect. Tikaya could not imagine standing beside him, knowing what she knew.

"So this may be a relative out for revenge? A daughter?" Amaranthe asked.

"Perhaps so. Though from listening to her speak with her own daughter, I believe events in her homeland forced her to leave. I may be an afterthought or an attempt to regain honor."

Amaranthe held up a hand. "The assassin has a *daughter* here?"

"A young child, yes." Sicarius's gaze flicked about the room—despite Tikaya's revelation that Rias might have been poisoned, everyone was riveted to this conversation. "I had an opportunity to kill the mage hunter, though she is crafty and may have evaded me, but I wanted your opinion on this matter before acting."

"Why?" Amaranthe whispered. "Why would anyone bring a daughter on an assassination mission?"

Tikaya bit back a question about why an assassin would *have* a child, remembering in time that Sicarius and Sespian might take offense, not to mention Amaranthe who apparently wanted a baby. Surely such offspring would be targets for anyone seeking revenge for the parent's kills. Then again... she considered Rias. He probably had more enemies in the world than Sicarius ever would, and that hadn't stopped Tikaya from wanting to have his children. Maybe it was because they *had* been targets more than once that her mind automatically went to that place. She had survived all of that, but only because she had had Rias at her side. To lose him would be... unacceptable.

She scooted her chair closer to him and linked her arm with his. When he met her eyes, she tapped a vein on the back of his hand. The assassin was a low priority, surely, compared to the plant and the poison that might be flowing in his blood. He gave her a nod, but responded to Sicarius and Amaranthe.

"If the Nurians exiled this assassin, she might have had no choice but to bring her child along." Yes, he knew all about exile.

"It was my intention to bring the mage hunter here for questioning," Sicarius said, "but I did not wish to apprehend her in front of the child. Knowing her skill, it might have been a bloody battle."

It surprised Tikaya to hear that he had considered the child at all. Amaranthe squeezed his hand, and he gave her a nod.

"She fled with the child when the soldiers came," Sicarius said. "She burned the building as a distraction. She was good. I didn't see her escape."

"Since you are her target," Rias said, "I'll leave you to deal with her as you see fit. If you want some men, let me know and I'll arrange it, though I sense you believe you can handle her better alone."

"Perhaps not entirely alone." Sicarius met Amaranthe's eyes. She tapped her chin thoughtfully.

"Handling her means killing her?" Tikaya asked, though she probably wouldn't have needed to, this being Turgonia. Murderers were given the death sentence here, and trials were nonexistent. Judges and magistrates alone heard and convicted criminals. She had already argued for Rias to make changes to the judicial system, and he had agreed that it would need reform, but there hadn't been time to do much yet. "What becomes of the child then?"

Rias turned his palm toward the ceiling. "A person cannot be absolved of crimes because he or she is a parent. There are orphanages, or perhaps Nurian relatives might be found, and she could be returned to her homeland."

Tikaya closed her eyes. Only Turgonians could speak so calmly and rationally about people's deaths.

"Because there are both male and female warriors and practitioners in Nuria," Sicarius said, "it is possible a mated pair may be slain in battle. There is an old tradition that the children of fallen combatants may be taken in and cared for by those who slew the parents, if there are no other kin. Sometimes even if there *are* kin. The Nurians considered it better to raise an enemy's child and shape his world view than to have that child grown up to hate them and take revenge upon them later."

"Are you saying this assassin brought her child along for *you* to care for in case you defeated her in some battle?" Tikaya found the notion mindboggling. She had read about that Nurian custom, but it was centuries old; nobody still *did* that, did they?"

Amaranthe's jaw had nearly dropped to her shirt during this discussion. It seemed her mind was boggled too.

"I do not presume to know the woman's motivations," Sicarius said. "I am merely stating that there is a Nurian precedent for adoptions by enemies."

Rias was rubbing his face, maybe as flabbergasted at the idea of Sicarius as an adoptive parent as Tikaya was.

"It is early to worry about this aspect of the problem," Rias said. "We have other matters to attend to." He clasped Tikaya's hand for a few heartbeats, then stood. "I had better not delay further on this electricity project. To build something in so little time, we need... serendipity. To build something at all will be a challenge." He huffed out a breath, his expression faintly daunted.

Tikaya hadn't seen the look on him often, and it worried her, but she gave him an encouraging smile. "You like challenges, love."

"Yes." He gave her a kiss, saluted the others, and left the room.

Mahliki and Sespian stood up, and Amaranthe and Sicarius, who had never sat, headed for the door. Tikaya cleared her throat.

"Wait a moment, please."

Everyone stopped and looked at her.

"My husband will put the city before his own health, his own *life*. I don't know if he's ingested some poison that will harm him or not, but I can't leave this up to chance. If I can figure out who the leader of this religious group is, will someone pay him a visit and find out if there's a poison and if so... what the antidote might be?" Tikaya refused to accept that there might *not* be an antidote.

She forced herself to meet Sicarius's cool dark eyes. He was the one who made the most sense, who could be the most effective in this scenario, though she certainly wouldn't refuse the assistance of the others. She didn't know how to ask him this favor specifically though. Would he do it for her? She had never spared him any kind thoughts. If not for her, would he do it for Rias? Sicarius *did* seem loyal to him. Strange, but in this moment, Tikaya trusted him more than Rias's own kin. Not strange, a matter of logic. He hadn't been here all winter, so he couldn't be the snitch. Besides, he and Amaranthe had been *targeted* by the snitch.

"I will go," Sicarius said.

Tikaya's knees weakened in relief and she gripped the edge of the table for support.

"*We* will go," Amaranthe corrected.

Mahliki spread her hands. "Father wants me to help with testing, but if there's anything I can do, I will."

"I know you will." Tikaya smiled at her daughter.

"But, uhm, how are you going to figure out who's in charge and where to find the person?" Mahliki asked.

"I," Tikaya said, flexing her fingers, "am going to camp out in that intelligence office and go over every piece of data Dak's men have gathered this winter, and woe to he who attempts to stop me."

"I could lend you someone forbidding to loom threateningly from behind your shoulder if you wish." Amaranthe leaned against Sicarius's arm.

He snorted softly but didn't object.

"I believe I can throw Rias's reputation around and get what I want from those men," Tikaya said, "but I will consider your offer if I have trouble."

"Ask Colonel Starcrest about the bomber who died of poison," Sicarius said. "A doctor was going to perform an examination, but I was never informed as to the results. Whatever poison he ingested was fast-acting, but it might offer a clue."

Tikaya nodded. "I will ask. Now my friends, I believe we all have work to do."

Tikaya barely heard the others preparing to leave. She was already heading for the door, already planning her assault on the intelligence office. She *should* have been in there all winter, instead of twiddling her thumbs and lamenting her place in this land. She only hoped she could find what she wanted, and that she hadn't waited too long.

CHAPTER 16

A S SOON AS AMARANTHE HAD Sicarius alone, she stopped him with a hand to his chest, then wrapped her arms around him and gave him the kiss she had longed to in the conference room. She dug her fingers into his hair, pulling him as close as she could, needing a moment where no distance stood between them. She thought he might be too busy thinking of this new assignment to take the time for sentimental dawdling, but she had been worrying about him all night and all day, curse his roaming ancestors.

Sicarius didn't break the kiss. He slid his arms around her waist and leaned his back against the hallway wall, a potted tree offering them a modicum of privacy, though for the moment, nobody else was walking on the floor. She was the one to eventually break the kiss, dropping her face to his neck, closing her eyes, and breathing in the scent of him.

Usually she enjoyed that scent, but... "Sicarius, have you been traveling in sewers lately?"

He snorted softly, his breath warm against her ear. "I believed it imperative to deliver that message, so I did not delay for bathing before reporting to the president."

"Well, maybe your new odor will prove useful in chatting with Ms. Sarevic. If you stand next to her, she'll be all the more eager to answer my questions, so she can escape sewer scents."

Sicarius's cool look suggested he appreciated her teasing less than her kisses. He released her and walked down the hallway. Amaranthe caught up to him by the time he reached the first floor. A security guard stood behind the counter as well as the receptionist now.

"The location of the prisoner," Sicarius said to them, his tone not making it entirely clear it was a question.

"Pardon?" the receptionist asked, adjusting her spectacles and choosing to meet Amaranthe's eyes instead of Sicarius's.

"Our friends Maldynado and Sergeant Yara requested a room for a plump matronly woman with a dress full of tools," Amaranthe said. "We'd like to locate them."

"Ah, one thirty-seven."

"Thank you." Amaranthe nudged Sicarius. "I'm not sure why *Basilard* is the only one who gets a translator around here."

Before they could head off to hunt for the room—or Sicarius could offer a rejoinder—Maldynado and Yara walked out of the hallway.

"We've secured the guest," Maldynado said, addressing a lazy salute toward Amaranthe.

Amaranthe wondered if Tikaya would find that an only-in-Turgonia statement. "We're off to question her. Want to join us?"

"Nah, I already asked her my question." Maldynado dug out the black disc he had found in the wreckage at the construction site. "She didn't want to answer, but I used my charms on her."

"You threatened to leave one of those vines tied to her chair as a housewarming gift," Yara said.

"Yes, but I smiled charmingly when I said it."

"How did that work for you?" Amaranthe had yet to strategize her own method for teasing answers out of Sarevic.

"It worked fine. She said this was part of a time-delay switch that could be wired to just about anything that needed to be delayed. She admitted that it had come out of her shop, but didn't admit that she had any idea what it had been wired to. At least I know what to look for now. She relented and drew a quick sketch of an undamaged switch. On account of my charms."

"Your threat," Yara said.

"My charming threat."

Amaranthe feared this would mean Sarevic would be in even less of a mood to be strong-armed into cooperation.

"Good luck with her," Maldynado said. "We need to go. We have another mission."

"We do?" Yara's eyes narrowed. "It doesn't involve nudity, does it?"

"I suppose nudity is an option, but I want to go out to the construction site for Sespian's building and stop whoever's been sabotaging it. I need the assistance of your honed enforcer investigating skills."

"I'm a patroller. I don't investigate; I shove criminals up against walls and throw handcuffs on them."

"You can handcuff the foreman if you want," Maldynado said. "He's a pest."

"Because he made you do work?"

"Because he snottily made me do work."

"I thought Starcrest wasn't making the building a priority right now," Amaranthe said, though Sicarius had already decided he'd had enough of the conversation and was heading down the hall. Maybe he intended to start wafting his sewer cologne at Sarevic preemptively.

Maldynado shrugged. "He didn't give me a more important job. I figure this is all tied in anyway. If I can catch the building saboteur, maybe he can lead me to the head priest you want."

"That's very responsible of you, Maldynado. Thank you." Amaranthe patted his arm before jogging after Sicarius.

She couldn't quite decipher Yara's sarcastic grumble, but gathered she already had a lot of work to do without going along on side trips with Maldynado. Amaranthe would have to find a moment to talk to her about the job she had passed up—or maybe hadn't yet passed up.

A soldier pressed into guard duty was standing outside of room 137 when Amaranthe arrived. The door was open, Sicarius having already gone inside. Starcrest must have sent the word down the chain of command that he was to be given free access to the hotel; either that or his glare worked as an effective key for opening guarded doors.

Amaranthe found him standing behind Sarevic, who had dumped her tools out on a desk and was sitting at the chair, using a screwdriver to clean her fingernails. She was ignoring Sicarius. Amaranthe thought about smiling at him and waving him closer, so she would catch the sewer scent, but he didn't seem to be in the mood for teasing, not with Starcrest's life at stake.

"Ms. Sarevic." Amaranthe dragged a second chair over for herself. "I hope you don't mind us interrupting your project for a moment—" she waved at the on-going fingernail cleaning, drawing a grunt from the other woman, "—but I was wondering if I could help you remember what exactly the thieves took."

"And their current location," Sicarius stated.

"I already told you what I know," Sarevic said.

278

"And you won't know more until you can get back to your shop and take inventory?" Amaranthe asked.

"Exactly. But I'm locked in here."

"Perhaps if you were to give us a more complete list of what threats we might be dealing with, I could talk the president into releasing you immediately," Amaranthe said, though she didn't know if she had that kind of sway.

That drew a flicker of interest from Sarevic, though she promptly returned her focus to her fingernails.

"The blasting sticks have already been used against us," Amaranthe said. "Were you working on anything else that could have... destructive uses?"

Sarevic sniffed. "Of course not."

"I've purchased wares from you before. There's no need to pretend you don't invent items that, however handy, can be put to ruinous use."

Sarevic peered more closely at her fingernails, then picked up a file, one designed to sand wood rather than parts of the human anatomy, but the roughness didn't seem to bother her.

Amaranthe leaned back in her chair. Time to try another tactic. What did Sarevic want, besides to be released to go about her business? Maybe Amaranthe could make her believe she wanted something she didn't yet *know* she wanted...

"Now that the president is aware of the special nature of your work," Amaranthe said, "I imagine it will be harder to attract some of your more... sophisticated clientele, folks who wish to remain anonymous and might worry that your establishment is being monitored. Of course, it was only a matter of time before things grew more difficult for you. The enforcers have been aware of your second set of shop hours for a while."

"I know," Sarevic muttered and filed harder at her thumbnail.

Amaranthe wasn't sure whether the comment represented acceptance over her argument or that the enforcers truly were aware of the clandestine side of the workshop's business. She had been bluffing; she hadn't heard about it herself until she had become an outlaw.

"But," she went on, "as any businesswoman knows, opportunity can often be found even in catastrophe. This could be a chance to put your special talents to work in meeting the president's needs. Working for him and those close to him would certainly come with perks, and you would no longer need to worry about watching your back for the law. I understand he has an engineering background. He might appreciate the uniqueness and quality of the items you produce."

Sarevic laid down the file and met Amaranthe's eyes for the first time. "You think he would hire me? As an independent contractor?"

Amaranthe wasn't in a position to make deals on Starcrest's behalf, but she lifted a shoulder and smiled. "If you were to help him thwart the priests who burglarized and assaulted you and who are also threatening him, I'm sure he would feel kindly toward you." When Sarevic's eyes narrowed, Amaranthe added, "And perhaps you could bring him some samples of your more recent work, especially if you have any ideas related to the generation of electricity. That's his priority right now." And he might not appreciate having some blasting-stick-creating tinkerer helping, but if it would get them the information they sought...

"They took the venom sacs out of my vault," Sarevic said. "I think they got my acid too."

"Your what?"

"The acid I made for dissolving metals. It works nicely, and doesn't burn if it gets on your hands."

Amaranthe met Sicarius's eyes over Sarevic's head, thinking of the submarine. Could some of this acid be stored in a small container or even under a uniform jacket and then casually dribbled onto the hull in passing? Still, if the submarine was being guarded now, someone would have a hard time getting close enough to do that. Unless one of the guards was their snitch... or working for their snitch.

"Royal water?" Sicarius asked. "President Starcrest made something similar to deal with the cubes."

Yes, Amaranthe had seen that in action herself.

Sarevic sniffed. "*My* acid does not burn skin. It's a groundbreaking discovery, I assure you. I also designed special containers and a launch device, so it wouldn't leak or be released without a suitable impact."

So someone could shoot it at the submarine from afar. That information would be important to deliver.

"I didn't know the president was mechanically inclined," Sarevic said, her expression growing less indignant and more thoughtful. "You say he has an engineering hobby?"

"It's what he studied in school and went into the service for," Sicarius said. "An early commanding officer steered him out of the engine room and onto the command deck."

"I understand he's built a number of submarines," Amaranthe added, thinking that might further endear the man to Sarevic. Surely designing such a craft was a clear sign of mechanical know-how.

"That use Kyattese magic for a power source." Sarevic's lips flattened.

Er, perhaps that hadn't been the best example.

"He is now seeking to find a mundane method of generating power for the crafts," Sicarius said.

"He is?" Sarevic peered over her shoulder at him, acknowledging his presence for the first time. "Interesting. This project would appeal to me. If I am to be a prisoner here anyway, perhaps I could be of assistance."

Amaranthe, recalling that their goal was to get all the information they could from Sarevic—not find her a new job—said, "I'm certain you would be useful on his team." Well, she wasn't *that* certain. "But the priority is to catch those who are conspiring against him. Are you positive you didn't overhear them speaking about a base they were returning to or some eating house where they were meeting?"

"Nothing like that," Sarevic said.

"Any distinctive stains on their clothing?" Sicarius asked. "Or identifying scents?"

Sarevic snorted. "They smelled better than you."

Amaranthe gave Sicarius a twisted smile. It was a good thought, but most people weren't as observant as he. Maybe if they went back to the workshop themselves and searched around, they could—

"Wait." Sarevic snapped her fingers. "Now that you bring it up, I do remember that the one who bent over me to tie me up smelled like... almost like perfume. Citrusy perfume."

"Interesting," Sicarius said.

Amaranthe raised her eyebrows. "Interesting that such a thing exists or interesting that a man would wear it?" She frowned at Sarevic. "Or *was* it a man?" Women could beat up and bind people too.

"It was a man," Sarevic said. "I remember thinking it was strange, because his breath stunk of sardines and wine. As long as you're slathering yourself in some scent to make you more attractive, wouldn't you brush your teeth as well? And why does someone going out to steal weapons need to smell good anyway?"

Most of the history of perfumes had to do with covering up unwashed body scents, but Amaranthe agreed that it was a strange thing to don before heading out to brutalize tinkerers.

"Are you sure it was perfume?" Amaranthe asked. "Maybe it was—"

"Describe the citrus," Sicarius said, his eyes intense as they bored into the back of Sarevic's head. If he realized he had cut off Amaranthe, he didn't show it. She didn't take offense, since he seemed to have gotten more of a clue from this revelation than she had. "Lemon? Orange? Something else?" he prompted.

Sarevic shrugged. "I don't shop at the fancy import markets. I'm not an expert."

Not on perfumes, just on venom sacs.

Though Sicarius never moved, never unclasped his hands from behind his back, Amaranthe had the distinct impression he wanted to throttle Sarevic for a more precise answer.

"Have you smelled it since you've been in the hotel?" he asked.

"Here?" Sarevic twisted in her chair to look at him again. "Why would it be here?"

Sicarius met Amaranthe's eyes instead. "The first night we were here, I smelled lemongrass incense being burned on the third floor."

"Lemongrass?" Sarevic nodded slowly. "That might be what it was."

"Then one of the men on that team of hooded people might be the snitch who is living and working here in the hotel?" Amaranthe asked. "You wouldn't expect such a person to risk being seen with those doing the dirty work."

"Incense is strong," Sicarius said.

It took Amaranthe a moment to figure out what he meant. "So... Sardine Breath could have simply been visiting the snitch and wandered past the burning stick?"

"Or the lemongrass incense is used widely among those of this religion."

"Such as in a religious ceremony?" Amaranthe found herself pacing—and thinking. Yes, that seemed more likely than inviting thugs into the hotel; all guests were signed in by security. But did that mean someone in the hotel had been performing ceremonies in his or her room? And to what end?

"What is she doing?" Sarevic asked.

Amaranthe realized she had stopped in front of the tinkerer's desk and started tidying her tool collection. Sicarius ignored the question.

Amaranthe stuck her hands into her pocket. "We need to ask Professor Komitopis if incense was used as a part of that religion. What was it called? Kriskrus?"

"Kriskrusian," Sicarius said. "We should also search the rooms on the third floor."

"We would have to get someone's permission for that."

Sicarius's eyebrow twitched.

"Well, I guess we wouldn't *have* to," Amaranthe said. "It's just that I feel like we should work on the side of the law now that we're staunch citizens of this new republic."

"You find the professor and ask about the religion; I'll investigate the rooms."

"Staunchly?"

"Yes."

Maldynado plucked a turd-brown hardhat out of the bin at the edge of the construction site and placed it on his head with a sneer of distaste. If one had to don costumes, he much preferred the sort that showed off one's finer attributes—such as chiseled muscles, a sublime facial structure, and luxurious brown locks. These workers—he picked up a shovel for further verisimilitude—needed to speak to their employer about more appealing hats and togs.

Basilard plunked a hat onto his own head without comment. Naturally he wouldn't mind covering up that scar-filled shaven pate.

"Thanks for coming along, Bas," Maldynado said. "I was hoping to lure Evrial out with me, but she had to go back to work." At least that was what she had said.

Basilard signed, *I am your second choice?*

"Of course not. She's simply the one I wish to..."

Impress with that hat?

"Ha ha, you're a one-man riot. No, I want her to see that I'm serious about working for Starcrest and getting a good job here in the city. I want her to realize it would be much better for us to stay here, rather than going back to that boring rural town she's from. What kind of job

could I do out there? We'd probably have to move in with her family."
Maldynado shuddered from boots to hat.

I heard about your first impression with them.

"You what? How—you weren't even in the country when
that happened."

Basilard's blue eyes twinkled. *I was on the way.*

"I'm surprised you arrived so quickly when you had that pretty little
translator to wake up to in the mornings."

Basilard's face resumed its usual morose cast. He shook his head. *She
is not... we are not... not.*

"It's fascinating that the human brain can be just as ineloquent with
hand gestures as with words," Maldynado observed, not feeling bad about
teasing when Basilard had started it.

Basilard took a shovel from the rack. For a moment, Maldynado
thought he might be contemplating a physical response, but he merely
propped it over his shoulder and shook his head.

"Do you find her attractive?" Maldynado asked.

The corners of Basilard's lips quirked.

"I'll take that for a yes. Have you told her you find her attractive? She
seems to understand all your made up gobbledygook." Maldynado waved
at Basilard's fingers. "You must have spent some time communicating
with her."

*Yes, but she's... she's the chief's daughter. It wouldn't be appropriate for me
to... proposition her.*

"Dear ancestors." Maldynado lifted his eyes skyward. "It's another
Sespian. Except he's young and as naive as a tadpole, so that's why he's
shy. You're older than me, Bas. And you had a wife at one point, so you
can't be that naive. Though granted, you Mangdorians sound like a
wholesome bunch with your peace-loving religion and all. Are any of
your people true bedroom warriors?"

Basilard's mouth had dropped open farther and farther as Maldynado
spoke. Was he being offensive? He just didn't know why all these perfectly
capable men were lacking in confidence. Sure Basilard had those scars,
but he had won an event in the Imperial Games, and now he was a
highfaluting diplomat. Finding a girl should *not* be a problem.

A one-handed, *I am* not *shy,* was Basilard's only response.

"Do you want me to ask the little flower if she likes you?"

Basilard dropped a hand like a steel vise onto Maldynado's forearm and shook his head firmly. He released Maldynado—though probably only because he needed his fingers for signing. *Do not bother her with your crude innuendoes. She is a professional woman and, as I said, the chief's daughter. She has traveled and studied in other nations. She is not a little flower or anyone to be... bothered with silliness.*

Maldynado lifted his hands. "All right, all right, I won't bother her, but courting isn't silly. It's part of being a human. One of the better parts, I should think."

Basilard glared.

"Here's an idea," Maldynado said. "I'm planning a dinner party to help Sespian and Mahliki get comfortable together, seeing as she's shyer with him than I expected from her, and he's... waiting for a clue to fall out of a tree and hit him on the head. Why don't you and your translator come? We'll make sure the wine flows freely, and when her tongue loosens up, maybe she'll lean close to you and whisper some... *unprofessional* words in your ear."

Maldynado couldn't remember seeing anyone shake his head firmly and look wistful at the same time, but Basilard managed it.

"It'll be after all this is over." Maldynado waved in the direction of the plant-besieged harbor. "And we'll invite some other couples, too, so your lady won't feel like she's in the center ring. Just a casual dinner party. What could go wrong?"

Will you be cooking?

Maldynado grimaced, thinking of the *last* time he had tried to cook for someone. "I'll arrange for it to be catered. Although if you wanted to impress her, you could play a role in the cooking. You have quite the gift for that. Perhaps you could contribute the dessert? Oh, but don't use any of those pee-soaked weeds you've been known to pluck from alleys. Just because something is edible doesn't mean it should end up on the plate."

I do not pick the pee-soaked ones, Basilard signed. *As for the rest... perhaps... I will consider it. If she's interested. She finds Turgonians brutish and violent, though she's too polite to say so. I don't know if she would care to spend a whole evening with them.*

"Mahliki isn't Turgonian," Maldynado pointed out. "Not really anyway. We can put her on your lady's right—oh, and you should tell me

285

her name at some point. It makes filling out place cards easier. Redheaded Mangdorian Woman is a bit much to write on there with calligraphy."

Basilard hesitated, then made a motion Maldynado interpreted as a woman combing her hair.

"That's... your gesture for her?"

She does it a lot. When she's nervous.

If she did it a lot around Basilard, that might be a good sign. So long as he made her nervous in a he's-cute-and-I-wonder-if-he's-interested way rather than an I-hope-the-brute-doesn't-kill-me-if-I-don't-translate-well way. "Woman Who Braids Her Hair When Nervous. That'll be even harder to put on the name cards."

Basilard snorted. *I'll write it down for you when—*

"What are you two shovel heads doing over there?" came the familiar—and grating—holler of the foreman. The barrel-chested man rolled toward them, black bags under his bloodshot eyes, the cigar clamped between his teeth more macerated than the most popular stick in a dog kennel. "Do you see how far behind we are? Quit yammering, and get your slagging butts over there and unload those I-beams."

He snatched the shovels out of their hands and threw them into the rack. They banged against others and fell down, knocking several down with them. Already walking toward—and yelling at—the next pair of idlers, he didn't notice.

"Guess we're not digging today," Maldynado said and headed in the direction the foreman had indicated. He hadn't truly intended to do work, merely wanting to observe and investigate, but allowed that they would be less conspicuous this way.

He didn't seem concerned that I'm not on an employee roster, Basilard signed. *Or that he's never seen me before.*

"As distraught as he looked, I bet he would try to put the president himself to work if he showed up next to the shovel rack."

For all the man's bluster, Maldynado didn't think the building could be that far behind schedule. Starcrest and Sespian might not have the construction site at the top of their priority list at the moment, but an impressive amount of progress had been made in the few days the crew had been working. The foundation had set, and the steel framework was already going up. The equipment operators and more experienced workers seem to be in charge of that; the "shovel heads" were dragging, pushing, and lifting materials around the site. Maldynado and Basilard joined one of those groups.

After exchanging a few meaningless comments and grunts with the natives, Maldynado asked, "Any more accidents on the site since the boiler blew up?"

Most of the people ignored him, though a beefy fellow grew loquacious enough to say, "No."

"Any plants pop up out of the sewer line that team is excavating?"

"No."

Maldynado shrugged at Basilard and told himself it was *good* that nobody else had been hurt and that no more equipment had been damaged, but he wanted to catch the culprits, and that would be easier if they were doing something... catchable.

Obeying someone else's points and grunts, Maldynado and Basilard picked up bags of mortar mix and carried them over to a forklift next to a parked lorry loaded with pallets of bricks. Nobody had started laying bricks yet, but this was going to be the station apparently. Maldynado took the opportunity to stick his head under the lorry and the forklift to see if any of Sarevic's timing devices had been placed under them. Best to catch a booby trap before it went off...

While he lay on his back under the lorry, wishing the cloudy afternoon sky offered more light, a pair of boots came into view on the opposite side. They didn't look like Basilard's footwear.

A throat cleared. A grumpy throat.

Maldynado rolled out from under the lorry as the foreman walked around to his side of the vehicle. "I would guess you were taking a nap," the man said, "but I don't think you're stupid enough to sleep under a moveable two-ton machine." He slapped his palms together, no doubt to indicate the degree of flatness a man might experience during such a nap.

Maldynado glanced around, wondering why Basilard hadn't warned him of the foreman's approach. He had been dragged off to help fasten a winch cable to a beam.

"I am happy to declare that this vehicle seems to be free of booby traps," Maldynado announced.

"Is that so? You know, you're awfully suspicious. If I hadn't seen you jabbering with Savarsin yesterday... who *are* you, anyway?"

"I'm Maldynado, of course." Given that he was still disowned and that his family had been portrayed poorly in the newspapers that winter, he doubted sharing his surname would help him here, so he went with the addition, "Friend of emperors, presidents, and ladies everywhere."

"Friend of the president. Right."

"He's the one who gave me this job."

"If he gave you this job, you're not his friend. This is the job he gives to convicts." The foreman thrust a hand toward a knot of workers unloading a lorry. They weren't in shackles and Maldynado didn't see a guard, but they wore gray and red prison smocks, and more than one had a gang brand on the back of his hand. "To rehabilitate them." The foreman's smirk was anything but friendly. "Maybe he thought you needed rehabilitation."

"I..." Maldynado hardly thought that was the case—he had *asked* for employment, after all—but a witty riposte didn't come to his tongue.

The foreman gave him a shove and said, "Stop pissing around, and get back to work," before walking off again.

Maldynado rarely fantasized about causing evil things to happen to his enemies, but he did find himself wishing the foreman would end up being the one sabotaging the site and that Maldynado could escort him to the magistrate personally. Basilard returned before his mind traveled too far down this path.

Are you all right?

Maldynado was still on the ground, so he stood and brushed himself off. "Yes."

What's next?

"What's the matter, Bas? Not enjoying the work? I know you're a fancy diplomat now, but this isn't anything worse than we had to do for Sicarius."

The work doesn't bother me. As for the rest... I haven't had much of a chance to practice diplomacy on anyone yet, so I'm not sure how fancy I can be considered. The president saw me and wrote down my people's concerns, but I think he's too busy with local matters to worry about international relations right now.

Maldynado found himself gazing at the prisoners again. How long had they been working on the site? Might one of *them* be tempted to perform sabotage? Especially if they were being paid or bribed somehow by men in green robes?

"I may have an opportunity for you to practice diplomacy right now," Maldynado said.

Basilard followed his gaze. *I had hoped not to have to practice that sort of diplomacy any more. As you noted, my people are peaceful. They wish their representative to be peaceful as well.*

"Who said anything about not being peaceful? Just because they look brutish doesn't mean we can't have a friendly conversation with them. Maybe you can offer to cook them something."

A pee-soaked weed?

"I thought you didn't use those."

Not in most *people's dishes.*

"Basilard, if you tell me you've gotten Sicarius to eat something doused by a dog, I might just kiss you."

Basilard's cryptic smile wasn't a solid confirmation, so Maldynado held back on a physical display of affection. He was, however, grinning like a birthday boy in a whore house when he sauntered up to the prison crew. This caused them to glower with suspicion.

He tamed his smile and offered a congenial wave. "Afternoon, gentlemen. The foreman said for us to help you."

Most grunted and ignored him. One said, "That street licker."

"He's the one who ought to be in prison, eh?" Maldynado picked up the corner of a crate two men were struggling with. Basilard got into line to receive a bundle of rods from a prisoner pushing things out of the back of the lorry.

"That's the truth," the talkative man said. He had a beard divided into six intricate braids that extended to his belt. The sign of someone with a lot of time on his hands.

"We don't get paid enough to put up with him," Maldynado said, hoping to establish some common ground with the men by complaining about the boss. That was an age-old tradition for the working class, wasn't it?

Braids glared at him. "*We* don't get paid at all."

Oops, so much for common ground. Maldynado walked back to the lorry to help with another crate. He caught Basilard's eye, wondering if he had any ideas for diplomacy. Basilard tilted his chin toward the worker unloading the vehicle bed. He wore the same unappealing uniform as the others and had a nondescript face. Tattoos ran up the backs of his hands, disappearing beneath his sleeves, but that wasn't uncommon in the group. A cigar dangled from his lips.

Maldynado shrugged at Basilard, wondering what he was thinking. Basilard pursed his lips. At first, Maldynado read that as a kissing gesture, but he realized it was more of a blowing smoke motion. The cigar. Maldynado took another look.

"Say," Maldynado said to Braids—they had grabbed a second crate to carry together, "if you fellows don't get paid at all, how did the man in the lorry get that cigar? It's a Bridgecrester, isn't it? That's an expensive smoke."

"None of my business." Braids squinted at him. "None of *your* business, either."

Maldynado caught the man in the lorry bed eyeing him. He wondered if his hunches had led him to the right place, or if this was simply someone who engaged in prison yard bartering. For all he knew, the man had received the cigar in exchange for taking someone's shift out here. Of course, Bridgecrest cigars cost enough that none of the other workers here were likely to buy them, either.

"You boys been working here all week?" Maldynado asked.

"You talk a lot," a new man said, walking over to block Maldynado's return to the lorry. He possessed all of Maldynado's height and breadth, plus an extra fifty pounds of fat he could throw into a fray. Neither the man or his heft concerned Maldynado, but he took it as a sign that he had been prying. How did Amaranthe get so much out of people without them *knowing* she was getting it out of them?

"Yes, I do," he said. "Some find it endearing."

"We don't."

"Why don't you head back over there, buddy?" the first man asked, pointing toward the pallets of bricks.

Maldynado hated to leave before he had more thoroughly investigated these men, but maybe he would have to observe from afar. With eight of them around the truck, picking a fight wouldn't be wise—besides, the foreman would probably blame *him* for starting it.

Maldynado lifted his hands in surrender. "Whatever you say." He nodded toward Basilard, then turned away from the big fellow.

Gravel crunched behind him, the only warning he got. He spun back, throwing up an arm in a block. When he spotted a thick board swinging toward his face, he changed his mind, ducking instead of blocking. The board swished past overhead without knocking his hat off.

He lunged at his attacker before the man had finished the swing. Maldynado threw his weight into a punch to the kidney. He didn't hold back, striking with enough force to send the brute tumbling backward. Aware of all the other men, he didn't follow the man to finish him. He expected more attacks to come in from both sides—he wasn't disappointed. Fortunately, Basilard had thrown himself into the burgeoning fray.

Knowing his friend was on the right, Maldynado concentrated on the two prisoners coming in from the left. He darted to the outside and threw a series of preemptive punches at the closest man. His opponent wasn't fast, but he was sturdy—he took several hard blows without so much as tilting backward, then launched a meaty fist of his own. Maldynado grabbed the punch out of midair—it was slower than forming ice when compared to Sicarius's lightning strikes—and pulled on the brute, simultaneously jamming a knee into his stomach with enough force to knock a tree off its roots. This time the big prisoner went down.

A shadow at the corner of Maldynado's eyes warned him of a new attack from behind. He ran forward instead of ducking, throwing himself at a target in front of him. Something—a shovel?—clanked into the gravel behind him. His new opponent had been watching that attack, perhaps expecting it to brain Maldynado, and didn't react quickly to the fist sailing toward his face. He took Maldynado's blow in the nose and staggered backward, clutching at the spattered proboscis.

Maldynado spun in time to catch the shovel man preparing a second attack. The iron blade swept toward his head. Maldynado stepped in, caught the shaft, and launched a side kick at the man's gut. His attacker stumbled backward, releasing the shovel. Maldynado kept the tool, brandishing it in case anyone else wanted to brawl with him.

Four men lay rolling on the ground—or were flat-out unconscious—at Basilard's feet. Only one convict remained standing, Braids. He lifted his hands and stepped back, clearly wanting nothing more to do with either of them. Or with Basilard more specifically, for it was Basilard he was stumbling away from, eyes wide. Maldynado didn't think Bas looked any fiercer than usual—he wasn't dripping blood from his teeth or anything of that ilk—but his hat had come off, and the scars did give him some natural menace, whether he wanted it or not. Maldynado would have to work hard to get that lady to hold hands with him.

The downed men were crawling away, the conscious ones anyway, so Maldynado lowered his shovel.

Basilard's shoulders slumped. *The diplomacy failed. I wonder sometimes... perhaps the chief merely wanted me out of the country. I am not truly fit to be a diplomat.*

"*You* didn't talk to them. I did."

This is true.

"I'm the one who isn't fit to be a diplomat. No surprise there." Maldynado pointed at a crumpled and unmoving form below the lorry bed. "That's Cigar Breath, isn't it? Let's search him and see if he has anything more suspicious than tobacco."

Basilard helped him turn over the big prisoner. His eyes were rolled back into his head. Basilard *did* make a deadly fighter, but that didn't mean he couldn't be a good diplomat with some practice. Maybe he would learn to use his scars and his reputation to his advantage. Starcrest certainly did that.

Basilard patted the convict down, then shrugged up at Maldynado. *No pockets.*

"Where does he keep his cigars, then?"

Basilard surveyed the fallen man, shrugged again, then pointed at his crotch.

"In his smallclothes?" Maldynado asked. "I'm not poking around in there."

Perhaps he was counting on people's disinterest in doing so. Basilard tilted his head. *It seems... large.*

Maldynado was torn between sneering, looking away, and telling Basilard to search the man. "Why don't you, uh, check then?"

Me?

"You're the one down there. Looking at... him."

This is your mission.

"Just search him, Bas. He's going to wake up soon."

Basilard stood back, folding his arms across his chest.

"I take it back," Maldynado grumbled, kneeling beside the supine figure. "You're going to be a lousy diplomat. A real diplomat would look in a man's pants for another man."

Basilard shook his head once.

Sighing, Maldynado unfastened Cigar Breath's belt. Best to get unpleasant tasks over with quickly... and before anyone else witnessed them. He lifted the man's trousers and smallclothes, peered inside, and pulled out two sweat-stained cigars with the tips of his fingers. He wished he had tweezers and gloves.

"Way to ruin a luxury smoke, buddy," he muttered and peered into the dark recesses again. "Ah, what's that?"

*You of all people should kno*w, Basilard signed. The amusement had returned to his eyes. Bastard.

Maldynado pulled out a folded piece of paper, the outside even more sweat-stained than the cigar wrappers. Wishing again for tweezers, he pried the soggy edges apart to read the five words within.

Place and set before midnight.

Basilard, reading around his shoulder, signed, *Place and set what?*

"Something of Sarevic's, I'm guessing."

Is that in there too? Basilard waved to the man's trousers.

"No."

You're sure? You didn't root around much.

"I rooted around plenty, but you're welcome to go exploring if you like." Maldynado stuffed the note into his pocket. "Maybe he's supposed to pick up one of those timing switches and install it somewhere on the site."

Maybe it's in the lorry.

Maldynado eyed the crates in the bed. They had stamps on them from freight stops, but nothing else indicated what might be inside. Perfectly legitimate construction-related items for the most part, he guessed, but someone could have arranged for something to be tucked in among the cargo, and since their fellow had been the one unloading, he would have been in an easy spot to see such an item.

Better hurry, Basilard signed. *The foreman is coming.*

"Dead, bloody ancestors, does that man's job consist of anything more than prowling the site and harassing workers?" Maldynado pulled himself into the lorry bed. "Distract him for me, will you?"

Only after he was pawing through the remaining cargo did he realize how hard that would be for Basilard, given that the foreman wouldn't understand a word he signed. Explaining a bunch of unconscious and missing workers would be difficult under any circumstances, especially when the foreman already found Maldynado suspicious. He needed to find some condemning evidence to share.

Most of the crates were sealed with nails. Maldynado had a knife on him, but the prisoner hadn't had one or any type of tool for opening the lids. He shoved the sealed crates aside, searching for something else.

"What in that twice blasted pile of slag is going on over there?" came the foreman's voice. It wasn't nearly as far away as Maldynado would have liked.

He glanced back to see Basilard jogging toward the man, but knew his search time was about to be cut short. He shoved aside a last crate and was about to jump over the side and search inside the cab, but he spotted a blanket jammed in the corner beneath a wooden bench that could fold down for seating.

"What's wrong with you, man?" the foreman growled. "Say something. Who started this fight? Why are that man's pants down? Is he dead? Shovel Head!"

"Be right with you," Maldynado called without looking back.

He grabbed the blanket. There was something lumpy inside. He hoped it was some evidence that would keep him from being kicked off the site—or hauled away by enforcers—and not simply someone's lunch bucket. He tore the blanket free and held aloft... a ceramic jug.

Maldynado's shoulders drooped. Aside from some garish artwork, it looked like the sort of thing one might use to store milk. He tried to unscrew the lid, but found it secured tightly. It was made of the same ceramic as the rest of the jug. Maybe it hadn't been screwed on at all, but glued.

"That's a little odd," he murmured.

Something heavy thumped on the end of the lorry bed. The foreman had pulled himself up. Maldynado had never seen his face that shade of red. It was almost a purple really...

"What are you idiots doing?" he roared, stalking toward Maldynado with a fist cocked. "I've sent for the enforcers. You're more of a menace than the prisoners. Baskun said you started the fight!"

"Not true," Maldynado said. "They swung first. We merely ended it. And if you call the enforcers, you'll want to have that man directly below the lorry arrested, as he's part of a conspiracy to commit sabotage on this site." Maldynado managed to sound confident, though he wasn't certain his milk jug was quite the condemning evidence he had sought. Perhaps in conjunction with the note...

The foreman lifted his balled fists, his face growing angrier—and darker—rather than enlightened.

Basilard stood on the ground, his hand on the edge of the bed. He was ready to help, his posture said, though his shrug said he wasn't sure if they should be beating this man up. Probably not.

Maldynado stood to his full height and lifted his free hand. "Listen, if you want to squabble, we can do it down there, but I'm not sure it would be wise to break this jug." He thrust it out so the foreman couldn't miss seeing it. At the least, maybe it would make him curious.

"What the blast is it?" The foreman didn't sound curious precisely, but at least he wasn't flinging those fists around.

"I believe it's intended to sabotage more equipment. Or perhaps the building itself."

Basilard's eyebrows rose.

"Unless it's full of black powder, I don't see how." The foreman glowered suspiciously at Maldynado, no doubt wondering if this was meant as some diversion to keep him out of trouble.

"Why don't we see what's in it?" Maldynado set it down in the bed, keeping his eyes on the foreman as he did so. Given the fellow's mood, he might be ready to kick Maldynado in the teeth.

The foreman jammed his fists against his hips but didn't do anything more threatening. Maldynado pulled out his knife and stabbed experimentally at the lid. There ought to be a seal or something he could break...

Basilard knocked on the side of the lorry for attention. *That looks like a bull's eye*, he signed.

"What does?" Maldynado asked.

The side. Look at it from a distance.

Skeptically, Maldynado leaned back and eyed the swirling patterns painted on the jar. There was a big yellow dot on one side, but he would have called it modern art rather than a target.

"Is that some sort of language?" the foreman asked. "What's he saying?"

"Mangdorian hand code. He's a diplomat." Maldynado returned his attention to trying to cut or pry off the lid, though he was wondering how wise of an idea that was, now that someone had mentioned black powder. The jar was big enough that there could be a few blasting sticks crammed inside. Perhaps attached to one of those timers or to a booby-trapped lid that would cause an explosion when someone opened it. Basilard's suggestion that the outside had a bull's eye on it was double cause for concern.

The foreman shifted his weight from foot-to-foot, harrumphing under his breath. Maldynado leaned back again and held up the knife, hilt first. "I don't suppose you'd like to try opening it?"

The man started to reach for the knife, but stopped with his hand in the air and eyed the jug while working his cigar back and forth in his mouth. "Nah, you go ahead."

"Lucky me," Maldynado muttered. The edge of his knife had some brownish gunk on it. He sniffed it, but it didn't smell like much. He scraped at it with a fingernail. "Some kind of glue, I think."

"Get the rest off," the foreman said.

Oh sure, *now* he cared about what was inside.

More gently than before, Maldynado slipped the knife into the crease again. He worked it along the edge, digging out more glue. Finally, he was able to jostle the lid. Using the knife to pry it upward, he eased it open a few hairs. He found himself leaning back and holding his breath, waiting for an explosion.

Nothing happened. He opened the lid the rest of the way. It wasn't powder, but some sort of viscous liquid inside, filling the jar to the brim. The glue might not have smelled, but this did. The acrid scent seared the inside of his nostrils.

"Whatever it is, it's not milk," he said.

"Over there," someone said from a few meters away. He was pointing at Maldynado's lorry.

Four enforcers had walked onto the site, three men and Evrial. He didn't know whether to find her presence comforting or not. She might throw him in jail even quicker than the others if she suspected him of breaking the law—or of stupidity.

Maldynado offered her a tentative wave with the knife. That was when he noticed the blade smoking.

"Uhh."

Something silvery dripped off the tip to land on the bed. Weird. The goo in the jar was more amber than silver. Unless... oh. His knife wasn't smoking; it was melting. Disintegrating before his eyes.

"That's... alarming." Maldynado held it so none of the goo would drip onto his hand.

Basilard pointed at the blade. *It's the section that was in the jar. What's in there? Acid?*

"Acid," Maldynado repeated. "That must be it. Like that stuff Tikaya used on those cubes in the..." He stopped because Basilard was holding a finger to his lips. Right, secret stuff.

"Maldynado," came Yara's sigh from behind Basilard's shoulder. She stepped up to the edge of the bed. "Why was I so certain this call for enforcers would have something to do with you?"

"No idea. Did you come because you wanted to keep me out of jail? Or because you wanted to throw me in jail?"

"Well, if you had to be thrown in jail, I thought it should be by someone who cares."

"Thoughtful of you." Maldynado shifted his attention to the foreman. He was staring in fascination at the melting blade; at least he had lost some of his bluster—and some of the alarming prune coloring on his face. "What do you think we should do with this?"

The foreman removed his cigar. The thing wasn't even lit, though it had been chomped down to a nub. Maybe Maldynado could win some good will from the man by offering him the two Bridgecrests. No need to mention where they had been stored.

"What do *you* think we should do?" the foreman asked, swiveling to face Yara and the other enforcers.

Maldynado propped a fist on his hip. *He* had found the acid. Shouldn't *he* be consulted?

"Is that something from Sarevic's shop?" Evrial asked.

Maldynado forgot his indignation. He hadn't seen the craftsman's mark, but maybe so. "Could be."

"Let's take it back to the hotel and see if she can tell us more about it."

"It should go to enforcer headquarters where someone qualified can examine it," one of the enforcers said, a man who also wore sergeant's rank pins. Too bad. Evrial couldn't simply countermand him.

"The person who made it would be a more logical examiner," Evrial said. "She can tell us exactly what it is, and she's being held in a secured room in the president's hotel."

"The president's hotel?" the second enforcer mouthed.

Yes, that's right. Evrial knew people. Maldynado smiled and picked up the lid. "I'll just ready this for transport. Any stalwart young enforcers want to volunteer to carry it?" He wasn't sure what the goo would do to skin, but he didn't want to find out, either. He hoped the remaining glue would prove sticky enough to keep the lid affixed.

Wait. Basilard held up a hand. *If that's the item that was to be placed for something to happen at midnight... someone will be expecting it to be there then.*

"Good point," Maldynado said. "These prisoners go back to their little jail cells at the end of the day, don't they? So they couldn't have anything to do with whatever happens at midnight."

"Midnight?" the foreman asked. "What midnight?"

Maldynado dug out the note and passed it around. When it made it to Evrial, she asked, "Where did you find this?"

Basilard smirked.

Maldynado pointed downward, though he couldn't see the man on the ground from his position. "In that unconscious fellow's pocket."

Yara looked down. "What fellow?"

"Did he crawl off?" Maldynado frowned at Basilard. "You didn't stop him?"

Basilard signed, *He disappeared when I was obeying your command to distract the foreman.*

"Which didn't work particularly well. Too bad. I bet we could have gotten some answers just by questioning that man. Well, maybe. They probably didn't tell him much. Just paid him to do a job."

"There are missing prisoners?" The foreman scowled and jumped out of the truck. "These were all men who were getting out within two months. I was promised they wouldn't be flight risks." He raised his voice and shouted for two of his workers to round up the rest of the prisoners.

"Cigar Breath must have decided that whatever he agreed to do would get him some extra months if he was caught," Maldynado said, though the foreman wasn't listening to him anymore.

We should set a trap with the jar, Basilard signed, *then return at midnight and see what happens.*

"If it's full of acid, it's probably meant to eat away a bunch of those support beams." Evrial waved toward the burgeoning building structure.

"So we should set a trap with an *empty* jar," Maldynado said.

Basilard nodded.

Maldynado glanced at the overcast afternoon sky. "We have time. We can take it to Sarevic and have *her* remove the acid." The woman could also let them know what its capabilities were, aside from melting knives. "Then we can bring back the jar and set something up." He gently pushed the jug to the edge of the lorry bed and climbed down.

"Does this mean we're not arresting him?" The enforcer sergeant pointed at Maldynado's chest with his baton.

"Not today," Evrial said.

"Should I be concerned that he looks disappointed?" Maldynado muttered to Basilard.

Probably.

"The foreman's assistant was adamant about him being a troublemaker," the sergeant said.

"I didn't say he wasn't a troublemaker," Evrial said, "just that we're not arresting him."

"I love it when she defends me," Maldynado whispered to Basilard.

You are lucky to have such a loyal woman.

True. If he could just figure out how to keep her...

CHAPTER 17

THE DOOR TO THE INTELLIGENCE office was open with the sounds of voices floating out, so Tikaya hesitated by the jamb before entering.

"...million people. Some are in hospitals, injured from the fighting this winter. Others are—"

"They don't have to be moved overnight. The plant isn't growing *that* fast, and there are plenty of army vehicles available for transport. You can figure it out." That was Dak's voice. "Here are the routes. Communicate with the enforcers and get their help."

"The enforcers have been swamped dealing with the plant."

"Tell them to leave the plant alone. They can't be any help with it anyway. We have a big team of specialists on it. They'll take care of it. Now, go. Let's try to make this as orderly as possible."

Big team of specialists. Rias and Mahliki? Maybe he was counting Sespian too...

A pair of officers walked out of the room, glancing at Tikaya curiously. She nodded to them and strode in, as if she had been in the middle of doing so all along.

Dozens of desks formed rows in the large room—it had been a gaming hall before being requisitioned for this purpose, and dartboards and tile tables had been stacked against the far wall. Several heads were bent over those desks, scribbling notes and pushing around paperwork, but Tikaya didn't see Dak. He must be there. She had been listening to him ten seconds ago.

"Help you, my lady?" a lieutenant at the closest desk asked. Most of the men lifted their heads to regard her.

Her determination to simply announce that she would be whisking through the office on a whirlwind, grabbing papers and rummaging through files at her pleasure, faded in the face of all the young soldiers.

She anticipated opposition. Best to start at the top and see if she could get permission before seeing how far her husband's influence would get her in a room of military officers.

"Is Colonel Starcrest still here?" Tikaya asked.

The lieutenant pointed to an open door at the side of the room. "In his office, my lady."

"Thank you."

Tikaya peeked through the door before knocking. Lanterns burned in the windowless room, but it still had a dim, drab feel, reminding her more of a cage than an office, even though wooden filing cabinets lined the wall and towering stacks of papers perched precariously at the corners of the large desk in the center. A few safes rested against the far wall, the steel doors all shut. Dak sat in a wooden chair that didn't look much more comfortable than a stump in the forest. His elbows were propped on the papers carpeting the center of the desk, and his hands cradled his forehead. He was either asleep or wanted to be.

"Come in, Lady Starcrest," Dak said without lifting his head.

More stacks of papers occupied the floor, and Tikaya had to follow a meandering alley to reach the clearing in front of the desk. She sat on the edge of a seat identical to Dak's and confirmed its lack of cushioning.

"I would like access to your files," she said. Perhaps she should have started by attempting to console him or at least with some friendly chitchat, but he was still on her suspect list, and she felt uneasy simply being in there.

"Which files?" He lifted his head with a wince. Ah, headache. Though Turgonians were trained to expect death and torture in the field, they seemed as susceptible to the small annoyances in life as the next person.

"All of them."

Dak stared at her for a long silent moment, long enough for Tikaya to wonder if he had something to hide somewhere in these cabinets or in the numerous others in the larger room.

"Rias sent you?" Dak finally asked.

A lie? Or the truth? If she lied, it would be discovered soon. He and Rias talked several times a day.

"Rias doesn't know I'm here." Tikaya lifted her chin. "I intend to find that which has eluded yo—all of your men." It might not be tactful to

301

suggest *he* had missed something important. "The names and whereabouts of those who are trying to kill my husband."

Dak's face revealed little. She might have read that headache, but she couldn't tell what else he might be thinking. Was he offended? Did he think her arrogant? Delusional? Maybe she was some of the latter. She didn't truly know if she could find the answers she sought, but she had to try.

"Lady Starcrest," he finally said, "you are... Rias's wife, of course, and not, as far as I'm aware, considered suspect in any matter regarding imperial—national security, but at the same time, you *are* a Kyattese citizen, not a Turgonian subject—citizen. Dear ancestors, I'm tired." Dak waved away the words of habit. "Forgive my dullness, please. My point is that while many of these files have grown obsolete of late, there are still national security issues that we would not care for any other governments to be apprised of, including the Kyattese government."

Though Tikaya had realized his objection right away, it took her a moment to formulate a response. Here she was suspecting *him* of being a threat to national security, and he was making the argument that *she* couldn't be trusted here? Maybe that was simply an excuse to keep her from prying.

"Colonel Starcrest," she said—though she had been thinking of him by first name since Rias introduced him thusly, she felt the utmost professionalism should be used in this meeting. "I suspect I already know all the secrets out there between your government and mine. Much was revealed twenty years ago, and Rias and I were the ones to dig up that history. But if it will make you more comfortable, I will swear not to reveal anything I stumble across to anyone except you or my husband."

"You, as a Kyattese citizen, would be comfortable taking that oath?" Dak's eyes had narrowed, and she sensed some judgment in there.

She leaned back in the hard chair. Blighted banyan sprites, what *was* in those files? Something about Kyatt that she would feel compelled to report about if she knew? "Do you know what I'm talking about from twenty years ago?" she asked. Maybe she hadn't been clear enough, or maybe he had no idea about those events.

"In regard to the truth about the colonization of the Kyatt Islands? Yes, I received one of Rias's letters."

"Oh." Tikaya had never asked who had been the recipients of the three copies of the letter that her president had authorized Rias to send. "I hadn't realized, er..."

Dak's lips twisted. Wryly? Bitterly? "That he trusted a twenty-year-old student that much? I think he just wanted someone young enough that the odds were he would still be alive when the letters were to be opened. Though with my combat record—" he pointed to his missing eye, "—that might not have been a good bet." He shrugged, then waved away the past. "My mother would have opened the letter if not me."

Tikaya didn't know how to respond to his bitterness—or the revelation that there might be deeper, darker secrets that Turgonians were withholding from her government and from the rest of the world. For all that Rias loved her and trusted her with his life, he hadn't told her every detail from his military career, nor had she asked. And who knew what the Turgonians had been up to in the last twenty years?

"Colonel, I'm not looking to dig up old secrets from a government that doesn't exist any more. I'm only concerned about the last three months. Those are the only files I need to see."

"Very good men have been analyzing those files all along," Dak said. "If there was something to find in them, it would have been found."

"I know that you and your officers are intelligent and wouldn't be employed in this branch of the military if you weren't, but I've spent my entire life deciphering logic puzzles and teasing out clues from crevices that others walk past without noticing. If you care about your uncle, why would you turn down a resource that might possibly make a difference?" Tikaya stared into his single eye, silently imploring him to accept her argument. It was a logical one. He must see that. Unless he had more to hide than old state secrets. That eye... it held mulish stubbornness. "Besides," she added, trying a lighter tone. "If Rias gets killed and someone else steps into office, you might find yourself unemployed."

Dak snorted. "Blast, woman, if someone could guarantee that, I'd strangle him myself."

This blunt statement—and horrifying image—startled her so much that all she could do was gape.

Dak shook his head, more in exasperation than apology. "Don't they have jokes on that tropical island of yours?"

"Not... about killing people."

"Sounds like a repressed place to live."

Tikaya was debating whether to point out all the ways Turgonians were far more repressed than her people when Dak stood up and walked around the desk. She stood as well, eyeing him warily. Though he hadn't been anything but civil with her—poor jokes aside—she remembered that he had enough fighting acumen to knock Rias across a gymnasium floor. Though the uniform hid his muscled form from sight, she wouldn't forget that it was there.

But he walked past her, heading for the door. Tikaya frowned after him. He wasn't going to leave, was he? Ignore her and hope she went away? Well, she had no intention of doing so. She would sit in his office until he returned, and maybe she would start browsing through those filing cabinets as well.

"Captain Banovitch," Dak called out the door. "See me."

Scarcely a second passed before a slim bespectacled man popped into the doorway, his uniform pressed, his short brown hair neat, and his face as earnest as a puppy dog. "Yes, sir?"

"Lady Starcrest has requested to see all of the files we've gathered since the president's inauguration."

Tikaya hadn't realized how tight her chest had grown until a lightness spread out from her heart. She hadn't learned anything yet, and Rias might yet be poisoned, but she had won the right to search for answers.

"Yes, sir. Uhm..." The captain glanced at Tikaya. "*All* of them, sir?"

"All of them."

"Er, yes, sir. Where shall we put them?"

"She can have my office for as long as she wishes."

"I... yes, sir." The captain lifted a folder with a three-inch-thick stack of papers in it. "Lieutenant Dodgecrest delivered these."

Dak accepted the folder. "Excellent, thank you."

"I'll just... go get some help for those files."

The captain surveyed the room before leaving. Looking for empty places for stacks of files? Tikaya was beginning to fear she had volunteered for an impossible task.

Dak walked up to her and held out the folder. "Want the first look? Lieutenant Dodgecrest was the night duty officer."

Tikaya opened the folder to the first sheet of paper and found a hastily penned page full of ink, about one in three words legible. From what she could make out, it was some soldier's report of what he had and hadn't seen from a spy position in the city. She flipped through a few more pages and found more reports filled out by other hands, some more legible than others. All thorough.

"This is all from last night?" she asked. There had to be more than two hundred pages.

Dak's eye glinted, not maliciously exactly, but close. "Yes."

Tikaya refused to look daunted, though her mind quickly did the calculation of ninety days times two hundred pages times two shifts a day, not to mention whatever else the office had gathered independent of its various spies and independent contractors. She couldn't quite refrain from a prim, "You know, Colonel, you're not as nice a man as your uncle is."

His dark humor faded, and she almost regretted her comment, for the weariness that replaced it gave him an air of defeat.

"No," Dak said, "I'm not."

Tikaya thought he might explain himself, justify his edge somehow, but he didn't. He picked up a pen and scribbled a few names on the top of the folder.

"Those are the men in hot spots who are most likely to have reported something useful. If you want to delegate some of your research, Darkcrest and Moorivich have quick minds and sharp eyes. They're out there." He waved toward the office. "I need to go outside and check in with the men watching that plant. I hear the cursed thing is snatching up people openly now. Why these idiots keep wandering close..." He growled something more under his breath and headed for the door. But he paused with his hand on the jamb and looked back. "Lady Starcrest, if you do find the answers that have eluded us, I'll have to resign my position in shame, but I shall hope that luck and your intellect favor you."

It was the first thing she could recall him saying without that rancorous edge to his tone. He was gone before she could thank him.

Tikaya sat down again, this time in Dak's chair, and laid the folder on the desk. She eyed the stacks of papers towering all around her and wondered how many days of reports they represented. One careless bump with an elbow, and a pile would topple to the floor.

Resolving to be careful with her limbs, she set to reading. The young captain and two enlisted men he had recruited made several trips into the office—with handcarts. She supposed she should start at the beginning but decided to continue with the latest night's work in hopes that it would hold new surprises. Oh, but what about that man who had died of poison? Could she find that report in the mess?

She stepped away from the desk and poked at the stacks of folders the captain had brought in. Dates were stamped on the fronts. Good. It had only been a couple of days ago, so it ought to be... yes, there. She found the folder for that date, then sifted through the reports, finally locating notes from the doctor. She skimmed through a description of the symptoms of death and then the details of an autopsy that sounded crude to her Kyattese ear. Mahliki's rant about the scientists in Turgonia not knowing what a cell was came to mind. By the time Tikaya reached the end, the verdict of death by "unknown poison" wasn't surprising. Someone had managed to identify the bomber and confirm that he was a local citizen with no known ties to Nuria. That was the most enlightening thing in the report, and it wasn't very enlightening.

Tikaya sighed. Her first dead end. She returned to the desk.

She had gone through a week's worth of reports when a diffident knock came at the door. "My lady?"

Tikaya had taken her spectacles off to squint at some of the fine print, and she donned them again. "Yes, Captain?"

"A woman wishes to see you. Amaranthe Lokdon."

"That's fine. Send her in."

"She's not cleared to enter this office, my lady."

"Oh. Am *I* cleared to be in this office?"

"You are now, my lady."

"Because the colonel said so?"

"Yes, my lady."

"You didn't stop me at the door before," she pointed out.

"No, my lady. You're the president's wife."

Tikaya gave up trying to wrap her mind around whatever logic motivated these military men. "I'll go see her in the hallway then, will that do?"

The captain smiled, perhaps pleased she hadn't asked him to break some rule. "Yes, my lady."

Tikaya's butt was already numb from sitting in the hard chair, so she didn't mind the break. She found Amaranthe in the hallway, shifting from foot to foot.

"Incense," she blurted before Tikaya could offer a greeting. "Was it a part of that old religion?"

"Yes, they burned sticks during their ceremonies, if I recall correctly."

"Lemongrass scent?" Amaranthe asked. "I know lemongrass isn't native to this area, but I wondered if they might have traded for it. The old spice road led from the south up into the lake areas, didn't it?"

"Yes, but that religion actually originated down near the Gulf and extended outward from there over a few centuries. Lemongrass grows wild down there."

"Excellent. Thank you." Amaranthe started to turn away but caught herself. "One more thing." She lowered her voice. "Is Colonel Starcrest working in there?"

"No, he left the building. Any particular reason?"

"We're following a new lead. We're going to be... performing an unauthorized search for incense on the third floor."

"In people's rooms?" Tikaya guessed.

"Possibly." Amaranthe's eyes crinkled.

"I believe I'll pretend I didn't hear that."

"Most wise." Amaranthe lifted a parting hand, then jogged for the stairs.

After she disappeared, Tikaya wondered if she should have had Amaranthe snoop into Dak's room while she and Sicarius were at the task. And Serpitivich's too. Cursed banyan sprites, someone ought to be searching all of the rooms in the hotel for proof of... snitchery.

Well, maybe the incense thread would turn something up. In the meantime, Tikaya squared her shoulders and headed back into paperwork miasma.

Sicarius followed his nose through the third-floor hallway. Though he remembered the area where he had smelled the incense before, he hadn't stopped to locate the room the scent came from at the time. Now, it wasn't being burned, and the trace odors had faded. He paused at the doors to take delicate sniffs and to listen as well. He might chance across some meeting in progress and not need olfactory proof to find the culprit.

Most of the non-essential staff and guests were being cleared from the hotel, and he detected the sounds of drawers closing and trunk lids thumping behind more than one door. He paused near the end of the hall, thinking he caught a faint hint of lemongrass. No sounds came from behind this door. He tested the knob. Locked.

As he withdrew his picks, the tread of light footsteps on the stairs at the other end of the hall alerted him to a visitor. He thought the gait familiar and nodded a silent greeting when Amaranthe walked into view.

"Lemongrass incense and the Kriskrusian religion," she said, "that's an affirmative."

Sicarius nodded and slid his picks into the lock. "I believe the scent originates with this room."

"Good, maybe we're about to find our snitch."

Soon, the lock clicked. Sicarius pushed open the door, then paused to analyze the room and scan it for traps, insomuch as he could by the light seeping in from the hallway. There weren't any lamps burning inside, and the shadows lay thick.

"This is the source of the scent," he confirmed.

"Oh?" Amaranthe leaned around his arm, peering inside.

Sicarius held out his arm to block her, for there was another odor inside, one he recognized well. Death. He stepped into the room first, igniting one of the lamps on the wall. It flared to life, revealing a man's body on the floor. The hood on his green robe had fallen away, leaving the red line across his neck visible.

"Garrote," Sicarius said, "from behind."

"I... see," Amaranthe murmured. She had seen enough death not to be horrified by it, though she never failed to look grim and regretful at its appearance. She picked up a pewter incense burner from a small table beside the door. It was engraved with crude images of animalistic creatures. The edges had been worn over the years—perhaps over the centuries. "I don't think this fellow is going to be able to give us answers or take us to his leader, but this could be our snitch. Let's see if we can figure out what he does for his day job." She headed for the armoire.

Sicarius knelt to remove the robe and search the body. He lifted the man's hand and checked his fingernails. "No skin," he observed.

"Pardon?" Amaranthe opened one of the armoire doors. Several military uniforms dangled from hangers.

"Whoever killed him was good enough that he wasn't able to claw at his attacker. Rigor mortis hasn't set in yet, either. This didn't happen long ago." Sicarius considered the height of the man and how the garrote had cut into his throat. "Someone taller than him as well." He thought of the Nurian mage hunter, but she was no more than five-foot-nine. "Unless the attacker stood on the bed or a chair." A possibility, as it would give a smaller person further leverage.

Amaranthe walked over to the window. "It's locked from inside, so nobody came in that way."

"Nobody went *out* that way," Sicarius corrected, then turned toward the hallway, for he heard footfalls on the carpeting near the stairs. He thought about jogging over and closing the door to ensure privacy, but their search was sanctioned—somewhat—since Professor Komitopis had asked them to investigate on Starcrest's behalf. This death would have to be reported soon, regardless.

"Good point." Amaranthe returned to the armoire. Busy scrutinizing the uniforms, she didn't notice the approaching footsteps. They were slowing. Two sets. Perhaps the people would go into a room before reaching this one. "Rank pins for a sergeant," Amaranthe said. "The name patch says—"

"Avigart," a voice said from the hallway at the same time as a tall figure stepped into the doorway, a key ring in his hand. Colonel Starcrest's face grew closed as he took in the dead man, Sicarius, and Amaranthe.

A lieutenant leaned into the doorway to peer inside as well. He wore the same uniform and patches as the colonel, though he didn't mask his features so well. His mouth fell open for a long moment before he snapped it shut. "I guess I won't need his room key, sir."

Amaranthe lowered her hands from the uniforms and gave the lieutenant a curious look.

Sicarius wouldn't have expected the officer to answer questions—or looks of inquiry—especially since Sicarius and Amaranthe might well be suspects in the murder until they explained themselves sufficiently, but the lieutenant said, "He didn't show up for his shift."

Colonel Starcrest walked into the room, his gaze flicking about, taking in details—it lingered on the incense burner for a moment. After a moment, he sat on the bed, his elbows on his knees, and sighed down at the corpse. "What did you get yourself involved with, Sergeant?"

"We thought he might be the snitch," Amaranthe said. "He's from your office, isn't he, Colonel?"

"What are you people doing in here?" the lieutenant asked, frowning not at Amaranthe but at Sicarius.

"Ms. Sarevic smelled lemongrass incense on the clothes of one of the robed men who tied her up," Amaranthe said. "Sicarius remembered smelling that same odor in these hallways." She pointed at the incense burner, a line of gray ash still nestled in its collection tray.

Though the lieutenant continued to glower at him, Sicarius stood with his hands clasped behind his back, saying nothing. He would let Amaranthe deal with the officers, for her words were more likely to assuage their suspicions. He gazed out the window where evening had fallen, eyeing the vines snaking out of the storm drains and sewer access holes, their tendrils streaking across the yard. Soldiers pressed into plant-slaying duty ran back and forth, doing their best to slow its growth. Brazen of an assassin to enter the hotel with all those people around and to kill this man during daylight hours.

Unless the assassin had come from within. Could there be more than one spy?

The colonel rubbed the back of his neck. "My room is two doors down. I smelled that stuff burning a couple of nights ago. I was in a hurry, between one meeting and the next, and didn't think anything of it." His mouth twisted in some inward censure.

"Is it likely this man could have been the snitch?" Amaranthe asked the officers.

"There's a snitch?" The lieutenant blinked. "Am I not... in the Tiles game?"

"Yes," Colonel Starcrest said, "it's been implied that information is coming out of our department. Though *I* don't seem to be in the Tiles game, either."

"We only know about things because we stumbled across some notes." Amaranthe offered a self-effacing smile and shrug designed to make the men less bitter and more comfortable. It seemed to work on the lieutenant, but the colonel's face only grew harder.

Sicarius thought about bringing up the flaws of the intelligence office spies, but that was not likely to endear the officers to them, either.

"I don't know all the details," Amaranthe said, "but among other things, someone told that Nurian mage hunter when Sicarius and I—and the submarine—were due into port. We had only spoken to the president and his wife, through the magical communication device."

The lieutenant blinked again, then he made a reflexive gesture, two fingers to the heart, to ward against "evil magics" as the backcountry folk said.

"Interesting," the colonel said. "Avigart didn't know about that."

"I didn't know about it, either," the lieutenant said.

Amaranthe gazed into the colonel's eyes. "Did *you* know about it, sir?"

Sicarius watched him as well. Though he suspected an intelligence officer as highly ranked as Starcrest would have practice in masking his features when answering questions, one never knew what might slip out to be revealed on the face.

"Yes," the colonel said, the twist to his lips wry this time.

He knew he was a suspect.

"I was there when Rias gave the order to have a slip prepared to the north of the plant. The vice president was there too. Also one of Rias's aides, Devencrow, and my men, Wrencrest and Merkoft." Colonel Starcrest scowled and stood up. "You could have had a much shorter list of people to investigate if you had simply asked me. Or Rias, for that matter. Ancestors' sake, is nobody including *him* in the Tiles game?"

"Professor Komitopis showed him the note we found, though she had to decrypt it first," Amaranthe said. "We're not the official investigators, either. The professor just asked us—asked Sicarius—" she waved to him, "—to find out if the president had truly been poisoned and to find out who is responsible."

And to find a cure. If President Starcrest had been poisoned, and there was a cure, Sicarius *would* find it.

"What *other* information has been leaked?" the colonel asked.

"There was a map of the hotel and details on security personnel and shift changes," Amaranthe said.

The colonel stood up and turned his back to them for a moment. His right hand curled into a tight fist. He took a deep breath, forcing his fingers to relax.

Amaranthe met Sicarius's eyes and she signed a few quick words. *He's hotter than molten ore about getting this information from someone who isn't on the payroll and hasn't sworn any oaths to anyone.*

Sicarius nodded once, understanding that perfectly. If the man had been made chief of intelligence, he must have assumed his uncle trusted him fully.

Should I be telling him all this?

I assumed you were trying to win him to your side.

Amaranthe's expression grew wry, but the colonel turned back before she could sign anything else. Just as well. His lieutenant had noticed the last flurry of hand signals.

"All right," Colonel Starcrest said. "That information would have come out of our office so Serpitivich might not have anything to do with this, though I'll keep an eye on him. The security shifts could have come from anyone on my staff. Maybe Avigart. He was a good man, though. I don't see him volunteering to betray the president. Maybe his death was designed to divert us from the true snitch. Or maybe he stumbled onto something and got caught, making this a frame. He also could have been blackmailed into doing something he didn't want to do. He has children..." The colonel winced again. "I'll have to inform his wife about this. Blast, Avigart. What were you thinking?"

The dead man did not answer.

Colonel Starcrest mumbled to himself, then headed for the door. "Everyone out of here. I'll have a team go over it. Lieutenant, find Wrencrest and Merkoft and hold them for questioning. Put a man on the vice president too. And his aides as well. Especially that smarmy one. Cursed civilians."

The two officers walked into the hallway.

Amaranthe signed, *Are you done?* to Sicarius.

Sicarius hesitated. He would have liked to search further and see if he could find evidence that might identify the murderer, but Colonel Starcrest stopped in the hallway, looking back at them. They were not, it seemed, to be allowed to continue investigating independently, not this room anyway.

Sicarius walked out, and Amaranthe followed him. The colonel closed the door and locked it.

"I trust this will remain locked until my investigation team makes it up here," the colonel said, eyeing them both. "I understand that you're... friends of the family, but as far as I'm concerned, you're unknown and uncontrollable elements that don't seem to answer to anyone. I haven't that luxury, and I must go forward by the book."

"We understand, sir," Amaranthe said.

Looking no happier than when he had walked in on the dead body, the colonel led his man off down the hall.

"It would not take long to pick the lock again," Sicarius said.

"And get caught snooping again?"

"I heard them coming; I could have avoided being caught."

Amaranthe snorted but didn't argue with the statement. "You could have told *me* they were coming. At least I was just looking at the uniforms and wasn't caught rummaging in his underwear drawer."

"I can more thoroughly examine the room, then station myself somewhere to overhear the comments made during the soldiers' investigation," Sicarius said.

"It sounds like you'd like to continue snooping around without me."

"I can also search the hotel for the murderer. He or she may still be on the premises."

"It *definitely* sounds like you wish to snoop without me." Amaranthe sighed at him. "I suppose this is what I get for taking up with an unknown and uncontrollable element."

Sicarius recognized her teasing for what it was and didn't respond.

"Well, then, I'll just go off and question someone I've been meaning to talk to since we returned. If past encounters are anything to go by, he'll be more open with me without you looming over his shoulder."

"Who will you see?" Sicarius asked, though he suspected he already knew.

"If anyone knows something about these priests that the intelligence office doesn't, it would be the journalists running the newspaper."

"Mancrest," Sicarius said, his tone going flat of its own accord.

"Yes, do you have any messages you'd like me to convey for you?" Amaranthe smiled brightly.

Sicarius glared.

"Yes, that's the one I expected. I'll let him know."

As she waved and walked away, Sicarius reminded himself that searching the room and finding the assassin were priorities. He trusted Amaranthe and trusted that she could handle Deret Mancrest if he tried anything untoward—which, he admitted, was unlikely these days—so there was absolutely no reason to follow Amaranthe and spy on her conversation with the newspaper man. To even contemplate it was illogical.

While removing his lock-picking kit again, Sicarius wondered why it irked him that he couldn't justify that spying.

CHAPTER 18

S ESPIAN TRIED TO IGNORE THE hacking and sawing—and the occasional blasting—that came from beyond the grimy windows of the old warehouse. It was hard with the green stalks wavering in the breeze outside those windows. Further, the floorboards creaked constantly, and tendrils sometimes burst up through seams or knotholes. It wasn't a great place to design a generator. It wasn't even a great place to ensure the continuation of one's life. Judging from the strained shouts of the soldiers outside, they would be pleased to leave at any moment.

But the sleek black form of President Starcrest's submarine lay in the center of the warehouse where the tugboat had delivered it. An engineering team under the command of a Major Rydoth was swarming inside and out, cleaning and repairing the damage from the blasting stick as well as the underwater immersion. The craft was too large to put on the back of a lorry for transport, so they had to work on it where it rested. At the time of delivery, the plant hadn't stretched this far south, but it was expanding its reach with every hour. Sespian couldn't help but think of Starcrest's comments on exponential growth.

A few clangs from a corner of the warehouse reminded everyone of the presence of the president. Starcrest walked over to the submarine to make comments to his engineers now and then, but his main focus was the table full of copper wires, magnets, batteries, and other bits of metal Sespian couldn't identify. Some of the things he *could* identify mystified him, such as the tub of tallow and the distilling equipment. And he had *no* idea why Mahliki was over there pulping severed bits of the plant in that grinder. Father and daughter had been working non-stop since setting up in the warehouse, each going about their tasks with nothing more than the occasional grunt to the other, and each ignoring the rest of the world. Sespian was glad his only job was to make the finished generator fit into the submarine, though even that seemed daunting, given the size of furnaces and boilers, not to mention that room would be required for carrying sufficient fuel. Sespian hated to bother the president, but he would need dimensions before he could plan further.

Leaving the drafting table someone had brought for him, he headed toward the cluttered table with a pen and pad of paper. One of his aides jogged through the door, passed Sespian, and veered for Starcrest first.

"Lord President?" the man said. "The vice president sent me to inform you that there's been a report of an incursion along the Kendorian border. It seems someone has heard of our distraction here in the capital and is attacking outposts."

Starcrest didn't put down his tools or do more than glance at the aide. "Give me the details."

"Can I help you, Sespian?" Mahliki asked, her voice strained.

She was still grinding away at the severed pieces of plants, turning them into a mushy green liquid inside a glass container. Judging by the way she had to throw her body weight into turning the crank, it wasn't an easy task.

"I came to get some dimensions," Sespian said quietly, not wanting to interrupt the president's conversation. He pointed his pen toward her straining arms—her sleeves were rolled up to her elbows and green splatters smudged her tan skin. "Can I help *you*? Do you want a break?"

Mahliki paused, shook out her arms, and eyed the contents of the jar. "Maybe for a bit. Not surprisingly, this is a lot harder than it would be for any other plant. Those blades came from a store that makes saws. The proprietor promised me I could stick a tree in this thing and grind it down." She shoved a few more cut vines into the feeder channel.

"Why are you grinding down the plant?" Sespian grasped the lever with both hands and promptly saw what she meant. It moved, but not without significant effort. "And is it... safe to do so?" He nodded at her spattered arms. "Those little bits won't grow into new plants, will they?"

Mahliki frowned at her skin. "I certainly hope not. I'll wash off if I feel anything trying to take root."

Sespian shuddered at the image of plants growing out of human flesh.

"As for the rest, we're making vegetable oil. Or alien plant oil. I haven't come up with a fancy name yet. I'm not sure if I'll be able to grind down enough to be useful, but Father grinned at the idea of using the plant against itself, and preliminary studies were extremely promising, so

I'm trying. There's tallow for whatever else we need. We're not planning any long voyages here—oxygen would be a problem for anything other than a short trip underwater—so we shouldn't need much."

Sespian kept nodding as she was talking, because he didn't want her to think him dull, but he felt more mystified than before she had begun. "The vegetable oil is going to... fuel the submarine?"

"The methyl esters are. We have to separate the glycerin out, though I won't be in a hurry to get rid of that, not after I saw how effective slime can be for escaping a graspy plant—" Mahliki wriggled her eyebrows. "Father said this would be a lot easier with petroleum, but nobody's locating and refining it in any serious manner yet, and given our time situation, we had to use what was easily available. Finding a Maker in the city would have made this all *much* easier, but even then, it would have taken someone days to create a power source like the one we had. Besides, my studies suggest this plant is going to create a fuel with a higher energy potential than wood or even coal."

Sespian had a vague notion that glycerin could be used to make soap, but the rest went over his head. He ought to take some science courses at the university, assuming the university was still around once this plant was done mauling the city.

"Good," he said, reluctant to ask more questions and make his ignorance obvious. He would ask Starcrest later. Odd, but it seemed more acceptable to appear young and ignorant in front of the president than in front of his daughter. Maybe because she was younger than Sespian. Shouldn't he know more, not less? "Do you know how big the finished generator will be? And, uhm, will steam still be involved in powering it or is this—" he tilted his head toward the green goop, "—going to eliminate that step?"

"Steam will still power the generator. Everything will simply be more compact because we won't need—"

A crack came from the floor, and boards beneath Sespian's feet bulged. He scrambled back. He had seen the plant grow up in other spots, only to be driven back by swords and small explosives, but it hadn't thrust up with such force, not since he had been there.

Nails shrieked and burst from their wooden homes as the first green tendril shot up through a seam, spilling dirt around it. While his instinct was to back away from the bulge, Mahliki ran forward. She knelt, a dagger in hand, and cut at the intruding vine.

"That's not going to do—" Sespian stopped himself. That was a very *familiar* dagger.

The black blade sliced through the emerging tendril, cutting it off at the base. The plant continued to grow though, shoving upward as if its life depended on it.

"Stay down, you stupid thing," Mahliki growled, cutting it off at the base again. The two severed tendrils bucked and writhed like living beasts.

Sespian grabbed them and stuffed them into the top of the grinding machine. Even in the short seconds he was in contact with them, one tried to curl around his wrist. He tore it free before it could firm up that grip and grabbed a crowbar—the closest thing on the table. Using it, he jammed the tendrils down into the chute, then dropped the tool and leaned into the grinding lever.

Mahliki had already cut another length of vine, and two more cracks sounded on the other side of the table.

"They seem to be coordinating an attack," Sespian said, grinding faster. "Does anyone else find that disconcerting?"

"Yes." President Starcrest stepped into view, holding something that reminded Sespian of a branding iron with two prongs on the end. Wires stuck out of it, running up his arm to a bulky metal contraption hefted over his shoulder. He walked behind the table and flicked a switch on the big device. Arcs of blue sparked in the air between the iron tips of the forked end.

"They can't know what we're doing up here, can they?" Mahliki was alternating between hacking at the plant and hunting around for something to block the hole.

Sespian left the grinding station—halting the incursion was more important than cutting up the pieces—and jogged toward a heavy crate against a wall. He didn't know if it would do anything to stop something that could push up through nailed floorboards, but he dragged it over, nonetheless.

"You wouldn't think so," Starcrest said, "but I wouldn't rule anything out, not with this plant's origins." He stopped in front of a second tendril that had pushed up through a knothole and snaked up to waist height in a matter of seconds.

This was the fastest yet that Sespian had seen the plant grow. He shoved the crate on top of the portion vexing Mahliki. One corner immediately started rising.

"That was helpful," Sespian grumbled to himself. The air tingled, and the hairs on his neck rose, as if someone were using magic nearby. "What the—"

Tzzzt-zipt.

"Hah," Starcrest said in the aftermath of the strange noise.

"Did it work?" Mahliki lunged to her feet. "Did you burn it?"

"Yes, though it takes a prolonged application at this voltage. It's not as effective as a bolt of lightning."

Sespian leaned across the table for a look. The tendril that had burst through the knothole had collapsed into a blackened strand. Smoke wafted from the shriveled carcass.

"It works," Sespian said. "That's brilliant."

"It works on a small scale," Starcrest said grimly, not showing any signs of the exuberance Sespian felt. He simply walked to the next vine, which had thrust a floorboard aside to enter the warehouse.

"But that's a start, isn't it?" Sespian asked. "It can be scaled up, or we can make packs like that to give to the enforcers, right?"

Starcrest prodded the vine with the forked tip of his tool and flicked the switch again. The streaks of blue electricity vibrated between the metal prongs. He touched them to the plant, and it jerked away, almost like an animal feeling pain. He pinned it to the floor, and the tiny streaks of lightning seared its flesh, blackening it as it had the first.

"It's a start," Starcrest agreed. "But to make enough of these to slay the plant faster than it can grow in the time we have—"

Glass shattered, cutting off his words. A dark shape burst through the window nearest to him. Starcrest leaped back, but not fast enough. A tendril the thickness of a man's thigh darted through the broken window like a tiger leaping after its prey. It wrapped around Starcrest's waist, lifting him off his feet.

"Father!" Mahliki screamed.

Sespian grabbed the dagger from her hand and leaped over the table. Somehow Starcrest had kept his grip on the electricity generator and, even as he was being dragged to the window, his feet dangling in the air, jabbed the prod against the huge green limb. Sespian landed by the window, slashing downward with the dagger. The weapon cut into the plant's fibrous flesh, but even the alien blade couldn't fully slice through, not in one blow. The thick vine pulled away before he could cut into it for a second time, hauling Starcrest past Sespian and to the window.

The stench of burning vegetation filled the air, but the plant continued to pull on its prey. Starcrest managed to brace his legs on either side of the window frame. Sespian ran to the wall and cut down again, trying to find room to saw through the impossibly thick vine. Noxious smoke filled his nostrils and stung his eyes. He kept cutting. Starcrest kept the prod pressed against the plant flesh.

"Over there," Mahliki barked to soldiers who had heard the fray and run inside. "Not everybody. Just people who can—you with the blasting stick. Light it and throw it through the window. Kill that plant at its base."

Sespian was too busy sawing at the vine—it would be easier to saw down a redwood tree—to check to see if the soldiers were obeying her. At the least, nobody dared push Starcrest's daughter to the side.

"Almost got it," Sespian yelled, hoping to keep anyone from doing anything drastic.

Starcrest was holding his position, one boot on either side of the window frame, though wood creaked and his thighs were quivering. More green shoots came into sight beyond the window.

"Don't tell me those slagging things are coming to help," Sespian growled.

The vine quivered, its flesh blackening. Sespian was halfway through. So long as no reinforcements reached through the window.

A uniformed figure darted beneath Starcrest's arm. Sespian glimpsed a burning fuse before the soldier threw a blasting stick.

Starcrest spat something in Kyattese, then switched to Turgonian for, "Cut faster, boy. I'm exposed here."

Sespian bore down, sawing with all his strength, but the vine snapped higher up, where Starcrest had been applying the electricity. He dropped to the ground, managing to twist and get his feet beneath him. He grabbed Sespian's arm and lunged backward, taking them both to the floor.

The blasting stick exploded outside the window. Wood pummeled Sespian, and all he had time to do was turn his face from the force before something hammered his back. The blow hurled him into the table, and it skidded away. Something would have crashed down on his head, but hands darted in and caught it. The crowbar. Shards of wood continued to rain down, though the big pieces stopped striking them. When Sespian dared glance over his shoulder, he found not only the window frame gone but a huge chunk of the wall missing as well. On the ground outside, vines smoked and writhed, retreating toward the nearby shoreline. Only the fat vine that had grabbed Starcrest, the one he had burned with electricity, lay unmoving.

"Dear daughter," Starcrest rumbled. "I appreciate your willingness to order soldiers into the fray to protect my life, but in the future, please consider the consequences of throwing a blasting stick between a man's legs. Nature put things down there that are intended to remain intact."

Mahliki tossed the crowbar on the table. "You've got three children. I didn't think you needed anything down there all that much anymore." Though she clearly meant the words to be light, her voice cracked. She flung her arms around her father for a hug.

Sespian, having landed in a pile with Starcrest, tried to extricate himself from the family embrace, though, between the upended table and the soldiers who had gathered around, it was hard to stand up. No less than six hands descended, trying to help Starcrest to his feet. Sespian decided not to be jealous that only one hand lowered for him, as he wouldn't want Starcrest's job for anything in the world. The more days that were between him and being in charge, the better he liked it.

Starcrest waved away the hands and climbed to his feet of his own accord. "Please return your attention to the plant, gentlemen. We've learned how to hurt it, but an injured beast fights harder than an uninjured one, and we must consider this more beast than plant."

Major Rydoth, a gray-haired man of fifty or so, gripped Rias's arm and guided him back to the workstation, saying, "Are you sure you need to stay down here, My Lord? I can finish the work on the submarine—we've already got most of your new weapons loaded onboard, don't we?"

"Yes, but I'm not leaving while there's work to be done."

"So long as I don't have to be the one to explain to your wife how a plant burst through a window and ate you."

When Sespian had stood, blackness had danced at the edges of his vision, and the effect was slow to fade. He groped about and braced himself on the table.

"Are you all right?" Mahliki asked, stepping past broken glass and rubble to take his other arm.

He thought about being manly and self-sufficient and waving away her concern, but it was rather nice having her at his side, supporting him. "I think I will be. Something hit me in the back. I need a moment."

She slipped an arm around his lower back. "Come over here and sit down."

That was nice, too—having soft, curvy parts pressed against his side. As he let her guide him around the table and past heaps of broken wood, he mused that it would have been nicer to be entangled on the floor with her than with her father. That thought gave him a guilty start, and he glanced around to find Starcrest, suddenly afraid that he might be watching. What would he think of catching Sespian gazing at his daughter with thoughts of tangled limbs dancing in his head?

But Starcrest was busy picking up his generator and dusting off debris. He clutched it to his chest and headed back to his impromptu laboratory, pausing only to give Sespian and Mahliki pats on their shoulders as he passed.

"Sorry about the blasting stick," Mahliki said, releasing Sespian long enough to pick a stool up off the floor for him. She dusted off the surface and gestured for him to sit. "I wasn't sure whether the dagger or the electricity would be enough, and... it seemed like a reasonable option at the time."

One of her braids had fallen over her shoulder, and she fiddled with the end. Shyly, he thought, though maybe that was his imagination. When she was around others, even strangers, she always appeared confident, especially given her age. She might be a couple of years younger than he, but she had been having world-spanning adventures since she was a toddler, whereas Sespian had been ensconced in the Imperial Barracks for much of his life, watching the world through the windows. It would be nice to find private time with her to ask her about some of the adventures that she and her parents had only hinted at.

Sespian wondered what she would look like with her hair down, streams of lush black locks falling about her shoulders. Of course, it was lovely in braids too. And somehow the plant guts spattered on her arms and face didn't detract from her beauty. Aside from the blue eyes, she had her father's features more than her mother's, but her nose and jaw were finer, elegant rather than handsome, and far more attractive overall to Sespian's eye.

He dragged his gaze away, reminding himself that her father was only ten feet away, and just because clanks and thunks were emanating from his space didn't mean he wasn't aware of his daughter being gawked at by a... a nobody. A nobody who didn't know what a methyl ester was. Sespian doubted Starcrest would care if his daughter developed an interest in someone who wasn't warrior caste, but he might be disappointed in someone who preferred using pencils for drawing rather than scribbling equations or cracking enemy encryption codes.

"It's fine," Sespian said, realizing Mahliki was watching him out of the corner of her eye, waiting for a response. "I mean, it certainly convinced that plant to leave us alone for the time being."

"Not exactly *alone*." Mahliki eyed the engineers still scampering in and out of the submarine, and the soldiers, many of who had stayed inside and stationed themselves close to the laboratory area.

"Maybe when this is all over, we can..." Sespian faltered when her gaze swung back to him, her eyes locking onto his.

"Yes?"

"Uhm." Why was fighting man-slaying plants easier than looking into a woman's eyes? Sespian couldn't get his real question out. "Where did you get that dagger?" he asked instead. "I didn't think Sicarius let anyone use it. I haven't even seen it in Amaranthe's hands."

"This one belongs to my father."

"I had no idea there was more than one in the world." Nor did he particularly care. Why couldn't he summon the courage to ask his true question?

"I'm not supposed to know about this, but there are heaps of artifacts from that race buried under a mountain up in your Northern Frontier."

"Ah, right. I did read those reports when I was... in my former occupation." Sespian winced. It seemed odd—or like bragging—to say, "when I was emperor," but his workaround only sounded awkward. "I didn't think many artifacts had made their way out though."

"They didn't, but my father was using the knives as tools to build something. I think he gave one to Sicarius as a distraction, to keep him from killing them. Or maybe it was the bat guano collection mission that was the distraction."

Sespian blinked. The reports he had read obviously hadn't been complete. "I hadn't realized he had been given that mission, to kill your father."

"Your emperor wasn't pleased that Father didn't come crawling back to be his good little attack dog when asked."

Sespian knew Sicarius had assassinated many people in the years he had worked for Emperor Raumesys, but he had a hard time imagining Sicarius seriously contemplating killing Starcrest. The president was one of the few people in the world—if not the *only* person in the world—he seemed to respect.

Mahliki nudged him with an elbow. "I have all *sorts* of interesting stories I'm not supposed to know about, if you'd like to hear them sometime."

That sounded like an invitation, like she might want to have conversations with him. In private. Alone. It would be rude of him to decline such an invitation, wouldn't it? Fierce and formidable fathers notwithstanding?

"Mahliki, when this plant issue is resolved, would you like to go—"

"Sespian?" Starcrest asked.

Sespian jumped off the stool, almost knocking it into Mahliki. He caught it before it pounded her in the stomach, even as he spun toward Starcrest. "Yes, sir?" he blurted, worried again that Starcrest had guessed his thoughts and wanted to interrupt anything before it started.

Starcrest had pulled open a panel on his portable generator and had his head stuck inside. He couldn't even *see* them. "Will you come give me a hand? If we're going to put a factory into operation to make more of these, they'll need a less cumbersome design. And you were ready for the specifications for the submarine machinery, weren't you?"

"Yes, sir." Sespian poked around under the table and found the pad of paper he had brought over earlier. As he walked over to join Starcrest, he glanced back, catching a wistful expression on Mahliki's face.

Maybe Maldynado had been right. Maybe she *did* like him. But what could he do about it when former Fleet Admiral and current President Starcrest was her father? Ask him for permission to court his daughter? What would he do when Starcrest frowned and said, "No, she's not for you, boy?"

"The plant's already growing back out there," one of the soldiers near a window observed.

Sespian hustled over to Starcrest's side. His love life would have to wait.

Maldynado cleared his throat and wriggled his fingers to get the attention of the hotel receptionist. The security guard behind the counter had already noticed him and leveled a glare at the suspicious jug. Basilard was standing in the lobby, signing comments to his translator. Maldynado hoped he was asking her out to dinner, but suspected Basilard was explaining that whatever diplomatic things they were supposed to be doing would be delayed further and that he wouldn't need her assistance for the rest of the day.

"Yes?" the receptionist asked, giving the jug a curious look.

"Nothing to be alarmed about," Maldynado told her—and the security guard. "It's empty. Although, ah, Ms. Sarevic is going to need a new room. The transfer of the jug's contents didn't go as smoothly as anticipated. We should have listened when she said that umbrella holder wasn't a sufficient receptacle, even though it did meet the requirements of being ceramic. I suppose, technically, it wasn't so much the problem of the holder as the less than steady hand of the person pouring the contents of the jug. It's not my fault though. You'd be twitchy, too, dealing with such caustic acid, and it's unnerving having those plants out in the courtyard, batting at the windows and such."

"Acid?" The receptionist lifted a hand to tuck a clump of hair behind her ear, but missed her target, and the clump fell into her eyes. She didn't seem to notice. "New room?"

"Yes, is the one next door available?" Maldynado asked, giving her his best smile. "Also, you may wish to put in a note to the maintenance people that her current room will need a few repairs, as it now has a view of the basement gymnasium. You can imagine the surprise of the wrestlers tussling down there."

The receptionist opened and closed her mouth a few times but nothing came out. Odd. Basilard's translator was heading for the stairs, so Maldynado left the receptionist, trusting she would figure out the room issues on her own—if not, Sarevic's security guard would doubtlessly be by soon, after he stopped batting at the smoking edges of that hole.

Sarevic kept telling him that the acid wouldn't start a fire, but he didn't grasp that.

Maldynado caught Basilard gazing—longingly?—after his translator. Her thick red hair bounced about her shoulders, and her hips had a nice sway to them as she ascended the stairs. Maldynado would have to find time to plan that dinner party soon.

"Ready to go back and set the trap?" Maldynado held up the empty jar. *Just the two of us?*

"Yara had to go back to work. Her dedication is admirable, but does alas mean she's not always available for last-minute fun, hijinks, and saboteur trappings."

Perhaps we should recruit help, Basilard signed. *If that jug was to be placed somewhere with a bull's eye on its side, it's possible an archer or sniper will be coming to break it open, someone who can avoid the nighttime security guard—and who would also be able to avoid us.*

"We can set up the target so the spots one could stand to shoot at it are limited," Maldynado said. "Then we wouldn't have much ground to watch."

Basilard started to sign a response, but paused with his fingers in the air and looked past Maldynado's shoulder. He lifted a hand in greeting, then changed it to a beckoning gesture.

Dressed in his usual black and wearing his usual humorless expression, Sicarius was trotting down the stairs, heading for the door. His gait was determined, like he was going somewhere important, but he spotted Basilard's wave. He eyed the door, as if he was thinking of ignoring the summons. Ultimately, he walked over to them.

We could use some help, Basilard signed, and Maldynado groaned inside. There would be no chance for fun or hijinks if Sicarius came along. *Were you going somewhere?*

Sicarius did not answer right away. When he did answer, it came out stiffer and more formal than usual. "I finished my task and intend to inform Amaranthe of the results."

"Oh?" Maldynado said, surprised they weren't together, since that seemed to be their normative state these days. "Where's she?" He would rather take her on a quest to capture a building saboteur.

"Out."

You don't know where?

326

"I know."

"You won't tell us?" Maldynado asked. Why did it seem like Sicarius was hiding something from them?

"No."

"What if Amaranthe gets in trouble and doesn't come back? We should know where she is so we can go look for her."

"Unnecessary."

Basilard swatted Maldynado before he could probe further. *We need help laying a trap that will be sprung at midnight tonight.*

Sicarius didn't look like he cared. Seconds ticked past, and he didn't volunteer to help. He was contemplating the door again.

"It's to save Sespian's building," Maldynado said.

That got his attention. Sicarius's eyes shifted back to the conversation, their full intensity locked onto Maldynado. He wondered when that gaze would stop making him twitch. It wasn't as if he was training with Sicarius any more; he didn't have to accept orders from him or perform impossible physical feats because that glare demanded it.

"Explain," Sicarius said.

The building Sespian designed for the president is being sabotaged, Basilard signed.

"We don't know if it's related to the assassinations, but some of the stolen goodies from Sarevic's shop are being used there." Maldynado held up the empty jug. "She just confirmed that the acid that was in here was her concoction. We're returning to the site to set up a trap for someone we expect to come by at midnight."

"Is Sespian involved?" Sicarius asked.

"He and Starcrest aren't prioritizing the building," Maldynado said. "Sespian is off designing submarine engines with the president. I don't think he's even heard about this yet." Maldynado pointed at Sicarius's chest. "But if you helped us stop the saboteur, I'm sure Sespian would be appreciative. You could wrap up the person responsible and deliver it to him like a present. A late Solstice Fest gift. I'm betting you were too busy having happy fun times on that submarine to get him a Solstice Fest gift. Am I right?"

Basilard covered his face with his hand.

"Amaranthe sent him a gift," Sicarius said.

"So, that's a no." Maldynado shook the jug. "Ready to join us?"

Sicarius gazed at the door one more time, but said, "I will come."

"Excellent, this will go well," Maldynado declared, then lifted a hand to his mouth and whispered to Basilard, "If he suggests light calisthenics to stay warm while we wait, don't you dare say yes."

Have you not been keeping up with your training? Basilard headed for the front door.

"Of course I have, but I've been getting enough exercise working for that vile foreman. And keeping my lady happy enough to stay in town." Maldynado elbowed Basilard. "You'll know what I mean once we get your translator thinking of you like the sexy Imperial Games champion you are."

Basilard glanced over his shoulder at Sicarius and gave an apologetic shrug.

For the conversation? Maldynado sniffed. Sicarius couldn't possibly mind the discussion of sex, especially now that he was having some. One assumed so anyway. Sicarius had never spoken of desires for happy fun times in the year Maldynado had known him. A strange man. Sespian never spoke much on the topic, either. A hereditary flaw? Maldynado tried to imagine a father-son conversation between the two on the subject of courting Mahliki. Awkward. It would have to be. Fortunately Sespian had turned twenty recently. He ought to be spared from such talks, under the assumption he already knew how things worked. An assumption that Maldynado wondered about, though he figured one couldn't be raised the son of an emperor and made emperor without sampling some of the offerings around the Imperial Barracks. And even if he hadn't... well, the Kyattese weren't shy about such discussions. Mahliki could probably draw him some diagrams.

Why are you smirking? Basilard asked as they crossed out of the plant-filled courtyard and into the street.

"Just thinking about the dinner I'm planning... and possible topics for conversation that night."

The streets were empty, with many citizens already having been evacuated to higher ground, or out of the city altogether. Amaranthe had heard about the evacuation, of course, but she had been so busy that she hadn't been watching it happen. The streets had an eerie abandoned feel to them, one made worse by the lack of lighting along the canal. Rustles came from alleys, proof that not everyone had left, and Amaranthe was glad she had grabbed her sword and dagger on her way out of the hotel.

Trolleys clanged now and then in the distance, but they had been rerouted away from the waterfront. After being forced to wait a long time at the stop near the hotel, she had discovered she couldn't get closer than two miles to the *Gazette* building, so she had walked the rest of the way. She hoped she wouldn't arrive only to find that the newspaper operation had been moved. The *Gazette* building was more than ten blocks from the waterfront, so she didn't think it would be in danger of being overcome by greenery yet. She hoped.

The old building came into view on the other side of the canal, and Amaranthe breathed a sigh of relief at the two lamps burning on either side of the entry steps. She didn't know if Deret would have the information she needed, so she would have hated to wander all over the city looking for him.

She crossed the bridge she had once swung beneath to sneak up on the building. The houseboats that usually lined the canal walkways were gone. She wondered how *they* had been evacuated, given that the lake was barricaded with a forest of greenery. Maybe they had left before it had grown so large. Their absence reminded her that she still needed to find and pay back the owner of the houseboat she had inadvertently burned down while fleeing from enforcers. Maybe she should be joining Maldynado in asking the president for a job.

Amaranthe glanced farther down the canal, toward the grate that covered the storm drain she had once used. A large green tendril dangled through the bars. She froze, one foot hanging in the air. By now, she ought to be used to that plant's ubiquitous presence, but finding it this far inland alarmed her.

"They're not evacuating the city for no reason," she muttered and wondered if she and Sicarius shouldn't be helping come up with a solution to get rid of it rather than dancing around, hunting for snitches, priests, and assassins. But what help would she be able to offer?

The clomp of footsteps on the sidewalk pulled her attention from the plant. Her hand dropped to her sword. She had a feeling most of the law-abiding citizens had obeyed the evacuation order. Those who were left might be looters—or worse.

But the figures walked in step and carried lanterns, their lights revealing enforcer uniforms. Amaranthe caught herself tensing, her hand tightening on her sword, then laughed to herself.

"You're not an outlaw anymore, girl," she murmured.

She headed for the stairs of the *Gazette* building. Not only did she not have to worry about being arrested—or shot—but she could stroll up to the front door and knock instead of sneaking in through some attic vent. An enjoyable realization.

The four enforcers veered from their path to stomp toward her though.

"Ma'am," a sergeant said. "This area has been evacuated. You need to gather your belongings and leave. Military transports are departing from Ninth and Scepter and the Bloodcrest Fountain on the hour all night."

"Thank you, Sergeant, but I'm here to visit Lord Mancrest and won't be long." Amaranthe pointed at the building's front door, but decided that sounded too casual and that they might grow more forceful if she didn't convince them she was on official business. "I'm staying at the president's hotel and am on a mission for his wife. I can't evacuate until they give me leave to do so."

"Is that Amaranthe Lokdon?" one of the enforcers in the back asked, stepping around his comrade to squint at her.

She hadn't yet reached the building's stairs, and there wasn't much light on the street. She hadn't expected to be recognized and wasn't sure how that would go over with the enforcers. There might not be a bounty poster out there with her face on it anymore, but there were probably people on the force who were holding grudges, knowing she had run with Sicarius and been responsible for Sergeant Wholt's death the winter before last.

"It is," she said, keeping her voice neutral.

The man jogged toward her, his sword and baton rattling on his belt. Amaranthe braced herself but kept her hand from straying to her own sword. The last thing she wanted was a fight with good people.

"Corporal, what are you doing?" the sergeant asked.

The man stopped in front of Amaranthe and dug into a pocket. "Wish I still had that article with me, but I've got... uhm, a napkin from Tarkon's Deli?"

"Pardon?"

He was clearly asking her a question, but she didn't understand what it was.

"For you to sign." The enforcer fished in his pockets again. "All I have is a pencil nub, but... Here, up in the light. Do you mind?" He jogged up the stairs to stand on the landing before the large timeworn double doors. He laid his paper napkin on the stone railing.

"I... suppose not." Amaranthe shrugged at the other enforcers, who were exchanging eye rolls with each other.

"I have all your newspaper articles," the corporal said as he climbed the steps to join her. "The ones where you're mentioned, that is. I can't believe one of us—" he waved at his fellow enforcers, "—helped stop those Forge people and put Fleet Admiral Starcrest on the throne."

Amaranthe had never seen a man swoon before, but this corporal might be in danger of it. She signed his paper, and he accepted it, then shook her hand heartily. For a moment, she worried he might kiss it, but he released her with an enthusiastic, "Thank you!" and skipped back down the steps. Well, it beat being greeted with swords and muskets.

"He's young," the sergeant explained, then gave her a salute and moved his team on.

"You've become a celebrity," came a voice from behind Amaranthe.

Deret Mancrest stood in the doorway. Wearing a green robe.

CHAPTER 19

MAHLIKI PRESSED THE SWITCH AND watched the tiny blue streaks arc out of the iron prod and into the severed section of green tendril. She kept an eye on the pocket watch on the table at the same time. After a few seconds, the inch-thick vine charred up and curled inward on itself. She turned off the switch and wrote a few notes. Next, she applied the electricity to a preserved pod, one of the ones that could spew those deadly spores. She was reasonably certain it wouldn't be able to do so after it had been cut open and spent two days in a formaldehyde bath, but she was prepared to leap over the table if it so much as twitched. But the pod succumbed to the electricity at the same rate as the other piece. She recorded this, then moved onto one of the rare leaves, green flat disks with shiny surfaces that could ooze that enzyme that broke up animal flesh. It proved sturdier, withstanding the electricity for twelve seconds before withering up. Some of that enzyme oozed out of its green pores before it fully succumbed.

"Are you learning anything useful?" Sespian asked, walking over to join her. He had finished helping Father design a portable version of the electricity generator an hour or two earlier and had been working in the submarine with the engineers the last she had heard.

"About what I expected so far." Mahliki waved at the charred samples, then fished a jar out of her bag on the floor. "*This* is the one I'm curious about."

"That's the root sample you risked your life to get, isn't it?"

"Yes, it's the last piece I have. I've already run so many experiments on it and the rest of the specimens that I'm surprised the mother plant isn't out there plotting my demise." She glanced at the demolished section of wall—night had fallen out there, and the plant's infiltrations had grown less frequent, but it was still keeping the soldiers busy.

"It seemed more offended by your father's ministrations," Sespian said.

"Yes, I think that's because he performed his experiment on *attached* parts of the plant. You would be more upset about someone trying to flambé your finger than a piece of hair you lost yesterday, right?"

"I imagine so. I'm comforted that it doesn't seem to know what we're doing to the pieces that have been severed. The way those bits can grow new plants of their own accord if they're not stopped..." Sespian shuddered. "The whole organism has a distressing ability to thrive against all odds."

"I wouldn't go so far as to say it's not aware of what we're doing in here to its severed bits." Mahliki secured the piece of root in the vise clamped to the table. "That first big attack came when I was pulping up one of its limbs, remember. Right now, I think it's focusing on growing big enough that it can ensure it wins when it attacks us next time."

"How... comforting."

"Let's see how it likes this." Mahliki prodded the root with the iron wand and flipped the switch. Within a second of turning on the electricity, the specimen burst into flame.

Sespian gaped. Mahliki caught herself gaping too. She *had* expected the root to be more vulnerable than the tough green flesh, but she *hadn't* expected quite so impressive a show.

"You... ashed it," Sespian said.

"Ashed? Is that a word in Turgonian?"

Sespian prodded the fine gray powder that was all that remained beneath the vise. "It is now. You tried burning it with flame before, didn't you?"

"I tried applying *everything* to it earlier. And to the other pieces as well. I just didn't have a way to make electricity at the time." Mahliki swept the ashes into her sample jar. "I suspected the root was most vulnerable when we learned that those priests wanted the *Explorer* out of commission—even though the plant has stretched several blocks inland, the only roots that seem to be accessible are down in the muddy waters beneath the docks. Which we should be able to get to soon." She nodded toward the submarine.

Clangs and clanks echoed from within. An hour earlier, her father had disappeared inside with as many engineers as could fit in there without anyone hitting anyone else with a hammer. Judging by the occasional yelps and cries of "ow" that came out, they might have crammed one or two too many inside. In Kyatt, most engineers would run for high ground if a man-eating plant invaded the harbor, but these people had been climbing over each other for the opportunity to work with Father.

"I'm glad the plant hasn't managed to harm the submarine yet." Sespian pointed to some of the broken floorboards and pushed up piles of earth around the craft and around the makeshift laboratory. Thus far, the soldiers who had come down with Father had been enough to keep the plant at bay.

"I know," Mahliki said. "It's our only chance at getting down there with enough weapons power to tear up the roots and electrocute them. Even if Father's handheld generator works underwater, I wouldn't want to send anyone out there in a diving suit." She shivered at the memory of her experience in the plant's grasp. "That would be a suicide mission. The plant has grown so much since then, there would be no pulling someone from its clutches."

Sespian glanced at the pocket watch. "Must be about time for the vice president's aide to show up again. It's been almost an hour."

"You've noticed his frequent reports today too, eh?"

"Every time he's burst in, he's brought up spot fires all over the nation that supposedly demand your father's attention right now."

"I know," Mahliki said. "Did you hear what he said the last time Father shooed him away?"

Sespian nodded. "You'll be sorry if you put this contraption above tending to Turgonia, the way a good president should."

"One wonders why the vice president can't handle some of those fires. Is he busy reading?" Maybe he was working on the report Mahliki had mentioned a few days ago. "I wonder if Serpitivich even knows his aide is coming down here. Maybe he's the snitch Mother has been looking for."

"I have a feeling—"

The front door slammed open, and a soldier raced inside as if a tiger were chewing on his heels. "My Lord President?" he shouted. "We have a problem!"

"The plant again?" Mahliki asked.

The soldier spun around. "Where's the president?"

"Here." Father thrust his head out of the hatchway, his gray hair sticking out in all directions, and his cheek smeared with grease.

Outside the walls, rifle shots blasted into the night, the soldiers firing at someone—or something. More booms erupted farther up the street. Blasting sticks? Mahliki couldn't tell whether their people were throwing them at some distant enemy, or if some distant enemy was flinging explosives at *them*.

Pounding sounded on the rooftop. Hammers? Or maybe footfalls? Had people climbed up there?

"My Lord President!" The soldier ran up to the sub and saluted, as if Father had time to waste on ceremony. "There are armored military vehicles coming down the street from either direction, and they're doing... doing..."

"Dump your ore cart, Private," Father said.

A tingle ran up Mahliki's arms and spine, stirring gooseflesh. "Someone's using the mental sciences," she announced.

Sespian ran to the front door to look out.

The soldier nodded vigorously. "Yes, magic. They threw flames at the ground around the building. At first, we thought they were trying to help, that someone had thrown explosives, not thrice-cursed m—magic. But it didn't bother the plants at all." The soldier's voice grew faster and higher pitched as he raced on with his report. "In fact, it riled them up, so all of a sudden, they started grabbing men, trying to pull them toward the water. We're so busy cutting them down, it's going to be hard to keep the lorries at bay."

"Yes, the plant has shown a propensity to defend itself when attacked," Father said, his face and voice utterly calm. "Someone must have noticed this and hopes to take advantage."

The soldier took a big breath and swallowed some of his hysteria. "Yes, My Lord. We'll keep defending, of course, but I thought you should know that we're going to have some trouble."

That sounded like an understatement. While the soldier finished reporting, Mahliki ran up to the front to join Sespian. She peered over his shoulder to see out the door. Not ten feet from the entrance, those plants writhed and twisted like living animals. The only time she had seen them so animated was when they had attacked Father, and there hadn't been so *many* of them then.

"I saw some of those vehicles this afternoon." Sespian pointed up the street, where two broad black army lorries blocked the way. "They were commissioned to help evacuate the city."

The tingle plucked at Mahliki's skin, warning of another Science attack. Expecting whatever practitioner was out there to try to rile the plants further, she wasn't ready when a ball of flame whooshed toward the front door.

Sespian reacted more quickly, hauling her away from the entrance. She almost tripped over one of the broken boards the plant had shoved upward, but Sespian kept her on her feet. Blinding flame washed over the doorway, and heat poured inside.

"Evacuate the city?" Mahliki squeaked. "It looks like they want to evacuate this *building*."

"More like incinerate this building. Those aren't soldiers out there. Someone snagged those vehicles somehow." Sespian's voice was almost as calm as Father's, though the flames crackling outside the door were certainly cause for alarm. "The drivers are wearing those green robes. A new fashion statement in the city, it seems."

"Mahliki," Father called. "It will ease my nerves if you come join us inside the sub instead of playing peep-and-hide with the enemy practitioners."

Mahliki straightened her clothing. "I'm a grown woman, Father. I *don't* play peep-and-hide."

"Understood," Father said, but she realized it was to the soldier who had finished reporting. "I'll come out and talk to Captain Eaglecrest in a moment, but tell him I want the supply lorry unloaded and those suits brought in before anything happens to them." He beckoned for Sespian and Mahliki to join him, then ducked back into the submarine.

"Suits?" Sespian asked. "Diving suits? I thought we'd decided they would be too dangerous? Or does that mean he's not going to have time to finish the submarine modifications?"

"I don't know, but it's going to be hard to finish anything with the roof on fire." Mahliki tugged Sespian toward the side of the building the blasting stick had blown away earlier. With luck, their enemies in the vehicles would be watching the front door and not the less standard exits. "Come on. Let's see if we can do something to stop those practitioners."

"I'll find a way to deal with them," Sespian said, though the glance he threw toward the door had a daunted quality to it. "You should stay in here and help your father."

"The *Explorer* will burst at the seams if anyone else goes inside."

Mahliki spotted the prototype generator by her table and grabbed it before veering for the hole in the wall. "We can be far more useful out there."

"Yes, but your father—"

"Can come out and visit if he's worried about me." Mahliki gave Sespian a wink and ran outside.

"Good evening, Deret." Amaranthe wondered if she should mention the robe. Would he know she understood the significance? Would he know she had been sent to find the leader of the organization? "I wasn't certain if I'd find you here or if the paper would have moved."

"It has actually. Up to the ridge."

Deret stepped aside to let her in. As usual, he managed to imply that his swordstick was an affectation rather than a crutch, at least when she was watching. Dubious green robe not withstanding, he had changed a bit, trading his shoulder-length wavy brown hair for a military-style cut. It looked good on him, leaving less to distract from his strong jaw and aquiline nose. He had different spectacles on as well, these with thinner frames than the sturdy old pair he had worn before. Suan's influence maybe, though Amaranthe was more concerned about the robe than his dating activities. It alone didn't unnerve her overly much—maybe there was a legitimate reason for it—but she did note that nobody else shared the building with them. Only a couple of lanterns burned on desks near the door. Too many shadows buried the back of the open building to see if there was still a gaping hole in the floor, a vestige of her *last* visit to the Mancrest establishment.

"I had a meeting down here tonight and decided to stop by for a few forgotten items," Deret added.

"What kind of meeting?" Amaranthe waved at his robe. "That's not your usual expensive warrior-caste clothing."

"Affording expensive clothing has been difficult of late. Someone demolished the *Gazette* building last winter, as you may recall, and it's taken a lot of money to make it suitable for printing again. Only my father's stubbornness kept the papers from being delayed. Now..." He huffed out an irritated breath in the general direction of the building. "I don't know if I care enough to rebuild again if that plant damages the place. I've been thinking of selling the paper."

"I'm sorry about your father." Amaranthe decided not to mention she had been twenty feet away from him when he had been killed. "I know you and he weren't close exactly…"

Deret snorted.

"But I'm sure he didn't deserve to be killed."

"He died the way he would have wanted—in a woman's bed. Albeit I had always imagined him dying in a much younger woman's bed, but I suppose screwing the president's wife was a conquest worthy of his penis."

"Er." Amaranthe didn't know what to say to his bitterness. Lord Mancrest had locked his son in the basement over a difference of opinion, so she hadn't expected tears over his death, but more… tact, perhaps.

"I apologize," Deret sighed. "That was crude. Please, come the rest of the way in and sit down." He waved toward a chair. "May I get you something to drink? There's… water from the tap—if that's still working—and water collecting in a bucket that's coming in through a leak in the roof."

"I'm fine, thank you." Amaranthe sat at one of the desks with a lantern on it. She wanted to ask him about the robe and this meeting he had gone to, but he looked like a man who needed a friend rather than an interrogation.

"Wait, I'm not sure if Needlecrest cleared out his entire collection. I may be able to offer you…" Deret fished around in the drawer of an adjacent desk, then held a dark bottle aloft. "Ah ha." He examined the label. "Starcrest Cellars. Now there's irony." He dragged a chair over to sit at the desk with Amaranthe, then tugged the cork out of the half-empty bottle of apple brandy. "Is it true he killed my father?"

Amaranthe had been in the process of holding up a hand to decline the drink, but she froze. "What? Who?"

"I hear you're staying in the president's hotel, so I figured you would know. Starcrest, my father. Because of the adulterous wife."

"No," Amaranthe said, "of course not. The president didn't even know he was still legally married to that woman until recently. Haven't you seen his Kyattese wife?" If Deret thought Starcrest's first wife still meant something to him, then he might not be the source of information she had hoped for. Perhaps coming hadn't been the best use of her time, though she had wanted to offer her condolences on his father's death anyway—for what little it seemed to mean to Deret.

He grunted. "Yes, though the old one is prettier. One thought that, now that he's back in the empire, er, the nation, and he could have anyone... Oh, I guess I haven't got the entire story. Starcrest has declined interviews, and there's been a lot of other stuff to cover."

"Such as why people are running around the city in green robes?" Amaranthe asked lightly, though she dearly wanted to know what his connection to the priests was.

Deret tilted his head curiously, then lifted his sleeve. "Oh, right. Sexy, aren't they? I had been trying to get someone into the organization for weeks—they didn't want to accept interviews, either—but they utterly ignored me until my father was killed. All of the sudden, I was an interesting commodity, probably because I'm now in charge of the newspaper. Weird, isn't it? After all the arguments we had—and the way he locked me up in the basement—he left the paper to me instead of my brothers. Maybe he knew I was the only one who cared enough to keep it running and who had the experience to make it work. Or maybe he simply filled out his will before we had our big tiff." Deret shrugged and took a swig from the brandy bottle. "Either way, the New Kriskrusians came knocking on my door, wanting to have a newspaper in their pocket. I wanted to know more about them, so I acted as if I might be open to the idea. Tonight was my first night being invited to a meeting."

Amaranthe relaxed back into the chair. "So you're not a recruit? You're simply... learning more about them?"

"More or less. I haven't decided what I'll do with the information yet. Like I was saying, I'm thinking of selling the paper, what's left of it. I'm tired of Stumps."

Since he didn't seem upset by his father's death, Amaranthe wondered if his malaise was a result of some *other* interpersonal relationship. "You might take a vacation. Go off somewhere with a pretty girl."

Deret grunted. "I would ask if you were offering your own company, but I understand you returned to the city with your dark shadow still attached."

"Yes, I was thinking more of Suan. Are you and she still on... good terms?"

Deret grimaced and took another drink. "I haven't seen her much since the funeral. At the time, I thought... well, let's just say that I think she was only looking for someone to stand between her and your friends in that factory last winter. She knew she was a prisoner and that she needed someone to protect her. She decided I could be that someone. For a time."

"Ah. And the girl you spoke of when we were blowing our way out of this basement?" Amaranthe pointed toward the floor.

"You mean the girlfriend I made up so you wouldn't think I was a castrated bull without any prospects?"

"Er, possibly?"

Deret set the bottle on the desk, propped his elbow next to it, and leaned his head into his hand. "It hasn't been a good winter for me."

Indeed, he appeared as weary as Colonel Starcrest. "Perhaps you can come to the dinner party Maldynado is planning. It's designed to get... a couple of young people together, but I imagine he could talk some extra women into coming along. You might have fun."

"There's a man-eating plant devouring the city, and Maldynado is planning a dinner party?"

"Yes," Amaranthe said. "Does this surprise you?"

"Not really."

"You'll think about coming?"

"Assuming we're all alive at the end of the week, maybe." Deret clinked a fingernail against the side of the brandy bottle. "Amaranthe, you haven't met my mother, but she's a strong, proud warrior-caste lady and doesn't know my father was... friendly with so many other women. She's been harping on my brothers and me—mostly me, because I live in the city—to avenge my father's death. I don't know that I'd go that far, but I would like to know what happened, so I can tell her that much at least. Do you know, if it wasn't Starcrest, who did kill him?"

Amaranthe realized she might once again be in a position to trade information with him. She had intended to ask about the priests, simply as a friend, but perhaps a trade would be more effective. If he didn't know what she needed to know, specifically who was in charge over there, he might feel obligated to find out, and it sounded like he was in a better position to do so than she...

"I'll tell you what I know on that front if you agree to help me find out who the lead priest is in that organization."

With his head still in his palm, Deret gazed thoughtfully at her. "Do you truly know what happened there?"

"Largely by unforeseen circumstance, I was downstairs in Sauda Starcrest's house when it all happened. Sicarius chased the assassin back to her lair."

"*Her* lair? Interesting."

"Yes." Amaranthe smiled and held out her palm, inviting him to take a turn at sharing information.

"I should have known you didn't come here because you missed my company."

"I *did* wish to offer my condolences on your father's death, though... it's true I might not have made it by quite so soon if I hadn't been hoping you knew more than the military intelligence office in regard to this organization. You journalists seem particularly fine at ferreting out information."

"I'll accept that as a compliment, because I haven't been getting many from women lately, but I think the intel fellows have things covered fairly well. They've got an informant working at the *Gazette*, so I don't know much they don't."

"They do?" Amaranthe asked. "How did you find out?"

"I wouldn't have except that he felt guilty about my father's death and told me he had been keeping the soldiers apprised of my father's goings on. Apparently his dalliance with that Forge woman left people suspicious of him. I read between the lines that I'm not entirely free of suspicion, either." He pushed a hand through his hair. "I need to get out of this city."

"If you sold the newspaper, you could hand these burdens to someone else, it's true. But you're not that much older than I am, still young enough to appreciate a challenge and want to do something important with your life, I should think. Running a solid, reliable newspaper that refuses to be influenced by outside parties... that would be a noble calling."

"Hm. Isn't settling down and starting a family a noble calling too? I've been thinking about that of late, which is odd, since I have no one to settle down *with*, but... if I did, I would hate to be spending sixteen hours a day at work. This isn't an easy job, even for the owner. Especially for the owner."

"You need to hire a good manager and delegate some of the work to underlings. Such as that fine fellow who's getting paid by Colonel Starcrest as well as by your coffers. A man getting paid twice really should be doing twice the work, don't you think?"

Deret smirked at this idea, though he shook his head in the end. "I'm not the type to delegate everything and ask someone to work harder than I do."

"You wouldn't delegate everything, just enough so that you could have time to do that which you love. Such as pursuing a fine woman at Maldynado's dinner party."

"Dear ancestors, I can only imagine who he would set me up with." Deret chuckled and took a drink—a smaller sip this time—from the bottle. He shook his head wryly—or maybe ruefully—at the label, then paused, his brow crinkled. "Did you say *Colonel* Starcrest? Not *President* Starcrest?"

"Yes, you didn't know he was running the intelligence department now?" Amaranthe was surprised how much Deret *didn't* know about what was going on with the president. She should have read some of the papers before coming by, assuming he would have useful information. Though, to be fair, she was living inside the hotel and sitting in on meetings with the Starcrests, a privilege nobody at the newspaper would have.

"No. I thought it was still Colonel Alpinecrest, though it makes sense that a new ruler—new *president*—would bring in new staff. Besides, I heard Alpinecrest was getting his pockets padded by Forge at one point." Deret rubbed his chin. "Colonel Starcrest. Huh. He's definitely kept quiet about that. I wonder how many of his informants even know who they're dealing with."

"Are you familiar with him? I had never heard of him before my return to the city."

"I don't know him well, but I covered the story of the border infiltrations ten, no that was almost fifteen years ago. It was before I went off to the military academy; I used to help my father at the paper after school." Deret grimaced, yet managed to look nostalgic at the same moment. Remembering better times for the family?

"Border infiltrations?"

"Yes, the major in charge of patrolling the southern border between us and Kendor was shot by a sniper. *Captain* Daksaron Starcrest ended up in charge because he was the ranking officer until Command sent out someone new, but they were dealing with more than the expected few smugglers and technology thieves that week. Kendorian shamans had concocted a virus that they were trying out down there, figuring there would be few witnesses. Well, they managed to kill a few of our patrollers, but they also had an accident and infected everyone in one of their own towns near the border. Damon Mokk. Do you remember hearing about that?"

Amaranthe shook her head. Deret was a few years older than she, so she would have only been a kid at the time. Following the newspapers hadn't been a big concern for her then. Of course, she had been too busy vacationing to keep up with them lately too...

"It was one of those ugly no-win military situations you hope you never get stuck in." Deret massaged his leg, perhaps remembering his own no-win military situation. "Dak Starcrest chose to go in and try to help the people of Damon Mokk. What exactly happened, I don't know. The minutes of the military trial were never shared publicly, and you would need a high security clearance to get a look at those records. What we at the *Gazette* were able to piece together was that he helped save the town, but he lost a number of his men in the process, men who wouldn't have been at risk if he hadn't chosen to cross the border and leave his post. Hundreds of lives were saved, but..." Deret shrugged. "If it had been a *Turgonian* town, it would have been a different story, but Emperor Raumesys wasn't the type to order soldiers across borders on humanitarian missions."

"No, he probably would have cheered, knowing the Kendorians had killed their own people in their attempt to harm us."

"Just so," Deret said. "Dak was demoted to lieutenant, and he switched from infantry to intelligence. I don't know whether that was his own choice, or if someone wanted to make him disappear. Either way, the average person didn't hear about him again. I crossed paths with him once shortly before I was discharged and again here in Stumps a couple of years ago. The first time, he was coming back from a mission in Nuria. The second, Kendor. He's been a field agent, I believe, spying and performing whatever missions the throne needed accomplished covertly. I got the impression he was good at his job and had refused promotions that would have meant desk duty. Sitting in an office in the bowels of that hotel must be driving him crazy. I doubt he would have accepted that assignment from anyone else but his famous uncle."

A spy. If Amaranthe had passed Colonel Starcrest on the street, she would not have guessed that, maybe because he looked more like an infantry thug with that missing eye. Still, that might make him an ideal person to gather information. Those who didn't know his last name might underestimate him, based on appearance alone.

"I had wondered..." Amaranthe stopped herself before mentioning the snitch; that wasn't information that should be shared openly. "I guess I was wondering how loyal he was to his uncle. He seems... bitter and resentful."

"Oh, he probably is. He's been in Rias Starcrest's shadow his whole life, even when Rias was out of the empire—and supposedly dead—for twenty years. That incident at Damon Mokk was one of a handful of commands that didn't go that well for him. He was—*is*—smart, but you got the impression he was trying too hard to be the hero his uncle had been, and he didn't quite have the same tactical savvy to pull off the impossible the way Rias so often did."

The front door banged open before Amaranthe could ask further questions.

Figures in green robes streamed inside, pistols in their hands. Amaranthe leaped from her seat to crouch behind the desk. Deret jumped to his feet, knocking over his swordstick, and cursing as he almost lost his balance. He caught himself on the desk. Amaranthe pulled him down beside her so they would have some cover, albeit not nearly as much as they needed against... eight, no, ten people spreading out in the entryway. Their hoods were all up, their faces hidden by shadows. They were all armed.

Amaranthe had pulled her sword out as she ducked behind the desk, but it would do precious little against men with pistols twenty feet away.

"Deret Mancrest," one of the figures said, his deep voice resonating as if it were echoing from the walls of a cave. "You will come with us."

"I'd rather not," Deret said. "I already attended the meeting tonight. The little sardine snacks weren't appealing enough to make me want to return again on the same day."

"Can we get out the back?" Amaranthe whispered, thinking of the door behind the presses as well as the unofficial basement exit they had made the last time she visited.

A clang came from the shadows in the back, and a cool draft whispered into the room. A moment later, six more robed figures strode into the light from behind.

"I think not," Deret murmured.

The desk offered no cover from these men, and they raised pistols as soon as they spotted Deret and Amaranthe.

"You *will* come with us," the speaker repeated.

Amaranthe didn't see many possible escape routes and none that wouldn't involve dodging fire. She admitted a certain curiosity as to where these people wanted to take Deret anyway. If she went along, she might find the leader she sought that very night.

Deret sighed and stood up, spreading his hands. "It seems I have no choice. Though I would appreciate it if you left this woman behind—"

Amaranthe elbowed him in the side as she stood up, also spreading her hands. "I'll not have you carted off by these strange men, never to be seen again," Amaranthe said. "Where you go, I go."

Deret glowered at her but didn't argue.

"Very sweet," the speaker said, the deepness of his voice doing nothing to muffle his sarcasm.

His voice sounded familiar, and Amaranthe thought it might belong to the priest who had called down the lightning. If so, would he recognize her? She hadn't done anything to stand out at that gathering. Like everyone else, she had been too busy gaping at the lightning strike and the charred plant.

The robed men at the back of the room shuffled forward until they were close enough to prod Deret and Amaranthe in the backs with their pistols. The proximity of those weapons made Amaranthe's shoulder blades twitch—and her instincts call out for her to do something—but she forced herself to do nothing more than walk in the direction the men indicated. She expected them to lead her and Deret out the front door, but they must have deemed that too public a route, even with the city largely abandoned. She and Deret were poked and prodded toward the back door, where Amaranthe had a chance to see that the floor had indeed been repaired. The big press she had hidden behind was gone—either disassembled and moved to the ridge location or maybe it had been smashed beyond repair when it had fallen into the basement. Poor Deret had inherited a mess. Even if he had helped create that mess, it had been her crazy idea that had prompted him into that destructive route. She told herself that his father had given them little choice, though she could definitely understand why he might want to take a break from the family business.

Outside on the loading dock, Amaranthe grew a little nervous when two of the men hopped down and opened a storm drain cover. This was a more secretive route than she had imagined. Stars gleamed between the clouds, and she eyed the rooflines, hoping to catch a dark figure crouched up there, spying on them. But she had left Sicarius hunting his own assassin. Whatever trouble she had gotten herself into tonight, she would have to get out of on her own.

CHAPTER 20

TEA DIDN'T REVIVE AND ENERGIZE one as effectively as coffee, and Tikaya couldn't believe the latter wasn't a popular drink in Turgonia. She wondered if it would be in her prerogative as a president's wife to request that shiploads of it be regularly imported to the capital to rejuvenate her—and Rias's staff, of course. As soon as she caught herself wondering that, she grumbled at herself to focus, and returned to the five thousandth report she had gone over. It was probably more like the five hundredth, but it *felt* like the five thousandth.

Outside of Dak's office, the sounds of chairs scuffing, papers shuffling, and throats being cleared had dwindled. She wasn't sure what time it was but knew that most of the staff had stayed late, so it had to be later yet. She rubbed the back of her neck and stood for a moment, giving her rump a rest from the hard wooden chair. She added a few calf and side stretches to loosen muscles tight from disuse. Though she shifted about, she didn't take her eyes from the reports. At least the one she was perusing now was legible. Mostly. Only one in four military intelligence officers seemed capable of passing a simple penmanship test. Tikaya couldn't bring herself to delegate reading them to anyone else, not being certain who she could trust, but there was so much chaff in the reports that she worried she was wasting her time. Almost worse were the interesting snippets among the chaff, for they could distract her, leading her down roads that eventually became dead ends.

Since it had grown so quiet in the outer office, when a knock came at the door, it startled her into tripping over the chair and falling to the floor. That was what she got for doing calf stretches while reading. When Dak walked in, he found her scrambling to her feet. Tikaya groped for the chair and straightened it.

"Good evening," she said. "I, ah, wasn't expecting company."

"Oh?" Dak eyed the section of floor she had vacated, the "what sort of floor exercises do you do when you *are* expecting company?" going unspoken.

Tikaya flushed, feeling like an idiot. She wished she could show him some piece of brilliance she had discovered, something that would justify any odd research habits.

"Here are a handful of names." Dak tossed a paper on the desk. "I've learned some of the information the snitch has been credited with relaying to others, and these are the only people who would have had access to everything."

"Oh?" Tikaya picked up the sheet. If she could simply skim the reports for mentions of those names, she would save a lot of time. Though... it was the information about the priests that she specifically sought here. She couldn't abandon that search. She read the short list. "Your name is on here."

"Yeah." Dak picked up a pen and wrote on a notepad on the corner of the desk. "Watch for this name too. Your friends found him dead upstairs. I think he might have been blackmailed, but I can't be positive he wasn't involved in something duplicitous of his own accord."

"Avigart?" Tikaya had seen something with that name on it recently. What had it been?

"Yes." Dak tilted his head. "Have you found anything interesting?"

He sounded genuinely curious. Maybe even hopeful.

"So far... I feel like I've been wasting my time. And yours. I haven't found anything." She straightened her own notepad and picked up her pencil; she wouldn't get anywhere if she allowed herself to be distracted.

"Hm." Did that hm sound skeptical? Maybe he didn't think she would tell him if she *did* find something interesting.

"Though, Avigart, I did see that name." Tikaya tapped the folders piled about her. "Not in here. Where was it? Oh, I remember." She pushed away from the desk and walked into the outer office. "I wandered around here, reading everything on the bulletin boards and walls when I needed a break a couple of hours ago." She stopped in front of a duty roster scrawled on a chalkboard. "Avigart requested a change of duty tonight. Instead of working the night shift here in the hotel, he wanted some patrol."

"He might have had an inkling about what was going to happen to him tonight," Dak said. "I wish he'd said something to me, or spoken to his lieutenant. Especially if he was being strong-armed."

"You would think that if he knew his own death was impending, he would have left the hotel, regardless of whether his duty shift was approved."

"True." Dak rested a finger next to scribbled initials on the chalkboard. "His request actually *was* approved."

"Not soon enough to help him, it seems." Tikaya removed her spectacles and cleaned the lenses as if the act would help her better see clues hovering in the air. "It's quiet in here tonight." They were the only ones in the office. "Or is it simply later than I realize?"

"An hour until midnight. We usually only have a couple of people staffing the office at night, someone able to raise the alarm if something happens in the city. The vice president collected some of the men to guard him as he moves his belongings to some friend's property, well outside of the plant-invasion area. He's not waiting for Rias to give the word to evacuate."

"Given that the plant is literally knocking at the windows, it's hard to blame him," Tikaya said. "Odd that he's moving in the middle of the night though."

"I thought so as well. I went to ask him about it, but he was mysteriously unavailable for questions."

"Do you find it... disconcerting that two of the people on your very short list of possible snitches made plans to spend the night away from the hotel?"

Dak gave her a sharp look. "Are you suggesting that it might not be a good night to enjoy a holiday in the Emperor's Bulwark?"

"I don't know. Rias isn't here, so if someone wanted to assassinate him, launching an attack tonight wouldn't do anything, not here anyway." Tikaya grimaced, thinking that Rias, for all the men he had taken with him to that waterfront warehouse, was a lot more vulnerable out there than he would be here. "There's nobody here worth expending effort to kill."

Dak's intense look hadn't faded. If anything, it sharpened further. "*You're* here."

Tikaya drew back, not sure what he was implying. "You're here too."

349

"Yes, but *my* death wouldn't devastate Rias so utterly that he would be unable to finish his submarine modifications."

"I wouldn't bet on my death having that effect, either," Tikaya said, though his point sank in. "He would finish the submarine and *then* mourn."

"Strangers might not guess that. Strangers might be desperate enough at this point to try anything. If they can't get at him directly..." Dak frowned, then cursed.

"What?"

"I originally came in here to tell you that I'm going down to check on Rias," Dak said. "I've had men reporting in every hour. Two hours ago, I got a schematic and orders to send that Sarevic woman out to a factory to start working with a team of people on making more electricity generators. One hour ago... I got nothing."

"Nothing?"

"No report."

Tikaya swallowed. "You think he's in trouble?" Rias and Mahliki were *both* down in that warehouse. Though they had been accompanied by a number of armed men, she would run back to the suite and find her bow if she thought she could help.

"I think he can take care of whatever trouble comes, but that doesn't mean it's acceptable to miss filing a report."

Tikaya couldn't tell if Dak was making a joke or not. She did sense that he was trying not to worry her. That made her worry more. "I can go with you." He opened his mouth, but she spoke again before he could start. "I've been in combat situations." Remembering she had demonstrated her ability to fall out of a chair not minutes before, Tikaya added, "I've been *useful* in combat situations."

"I've heard about your bow skills. What I was going to say is that you should pack a bag too. I'm going to put out orders to evacuate the hotel. Just in case."

"Based on our hunches? That seems drastic."

"It was going to have to be evacuated soon anyway." Dak jogged for the door, but paused before turning into the hallway. He looked back at her. "Don't take too long packing that bag."

When Maldynado had imagined setting a trap and catching the villain responsible for sabotaging Sespian's building, he hadn't imagined himself crawling out on a six-inch-wide steel beam twenty feet above the ground. If he dropped the jug cradled under his arm, he hoped Basilard would catch it before it crashed to the dirt below and broke into a thousand pieces.

"Should have delegated this to Sicarius. He *likes* this sort of thing."

Maldynado had no idea which section of the framework would be most structurally crucial, but he doubted the cigar-smoking prisoner would have known, either. This had probably been intended to be one more bit of mysterious sabotage to set back construction, not the ultimate disaster that would halt work permanently.

"How's this look?" he called down, trying to keep his voice low. They had more than an hour until midnight, so he doubted the sniper they expected would be out there yet, but there was a security guard roaming around the site, a lantern bumping and banging against his thigh. As quiet as the city was tonight, Maldynado had been able to hear it from a hundred meters away. He had timed his climb to avoid being spotted. Even if he was on the side of the law here, explaining his current position might prove difficult, especially to the foreman.

From the shadows below, Basilard waved and pointed. Of *course* he thought the jug should be moved ten feet farther out on the beam. *He* wasn't the one sliding along the narrow perch on his belly.

"You better not be having fun with me," Maldynado whispered, scooting farther out. His shirt was rucked up around his ribs, so the cold metal scraped his bare stomach. He couldn't see any difference between his chosen spot and the other. "All right, what about here?"

Basilard gave him an affirmative, then waved with urgency and pointed toward the south side of the lot. Maldynado couldn't see anything over there, but he scooted backward, assuming the guard was coming. Or maybe their guest had shown up early. If the sniper spotted Maldynado up on the beam, he would know something was wrong and would flee without ever taking a shot.

"Or he'll take a shot at *me*," Maldynado grumbled.

As he reached the closest vertical support post, a lantern came into view around the corner of the building. Yup, that night watchman was ambling along at a good clip. Maldynado skimmed down the post, ignoring the rivets bumping at his legs through his trousers, and landed on the cement slab at the bottom, careful to slow down for a soundless landing.

Without any lights on the site, Maldynado would have expected the shadows to hide him, but a bright three-quarters moon had risen, and the guard was squinting in his direction. Someone must have chosen the midnight hour for sabotage, knowing it wouldn't be too dark for the sniper to see his target. Good for the sniper, bad for Maldynado. He slipped behind the thick steel post, hoping the guard wasn't certain he had seen something. Basilard had already melted into the shadows somewhere.

But the guard dropped a hand to a pistol and changed his path, heading straight for the post. Maldynado was debating whether to flee or to attempt to explain himself when the man spun about, facing in the opposite direction. He raised his lantern and pulled the pistol from its holster.

Maldynado didn't know whether he had Basilard or Sicarius to thank, but he took off in the opposite direction, using the shadows beneath the looming framework to hide his retreat. By the time the guard turned around, Maldynado was out of sight behind the dumpsters at the corner of the lot.

A moment later, Basilard joined him there.

"Are you the one I have to thank for that distraction?" Maldynado whispered.

It was too dark to see Basilard's response, but he pointed toward an alley across the street. Yes, good idea to leave the site—and the guard who was poking his head around posts and beams, looking all over the place now. They ran across the street, then followed the shadows along the buildings until they reached an alley that had a view of the jug. It would have a view of it for someone with eagle eyes anyway.

"Can you see that from here?" Maldynado asked.

Basilard pointed at the beam.

"That smudge? Are you sure?"

Unfortunately, the alley was also too dark to read his signs.

"It will be easier to see from a rooftop," Sicarius said from behind them.

Maldynado nearly jumped out of his boots.

You invited him, he reminded himself. No complaining about stealthy approaches.

"A sniper may choose to shoot from the building to our right or the one to the right of it. The lower roof to our left would provide a poor angle."

"Guess that means he can see it too," Maldynado said.

"Someone approaches," Sicarius said.

"Someone with a bow or a rifle who's obviously here for heinous purposes?"

"It's Sergeant Yara."

"Oh, probably not then," Maldynado said.

"I will watch the rooftops for the approach of this saboteur."

Maldynado tried to decide from Sicarius's tone if he thought this mission a waste of time. He definitely gave the impression he had somewhere else he would rather be. Of course, emotionless features and monotone voice notwithstanding, Maldynado usually sensed that from him.

Several seconds later, the soft clinking of handcuffs bumping on a utility belt foretold Evrial's approach. Maldynado stepped out of the alley to lift a hand toward the shadowy figure, though he would not have been certain it was she and not some other enforcer if not for Sicarius's warning. Maldynado wondered how he could tell—her height was tall for a woman but not for a man, and the bulky uniform jacket hid her curves. He trusted Sicarius's instincts though.

"Good evening, my lady," Maldynado said. "Did you come because you were unable to sleep after your shift, due to the cold emptiness beside you in bed?"

"I came because I was sure you would be arrested by dawn if I didn't." Yup, that was Evrial.

Basilard signed something, though Maldynado could only pick out a couple of the gestures. He got the gist though. Basilard's vote was for Maldynado getting arrested well *before* dawn.

"I also came to tell you that our block has been added to the evacuation list," Evrial said. "You might want to come back to the flat and pack whatever belongings you don't want to see devoured by the plant."

"I can't leave until we've found out who's behind the sabotage here."

"I'm not packing your hat collection for you."

"I don't need you to. I'll risk the loss."

"Fine," Evrial said. "Though I don't see why you're so worried about this building. I can't believe they're even continuing with construction in the face of everything that's going on."

"Because..." Maldynado turned around, intending to ask Basilard to give them some privacy, but he had already slipped away, joining Sicarius on the rooftops perhaps. "Because this is my chance to prove myself to Starcrest. He thinks... well, I don't know what he thinks, but I'm guessing he believes me a tad... superfluous."

"I doubt that's the word that comes to his mind when he thinks of you."

"Whatever it is, I'm sure it's not flattering. I haven't had a chance to make a good impression on him yet. If I can solve this problem, this is my chance to show him I'm... useful."

"Still angling for a statue?" Evrial asked.

"No, a job."

She was silent for a moment, gazing toward the building site, watching the guard, his lantern bumping at his side as he made a new circuit. "A job in the city, I assume."

"I imagine I would go wherever he might want to send me."

"Which probably wouldn't be to a little rural town with two streets."

"Two streets?" Maldynado asked, trying to lighten her somberness. "Were there that many?"

It didn't work. Evrial folded her arms and continued to stare across to the construction site. "Do you truly want a job or is this just some... strategy to get me to stay. You can't leave because you have this important government work to do, so naturally I would be the one who would have to give up my dream?"

"Uhm." Maldynado might have been thinking along those lines, but he hated to admit it. "Are you so determined to leave Stumps? Isn't there any way...?"

"Maldynado, this promotion... it's all I ever wanted, all I ever worked for. To be one of the first women at the top of the enforcer ranks."

"I thought..." Maldynado cleared his throat. "I had hoped that if I got a good job here, you would be open to staying. I know there's a promotion for you there, but you have a job here, too, and you're good at what you do. You would get a promotion here sooner rather than later, I'm sure of it." Especially if Maldynado could indeed get in with the president. "I just can't see myself in your little town. With all your relatives."

"They would get used to you."

"But what would I *do* there?"

Fortunately, she did not point out that he wasn't *doing* much here. "I don't know, but it stings that you would be willing to go wherever

Starcrest tells you, but you won't even think about going where I... Never mind. I guess I knew from the beginning that we're... too different."

Maldynado slumped against the cold brick wall. Was he selfish not to consider it? It wasn't *that* far away from the city. Or was it less about being selfish and more about sensing that deep down, she had had enough of him?

"I thought the differences made things interesting," Maldynado said.

"They did. They do. But is 'interesting' enough to base a life around?"

Maldynado shrugged helplessly. He hadn't realized she had been planning the rest of her life. He had thought they were still just having fun.

"I need to go back and pack," Evrial said. "Good luck with your trap. Be careful."

Maldynado didn't say anything as she walked down the alley and disappeared around the corner. Maybe instead of trying to arrange love lives for Sespian and Basilard, he should have been worrying about his own affairs. Or maybe it had just been easier—safer—to deal with someone else's.

CHAPTER 21

SESPIAN CROUCHED AT THE CORNER of the building with Mahliki. Two lorries barricaded the street to the north and the south, military lorries that should have been there to defend Starcrest. How had those religious zealots acquired them?

On the other side of the building, a few soldiers were rushing to drag in the diving suits the president had ordered while others covered them, hurling blasting sticks into the riled up greenery. Spot fires burned, but the plant itself never caught flame. Craters dotted the ground around the building, and it was as if they were in the middle of a battlefield rather than on the waterfront in the most populous city in Turgonia. But midnight had come, and the citizens had been evacuated, so the only witnesses to this battle were the combatants and the moon above.

On the rooftop, more soldiers knelt or lay on their stomachs in sniper positions, taking shots at the lorries and the robed figures inside. In the few seconds Sespian watched, bullets that should have cut through the glass windows of the cabs bounced off.

"The Science?" he asked.

"Yes." Mahliki waved toward the nearest vehicle. "Someone is maintaining shields—the vehicles don't have the feel of Made devices. The practitioners out there feel clunky—like they're expending a lot of effort to perform small tasks—so I don't think they're particularly well-trained."

"They don't need to be to make trouble for us, seeing as we lack anyone with those talents."

"True, but there aren't that many of them. Maybe three or four with any skill. The rest of the robed men are bruisers acting as bodyguards and cannon fodder for our soldiers. If we can get to the practitioners and knock them out or take them out of the equation somehow, then this simply becomes a firefight between two parties of mundane warriors."

"Do you think you can identify the practitioners?" Sespian asked.

"They're in the cabs, those two, I think. I wonder if they're only shielding the fronts of the lorries or if they've thought to extend their defenses to the bottoms as well. A well-placed blasting stick..." Mahliki looked Sespian up and down in the dancing shadows from the nearest fire. "I don't suppose you brought blasting sticks?"

"No, sorry. Those are *our* lorries after all, the military's. I didn't think blowing them up would be a goal."

"Better them than the *Explorer*. Sespian, if Father doesn't get that sub fixed up and down in the water... those priests are going to be the only ones who can harm the plant, and I don't think they realize the magnitude of the problem. A few lightning strikes will be like stealing grains of sand from the beach. Even if they do understand and have something great planned, do we want to be rescued on their terms?"

Though Sespian wasn't sure Starcrest would approve of his seventeen-year-old daughter running into the middle of this danger, he couldn't deny her argument. The soldiers had orders to stand their ground and protect the president—and the submarine. He and Mahliki might be the only ones who could try to sneak behind enemy lines to stop the practitioners.

"I'll get some blasting sticks," Sespian said.

Mahliki flashed a smile. "Good."

He darted back into the building through the gaping hole in the side. The fire at the front door had been put out by some of the men on the roof, but the priests were still targeting that area—some of them had rifles as well. Clangs and clanks continued to echo from within the submarine, the sounds faster and more frenzied now. Sespian hoped Starcrest was almost done in there, but at the same time, he was relieved nobody was outside the craft to notice him racing back through the hole with matches and an armful of blasting sticks. He didn't want to have to explain, "Uh, yes, My Lord, they're for your daughter."

He almost tripped and sent the explosives flying when he ran outside to find Mahliki with her back to the wall and two thick vines swirling in the air around her head. She jabbed at the closest one with the electrifying prod. Like a living beast, it jerked away from the attack before she could deliver more than a quick jolt. The lightning scorched it, but didn't slow it down.

Sespian set down the blasting sticks and raced to join her. He yanked the black dagger out of his belt, jumped, and grabbed the nearest vine.

With one hand, he hacked into it, and with the other, he tried to wrestle it to the ground. The tendril, as thick as his forearm, was as unyielding as a tree trunk. Only after he sliced into it several times, cutting halfway through the meaty stalk, could he push it to the ground. It took all of his body weight.

He thought Mahliki was busy with the other vine and that he would have to saw the top of his off by himself, but she pounced like a cat, trapping the tendril with the forked tip of the steel prod. Lightning poured from the tool, searing the plant.

It shocked Sespian as well, and he leaped free, feeling as if his heart would shoot out of his chest. The singed scent of the vine tainted the air, mingling with the wood smoke from the charred building. Soon the attacking vine went limp, its flesh shrunken and black. Mahliki had managed to take down the other tendril as well. More of the green stalks writhed scant meters away. They reminded Sespian of hissing cats backed into a corner.

"We might not want to stay here," he said, gathering the blasting sticks.

"I know. I wish we could circle around somehow and get behind the lorries, but I'm not going through that jungle." Mahliki peered into the gloom behind the building—the dark lake waited back there, along with the remains of the dock where the submarine had been unloaded. The plant had since destroyed most of the structure and taken over the shoreline. "We'll have to dart across the street. Let's head for that alley. If we can slip between those buildings and get onto the next block, it'll be dark over there. Maybe we can sneak up on them from that direction."

Sespian wondered if he, as former emperor, should be giving the orders here. You're not anyone now, the voice in the back of his head pointed out. Besides, he didn't have a better idea. "Hold on." He dug out a match. "I'll throw a blasting stick in either direction, and we can run across the street while they're busy staring at the explosions." He wished he could hurl one as far as the lorries, but the drivers must know their magical protection would only do so much good—they were staying back far enough that none of the explosives hurled from the soldiers had gotten close.

"Good idea," Mahliki said.

Sespian was about to strike the match when a voice from above asked, "What are you two kids doing down there?"

A soldier knelt at the edge of the roof, a rifle across his knees. He had an eye toward the nearest lorry, but he was clearly talking to Sespian and Mahliki.

"Plotting an incursion behind enemy lines," Mahliki announced.

Her honesty surprised Sespian. "I would have lied," he whispered.

"It's not like he would have believed we're going out for rum and haupia."

"For what?"

"It would probably be cider and flat cakes here."

"Does your father know about your... mission?" the soldier asked. Though he was addressing Mahliki, Sespian found the notion that he had to ask for parental permission a strange one after so many years of taking care of himself.

"Light the blasting sticks," Mahliki whispered to Sespian, then raised her voice to tell the soldier, "My father raised me to be a creative thinker and an independent soul."

"That sounds like a no," the soldier said.

Mahliki nudged Sespian. Shaking his head, he lit the two blasting sticks. The flames danced on the fuses.

"What are you two doing?" The soldier lowered his rifle and gripped the edge of the roof, as if he were going to jump down.

"Now," Sespian whispered and leaned around the front corner of the building. He tossed one stick into the street to the north and the other to the south.

A rifle cracked in the distance, and he jerked back. A bullet smashed through the corner of the building, and shards of wood dusted Sespian's head.

"A little cover fire would be welcome," Mahliki called up to the soldier.

Whatever his response might have been was lost in the explosions, first to the north and then to the south, one after the other. Mahliki raced from cover, the awkward electricity generator not slowing her at all. Sespian sprinted across the street after her.

To his right and left, clouds of smoke billowed from the blast sites, obscuring the lorries. Broken cement and dirt thudded down in all directions, but nobody fired as Sespian and Mahliki sprinted across the street. They reached the alley without trouble, though they hadn't run more than ten paces down it before two robed figures appeared at the far end. Two figures with rifles.

With the flames lighting the sky behind Sespian and Mahliki, he knew they would be easy targets. It would take time to light another blasting stick, and it might bring down one of the buildings anyway. He still had the black dagger and snatched it from his belt, leaning around Mahliki to hurl it at the closest of the figures.

"Look out," she whispered to Sespian and lunged behind a garbage bin.

As soon as the dagger flew from his hand, he followed her example. A rifle fired, cracking into brick inches above their heads. The closer man never got a shot off. Sespian hadn't taken more than a split second to aim, and had thought he would distract his target at best, but the dagger slammed into his shoulder. The robed figure spun backward, then tripped over his own feet and toppled to the ground.

"What the—" the other priest blurted, glancing at his downed comrade.

Mahliki sprinted from behind the garbage bin, charging straight at him.

Sespian cursed and ran after her, afraid the priest would have far too much time to recover before she reached the mouth of the alley. He noticed her racing at him and raised his rifle again. Sespian didn't have anything else left to throw.

Mahliki must have flicked the switch on the generator, pushing it to full power, for blue streaks of lightning arced through the air in front of her. The man stepped back, his eyes bulging open. For a moment, his rifle lowered. He shook his head and recovered, jerking it up again, but he was too late. Mahliki leaped the last few feet, swinging the prod at the rifle. Metal clanked against metal. Lightning ran from the prod up the rifle, and the man yelped and released his hold. Mahliki kicked him in the groin.

Sespian intended to leap in to help, but the first priest was rising to his feet. He yanked the dagger out of his shoulder with a pained grunt, one that turned into a snarl of fury. He lifted it toward Mahliki, then saw Sespian run out of the alley and changed his target.

The inky dagger slashed toward him. The darkness made it hard to judge the attack, and Sespian chose to dodge rather than block it. The armful of blasting sticks made throwing out blocks—and punches—difficult, regardless. He kicked upward, catching the side of the man's arm. It was enough to get him to drop the knife, the blade clanking as it struck the cement. Without lowering his leg all the way to the ground, Sespian shifted his hip and launched a side kick. His heel slammed into the priest's ribcage. Sespian followed the attack with a palm strike to the solar plexus. The man reeled back, clutching his chest. He dropped to his knees.

In the poor lighting, Sespian couldn't see the dagger, but he spotted the bigger weapon, the man's rifle. He grabbed it and pressed the muzzle into the priest's back before he could recover.

Mahliki was finishing her foe, too, and Sespian had time to see her punch the man in the gut, throwing all of her weight behind it like a hand-to-hand specialist, not a teenage girl. Sespian would compliment her later. For now...

He pressed harder with the rifle. "Take a long walk, friend. There's nothing but death for you here."

The priest staggered to his feet and glared at Sespian, but shambled off without argument. Sespian hoped he wasn't making a mistake in letting him go, but they couldn't stop to tie up everyone they crossed. He hadn't even thought to bring rope.

A heavy thud came from behind him. When Sespian turned, he found Mahliki's opponent unmoving on the ground.

"Mine didn't want to walk," she said.

He smiled at her. "Sometimes they don't. You have impressive fighting skills." He hoped his own hadn't embarrassed him. It was hard to throw knives, kicks, and punches while cradling blasting sticks to one's chest.

"Thank you. Though that smarted." Mahliki shook out her hand. "Only in Turgonia can you find priests with abdomens harder and more muscled than those of the soldiers."

"Well, we have a long history of being warriors." Sespian patted around on the ground and found the dagger. "Religion on the other hand is just catching on after a long break."

"Take this one's rifle," Mahliki said. "It's one of those new ones that fires multiple rounds without needing reloading. I'd take it, but the generator is all I can manage, and we might need it if we encounter plants."

"Got it," Sespian said after he had grabbed the rifle and tugged the man's ammo pouch off his belt—this elicited a groan but nothing more. "By the way, how did you get so used to ordering people around in combat situations?"

"I've been ordering my cousin around since I was four." Mahliki nodded toward the street, and they walked along, paralleling the waterfront. "Granted," she added, "those were mostly in bug-collection situations, but sometimes they grew quite hectic."

"Somehow I'm not surprised. Do you—"

Mahliki hissed and dropped to one knee. At first, Sespian thought she sensed some danger and was ducking out of the way, but the generator dipped off her shoulder and clunked to the ground. She clutched at her head with both hands.

"What is it?" Sespian whispered, putting a hand on her back, though he was already scanning the street for an attacker. He didn't see anybody.

"Practitioner," she got out between clenched teeth.

Sespian grimaced. How could he defend her from an opponent he couldn't see?

Sicarius crouched in the shadows, his fingertips pressed to the coarse tarpaper rooftop. He heard but paid little attention to Maldynado and Yara's conversation. Instead he trained his ears toward the city around him as he watched all possible routes leading to the buildings and the construction site. If he were a sniper, commanded to strike that jug from afar, he would choose a spot near the edge approximately ten feet in front of his current hiding spot. He had climbed to the top of a water tank at the back of the building and dismissed it—an intervening chimney would make the shot to the jug less than ideal. Yes, this was the spot he would choose. Though he could not imagine accepting such an asinine task. Even full of acid, the broken jug would cause little significant damage. A few beams and posts would have to be replaced, but it would set the workers back no more than a few hours. Sicarius believed Maldynado had misread whatever clues he had discovered that had led him to believe someone would be coming tonight. Nonetheless, he listened.

He heard the end of Maldynado's conversation with Yara. She strode out of the back of the alley they had shared, crossed the street, then stopped and leaned against a building. Sicarius could not see her, but knew she hadn't continued on. He did not suspect her of having anything to do with the saboteurs so assumed the conversation had affected her and made her pause. He was aware, too, of Basilard scouting about, first in the alleys and then on the adjacent rooftop. Sicarius trusted Basilard to remain hidden from an approaching sniper. Yara was less worried about hiding. She might become bait for an unintended trap if she did not move on. But after a few minutes, she pushed away from the wall and left. Good.

By the stars and the moon, Sicarius judged the passing of time. Midnight drew closer. He thought of walking a circuit to more fully see everything below, but he trusted his senses. He would remain hidden for now. And wait.

Eventually, the feeling of being watched came over him. That sense was not as reliable as taste or touch or hearing, but he trusted it well, and he knew the moment he was not alone. He shifted his head minutely to watch the rooftop of the building across the street behind his. The flat structure was lower than his own, and he had dismissed it since it would not provide a view for a sniper, but something about a lightning rod on that roof had changed. The narrow rod would not prove sturdy enough for him to climb, but for someone lighter, perhaps... Yes, a shape bulged out from the vertical shaft. A boy? A woman?

The Nurian mage hunter?

Would someone with her skill have been given such an uncritical task? He wouldn't think so, but those people *were* using her. The note had said as much. Using her like a hound until she ran into a grimbal that would eat her.

Sicarius shifted his gaze so he was not staring intently at the lightning rod, knowing she, like he, might sense another's eyes. One trained as a mage hunter might have even more refined mundane senses, all the better to detect the use of the Science. She might already know he was there.

Deciding to wait for her to make the first move, Sicarius remained in his position, his back to a chimney, trusting his form was indistinguishable from the dark bricks. He kept to his toes, ready to spring away, in case an exceptionally fine pair of eyes picked him out of the shadows. The figure on the rod remained still, too, so still he began to suspect the bulge was some object fastened to the shaft rather than a person. But he had surveyed that roof when he had first come up to this one. The bulge hadn't been there then.

Between one blink and the next, the shape dropped from its perch, landing on the roof and disappearing from his line of sight. Sicarius waited. The street was too wide to leap across. If she descended from the rooftop, she might encounter Maldynado. Sicarius listened for signs of an attack—Maldynado would likely need help against this opponent.

But the sniper didn't climb down from her building. She sailed out of the night, tucked into a ball, a long pole held horizontally as she somersaulted down onto the lip of his rooftop. Impressive. If Sicarius had been closer to that back edge, he might have attacked then, before she landed and recovered from the flight, but he was closer to the front, to the view of the construction site.

The woman crouched, laying the pole on the roof without a sound. She shifted a bow stave off her back. She would have to string it. Recognizing a moment when she might be slightly distracted, Sicarius slipped away from the chimney. The flat roof offered no contours to hide behind, but there were other chimneys, as well as vents, and that water tank at the back. He used every scrap of cover, drawing closer to her.

Her head came up, and he froze, standing tall, pressing his back against the side of the water tower. For a long moment, the woman didn't move, though he could feel her gaze raking the roof, searching for whatever she had sensed. He hadn't made a sound, but she knew he was there, nonetheless.

When her head shifted slightly, pointing toward the chimney where he had been before, he eased behind the water tank. At some point during his stalking, his black dagger had found its way into his hand. Apprehending her without killing her would be difficult, but he might strike a grievous blow without making it a mortal one. If her attention was still focused elsewhere, he would be close enough to attack when he reached the far side of the tank. He thought of climbing it and leaping down from above, but he would be silhouetted against the sky then. Also, once one jumped, it was difficult to alter one's direction, and impossible to change one's momentum, if an opponent on the ground reacted.

Sicarius listened before coming out of cover and didn't hear anything, but his senses told him he had taken too long. He eased his head around the side of the tank.

The woman was gone.

She had either sensed his approach or had finished stringing her bow and continued on to the front of the rooftop. He didn't see her anywhere. The moon had gone behind a cloud, stealing the shadows, the contrast. She wasn't wearing white tonight. If she were crawling across the roof on her belly, he might not be able to distinguish her from the tarpaper. He looked up, on the chance that *she* had chosen the top of the tank for an attack. With a projectile weapon, it made much more sense. But no figures were silhouetted against the cloudy sky.

A crack sounded in the distance—from the construction site. The jug.

A crash followed the crack, the ceramic shattering on the ground below its perch.

Sicarius forced himself not to sprint to the edge of the roof, though the knowledge that she had gotten by, and that he might miss her altogether, threatened to muddle his calmness with urgency. He went the rest of the way around the water tank, intending to stay behind cover and pick his way to the front again. His foot brushed something, and he chastised himself. The pole. He had forgotten it and almost kicked it. Such noise would be unforgivable.

He was going to step over it, to leave it so she wouldn't know for sure someone was up here with her, but his senses and his mind melded, throwing an alert to the front of his brain. The sounds... the way the arrow had clunked against the jug instead of cracking solidly into it, the way the ceramic had landed, off to the side on the dirt instead of on the cement directly below it. She hadn't shot from an ideal position. She had glanced it. She—

Sicarius crouched and spun. A figure knelt on the top of the tank, raising its bow at him.

The string was dampened somehow and didn't have a telltale twang—otherwise he would have heard that with the first shot and known the shooter's location right away. He lunged to the side, dodging the arrow and launching a throwing knife in the same breath. The arrow thunked into the tarpaper inches from his head. His knife almost caught her—in the shadows, she hadn't seen him fully, and he had kept the movement of the throw compact. He expected her to roll away from the edge, to use the top of the tank for cover, forcing him to climb the side to attack her again. But she dodged and jumped at the same time. The clouds shifted, and the moon came out. Its beam reflected off steel in the woman's hand, a short Nurian sword that he knew would have a razor edge. Its length would give her the advantage in a blade fight.

Instead of grabbing another throwing knife, Sicarius snatched up her discarded pole. He jerked it up, pointing the tip at his descending foe.

She saw it, and tried to twist to evade it, but he tracked her. He jabbed the pole upward to take her in the stomach. It wouldn't be a killing blow, but with her momentum, it would bruise or break ribs. The pain should distract her in a fight.

The pole caught her, sliding into her gut more than he expected. The scream was unexpected as well. A mage hunter should have been trained not to cry out and certainly not to do so loudly enough to announce her position to the world.

Sicarius thrust the pole—and her—away from himself. He expected her to find a way off it, to leap away as she landed, but she didn't, and he reached her as soon as she dropped to the roof. She tried to roll away from him, but he knelt, pinning her. Perplexingly, she gave him the time to drop his dagger to her throat, resting the blade against vulnerable flesh. Then his nose caught the telltale scent of blood and he understood. The pole had done more than bruise ribs. Or had she been surprised into cutting herself with her own blade somehow?

He didn't take his eyes from her, but in his peripheral vision, he considered the pole. The moon was still out, and he could make out more under its revealing light, including the bloody tip of a six-inch-long stabbing blade on its end. An unexpected tool for springing from building to building. Ah, and there was her own sword. She had dropped it as she fell, but it too had blood on the blade. He would not feel smug at this awkwardness in her defense, for she had nearly succeeded in outmaneuvering him.

The fallen woman gasped, clutching her stomach. She seemed oblivious to the weapon at her throat.

"You are Ji Nah, the Nurian mage hunter, correct?" Sicarius asked. He did not believe she would die immediately from the gut wound, but he would extract what information he could in case she did. He did not currently know the location of any healers in the city, and she might die before he could reach a doctor, regardless.

She lifted her arm, and he pressed the dagger harder against her throat, wary of an attack. If she knew she was dying anyway, she might try anything to take him with her.

But her shaking fingers clutched weakly at the air, then locked onto his arm. "Your son... he—" she coughed, trying to clear her throat, but phlegm—or blood—made it a rough gurgle. "He owes me... favor."

"I am aware of the arrow you shot at him," Sicarius said. He did not believe Sespian considered himself indebted to the woman, but he did not say this. She had few words left. He would hear them to see if they contained useful information.

She licked her lips and spat blood. Struggling to enunciate clearly, she said, "Three-seventeen Dee-Four Windy Lane."

Sicarius said nothing, waiting for more.

"Tell—you will tell him?" she asked.

"I will tell him."

"Tell..." She had a coughing fit, and Sicarius leaned back, removing the blade from her throat. She was no longer a threat. "Tell Serpitivich... he's... a bastard. I'll... haunt him... 'til he dies."

The vice president? He was among those who were plotting against the president? Did Colonel Starcrest know? Or maybe this woman had some other grievance against Serpitivich. Sicarius thought to ask for clarification, but her grip on his arm slackened, then fell away. He touched his fingers to her throat, felt the last beats of her heart, then stood, aware that he hadn't been alone for the last minute.

Basilard stood a few meters away. Someone else was climbing a ladder on the side of the building—Maldynado, judging by the weight of the tread on the rungs. They all would have heard the woman's screams.

"She is dead," Sicarius announced.

When Maldynado clambered over the side of the building, he had a lantern with him. He walked over, the light telling Sicarius nothing he didn't know. It did, however, allow Basilard to communicate with them.

What's at Three-seventeen Dee-Four Windy Lane?

"My guess is a seven-year-old child," Sicarius said.

CHAPTER 22

W HEN THE PRIESTS HAD SHUFFLED Amaranthe and Deret into the sewer tunnels, she had thought the plants might leap out and devour the green-robed men, but they had encountered nothing except for a few blackened husks, meaning someone in the group must be a lightning-summoning practitioner. Based on that—and Amaranthe's hope that she and Deret would be taken to the leader of the outfit—she didn't try to escape.

The detour through the tunnels was short, followed by a climb to street level and into the back of a lorry, along with most of the robe-wearing crew. The lemongrass odor lingering about them didn't quite block out the scent of unwashed bodies. Whatever naughtiness they had been engaged in lately apparently precluded time for bathing.

The men had kept their hoods up in the back of the lorry, so she didn't catch any faces, though given the height and breadth of the bodies packed against her on the wooden bench, most of the priests were male. They kept their pistols pointed at Amaranthe and Deret for the duration of the ride, a gesture that made her nervous when they left the smooth city streets to bump and jolt up a dirt road. The back flap had been pulled down, so she couldn't see where they had gone, but the earthy scents of vegetation—*natural* vegetation—drifted to her nose over the sweat and lemongrass potpourri. If she and Deret managed to escape, they would have a long walk back to town. The priests had let Deret bring his swordstick with him to navigate the sewers, but she wasn't sure if he still had it. Several men separated them on the bench, and she hadn't tried to speak with him. Given that it was a weapon as well as a cane, she thought they might take it from him, but maybe they hadn't noticed its dual functionality.

The lorry made a turn onto a rutted dirt road worse than the last. It jostled the priests into each other—and Amaranthe—and almost tossed her onto the floor a couple of times. She was relieved when the vehicle finally slowed down. The scent of wood smoke crept into the mix. She hoped that whatever rustic homestead they had arrived at included the leader of this old/new religion, so she could attempt to talk him into giving up his felonious ways. And if that didn't work, she would settle for painting a target on his back for some sniper under Dak Starcrest's command. Amaranthe wondered if the colonel had any idea about this place.

The lorry halted, and someone pushed up the tarp. A few men piled out, but others remained inside, keeping their eyes on Amaranthe and Deret.

"Where are we?" She didn't expect an answer—the men hadn't proved a garrulous lot thus far—but one never knew.

"Your final destination," one said.

"That sounds ominous."

"Good."

Before Amaranthe could come up with another question that might or might not be answered helpfully, the muzzle of a pistol jabbed her ribs. "Get up. Get out."

"You too," someone said farther down, addressing Deret.

A door slammed somewhere in front of the lorry—someone coming out of the house? A conversation started up, but the speakers were too far away for Amaranthe to distinguish the words. She let the man with the pistol guide her out of the lorry. When she hopped down, she almost twisted her ankle on mud that had melted during the day and refroze after dark. A moon had risen, illuminating an orchard with rows of apple trees stretching away to either side of the road, their branches still mostly bare from the winter. A few lanterns drew her eye toward the buildings in front of the lorry. This was more than a "rustic homestead."

Two houses, barns, and numerous equipment sheds formed a loose semi-circle around the driveway. All of the buildings had modern designs with unique angles and oddly sloped roofs that didn't fit Amaranthe's idea of a farm—or orchard. There was a wrought iron fence around the largest house with sharp spikes pointing toward the night sky. Interesting, but the speakers in front of the main house demanded most of her attention. Two were robed and had probably come out of the lorry, but a pot-bellied man with gray hair wasn't wearing any sort of disguise, though the poor lighting made it hard to see the details of his face. Amaranthe tried to sidle closer without being obvious about it.

"Stop." A pistol jabbed her in the ribs again.

"Just trying to stretch my legs," Amaranthe said innocently. She found Deret in the shadows. He was paying more attention to the buildings than she, and she wondered if they might be a clue. Given the circumstances, she doubted he was simply admiring the craftsmanship.

She shook out her legs to give credence to her statement and managed to get a little closer to Deret without getting another bruise from the pistol. Maybe the priests didn't care if they stood next to each other, only if they tried to approach the speakers.

"Know where we are?" Amaranthe murmured. She wished Deret could understand Basilard's hand code, as even the soft words drew the attention of a nearby priest. No less than six pistols were pointed their way. Who did these people think they were dealing with anyway? Deret might be a former soldier, but with his limp, he shouldn't seem threatening to a group this large, and she didn't think anyone knew who she was, not that she could threaten a group this large, either, not unless Sicarius had followed her out here, and she deemed that unlikely. Silly her, she had decided she should visit Deret alone.

"Edgecrest Orchards," he said.

"Edgecrest... that's not the first time I've come across that name of late."

"It's on a lot of apple cider and brandy labels in the satrap."

Amaranthe shook her head. "It's more than that. I've seen it recently. There was a Ploris Edgecrest in Sauda's date book. And Tikaya had seen another Edgecrest as an entrant to the building design contest."

"Ah, Oddak. I don't think he has anything to do with the family orchard. He's an architecture professor at the university. He must have designed these buildings." Deret cocked his head, considering the style. "In his youth."

"Is that Ploris, then?" Amaranthe nodded toward the gray-haired man, who was now pointing toward the barn. She had a hard time imagining the attractive Sauda spending time with the double-chinned, pot-bellied man. Of course, her note had mentioned scintillating conversation rather than scintillating looks.

"Yes. He's the eldest of several brothers. He's the one who runs the orchard. The paper has done a few write-ups for the food and drink section."

"So is he the lead priest, or is he just letting the clan use the estate for meetings?"

"I don't know," Deret said. "The earlier meeting tonight was at the library."

"The *library*?"

"Yes, you were expecting a different locale?"

"For a group of people reviving an ancient religion?" Amaranthe asked. "Yes. Something oozing with history, decorated with cobwebs, and perhaps embellished with blood-spattered walls."

Someone nearby snorted, reminding her that their private conversation wasn't that private. Either Deret hadn't said anything that was terribly secret yet or... these people weren't planning on letting either of them go, so what he revealed didn't matter.

"If you leave enough in the donation jar by the door, the librarian might have a decorator come in for you," Deret said.

"Funny."

"Yes, it's wit like this that keeps the women flocking to my door."

"You and the colonel should spend time together," Amaranthe said, leaving off Starcrest's name since it hadn't sounded like it was widespread knowledge that he was working intelligence for the president. "You can marinate in each other's bitterness."

"Does he have trouble getting women too?"

"I'm not sure, but I haven't seen any hanging on his arm."

"Will Maldynado be finding him someone at his dinner party too?" Deret asked.

Now Amaranthe snorted, imagining Maldynado hustling the dour one-eyed colonel out onto the dance floor. "I don't think he was planning to, but perhaps I should mention it. He's not easily daunted when it comes to finding women."

"I've noticed."

The gray-haired Edgecrest went back inside the house, and the priests he had been talking to returned to the lorry. One pointed at Amaranthe and Deret. "Put them in the press building."

Press. Amaranthe didn't care for that word. She imagined her limbs being fed into a massive apple pulper. Pistols prodding her in the back didn't give her any choice but to go along with the order. The entire group of priests came along. She wished a few of them would wander off to pray or practice magic or take baths, so more escape opportunities might present themselves.

She and Deret were ushered into a building filled with equipment and vats, including a hulking steam-powered press. Yes, that machine appeared perfectly capable of pulverizing limbs.

"Sit them down."

Two priests brought out casks that had been sawn in half. They upended them, creating chairs of a sort.

"I'll stand," Deret said.

Someone kicked his swordstick off the ground. He lurched, but caught his balance, leaning more heavily on his good leg.

"Sit," the deep-voiced priest growled.

Deret flexed his fingers, looking like he'd had enough of going along with the priests' machinations. There were too many, though. This wasn't the time for a fight.

Amaranthe sat down on her cask and wiggled her butt. "It could use a cushion, but it's not bad."

Grumbling under his breath, Deret joined her, doing his best not to display his limp. She wished he would display it and then some—the more helpless these people thought they were, the more likely some of them would wander off, leaving only a small detachment of guards Amaranthe and Deret could overcome. That was how she imagined the scenario anyway. In reality... all of the priests, all sixteen of them, queued up along the nearest wall, their pistols in their hands.

"Are we waiting for someone?" Amaranthe asked cheerfully, still hoping someone might spill something useful. It was hard to gaze imploringly into someone's eyes to gain sympathy when they had hoods pulled low over their foreheads, hiding their faces. None of them answered.

"I would apologize for getting you into this," Deret whispered, "but I did try to have you left behind."

"Yes, that was noble of you. Thank you." Amaranthe's choice to invite herself along hadn't been premeditated, and, in reflection, she should have seen if they would let her go out the front door. From there, she could have followed the group, jumped onto the back of the lorry, and ridden along in secret, where she might now be in a position to free Deret and snoop around the premises... She sighed and told herself the priests probably wouldn't have let her go anyway. She didn't know if that was true, but it made her feel better.

"I'm also not entirely sure this is all about me," Deret said.

"You think they came to kidnap *me*? You're the one wearing their robes."

"Exactly. I thought I was... on the inside."

"Maybe you thought wrong," Amaranthe said.

"Possibly, but you know the president. You'd be a more appealing hostage." He kept his voice low so the priests shouldn't overhear, but Amaranthe wished he would keep his mouth shut on the matter, in case they *didn't* know who she was and whom she knew.

She turned her head away from him, hoping he would take the hint, and examined their surroundings more carefully. In addition to the machinery, giant fermenters and tanks lined one of the walls. Though she wouldn't care to duplicate the deadly results of her molasses tank explosion, she wouldn't be above drenching these priests in alcohol if she could figure out a way to do so. If she had a few minutes unwatched, she ought to be able to rig something...

A door creaked open.

Amaranthe twisted in her seat, expecting the gray-haired Edgecrest to walk in. Instead a handsome older woman entered, her long black hair pulled away from her shoulders and face in an elegant coiffure held in place with ivory combs. She wore a luxurious leopard-fur cloak swept back from a suede dress that hugged her hips—and other curvy parts as well.

It might have taken Amaranthe a moment to identify the woman—after all, she had spied on the *house*, not the owner—but Deret stiffened with recognition—cold recognition—as soon as she walked in.

"Sauda Star—Shadowcrest?" Amaranthe whispered.

Deret nodded curtly as the woman approached. "Yes."

"Good evening, Deret," Sauda said, stopping in front of him. "My condolences on your father's death, though I assure you it grieves me as much as it does you."

The woman didn't sound aggrieved. But then neither was Deret, so maybe that was the point of the comment.

"I'll bet," Deret said.

"Aren't you supposed to be in jail?" Amaranthe asked.

"Why have you brought us here?" Deret asked at the same time.

"Us?" Sauda gave Amaranthe a curious look. "*You* were brought here because I have an offer for you, Lord Mancrest."

"Yes?"

"Your father wasn't as amenable to putting his backing—the *newspaper's* backing—behind the new regime as I had expected he might be, given the proper persuasion. Indeed, I spent many nights *persuading* him, but in the end, he wasn't willing to cross Rias."

New regime? One run by the Kriskrusians? Amaranthe itched to take over the questioning, but Sauda didn't have any interest in *her*, and she still thought remaining incognito would be best, if she could.

"*My* father?" Deret asked. "He didn't show any scruples when it came to jumping into bed with Forge and the Marblecrests."

"Precisely why I thought he would be amenable to a new offer. It is much easier to recruit for a new religion when it's being endorsed by the oldest paper in the capital, as well as the new president."

New president? Amaranthe nibbled on a fingernail. If Rias were to... disappear, Serpitivich would take over the position. She didn't know the man well, but she wouldn't have guessed him as someone to be in league with religious zealots. With his academic interests and mannerisms, he reminded her of... Books. Someone who would be happier researching in a library than running a nation. But he *had* run against Starcrest in the elections. And he had garnered a lot of support, coming in second. Maybe that second place position had rankled.

Deret recovered from a stunned moment of silence and asked, "My father wouldn't take your offer?"

"Even after twenty years, few people will cross Rias." Sauda's lips were a little too full—or perhaps she was too refined—to manage a hard sneer, but she conveyed the feeling, nonetheless.

"So you had him killed?"

"He knew too much. Admittedly, they weren't supposed to have him murdered in my *bed*—" Sauda sent a withering glare toward the priests. "That proved quite nettlesome. I hadn't been planning to be a *suspect* and spend days in jail, surrounded by mouth-breathing miscreants. I can't believe Rias didn't come down to help me out."

"Perhaps he believed you were guilty," Deret said.

Sauda sniffed.

"How *did* you get out?" Amaranthe asked.

"Let's just say that I am now fully committed to the *next* president. I've given my word."

And had someone bought that word in exchange for arranging her pardon? "To whom?" Amaranthe asked. It was possible these priests planned to kill Starcrest *and* Serpitivich and had a completely new candidate in mind. But if that were true, how could they ensure his election?

Sauda merely smiled.

"What do you want from me?" Deret asked. "I grew up in this town and grew up in this business too. I'll be distressed if your people believe *I* can be bought."

Amaranthe wished her cask were close enough to his that she could nudge him. It might not hurt to go along with Sauda, at least for tonight. Refusing her outright could be a bad idea.

"Why, I don't want to buy *you*, dear. I want to buy the *Gazette*."

Deret's jaw dropped.

"I understand you've been considering selling. Quite recently, in fact." Sauda raised her eyebrows at Amaranthe.

Had one of these priests been listening in on their conversation at the newspaper building? She hadn't heard or seen anyone lurking in the shadows, but if one was a practitioner, he might have more effectively hidden himself.

"I'm prepared to make a reasonable offer," Sauda said. "The Shadowcrests weren't embroiled in this succession war, nor do we have waterfront property that's been affected by this tedious plant invasion. I have the funds to pay you what the paper's worth, and I have a brother who's interested in taking over the running of it. There's no need for you to worry about your ethics or fear reprisal from Rias. I assure you he isn't a vindictive man."

"What's in it for you?" Amaranthe asked. "What do *you* care about this religion and whether they're well represented by the paper? Surely *you're* not practicing."

Sauda raised an elegant, finely plucked eyebrow.

"Are you?" Amaranthe added.

Wouldn't the president have known if his first wife had tendencies toward studying magic and ancient multi-headed gods? Of course, if it had been two decades since they had spoken... People could start a lot of new hobbies in twenty years.

"I will be the wife of the president," Sauda said. "One way or another." So if she couldn't have Rias...

"Serpitivich is that good in bed?" Amaranthe asked, hoping she could startle a verification out of the woman.

Sauda smiled. "I do not believe you'll be leaving tonight, but in the event that I'm incorrect, I'll keep that information to myself." While Amaranthe was trying to decide if Sauda had just verified her guess or not, the woman opened her cloak and withdrew a rolled parchment. "Here's my official offer for the paper, Lord Mancrest. I have a pen should you wish to sign tonight."

"Why would I sign anything to help you? Do you believe *I* won't be leaving tonight, either?"

"That's up to you. You can choose to sell the paper and walk away from the journalist's life, or you can remain here. Indefinitely."

"I wouldn't have thought President Starcrest would have married a murderer." Amaranthe watched the woman's face, trying to see if she was bluffing.

Sauda pressed her manicured and maroon-painted fingernails to her chest. "*I* have not murdered anyone."

The way she sent a long look toward the head priest told Amaranthe enough. She might not be murdering people, but she had no trouble standing back while others did the task.

"The only thing I need to accomplish is to gain control of the *Gazette*," Sauda said, "and then I'll have my marriage. I'll trust my husband-to-be to handle the more onerous task of becoming president."

"Unless he's willing to wait five years, that can only be accomplished with Rias's death," Amaranthe said, deliberately using the president's first name. While she could believe that marriage might turn some types of people from lovers to mortal enemies, she had a hard time imaging a former lover—wife—loathing Starcrest enough to design his death. Reputation aside, he struck Amaranthe as a likable, genuine person without any malice in his heart—or any irritating tendencies that might cause said malice to develop in the hearts of others. Even his mortal foes from enemy nations were reputed to think of him as an honorable opponent.

"Rias made his choice," Sauda said. "He should have stayed on that tropical island instead of coming back here with that vile blonde woman. No ruler of Turgonia has ever taken a foreigner for a wife, especially one who hasn't renounced her citizenship in her own land. It's loathsome and unacceptable."

But a scheming xenophobic murderer of a wife was perfectly acceptable, apparently.

"Why not simply wait until the next term?" Amaranthe asked. "There's no need for murder. Five years isn't so long, and your would-be husband can run then."

Sauda didn't answer. Actually, she didn't seem to be paying attention. One of the priests walked over with a pocket watch in his hand, and she nodded to him.

"Lord Mancrest," Sauda said. "The paper. Will you sign it over to me? As you can see, I've made a reasonable offer. You can retire young, and you need not suffer financial problems ever again, if you're wise with your investments."

"How thoughtful of you to consider the financial future of a stranger while you're plotting your husband's death," Deret said.

"As I've told you, I'm not plotting anyone's death."

"Maybe she's going to offer Starcrest a chance to sign away the presidency in exchange for his life," Amaranthe murmured.

Deret crumpled up the parchment and tossed it at Sauda's expensive silk shoes. "I would rather give the *Gazette* to one of my idealistic young interns than sell it to the people plotting against the president."

"How noble," Sauda said. "And how foolish." She nodded to the priest with the watch. "Put him somewhere that'll let him think about changing his mind."

"What if he doesn't change it?"

Sauda lifted a shoulder. "Accidents happen."

Maldynado wasn't sure how he had gotten stuck carrying the body, or why they were taking it back to the hotel at all. It wasn't as if the Nurian assassin could answer anyone's questions *now*. Sicarius would have left it on that rooftop, but Basilard had pointed out that they might need proof to explain what had happened at the construction site—not to mention that even a Nurian should have a funeral ceremony, rather than being left to rot on a barren rooftop until the crows came. Somehow *he* hadn't ended up carrying the body though. He was carrying the dead woman's weapons and the pole that had eviscerated her.

"Sicarius could have helped us tote everything back to the hotel before disappearing," Maldynado grumbled. He looked forward to reaching Colonel Starcrest's office, where he could foist his burden off on someone else. "Especially since *he* killed the woman, a woman with a child apparently."

It was not intentional, Basilard signed. *I saw the end of the conflict.*

They had reached Seventh, the broad street that led to the hotel, and unlike many of the roads closer to the waterfront, its gas lamps had been lit for the night, so Maldynado could make out Basilard's gestures.

"I wonder where he ran off to that's so important. You don't think Amaranthe is in trouble, do you? He wouldn't have come with us if that were the case, right?"

Unlikely.

"I hope he didn't go to check out that address. He is *not* the type of person a child wants to have appear out of nowhere in the middle of the night. That would be worse than a makarovi popping out of the closet."

I wonder why the woman thought Sespian would be a good choice to care for a child.

"Maybe the least bad choice out of a whole pile of bad choices. If she doesn't know any people here... or if there's no way the kid can be sent back to Nuria..." Maldynado shook his head. "I can't figure out why someone would take a child into enemy territory, especially when she was there to kill people."

More enemies left at home, perhaps.

"That's hard to imagine. I—"

Something snagged Maldynado's ankle. Startled he jerked back, almost dumping his load. Whatever had him didn't let go. He and Basilard were in the shadows between street lamps, and he couldn't make out anything on the sidewalk at his feet, but he had a hunch as to his captor.

"That blasted plant. A little help, Bas?"

Basilard drew a knife and crouched. The tendril—it must have been two inches thick—tightened around Maldynado's ankle. He shifted the dead assassin off his shoulder and pulled out a dagger of his own. Clouds had obscured the moon. He wished he had a match so he could see what he was doing. Or maybe a blasting stick. He had heard explosives, Sicarius's black dagger, and lightning strikes were about the only weapons that made a dent in the plant's green armor.

"I'm coming down to help," Maldynado warned, not wanting Basilard to mistake one of his fingers for the plant.

He patted around his calf and found the thick tendril, its flesh smooth and slick in the night air. Vibrations coursed through it—Basilard was sawing at it a few inches from Maldynado's leg. Maldynado poked with his own blade, trying to get it between the vine and his calf without cutting himself. His stabs proved ineffective. If anything the plant tightened its grip.

"It hasn't attacked people so quickly before, has it?" Maldynado was sure he hadn't stepped on anything; that vine had slithered out of some crack to snap around his leg like a hunter's snare. "I mean, I know some people got caught but—" he hissed as the tendril tightened yet again, "—I thought it was because they were slow. Or being stupid. Or—ouch, this thing is going to squeeze my leg right off. Bas, I hope you're making some progress."

Basilard couldn't sign and cut at the same time—and in the shadows, Maldynado wouldn't have been able to interpret his gestures anyway. Maldynado redoubled his efforts at prying the thing off, no longer worrying if he cut himself. This time, he simply sawed at the vine. The rasps of Basilard's dagger—he must be using one of the serrated ones—were comforting, but he couldn't tell how many millimeters were being shaved away—if any.

Maldynado resisted the urge to start yanking his foot around, certain it would mess up Basilard's cuts, but he couldn't feel his toes any more, and urgency and desperation were encroaching. He glanced around as he continued to cut, his blade doing next to nothing on the rubbery vine, hoping some steam vehicle might turn down the street and run over the plant a few times for him. Instead, he spotted movement in a nearby alley and heard a soft rustle, like that of snakes whispering through the grass. Except there were no snakes in the city—and no grass on the street.

"More are coming," he whispered. "What in the universe *is* this vile plant?"

Basilard's rasps grew faster. He felt the urgency too. Maldynado grimaced as some new sensation came to his leg, something damp seeping through his clothing. He probed it with his finger, then jerked his hand back. The dampness had... *bit* him. He wiped his finger on his jacket and dug his knife into the vine again. The blade slipped on its slick flesh. The ancestors-cursed plant was oozing something caustic.

The rustles grew closer, even as the acid bit into his skin. Maldynado cursed, hardly believing that after all he had survived, he was in danger of being killed by a plant on some random street corner.

"Bas, get out of here. More are coming. Don't let them grab you. Tell the others—tell Evi... I was wrong. I should have gone to the country with her. I—"

Basilard slapped him on the chest. What was *that* supposed to mean? Maldynado pulled on his leg, not expecting anything to happen. But it came away from the sidewalk. The tendril still had a death grip around his calf, but he could move.

"You cut it off? Basilard, you're—"

Basilard grabbed him and hauled him several feet down the street. He pointed at the alley.

"Right, right, more coming. Let's go."

Basilard ran back for the body. Maldynado hoped more tendrils hadn't already wrapped around it—he hadn't been worrying about preserving it when he had dropped the corpse, but the dead woman had already suffered enough tonight. Nobody deserved to be eaten street side by some mutant plant.

Basilard slung the body over his shoulder and jogged away from the alley. Maldynado tried to run after him, but he still couldn't feel his foot, and he pitched forward, almost grinding his face into the street.

"Gonna need a medic—or a logger—to hack the rest of this thing off me when we get back to the hotel," he growled as he grabbed the pole to use as a crutch.

Basilard only shook his head, his face grim as they passed through the light of the next street lamp. Carrying a body didn't slow him down, and Maldynado struggled to keep up. He was starting to worry that the vine would act like a tourniquet and that he would lose his foot if he didn't find a way to get the rest of it off soon. That spurred him to keep up, the pole clacking loudly on the cement with each awkward step.

His breath whooshed out in relief when the lighted stone wall of the hotel came into view. Someone in there would be able to help.

Basilard led the way, pounding toward the front gate. A gate that was usually guarded by two men. Nobody stood beside it now, and it was open, inviting anyone to enter. Strange, but Maldynado would worry about it later. He would—

A thunderous boom blasted from within the hotel, and a volcano of light burst through the roof and poured into the sky. Even on the street fifty feet away, Maldynado felt the power of the explosion. It hurled him onto his back, and the pole spun out of his hands. Basilard staggered but somehow kept his feet, not even dropping the body hanging over his shoulder. Maldynado rose to his knees, staring in astonishment at the scene through the gateway. The explosion had left a hole the size of five rooms in the center of the roof, and walls were crumbling on every side, bricks tumbling to the ground like water streaming over falls. Flames leaped from doorways and broken windows. Glass and wood littered the grass and the upturned earth. Thanks to the plant, the entire yard of the beautiful old hotel looked like giant gophers had been using it for a playground, but those vines were oddly absent now.

"Bas," Maldynado croaked. "Is there... Do you see... Could anyone have survived that?" He didn't see anyone. Wouldn't *some* people have made it out? Beyond the windows, curtains and furniture burned in some rooms. In others, it looked like the floor had been blown away, and everything had tumbled to the levels below.

Basilard had been staring at the fire, his gaze transfixed. He shook away whatever thoughts had claimed his mind—concern for Amaranthe? his translator? the others?—and looked around the yard and to the street as well. Not another soul was out there with them.

The guards, Basilard signed. *They were not here.*

"Do you think maybe... *nobody* was here?" Maldynado hoped for all of their ancestors' sakes that his question proved true, that everyone inside had somehow gotten warning of this catastrophe and fled the building in time.

A clank sounded, rising over the cracks of breaking wood and the snaps of the fire consuming the hotel. A burned and blackened man staggered out the front door, tripped on the steps, and pitched to the ground.

"Dear ancestors," Maldynado breathed, stumbling as he tried to walk forward to help. The others might not have made it out after all...

CHAPTER 23

FROM THE BACKYARD BY THE carriage house door, Tikaya stared at the flaming roof of the hotel, shielding her eyes with her arm. Smoke buried the moon and clouded the air around the burning structure. A broad expanse of pockmarked grass stretched between her and the fire, but she could feel the heat, nonetheless. She had expected... She didn't know what she had expected, but the realization that she had been inside that hotel not five minutes ago made her shudder. The weight of her bow, strung and hanging from her shoulder, reminded her that she had taken the time to return to the suite and pack—she was lucky her choice to delay hadn't ended her life.

She hadn't believed anything would come of her random observation about the "suspects" who weren't in the hotel tonight. This was... unthinkable.

Clanks and thuds came from the carriage house behind her, Dak's men and the hotel staff preparing vehicles to drive them off the premises before the fire spread. Five minutes earlier, the men had been groggy and grumbling. They were all wide-awake now, their eyes as haunted as Tikaya's must look.

A familiar uniformed figure stepped out of the smoke. "Lady Starcrest," Dak rumbled. "I believe I owe you my life."

"No more than I owe you mine," she said. "I think perhaps we can call each other by first name now."

"If you wish." Something in his tone suggested he probably wouldn't.

"Everyone didn't make it out, did they?" Tikaya had heard a few screams after the explosion.

"We warned everyone," Dak said. "Some people packed and left. Some people ignored us, or were too slow. There wasn't time for hand-holding." He pulled out a pocket watch and shook his head. "If I had known how little time there truly was..." Another head shake, this one almost violent, full of disgust. "I should have known about this, should have uncovered... whatever there was to uncover. We won't know until the fire is out and a team can investigate. Explosives in the basement, or maybe lower. Someone might have tunneled in past all those cursed plants. I don't know."

An image of Serpitivich in the library flashed into Tikaya's mind. "A couple of nights ago, I saw the vice president with blueprints for the hotel and maybe the underground infrastructure too. He said he'd been assigned the task of keeping that plant out of the sewers."

Dak grunted. "*I* didn't give him that task. Guess we can't ask him about it since he's not here. Conveniently."

A man in a bathrobe broke a bottom floor window with a chair. He knocked out the glass and stumbled from the building. Coughing, he almost collapsed, but he wiped his face and lifted a hand toward the window. A woman in similar attire half climbed and half fell out after him.

"Baskic," Dak called to a corporal, then pointed to the figures. They were stumbling away from the building, coughing and wheezing for air.

The soldier jogged toward the couple to help.

"I sent some soldiers to round up the fire brigade," Dak said. "They'll put out the fire, and my men will help them pull out anyone else who's alive."

Tikaya nodded numbly. "I feel useless standing here staring, but—"

"You would only endanger yourself if you tried to go back in there. Let the professionals handle it. You've already helped more than anyone else—we'd all be stuck in there if you hadn't had that hunch."

Tikaya wanted to shrug away this praise. She had only pointed out a piece of data that might suggest something. Dak had been the one to figure out what the something might be, not to mention having the audacity to force an evacuation when nothing might have happened.

"I'm also moving Serpitivich from my short list to my special list," Dak said.

"What happens to people on your special list?"

"They get shot on sight."

"I... see. Is anyone else on it?"

Dak snapped his pocket watch shut. "Rias might be if his report doesn't arrive soon."

"Those vehicles your men are readying, are any for checking on him?"

Tikaya hadn't forgotten the reason she had packed and dressed, throwing on boots, trousers, and a jacket, along with grabbing the bow and a knife. She had tried contacting him via the communications sphere they had in their quarters, too—as far as she knew, the other half was still in the submarine—but nobody had answered. She had stuffed it into her pack to try again later.

"Yes," Dak said. "We'll leave as soon as the fire brigade shows up."

Tikaya would have started walking to the submarine warehouse at that moment, but there was little point when the vehicles could get her there ten times as quickly. As soon as the water in one of the boilers heated enough to be operational, she *would* go, fire brigade or not.

"Sir?" someone called from around the side of the building.

Two soldiers came into view, and they were escorting two other men, one carrying something large over his shoulder and one hobbling and leaning heavily on a pole.

"Bring them here," Dak yelled, then lowered his voice. "That's the Mangdorian diplomat, isn't it?"

Tikaya squinted into the smoke. "Yes, that's Basilard and Maldynado. Basilard is carrying... someone. Were they caught in the explosion?"

Dak jogged forward to meet the pair, and Tikaya followed, though not before casting a long look toward the vehicles. Soldiers were shoveling coal into furnaces. Surely one of those lorries would be ready soon.

"Hello, good Colonel," Maldynado said, a deep grimace making the words come out oddly. "I don't suppose you have a medic around, do you? While I'm sure there are survivors here who need assistance, I really need someone to remove this vine from my leg before I lose my foot." He sounded like he was trying very hard to be polite and not to start screaming—or throttling someone—but given the tightness of the green tendril wrapped twice about his leg, he had to be in a lot of pain. Though a foot of it trailed behind, the rest severed somewhere along the way, what remained hadn't loosened its grip. In addition, it had eaten away his clothing with its enzyme, and that must be burning into his flesh as well.

Basilard lowered the person he had been carrying and went to help his friend, drawing a serrated knife and motioning for Maldynado to sit down.

Tikaya gaped at the burden Basilard had dropped. It wasn't a survivor from the hotel fire, it was a woman, a *Nurian* woman, her almond-shaped eyes frozen open in death, her dark clothing saturated with blood that hadn't yet dried.

Dak had pulled out a knife, looking like he intended to help cut Maldynado's plant off, but he froze when he noticed the dead woman's face. "Is that...?"

"The Nurian assassin and sometimes sniper?" Maldynado asked. "Yes, and how we got her is a fabulous story that I'd be delighted to tell once someone saws this off my leg."

Quit moving, Basilard signed.

"I'm sorry, but my leg *hurts*. The parts I can feel anyway."

Now Dak looked like he wanted to throttle someone, but he started cutting into the vine on the opposite side of Maldynado's leg from Basilard.

Maldynado watched the knife work with concerned eyes. The blades were slicing quite close to his skin. The couple of times Basilard looked away, gazing toward the hotel and searching the yard, Maldynado swatted him on the shoulder and pointed at his ankle for emphasis. The knives didn't have much of an effect on the rubbery plant. Tikaya thought of Rias's black dagger—it would slice through the vine more easily—but she hadn't seen it when she had packed her bag. He must have taken it with him.

"Easy," Maldynado said, "easy, please. You're getting close to tender flesh. Colonel, are you sure you're qualified for such a delicate procedure? I only ask because you're in intelligence, and I imagine that involves using pencils as weapons rather than blades. And a man's foot is at stake here. His favorite foot."

"I didn't think one typically had a favorite foot," Tikaya said, hoping to take Maldynado's mind off the procedure. The way he was squirming, it wouldn't be either of the men's fault if they *did* cut him.

"I didn't, either," Maldynado said, "until I was in danger of losing this one. Now I'm positive. It's definitely my favorite." He flinched when one of the blades brushed his trouser leg. "And it's sensitive. Careful there... careful..."

"Does he always complain this much?" Dak asked Basilard.

Basilard nodded. *Usually more.*

"I'm not complaining, I'm advising."

I haven't noticed a difference.

Maldynado prodded him. "Don't stop cutting to gab. What? Don't

386

look at me like that. It's not my fault you can't talk and cut a vine off a man's leg at the same time."

That earned him a glower, and Basilard kneeled back for a moment. *Professor Komitopis, do you know if my translator was in the hotel tonight? I had told her... that I didn't need her with me, that she could have the evening off. But I don't know if she would have left to explore the city with so much of it closed down or abandoned or...* His fingers faltered as his gaze raked the yard again. The fire brigade's lorries were rolling into position around the smoking building, but Basilard probably didn't see them, not when he was looking for a sole person.

Maldynado's fingers twitched toward Basilard, as if he wanted to wring his friend's neck to force him back to sawing, but Dak was getting close to breaking through. His blade kept brushing Maldynado's clothing, something that transfixed his attention, though Dak had yet to slice so much as a thread.

"Dak," Tikaya said, "do you know if Basilard's translator was warned? The red-headed Mangdorian woman?"

"Everyone was warned."

"I don't suppose you know if she... heeded that warning promptly?"

"I don't know." Dak knelt back, raising his knife. "There." He flicked the severed ends of the vine away from Maldynado's leg.

"Oh, thank you, Colonel. Allow me to revoke all those nasty comments about the uselessness of intel officers."

"You didn't make any such comments."

"Didn't I? Oh good."

"Though you were rather derogatory toward my pencil." Dak stood, strode into the carriage house, and yelled, "If there's not a lorry ready by now, I'm going to start throwing privates into the furnaces."

"I'm beginning to suspect that man of having a sense of humor," Tikaya said. "A coarse one."

Maldynado was too busy unlacing his boot and frowning in concern at his foot to respond.

I'm going to help the fire fighters, Basilard signed and trotted off.

A whistle sounded, releasing a screech of steam. Tikaya hoped that was the sign that a vehicle was ready and they could check on Rias now. She was about to run for the carriage house, but a large armored lorry rolled out first. With cannons mounted on the roof and harpoon launchers below the cab, nobody would mistake it for anything except a military conveyance. It braked with a squeal of steam, and a squad of soldiers piled into the back, men armed with rifles and swords. Dak was standing in the cab next to the driver, and Tikaya climbed in beside him, glad to finally get going.

"You too, Marblecrest," Dak called.

Maldynado was holding his boot and a sock up with one hand and prodding his bare foot with the other. "Pardon?"

"I want that body explained."

"Now?" Maldynado pointed at his poor foot. "I've been grievously injured, and I'm quite certain I've done my piece for the president tonight already."

"*Now*, Marblecrest."

Maldynado sighed dramatically, picked up the pole, and limped to the lorry, his sock and bootlaces dragging on the ground. Tikaya wondered if she was grinding her teeth as audibly as Dak at his plodding pace.

When Maldynado finally maneuvered himself inside, he said, "I'm disowned, you know. I'm just Maldynado now, not Maldynado Marblecrest. If you've a passion for surnames, you could use Montichelu. That's what I'd like on my statue." He stretched a hand out, as if stroking a plaque etched with his name. "Maldynado Montichelu. There's really no reason to mention my father's line at all. Dreadful people most of them."

"Marblecrest," Dak said. "The *body*."

Tikaya fingered her bow as the lorry rolled out of the hotel's courtyard, the dark city streets replacing the bright flames of the burning building. A part of her wondered if Dak would get the story out of Maldynado before they reached the warehouse. The other part was too concerned about Rias and Mahliki to care.

Mahliki clutched at her temples, trying to gather her wits, to find a way to fight the mental assault. It felt like mallets were slamming into the sides of her head, treating her like a gong. She squinted up and down the street, trying to pick out her attacker. She was aware of Sespian touching her back and asking what was wrong, but she couldn't see anyone else on the street. He had to be out there somewhere. A good practitioner might be able to target someone out of sight and at a distance, but these Turgonians didn't seem that adept.

"Adept enough to hurt you," she grumbled, wincing.

"What?" Sespian asked. He was searching the street, too, that dagger clenched and ready.

Mahliki jerked her hand to dismiss the comment. It had been in Kyattese, and her head hurt too much to reformulate it into Turgonian. She tried to push herself to her feet. Maybe if she could put a few blocks between her and her assailant, she would escape his range.

Sespian's hand tightened on her shoulder. "Stay here," he whispered. "I see him. I'll pretend I don't."

"Where?" Mahliki asked.

"Roof." He squeezed her shoulder, then ran across the street and into an alley.

Mahliki hunkered down, slumping against a building. If she appeared more incapacitated than she was, maybe the person would come down to check. She would pretend she couldn't move. It didn't take much pretending. She had never had much interest in studying the mental sciences, but she had been regretting that choice these last few weeks. If she knew how to call lightning from the sky, her father wouldn't have to be risking his life, trying to invent new machines while under fire—and *she* might know how to thrust this Turgonian bastard from her head. Even better, she could return the attack.

Well, maybe she could do that anyway.

She had dropped the electricity generator, but it wasn't a long-range weapon anyway. She inched her hand to her belt and drew a dagger, careful to hide it from above with her body. Knife throwing wasn't her specialty, but she and her siblings had sat around numerous campfires, tossing blades at driftwood stumps with Father while waiting for dinner to cook. At the least, she could distract a practitioner by hurling one close enough to worry him. For that, she had to locate him first.

With her head down, Mahliki couldn't hear much. She listened, trying to pick out scuffing above that might indicate someone moving closer, but the shouts and rifle shots from the waterfront drowned out lesser sounds. Hoping the shadows would hide her, she risked a glance upward. A hooded figure knelt at the edge of the roof right above her. She winced, certain the person had seen her look up, but his attention seemed to be toward the alley Sespian had run down. He drew a short sword. Maybe he thought that, with Sespian gone, Mahliki would be helpless and he could finish her off.

"Try it," she whispered.

Blackness pulsed at the edge of her vision, and she struggled to focus on the figure, but she did her best to push the pain aside. When the practitioner dropped off the edge of the roof, Mahliki jumped to her feet. The blackness almost swallowed her sight completely, and she had to grab the wall to keep from losing balance. She gave herself a half second to recover, then threw the dagger at the figure.

A clank sounded. She was sure she had missed and that the blade had struck the wall, but the mallets banging on her head disappeared. The resulting relief gave her a surge of energy, and she lunged for the man, ready to throw a punch. But he crumpled to the ground before she reached him.

Confused, she stood there for a long moment, her fist cocked. Had her knife struck after all? The darkness made it hard to tell, but she was certain she had missed. The way he had fallen against the wall made it seem more like...

Mahliki glanced toward the roof on the opposite side of the street. Sespian dropped his hand to the gutter and hopped down, landing lightly on his feet.

"That wasn't quite how I imagined it," he said, "but I guess it worked. Are you all right? Is he, erm, was my throw accurate?"

Mahliki checked the man's throat, her hand brushing against the hilt of the black dagger—and a lot of warm blood. The blade was embedded in the man's neck and must have severed his spinal column as well. "Very accurate," she said, struggling for detachment. She wiped the blood off her hand, though she tried not to be obvious about it. She didn't have the bloodthirstiness of her Turgonian ancestors and always preferred subduing a man without killing him. She reminded herself that this one had meant to kill her and had been using his craft to delay Father when he could have been helping the city instead.

Sespian sighed. "I don't usually aim for throats, but I saw him over you with the sword, and was afraid to dither around."

"Given the situation, I appreciate the non-dithering approach." Mahliki tried to decide whether it would seem weak-kneed to ask him to retrieve the knife, since he had been the one to throw it. She didn't care for the crunch of bone that came from pulling a spear out of a boar's side when the family was hunting. The crunch of a human being's bones was even less pleasant.

Sespian retrieved it before she had to ask, wiping the blade on the man's robe. "Two more practitioners to go?" he asked.

"That have shown themselves so far, yes. I saw two separate ones throwing fireballs from the cabs of the lorries. I think they're still there and that this was a third. He might have been placed on guard because he has—had—a different specialty."

"Like attacking women's minds?"

"Maybe so. There could be others back here like this." Mahliki picked up the electricity generator and pointed up the street. "Let's keep going, but keep an eye out."

As she led the way, she realized she had given him another order. When he had asked that earlier question about where she had learned to order people around, she had worried it had been a criticism, or a hint that he didn't care for following the commands of women who were younger than he. Especially when he had been groomed to be emperor all of his life. His tone hadn't sounded irritated, but Sespian could be as hard to read as his father at times. His face was far more pleasant and his eyes much warmer, but that didn't mean one knew his thoughts.

"You can lead if you want," Mahliki said as they passed another alley, the front of one of the enemy lorries visible at the other end.

"And thus be the target for the next practitioner launching mental harpoons?" Sespian asked.

"No. I just meant... I wasn't sure if... well, you have more experience giving orders. I'm just headstrong and used to bossing my younger siblings around and being fairly independent."

"Yes, I gathered that." He sounded... amused. Well, that was better than irritation.

"But if you think you would be a better leader or if you have a better plan—"

Mahliki halted, catching a hint of movement in a recessed doorway ahead. A tendril snaked out of the nook, and she spun toward it, throwing the switch on the generator. The vine moved unbelievably quickly for a plant, but the little streaks of electricity gave her enough light to see it and catch it with the forked tip. She pressed the vine against the wall. Fortunately, it wasn't as big as some of the others. The scent of charred vegetation soon stung the air.

"I think you're doing fine," Sespian said, watching the street—and the roofs—as she finished toasting their botanical attacker.

"Leading or planning? Or mutilating plants? Did you see how fast that tendril shot out?"

"Yes to all."

"Let's see if we can sneak up on these practitioners and knock them out then." Mahliki backed away from the alcove, leaving the smoldering vine for dead. "This plant is going to fight hard to stay alive. Even without the delays, I worry that we might already be too late." What kind of jungle might have already grown up in the harbor in the days since she had collected that first root sample? Would the submarine be able to get close? What if the plant smothered it faster than Father could wield whatever weapon he was creating? What if the enzymes that broke down skin could also break down the hull of the submarine?

"We'll succeed," Sespian said. "Don't underestimate your father. He's won a lot of wars."

"Against humans, yes. This is something new. Something... alien and inexplicable."

"Then we better hurry up with our self-appointed mission, so he has more time to plan crafty things."

Mahliki nodded, thankful for his optimism, and continued down the street. She would focus on their first problem—the human element. They passed two more alleys and stopped at the third, one so narrow that they would have trouble walking side by side. The sounds of the battle raged on, but there were no lights or fires burning at the other end.

"This should be far enough," she whispered.

"I'll go first." Sespian stepped into the alley.

Mahliki started to object—leaders should lead, after all—but he raised the black dagger.

"I have the more logical weapon for dealing with people," Sespian said. "If any plants wrap themselves around my neck, I'll trust you to take care of that. Without dithering."

"Understood."

Though she let him lead, Mahliki followed no more than a step behind. When he stopped at the end, she stood on her tiptoes, trying to see past him and around the corner. They were about the same height, and she might have struggled—he was looking around the corner, too—but he crouched down a few inches.

Not far away, the two closest lorries idled side-by-side, blocking the street from any other vehicular traffic. Not that there *was* any traffic. Nobody knew Father and his team were down here except for Dak and maybe a couple of others. Unfortunately, that meant nobody knew they were under attack, either, unless one of the soldiers had slipped through enemy lines to deliver the message. On the rooftop of the building, Father's men seemed to be holding their ground, but more of the structure was burning now, despite the soldiers' efforts to quench the flames with buckets of water. With the agitated plants grasping at people with their thick tendrils, the men risked their lives every time they hopped down from the roof to fill those buckets.

"Four guards in the back," Sespian murmured, nodding toward the backs of the lorries.

Two robed figures leaned against each one, rifles cradled in their arms as they alternated gazing up the street and out toward the plant-infested water. Darkness sheathed Mahliki and Sespian, so she doubted they could see them, but when their eyes shifted in her direction, it made her uneasy, nonetheless.

"The plants aren't bugging *them*, I see," she whispered. Those four weren't the practitioners, but they would make it hard to *reach* the practitioners. It might be dark in the alley, but as soon as Mahliki and Sespian crept out and tried to sneak up on the men, they would be spotted. They could approach via the roofs, but Mahliki had a feeling they would find more lookouts up there. Someone might already be missing the practitioner.

Sespian pointed. "It looks like they scorched—or maybe electrified—the earth on the waterfront side of their vehicles. Warning the plants to keep back."

"Father scorched some, too, and it only irritated them."

"True. Maybe the plant senses he and the submarine are more of a threat than the priests."

"Maybe," Mahliki said.

"You don't think the priests could have some sort of... alliance with the plant, do you? It almost seems... smart enough that one *could* reason with it, if one knew how."

That notion filled Mahliki with dread, but when she shook her head, it was with confidence. "Given its origins and what I know of the race that made those seeds, I find it doubtful the plant would see humans as anything other than food. I think the priests are just opportunists."

One of the guards turned his head and called to someone in the cab. Mahliki leaned out to peer down the street in the other direction. Her shoulders slumped. Another lorry was rolling down the street with a robed figure at the controls.

"Great, that's all they need. Reinforcements."

"Those aren't reinforcements," Sespian said, a curious note in his voice. Pleasure? "That's our ride."

Mahliki grasped the idea immediately. "Jump on the back so the guards don't see us coming?"

"Or maybe underneath." He glanced over his shoulder at the bulky generator. "You might want to leave that in the alley. Here, take the dagger. I have a knife and the rifle."

Mahliki was reluctant to leave her father's prototype where it might be captured or damaged, but she would have a hard time jumping on a moving vehicle with it weighing her down. And she would never fit *under* the lorry with it strapped to her back. "All right."

By the time she wriggled out of it and leaned it against the wall, the lorry was already even with them.

"Get ready," Sespian whispered. He waited until the cab passed and its bulk was blocking the alley from the guards' views. "Now."

Though Mahliki ran out right after him, he proved the faster runner and reached the back first. He leaped, catching the bed gate, and swung himself under the vehicle in one smooth motion, disappearing so quickly he almost seemed to vanish. The rifle on his back didn't so much as clack against anything to alert someone. Mahliki leapt on—the lorry was slowing to stop behind the others—and hurried to scramble onto the framework beneath the vehicle. She smacked her knee against the axle and cracked her head on a bar, but she made it without scraping any skin off her back on the cement. The vials and tools she kept inside her jacket—*why* hadn't she thought to leave those behind?—jangled with alarming vigor as she locked her legs around a bar. The noise shouldn't be audible over the hissing of the steam brakes. She hoped.

Sespian had already climbed hand-over-hand to the wheels at the front end of the lorry. He might not want to admit to his relationship with his father, but he had definitely inherited that agility. Mahliki supposed she was lucky she had some of *her* father's athleticism—her little sister had more of Mother's accident-prone tendencies.

The vehicle slowed to a stop behind the two lorries in front. Boots came into view—men jumping down from the cab and others—those of the guards—walking around to the bed to unload something. Mahliki twisted her head to watch Sespian. A dark lump between the front wheels, he wasn't moving yet.

A flash of light and an explosion came from a few meters in front of the first truck—the vehicles blocked Mahliki's view for the most part, but she knew the sound—and the earth-shaking feel—of a blasting stick going off by now. She almost lost her grip and fell on the ground.

Though the blasting stick hadn't landed close enough to damage the vehicles, the nearby men cursed anyway, lurching and grabbing the lorry for support. Shards of broken cement pattered down on either side.

Sespian dropped to the ground and scurried out on the waterfront side of the vehicle—there was only one pair of boots on that side. Mahliki scrambled after him to help. He popped up behind the boots, but the man spun toward him immediately. The sounds of a scuffle reached her ear.

She crawled out beside the back tire, intending to help Sespian, but another man charged around the corner. He almost tripped over her. Mahliki reacted quickly, stabbing her dagger into a robed thigh before the man could pull out his pistol. The black blade dove in with alarming ease. He started to scream, but she leaped to her feet, using her upward momentum to slam the heel of her palm into the bottom of his jaw. Teeth cracked against teeth, cutting off the cry. She jammed her elbow into his gut to drop him to the ground.

A thud sounded—someone jumping out of the lorry bed—and a third man ran around the corner. Mahliki yanked her dagger free, prepared to defend herself, but the butt of Sespian's rifle whizzed past her ear. It slammed into the priest's head, and he dropped like a steel ingot. Sespian left him to jump around the corner and scurry up into the lorry bed. With the flap down, he couldn't know how many men might be waiting inside, but he didn't hesitate. Mahliki paused, torn between following him to make sure he wasn't overwhelmed and wanting to rush straight for the practitioners in the lorries up front. If they figured out they had enemies in the rear, they would soon turn their attention in this direction.

A stirring of the hairs on her arms made her decision for her. Someone nearby was about to use the Science—and she might very well be the target.

Dagger in hand, she ducked low to check at how many sets of feet were visible on the other side of the lorry. She spotted one pair of boots and one pair of sandals walking back toward her. A fighter wouldn't choose sandals. She waited in her low crouch, ready to spring up and attack, but from the way the men slowed down, they had to be expecting trouble. Better not to be where they were anticipating someone.

A thud, then a crack came from behind the flap. Sespian definitely wasn't alone in there, but she would trust him to hold his own. Mahliki slithered under the lorry, thinking she might stab the sandaled man in the unprotected feet. If he *was* a practitioner, the pain would make it hard for him to concentrate on flinging fireballs at anyone.

But the men must have sensed something, for they halted abruptly before rounding the corner of the vehicle—or maybe they heard Sespian in there, thumping people around. Mahliki eased a little farther toward the front. The boots were facing her, but she didn't think she had made a sound. Another crack came from up above her. Sespian.

"That doesn't sound like our people," one of the men said.

"No."

They both turned for the corner. Mahliki rolled out from under the lorry behind them, springing to her feet as soon as she cleared the vehicle. The robed men's backs were to her. One was already darting around the corner. She lunged after the second, slamming the hilt of her dagger into the back of his head. He staggered forward, but didn't go down. He clawed for his pistol. Mahliki kicked it out of his belt before he could draw it. The weapon clanked to the street and skidded away.

"You dumb—"

Mahliki's second kick, this time to the groin, distracted him from whatever he had meant to say. He pitched forward, one hand belatedly protecting himself and the other trying to grab her foot. She could have stabbed him with the dagger, but remembered how easily that blade slid into human flesh and hesitated. She hadn't come out here to *kill* people.

The sandaled man stole her time to think about how to subdue his buddy. He appeared around the corner, a hand raised. The hairs that had been wavering on Mahliki's arms stood to upright attention. She leaped back an instant before the practitioner unleashed his attack.

Fire swallowed her vision, the blast so close to her eyes that she thought she had been hit. The heat *did* pound her like a jackhammer, but it didn't bring pain. She had scrambled backward in time. An ear-splitting scream erupted in front of her. Her stomach clenched in sympathy. *Someone* hadn't backed away in time.

The flames were extinguished abruptly. Mahliki raised her dagger, ready to attack, but the light had blinded her, and the spots swirling through her vision offered poor targets. A hand clamped onto her upper arm. Assuming it was the practitioner, she swung her blade at him. Another hand caught her wrist though.

"It's me," Sespian whispered. "There are more coming. This way."

Mahliki stumbled after him, blinking furiously, trying to regain her vision. She tripped over something—a body. Had Sespian killed the practitioner? Whimpers of pain came from the side, and the smell of scorched flesh tainted the air.

"That idiot hit his own man," Sespian grumbled, his voice coming from an elevated position.

He was climbing back into the lorry bed. Mahliki groped her way after him, the flap hitting her in the face as she crawled over the gate. Her hand landed in something wet. Water? No, blood.

"All you all right?" Sespian whispered. "That didn't go as smoothly as I'd hoped. They're going to figure out someone's attacking them back here soon, if they haven't already."

Mahliki wiped her hand on her trousers. Her eyes were finally adjusting to the darkness again, but she wasn't sure she wanted to see what was inside with them. Bodies, she suspected. When she had run from the warehouse, intending to help her father by knocking out the practitioners, she hadn't considered how much fighting they would have to do to *reach* those practitioners. How could she tell Sespian that she had already had her fill of stabbing people with daggers and she wanted him to take over the leadership role? More than that, she wanted her

Father to come out here and fix everything, so there was no more need for leading—or being led—into battle. She had seen combat before and death a few times as well, but she had never been in a position where she had to mow through so many men to reach such a dubious goal.

This is for Father, for the submarine, and for the city, Mahliki reminded herself. Staying in that building and hiding wouldn't have accomplished anything. It was these priests' fault she had to attack them, to hurt them.

"I'm uninjured," Mahliki said, because Sespian had started patting her down, checking for wounds. "Just got stunned and blinded by that fireball."

"Yes, that was close. I wasn't expecting a wizard back here."

"I think my sight is returning, or at least... there are fewer dots of white swimming through it."

"There's not much to see in here," Sespian said. "It's dark. Though you'll want to note this."

He took her hand and guided her a couple of steps, then laid her palm on something cold and metal. She couldn't see anything except a dark shape against a dark interior, but she followed the smooth curved object, found a couple of wooden wheels, and soon guessed what it was. "A cannon?"

"Yes, a military one. These priests are stealing all sorts of equipment."

Mahliki frowned, imagining their enemies firing cannonballs at the warehouse. The submarine might be sturdy, but she doubted it could withstand an attack of that magnitude. Not to mention that any of her father's men who got in the way wouldn't withstand cannonballs well, either.

"I'm beginning to loathe these people," Mahliki said.

"Me too." Sespian shifted his weight, and soft metallic *chings* sounded. He was reloading the rifle. "Stay low. Like I said, I expect them to come back here any moment. They must have heard that scream, and I think I heard one of the men we downed in the beginning climb to his feet and run." He shifted the flap aside. "I'm surprised they haven't already... Oh."

"What is it?"

Mahliki crawled over an inert body to the other side of the gate and peeped past the flap on that side. Two more vehicles were rumbling down the street, headlamps burning in the night like fiery eyes. She slumped. "Not *more* reinforcements."

The pistol poked Amaranthe in the back again, guiding her toward the large tanks at the back of the cider mill. Deret walked at her side, being similarly nudged along with weapons. Several robed men followed behind those doing the nudging, and though Sauda had left, the line of zealots along the wall had not. Those people, too, remained armed with pistols.

Amaranthe doubted she was being taken anywhere longevity-promoting, so she was going to have to risk getting shot if she saw even the remotest chance to succeed at escaping. She tried to catch Deret's eye, to give him a silent signal about her intent, but he was limping along, his gaze toward the cement floor. There was nothing down there more interesting than cracks, so she worried he had given up and wasn't thinking of escape at all.

"You all have an evacuation plan?" Amaranthe asked, figuring she ought to try reasoning with someone before resorting to starting a brawl with the pack of people pointing pistols at her. She had gone out of her way not to mention her name and whom she knew—no one had tried that hard to get the information—but maybe that had been a mistake. When no one responded to her question, she said, "I only ask because my friend will track me down as soon as he realizes I'm missing, and if he finds me dead... well, I'd feel bad if *all* of you got killed because of some dubious plan your boss schemed up."

The man behind her snorted.

Well, that was a start. At least she knew someone was listening. None of them was curious enough to ask her who her friend was.

"He's actually more than a friend, I must admit, and he's oddly fond of me. I haven't figured out why, since I talk a lot, and he's more of the quiet, deadly type who prefers silence. Still, he's killed for less virtuous reasons than avenging a lover. He'd probably flatten this entire compound in less than an hour. Not that I encourage these actions mind you—I'm the reasonable one, you see, and I try to stop him from wholesale carnage. But if I were dead, I suppose it wouldn't matter much to me. Even if it did, what would I be able to do to stop him?"

The man behind her shoved her in the shoulder. She caught herself on a ladder that climbed the side of a large fermentation or storage tank. The modern steel contraption stretched at least twelve feet wide at the base and rose two-thirds of the way to the thirty-foot-high ceiling. Narrow pipes ran behind other tanks on either side. A larger pipe stuck out of this tank halfway up and attached to a big vat farther out in the room. Near the base of the ladder, there was a wheel and a couple of gauges for reading the level of liquid inside the tank. Right now, it was one-third full.

"You think Sicarius can find us?" Deret twitched an eyebrow at her. The gesture might have meant she should have used his name from the beginning, or it might have meant he didn't think this ploy had a chance at working.

"He once tracked me five hundred miles into a jungle. I was on a... dirigible—" though these people might have seen the alien craft that had crashed last winter, it still sounded too far-fetched to mention, "—and there's no way he *should* have been able to follow me from the ground, but he did, nonetheless. He has instincts that scent-hounds would envy."

One of the men at the back of the pack shifted his weight, and he glanced at the fellow beside him.

"If I hadn't sent him off on another task earlier tonight, he would have been at the *Gazette* building with me," Amaranthe went on pleasantly, trying to ignore the fact that they had halted at this ladder, "hovering over Deret's shoulder and glowering as Deret shared his brandy with me."

"A shame he couldn't make it," Deret muttered.

"Sent him on a task?" one of the priests asked, snorting again. "Who do you think you are, Amrenth Lokdon?"

Amaranthe blinked, not so much because the man had heard of her, but because it had finally gotten out that she had been in charge of the group who had defended Sespian and fought Forge—and that Sicarius had been working for her. She had dismissed the odd signature request here and there, but maybe she had Deret to thank for stories that had informed the public of her deeds. Had he written more about her team while she had been away this winter?

"It's Am-ah-ranthe, you slag-head," Deret said. "And who else did you think would be foolish enough to wander around in the plant-infested evacuated part of the city at night?"

"We thought she was your girlfriend," someone said.

"No, my girlfriends are all brighter than that." Deret's eyes glinted with gallows humor—or maybe a challenge.

Amaranthe couldn't tell if he was simply being a pest or if he hoped to start an argument with her to distract their captors. "Are these the nonexistent girls you make up when mercenary leaders innocently ask how you've been doing?"

"I—"

One of the priests shoved him. Amaranthe received a simultaneous prod in the back.

"Get climbing. Up the ladder and through the hatch at the top. Tsitsiv, Baknoch, go cover them from the other tanks. Make *sure* they climb in."

"You sure you don't want to heed my warning?" Amaranthe turned to face the men, raising her hands imploringly while she shifted to stand in front of the gauge on the side of the tank. "You might have time to escape now if you took to the orchards. Once he learns you were here and that you took part in my death... he'll hunt you down no matter where you run."

"Nobody here's taking part in anyone's death," the priest said. "You were simply out here snooping around when you fell in the tank and drowned. Very unfortunate."

"Please, Sicarius has seen me tread water for a half hour with a ten-pound brick over my head. While he might believe that I was out here snooping..." Amaranthe leaned one hand against the gauge and pointed toward the wall and orchard beyond with the other, causing several men to look in that direction for a moment. "He would never believe that I drowned." Covering her actions with her body, she unscrewed the glass face of the gauge and fumbled with the dial. She wished she had Ms. Sarevic's collection of tools in her pocket, not to mention a second hand to use. Just breaking the gauge wouldn't do anything. "I know you think I'm simply trying to save myself—I can see it in your faces, er, in the way the shadows under your hoods hide your faces—but I don't want your deaths staining my soul, either. Enough people have died at my hands. Is all of this worth it? All this killing? To put someone in the president's chair who will only be there for five years anyway? How much can he do in that time?"

"Get our religion legitimized and allow magic to be practiced in Turgonia again," a priest said, his voice full of longing. He probably cared about the religion; Amaranthe wondered how many of the others did and how many were simply along because they had been promised power and status by someone with a smooth tongue.

"That would have happened anyway," Amaranthe said, fiddling with the needle on the gauge. "Why didn't you simply proposition Starcrest? His children practice the mental sciences. I can't believe he would be opposed to legalizing them here in Turgonia."

"We *did* ask him. He said let's wait and look at that in another year. He said the people have already stomached a lot of change in a short period of time. We could see what *that* meant. He was going to put us off, give us no more than the emperors ever did."

Amaranthe doubted that. If these impatient zealots had simply waited, they might have seen for themselves. "You should have given him a chance. If you waited a year and he continued to reject your proposition, then you would have found grounds for peaceful protest." She screwed the cap back on the gauge as she continued to speak and to gesture with her free hand. "But not for plotting his death. Or anyone else's for that matter."

"We don't *have* to wait. We found someone who will endorse our religion and our ways *this* year."

"Serpitivich has sure made a lot of promises," Deret observed. He was still standing by the ladder, leaning his shoulder against it.

"I understand that's the nature of politicians in nations that use an electoral system," Amaranthe said. "Listen, do you men really want to start off the rebirth of your religion with blood on your hands? Instead you could be helping the president to save the city from that plant. One of you has demonstrated an ability to harm it. You could be out there being heroes now and showing people that your religion is noble. Instead, you're waiting until someone murders—"

"Enough jabbering." The priest with the deep voice stepped forward, grabbed Amaranthe's arm, and shoved her toward the ladder. "Climb. Both of you."

"What if we don't?" Deret asked. "Your they-got-drowned-while-snooping story will be a harder sell if we're found with bullet holes in our heads."

The priest slapped his pistol against his palm. "Then maybe you won't *be* found."

The men against the wall were shifting about, murmuring to each other. There was doubt among them. If Amaranthe and Deret balked, they would come together to fight the resistance. If they went nobly, maybe the seeds of doubt would continue to spread among the priests and one of them, once released from this large group, would return to help. Also, she didn't like the way the leader's finger was tightening on the trigger of his pistol. He seemed to realize he had let her talk too much. Maybe he was thinking of fixing the problem before any dissent could arise.

Amaranthe touched Deret's shoulder to move him back a step, then climbed onto the ladder. She rose up with her head held high, like a martyr going to her death, though she kept an eye on her surroundings as well. If she had the chance to simply jump from tank to tank and perhaps escape in the maze of machinery in the mill...

But at the leader's earlier order, two priests had gone up on the tanks on either side of this one, both taking rifles. They knelt up there, the weapons aimed in her direction.

Soft clangs drifted up from below. Deret was following her up the ladder.

I hope I'm not leading you to your death, my friend, she thought.

Two priests climbed up the ladder after him. At the top of the tank, Amaranthe found a big round hatch standing open. Utter darkness waited within. The pungent smell of hard cider drifted out, already fermented and ready for the bottles. Darkly, she imagined some future food inspector complaining about the bits of dead people floating around in the latest batch.

"In," the leader called up from below.

Deret climbed over the edge of the tank. Sweat bathed his brow. He hadn't been allowed to take his swordstick up, not that it would have helped him on the ladder anyway. He met her eyes, tilted his head toward each rifleman and glanced at the other two climbing up, then raised his brows.

Amaranthe nodded back. They had to try to escape. She wasn't confident that her fiddling with the gauge had accomplished anything, and even if it had, it wouldn't free them from inside the tank once the hatch was locked. If they could avoid being shot, and if they could grab these men's weapons... the people on the ground would have a hard time finding the right angle to hit them. She hoped.

One of their guards had already joined them on the top of the tank, and the second was about to climb over.

Deret chose that moment to attack. He kicked the man still on the ladder, taking him in the face. It was a solid blow, though not enough to knock the priest free. Worse, Deret's weak leg wouldn't support his weight while the other was in the air, and he hit the deck without grace. It might have saved his life though, for a shot rang out from one of the other tanks. It whizzed past without hitting him.

As soon as the second guard was distracted by Deret's maneuver, Amaranthe threw her elbow, taking him in the side. She jumped behind him, clapping her hands over his ears, then grabbed him by the shoulders and spun him toward the second rifleman. The weapon seemed to crack over there at the same instant as a bullet pounded into the chest of Amaranthe's man. And then a second. She hadn't forgotten about the ability for those new firearms to shoot multiple rounds, but she hadn't grown accustomed to it yet, either.

Weapons fired from the floor as well, and Amaranthe dropped into a crouch, pulling the wounded man down with her, though he was gasping and trying to tear free. To keep him there as a shield seemed cowardly, but there was nothing else she could do, not if she wanted to escape this stupid situation. She tore his pistol from his hand, wondering how she had gotten herself into another bloody predicament.

More shots rang out and she wriggled toward the open hatch, trying to use it as cover for her back. Another bullet pounded into her human shield. Didn't these people care that they were shooting each other?

Shots came from Deret's side of the tank, followed by a meaty thud. She hoped that meant he had taken care of the other guard.

Amaranthe fired at the closest rifleman. The pistols lacked the accuracy of the longer weapons, and her bullet screamed uselessly past the man's ear. At least it made him drop to his belly. The hatch on *his* tank wasn't open, so he didn't have anything to hide behind.

She took more time to line up the second shot, but the injured guard was still alive and thrashing about. His elbow slammed into the side of her jaw, and pain shot through her head. Frustrated, she shoved him away. The rifleman used her distraction to shoot again, but his wounded comrade was just as much of a distraction for him. The bullet missed her and clanged off the hatch. Amaranthe exhaled and waited a second for the steadiness she needed, ignoring the ringing of boots on the ladder, and fired.

The bullet slammed into the rifleman's eye. He jerked, his weapon clattering free, and slumped onto the tank. Amaranthe shifted around the hatch to check on Deret's fight, only to see him at the edge of the opening, clutching his shoulder, his hand washed in blood. The remaining rifleman was kneeling, prepared to shoot again.

Without taking time to aim, Amaranthe fired at the sniper. The bullet hammered into his chest, and he flew backward, the rifle escaping his grip. It banged on the edge of the tank and dropped off, falling to the ground twenty feet below.

Deret was trying to get to his feet, but that wasn't a good idea, not with people firing from below.

"Stay down," Amaranthe said and reached for him.

"I—" He jerked back to avoid someone's fire, but he was already on the edge of the hole. His foot landed on empty air and he pitched backward.

Amaranthe had been using the hatch for cover and had to lunge around it. She didn't reach him in time. He disappeared through the hole, banging his head on the way through. A splash came up from below—*far* below.

While she had been trying to grab him, the first of the reinforcements had climbed over the edge of the tank. There wasn't time to leap over the hole and try to kick him off the ladder. He was already raising his pistol to shoot.

If she had been alone, Amaranthe would have thrown her weapon at him and jumped to the next tank, trying to find an escape route through the equipment-filled shadows below, but Deret might be drowning at that very second.

She grabbed the hatch and jumped into the hole, pulling it shut behind her. The resonating clang came at the same time as utter darkness swallowed her.

CHAPTER 24

O NE OF THE FRONT DOORS of the *Gazette* building stood open, creaking in the breeze. The lanterns on either side of the entryway had either burned out or had never been lit. Sicarius's first impression was that the building had been abandoned as part of the evacuation, but would the newspaper employees have left that door open? He doubted they could have cleared out all of the printing presses and supplies in the hours since the evacuation had been announced. They should have locked up to protect against looting.

After ensuring he was alone on the street, he jogged up the stairs and slipped past the partially open door. Darkness waited inside as well, though a number of odors lingered, suggesting recent occupancy. The scents of kerosene mingled with those of stale sweat, lemongrass incense, and—he wandered into the big office area a few paces, sniffing gently—apple brandy. A bottle had been left open on one of the desks, a desk with two chairs beside it instead of one. One had been tipped over and the other pushed back crookedly. Sicarius ran a hand lightly over the standing seat and found a strand of hair caught in one of the metal fasteners. He hadn't lit a lantern and couldn't discern color, but it was the right length to belong to Amaranthe.

So, she and Deret had been drinking when some of those robed priests had come in the front door. Or perhaps only Deret had been drinking. Unless Amaranthe was trying to woo someone to her cause, she wasn't the type to swig from a bottle with another.

Sicarius examined the other chair, but it did not give any clues. He surmised that the priests had burst in and kidnapped Amaranthe and Deret, but where would they have been taken? He walked around the rest of the floor and checked the basement as well, but determined that the group had merely passed through. The back door wasn't flapping in the breeze, but it *was* unlocked.

The night air had swept away the scents of those who might have walked across the loading dock and into the alley, but he found a manhole cover ajar. He fetched a lantern from the building before heading into the tunnels, knowing the strong underground scents would similarly hide the subtler nasal clues. He would have to rely on sight and perhaps touch to track people through the subterranean passage, but he would do it. That many men would leave a sign, a scrap of cloth on a jagged wall stone, a patch of mildew smeared by a boot print, a discarded cigarette stub. He would follow them, he would find Amaranthe, and if he found out Deret had in any way facilitated this kidnapping, he would kill the man.

Sespian pulled two blasting sticks out of his shirt where he had insanely elected to store them while he had fought with the priests. Though Ms. Sarevic's explosives seemed more stable than many, he felt fortunate he hadn't taken a serious hit to the chest.

"There are cannons mounted on that lorry," Mahliki whispered. She was on the other side of the lorry bed, watching the military vehicle approach. Neither of the priests Sespian had knocked out had stirred; he hoped he hadn't killed either one. Though it was hard to muster sympathy for men who had intended to blow up the president with cannon fire, they *were* Turgonians, however misguided, not enemies from some distant land. Besides, Mahliki had clearly been uncomfortable after Sespian had killed the last man, despite her light words. He had seen through that attempt to show him she was fine. She might have experienced all sorts of dangers when roaming the world with her father and mother, but Sespian wagered Starcrest had been clever enough to extricate his family from trouble without killing people. Why couldn't *he* be that clever? All he had been thinking was to protect her, but he dreaded the idea of her looking at him and seeing Sicarius.

"Harpoons too," Mahliki added. "That warehouse is doomed if we can't take over that lorry or divert it somehow."

"I have a blasting stick here," Sespian said. "That ought to divert it."

"Think they'll be smart enough to jump from the cab when they see it land in front of the lorry?"

"Yes." Maybe.

While he didn't *want* to kill anyone else, he wasn't sure how sympathetic he would feel toward anyone dumb enough *not* to jump out of the way at the sight of a lit blasting stick. He was still appalled that the practitioner had roasted his own comrade. From their actions, and Mahliki's words, Sespian suspected they were dealing with a bunch of self-taught Akstyr types.

He scraped the match along one of the rough fold-down benches, and the bulbous head flared to life. After a quick glance to make sure the vehicle had come within range, he lifted the stick to light it.

"Wait," Mahliki blurted, lunging over to catch Sespian's arm before he touched match to fuse. "Those aren't priests."

"Then who?" Dare he hope the actual *military* was driving that military vehicle?

"That's Dak and..." Mahliki jumped to her feet. "Mother! What is she doing down here? She has her bow."

Sespian extinguished the match and pushed aside the flap. "I hope they have a bunch of soldiers too."

An explosion sounded, and for a crazy instant, Sespian thought he had somehow managed to light his blasting stick. He snorted at himself. "It was a little farther away than that."

He poked his head outside and risked leaning around the corner of the vehicle, figuring that the priests would be too busy looking at the explosion to be worrying about the people in the back of their new lorry. But in the already fading light, he couldn't see beyond the front two vehicles. The soldiers must be attacking the lorries, boxing in the warehouse from the opposite end of the street. Maybe they had figured out a way to extend the reach of their blasting sticks.

Another boom came from that direction. Glass shattered and crashed to the ground somewhere, and shouts came from the priests in the nearby lorries, though Sespian couldn't make out the words. He hoped they were orders to retreat.

"Looks like Dak and Mother are thinking about firing in this direction," Mahliki said. "I'm hopping down to join them. You coming?"

"If they don't know we're here and they're planning to fire at us? Absolutely." Sespian had probably already risked his neck by sticking it out there. It was dark enough that Tikaya and Dak wouldn't be able to tell who he was by the back of his head. "Not being that smart tonight, Sespian," he told himself and climbed outside.

Mahliki had already climbed down. After a quick check to make sure she wasn't in anyone's line of fire, she ran toward the approaching vehicle, waving as she went. Sespian trotted after her, making sure to keep the rifle pointed downward until he was sure he was close enough to be recognized. Tikaya pushed open the door to the cab, grabbed her daughter before she had finished swinging up, and engulfed her in a hug. Sespian climbed in behind the driver, a corporal who didn't look any older than he, and almost tripped over Maldynado on his way to report to Colonel Starcrest.

"Ouch," Maldynado moaned when Sespian caught a toe underfoot. Why was the man barefoot? And sitting on the floor?

"Sorry," Sespian said.

"No, no, that was great. I *felt* that." Maldynado beamed up at him.

Before Sespian could attempt to decipher that, Dak gripped his shoulder. "Good to see you two. Rias still in the warehouse?"

"Yes. We came out to... There were practitioners, that is, and we thought it would be a good idea to keep them busy."

"It was my idea," Mahliki said, pulling away from her mother's embrace. "Sespian was good enough to come along and keep me from getting myself killed."

Another explosion rocked the street. Sespian wished he could see around the lorries in front of them to the warehouse and the vehicles beyond. Were the president's men throwing randomly, or had someone with an exceedingly good arm come out who could reach the lorries with the sticks?

"Your father approved of that?" Tikaya frowned.

"Father... was busy in the submarine."

Tikaya turned the frown onto Sespian, as if *he* could have stopped Mahliki from risking her life. He raised his hands, pleading... if not innocence, then an inability to sway her.

"We have no allies we have to worry about in those three lorries?" Dak pointed at the vehicle Sespian had left and the two in front of it.

The robed figures must have all ducked into the cabs at this fresh barrage of blasting sticks, for no one occupied the street around them. Except for those who had fallen to Sespian's and Mahliki's hands. He eyed the unmoving practitioner and the man he had burned. "No," he said grimly. "No allies."

"Cannons," Dak told the driver. "Clear the way."

The corporal reached for the switches on the weapons control panel, but hesitated, chewing on his lip. "Are you sure, sir? Those are *our* vehicles."

"Quite sure." Dak's smile seemed a touch vindictive. "I'll hand Rias the bill." He seemed to anticipate Tikaya arching her eyebrows in his direction, for he told her, "As punishment for being late on his hourly report to me."

The corporal paled, perhaps thanking his ancestors that *he* had never been late with a report.

"You didn't receive a message?" Mahliki asked. "We thought one of the men might have gotten away to deliver one. How did you know we were in trouble?"

"By the *lack* of a report." Dak tapped the back of the corporal's chair. "Those cannons, if you please."

"Yes, sir." This time, the soldier didn't hesitate to pull a lever and punch a button labeled "Ignite."

The truck reverberated with a soft thud, and before Sespian fully realized the weapon had launched, the back of the lorry in front of them exploded in a blaze of brilliant yellow and orange so bright he had to shield his eyes.

"What was *in* the back of that lorry?" Maldynado asked. He had managed to find a standing position, though he was leaning heavily on a pole.

"A cannon," Mahliki said.

"And several kegs of powder," Sespian added.

Mahliki raised her eyebrows at him. "You didn't mention that."

"They were in the front of the bed." Sespian would have had to lead her across another inert body and had decided she didn't need that experience.

"Glad I won't be the one handing the president that bill," Maldynado said as the flames died down, revealing the utter obliteration of the vehicle.

"It was his idea to employ me here." Dak pointed. "The next lorry, Corporal."

"Yes, sir."

This time, the target didn't blow up. The ball plunged straight through, crunching metal, and disappearing into the cab. Sespian was relieved there wasn't a big explosion, because he was certain there were people in the front of the vehicle. They ought to have a chance to surrender.

"Watch the plant." Tikaya waved toward the shoreline, where the green swaying stalks rose so high that they blotted out the sky in that direction. "I'm sure it's my imagination, but it almost seems like it's being drawn to us."

"It's not your imagination, Mother. A huge vine smashed in the window of the warehouse and grabbed Father after he charred a lesser one with his electricity generator. The plant has been extremely feisty tonight."

"Tell me about it," Maldynado said, flexing his toes.

"Oh, that reminds me. I'll be right back." Mahliki squirmed past Maldynado and Sespian and darted into the alley where she had left the generator.

"Fire, Corporal," Dak said, though he was watching Mahliki, leaning in that direction as if he meant to retrieve her himself if she didn't return promptly.

Only a few seconds passed before she reappeared at the mouth of the alley. She glanced both ways before running back to the lorry and climbing into the cab. "Can't lose Father's prototype. He didn't exactly approve my taking it."

"He didn't approve or he wasn't *aware* of?" Dak asked as another cannonball shot away.

"It was one of those two scenarios, yes."

Dak gave her a look that could have withered a mighty warrior.

Mahliki smiled.

Sespian bit back a smile of his own. She wasn't daunted by much, not even the surly colonel.

"Are there any other reinforcements coming, sir?" Sespian asked.

"The rest of my men are busy putting out the fire at the hotel," Dak said.

"The what?"

"The hotel exploded like a big fiery ball of naphtha," Maldynado said.

Sespian swallowed. "Were... a lot of people in it?"

"Some," Dak said, "but we warned everybody to get out before the bomb went off. Most did."

"Bomb?"

"That's my surmise. The fire brigade and the rest of my men will investigate when the flames are out."

During the discussion, the corporal continued to fire. A few robed men jumped out of the cabs, but more seemed to be hunkering down, enduring the barrage. Or they were until a cry of "Look out!" came from two-dozen meters ahead.

The sky lit up in a white flash at the same time as another explosion roared, this one closer than the others. Sespian squinted and looked away. Debris rattled against the glass front of their lorry and clanked and thudded to the street all around them. Something smashed into the top of their cab and bounced off. Sespian gaped up at the dent in the roof, then, still gaping, watched as a tire thunked down beside them.

"That... wasn't our cannonball, sir," the corporal said.

The entire lorry on the right had disappeared, leaving nothing except a few pieces of twisted, smoldering metal in its wake. Sespian had no idea where the *rest* of the tires had gone.

"It was Father," Mahliki cried, pointing to the warehouse, which, with the lorry gone, was now visible.

The wooden walls were singed and littered with holes, and beams had been knocked or burned down so the roof sagged in places, but the soldiers remained on top with their rifles. In addition, President Starcrest knelt in the back with some kind of hastily made apparatus for launching blasting sticks farther than a man could throw. The lorries that had been barricading the building from the other end of the street were also gone, with nothing except rubble where they had been.

"Watch it." Dak gripped the back of the corporal's seat. "He's turning around."

The remaining lorry on their side of the street was on the move— sort of. The tires wobbled—one was flat—and the whole vehicle looked like it could tip on its side at any moment. In addition to the flak from the explosion right next to it, it had been the recipient of more than one cannonball.

"Shall I fire again, sir?" the corporal asked.

Up on the rooftop, a soldier pointing at the lorry seemed to be asking the same question. President Starcrest lifted a staying hand and set down his apparatus.

"We've had enough blood here. Let him go," Tikaya said, "so long as they aren't preparing any parting shots."

"How... would one know?" the corporal asked. "They're wizards."

"Someone raising a hand with flames dancing on his fingers will be a clue," Mahliki said.

Sespian grimaced, their encounter with the fire-slinging practitioner fresh in his mind. Dak grabbed a rifle and raised it toward the driver's seat—the vehicle had managed to turn around and clearly wanted to limp past them. He jumped out, and Sespian frowned at this countermanding of Tikaya's and the president's wishes.

The driver, the only person visible in the cab, ducked and tried to charge past them. His wobbly vehicle lurched into a pothole made by the explosions, and when the man swerved in the opposite direction, it went up on the curb. Metal squealed as the lorry raked against a brick wall. With the vehicle limping along at three miles an hour—and hitting everything in its path—Dak had no trouble jumping into the cab. He pointed the rifle at the driver and barked an order. Sespian couldn't make out the words over the bangs and clunks of the vehicle. A moment later, the man stepped out, his hands clasped behind his head. He twisted his ankle on the uneven pavement and nearly pitched into a pothole himself. When he recovered, he trudged down the street away from the warehouse, his hands still locked behind his head, his gait as lopsided as the vehicle's.

Dak searched the rest of the lorry, but nobody else remained. He slung the rifle over his shoulder and strode back to Sespian and the others. When he hopped into the cab, he met Tikaya's inquiring frown without flinching.

"Those are *our* vehicles," Dak said.

Maldynado looked at the lorry, which was currently parked half in the street and half on the curb, like Dak had just fought off the vultures for a particularly old piece of roadkill for the stewpot. "Would have been a shame to lose such a fine conveyance."

"Rias can fix it," Dak said.

"In his copious free time?" Sespian asked.

"He's only in office for five years." Dak waved at the vehicle—it had started smoking alarmingly from numerous orifices. "He'll need hobbies to keep him busy after he retires."

"Have I mentioned," Tikaya asked, "that you're not a very nice man, Colonel?"

"Not since the day before yesterday." Dak prodded the corporal. "Take us over to that warehouse. I hope that blasted submarine has fared better than the rest of the vehicles on this street."

"Me too," Sespian murmured.

Mahliki came over to stand next to him and eyed his chest. Since he was covered in soot, blood, and grease, he doubted she was admiring his fashion sense—or his physique—but he wouldn't have minded a feminine compliment.

"Do you still have the blasting sticks in your shirt?" she asked.

Not a compliment so much as a reminder about his foolish storage system. Sespian had left the one he had been about to light in the lorry—in fact, it had probably lent itself to that first stupendous explosion—but one did indeed remain nestled against his breast. He fished it out.

"Careful there, boy," Maldynado said. "Sicarius put a lot of effort into keeping you alive against all those villains trying to oust you. He'd be disappointed if you blew yourself up of your own accord."

"Yes, I would feel foolish if that happened. Or rather my eternal spirit would."

Mahliki smiled and leaned against his arm. That was even better than a compliment about his physique. Something about their closeness made Maldynado smirk.

Sespian cleared his throat. "Speaking of foolishness, why are you only wearing one shoe?"

Maldynado wasn't even wearing a sock on the unprotected foot—the textured metal floor of the cab had to be cold. Not to mention there were crazy people waving blasting sticks around. Footwear had to be considered wise.

Maldynado lifted his bare toes. "It's still waiting for the attention of a medic."

His foot *did* have a red and swollen aspect to it.

"What happened?" Sespian asked.

"I saved your building," Maldynado said smugly.

"You did?"

"I thought you said Sicarius killed the assassin," Dak said.

"Yes, but *I* talked him into coming with us," Maldynado said. "I set up the whole trap. I'll tell you all about it later."

"You better tell him about the other thing first," Dak muttered.

"Oh. That should probably wait until... later. For Sicarius. Yes, this is definitely the sort of talk one should have with one's father."

"Uh, all right..." Sespian frowned around the cab, wondering who besides Dak knew about... whatever this was. Tikaya wore a thoughtful expression. Sespian thought about pressing the matter, but the vehicle had stopped, and Dak was hopping out. Maldynado hustled after him. "In the meantime," Sespian said to Tikaya, "how alarmed should I be?"

"It will depend on what you do with the information," she said. "Parenthood is a tremendous opportunity, but a life-changing choice as well."

"*Parenthood?*"

When Sespian climbed out of the lorry, he wobbled and stumbled as much as the priest Dak had ushered down the road. Parenthood? He hadn't even... Could they be talking about his cat? That was the only thing he could think of, that Trog had been... cavorting in the neighborhood.

CHAPTER 25

"DERET?"

Amaranthe paddled around the icy cider-filled tank, groping in the darkness. He had been shot *and* hit his head falling in; she didn't know if striking the liquid would have revived him—or not. She also didn't know if those priests would open the hatch and start firing at them from above. If so, they would be easy targets. The darkness might cloak them somewhat, but it wasn't as if they could *go* anywhere. They could duck into the six feet of cider in the tank, but she doubted the liquid would stop a bullet. It would only be a matter of time before someone's shot hit...

"Here," Deret said from one side of the tank. "I'm sorry. That was idiotic."

"Getting shot or falling in? Or hitting your head as you fell in?"

"Dear ancestors. Don't remind me. I used to be... maybe not an elite warrior, but I could hold my own on the battlefield. You'd think I would know how to compensate for the cursed leg by now."

Something thunked hollowly against the side of the tank. At first, Amaranthe thought it was the hatch being opened, but it had come from below. Deret bumping the wall with his elbow. Or maybe his head.

"It takes a while to reteach muscles that have memorized moves a certain way," Amaranthe said, wishing she could touch the bottom and didn't have to tread water—cider. Just because she could do it—with a ten-pound brick over her head—didn't mean she preferred to. "How often have you had to fight since you received the injury?"

"Oddly it only happens when you show up."

"It's clear you need more practice being shot at. I'll have to come by more often."

"That would be nice. The coming by, that is. Not the being shot at."

"I understood," Amaranthe said.

"I suppose Sicarius would object to that."

"You being shot at? No, that wouldn't bother him."

Deret grunted.

"How injured are you? You sound a little pained, but your voice is more even than mine."

"I'm able to stand on the bottom. Barely. I was hit in the shoulder. It hurts, but it won't kill me. A second shot wouldn't feel good though. I keep waiting for them to open the hatch and finish us."

As if someone outside had been waiting for this statement, thumps sounded on the roof of the tank, then a squeaking.

"I believe they've decided to lock us in instead," Amaranthe said.

More squeaks came, this time from the other side of the tank, somewhere behind Deret. Gurgles sounded from above. Amaranthe thought of the pipe from the vat to the tank. She wasn't surprised when cider started gushing through, splashing her shoulders as it poured down.

"And drown us," she added.

"As the night goes on," Deret said, raising his voice as if he expected the people outside to hear, "I'm more and more happy I didn't vote for that smiling shrub!"

"Did you vote for Starcrest?" Amaranthe had left before the final votes had been tallied, but she remembered four people running for the office.

"Yes. I almost didn't because I didn't want to show warrior-caste favoritism, but I ultimately thought he was the best man for the job, and that he would usher in a period of peace and prosperity." He raised his voice again to yell, "And I didn't want idiotic religious fanatics in charge!"

He sputtered the last few words, not out of anger, Amaranthe realized after a moment, but because cider had flooded his mouth. The liquid level was already rising.

"How long can you tread water?" she asked, wondering about his leg. Would it trouble him as much in water—cider—as on land?

"Probably longer than it takes for the tank to fill up," Deret said grimly. "I never thought I'd be in a position where I was hoping an assassin would come save my life."

"In the event that he arrives late, we might want to see if we can find a way out on our own."

"I'm open to ideas." He hissed, then gurgled and spat. "I may have to revoke my earlier statement. The bullet grinding against my shoulder bone is making treading water very painful."

"I'll see if I can figure something out."

Amaranthe didn't think they would have many options until the cider filled enough to let them reach the hatch. Maybe she could find a way to break the seal at that point, but the priests had taken her sword and dagger, and she didn't have any tools secreted away. Not that a lock-picking kit would work on the bottom of a hatch anyway, but her fingernails weren't going to do the job. Maybe when they reached the pipe, she could plug it with a boot or sock and stop the flow of cider coming in. In the meantime, she ducked beneath the surface, probing the dark cold bottom with her hands, hoping to find some weakness or some fallen tool she might use to pry a way out. On the third try, she found the pistol she had forgotten about. It had flown from her hand when she hit the cider.

"Found my pistol," she said when she broke the surface. "I doubt it'll fire, but maybe I can bang a nice medley on the wall for someone."

"It might," Deret said. "That's one of the new guns... with self-contained... bullets, right? The powder... might still be dry."

"Well, I don't think shooting it while we're in a sealed metal tank would be a good idea." Amaranthe imagined a bullet zipping all over the place, clanging off walls and finally lodging in someone's flesh. "We're almost up to the pipe. I'll try blocking the outlet."

"Good."

With Deret's words more labored now, his breathing ragged, Amaranthe worried about him. She swam over and caught him beneath the armpit, trying to give him some support.

"Shouldn't you... be removing your socks... to stuff in that pipe?" Deret grumbled. He didn't push her away though.

"I can't reach it yet. The cider is rising quickly though. It shouldn't be long."

"Great." Deret spat out a mouthful. "If we get out of here, I'm not touching this stuff ever again."

"We'll get out of here."

Deret didn't respond. It was probably wiser for him to save his energy for treading water.

As soon as the cider level rose enough, Amaranthe paddled to the pipe. It was about six inches wide. It would take more than a pair of socks to staunch the flow.

She debated on the rest of her clothing, then started unbuttoning her shirt. If this didn't work, she would try the trousers, but those would be hard to get off without removing her boots, and she didn't want to be running around the compound barefoot if they managed to escape. "Won't be the first time I've taken off my shirt in recent weeks," she supposed.

"What?" Deret asked.

"Nothing."

"I thought you were offering to go topless for me in my dying moments. I was going to approve of the notion."

"What does it matter when it's dark?" Amaranthe pulled off the shirt, shivering as the cold cider bathed her bare arms. She had a light sleeveless undergarment, so at least she wouldn't be running around completely topless if they escaped. *When* they escaped.

"Didn't Sicarius tell you? Men have wonderful imaginations when it comes to these things."

Amaranthe wadded up the shirt and stuffed it into the pipe. Cider sprayed her face, and the flow dumped the garment out onto her again. She huffed in frustration and groped around for it. Fortunately, she found it before it sank. She returned to the wall beside the outflow, deciding the task might be easier once the level in the tank rose to the pipe.

"We don't talk about his imagination often," she said, though he *had* admitted to speculating about her a few times, after she had breached the topic of becoming "bed friends"—her silly words—and before he had agreed that this would be a "desirable event"—his words.

"What *do* you talk about?" Deret asked. "It's hard to imagine—" he sputtered and coughed. "Hard to imagine... you being a part of... such a... mute relationship."

"It's not mute. *I* talk plenty." Amaranthe tried the shirt again. They were floating even with the pipe now, so maybe she could get a better angle. "Ugh, the flow is too hard. This won't work unless I can glue it to the walls somehow. Or maybe with a bigger, heavier shirt. I don't suppose you would like to shed?"

"At the risk of sounding... even more unmanly than I've already been... I think I might pass out if... I tried to remove it. My shoulder...

is already unhappy... and I'm a little... dizzy. Not sure how much... blood I've lost. Also... I doubt you could... hold *both* of us up... indefinitely."

"Ah, don't risk it then. I'll just strip off more of my own clothing." She would have to try the trousers. Maybe the two pieces combined would be enough to stop up the flow.

"Just so long as... you don't tell Sicarius... that was my idea... if he shows up."

Amaranthe would risk running into him in her undergarments if it would stop the cider from rising. She struggled to remove the trousers without losing the shirt or her boots; they had to be ten or twelve feet from the bottom now, and she didn't want to go diving for her garments. She wadded them into a ball and stuck them in the pipe again.

For a moment, the flow lessened. She was on the verge of spouting her success when they slipped free, gushing into her along with the pent-up cider.

She snarled in frustration and tried again, but it was as if the walls of the pipe were greased. Her clothing wouldn't stick.

"It would be nice if... floating were easier," Deret said. "Is it just my injury speaking or... is it harder to stay up in this... than it would be in water?"

"No, it's harder." Amaranthe almost said that if Books were there, he could explain the science to them. She pushed away the sad twinge the thought evoked.

"I can't believe there's... not a ladder on... one of the sides. You'd think... someone has to climb down... to clean this place... now and then."

"That's the first thing I checked for. Maybe they took it out, knowing they would have guests." Amaranthe wished he would stop talking and save his energy. Maybe if she stopped talking, it would discourage him from continuing to do so.

"Unfortunate," Deret said. He did indeed fall silent after that.

Amaranthe tried stuffing her clothes in the pipe several more times, but the cider level continued to rise, and all she did was wear herself out diving down over and over again. She finally gave up when she lost her shirt, the sodden garment disappearing in the current and sinking somewhere in the darkness. After a vain search for it, she swam back to the top.

"Still with me?" she asked, remembering Deret's comment about dizziness. It had grown quiet once the gushing of cider from the pipe fell below the surface. The quiet was more unnerving than the splashing somehow. Maybe because it meant they were getting close to the top and running out of time.

"Yes," he rasped.

"We're two-thirds of the way up."

"Glad you're... keeping track."

"It's just that... well, if my fiddling with the gauge had worked, someone would have seen the tank as full now and turned off the cider."

"Maybe they all left."

Amaranthe stretched her hand up, wondering how far they were from the top of the tank. Her fingers brushed only air.

Faint squeaks arose from somewhere below. She held her breath, afraid to hope that was the cider being turned off.

The squeaks ended. It had already been quiet, but it grew quieter.

"Be right back," Amaranthe whispered, then took a deep breath and swam down to the pipe, or where she thought the pipe was. The current had stopped, so she had trouble locating the opening. She laughed to herself. What did it matter? The current had *stopped*.

"They turned it off," she said when she came back up.

"Good." Deret sounded tired, no, exhausted. "Can you reach the hatch?"

Amaranthe stretched up again, kicking this time to thrust herself out of the cider. She dropped back down without touching anything. "No. I'd better be careful about splashing and sloshing too. If they hear us chatting, they'll know the tank hasn't filled all the way."

"Right."

Amaranthe guessed whoever was out there would wait a few minutes, to make sure they had drowned, then come up top to check. She wished she could have set that gauge to wait a few more feet before showing the tank as full, but she hadn't even been looking at it, so what could she expect?

She stuck the pistol in her mouth and tugged on her trousers. She didn't want to be caught sans leg wear by the enemy. It was more of a struggle than the swimming, diving, and treading had been. She gripped the pistol, ready to test Deret's thought about waterproof bullets on whoever stuck his head through the hatch.

Soft tinks drifted through the wall.

"Someone's climbing the ladder," Amaranthe whispered.

"Do we shoot him or play dead?"

Amaranthe considered. If they lay face down in the liquid, would the priest be fooled? Would he stick a pole in and try to pull them out? No, they weighed too much for that. He would probably just shut the hatch again and turn the flow back on. To make sure.

"I don't know. I'll figure out what to do when the hatch opens."

Deret snorted.

Squeals drifted down from above, the hatch being unscrewed. She wished Sicarius would be standing out there, waiting to help them out, but they never would have heard his light feet on the ladder.

The hatch lifted, and the faint yellow of lantern light seeped through the hole. Someone crouched by the opening and peered inside. He frowned straight at Amaranthe, though she doubted he could see anything. It was one of the robed men, though his cowl had fallen back, and she could make out short brown hair and a large nose. She didn't recognize him.

She treaded water quietly, not certain whether to talk to him or pretend she and Deret had long since drowned.

Perched on the edge of the hole, he started to lower his lantern inside for a better look, but his head jerked up. He froze like a rabbit, staring in the direction of the door.

At that moment, Amaranthe knew she had an ally. He wasn't supposed to be there.

When she spoke, she kept her voice low, not certain if other priests lurked about. "I don't suppose you'd like to drop a rope or something down here?"

The man jumped back, disappearing from view. The light faded too.

"Hm."

"You scared him away," Deret said. "You should have told him you were... shirtless and trouser-less."

"Actually I got my trousers back on."

"Ah, so he left in disappointment."

"Every time I start to feel sorry for you because you sound like you're on the verge of passing out and drowning, you make jokes."

"My father always found my humor... inappropriate too," Deret said.

Something fell through the hole.

Amaranthe lurched backward, images of blasting sticks and grenades filling her mind, but her eyes caught up with her imagination. A rope dangled down from the hole.

The priest hadn't reappeared. Maybe he wouldn't.

Amaranthe tugged on the rope and found it attached to something sturdy up there. "I'll go first."

Deret grunted. "I'll go... whenever this bullet works its way out of my shoulder."

"Ah, maybe I can pull you up."

"I weigh two hundred pounds. We better hope our helper up there hasn't wandered off."

"I'm sure I can figure something out if he has. A block-and-tackle system or... a fast-acting diet program."

"Funny, Lokdon. Funny."

After making sure her trousers were securely belted again, Amaranthe shimmied up the rope.

"It's all muscle," Deret called up after her.

Amaranthe had reached the hatch and didn't respond. She poked her head over the lip, twisting her neck for a three-hundred-and-sixty-degree view before climbing the rest of the way out. The robed man who had dropped the rope was crouching by the ladder, watching the rest of the mill. A lantern burned by the door and at his side, but the rest of the lights—and the men holding them—were gone. Somewhere in the distance, machinery—or perhaps vehicles—let off blasts of steam, but silence had come to the mill.

"Thank you for the rope," Amaranthe said. "Do you mind helping again? My friend is too injured to climb out on his own."

"I thought he was dead." The man returned to the hatch. "I thought I'd be too late and that you would both be dead."

"That would have bothered you?"

"Not so much before you started talking, but then..." He grimaced. "I'm only twenty-three. I don't want to be killed by an assassin."

"I hear it's unpleasant at any age."

There was a long coil of rope, with only the last few meters dangling into the tank from a bolt hole, so Amaranthe waved for Deret to wait a moment, and untied the knot. She slung the rope over a beam above them and directed the tail back into the tank. Not exactly a block-and-tackle, and Deret still wouldn't be light, but it ought to be easier pulling him out that way. She handed the end of the rope to her new ally and gripped a section for herself.

"Say when you're ready, Deret," she called softly, not certain whether guards might be roaming around outside the building. "I'm Amaranthe," she added over her shoulder. "What's your name?"

"Verosh. They sent me back in to turn off the cider when it was done. When I saw the gauge already at full, I thought I'd be pulling out two corpses."

"Gauges can be faulty," Amaranthe said.

"Ready," Deret called up.

"He's two hundred pounds and refuses to diet, Verosh. Pull hard."

"Yes, ma'am."

"One-two-*three*," Amaranthe said and pulled on three.

The rope scraped a few inches over the square beam—it *definitely* wasn't a block-and-tackle. She and Verosh repeated the move countless more times before Deret's head appeared, his short wet hair plastered to his skull. He was only holding the rope with one hand and had the other arm tucked into his chest. Seeing that he would struggle to lever himself out like that, Amaranthe ordered several more pulls, not stopping until his legs rose above the hole. She left Verosh leaning back, holding their burden aloft, then jogged to Deret's side and pulled him onto the tank.

"I told you," Deret said, "it's muscle."

Even with the weak lighting the single lantern offered, the paleness of his face was visible. Treading cider with one good leg and one good arm couldn't have been easy, and he had to be in a lot of pain.

"Let's get you down from here." Amaranthe kept her second thought, *and steal a vehicle to drive back to the city*, to herself. There was probably a limit to how much help their sympathetic priest was willing to give.

"The door is open." Verosh dropped the rope and backed away from the lantern, his gaze skimming the darkness. "It wasn't a minute ago."

A cool draft whispered against Amaranthe's damp, bare arms. "Someone checking up on you?" she asked.

"Maybe."

She handed Deret the pistol she wasn't sure would fire. "I'll go down first."

He nodded with understanding and stood at the edge, ready to cover her.

Amaranthe hated putting her back to the open room to climb down, but she had little choice. She skimmed down the rungs as quickly as she could. At the bottom, she put her back to the tank and watched the dark nooks and alcoves between the other tanks and the machines. Deret tossed the pistol down to her, then followed her to the ground. Nothing stirred out there in the shadows, but more than the cool draft was raising gooseflesh on Amaranthe's arms. She sensed they were being watched.

She felt better when she and Deret stood on the ground, but wished they had their own weapons. Up top, Verosh knelt by the ladder and chewed his lip, as if he wasn't sure coming down would be better than staying up there and maybe tossing himself into the tank. Then he could pretend to be a victim rather than an accomplice when someone noticed the prisoners roaming the compound.

Ultimately, he grabbed the lantern and came down.

"Any chance you know where our weapons are?" Amaranthe asked. "Deret's... cane especially?"

Deret scowled at her for calling the swordstick a cane, but if Verosh didn't know it held a blade, he might be more willing to share the information. Who would deny a lame man his walking aid?

"I can't tell you." Verosh stepped away from the ladder—away from *them*—his hands spread. "I've already done more than I should. Please go. Follow the dirt road, then take a right at the main road. It'll take you back to the city limits in ten miles."

Amaranthe had no intention of walking that ten miles, soaking wet and in nothing but her undershirt. "Are you sure you can't let us know? If you don't, we're liable to wander around the compound and stumble across who knows what secret information before leaving."

"I'll already be in trouble," Verosh said, taking another step back, clearly fearing they would attack him. "I can't tell you."

A shadow moved behind him, and a black blade came to rest against his throat.

Deret flinched almost as much as Verosh.

"Can you tell us now?" Amaranthe asked.

Verosh gulped. "Big house. I think they're in the room to the right of the entryway."

Amaranthe lifted a hand toward Sicarius, who was barely visible in the poor lighting. "He helped us escape. Please don't exsanguinate him."

"Tie him up?" Sicarius asked.

Verosh didn't look happy at the idea, but Amaranthe nodded. "Maybe it'll keep him from getting into trouble with his boss."

Sicarius had brought along his own rope and quickly took care of the task. Amaranthe was glad. Though she didn't think the tank experience had drained her as much as Deret, her limbs were heavy with weariness, nonetheless. Deret hobbled around until he found a pole he could use to lean on.

Only after Sicarius finished tying Verosh and they were walking toward the door did he give her bare arms and thinly covered chest a raised eyebrow. She blushed, wishing she hadn't lost her shirt, especially when that plan hadn't worked.

"Was there a snake?" Sicarius asked mildly.

Remembering the last time she had been running around shirtless, Amaranthe blushed further. "No."

"I see." He paused, perhaps considering other possible explanations. "An explosion?"

"No." She thought about blaming Deret, but the cool gaze Sicarius had leveled at the man when he had returned with his pole had already implied that he was in more danger of feeling an assassin's blade than the young priest had been. "A true gentleman would offer a cold, wet woman his own shirt rather than... interrogating her so."

"It's true," Deret said. "I would have offered her mine, but it's just as wet. And it's bloody."

Sicarius considered this, doubtlessly weighing the benefits of keeping his shirt, which allowed him to blend into the night nicely, against pleasing her. Ultimately, he decided in her favor and removed a knapsack and unfastened his throwing knife sheath from his arm. He took off his shirt and handed it to her. She wasn't too proud to accept it, not when it was this early in the spring and the coldest part of the night awaited them. She pulled it over her head, glad for the warmth of his body heat.

Deret eyed Sicarius's lean muscular torso with disgust.

"Rethinking your definition of all-muscle?" Amaranthe asked.

"I never had a chance at that park, did I?"

Amaranthe couldn't think of a way to say he would have if she had never known Sicarius, especially with Sicarius standing right there listening, so she merely shrugged.

"I brought a vehicle." Sicarius pointed through the door and toward the orchards. "It is hidden. Mancrest may wait in it."

"Just me?"

"You are injured."

"He's intuitive too," Deret muttered to Amaranthe.

Sicarius's eyes narrowed slightly.

"Intuitive enough to know I want to snoop around." Amaranthe patted Deret on his good shoulder. "We'll fetch your swordstick. Go rest and keep the vehicle running in case we need to escape in a hurry."

"So by 'go rest' you mean go shovel coal into the furnace to keep the fire going."

"Yes. Doesn't that sound peaceful compared to the rest of the night?"

"I think... perhaps I've been mistaken in envying your assassin this last year."

Amaranthe smiled. "Likely so."

Sicarius pointed toward a path, and Deret limped off in the indicated direction. They waited to make sure he reached the trees before heading off to "snoop."

Amaranthe gave Sicarius a hug before he could lead the way deeper into the compound. "Thank you for coming. How did you find us?"

"A competent tracker always finds his prey."

"Even when his prey was driven ten miles in a lorry?"

Sicarius withdrew something from a pocket and pressed it into her hand. Amaranthe couldn't see much in the darkness between house lamps, but she rubbed it between her fingers. It felt like an apple stem that had been mashed by the tread of someone's boot. She was skeptical that he had decided they had been taken to a local orchard on that clue alone, but they were drawing close to the main house, so she left him his secrecy.

"I'm glad you decided to look for me," she said instead. "I hadn't planned this much excitement for the night."

"It was urgent that I find you promptly," Sicarius said.

"Oh?" She could envision all sorts of problems back in the city. Had the plant become more aggressive? Had the assassin caught up with Starcrest? "Trouble?"

"Sespian may soon be expected to take on the role of father."

"*What?*" Amaranthe almost tripped over a root—or maybe her own feet. "I didn't think... I mean... Maldynado said Mahliki liked him, but I didn't think they had... *have* they?"

"I am unaware of what you are speaking about in regard to Starcrest's daughter. The Nurian mage hunter is dead. With her last breaths she gave me a message—an address—to deliver to Sespian, and reminded me that he owes her a favor."

Amaranthe's mind, which had hiccupped to a stunned stop, started working again. "Oh. I... huh."

"Indeed. It seems she studied him and found him a more likely adoptive parent than I."

"Er." Amaranthe couldn't imagine either of them as someone's choice for an adoptive parent—Sespian might do in another ten years, but now? It seemed a bizarre decision. But she didn't have the experience with Nurians to truly understand their culture, either. Maybe there was some cachet attached to properly raising an enemy's child, so people tended to do a good job when presented with the opportunity. Or maybe the Nurians deemed honor the primary factor in considering suitability. She *did* know that was a key component of their culture. And Sespian was honorable; as far as she knew, no imperial enemy had ever disputed that. "Have you checked on the child yet?"

"No. That is why I came in search of you first."

"Oh," Amaranthe repeated, feeling a numbness that had nothing to do with the cold air needling her skin through her wet trousers. "Yes, you probably shouldn't be the one to go to the child first. Especially since... er, I assume you killed the—" she stopped herself from saying *mother*, as that seemed far too condemning, "—the assassin?"

"She attacked me."

"Sespian isn't quite as intimidating a figure as you, so maybe he wouldn't... alarm the child."

"He is busy working for Starcrest," Sicarius said.

And the girl couldn't be left in an apartment by herself indefinitely, right. She rubbed her face. What had that Nurian woman been thinking? To foist a child on someone so young, someone who was, at the moment, barely earning enough to pay for food for himself and his cat. Maybe the Starcrests would take the child in or some Nurian kin could be found.

"We'll pick her up in the morning," Amaranthe said. "In the meantime... there are more pressing matters to attend to."

"Mancrest's swordstick?"

"My snooping."

Tikaya watched with concern as Sespian walked away from the vehicle. She hadn't handled that well, but she had been distracted by Rias jumping down from the roof of that smoldering warehouse. Sespian would hear the full story soon and have an opportunity to decide what he wanted to do. She found it perplexing that an enemy of Sicarius had wanted his son to care for her daughter. Perhaps they would find the child had been sent away already and someone else waited at that address.

"Tikaya," Rias rumbled, brushing past the entourage of people who were congratulating him on surviving the battle and who wanted to know if he had completed the submarine so he could be ushered off to some new military headquarters where he could be kept safe.

Tikaya was more interested in checking him for wounds. She stepped down from the lorry, but he wrapped her in a hug before she could pat him down. Given the fierceness of the hug, she guessed Dak had delivered a quick report on the status of the hotel before hustling inside to bark orders. She was happy to return that hug with equal ferocity—what *had* he been doing up there on the roof, dodging fire and hurling blasting sticks as if he were some young private?

Mahliki gave them both a quick hug before heading into the warehouse.

"We'll be discussing a few things later, Mahliki," Rias called after her, a warning in his voice, one Tikaya had heard as many times as Mahliki and which she doubted would worry their daughter much.

"I hope you didn't need to put that bow to use here," Rias murmured in a gentler tone, brushing a strand of hair away from Tikaya's face.

"No, your nephew had cannonballs, so my arrows seemed superfluous."

"Good. The role of a president's wife hasn't been fully established yet, but I don't think that shooting his enemies full of arrows will be part of the description."

"What about snooping around his intelligence office?" Tikaya figured she should mention that new hobby before Dak beat her to it.

LINDSAY BUROKER

Rias arched his eyebrows. "Is that an interest for you? You certainly have the qualifications."

"I didn't know being able to piece together potsherds and read two-thousand-year-old languages qualified one to work in military intelligence."

"You know what I mean. Aside from decrypting intercepted messages, we could use someone who's an expert on..." Rias waved toward the thick stands of green stalks all around the warehouse; the priests may have been defeated but the plant remained. "I'm sure we haven't seen the last of artifacts and legacies from that civilization."

"I—"

"Look out," came Maldynado's voice from behind.

Tikaya found herself shoved to the side at the same time as a dark shadow reared at the edge of her vision. Sespian sprinted over to a thick vine flicking toward them like the end of a whip. He jumped, a black dagger in his hand. He landed atop the vine as if it were a donkey waiting to be ridden—a rearing and bucking donkey.

Rias should have taken cover inside the building, but of course he ran over to help. The sharp knife cut into the vine, but even it couldn't slice through that many inches of tough flesh in a single swipe. The thick tendril ought to have been forced to the ground by Sespian's weight, but it continued to whip back and forth. At first, Tikaya thought it was trying to knock Sespian off, but the tip was lashing toward Rias instead.

"Mahliki," Rias called, "where's my generator?"

Mahliki had gone into the warehouse, but she ran back out at his call. "Sorry, I borrowed it," she yelled and jumped back into the cab. She dragged the metal contraption out.

"Can I help?" Tikaya almost slung the bow off her shoulder, but her arrows wouldn't do more than scratch the monstrous thing.

"We can handle it," Mahliki called, running toward the whipping plant. "We've been doing this all night."

Maybe so, but that didn't keep Tikaya's nails from digging into her palms. She wished she had figured out some way her knowledge of the ancient language could help. Dak ran out, a blasting stick in his hand.

"You're not throwing that anywhere near them," Tikaya ordered.

After trying several times to stab the whipping top section of the vine with a long iron fork, Mahliki ran around Sespian, closer to the base of the plant. This time she caught the fork against it. Before Tikaya could ask what good it would do, streaks of blue electricity leapt from the tool. After a moment, gray smoke poured from the vine, and the green flesh grew charred.

"Got it," Sespian said a second before the sawn-off stump dropped to the ground. The several-feet-long tip that had been lashing toward Rias continued to flop and flail, but the rest of the plant slumped down. The charred area spread up to the stump and back to the base, and it soon appeared as limp and dead as bougainvillea after a freeze.

"Well done," Rias told Sespian and Mahliki. He flicked a hand to wave away Dak's blasting stick. "I've had enough of those thrown near me for one day."

Dak shrugged and went back inside.

Tikaya strode forward, grabbed Rias firmly by the back of the arm, and propelled him toward the door as well. "Just what do you think *you* were doing there? You clearly didn't have a weapon capable of harming it."

"I... was distracting it so it wouldn't focus on Sespian and Mahliki."

"Please. You were risking your life needlessly. It wanted you." A fact that Tikaya found alarming. It seemed as if this plant was gaining in sentience as it gained in mass. How were they going to destroy the thing *now*? "You're going to march inside and leave the fighting for the young people."

"Yes, ma'am," Rias said sheepishly.

"It's strange hearing him... reprimanded," Sespian whispered to Mahliki.

"It doesn't happen often," Mahliki said. "Just when he deserves it."

Tikaya snorted and followed Rias into the warehouse. She was tempted to order her daughter inside, too, but Mahliki and Sespian seemed to be the only people with tools capable of fighting the plant. She would have to trust that Mahliki could handle herself in this matter.

Inside, a swarm of engineers in uniforms had already accosted Rias. Tikaya continued to find it strange that this nation's brightest minds all came from the military. She supposed the odds would naturally go that way when nearly all of the able-bodied young men signed up to serve, at least for a time.

She walked over to examine the *Explorer*. Maldynado was already there, lying on the top of the hull with his head stuck inside. He had finally put his boot back on. His foot had either recovered enough to do so, or maybe his toes had simply gotten cold. He slid to the ground in front of Tikaya, wincing as his left foot touched down, but he was able to stand on it without an aid now.

"You're walking. Dak must be a better medic than advertised." She walked around the *Explorer* as she spoke. There was no sign of any damage on the outside. There were cables attached to the craft for hoisting it over to a pair of rails that could presumably take it out to the water—so long as that water wasn't completely blocked by the plant. Though she knew the submarine was sturdy, she shuddered at the idea of riding into that dense stand of irritated foliage.

"Hardly that," Maldynado said. "I simply have a fantastic constitution."

Rias strode over with Dak, the engineers and a dozen soldiers trailing behind them. "It's time to assemble the team."

"The team?" Tikaya asked. "Tonight?"

"Given the plant's accelerated growth rate of late, delaying even a day could mean the difference between success and failure."

Tikaya wondered if they had already delayed too many days to succeed. Mahliki almost hadn't escaped from the last underwater excursion, and the plant had barely been out of the harbor then. It had also been far less aggressive. She kept the thoughts to herself. These men were nodding at Rias. They wanted encouragement not pessimism. It wasn't as if there was a viable alternative, short of abandoning the city—maybe the continent. *Someone* had to go down.

"I hope you're planning to appoint some hearty young men to the task," Tikaya said, "while you remain here on dry land to attend to your presidential duties."

Rias had the look of a man bracing himself for a battle. Tikaya realized she would be his opponent in this and stared at him with chagrin.

"Nobody knows the controls like I do," Rias said, "and there's not enough time to teach anyone."

"Amaranthe and Sicarius know them."

"They're not here."

Tikaya started, realizing she hadn't seen either person all day. "Where—they didn't get caught in the hotel, did they?"

Dak shook his head. "I didn't see them when I was warning people."

"Amaranthe went off to see Deret Mancrest, last I heard," Maldynado said. "But she didn't come back, and Sicarius went to look for her."

Rias spread his hand. "They have troubles of their own. Other people can run the government. I'm the only one for the submarine."

"*Other* people? If that were true, they wouldn't have sent a letter three thousand miles asking for *you.*" Tikaya tried not to sound shrill and frustrated, but it was hard. Her fear of losing him came back full force, the emotion rising into her throat and lodging there.

Rias stepped closer to Tikaya, drawing her aside for a private moment. Dak lifted his hands, ushering the other men back. He didn't say anything, but Tikaya guessed what they were all thinking. *Let him calm the woman, so we can get about our work...*

"Do you remember how we electrified the hull of the first submarine we made?" Rias asked. "To fight the overeager sea life in your harbor?"

"Yes."

"In addition to making other weapons, I ensured that feature works even without the artifact. I'm not planning a suicide mission."

Tikaya thought of the way Mahliki had been forced to apply the electricity for several seconds before that single vine started to char and wondered how much power it would take to drive back the jungle in the waters below, especially now that the plant appeared quasi sentient. She imagined the huge limbs batting the submarine around, each one contacting the hull only briefly, not long enough to be damaged. How would they fight that?

"You look grim." Rias's eyes crinkled, as if this were some game. "No faith in an old admiral who's survived a lot of battles over the years?"

"This is different. Even after twenty years of studying that race, I hardly know..." Tikaya sighed and laid her hand on his arm.

"We've defeated it before."

"We guessed the combination lock on one of their security systems. That's not exactly the same as *defeating* the technology."

"I was thinking more of the ship you blew up, love."

"That wasn't defeat, either," Tikaya said. "That ship had a self-destruction program built in. I simply turned it on."

"Maybe the plant has a self-destruct command programmed into its cellular punch cards."

Tikaya shook her head. "If it's there, I wasn't able to find it. While Mahliki was experimenting with the physical body, I tried everything I could think of with the sphere. I wouldn't know how to... *transmit* any orders if there were some."

"Then we'll have to do it this way." Rias patted the submarine hull.

Tikaya stepped in closer, leaning her head against his shoulder. "Is it horrible of me to wish Sicarius had never sent that message to you?"

"Abysmally horrible, yes." He wrapped his arms around her. "But I love you anyway."

They held each other for a couple of long moments, then, when Rias pulled away, Tikaya let him go.

"We don't have a lot of room for a big team," Rias said, returning to the waiting men. "I could use an engineer and a couple of people who have experience with the diving suits, in case we're not able to get close enough to the roots with the submarine."

Tikaya lifted her fingers to her lips, horrified anew at the idea of someone walking out in that man-eating jungle with nothing but a canvas suit for protection. Though Mahliki had downplayed the danger of being captured by the plant, Tikaya could guess how close her daughter had been to dying, based on Dak's report, and the way he had avoided her eyes when answering her questions.

"I'll only take volunteers," Rias said.

Every single engineer's arm shot up. Several of the soldiers said, "I haven't been in a suit, but I'm sure I could learn it," or something to that effect.

"Rydoth." Rias pointed to a graying engineer with major's rank pins. Unlike the more eager men who were waving their hands and proclaiming their fitness for the job, he had merely raised a finger, his face grave.

A throat cleared behind Tikaya.

"Uhm," Maldynado said, a tentative finger poking in the air. "I've spent time in the suits. And fought a battle underwater."

Tikaya thought Rias would dismiss him instantly, since he wasn't military, and twenty minutes ago, he had been whining like a rusty wheel about the likelihood of his toenails falling off.

But Rias considered him thoughtfully. When Maldynado wasn't opening his mouth and offending people or talking about sexual conquests, he *did* appear a formidable warrior, and if he had trained and fought with Amaranthe and Sicarius for a year, he was probably as battle-hardened as most soldiers.

"Are you simply volunteering that information, or are you volunteering to go?" Rias asked.

"I could go," Maldynado said. "I owe that plant a lick or two. Besides, I'd like another chance to protect necessary people." He nodded toward Mahliki.

"She is not going," Rias said.

"What?" Mahliki propped a fist on her hip. "Nobody knows more about that plant than I do. You'll need an expert along."

Tikaya's heart sank at the argument. When Mahliki hadn't raised her hand, she had thought maybe her daughter had enough of a self-preservation instinct to wait out this fight, but she must have assumed she was on the team to start with.

"Your mother is already put out with me for volunteering," Rias said. "I doubt she would speak to me—or my spirit—again if I took us both on a journey from whence we didn't return."

Fancy way of saying, "If I got us both killed," Tikaya thought bleakly. Maybe Rias had been destined to be a politician after all.

"So whether or not I go is Mother's decision?" Mahliki asked.

"No," Rias said. "I want you back here, safe."

You implied this wasn't a suicide mission, dear...

A floorboard popped up in a corner, and a thin tendril rose through the crack. Sespian ran over to deal with it, the black dagger in hand.

"It's not exactly safe here, either," Mahliki said.

"Safer," Rias said. "Dak will take everyone to our backup headquarters, three miles from the waterfront. I'll bring up the submarine somewhere less strangled with vegetation—the Fort Urgot dock if it's still free—so there's no point in waiting here."

Dak propped his arms over his chest, frowning at this assignment. Surely he hadn't been expecting to be invited on the team as well? What was wrong with these Turgonians? Were they all so eager to die? No, she realized, they were just so eager to help Rias. This was what she got for marrying a national hero and returning to his homeland.

"Mother?" Mahliki asked, the age-old trick of asking another parent when the first said no. Strange to see it played here, especially with Rias looking on.

Naturally, Tikaya's instinct was to squash the request and keep her daughter safe, but Mahliki *was* the foremost expert on the plant here. Her knowledge might be crucial in defeating it. More than that, Rias might sacrifice *himself* for some noble cause, but he would move mountains to make sure his daughter survived. And if they were on the same vessel together, they'd both have to survive, now wouldn't they?

"I had assumed you would be a necessary member of the team," Tikaya said.

Mahliki had her finger raised and her mouth open, an argument on her lips, so she sputtered a couple of times before managing, "You did? So I can go?"

"No." Rias scowled at Tikaya.

He had probably followed her train of thought as easily as if she had spelled it out on a page.

"You promised me it isn't a suicide mission, love," Tikaya said. "Why wouldn't you take one of your greatest assets?"

Mahliki beamed at this designation, or maybe the fact that Tikaya was arguing on her behalf. Inside, Tikaya wanted to wail against the idea of letting either of them go and cry out that it wasn't fair that *her* loved ones had to take these risks. Outside... she smiled calmly at Rias.

"It'll still be dangerous," he grumbled, though he couldn't fight much harder, not without invalidating the very argument he had used to talk her into letting him go.

"Fine," Rias said, his tone clipped. "We have our team."

"I, ah..." Sespian raised a hand. "I have that fifteen minutes of experience with the suits. Maybe I can come too?"

"Very well. There's no time to spare. Let's get going." Rias headed for the submarine.

A number of the engineers and soldiers glowered at Sespian and Maldynado, clearly disgruntled that a couple of civilians had been chosen over them. Rias ordered a few men to help prepare the submarine to launch and told Dak to take everyone else to the backup headquarters. Dak issued a few orders of his own but didn't hurry to the lorries. Like Tikaya, he seemed to want to see Rias off before leaving. The soldiers had to fight off a few more attacks from the plant as well. Tikaya could only imagine—with nightmare-like vividness—what sort of battle it would offer once the submarine was in the water.

When the suits and men—and Mahliki—were in the craft, Rias came to her for one last hug. "I saw that the Kyattese communication device is still in our cabin. Did you by chance pack the complementary half before you left the hotel?"

"Did you also see that there was a message on it for you?" Tikaya arched her brows.

"A recent one?"

"Yes."

Rias shook his head. "I haven't looked in the cabin since my original walkthrough this morning."

"Never mind then." Technology, only helpful when used... "I do have the other one," she said. "It's in the lorry."

"Good. I can send Dak reports."

"You better send *me* reports." Tikaya stood on tiptoe to kiss him, but paused. His skin was oddly warm. She squinted at his forehead. Small beads of perspiration filmed his skin. The poison. Dear Akahe, what if it hadn't been a bluff after all?

He started to turn away from her, but she gripped his arm.

"Rias?"

He sighed softly. He knew. "Yes?"

"How are you feeling?"

"Tired. It's been a long night."

Her grip tightened. "You know what I mean."

Another sigh. "I've had a fever and some other symptoms for the last few hours."

"The poison?" she whispered.

"It might simply be a virus."

He had grown blurry. No, that was her vision. Tikaya blinked rapidly. "I'll find Amaranthe and Sicarius. I asked them to locate the head priest, to look for an antidote."

Rias nodded. "Good. I have to take care of this."

"I know."

The blinking didn't help. Hot tears ran down Tikaya's cheeks as he returned to the submarine.

CHAPTER 26

Sicarius stood with his back to a thick oak, the cool breeze whispering across his bare chest. Amaranthe leaned against his arm, smelling of brandy. He thought about teasing her that her new perfume was much worse than his earlier sewer scent—especially since he had washed before going to the construction site with Maldynado and Basilard—but she was shivering, so they ought to get on with the mission.

He eyed the wrought iron fence surrounding the large masonry house, razor-edged spikes protruding toward the night sky. Bypassing them would not be difficult, but doghouses leaned against one of the gray stone walls, and he had heard a few wuffs and snuffles during his initial scouting of the compound.

"Who would have thought a house in an apple orchard would need such security measures?" Amaranthe mused.

"Judging by the rust accumulation and weathering, the fence is approximately ten years old."

Amaranthe looked up at him, though the shadows hid her face. "You were dating the fence while I was drowning in a vat of cider?"

Sicarius had only meant to relay information on the age of the security apparatuses and could not tell if she was truly irked with him. "I was unaware of your location at the time."

"I'm going to forgive you since you were kind enough to lend me your shirt."

"You may consider it a permanent exchange." Sicarius could not imagine what degree of washing would be required to remove the brandy vapors.

"Very generous."

"If you wish to enter, I recommend going over the fence there, downwind of the dogs, and climbing up the roof to that attic entrance. The house has been quiet since I arrived, so the residents may be sleeping.

The bunkhouse over there contains more than twenty beds. I believe most are occupied."

"There's still a light on there." Amaranthe nodded to a window.

"Yes, it has not been long since the men left the mill. Some went in the bunkhouse and others took a lorry and left the premises. Someone will likely come out to check on the missing man before long," Sicarius added to remind her that they had better do their infiltration quickly. "I can go in on my own while you wait here if you wish."

"Would you remember to get Deret's swordstick?"

"I would not consider a swordstick a priority." The only thing Sicarius wanted that he thought might be in the house was information identifying the key members of this religious organization. If a poison had indeed been used on the president, one of them would know which one.

"That's what I thought." Amaranthe waved to the back of the house. "Lead the way."

Sicarius did so, making a circuitous route to avoid the dogs. He hopped onto the side of the fence, catching the bars near the top, his nose less than a foot from the barbs. A faint odor wafted to his nostrils and he froze, his legs dangling three feet above the ground. The barbs smelled like a mix of juniper berries and the *laddakal* plant, a combination he recognized, for the compounds were mixed to create a deadly poison.

"Interesting," he murmured.

"What?" Amaranthe whispered up to him. "And you know that's a rather strange position to be experiencing introspection from, right?"

"The tips of the fence are poisoned. Proceed with extreme caution." Sicarius had lost his momentum when he paused, but he still pulled himself up and over while giving the barbs a wide berth. He landed and waited for Amaranthe. Though he believed she could avoid the trap, he would offer assistance if needed.

She grumbled to herself but climbed to the top and over without brushing the tips. In her eagerness to avoid them, she dropped to the ground more heavily than normal, and her landing was audible.

A shift and a canine yawn came from one of the doghouses around the corner. Sicarius held up a hand, and they waited in silence for the canine to return to slumber. From behind the building, he couldn't see the bunkhouse or the mill, so he listened for steps or creaking doors that would mean someone was going to check on the missing man. Nothing yet.

Sicarius pointed toward the attic, then climbed atop a rain-catchment barrel and pulled himself onto the roof. He and Amaranthe padded across the ceramic tiles and up to the vents on the top story. He withdrew a hook from his lock-picking kit and unfastened an inner latch. Inside, Sicarius stretched out his senses, his fingers to the dusty floor, listening for people awake in the halls below. The attic smelled of cloves and cinnamon, the scent strong enough to blunt any lesser odors in the area.

"A question," Amaranthe whispered before he could start searching for a trapdoor down. "If the fence is poisoned, is it likely these people have an extensive collection of concoctions and might have used them elsewhere?"

"Such as for poisoning a president?"

"That's what I'm thinking."

"It's possible," Sicarius said.

"I don't know if one of the Edgecrests is involved in the religion, but for whatever reason, this seems like a stronghold for the priests. If they do make poisons, they could be here. Along with antidotes."

"Yes."

"By the way, it seems the priests also have Serpitivich under their sway, or perhaps it's the other way around. He's probably been our snitch all along."

"How did you come by that information?" Sicarius had never spoken to the vice president, indeed, had rarely seen him at all. He didn't think Amaranthe had spent any more time with the man.

"Starcrest's former wife is in bed with him. She's here on the compound tonight. Or she was earlier."

"Was she not just sharing a bed with Lord Mancrest?"

"Yes," Amaranthe said, "she seems to visit a lot of beds."

"A curious hobby."

"I'm glad you think so. She and Serpitivich both want Starcrest out of the way. Permanently."

"Is he here?" Sicarius hadn't intended for his voice to sound hard and chill when he asked, but if the vice president was plotting against Starcrest, he would take care of it in a blunt manner.

"I haven't seen him."

"Retrieve the swordstick," Sicarius said. "I will check the rest of the house."

For a moment, Amaranthe didn't answer. Sicarius waited to see if she would admonish him about assassinating people, but she either hadn't understood his intent or couldn't muster a defense for the man trying to kill Starcrest.

They hunted around and found a trapdoor. The hallway below lay in shadows, without any light seeping beneath bedroom doors. Sicarius dropped to the floor and started listening at doors, trusting Amaranthe could find the swordstick and her own weapons without his help.

He did advise, "Watch for more traps," before she disappeared down the stairs to the first floor.

She waved a hand in acknowledgment.

Most of the doors weren't locked. When Sicarius opened them, he found empty bedrooms, closets, and storage rooms stacked high with apple paraphernalia. Whatever else might lie within these walls, the orchard and mill appeared to be legitimate operations. A few bedrooms held sleeping figures, an older man and woman in one, and some younger single forms. Parents and adult children, he guessed. Those who ran the orchards? He didn't smell the hints of the lemongrass incense that had lingered near the bunkhouse.

Sicarius came to a locked door near the end of the hall and heard breathing that bordered on snoring coming from within. It was feminine, he thought, but he couldn't be certain. He started to pull out his picking kit, but hesitated, detecting a hint of kerosene in the air. He hadn't caught the scent farther down the hall. Someone had been that way with a lantern recently. Heading to a bedroom? Or elsewhere?

The hallway dead-ended with a large framed painting occupying the wall. Sicarius drifted toward it, then felt around and under it for hidden passages. He found a switch between the creases in the wood paneling near the ceiling. The wall popped open. He expected another hallway or a stairwell, but cool metal met his fingers. He probed side to side and up and down, outlining the contours of a vault door, a sturdy vault door. In the darkness, he couldn't tell if it was new or, like the fence, had been there for some years. He also couldn't tell how to get in. Maybe someone in the house would have the combination.

He took out his picks and returned to the locked door. It was unlikely

441

Starcrest's first wife would be sleeping in the bunkhouse, and this was the last bedroom to check. While he worked, he debated what he would do if he found her within. If she was plotting against Starcrest, she might deserve a fate similar to Serpitivich, but would Starcrest wish death for her? If not, he might be displeased with Sicarius if he killed the woman. Sicarius nodded to himself. He would only question her.

He did not hear Amaranthe climbing up the stairs, but the scent of brandy preceded her return. Her silence pleased him, but he chose not to whisper more than, "Here," in the quiet hallway.

Amaranthe joined him in front of the door while he finished picking the lock.

"I found the swordstick and my dagger," she whispered, "as well as a rapier I didn't recognize. Maybe Deret and I weren't the only people kidnapped tonight."

The lock released and Sicarius withdrew his tools. The heavy even breathing continued, so he eased the door open. Some starlight filtered in through the bedroom window, enough to pick out a single form under the blankets on one side of a bed large enough for two. The covers were rumpled on the empty side.

Amaranthe padded over for a look. "Sauda," she whispered.

Somewhere outside of the house a door banged open. Sicarius and Amaranthe were running out of time to explore without the compound being aware of them.

"I will restrain her," Sicarius whispered. "Get the vault combination from her."

"Vault combination?"

"Yes."

Sicarius pulled the woman out of bed, clasping a hand to her mouth and pressing his dagger to her throat. She struggled for a startled moment, then her mind awakened to the presence of the cold blade.

"Amazing you can sleep so peacefully," Amaranthe said, "when you believe people are drowning in the next building over."

Sauda said nothing, though that might have been a growl.

"What's the combination to your vault?"

Surprise stiffened the woman's limbs. "My what?"

"The vault at the end of the hall behind the painting," Sicarius explained.

"I don't know what you're talking about." Sauda twisted around as much as Sicarius's grip would allow. "Where's Serp? What did you do with him?"

So, the vice president was here as well. Good.

"Give us the vault combination and we'll tell you," Amaranthe said.

"I don't know anything about a vault. I'm just a guest here."

Possibly true. Just because she was sleeping with the vice president didn't mean she knew all his secrets.

Amaranthe walked over to a desk and lit a lamp. "Does he work here?" she asked and rummaged through drawers.

"I don't know," Sauda mumbled. "Let me go, and I'll find him so he can answer your questions."

"I don't think so." Amaranthe opened a book stuck in the bottom drawer and let the pages dangle downward. She fanned them, and a slip of paper fluttered out. "This has three symbols on it. Did the vault have numbers or something like this?" She walked to Sicarius and held up the paper.

"Symbols." Sicarius hadn't been able to see out there, but had run his fingers across the etchings around the lock wheel.

Another door banged outside and someone shouted from the direction of the mill.

"What?" came a response from the bunkhouse.

"I said, they're gone!"

A dog barked in the yard, and the others soon took up the chorus.

"You're about to be captured," Sauda said, "but I can help you escape. Keep me alive, and I'll tell you a secret way out of here."

"I don't believe we're ready to go," Amaranthe said. "Got any rope left in that pack?"

"Yes," Sicarius said.

He pushed his prisoner toward Amaranthe. Sauda opened her mouth to scream, but Amaranthe caught her, clamping her mouth shut before a single syllable escaped. Sicarius pulled out twine to tie the woman, then cut a gag from the bedspread. They left her trussed in a corner.

"Let's see if these symbols do anything." Amaranthe grabbed the lamp.

The dogs were still barking, and footsteps sounded from other rooms in the house—sleepy people climbing out of bed to check on the commotion. Though aware of the need to hurry, Sicarius studied the slip of paper before rushing for the door. Some of the symbols were similar to Turgonian letters. Others he had never seen, and a couple had a vague familiarness.

He pointed to one. "That's etched in stone at Pyramid Park. Near the altar."

"Kriskrusian?"

"Perhaps."

Sicarius opened the door, but waited before sticking his head out. Yellow lantern light swayed and wobbled farther down the hall—someone leaving a bedroom and heading for the front of the house. He waited until the illumination disappeared before slipping out and opening the secret door again. Amaranthe held up their lantern so he could see the symbols clearly. There were more he recognized from the pyramid.

He turned the wheel in the standard left-right-left manner of opening a safe, though he didn't know if Turgonian standards would apply.

The front door to the house slammed open. "Lord and Lady Edgecrest?" a man called. "Vice President? Are you here? The prisoners escaped."

"We're going to have to go out a window if that doesn't open," Amaranthe whispered. "We might want to go out a window anyway. Getting locked in a vault... Judging by Ms. Sarevic's story, that doesn't make for an enjoyable day. Or week."

The vault lock clicked. Sicarius pulled on the wheel. The thick door was heavy, but it swung open.

"Wake up Sauda and Serp," someone called.

Boots hammered the stairs.

Amaranthe snuffed the lantern. "Sicarius..."

He stepped through the vault door and tugged her in after him. He pulled the vault door shut from within—a rope attached to the inside allowed for this, but the hinges groaned and the ponderous door wouldn't be snapped shut quickly.

Gunshots fired. Metal rang out as a bullet clanged against the outside. Finally the door thudded shut, the lock engaging. A couple more pistols fired, but the thick metal muffled the bangs. The bullets made faint pings striking the door, hardly anything to be concerned about. Of course, there were other concerns to ponder. Sicarius slid his fingers across the cool metal of the door. Aside from the rope handle, it was smooth. If there was a way to open the door from this side, it wasn't apparent.

"Sicarius," Amaranthe said slowly, "did you just lock us into a room with no way out?"

"Given the temperature, moisture in the air, and musty smell, I believe it's an underground complex."

"Fine. Did you just lock us into an underground complex with no way out?"

"Unknown."

"It's not that I'm judging you," Amaranthe said, "it's just that I'm usually the one who does such rash and impulsive things, not you."

"Serpitivich went this way."

"Meaning, he'll know a way out?"

"Meaning, he's the one behind the attacks on Starcrest. I will kill him."

Sicarius thought Amaranthe might object to his bluntness—or rather his intent to kill the man—but all she said was, "After he tells us how to get out, I hope."

The submarine tilted, scraped on the warehouse floor, then swung in the air like a pendulum. Maldynado decided it would be unheroic to get seasick before the craft touched the water. Another soft scrape sounded as it bumped down on the rails. Someone must have already shoved open the back doors of the warehouse—they weren't quite as charred as the front, but the plant had smashed many holes into them—for the craft immediately started moving. A series of muffled booms penetrated the hull—soldiers hurling blasting sticks into the lake around the warehouse, trying to clear an entry path.

Maldynado sat on the cold metal floor, his back against the bulkhead, his fingers tapping a nervous rhythm on his thigh as he wondered what in all the lands in all the world he had been thinking. Even before Starcrest and Tikaya had gotten all teary and clingy, he'd known the odds were in favor of this being a one-way trip. Some genius scientist from a race a billion times more advanced than humans had made that plant. To think they could defeat it with a submarine and a couple of diving suits was hubris. Madness. Insanity.

Sespian settled down beside him, his legs scrunched in. This was the only spot to stay out of the way as Starcrest and the engineer jogged back and forth from navigation to the bulging miasma of machinery that comprised the new engine room.

"I know why I'm here," Sespian said. "Why are *you* here?"

"The president and his daughter have the seats up front, and the sleeping cabin is full of metal thingies... weapons, I guess. And crates. And fuel cans."

Sespian snorted softly. "I mean why did you volunteer for this? Amaranthe usually talks you into risking your life, doesn't she? It's not something you typically sign up for of your own accord."

Maldynado twitched a shoulder. "I don't know. It was an impulse."

Sespian studied him, not believing a word of that, Maldynado could tell.

"Fine, it was Evrial."

"You want to prove something to her?"

"No, I already did that in staking out your building site and fighting the saboteurs. At least that's what I was trying to do. She wasn't... I don't know. I'm pretty sure she's leaving me to go back to her town and her family, and some stupid career opportunity. I mean, it's not stupid. It's just... I think she was using it as an excuse. She didn't really want..." Me, Maldynado thought, but couldn't say it out loud. He had already admitted more than he intended to.

"Ah."

Thankfully, Sespian didn't probe further or point out how funny it was that Maldynado, the man who had no trouble getting women to sleep with him, couldn't convince one to stay with him for more than three months.

"Why are you here?" Maldynado asked, not wanting to linger on his own mess.

"Hm?"

"You said you knew why you were here."

Mahliki jogged past carrying a clipboard and a plant specimen in a jar. She jangled as she moved, glass vials clinking inside her vest. Sespian's gaze followed her, and Maldynado had the answer to his question before Sespian responded.

"Never mind," he said.

Sespian blushed. "I wasn't planning to, but then when she joined the team... it seemed cowardly not to volunteer when a girl had."

Hah, liar. That wasn't the *real* reason. But maybe Sespian hadn't figured out his feelings yet. Maldynado wondered if they would survive so he could throw his dinner party. While he had been waiting in the shadows at that construction site, he had decided on a caterer and a drum group, the latter to ensure some lively dancing at the end. Dancing that would inspire all those shy couples to thump some body parts together. Something he would gladly do, too, if Yara would come. Would she even be in the city by then?

"So the building is continuing on schedule?" Sespian asked. "I haven't been by since... I don't even know what day it is. Or when I slept last."

Maldynado yawned. "I know the feeling. This has been the longest night ever. I still don't know who the lead saboteur is, but at least that crotchety foreman won't have any fresh trouble in the morning."

"Good. Thank you. I feel as if I should have been out there with you. Starcrest asked for my help, but I don't know how imperative a part of the team I was. Though—" Sespian brightened, "—I do believe I kept Mahliki from having her eyebrows torched off."

"A noble act."

"Of course, if she hadn't been following me to that lorry, they might not have been in danger of being sizzled..." Sespian prodded thoughtfully at the light brown stubble fuzzing his jaw.

"Nah, I'm sure that girl would have thrown herself into danger one way or another tonight. It was good you were there to look out for her."

Mahliki jogged back past them again, this time heading to navigation. She glanced at Maldynado, and he wondered if she had heard his comment. If so, she didn't attempt to deny the statement. Maybe she was too busy to bother.

The hull lurched under them, and a faint splash sounded. Maldynado planted his palms on the deck, bracing himself—or maybe his stomach.

"We're in." Sespian pointed toward the oval viewing window above the navigation controls.

Maldynado couldn't see much from the deck, but he wasn't sure how much he wanted to see. A line of water stretched across the display with the night air visible above and black water below. The horizon was blocked by dark sinewy shapes rising in the distance. The blasting sticks might have cleared an area, but he had no idea how they would get out into the lake and to open water. Maybe they didn't need to. Nobody had yet briefed him on the plan, beyond the possible need for diving suits. And bodies to go into them.

Sespian pulled out the black dagger and a rag for cleaning it.

"You better do that *after* we finish fighting," Maldynado said. "And before Sicarius sees all those crusty plant bits plastered to the blade."

"This is the president's knife."

"There are two?"

"Apparently they got them at the same time."

"Huh." Maldynado scratched his chin. "I didn't know they had a connection from the past."

"Twenty years in the past, when a young Sicarius was sent to make sure Admiral Starcrest obeyed the emperor's orders in some ancient and very deadly tunnels."

"Huh," Maldynado repeated, his mind boggling at the idea of a *young* Sicarius still working for the emperor. He'd had the warmth and personality of a block of ice when Maldynado first met him; it was hard to imagine an even more humorless version. "Well, I doubt Starcrest would want his knife returned with plant crusties sticking to it, either."

"That is likely."

"We're lucky he even chose us to come along." On second thought, Maldynado didn't know if *lucky* was the right word, but he went on, nonetheless. "Sure, we've been in the suits before, but I'm surprised he didn't think his soldiers would be more... reliable."

"You mean more likely to obey him without arguing?"

"Not exactly. He doesn't seem to think highly of me. At least that's the impression I get. But maybe he's changing his mind. I *have* been helpful of late." Though Maldynado didn't know if anyone had briefed the president on that helpfulness yet. Had he heard about the saved building? Admittedly, it was a low priority, but surely the president would appreciate having a new residence to move his family and offices into once the rest of this mess was cleared up...

"Hm," Sespian said.

Maldynado squinted at him. "You have something else on your mind?"

"It may be my imagination, but he seemed to be studying everyone who volunteered, eying them from head to toe. I'm wondering if we were just the two people who looked like we would fit in the diving suits his men had loaded into the submarine."

Maldynado snorted. "You're a pessimist, aren't you?"

"Maybe so. I have my reasons to be one."

Maldynado supposed having Sicarius for a papa would sour his outlook on life too.

Sespian put away the dagger and pushed to his feet. "They've stopped running back and forth so much. I'm going to take a look at where we're going."

Maldynado didn't know if he wanted to *know* where they were going, but he had never enjoyed having only his own company for entertainment. He trudged into the navigation chamber after Sespian, though he wondered if they would be kicked out. There wasn't much room up there. Starcrest and Mahliki sat in the two seats, their hands resting on the controls. Maldynado had only been in the submarine once, for a very brief ride across the lake, so he wasn't sure how anything worked, but Starcrest had the more complicated control panel. A number of gauges on the side held his attention for the moment. Maybe he was worried about whether his modifications would work. Nothing had been tested.

"Light," Starcrest said.

Mahliki flipped a switch. Some exterior lamp brightened, shining a cone of yellow ahead of the nose of the craft. Green foliage and vines stretched all along the lake bottom below them, leaving only a few spots where the sand and pebbles were visible. Stubble poked a few inches out of the earth, but many of the small vines had been shorn off. Courtesy of the blasting sticks, Maldynado guessed. The vines would probably grow back within the hour.

"We're still at the surface?" Sespian asked. Occasionally a wave came, and the water line dropped below the top of the viewing port.

"Yes," Starcrest said. "We can't be frivolous with our oxygen with this new system. We'll stay on the surface until we reach the original spot in the harbor."

"Why the harbor? Aren't there roots we can attack anywhere?"

"That's where it started," Mahliki said, "and that's where all the rhizomes branch out from. Based on my experiments earlier today, they conduct electricity. Not the plant itself, mind you, but the rhizomes. Father's weapons are predicated on that." Her voice dropped to a mutter when she added, "So I sure hope my experiments were right."

"So if we apply electricity to the core roots, it might carry to more distant plants?" Sespian asked.

"That's the hope."

"What's a rhizome?" Maldynado whispered to Sespian.

Mahliki answered in a distracted tone, as something outside had caught her attention. "A continuously growing diageotropic subterranean stem that sends out adventitious roots and lateral shoots from its nodes. Though I'm not sure I'd consider anything this plant does adventitious. We're reaching the end of the area the soldiers cleared with blasting sticks, Father."

"I see it."

"As I always used to tell Books, the definition of a word shouldn't require the definitions of three other words," Maldynado said, making his whisper lower this time so Mahliki wouldn't hear it.

"Three other words?" Sespian asked. "I was only stumped by one of them."

"Books would have liked you."

"I barely got a chance to know him. I wish..." Sespian shrugged.

"Me too. I just hope they don't expect me to do more than shoot at a target out there. Or cut at it. Or whatever we'll be doing in those suits."

"If we're lucky, we'll be able to cut through to the roots without leaving the *Explorer*," Starcrest said.

"Are you going to test the weapons?" Mahliki pointed out the viewing port. They had run out of stubble, and thick vines stretched from the shallows, more than one shifting toward them.

"The electrification of the hull," Starcrest said. "We have to cut a path at some point."

"You don't think we should test the weapon too?"

"Let's not show our tiles before we play them."

"Do we... think this plant is a Tiles player?" Maldynado asked.

"It's proven itself far more intelligent than any other plant I've met," Starcrest said, "if that word can be applied to plants."

"Not generally," Mahliki said, "though they have demonstrated sophisticated behaviors for propagation and self-defense. They're able to sense and respond to many environmental variables, and some scientists have suggested that some brain-like system may exist for processing information and coordinating a plant's behavioral response."

Maldynado eyed Sespian, wondering if these spoutings of biological babble would make him second-guess his interest in spending extended periods of time with the girl, but he seemed... enraptured.

"That's with plants from *our* world though," Sespian said. "I assume this one breaks the rules."

A thud came from the side at the same time as the submarine lurched, the deck tilting. Maldynado grabbed the ceiling to catch himself. "It's breaking *something*."

"One of those vines has wrapped around us," the engineer called from the back.

"This is opportune," Starcrest said and flipped a switch.

"Opportune," Maldynado muttered. "Not the word I would have chosen."

The hair on his arms stood up. A faint blue glow seeped through the viewing display. The air crackled with energy, and Maldynado was certain he could have given someone an electrical shock without shuffling his socks along a carpet.

Mahliki jumped from her seat to dart between Maldynado and Sespian. She ran to a porthole cover on the side of the craft and unbuckled it.

The deck shifted back to level.

"That did it," Mahliki called. "It let us go."

"Does it appear damaged?" Starcrest asked.

"You can't really see any charring, but it's... limp."

"Good. I'm hoping that as we go forward, it'll learn to avoid us altogether, maybe even part for our passing."

That sounded optimistic, but Maldynado would hope for the same thing. A smooth slaying of the giant plant and home for breakfast would be fine with him.

"Were you this idealistic when you were commanding vessels at sea, Father?" Mahliki asked.

"No, but the men who served under me were prepared to die every time they left port. I didn't have civilians on board whose spirits I needed to keep up."

"Are you talking about me or Maldynado?" Mahliki asked.

"My spirits are just fine," Maldynado said. "Sespian, do I not look like I have spiritual fortitude?"

"It's possible he's judging you based on your... fortitude level when you had that little vine wrapped around your ankle," Sespian said.

"It wasn't *little*. It was like a boa constrictor, thank you very much. And wait. President Starcrest wasn't there. How could he know?"

"The colonel may have whispered a report in his ear."

"I knew I didn't like that man," Maldynado said.

The submarine shuddered.

Maldynado gripped the ceiling again—with fortitude. "Another vine?" He kept his voice casual. He wasn't worried, not him.

"It brushed us and jerked back," Starcrest said.

"You're leaving the hull electrified?" Mahliki asked.

"We're moving into the thick of them now, so yes."

"Does it... take a lot of power?"

Maldynado glanced toward the engine room where the machinery hummed. Nothing sounded strained, but who would know with these fancy new upgrades? Only Starcrest.

"Yes," Starcrest said. "But we have it." His voice lowered and Maldynado almost missed the rest. "For now."

Nothing but green stalks and swaying tendrils occupied the water beyond the viewing port now. They were floating along near the surface, but the verdant jungle made it impossible to see more than a few feet ahead. The taps and bumps of the plant brushing the hull—*testing* the hull—were audible inside. Maldynado found himself holding his breath to listen, concerned some crack or other weakness would be discovered and those tendrils would damage the craft irrevocably. It had grown silent all around, and he had a feeling *everyone* was listening.

Though sweat glistened on his forehead, Starcrest's face remained calm as he alternately watched the route ahead and checked his gauges.

If *he* was calm, then there shouldn't be any reason to—

The submarine lurched. Bubbles rose outside the viewport.

"We're descending," Mahliki said. "Rapidly."

"They're pushing against us from above." Starcrest's fingers flew across the controls, prodding levers and turning a small wheel. "Attempting to compensate."

The hum from the engine room increased to a loud thrum. The deck vibrated beneath Maldynado's feet. A thump coursed through the craft, and they stopped descending. The submarine had struck the bottom of the lake.

"Did the electrical hull thing stop working?" Maldynado asked.

"It's still active." Starcrest pointed out the front, even as a six-inch-thick vine slapped down, cutting the view in half. Blue electricity crackled around it, and it grew charred. While it withered before their eyes, three more vines landed atop it. Then smaller ones swept across from the sides. The interior grew darker as the illumination from the running light was snuffed out. "It's dropping on us in layers," Starcrest said. "Sacrificing the vines closest to the hull to immobilize us."

"My Lord President," called the engineer from the back. "We're overheating. We can't move with all of this atop us. The ballast tanks are completely full of air, but it's not doing anything."

"Turning off propulsion." Starcrest pulled another lever. "We'll have to find a way out of this snarl before we try moving again."

"We can do that, right?" Maldynado asked. "There's a plan for this, isn't there?"

He didn't like the grim looks that Starcrest and Mahliki exchanged, not one bit. Oh, how he wished he were in bed with Evrial right now, somewhere far, far away from sentient plants. Her quaint little village, perhaps. Why had he ever thought that place too dull for his tastes?

CHAPTER 27

FTER THE SUBMARINE LAUNCHED AND disappeared from sight, Tikaya followed the men back to the lorry. With no further reason to defend the warehouse, the soldiers piled into the bed of the vehicle. Tikaya joined Dak in the cab, along with the same corporal who had driven before. It felt too spacious, too lonely, without Mahliki, Sespian, and even complaining Maldynado in there with them.

She dug into her backpack to pull out the communications orb. It glowed a soft yellow, and the corporal gave it a few uneasy glances. She thought about testing it, but Rias would be busy—and focused. She didn't want to be a distraction. She would simply keep it close in case he chose to send them a message. And he *better*.

"To the new headquarters, sir?" the corporal asked.

"Back to the hotel," Tikaya said.

"Er?"

Dak raised his eyebrows at her.

"I need to find Amaranthe and Sicarius," Tikaya said. "They're the ones I tasked with finding a cure for that poison." Among other things, she admitted. What were the odds that they had figured everything out in a few hours? "I don't know where they are, but they'll check in back at the hotel when they have something." What was left of it...

"The poison isn't what's on Rias's mind right now," Dak said.

"It may not be on his mind, but it's taking effect in his body."

He frowned at her. "You're sure?"

Tikaya rubbed her fingers where she had touched his face. "Yes."

"I'll need to get to the new headquarters," Dak said, "but we can drop you off at the hotel."

"That's fine."

It would have to be. But what would she do if Amaranthe and Sicarius weren't there? How long could she wait? If the entire intelligence office hadn't been blown up, she might have continued to research on her own. Maybe she could have come across some hint of what poison had been used. That alone would give her the information she needed to find out if there was an antidote or not. She knew some of his symptoms. Perhaps she could research in a book. But those symptoms... they were vague. Surely thousands of viruses and poisons could cause them.

"It looks like they've got the fire out," Dak said, rousing Tikaya from her thoughts.

They were already turning up the street to the hotel—to what *remained* of the hotel. Two fire brigade vehicles were parked in front of the gate with smoke billowing from their stacks, but the roiling black clouds pouring from inside the compound had disappeared, and night's shadows had returned to a block previously alight with the flames. There were also medical vehicles, and Tikaya spotted Basilard near one, his buckskin clothing standing out among all the black uniforms. He was trailing a pair of medics carrying a stretcher. Was that his translator lying on it? If the woman had been caught in the explosion or fire, Tikaya hoped she would recover.

"Stop right there, Corporal." Dak pointed at the front gate.

Tikaya expected to be discharged and left on her own at that point, but a soldier jogged out of the compound, heading straight toward them.

"Sir!" he called, veering toward Dak's side of the cab. "You're back! I have a message."

"From whom?" Dak leaned out to accept the folded note.

"Sicarius." The young soldier's face blanched, as if dealing with the assassin had been a heart-stopping experience.

Dak opened the furnace door to read by the light. Tikaya leaned over his shoulder, clenching her fingers into fists to keep from ripping the note from his hands.

"Amaranthe has been kidnapped by a group of priests," Dak said. "They took her to Edgecrest Orchards. I am following." He lowered the paper, his brow wrinkling. "Edgecrest *Orchards*?"

"Is it far away?" Tikaya asked. If the priests had their headquarters there, maybe information about the poison would be there too.

"Not that far. That's where the vice president went tonight. I wondered if I should have had him followed, but—gah." Dak scowled down at the letter. "Maybe Sicarius *should* be Rias's right-hand man."

"You're not experiencing feelings of inadequacy, are you?"

"Of course, I am. Haven't you read my files?"

"No."

"No?" Dak asked. "I thought that would have been one of your first stops, me being a suspect of late."

Ah, he had figured that out, had he? "I'm sure I would have gotten to them if the building hadn't blown up. Are you still going up to headquarters?" Tikaya tapped the note. If he was, she would request a vehicle and a driver who knew where these orchards were.

Dak read the words again, then prodded the driver. "Take us out of the city, Corporal."

"Yes, sir."

The crackle of electricity beat against the hull of the submarine like rubber bands snapping. Mahliki could feel it on her skin and in her mind, almost like the sensation one received from the mental sciences being plied nearby. Two types of energy, both inadequate against those vines, at least on such a grand scale. For every charred husk that floated away from the viewing windows, others pressed in to replace it.

"I have batteries I can deploy," Father said, "but I wanted to wait until we reached the harbor."

"I know," Mahliki said.

"We're on the lake bottom now. I have digging tools. Will the roots here be susceptible?"

"They should be." Mahliki wasn't as confident as she sounded—after all, she had only tested one small section of a root bulb—but she hoped her words would prove true.

"I'll see what I can dig up with all that greenery smothering us."

Father left his seat, passing between Maldynado and Sespian to access the small science station nook between navigation and the engine room. Controls there allowed for the collection of specimens. Mahliki hoped the drill would be up to the task of piercing the layers of protection that would exist above the root. When she had collected her sample, she had struggled to pry her way past not only earth but a filmy yellowish-green shield around the subterranean nodules.

"Are we going to need to go out in the suits soon?" Sespian asked.

"I'm sure you remember that it takes a while to put that cumbersome gear on, so we'll need a little warning."

"Don't sound so eager," Maldynado whispered.

"I didn't think I was."

"Well, maybe I assigned you eagerness based on the fact that you brought it up at all. Going out there looks like suicide to me."

"Sitting down here would eventually be suicide too," Sespian pointed out. "When we run out of air."

"While you're at it, why don't you say a few more things I don't want to hear?" Maldynado asked. "Such as that Evrial will never come back to me, and I'm destined to live a lonely and unfulfilled life. All thirty minutes of it that are left."

While they sniped at each other, Mahliki leaned back in her seat, twirling the end of a braid around her finger and searching the control panel for inspiration. She thought about sending Maldynado back to help the engineer—somehow his babble was more distracting than Sespian's—but Major Rydoth had problems enough already.

"You can't go out there until we're back on the surface," she said. "We don't have a lock-out chamber on the *Explorer*."

"So there's no way to get out there without flooding the whole place?" Sespian asked.

"Right. The big research submarines Father has built have them, but this is our little family exploration craft. We didn't—"

Something snapped in the rear of the sub.

"My Lord," the engineer called.

"I see it. Mahliki, you'll have to handle the drilling."

"Got it." She jumped out of the seat. "You two, watch the gauges and holler if you see any trouble—any *more* trouble than we're already in."

Maldynado pointed. "Like that gauge with the needle bouncing around the red?"

"That's our *current* trouble," Mahliki called back as she ran to the science station. "I'm only interested in new trouble."

Air hissed somewhere in the rear, but Father could handle the problem better than she. If it *could* be handled. She had no idea how much pressure that plant was exerting but wouldn't be surprised if it equaled that of water in the deepest parts of the ocean.

Mahliki slid onto the edge of the seat and checked out the viewport above the narrow control panel. Green vines plastered the glass. She was glad that glass was a Made item, reinforced to withstand deep-ocean pressures. Even so, she wondered how long it could hold up under this assault.

"Concentrate on your task and get rid of the plant then, eh?" Mahliki checked the drill. Father had already deployed it from the hull, but he hadn't turned it on yet. The tool dropped out from a compartment below the science station, so it wouldn't have to pierce the vines. It *would* have to dig through the lake floor and pierce the protective film around the roots.

She pressed the power switch, and the whirr of the rotary blades hummed beneath her. With the viewport covered, she couldn't see a thing, but a gauge next to the controls displayed the tool's depth. The bit burned through the first four inches of earth without trouble, then slowed down and halted. The blades kept spinning, but they stopped making progress. She let the drill continue for a few more seconds—she had cut through coral and rock before with this bit and knew hard substances took time—but then turned it off, letting it cool for a moment. Normally the chill water would keep the friction from heating to dangerous levels, but she wasn't sure how it would handle beneath the earth. With the submarine pressed to the bottom, there might not be any water seeping into that hole.

The low voices of Father and the engineer drifted to her ears. They were talking too quietly for her to make out the words, but the urgency didn't fail to come through. They needed this to work so they could get out of this vile embrace.

Sespian crouched beside her. "Any progress?"

Mahliki glanced at him, shook her head, and flipped the switch to try again.

"Maldynado is watching the gauges. Forgive my intrusion, but I thought if the drill didn't work, there might be a way to..." Sespian held up the black dagger. "Replace the bit?"

"There *is* a way to bring the tool inside to change out broken bits," Mahliki said, "but that's not exactly the right shape. I don't know if we could figure out a way to clamp it on there. I would hate to lose it."

"—have to do *something*, My Lord President," the engineer was saying.

Mahliki tapped the drill gauge. "It's sunken in another quarter of an inch. It's making progress. If we can just—"

A dull snap echoed from below.

"Blighted banyan sprites," Mahliki growled. "The bit snapped."

"Bring in the tool. We'll try the dagger."

"It's not going to fit." Mahliki reeled in the drill—she had to change out the bit, regardless. "Unless you brought some extra strong water-proof glue."

"We'll improvise."

"The force applied to the drill will ensure a shoddy improvisation will simply snap off."

"I wasn't planning to improvise shoddily," Sespian said a little stiffly.

She gave him an exasperated look. Anything they tried to do out here in the field would be shoddy.

"Just let me look at it," he said.

Mahliki drummed her fingers while the small airlock that allowed the tools to be changed out and for specimens to be brought in ran through its cycle. They were only twenty feet below the surface, if that, and she wasn't worried about water pressure or making a puddle on the floor. The machinery cycled as precisely—and slowly—as ever, and Maldynado had time to make a few moans and groans from the front before she could get her hands on the drill. The needle on that gauge up there must be getting worse. Or maybe needles on more gauges had pressed into the red.

"Here it is." Mahliki pulled out the broken bit and moved aside so Sespian could look at the tool while she hunted in a drawer for a new bit. Unfortunately, they had already been using the hardest one they had, the steel blade with the diamond edging.

"How does one fit an oval knife pommel into a square hole?" he mused.

"There's some twine in the cabin if you want." Mahliki waved a sarcastic hand toward the sleeping quarters that had been turned into a storage room.

"How about a screwdriver and some pliers?" Sespian sounded serious, not sarcastic.

"You have an idea?"

"Maybe. Let me show you on a piece of paper." He patted himself down and produced a pencil stub from a shirt pocket, then dug a little notepad out of a trouser pocket.

"You came prepared."

"I know you're not teasing me, not when you carry glass vials in your vest." Sespian frowned at the broken lead on the tip of his pencil and applied the knife to trimming and sharpening it.

"I wasn't teasing. It was an observation." All right, she *had* been teasing, but she wouldn't admit to it.

"Oh." Tongue peeking out of one side of his mouth, Sespian started drawing at a speed usually reserved for the reckless scribbling of toddlers.

Mahliki had the new bit out, but she waited before sticking it in the drill. Sespian's design came out in seconds, and she found herself reaching for it as soon as his pencil left the page. "That's interesting. I... maybe."

He smiled and handed her the dagger.

Boots clomped on the deck—Father jogging out of engineering. He paused to look at the problem and the sketch, tapped it with a finger, and said, "That's a good idea," then continued his jog. In navigation, he leaned over Maldynado's shoulder. The sound of switches being flicked drifted back.

Mahliki dug out a toolkit and set to work, the creaks and groans of the hull spurring her to alter the tool as quickly as possible. She envied Sespian's hand speed and precision.

Father jogged back in the opposite direction, issuing a grunt of approval, then disappearing into the engine room again.

"That figures," Mahliki muttered.

"What?" Sespian asked.

"You got articulate praise. I got a grunt." She grabbed the dagger and fastened it with the improvised locking mechanism.

"I'm not sure how articulate 'good idea' is."

Mahliki twisted and torqued their new "drill bit" as much as she could with her hand, but there wasn't a real way to test it without putting it back out there. At least the station had a grabbing tool as well. She ought to be able to get the dagger back if it snapped away. So long as one of those vines didn't dart in and snatch it first. She bared her teeth at the notion.

"If it's any consolation, I rarely get more than grunts from my own father," Sespian added.

"It's fine," Mahliki said, realizing he must think her bared teeth applied to their silly conversation. "I was joking. Let's try this."

They waited an eternity for the airlock to cycle again. A soft click sounded.

"Ready." Mahliki aimed the drill, choosing to go in at an angle instead of straight down this time, and flipped on the power.

Clacks and clunks pelted the hull beneath them. Mahliki didn't know whether to consider that promising or alarming. The gauge showed the drill digging deeper though. It hit the three-inch mark... then continued to descend.

"Good..." Five inches. "Good..." Six inches. "I wonder how far down the roots are. The one I dug up earlier was only—"

An ear-cracking snap came from below. Mahliki started to groan, certain the dagger had broken or snapped off, but the light level flowing in from the portholes increased. She looked up in confusion.

"The plant is letting go," Maldynado shouted. "No, no, it's *disintegrating*! What did you do? It's totally—that's brilliant. All of those vines are turning black and falling apart."

Mahliki slumped back into the chair, every vertebra in her back going slack with relief. She might have oozed all the way out of it and onto the floor, but Sespian leaned forward and hugged her. Delighted, she hugged him back, then surprised him—and herself—by kissing him. She might have lingered there, her lips pressed to his, but she was aware of his eyes bulging open... and her father jogging out of the engine room again.

She pulled back and thumped Sespian on the shoulder. "That sketch was perfect, just what I needed."

"Uh." He touched his lips. "Good."

Father didn't grunt this time when he passed them. Mahliki hoped that meant he was too busy checking on something to be aware of them or any... touching that had occurred. Her cheeks were wickedly hot, as if she had been zapped by electricity herself. Sespian had been too surprised to kiss her back—unfortunately—so she attributed her flushed cheeks to embarrassment. Or mortification. Something like that.

"I'll just pull our new drill back in before the plant sends in a new vine to snatch it up," Mahliki said.

"What happened exactly?" Sespian asked.

For a confused moment, Mahliki thought he was asking for an explanation as to why she had kissed him. "You mean with the plant," she reasoned.

"Yes..."

"I'm assuming the knife hit the root and acted as a conduit for the electricity coursing along the hull."

"Ah, nice."

"Very nice." Father must have checked what he needed to check, for he walked back to them. He patted Sespian on the shoulder and gave Mahliki a hug.

She hugged him back, asking, "Did you fix whatever popped off back there?"

"It did not *pop* off," Father said, using that affronted tone that only came out when he perceived some insult to one of his creations. "A recently installed component was damaged due to the excessive external pressure. It's to be expected, given that we weren't able to do any testing before launch."

"I know. I was teasing." She kissed him on the cheek.

Father harrumphed. "Keep that dagger-drill handy. We cleared the plants for approximately fifteen feet around us, but we still need to reach the harbor."

"I understand."

When Father withdrew and headed back to navigation, Mahliki caught a perplexed expression on Sespian's face. He masked it as soon as she met his eyes and stood up.

"I better go check on... Maldynado."

He strode off, leaving Mahliki perplexed as well.

She sighed and returned to the controls. She wasn't sure how far it was to the harbor, but guessed she would have to drill a lot of holes to expose a lot of roots before they got close. She hoped the plant didn't grow wise and figure out a way to protect itself before they reached their goal.

By the time Amaranthe relit the lantern, Sicarius had disappeared into the shadows ahead. Or rather, the shadows *below*. Beyond a five-foot-long stone landing, a narrow stairway descended, the walls made from worn stones and cracked mortar. Sicarius had identified the scents accurately—the cool passage smelled of must and mildew, and age as well. If not for the dampness in the air, she might have thought they were in one of the university library's subbasements. It was probably her imagination, but the passage seemed to smell of death too. Nothing fresh, like a battlefield or butcher shop, but old death. Bones.

"I'm guessing this isn't the family's root cellar." Amaranthe kept her voice low, since their missing vice president was supposedly wandering around down here, and she knew Sicarius's keen hearing would catch her words anyway.

Figuring he might appreciate a little light, Amaranthe walked down the stairs after him. The stone slab steps were as worn as the walls, the centers hollowed out by the passings of countless feet. Whatever this place was, it long predated the farmhouse.

The stairs descended more than one standard level, and the temperature dropped a few degrees before the passage leveled out. Tunnels turned to the left and right as well as continuing straight ahead. Thick cobwebs draped the side passages while the forward route lay clear. Someone had been that way recently, someone besides Sicarius. He could probably walk through a tunnel without stirring a cobweb. Amaranthe was relieved to see him waiting by some large wall niches up ahead. This house had gotten a lot creepier in the last couple of minutes, and she didn't want to roam these passages alone.

He gazed back at her, waiting. She brought the lamp, though she halted before she reached him. The contents of the niches had come into view.

"Are those bones?" she whispered. "*Human* bones?"

"Old ones, yes."

Amaranthe leaned past him. More niches lined the walls ahead, continuing for as far as her lamplight reached. "Any idea why they're here?"

"Presumably this is a crypt or ossuary created for religious purposes."

"Oh." Amaranthe relaxed a few iotas. "From a religion that doesn't do funeral pyres." She had heard of burials and tombs, of course, but could not imagine why such a practice would be customary. The idea of having her remains rotting beneath the earth with insects and worms and who knew what helping with the decomposing... She looked at the bones and shuddered. "Was this standard practice in the Kriskrusian religion?"

"I have not studied the rites or religion."

Books would have known. She kept the thought to herself, missing him anew in this place of the dead. Turgonian custom—she couldn't call it a religion since all religions had been outlawed for so long—said that it was through the burning of one's remains that one's soul was released into the spirit realm. She had never been certain she believed those stories, but seeing these skeletons laid out in the stone alcoves made her wonder if their spirits had been released or if they lingered, unhappy without rest, lurking ancient and bitter. Some Turgonians believed that happened to those who committed suicide, and most ghost stories centered around such instances.

"Someone has walked this way recently." Sicarius pointed to stirrings in the dust on the floor.

Always the practical one, it surely wouldn't occur to him to worry about ghosts or hauntings.

"Lead the way." Amaranthe extended a palm. "And if you see a possible exit at any point, that might be worth noting too." She did *not* want to be locked down in this place indefinitely.

"Serpitivich will know the way out."

"What makes you so certain he came down here? Granted, he was missing from his bed, but did you see him come this way?"

"A lantern had been burned near the vault."

Amaranthe stared at the back of his head. "That's it? We're down here in a creepy, eerie dark crypt because you caught a whiff of kerosene in the air?"

Sicarius looked back over his shoulder, giving her one of his cool stares. "Yes."

Those stares no longer intimidated her the way they once had, but she didn't question him further. What could be done at this point anyway? If nothing else, they could dig their way out before they died of thirst. She eyed the stone walls and the masonry arches overhead. She *hoped* they could dig out anyway.

As they walked farther, more tunnels opened up to the left and right, some with broken cobwebs, others still shrouded in dust and age. Bone-filled niches lined the walls of each passage. Sicarius stuck to the main corridor. Now and then he paused to listen or smell or whatever he did while gazing into the darkness. She bit her tongue to keep from asking if he caught the scent of a lamp being burned recently. Their own lamp would probably cover any such odors, regardless.

The passage ended, and Amaranthe gulped, for more than stone comprised the back wall. Rows and rows of skulls stared at her with hollow black eyes. Stacked from floor to ceiling, there were hundreds of them. Maybe thousands. A stone altar stood in front of the bone wall with more skulls stacked beneath it. They were dusty and yellow with age, but that didn't make them any less disturbing. A copper basin rested on the altar along with four more skulls that had been sawn in half, the rounded tops turned upside-down and used for candle holders. At the back of the altar, two squat figures with far too many limbs gazed out over the basin. Dagu and Magu, presumably.

"There's no dust on that bowl," Amaranthe whispered, pointing at the basin.

"No," Sicarius said. "There's blood in it."

Amaranthe crept forward, thinking he meant dried blood, but her stomach sank when she drew even with him. Several ounces of dark liquid pooled in the bottom of the basin. Sicarius picked up a couple of vials and small ceramic jars from behind it.

"Some sort of... spell components?" Amaranthe asked. As far as she knew, there were no such things as magical spells, at least not in the way superstitious Turgonians perceived of the notion, but Makers did *use* physical components to craft constructs. She recalled her first experience with one of the supernatural creatures and investigating the kiln that had been used to Make it.

The vials were empty with dried blood smeared on the inside. Sicarius examined the contents of the jars, which each contained a different color of powder. Then he stuck a finger in the basin and held it to his nose.

"If you lick that, it's going to be a long time before we resume bed-friend activities," Amaranthe said with a grimace.

"That would be unwise." Sicarius pulled out the rag he used for cleaning his knives and wiped his finger. "Someone has been mixing poisons."

"Like the one on the fence points?"

"Yes." Sicarius returned the lid to a jar filled with yellowish powder and set it down. "Others as well. Daikus root is often used in food-based poisons because it has the ability to deceive the palate, taking on the flavors of the components around it."

"Dear ancestors, the note Tikaya deciphered.... Does this mean Starcrest truly was poisoned?"

"Termite Paste can be made from these components," Sicarius said.

"That... doesn't sound like that inimical of a name."

"Used as a sticky paste, it was originally employed as a pesticide. Termites would walk through it and carry it back to their colony where it would be spread around, so the queen would track through it as well. Because it needed to be taken back to the queen, it was designed to have a delayed effect. A couple of days after contact, the entire colony would be killed."

"And then someone figured out it could harm humans as well?" Amaranthe guessed.

"If ingested in sufficient quantity or taken up into the bloodstream."

"And it's deadly."

"Within a couple of days." Sicarius's tone had changed as soon as he started speaking of the poison, his usual emotionless monotone growing clipped and cold. They didn't know exactly when Starcrest had ingested the poison, but that note was well over a day old, so it would have had to be sometime before that.

Amaranthe pointed at the jars. "Is there an antidote?"

"No."

She stared at him. "What do you mean no? There *has* to be one. Isn't there always such a thing? In case the person making the poisons accidentally poisons himself?"

"There is no known antidote to this poison."

CHAPTER 28

A S THE LORRY BUMPED DOWN a dirt road, Tikaya fiddled with her bow and tried not to worry about Rias and Mahliki, though she couldn't help but glance at a pocket watch. It had been thirty or forty minutes since the submarine descended into the lake. Had they reached their destination in the harbor yet? Or had they been delayed by all those grasping vines? Was the submarine even now hopelessly mired at the bottom with their precious air being breathed away? The communication orb remained dull and dormant.

"We're almost there, sir," the driver said. "I see lamps ahead, over to the left of the road. Someone is awake."

"Naturally," Dak said. "Kidnappers, rebels, and usurpers don't keep normal hours."

The corporal glanced over his shoulder. "We're not keeping normal hours, either, sir."

"*Because* of the kidnappers, rebels, and usurpers." Dak pointed. "Focus on the road."

"Yes, sir."

"Do we have a plan?" Tikaya asked.

"We have an armored lorry with cannons, harpoons, and fifteen armed men in the back." Dak touched a cargo pouch attached to the back of the cab. "We also have that blasting stick that Sespian left in here."

"So our plan is to barrel into the complex and blow things up?"

Dak gave her a wolfish smile.

"Are you going to send Rias the bill for this too?" Tikaya asked, reminded that all they had was Sicarius's note to go on. If they blasted their way across some innocent family's orchard... that wouldn't be good publicity for this new government.

"We'll assess the situation first," Dak said.

The corporal slowed the vehicle and turned onto a muddy road with canyon-sized ruts. Trees stretched away to the north and south in tidy rows, though something glinted between two of those rows. Some bit of glass reflecting the light of the lorry's running lamps?

"Slow down," Dak said.

"I see it, sir. It looks like another lorry."

"Pull us off to the side," Dak said. "Under the cover of the trees as much as possible. Cut off our lights too. No need to announce our arrival."

By now, Tikaya could make out a large house and several outbuildings at the end of the road. Someone raced out of a big, tall building. Her breath caught. A dark robe flapped about the man's legs as he ran.

"This might be the right place," she whispered. Dare she hope the people who had sent that encoded note—and mentioned poisoning Rias—would have their headquarters here?

She wanted to drive straight to the end and start questioning people—or perhaps perforating them with arrows until they volunteered information—but Dak had hopped out of the cab, a rifle in his hands. He called someone's name softly, and two soldiers climbed out of the back and joined him. They headed into the gap between the rows of trees.

The glass Tikaya had seen did indeed belong to a lorry, one backed several meters off the driveway and into the shadows. She thought she spotted movement in the front cab but couldn't be sure. Though she doubted the soldiers would need her help, she stepped outside with her bow to cover them in case they received more trouble than anticipated.

Frost crunched in the short grass beneath her feet.

"Stop right there and identify yourselves," a man called from the parked lorry, his voice stern. He sounded like another soldier, but who else would have seen Sicarius's note and come out here? "I've got you in my sights."

Tikaya didn't see a pistol, bow, or other weapon sticking out of the cab, but maybe the person intended to shoot through the glass window. The two soldiers had their own rifles up at this point, with the cab, if not the person within, in *their* sights.

"We're soldiers in the president's employment," Dak said. "That's all you need to know. Toss out your weapon and step out of the vehicle."

A few seconds dribbled past, then something was thrown from the cab. Tikaya frowned. It looked like a crooked stick, not a rifle or other weapon.

"Throw out your *weapon*," Dak repeated.

"That's all I've got," the man responded, the sternness gone out of his voice. He sounded tired. Beleaguered.

"A stick?"

"A stick."

"You had us in your sights with... a stick?" Dak asked.

"Yes, I hope you were suitably quaking with terror."

"Go get him," Dak told his men.

The pair of soldiers walked forward, keeping their weapons trained on the cab, but the man who slumped out of the vehicle didn't look like much of a threat. He favored one leg and hissed and clutched his shoulder when he bumped the doorframe.

"I'm Deret Mancrest," he said. "And I'm injured, so I'd appreciated it if you forwent the manhandling and simply escorted me to your vehicle, if that's your intent."

One of the soldiers had been about to grab him, but stopped at the name, and looked to his colonel.

"The journalist?" Dak asked.

"Journalist and owner of the *Gazette*," Mancrest said. "I believe we've met before. In the service. Colonel Starcrest, isn't it?"

"That's right."

"I served in the Twenty-Third Infantry Battalion, under General Bearcrest."

"I must not have made a good impression on you if you were keeping me in your stick's sights."

Mancrest grunted.

"You were at the funeral for Professor Mugdildor," Tikaya said. In the poor lighting, she couldn't see the man's face, but she remembered the name. They hadn't spoken, but he had been a friend of Amaranthe's, hadn't he? "You know Amaranthe?"

"Yes."

"Is she here? The note said she'd been kidnapped."

"The note?" Mancrest asked.

"From Sicarius," Tikaya said.

"No mention about *me* being kidnapped as well?"

"No."

"That figures. Look, she and Sicarius were going to sneak into the compound to snoop." Deret pointed in the direction of the house. "I was supposed to keep the furnace hot in the lorry. They've been gone a while, and people started banging around, yelling about escaped prisoners about fifteen minutes ago."

"How many men are in there?" Dak asked.

"At least twenty in the bunkhouse, plus whoever lives in the house."

"Armed?"

"The priests all had pistols," Mancrest said.

"All right. You want to come with us or stay in that lorry?"

"That depends. Do you have a medic with you?"

"Shovak, anyone in your squad got training?" Dak asked one of the soldiers.

"I think Drogo had basic first aid, sir."

"Maybe I'll just stay here and bleed."

"We're going to go blow things up," Dak said. "You might want to come along and help us avoid hitting your friends."

"Friend. Singular." Mancrest bent, grabbed his stick, and used it as a crutch as he walked toward Tikaya. He nodded at her bow before he climbed into the cab. "Your stick is more impressive than mine, my lady."

"Not something a man should ever say to a woman," Dak muttered, hopping in after him.

"It *is* made from the finest Kyattese onyx wood," Tikaya said.

Dak took up his position behind the driver's seat. "Let's go, Corporal."

"Shall we... drive straight up to the door, sir?"

"I thought we'd start firing before then," Dak said.

"I see you're applying your infantry background to your intelligence career," Mancrest said.

"Actually that's my artillery background. We practiced everything down there on the border."

The corporal shoveled some coal into the furnace, checked a gauge, then thrust the forward lever on the lorry.

"Any suggestions for targets, Mancrest?" Dak asked.

"As much as I'd like to see you blow up that cider mill, the bunkhouse is where most of the robed fellows live. You might catch some inside still. Assuming you don't want to take them prisoner."

"Their friends spent the night trying to blow up the president," Dak said. "If they beg to be taken prisoner, we'll do it. I would be just as happy if they didn't."

"I see," Mancrest said. "Should we... be taking his wife along for this... carnage?"

"It's not my first carnage, Lord Mancrest."

"You can call me Deret, my lady."

"Then you can call me Tikaya."

"Uh," Mancrest said. "I don't really think I can. But thank you."

"I address my Kyattese president and his wife by first name," Tikaya said.

"Yes, but your people are... special."

Dak snorted. "Tactful, Mancrest."

"What did you expect from the man who threatened you with a bent stick?"

"We're getting close, sir," the corporal said. "Someone saw us and ran into the bunkhouse."

His tense tone stole the mirth from the air. Tikaya continued to hold her bow, though she imagined the soldiers would take care of things with their superior firepower.

The trees ended, giving her a better view of the compound. Someone slammed a wrought iron gate shut in a fence that surrounded the house, then ran inside and slammed the front door shut as well. The person who had seen them was running toward a carriage house behind the bunkhouse.

"They'll have lorries of their own in there," Mancrest said. "They kidnapped us in one. I don't know if they're armored."

"Carriage house first, Corporal. We don't want anyone leaving before we give them our permission."

"Yes, sir." The corporal reached for the cannon controls. "Should we warn them first, sir? Give them a chance to surrender?"

The bunkhouse door flew open, and a green-robed man thrust his arm out.

"Practitioner," Tikaya barked, the intense prickling sensation on her skin promising a big discharge of energy.

"No warning, no," Dak growled and grabbed the blasting stick.

"Duck," Mancrest said.

Red energy danced in the air around the priest's fingers. Tikaya stepped past Mancrest and yanked out an arrow. She loosed it at the same time as the priest hurled the fireball. Someone grabbed her from behind, pulling her to the floor, and she feared her shot was thrown wide.

Rifles fired behind her—someone leaning out of the bed of the lorry—but Tikaya couldn't see anything except the padded roof of the cab. Then heat washed over her, and the orange and red of flames drove away every shadow. The fireball struck the front window. Glass cracked under the intensity, and Tikaya lifted her arm, afraid shards would pelt them. But the heat faded without anyone crying out, and she dared hope the window had blocked the brunt of the attack.

A match hissed in her ear. Tikaya tried to sit up, but someone bumped her with an arm.

"Sorry," Dak grunted.

Everyone was trying to stand up at the same time. No, Dak was doing more than that. He had hurled the blasting stick at the bunkhouse. It struck before she got her head high enough for a view, but she heard glass crack in the distance. He must have aimed at a window instead of the door. Good thinking. The practitioner might have come up with a defense if the projectile had been arrowing straight toward him.

A boom split the night, loud enough that farmers on parcels fifty acres away were sure to bolt from their beds, clutching at their hearts. The wooden bunkhouse didn't stand a chance. Burning boards flew fifty feet into the air, and slammed into the first row of trees in the orchard. Tikaya looked away, not wanting to see if bodies—or body parts—flew into the air as well.

"Did you get the practitioner?" she asked when the flames died down.

"*You* got the practitioner," Dak said.

"Nice reflexes," Mancrest said from the floor. He propped himself against the wall by the furnace, not looking like he wanted to rise further. In the better lighting, the blood staining the shoulder of his shirt was visible.

"Yes, I was too busy throwing myself down for cover to shoot anything," Dak admitted. Interesting, she had never seen a sheepish expression on him before.

"I'm sure if it had been a gunman, you two would have both fired more quickly," Tikaya said. "Magic seems to alarm Turgonians, doubtlessly because you've had so little experience with it."

"I've had more than the average Turgonian's experience with it, but I'll accept your excuse," Dak said.

A few men with singed and tattered robes staggered out of the back of the bunkhouse—the only side with a wall still partially standing—and hobbled toward the trees.

Dak thumped on the back of the cab. "Go round up those men."

Judging by how quickly a team of six soldiers shot off into the orchard, they had been ready and waiting for the command. Another squad jogged up to the driver's side of the cab.

"Should we take the house, sir?" the leader asked.

"Corporal, see if you can open that gate for them," Dak said.

"Yes, sir." The man smiled, no longer hesitating to reach for the cannon controls. Apparently once a wizard spat a fireball at them, Turgonians felt justified in commencing bloodshed.

The cannonball launched, spinning *through* the iron bars instead of into the gate, and the corporal lost his smile. It smashed into a planter under a window and tore into what was probably those people's living room. "Sorry, sir."

Dogs streaked out of little houses on the side and started barking.

"A little to the right," Dak advised.

"Yes, sir."

The second cannonball clanged into one of the hinges, tearing the gate from its mooring. That proved too much noise for most of the dogs; they streaked through the broken gate and into the field behind the house.

"That ought to be enough," Dak said. "Go get them, men."

"Watch out for a woman smelling of brandy and wearing a man's shirt," Mancrest called after them.

That earned a strange backward glance from the squad leader and a quirked eyebrow from Dak as well.

"It's a long story," Mancrest said. When the quirked brow didn't lower, he added, "It's been a harrowing evening. If we hadn't been lucky, you might have pulled our bodies out of a tank full of apple juice."

"I was wondering about the odor," Tikaya murmured.

The corporal drummed his fingers on his leg. "Shall we target that big building over there, sir? None of our men have gone in that direction."

"That's the cider mill," Mancrest said. "I don't think anything is in there except a lot of expensive equipment. And maybe a man Sicarius tied up, though I would guess that his comrades have found him by now. That's probably what alerted everyone out here."

"Hold steady until our men return," Dak said.

The soldiers were already marching prisoners out of the orchard and past the remains of the smoldering bunkhouse. Several men and women left the main house via the windows, only to run into their own iron security fence. The team who had remained outside the dwelling captured these people without trouble—most of them were in nightclothes, with more than one running around barefoot. Tikaya wondered what had prompted them to allow the priests to set up on their property. Or had blackmail been involved?

A soldier jogged up to the lorry. "Sir, should we also tie up the people from the house?" The captured priests had been bound and ushered into the cargo bed. "They're not wearing robes. One said he's Lord Edgecrest, and that we'll be in trouble for trespassing on his property."

"Truss him and toss him in too," Dak said.

"Yes, sir." He jogged off, but was met by a second soldier before he could return to the house. They had a quick conversation, and the first man returned. "Uh, sir? One of the people in the house is... uhm."

"What?" Dak asked.

"I bet I can guess," Mancrest said. "You ever meet your uncle's first wife, Colonel?"

"Sauda?"

The soldier nodded. "Sauda Shadowcrest. The men are bringing her out now."

"She's here?" Tikaya asked. "I thought she was in jail."

"So did I," Dak said. "In fact, I told Rias to visit her after... was that just yesterday we had that meeting?"

"I think so. Time has become a blur."

"A lot has become a blur," Mancrest said—he was still sitting on the floor. "I'm not sure if it's because I'm tired or because I hit my head falling into that tank."

He didn't look well, but there wasn't much that could be done at the moment. Tikaya doubted the lorry had blankets or any supplies meant to make men comfortable. Turgonian military vehicles all seemed to run toward the sparse and utilitarian.

The front door opened, and the raven-haired woman who walked out managed to look regal even in a robe and with two armed men escorting her. The men marched her out to the lorry. Tikaya didn't know if the woman would recognize her. Sauda gazed into the cab for a moment, then dismissed everyone with a haughty sniff.

Before Dak could question her, another soldier trotted out of the house.

"Sir, there's a vault door at the end of the upstairs hallway, and it looks like someone has been shooting at it."

"A *vault* door?" Dak asked.

"Yes, sir. Like you would find in a bank."

"Sounds like where Amaranthe might have run off to," Mancrest said. "Based on the bullets. She has a knack for getting herself in trouble."

"Sauda, do you know what's behind the vault door?" Dak asked.

The woman crossed her arms, sniffed again, and gazed toward the orchards.

"Answer him." One of the soldiers gripping her arm gave it a shake.

Dak lifted a quelling hand toward the man. Maybe there were rules against physically interrogating warrior-caste women. Tikaya wouldn't mind giving her a shake... *more* than a shake. A few arrow perforations might loosen her tongue.

"He never took me there, nor told me what he did when he spent time inside," Sauda said.

"He?" Dak asked. "Is this Serpitivich, by chance?"

Tikaya frowned at him. "The vice president and... this woman? But where did Lord Mancrest, the *elder* Lord Mancrest, come in? I thought they were... sharing hammocks."

"Oh, I'm guessing she was sharing hammocks with a lot of people," Dak said.

Sauda gave him a scathing look, but did not refute the comment. Tikaya remembered Rias describing his former wife as unfaithful, though he had blamed himself—or at least accepted some of the blame—due to his long absences at sea. Maybe the woman simply had a pathological flaw.

"She was trying to bribe my father," Deret said. "She wants control of the *Gazette* for Serpitivich and his priest goons."

"Goons." Sauda sniffed. "Hardly that. With their connections, they almost handed him the election. Against anyone except Rias, Serp would have won."

"And he still intends to win," Deret said, "isn't that right?"

"We'll see." Sauda smiled slightly. "The night isn't over. You people haven't won yet."

Tikaya thought of the plant, of Rias and her daughter. Did the woman know something she didn't?

"Tell us about this vault," Dak said. "Is Serpitivich there now? And what does he do inside?"

"If he's responsible for the poisonings," Tikaya said, "maybe it's where he keeps his collection."

Sauda shrugged a narrow shoulder. "I have no knowledge of the vault's contents. Perhaps the priests would know. They are his zealous followers."

"You're only here for the social status of being seen with him if he becomes somebody, is that right?" Dak asked.

Sauda, gazing toward the orchards again, did not respond. It was as if she couldn't care less what happened here—what happened to *her*. Maybe she had some plan already. She had escaped from jail once, after all.

Dak ground his jaw back and forth for a moment, then waved toward the rear of the lorry. "Put her in with the other prisoners, and make sure there are plenty of guards back there."

"Yes, sir."

The soldiers ushered Sauda away.

"What do you think?" Dak asked Tikaya.

"Me? About what?"

"Is she lying, misdirecting us, or hiding something?" Dak shrugged. "Knowing any of those things would be useful."

"I've never spoken to her before and don't have a baseline by which to judge. I couldn't tell if she was lying, but she certainly didn't seem trustworthy."

"Ah," Dak said. "I thought you might have some insight, since you two married the same man."

"You don't know much about women, do you?"

His expression grew wry. "Not... as much as I'd like." Dak waved to one of the other soldiers. "Brekker, show us to that vault, will you?"

"Yes, sir."

Dak hopped down and invited Tikaya along with a wave. "Perhaps what she won't tell us we can find out for ourselves. Mancrest, you want to stay in there?"

"Yes, but if someone helps me to my feet, I'll come anyway. This story will have to be in the paper as soon as possible."

"I could have one of my men write up a report with the pertinent details," Dak said.

"I've read your men's reports," Tikaya said. "You're offering him a punishment, not a good turn."

"That's... probably a fair assessment."

Dak and Tikaya helped Mancrest up, and the soldiers led them past the gate and through the front door where a final young man was being shoved out, his wrists tied behind his back. He glowered sullenly at Tikaya's group. Dak glowered back, and the young man lost some of his menace, shrinking away from the big colonel.

"You should have tried that glare on Sauda," Tikaya murmured as they continued inside.

"I did. She either wasn't paying attention or didn't find me intimidating."

"I assure you you're quite intimidating."

"I'd take that as a compliment coming from a man, but I'm not sure I want women to find me intimidating."

Tikaya and Dak jogged through a living area, up a set of wooden stairs, and into a hallway with floorboards that creaked beneath their boots.

"In that case," Tikaya said, "you might want to get a nice eye patch to wear. That scar gives you a sinister cast."

"I tried eye patches. They made my hollow sweat and itch. Besides, having a sinister mien isn't a bad idea if you're the chief of intelligence. It intimidates the enemy. And helps keep your own men in line, right, Sergeant?"

"Yes, sir," the man leading them said before stopping at the end of the hall. A secret panel was propped open, revealing the silvery metal of a very modern vault door.

Dak touched a splintered hole near the edge of the panel.

"Bullet?" Tikaya asked.

"Yes." Their soldier guide pointed to a tiny dent in the metal vault door, then walked back down the hall to a place where wallpaper had been gouged free. A bullet was lodged in the wood paneling underneath. "It ricocheted. It looks like they shot a couple of times before realizing they were more likely to hurt themselves than the vault door. Judging by the reactions of a couple of the people we dragged out of bedrooms, they didn't even know there was a vault door *here*."

The soft scrapes of a pencil on paper drifted into the thoughtful silence that followed. Somewhere, Mancrest had acquired a notepad. He had already filled up the first page.

"Your threat to offer him a report seems to have inspired him to write," Tikaya said. "Copiously."

"Impressive since he didn't even have a notepad before." Dak plucked up a lamp that had been lit and left on a narrow hallway table, and walked to the vault door.

"I did have one, but it fell out in the tank," Deret said, his pencil never slowing. "Just as well. It would have been too soggy to use."

Tikaya noticed symbols etched around the wheel in the center of the metal door and moved closer as well.

"Those aren't the usual numbers one expects," Dak observed.

"No, they're symbols from the Kriskrusian language. Old symbols used in religious ceremonies. Later on, by the time your ancestors came, they had switched to an alphabet." Tikaya spread her hand to cover five of the symbols. "Those are the names for the gods. That one represents a house or one's homeland. That one is the sun. There's the moon."

"You know them all?" Dak asked.

"Yes, I believe so."

"Does that give you any insight into how to open the lock? Because I'm guessing we want to get in there." Dak touched one of the dents the bullets had left.

"Er, no," Tikaya said. "I don't think so."

"Sergeant, grab a couple of men and start searching the rooms. Edgecrest's room first, then Sauda's, and anyone else's that looks promising. See if you can find the combination."

"Ah, shouldn't we just..." The sergeant cleared his throat and studied his commanding officer's boots.

"What?" Dak asked.

"The woman may know the combination, sir. We could question her more forcefully."

"I doubt she knows it," Dak said. "Besides, the president might not be happy about having his first wife questioned forcefully."

"Yes, sir. I'll get my team searching."

"You should also have them search for signs that someone has been making poisons," Tikaya said. If the antidote to Rias's illness wasn't here in this compound somewhere... This would all have been a waste of time, leaving her farther away from helping Rias than ever.

Dak nodded. "As she said, Sergeant."

The soldier jogged off, and doors and cabinets were soon banging up and down the hallway.

Dak removed his cap and pushed a hand through his short black hair. "Was that the right decision?"

"What?" Tikaya asked.

"Not interrogating Sauda."

"I don't think Rias would care to have any woman interrogated in the Turgonian way." Tikaya shrugged. "If we don't have any luck, we can always try later. I think you're right, though, in that she wouldn't know. I don't get the impression she's... bright enough to have masterminded all of this. Serpitivich is probably using her."

"Yes. Good."

Good that he was using her? Or good that Dak wouldn't be expected to torture a woman for information? The latter, Tikaya suspected. It pleased her that the notion bothered him. With Turgonians... one never knew. She supposed he wouldn't blink at the idea of interrogating a man. Such a strange people.

Mancrest shuffled forward to examine the symbols. "In the meantime, we could try guessing the combination."

"There are more than thirty symbols," Dak said. "That makes for thousands of permutations."

Rias would have given the exact number of permutations. He liked solving quick puzzles like that in his head—and showing off that he could do so, or so Tikaya had always thought. He never admitted to such vanities of course.

"I'm going to see what tools we have in the lorry. Maybe something can open this, lock notwithstanding." Dak waved for them to stay and jogged for the stairs.

"May I borrow your pencil and a piece of paper?" Tikaya asked Mancrest. "If I write everything down and play with them a bit, maybe I can guess a logical combination."

"Without trying thousands of permutations?" Mancrest handed her the pencil and tore off a sheet from the back of his pad. The first page had someone's grocery list on it; he must have pillaged it from the homeowner.

"Thousands supposes it's a random combination. Humans are rarely random."

"My night has certainly felt random." Mancrest leaned against the wall and closed his eyes.

Tikaya felt sympathetic, but she soon forgot about him, her focus consumed by the symbols. She doubted opening the vault would reveal rows of poisons—and antidotes—lining the insides, but she worked on cracking the code as if that were the case.

Sespian sat beside President Starcrest, watching him steer the submarine while Mahliki operated the drill from the science station. He alternated between feeling useless, because he didn't know what any of the switches did or what any of the gauges meant, and feeling guilty, because Mahliki had kissed him, and he was fairly certain her father had seen. Every time Starcrest looked in his direction, Sespian anticipated a glower and a stern my-daughter-is-not-to-be-pawed-over-by-the-likes-of-you lecture. But every time, Starcrest only moved a lever or pressed a switch, then returned his attention to the lake floor creeping along ahead of them.

Every ten or twenty meters, they had to stop, drill down to a root, and electrocute the surrounding swath of plants before they could travel forward again. So far it was working, but recent reports—they were more expletives than reports—from Mahliki said the vines were snaking in and trying to break off the dagger. If they lost that, Sespian didn't think they had anything else on board that would cut through to the roots. At least the rhizome structure was working in their favor and blasting one root with electricity sent deadly energy through to the neighboring ones. He began to have faith that the Starcrests' plan to electrocute the original root mass in the harbor might work, especially if they delivered a larger charge. The equipment stacked high in the sleeping cabin was presumably for that.

"I pulled in a sample from the last root we zapped," Mahliki called. "It doesn't have the symbols and structure of that original one I cut. These later generations are less sophisticated."

480

"Let's hope the same tactic works on the original generation," Starcrest said. "At present speed, we should reach the harbor in twenty minutes."

Maldynado shuffled up behind Sespian's seat. "Sounds promising. Maybe we won't need to suit up."

"You wouldn't mind if you came along and ended up simply being decorative?" Sespian asked.

"Nah, I specialize in being decorative. It's hard not to when you're this handsome."

Starcrest glanced at him, but didn't say anything.

Maldynado chewed on his lip. Sespian wondered if he would ever figure out that saying such things tended to make people take him less seriously. If he truly wanted a career working for Starcrest, he ought to forego the dandy act, at least around the president.

"It's a bit of a curse, I'll admit," Maldynado added. "People don't think you have a brain or any thoughts in your head. But that can be advantageous at times. Those same people will say things around you that they wouldn't around a keen-eyed military intelligence officer."

"Maldynado?" Starcrest said.

"Yes, My Lord?"

"Are you truly lobbying for a job while we're in the middle of all this?"

A call came up from the engineer. "We're running low on oxygen, My Lord. We better go up for a few minutes before heading into the harbor."

"Understood," Starcrest responded.

"Not lobbying exactly," Maldynado said. "Just... trying to fill the air with something besides tension."

Sespian's ears popped as they rose toward the surface. Faint light drifted down from above. Dawn must have come while they had been plodding along the lake bottom. They plopped up, and rivulets of water ran down the viewport.

A slender tendril drifted into view from the side, a green one, not one of the many charred ones that were clogging the water.

"Is the dagger back in?" Starcrest asked.

"Yes," Mahliki said.

"Let me know when we can descend again," Starcrest called back to the engine room.

"Yes, My Lord President."

"I don't like giving it time to think," Starcrest said. "Now that I'm convinced it does so."

"I agree." Sespian watched that tendril veer in close, not close enough to touch the hull and get shocked, but close, as if it were some enemy periscope, sent to survey them.

"Me too," Maldynado said.

"Ready, My Lord," the engineer called.

Starcrest took them down again, back into darkness pierced only by the running lamp. The ground that had been cleared of plants a moment before was covered with green now. Not tall new stalks that had grown up, but some sort of carpet formed from existing plants sending vines in from the sides.

"Uh," Maldynado said.

"Landing on it," Starcrest said.

Mahliki jogged up and leaned on the back of his chair. "How thick is that? I wonder if they're trying to protect their roots the same way they smothered us earlier—sacrificing the top layer."

The submarine settled on the bottom again, the lakebed pillowed by those cushions of vines. The blue energy crackled outside of the hull, and charred bits of plant flesh floated away, but the greenery didn't move away from the craft.

"It looks like it," Starcrest said. "I'll take us up again. In lying down, these have cleared a path for us. The ones in the harbor are our priority."

"Won't we have to deal with the same thing there?" Sespian asked. "If we can even get there?"

"Yes, but we have more weapons to deploy, weapons the plant hasn't seen yet."

Nobody pointed out that the vines didn't have eyes.

The submarine rose to the surface again, pushing through stalks that remained upright. For the moment, they were parting to avoid being singed. Maybe they felt they had won a victory by denying the sub access to the roots and they needn't sacrifice as much up here. Maybe they just hadn't collectively figured out what the sub was up to yet. Maybe Sespian needed to stop thinking about this plant like it was a human enemy. Or... maybe not. It had certainly proven itself crafty.

Maldynado whistled as they sailed farther, the stalks rising up from the lake bottom now stretching twenty feet into the sky and blotting out the promise of dawn. "Those things are almost as big as my—" he glanced at Mahliki, "—backyard trees."

She wrinkled her nose at him.

"Aren't you living in a flat?" Sespian asked, knowing full well that *trees* hadn't been what Maldynado had intended to mention.

"Yes, but as a boy on my parents' estate, we had lots of trees," Maldynado said. "Many well-endowed."

Trees actually *were* what came to Sespian's mind when looking at the towering forest. Before the stalks had been as thick as arms and legs. Some of these were broader than hundred-year-old cedars. Sespian would hate to have to try and cut one away from him with nothing but a knife, however sharp the edge.

"We're almost to the harbor," Starcrest said. "Another thirty, forty meters, and we'll dive again. We may not need the suits."

"That'll be a shame," Maldynado said.

Though Sespian didn't comment, he couldn't help but feel relieved as well.

"The sooner and more effectively we get this done, the better," Mahliki said. "Mother will be worrying about us."

"Yes, I should send a message," Rias said. "As soon as—"

"Look out," came a cry from engineering. "To the port. It's falling!"

Nothing was visible through the navigation viewport, but Rias pushed on the main lever. The submarine surged forward. Something slapped the surface of the water behind them, the sound almost deafening, as if a mountain had fallen. Or a towering tree.

Water sprayed, and a huge wave swept the *Explorer* into the air. The deck lurched, and Sespian was almost thrown from his seat. He caught himself on the control panel. Someone else—Maldynado?—was less lucky, tumbling to the deck behind him.

The submarine landed with a jolt and massive green stalks filled the viewport. The vessel crashed into the side of one. Like a tree, it didn't yield at all. Though streaks of blue lightning bit into anything that touched the hull, that didn't keep the craft from ricocheting around, slamming into two more unyielding stalks, before settling back down.

"Remarkable," Mahliki said. "I knew the vines were flexible, but I wouldn't have guessed these huge trunks could change physical properties so quickly. To go from a tree-like structure to a flaccid..." She must have noticed Maldynado gaping at her from the deck, for she cleared her throat and said, "Never mind. That's not important now."

Starcrest's hands were flying across the controls. "Any damage, Major?" he called back to the engineer.

"Nothing showing up yet, My Lord."

"What happens when one lands *on* us?" Maldynado asked.

Another trunk went limp, this time directly in front of them. Rias veered the craft to the left, but the stalks in that direction didn't yield as the earlier ones had. The submarine might as well have crashed into dock pilings.

"Brace yourselves," Starcrest ordered.

Sespian still had a death grip on the control panel. It didn't help much when the massive stalk struck with the force of a falling redwood. He was thrown upward, even as the submarine plunged downward. He flung an arm up to protect his head from hitting the ceiling. When gravity caught up, pitching him in the other direction, he missed the chair. His butt struck the control panel, then he tumbled into Maldynado. Mahliki had fallen to the deck as well. She sat crumpled against the bulkhead, rubbing the back of her head.

"Who's driving up there?" the engineer cried, the "My Lord President" address forgotten.

"I'm taking us down again," Starcrest said. "We'll be safer down there. From that attack anyway."

"Comforting," Maldynado grumbled.

"Judging by the rapidity with which we descended and the water displaced, I judge them about half the density of a typical hardwood tree." Rias left his chair to help Mahliki up—apparently this random information was for her. Sespian certainly wasn't in the mood to find it interesting.

"Yes," Mahliki said, "when I examined the cell makeup of the stalks, they reminded me more of cane than wood."

"I hope that means it didn't do as much damage as it could have," Maldynado said.

"This craft was designed to be sturdy," Starcrest said. "To weather storms and enemy attacks if necessary."

"What about irate giant plants?"

"That was, alas, not anticipated by the designer."

"A shame," Maldynado said.

Starcrest returned to his seat. "Let's see if we can navigate through these last twenty meters underwater."

Sespian waved for Mahliki to take the other seat. She could do more good there than he.

"Sespian, Maldynado," Starcrest said, "get those batteries out of the cabin, please. We'll prepare to deploy them."

"Yes, sir," Sespian said.

They walked back to the only cabin in the place, one usually reserved for sleeping. The bunk was buried beneath unrecognizable mechanical paraphernalia, gray metal boxes, and crates of tools and spare parts. Spare parts for what, Sespian didn't know. He was being generous with his identification—his first thought was to consider the contents scrap metal.

"Do you know which of these things are batteries?" Maldynado asked.

"I'm going to guess these." Sespian picked up two of the gray boxes, though he doubted he had any more engineering or mechanical know-how than Maldynado.

"I hope you're right. I doubt the president will be happy if we throw storage chests full of his wife's smallclothes out the hatch."

"I doubt there was room to pack *anyone's* smallclothes with all this stuff that's been piled in." Sespian didn't know whether the batteries would be deployed through some airlock at the science station or if they would have to go to the surface, open the hatch, and chuck them overboard, so he laid them next to the bulkhead in between the two spots, then went back for more.

"That's too bad," Maldynado said, "because we've already had a couple of moments where... let's just say I wouldn't mind having a change of smallclothes down here."

"Maldynado..." Sespian dragged two more batteries out of the cabin. "Does your brain ever think things like... Oh, this fellow is a president or a former emperor or some other type of vaguely important person, so maybe I shouldn't share my hygiene issues out loud with him?"

"I share with everyone. It's part of my charm." Maldynado raised his voice. "My Lord Prez, are we digging out *all* of these batteries? Or saving some for later? Also, the batteries are these gray things, right?"

"Yes, and yes," Starcrest responded.

"Not that I didn't trust you." Maldynado slapped Sespian on the chest. "But the smallclothes thing would surely get me in more trouble than comments about my hygiene."

"Surely."

Something struck the side of the submarine, causing it to tilt to the side again, but the blow lacked the force of the ones from above. With the last of the twelve batteries lined up, Sespian and Maldynado returned to the navigation chamber. They had to stop in the hatchway, because Mahliki had laid a big map of the harbor and the city out on the deck. Green lines and arrows had been drawn all over it.

Starcrest was bending over the side of his chair, leaning his elbow on his knee. Sweat bathed his forehead and dampened his collar. It wasn't warm in the submarine—if anything the chill air seemed to match that of the water outside—but maybe he was running around more than the rest of them and had to deal with the pressure of navigating the craft through all these attacks. Still, it was hard to imagine former Fleet Admiral Starcrest breaking a sweat because of a little enemy interference.

With sudden chilling clarity, Sespian realized what he was seeing. A man poisoned. They hadn't been sure about the note, but it must have spoken the truth. Did anyone else know?

Tikaya. That hard hug and long look she had given Starcrest before leaving. Had that been more than concern over the mission? Dear ancestors, was there an antidote anywhere?

Starcrest tapped a spot in the water on the map. "That's where we are."

"I have no idea how you can tell our position right now," Mahliki said, waving at the disorientating stalks of green that thrust up in all directions around them, "but I'll trust you on it."

"There are contour lines on the map," Starcrest said.

"Was that an explanation?" Maldynado whispered to Sespian.

"I think so."

"From my studies, I believe this is approximately where the initial plant sprouted." Mahliki pointed to a spot near Dock Eighty-Three in the harbor.

Sespian hadn't heard about these studies, but that wasn't far from where she had taken him to draw the plant that first day. She must have been watching it from the beginning.

"Judging by the collective intelligence and a few other factors,"

Mahliki said, "I believe every other plant, in the lake and coming up under the land, is connected to the original sprout."

Sespian almost choked on the idea of classifying any part of the plant in any stage a *sprout*.

"This root ball is going to be our target, and we'll use our strongest weapon on it, one capable of... how many volts was it, Father?" She crinkled her brow. "Was that the right term?"

"It'll depend on the resistance, but if the rhizomes conduct electricity the way they've demonstrated so far, I believe there'll be enough voltage and amps to carry the current several miles."

"We're ready to attack then?" Mahliki asked.

"Yes."

"Are we going to use these batteries to make a safe area within which to work?" Sespian asked, imagining them strung together in a circle.

Starcrest nodded. "That's the idea."

"Can we deploy them from in here?" Maldynado asked.

"Mahliki?" Starcrest bent further and turned over the map to write on the back with a charcoal stick. "They need to be placed about ten feet apart and hooked together to make a complete circuit. Do you think you can handle that with the tools in the science station?"

"Uh, that'll take some precision that will be hard to achieve with the grasper. It would be a lot faster if I went out there in a suit and could use my hands."

Starcrest grimaced. "You won't have the protection of the hull out there. You would be vulnerable."

"Yes, but we've seen how fast this plant is adapting to our tactics. If it figures out what we're doing..." Mahliki shrugged. "We're talking about five minutes to do something by hand versus thirty minutes to *attempt* to do it with tools."

Sespian exchanged long looks with Maldynado. He hated the idea of going out there—hated the idea of letting *Mahliki* go out there—but the situation seemed to be going that way. What else could they do? This was why he had come along.

"Try it from in here first," Starcrest said.

"Father, are you letting the fact that I'm your daughter affect your decision? I can't believe you would make this choice if you had a soldier to send out there. Or if it were Sespian. Or Maldynado."

"I was contemplating sending Maldynado out earlier, to get some quiet in here," Starcrest said, though he smiled at Maldynado as he said it, and there was no malice in his tone.

Maldynado's snort didn't sound offended; he must have heard similar comments countless times.

Mahliki didn't snort or smile. She jabbed her fist against her hip and frowned.

Starcrest tugged out a kerchief and mopped his brow. Judging from the limpness of the cloth, he had done so numerous times already. Sespian wondered if it would be received poorly if he suggested to the president that he had a fever and should be drinking more.

"Try it from in here first," Starcrest repeated, a mulish set to his jaw. A vine thumping against the viewport distracted him.

Mahliki stalked out of the navigation area. Sespian followed, finding her scowling out the porthole above the science station panel. He didn't know what to say, so he put a hand on her shoulder.

"I'll help you with the grasper," Sespian said. "I'm fairly dexterous when it comes to manipulating tools. Real ones, not just pencils."

"He's not being logical," Mahliki said. "He's being emotional."

"That's a thing fathers do when their children are involved. I hear even mine got slightly illogical a couple of times when my life was in danger." Sespian decided not to mention all the Forge people Sicarius had killed during one of his "illogical" moments. He might understand his father more now, but memories of such events still chilled him.

"Whatever." Mahliki strode into the cabin and grabbed a reel of cable.

For the first time since Sespian had met her, she seemed sulky and... a little immature, almost reminding him of Akstyr. She was only seventeen, he reminded himself. Besides, who was he to judge? He'd had his own sulky and immature moments in the last year, especially in accepting Sicarius as his father.

He knelt beside Mahliki as she sat in the seat, preparing the batteries and cable. "You know he's dying, right?" he murmured.

She dropped the cable. "What?"

"He probably wants to make sure *you* make it back, especially if there's a possibility he won't."

"What are you talking about?"

"The poison, remember?"

"What? I thought that was a bluff, that..." Mahliki stared toward the navigation area, where the back of her father's head was visible. She said a single word in Kyattese. It sounded like a curse.

Sespian picked up the cable reel. "Here. Or do you want me to do it?"

"Yes. No. I don't know." She huffed in frustration and grabbed the reel. "Might as well drop this first. Father," she called, "are we over the spot?"

"Yes."

Boots clanked on the deck behind Sespian. It was Maldynado wearing the bottom half of the diving suit, the top bunched around his waist.

"Getting ready, just in case." He shrugged, but his face was bleak. He expected to go out.

"You might want to get ready too," Mahliki told Sespian, glancing at navigation again. "I'll try to attach all the batteries from in here, but..." She shook her head and went back to work.

Sespian thought about volunteering to help again, but maybe that was arrogant of him. She had operated the tools before. She was probably the logical choice to do so now.

He stood, patting her on the shoulder before leaving.

"Prepare my suit, too, please," Mahliki said.

This time, Starcrest was the one to glance back, but he didn't say anything.

Sespian headed for the cabin where the suits had been dumped along with all the other gear. There were three remaining, a large, and a couple of mediums. Since Mahliki was as tall as he was, Sespian laid out one of the mediums for her and took the other for himself, as well as a helmet.

"Where's the tubing?" he asked. "That connects us to a pump on the surface—or wherever on the sub that might be?"

"Ah." Maldynado shuffled in after him and pointed to cylindrical tanks on the bunk. "I used ones like this before. They were from Kyatt or some place that used a little magic to make it all work. It's all self-contained. The air is in those tanks."

"Where did Starcrest *get* them?" They hadn't had access to these before, and Sespian couldn't imagine Turgonian vessels using equipment that employed magic, however handy it might be.

"I don't know, but there have been quite a few foreign ships visiting since the change of government. Maybe he traded for them. Last time, we found them on a wrecker all kitted out for underwater treasure hunting."

"Well, good." Sespian grabbed a pair of boots. "I had visions of those vines sweeping in, wrapping around the tubes, and cutting off our air supply."

"They'll just wrap around our necks instead."

"You're a cheery fellow, aren't you?" Sespian knocked on the sturdy helmet. "These should protect our necks somewhat."

"Let's hope so." Maldynado tugged the upper portion of his suit over his shoulders. "I wish I had a weapon to take out there. A *useful* weapon. Think you can get that black knife back?"

"Maybe. I'm hoping that hand-held generator can work down here too. I designed the casing to be waterproof." Sespian tugged his own suit up, feeling the weight of the heavy canvas. An unwelcome yawn cracked his mouth, and his eyes watered. A man ought to take on megalomaniacal vegetation after a full night's sleep and a hearty meal. He hadn't had either in some time.

"Am I forgetting anything?" Sespian waved at his ensemble. They would wait to fasten the helmets until it was time to go.

"Yeah, to kiss the girl."

"Er, what?"

"She kissed you," Maldynado said. "Now you kiss her back before flinging yourself into danger. That's how it works."

Sespian's face heated enough that he wished he already had the helmet on to hide the flush. "She's going to be flinging herself into danger too."

Maldynado opened his mouth to respond, but someone else spoke first. "No, she's not." Starcrest stood in the hatchway.

Dear ancestors, how much of that had he heard? Sespian stepped back to the wall and sucked in his belly, not sure whether it was to make room for Starcrest to enter or to try and make himself invisible.

"Pardon, My Lord?" Maldynado asked.

Starcrest stepped into the cabin and grabbed the large suit. "I designed the equipment. I know it best. I'm going out with you."

"Uh," Maldynado said.

Sespian couldn't manage anything more articulate. Even if he weren't poisoned, wasn't Starcrest a little... *venerable* to be cavorting around the lake floor, fending off attacks from killer plants?

"Are you sure that's wise?" Maldynado asked. "Given your condition?"

Starcrest gave him a cool stare. Sespian stared too. Had Maldynado realized Starcrest was feeling the effects of the poison before he had? If so, Sespian felt... obtuse.

"Given my condition," Starcrest said, "I'm probably the *only* one who should go out. But I may need someone to keep those vines off my back while I work. It's *going* to try and stop us."

"Did you ask Mahliki?" Sespian said before realizing how stupid that sounded. As if he needed his *daughter's* permission.

"We discussed it and agreed I was the logical choice to go out. She'll watch us from within the submarine and do what she can to help."

"Did she actually agree," Sespian asked, "or simply say 'whatever'?"

Starcrest smiled faintly. "She said 'whatever,' but she handed me this and hugged me." He held up the black dagger, then flipped it and extended it toward Sespian, hilt first. "Maldynado, take the generator." He pointed at the box Sespian and Mahliki had used on the street. "You're strong enough to carry it and your tank. Flip that switch to activate it."

Sespian felt a twinge of disgruntlement at hearing Maldynado get the strength compliment, but admitted Maldynado was bigger and brawnier than he. Besides, he would rather wield the dagger. Whipping daggers around was in his blood, after all, wasn't it? He wondered if it was petty of him to wish Sicarius were there with him instead of Maldynado. Or maybe it was just that Starcrest had gotten a hug from his daughter and a chance for a farewell, and Sespian... didn't even know where Sicarius was.

The deck vibrated. The sub was ascending.

"Time for final preparations." Starcrest waved Sespian over. "I'll fasten your helmet."

"Yes, sir. Thank you, sir." Sespian turned around.

"By the way, son," Starcrest said, resting a hand on Sespian's shoulder for a moment. "No matter what happens out there... you have my blessing if you want to court my daughter."

"Erp?"

"Or whatever your generation calls it these days." Starcrest patted him, then worked on the fasteners.

Maldynado sniggered. "We call it—"

"Courting," Sespian blurted, not wanting to hear Maldynado's lewd interpretation. "Courting is good."

"Just don't let *him* anywhere near her," Starcrest added.

"No, sir. I would skewer him myself, should he have any impure thoughts about her."

"Thoughts?" Maldynado asked. "A man can't be skewered for *thoughts*." He stepped back, his tank bumping against the hull. "Can he?"

"We're at the surface," came Mahliki's voice from navigation. "You better get going before that plant starts hurling trees onto us again."

"Understood," Starcrest said. "Gentlemen? It's time."

CHAPTER 29

"THERE HAS TO BE AN antidote," Amaranthe said, "or some... concoction that can nullify the effects."

Sicarius gazed into one of the dark tunnels stretching away from the altar, his silence more alarming than that of the ancient ossuary. Had he already accepted Starcrest's death as inevitable?

Amaranthe gripped his arm. "What about a practitioner? Like the shaman who healed me of that infection. Couldn't someone skilled in the medical sciences cure a man of a poison?"

His gaze lowered, locking onto hers. "Possibly."

"Then one of these priests... one of the ones who knows the Science. We can question them until we find someone suitable."

"Their craft is crude," Sicarius said. "It is likely they've always practiced in secret and only among themselves. Finding a healer—"

Amaranthe's grip tightened. "We have to try."

"Yes," he agreed. "Put out your lamp."

"Uh, what?" The last thing Amaranthe wanted was to be in the dark when she was stuck in a crypt.

"Someone is coming."

After a quick check to make sure she had matches, Amaranthe extinguished the lamp. Sicarius took her hand and led her into one of the side tunnels, one where the cobwebs had already been broken. Though she trusted him, and had grown used to his uncanny ability to navigate in the dark, she kept her other hand extended, afraid she would crash into a wall—or trip over some bone that had fallen from one of the niches.

He slowed down, let her find a corner with her groping hand, then turned around it. He stopped there, and they turned to peer back the way they had come. The dark was gray rather than absolute, and it grew lighter as they watched. A lantern appeared. It was farther back than the altar, perhaps around a corner similar to theirs. It drifted closer. Amaranthe squinted, trying to see who held it. Serpitivich? Or was someone else down here with them?

As the lantern drew closer to the altar, a sense of dread stirred within her. She wanted to speak, to ask Sicarius if her eyes were fooling her, but she dared not lest someone—or *something*—hear. The lantern was floating toward them without anyone holding it.

It paused at the altar and hovered there, then rotated in a circle, as if it were *looking* for them.

Stop your wild imagination, girl, Amaranthe told herself. It was some levitation trick by a practitioner. They had *wanted* to find a practitioner, hadn't they? This might be *good* news. Except that if they were dealing with a practitioner, vanquishing him might be much harder than simply capturing some sixty-year-old politician.

The lantern hovered over the altar, and its glass door creaked open. It tilted, lighting each of the four candles.

Sicarius eased back from the corner. "Watch for him here," he whispered in her ear. "I'll circle around to find the practitioner. Concentrating on that trick will be distracting him."

Amaranthe patted his shoulder in acknowledgment. As soon as he left her side, she drew her dagger. She didn't know how effective it would be on floating lanterns, but she felt better with the leather-wrapped hilt in her hand. If she needed a bigger weapon, she had Deret's swordstick laced through her belt as well. She put her back to the wall on the opposite corner, so nothing could sneak up on her. From there, she could lean her head into the tunnel and keep the altar in sight.

With the candles lit, the lantern settled down on the side of the basin. Just as she was thinking the scene was returning to normal—or as normal as a blood-filled bowl in front of a thousand human skulls could be—a soft grating sounded, then a clunk. Something rolled down, bounced on the altar, and landed on the floor. A skull. Amaranthe jumped despite her certainty that this was the result of someone practicing telekinesis. It had nothing to do with hauntings or the spiritual residue from old religions being practiced. She was positive. Mostly.

Something stirred beneath the altar, then a yellowed object drifted out of the darkness. A human femur with a stone or ceramic spatula attached at the end. It rotated to a vertical position and hovered over the basin. A lid on one of the jars rose and was laid to the side. Then the jar itself lifted and tilted, dumping some of its contents into the blood.

Amaranthe shifted, aware that it was the powder Sicarius had pointed out. When a second jar was unfastened and lifted to dump some of its contents, she developed an uneasy certainty that the practitioner was making some of that poison.

She ought to stop it. Stride forward and kick the bowl off the altar. Why not? The practitioner already knew she was there. He wouldn't bother with a show otherwise. Surely all of this was more easily done by hand.

Yes, let him come out and face her. She wouldn't be cowed by this display. Amaranthe took a step toward the altar, but a clunk came from the passage beside her, the one parallel to the entrance tunnel they had traveled down. Sicarius had gone down it to circle back, but she doubted that noise had been a result of anything he had done.

Another clunk sounded, followed by a prolonged scuff, like something being dragged over the floor. She fingered her lamp, tempted to light it, step in that direction, and take a look. It wasn't as if the *spoon* could see her. The practitioner was probably standing somewhere farther down the tunnel in the opposite direction.

Except the spoon was already stirring the concoction in the basin. Maybe she ought to knock it over before it made any more progress. So long as she didn't eat the poison or get it into her bloodstream, she ought to be fine, wasn't that what Sicarius had said?

Another clunk came from the darkness to her side. Whatever had made the noise was closer now.

She wavered, torn about which problem to address first.

"Hurry up over there, Sicarius," she muttered.

She had no sooner said his name than the spoon dropped, the heavy bone handle clunking on the basin. One of the jars that had been in the air also thunked down, powder flying. The candle flames wavered but didn't go out.

"Someone was distracted," she breathed and smiled.

A huge clatter arose from the opposite side of the crypt, the sound of rocks falling. Many, *many* rocks. The stone floor shuddered. Dust flowed out of the tunnels and dimmed the light from the candles. The ceiling must have caved in. Amaranthe lost her smile. That couldn't be a coincidence, not in a crypt that had stood for centuries without any signs of such destruction. She was tempted to call out Sicarius's name, but he would return to her when he could. *If* he could.

No. She couldn't think like that. It might have been Sicarius dropping the ceiling on the practitioner, not the other way around.

But would he have done that? After they had discussed needing a practitioner to heal Starcrest?

On the altar, the spoon lifted and returned to stirring.

The scuffing from down the dark tunnel grew audible again. Amaranthe didn't know if it had stopped, the same way the spoon had, or if the rockfall had simply drowned out the noise. Either way, the sound was closer now.

She opened a storage cache on the bottom of her lamp and pulled out a match. If something dangerous was creeping up on her, she wanted to know what.

Amaranthe eased a couple of steps into the tunnel, so she wouldn't be visible from the altar—or to anyone standing farther down that passage. She struck the match head to the wall. Light flared.

She gasped and dropped the match, staggering backward. A decapitated man in a bloody soldier's uniform was shambling toward her, arms outstretched.

She almost screamed, but bit down on her tongue instead. There was a logical explanation. There had to be.

In the meantime... she sure as winter wasn't going to let the thing catch up with her.

She wouldn't run toward the altar, so she ran in the opposite direction of it, heading down the only tunnel without anything strange happening in it, so far as she knew. Since she had dropped her match, she crashed into the wall at the end, almost smacking her forehead on the unyielding stone. She caught herself with her hands, wincing at the sound when the lamp banged, and felt around. It wasn't a dead end. There was another tunnel that paralleled the main one. Good.

She glanced back the way she had come, and her heart rate doubled again. The headless figure had come out of the side passage and was outlined by the candlelight from the altar. It had turned toward her—it was *following* her.

"An illusion," she whispered. It had to be.

If so, she ought to be able to walk right through it. Before she took a step, she spotted the scabbard at the figure's hip. A sword scabbard. She remembered the rapier she had seen in the room with Deret's swordstick, and her comment about another prisoner. Her stomach gave a sick lurch. That blood in the basin... she hadn't asked Sicarius, but she bet it was human blood. The soldier's blood. There had been a nametag on the uniform. Rydor? Rydak? Rydoth, that was it. With a sinking certainty, Amaranthe knew: the figure shambling after her wasn't an illusion. She didn't know if it was simply a corpse being levitated or something... more disturbing, but she didn't want to try and fight it. If it was already dead, what could she do to deter it?

Kill the practitioner controlling it.

Amaranthe took a few steps down the new passage. Cobwebs licked her face. She batted them away and struck another match. If anything creepy was heading at her from the opposite end of this tunnel, she couldn't see it yet through the wispy white shrouds dangling from the ceiling. This time, she managed to get the lamp lit. She headed off, aware of the scuffing sounds of the corpse following her. She would circle around and find Sicarius. By now, she was probably too late to do anything about the concoction in the bowl. It had already been mixed.

She reached a spot where she could turn right. More cobwebs draped the passage, and nothing but darkness lay ahead, but it *should* take her back to the main corridor. So far, everything had been laid out on a grid with the tunnels crossing at right angles. She checked behind her, expecting the headless corpse to be following her still, but there was no sign of it. The influence of her light didn't stretch back as far as the corner, so it might be waiting for her and she would never know.

"Let it wait."

Amaranthe pushed on down the new tunnel. More passages crossed it, some with cobwebs, some without, but she continued straight, believing her route would bring her back to the main one. She kept glancing right, checking for the candles and altar, but all she ever saw was darkness. The uneasy feeling that had never been far from her that evening returned as she grew more and more certain that she had walked too far. Somehow she had missed that central passage. Maybe the practitioner had snuffed the candles and she had passed the altar without realizing it. Or maybe... she crouched and eyed the floor ahead of and behind her.

"Bloody ancestors, I've been going down."

She was on the verge of turning back when something glinted up ahead. She took a few more steps, and a door came into view. The sturdy oak boards and thick copper hinges fit the theme of the crypt—with skulls etched in the metal and bones carved in the wood—but lacked the age of the rest of the place.

"New addition?"

Amaranthe tried the latch. She had to throw her back into opening the door, but it *did* open.

The mingled scents of chemicals, herbal components, and incense wafted out. Before crossing the threshold, she eyed the walls and floors for traps or trip wires. The vault door upstairs probably offered enough security for Serpitivich or whoever roamed around down here, but one never knew.

Warily, she stepped inside. A single room waited, a workshop lined with stone shelves on every side. A table with legs made from bound bones stood in the middle. A black box and all manner of vials, jars, and bowls were spread out upon it. A thick book with yellowed pages rested in the center, open to a page near the front. Amaranthe couldn't read any of the words but thought the symbols matched some of those on the vault door. She wondered if it might be a book on poisons, and, if so, would it contain information on cures? Mundane, magical, or otherwise?

She tried lifting the lid on the black box in case some useful solution waited within. It didn't. Amaranthe leaped back, stifling another scream.

"Should have known," she panted. By the size alone. The young soldier's severed head was inside, stored for what purpose she didn't want to contemplate. "You're a sick man, Serpitivich. I can't believe Mancrest almost voted for you."

"Perhaps if he and a few others had," came a voice from behind her, "you wouldn't be stuck in this situation, about to die."

Amaranthe turned slowly, keeping the desk between her and the door, irritated with herself for not having heard the man coming. Serpitivich wore a smock rather than his typical pressed suit, and bloodstains spotted the front, some old and brown, some fresh and crimson. Underneath the smock... he wore one of those dark green robes. Not surprising at this point. He wasn't working with them or for them—he was *one* of them.

Instead of carrying a book, as he usually did, he held a pistol. It was aimed at her.

"You're not going to kill me with magic? Or poison?" Amaranthe asked. "That's disappointing, as I've been admiring your art all night." She wanted to ask him about Sicarius, but was afraid of the answer. If he was here, maybe Sicarius had already been... dealt with. It seemed impossible to imagine him thwarted by a sixty-year-old politician after all the enemies he had slain, but Serpitivich was obviously more than they had all thought. Was he just a poison maker, or was he a practitioner as well?

"The poisons are... simply a hobby," he said. "I never thought to use them on anyone, but this year has been... eventful." He adjusted his spectacles, looking far more like a schoolteacher than a murderer. "It's a shame you and your knife-flinging friend concerned yourselves with my affairs. I had no particular distaste for you—indeed, you did us all a favor by getting rid of the corrupt and inflexible empire and creating new opportunities for everyone."

"Glad to hear it."

"Now that your friend is dead, I'm afraid it's time for you to join him. This is a sacred place. Visitors aren't allowed. Step away from the box, please. I've already started working on the head. I would hate for you to damage it with your death throes."

Uh huh. She would be sure to accommodate him so he could more easily shoot her... Amaranthe was beginning to see why Starcrest had put these people off. Maybe he'd had some notion of the grisly rituals that went along with the religion.

"Are the human sacrifices necessary?" she asked. "You might have trouble finding followers and gaining mainstream acceptance if that's required for your religion."

"Oh, I don't know about that." Serpitivich strolled into the room, perhaps trying to step around the clutter-filled desk, so he could target her chest more easily. "We Turgonians are a bloodthirsty lot. Just look at how many sign up for the military. A career that makes killing people socially acceptable."

"Yeah, but those are usually people on the other side of a war." Amaranthe stepped around the end of the desk to keep it and his precious box between them. Her hand drifted to her dagger—with all the books and jars in the way, he shouldn't see the movement—but she hesitated. The swordstick might serve her better. *If* she could remove it from her belt without being obvious about it. Too bad she had stuck it behind her back where it wouldn't impede her.

"There are plenty of murderers and criminals who can also be put to death without disturbing the general populace." The corner of Serpitivich's mouth twitched as Amaranthe continued to keep the desk between them. Irritation? He stopped and shifted his weight—he wasn't going to let her maneuver toward the door.

"Is that what this fellow was?" Amaranthe pointed to the head. At the same time, she loosened her belt with her other hand. "A criminal?"

"He was one of Starcrest's men we captured for bargaining purposes, until he tried to escape."

"In other words, he was a loyal soldier."

"I believe we've chatted long enough, Ms. Lokdon."

"I'm having that feeling too." The swordstick dropped to the floor, cracking on the old stone.

Serpitivich frowned downward, distracted for an instant. Amaranthe ducked down, grabbing the stick. A shot fired, but she was already below the table. The bullet struck the wall and ricocheted into the room.

Serpitivich cursed. Good. She hoped the bastard had shot himself. She popped up and hit the release on the swordstick. The wooden case flew across the table, striking the man in the shoulder, and leaving Amaranthe with the bared blade ready to use. She raced around the table herself, knowing she had to reach Serpitivich before he sent some mental attack at her.

He recovered quickly, whirling toward her and lifting the pistol for another shot. She used the rapier to knock the box toward him, sending a silent apology to the dead soldier. Whatever Serpitivich had been doing to that head, it must represent a lot of work, for he reflexively lunged to catch it before stopping himself and whipping the pistol toward Amaranthe again. By then, she had run around the table. She slashed the sword across, knocking the pistol away and cutting into his hand. She stabbed him in the gut before he could jump back. If not for the fact that Starcrest was out there somewhere, dying of poison, she would have run him through for the garish things he was doing down here.

"You cursed bitch," he snarled, stumbling back. He snatched at a jar on the table and threw it at her.

Amaranthe ducked it easily and stabbed him again, wanting him incapacitated enough that he wouldn't be able to concentrate on magic. When he grabbed for something else, she kicked him in the shin. He pitched into the table. She jumped over the fallen box—and its gruesome contents—to land behind him. She grabbed him by the shoulder and laid the blade on the side of his neck.

"Time for you to lead me out of here," she said. "And why don't you show me where you dropped that pile of rocks on the way out?" She wouldn't believe Sicarius was dead until she dug his cold body out herself.

He snorted. "I don't think so. You'll die with the thousands of others who have died down here."

"You're awfully confident for someone whose pistol is..." Dear ancestors, it had fallen in a pile of brains that had tumbled out of the box. Amaranthe clenched her fist. She wanted to ram the sword right through Serpitivich's back and out the other side. "Start walking."

For a long moment, he didn't move. Amaranthe pressed the blade harder against his neck. He tried to jerk away, but she still held him with her other hand, so she dug her thumb into the pressure point between the tip of the shoulder and the spine. He flinched, pulling in the other direction, toward the blade. Skin tore, and blood dribbled down to his collarbone.

"I've had a long, rough night," Amaranthe said, "and it's making me crabby. Start walking *now*."

This time, he complied. He walked slowly toward the door, and Amaranthe didn't let him out of sword's reach, though she did grab the open book in case Tikaya could read it and find anything useful within. Since she needed to carry the lamp as well—and keep Serpitivich from making trouble—she stuffed it into her shirt. Sicarius's shirt actually, which was fortunate, because it was baggy on her and had room for fat musty tomes that made her skin itch. She needed a bath badly. And another vacation.

Serpitivich walked through the door and started up the tunnel. After only a few feet, he halted so quickly Amaranthe almost jabbed him with the sword again.

"What—" she started, then stopped, her jaw descending.

Sicarius stood in the shadows, a robed figure draped over his shoulder. Dust made his blond hair a shade paler, and a few scrapes were visible on his face and hands. He must have been caught at least partially in that rockfall. He hardly appeared *dead* though, something Serpitivich clearly deduced as well, for his shoulders slumped. Had he been hoping that the other robed fellow would come help him?

"You did not wait at the appointed location," Sicarius said.

Though she'd had a good reason not to wait, she blushed at his statement, nonetheless. Amazing how a man speaking in an utter monotone could convey that he had, in exasperation, walked all over a crypt with an unconscious enemy slung over his shoulder to find her.

"Sorry," Amaranthe said. "I was being chased by a headless corpse."

He gazed at her, his face expressionless.

"It's true," she said, though if he hadn't seen the corpse himself, she could understand where skepticism would arise... "Who's your friend?"

"The practitioner," Sicarius said.

"Oh? I thought *he* was the practitioner." She nodded toward Serpitivich. And if he wasn't, Amaranthe had poked him full of holes unnecessarily. Oddly, she couldn't manage to feel bad about that.

"He Makes artifacts; I make poisons," Serpitivich said.

"Do you also make antidotes to poisons?" Amaranthe asked.

"No." The bastard sounded smug. He knew he had won, that he had succeeded in having Starcrest poisoned. He must. Maybe he had some plan that he thought would continue on even if he were jailed or killed.

Amaranthe would make sure it didn't happen, whatever it was.

"Serpy here is about to show us the way out," Amaranthe told Sicarius.

"I have no wish to leave," Serpitivich said. "You will have to torture me before I'll show you how to open the door from within."

Sicarius stared at him, his eyes appearing black in the dim lighting. Black and hard like chips of obsidian. "Good."

Tikaya was tinkering with combinations of symbols while Mancrest sat at a hallway table, diligently scribbling his notes. With the prisoners taken out, the house had fallen quiet.

"A typical Turgonian safe uses how many numbers?" Tikaya asked. "Three? Four?"

"Three," he said.

"All right. I have a few ideas here. I'm going to start trying them." She headed for the vault door.

"Are you warning me in case you trigger a trap, and an explosion shoots out of the wall with enough force to burn us both to cinders?" Mancrest asked.

"Er, no. I just talk aloud sometimes when I'm working." Tikaya had her hand up, ready to try the lock, but she paused. "Is that... a common thing here? Booby-trapped safes?"

"It was a joke, sorry." He yawned and rubbed the back of his neck. "Though... I suppose it isn't *un*common. Foreigners have told me before that we're a paranoid people."

"Yes, I've told my husband that as well."

"That he's paranoid or that Turgonians in general are paranoid?"

"Yes to both." Tikaya smiled and returned to the safe. She would risk trying the combinations she had strung together. It would irk her to no end if she had possible solutions to a problem and *didn't* try them.

She was on the fourth or fifth one when heavy footsteps sounded on the stairs. One of the soldiers, she assumed, but glanced back to make sure. Some of those priests might have eluded their pursuers.

Dak strode toward them, an unwieldy long metal tool with a giant wheel balanced over his shoulder. He had donned a padded vest and thick gloves.

"That's... big," Tikaya observed as he set it down on the floor.

"An Aspencrest hand power drill," Dak said. "It'll cut through granite. I'm not sure about steel, but we can try. There's no way we're getting a water- or steam-powered drill up the stairs."

"That door has to be six inches thick," Mancrest said.

"I just need to drill through the lock face to get to the lever or drive cam."

"So, what? Through three inches of steel?"

Dak waved Mancrest to the side. "Sit over there and write your words, newspaper boy."

Mancrest lifted his hands and returned to the desk.

Tikaya eyed the drill. Dak sounded like he knew what he was doing, but... drilling into the lock might render the door inoperable—permanently—if it were done wrong. "Let me try a few more combinations."

She expected an argument, but Dak extended a hand toward the door. "As you wish, my lady."

"You Turgonians can be quite polite when you're not being brutal." Tikaya tried the sixth combination on her sheet of paper.

"We can also be polite *while* we're being brutal," Mancrest said. "Those of us with proper warrior-caste upbringing anyway."

"I saw that look, Mancrest," Dak said. "My upbringing was fine."

Tikaya continued trying combinations, running down her list. She was aware of the men watching her and the time bleeding past. She wondered where Rias was and if his condition had grown worse. Did the others in the submarine know he was sick? Should she have warned someone? Mahliki? Sespian? A surge of guilt flooded over her. She hadn't checked the communication sphere since leaving the lorry. There had been so much going on that she hadn't thought of it. What if he had sent a message and she hadn't responded? She vowed to run out to the lorry and dig it out of her pack as soon as she ran out of combinations to try. Dak could drill.

"Last one," she murmured.

Dak and Mancrest leaned in her direction, watching with intent eyes. The dial spun, left-right-left, and landed on the last symbol. She tried to pull open the latch and... nothing happened. The same as with the other twenty attempts.

Tikaya sighed. "Sorry, gentlemen."

"That Serpitivich is a crafty bird," Mancrest said. "He seems like a nice scholarly fellow, but underneath... he's plotting the president's death. And starting a Kriskrusian cult."

"Oh," Tikaya said, an idea sparking in her mind. "A cult. So he would be the cult leader? He has probably read the holy texts then, right? And is familiar with the animal symbols that represent leadership?"

Mancrest and Dak shrugged.

"I wonder..." Tikaya didn't bother putting her idea down on paper. She simply tried the symbols for the lion, the wolf, and the dagger-toothed lizard. They were all on the dial. "Not that order. Only six options though..."

On the third try, the lock emitted a soft click.

"Hah." She kneeled back, stretching legs that had started to ache from their long crouch.

"I don't have any idea what you were just talking about," Dak said, "but that click sounded promising." He grabbed the wheel and pulled.

The vault door swung open.

Dak pulled out a pistol and pointed it at whatever lay inside. He didn't fire though. His brow furrowed and he uttered an, "Uh?"

Not sure whether that signified something good or an impending explosion, Tikaya wasn't sure if she should look or not. Her curiosity took over though, and she stuck her head around the edge of the door.

Serpitivich himself faced her, standing at the top of a stone landing surrounded by old brick-and-mortar walls. Tikaya noticed the architecture first—and that it didn't fit in with the style or age of the house. It took her a moment to spot the blood trickling down Serpitivich's neck and the sword pressed against it.

"Can we come out?" a familiar voice asked from behind the politician.

"Amaranthe?" Tikaya asked.

"Yes, and I'm carrying a bunch of awkward stuff, not to mention pushing this awkward prisoner along. Sicarius is with me too. His burden is also awkward."

"Yes," came Sicarius's emotionless voice.

"Is there a chance any of your, ah, stuff has to do with antidotes for Rias's poison?" Tikaya asked.

The silent moment that followed lasted far too long for her tastes.

"Has it been verified that he's been poisoned?" Sicarius asked.

"Yes." Tikaya swallowed. "I can verify it."

Serpitivich smiled.

"Sicarius identified the poison," Amaranthe said, "and says... er, he believes there might not be an antidote, but we thought Serpitivich or his practitioner friend here might have a way to cure the president. It seems they dabble in the Science."

No antidote. Tikaya gripped the wall—it was the only thing that kept her from dropping to the floor, for her legs had grown rubbery and couldn't support her. She heard Amaranthe's other words, but couldn't muster much hope. It would take a healer, and those who specialized in the arts these priests were flinging around—fire and weather manipulation—rarely put the years in to master healing.

"Well, Serpitivich?" Dak asked. "Do you know a cure?"

"The ability to know a thing is not the same as the ability to execute a thing." Serpitivich glanced at the inert man draped over Sicarius's shoulder.

"Fine, do you know how to *execute* a cure? Your buddy there can help."

"If I knew how once, I may have forgotten since."

What did *that* mean? Did he know or not? Tikaya wanted to wring his neck.

"We were... Sicarius was just about to... interrogate him for information on how to open the door," Amaranthe said. "He would probably be willing to offer his services in relation to this matter too."

It was a measure of Tikaya's distress that she didn't find the notion of interrogation—*torture*—so unappealing at the moment.

Dak grunted and ripped a piece of paper from Mancrest's pad, then took the pencil from his hand.

"You're welcome," Mancrest muttered as Dak used the wall to write a few lines.

Dak handed the paper to Serpitivich. "I ask again, do you know how to execute a cure?"

Serpitivich stared down at the paper for a long moment. His shoulders slumped. "I... yes."

Hope rushed into Tikaya's breast.

"Put him and his friend in the lorry," Dak said.

Amaranthe pushed Serpitivich into the hallway, and two soldiers appeared out of the woodwork to add a few more weapons to the escort duty. She paused to hand Tikaya a book on her way past.

"I don't know if there's anything useful in it, but in case he isn't as helpful as we hope..." Amaranthe shrugged and continued down the hall with her prisoner.

Sicarius stepped through the doorway, his own prisoner still dangling over his shoulder. "Even bound and gagged, a practitioner may prove troublesome if not watched closely," he told Dak.

"Yes, thank you for agreeing to do that on the way back." Dak pointed down the hallway after Amaranthe.

Sicarius stared at him for a moment, and Tikaya expected a protest or a statement that he wasn't one of Dak's soldiers. But Sicarius walked off without comment.

"You're lucky he didn't castrate you," Mancrest told Dak. "Even

Amaranthe smiles and shines her big brown eyes at him when she gives him work."

Dak grunted. "I'm sure Rias's right-hand man knows better than to turn his nephew into a eunuch. You better head out, too, before I give you half of this drill to carry."

"My injury precludes such labor." Mancrest plucked his pencil out of Dak's grip and hobbled toward the stairs.

Dak grunted again, this time in response to picking up the heavy tool. "After you, my lady."

Tikaya took the lead but asked over her shoulder, "What did you write on that note?"

"The address of his daughter in Port Gamouth."

"You had it memorized?" That city was on the coast, almost two thousand miles away. Serpitivich must have believed his kin safe from his maneuvering in the capital.

"He's been on my short list for a long time."

Tikaya remembered Dak warning them they should keep an eye on Serpitivich several days ago, when word of the snitch had first come out. She regretted that she had treated him as a suspect rather than a confidant. They probably could have pinned Serpitivich down earlier if they had worked together. But how could she have known?

"Could have trusted Rias," she muttered.

"What?" Dak asked.

"Nothing, I was just thinking we better find Rias. I hope he's... still in a position that a cure will be of use."

"So do I," Dak said. "So do I."

Mahliki sat in the main navigation seat, Major Rydoth standing behind her. It seemed strange being in charge with a trained officer thirty years her senior two feet away, but she had been working the controls of her father's submarines since she was a little kid. Besides, given what was at stake, she would have gnawed off his hand if he tried to take control. He kept jogging back and forth between navigation and the engine room, so he didn't seem so inclined, but he was up here now, chewing on his fingernails while he watched the men in diving suits drop into the water and swim away.

"The hatch is closed, the batteries and cable have been dropped, and we're ready to descend," he said.

Mahliki nodded and pushed the lever that released the air in the ballast tanks. "Electrifying the hull again, and following them down."

"If trouble shows up, are there any weapons left we can use besides that drill? You gave Starcrest the dagger, didn't you?"

Meaning the drill would be completely ineffective now. She knew it all too well.

"We've got a couple of weapons we can try." Mahliki touched a panel to the side of her seat, though the idea of firing Father's charged torpedoes while he was out there didn't sit well with her. That much electricity could kill human beings as well as vegetation. "He was holding them in reserve, not wanting to warn the plant beforehand."

"Warn the plant. That will never sound normal."

"No, I suppose not." Mahliki turned the rudder and added a bit of thrust to follow the divers. With their belts weighted, they sank rapidly.

Maldynado was the first to land, his body weight and the addition of the generator bringing him down more quickly than the others. Mahliki tensed as his boots hit the green carpet of vines smothering the lake floor. Nothing happened. For the moment. Good. The more moments they had to work with, the better.

Sespian and Father alighted, too, and all three of them strode across the bumpy green floor to the area where the gray battery boxes had landed. The plant hadn't disturbed them yet, either. Mahliki had envisioned them swallowing the batteries as soon as they struck down, and had almost suggested the men carry them by hand, but they were too big and bulky for that.

Father wasted no time. He pointed for the other two to space the boxes while he knelt and affixed cable to the first. Seeing the canvas knee of his suit touching those vines made her shift uneasily. All too well she remembered the enzyme that could seep from the plant's pores and eat through clothing.

A shadow stirred at the edge of the viewport.

"It's going to attack them," the major said.

"I see it." Mahliki grabbed the control stick for the torpedoes, lining it up with her target, as she had seen her father do before. She jabbed the button before she could second-guess herself.

"Whoa," the major blurted as the sleek black cylinder darted away.

Mahliki had seen them shoot out before. She was more concerned about her aim—and her father's modifications. If all the torpedo did was disappear into the stalks, then that sleekness wouldn't help them.

It clipped the vine she had been targeting, and she groaned. She needed a cutting tool or something she could sweep out with, or maybe—

The side of the vine blackened, and the rest of the flesh followed. It fell limply out of sight. The torpedo itself disappeared between two stalks at the front of the forest, but seconds later, a flash of white with blue streaks of energy erupted. The brilliant light dwarfed the illumination from the running lamp. More importantly, it burned the green off a swath of plants. Blackened stalks disintegrated into the water, clearing a stretch several meters wide.

Down below, Maldynado looked toward the sub and gave a gesture of approval. Father kept wiring the batteries, but Mahliki thought he gave her a helmet nod as well.

"How many of those do we have?" Rydoth asked.

"Not that many. We should save them. Next time, I'll try to steer the sub over and intercept any vines with the electrified hull."

"Like that one?"

"Erg, yes." Mahliki took them forward and down, blocking this new vine's attempt to veer toward the men. It thumped against the side of the sub. "Wish this thing had more windows. Major, want to keep an eye out at the science station? Let me know if anything comes in from that side."

He gave her an indecipherable look—one that probably meant he wasn't used to taking orders from a kid—a girl kid at that—but he did head back there.

Mahliki navigated around the clearing, using the craft's electrified hull to keep back any vines that encroached, but some of the ones matting the lake floor were starting to shift about. A tendril drifted up behind Sespian, angling toward his boot. He was busy placing the last of the batteries and didn't seem to notice it.

"Look out," Mahliki said, though he couldn't hear her. On impulse, she flicked the sub's running lamp on and off.

All three men's helmets tilted up. She wasn't sure if they could see through the viewing port and into the cabin, but she pointed behind

Sespian, nonetheless. Maldynado, placing batteries on the other side of the circle, saw the vine and pointed too.

Sespian spun in a circle and spotted the tendril when its tip was inches from his leg. He swiped down with the dagger. Fortunately it was a thin vine, and it only took a couple of slashes to hack the end off. It drew back, its severed tip wavering at his eye level, and hovered there. More of the vines were standing up all around the clearing.

"Hurry up, Father..."

As if he heard her, Father bounced along the bottom more quickly than he could have walked, arms stroking to add speed. The wire reeled out behind him. He only needed to connect the last two batteries. And then... then they got to find out if this field would work to drive away the vines. If it didn't swallow them first.

Mahliki tapped a finger on the torpedo controls. She didn't want to fire anywhere close to her team, but it would be a way to quell the plant for a while. Maybe if she could convince the men to float up to the top, she could target the ground beneath them.

But Father hooked up the last battery, creating a ring around their work area. He waved to the others, then bent and hit whatever switch he had made for the boxes. Without waiting to see if anything happened, he moved on to the next. Sespian and Maldynado, on the opposite end of the circle, turned theirs on, though they had to stop to deal with more intruding vines. None had attacked Father yet, but Mahliki kept an eye on him—since he had given Sespian his dagger, he didn't have a weapon capable of stopping the plant.

One reared out of the matting behind Father, more than one. Three vines veered toward him at the same time.

"He needs help," the major called.

"I see it." But she couldn't launch a torpedo, not with Father right *there*. She nudged the *Explorer* forward, hoping to intercept the vines before they snaked around him.

Father flipped some final switch and bounded forward of his own accord. His helmet tilted up—he had noticed her coming—then twisted to peer over his shoulder. He saw the trouble. Good. He jerked a wave to Maldynado who was fiddling with a final battery on the far side. Sespian ran toward Father, his dagger out. Something rose up and tripped him though. Mahliki chomped on her lip. She wasn't going to get there quickly enough.

Maldynado flung an arm up. The circuit was complete. Mahliki held her breath, expecting some grand explosion of light and electricity. But Father was waving to get everyone's attention and pointing up. Maldynado fiddled with his weight belt, then rose from the lake bottom. Father rose as well.

By now the submarine had reached the far side, and Mahliki shifted it to block those three vines. Father had something in his hand. A controller? A fine wire attached it to one of the batteries. He was waiting for something. Oh, Sespian. His boots were still on the ground as he worked to pry free the vine that had grasped him. Maldynado swam down, waving the wand from the generator on his back. He stabbed the vine attacking Sespian and a blue streak of lightning shot out.

"Huh, it *does* work underwater," Mahliki said.

Sespian patted Maldynado on the arm, and they rose from the bottom together. Father did something with the controller. Ah, there was the surge of energy. She didn't see much, but the effect on the plant was immediate. Everything on the ground around the battery circle, and inside it as well, grew black and started to disintegrate. The affected area stretched out nearly fifty meters in every direction.

Father landed near the middle and pulled a big black box out of his own pack. Sespian and Maldynado touched down on either side, facing outward, ready to protect him. The ground was bare of the plant though, with small black debris drifting away on the current. At a wave from Father, Sespian knelt and started digging with the dagger. Would he be strong enough to cut into that film? Mahliki waited, not certain if she would be called over to help drill. While Sespian dug, Father set up his final weapon. She didn't know what it was, another battery of a sort, but he had warned her he would have to attach it to some special connector on the submarine so it could utilize the engine's power.

He stood and waved for her to come down. Mahliki let air out of the tanks to descend again, nudging the nose in Father's direction. But too much air was pumped out of the tanks, and the craft lowered more quickly than expected. The steering grew sluggish and unresponsive as well. Instead of turning toward Father, the submarine picked up speed and traveled straight ahead, toward a rocky outcropping beyond the battery circle.

"What the— Major, can you check the ballast tanks? Is something going on back there?"

Even if it was, the steering shouldn't be affected. It wouldn't be controlled from back there. Mahliki scowled, trying to compensate for both problems. With her focus on the control panel, she didn't notice the major coming up behind her until something moved at the edge of her vision. It moved *fast*.

She started to turn, but it slammed into the back of her head. The pain of a sledgehammer blow rang through her skull, and she pitched forward. She tried to catch herself before tumbling out of the seat, but her limbs reacted too slowly. Everything seemed to be happening slowly as she clunked to the deck and banged her head one final time.

CHAPTER 30

MALDYNADO LIKED THE PLANT ZAPPER, as he had dubbed the generator with its long metal fork. He almost regretted when the gray boxes were activated, forming that field that destroyed all of the greenery around. More vines waved in the far distance—in the dark water, the visibility was poor, but the powerful submarine lamp helped illuminate the surroundings. He had an urge to trot over and zap a few more of them for fun, but Starcrest might yet need his help. Things looked to be under control—he had just waved the submarine down to help with some final task—but one never knew. Besides, Maldynado had a feeling he might get zapped himself if he tried to step over the battery line. If that electricity could shrivel a tree-sized plant into ashes, he didn't want to know what it might do to a man's love apples.

Sespian tapped him on the shoulder and pointed at the *Explorer*.

Odd, it wasn't coming close, the way Starcrest had gestured for it to. It was dropping quickly and veering toward a large rock outcropping that had been revealed when the plants had been seared away.

"What's Mahliki doing?" Maldynado wondered, though Sespian wouldn't be able to hear him underwater. He could sign the question, but doubted he needed to. They must all be wondering the same thing.

Starcrest's waves had grown larger and more urgent, but the submarine cruised past him without slowing. It was about to cross over the battery line. Maldynado didn't quite know how that thing worked— would something swimming above it be as affected as something walking close to it?—but was sure the vessel disappearing into the lake depths, *or* smashing into those rocks couldn't be a good thing.

Sespian jogged in that direction, and Maldynado bounded after him, pushing at the water with his hands to gain greater momentum. Starcrest dropped a copper cube he had been holding and halted Maldynado and

Sespian with a raised hand before they could get near the circle. Right. Shriveled love apples.

The submarine crossed over the line, no more than a few feet above the ground, and great sparks and streaks of lightning flew from the dark hull. Maldynado didn't know if it indicated damage—it sure looked impressive—or simply a meeting of two electrical fields, but he doubted it was good either way.

The craft's running lamp flicked out. Darkness swallowed the lake bottom.

Maldynado hadn't realized how much they were depending on that light to see what they were doing. A great crunch and scrape came from the rock outcropping. He stared, trying to pick out the submarine in the gloom. It was clear what had happened, but he couldn't tell if the craft had been breached. Were Mahliki and the engineer in danger? There weren't any more diving suits in the cabin. Of course, the surface ought to only be twenty or thirty feet up at this point in the harbor, so they could swim up before running out of air, but only if they were conscious and weren't pinned by wreckage.

Maldynado's thoughts took him forward again, but he halted, remembering the barrier. How were they supposed to get over there to help?

Sespian tapped him again and pointed. Starcrest had recovered the controller he had used to turn on the batteries. Yes, of course. He ought to be able to turn them off again. Maldynado didn't know what would happen with the plant—with *them*—without that protection, but there was no choice. They had to check on the sub.

Indeed, Starcrest was already running for it. When he bounded across the cable without any of his favorite parts being zapped off, Maldynado assumed it was safe. He raced after Starcrest. Sespian charged along beside him.

Maldynado's eyes adjusted to the dimness. Some light filtered down to the bottom from the sky above, enough to make out the dark cylinder of the submarine jammed against the rock. It wasn't enough, however, to judge the damage from a distance. Starcrest had already reached the submarine. Maldynado thought he would go straight for the hatch, but he swam around to the viewing port instead. Of course. If he opened the hatch, it would flood the interior with water. Anyone inside would *have* to go up at that point. And how could they finish the mission without the rest of the team? They would have to go up and try and help Mahliki and the engineer—even if they were only fifty or a hundred meters from shore at this point, there was no way two swimmers could make it past all those plants without being impeded—or snatched up by boa constrictor-like vines.

Starcrest pounded on the viewport. Maldynado stopped in the sand by the submarine's side. He didn't know what Starcrest saw, but those choppy hard blows looked angry. Maldynado was surprised he wasn't being shocked from the electrified hull, but maybe the crash or sailing through the battery barrier had caused it to stop working, like the lamp.

Sespian pointed, then pushed off, half swimming and half climbing to navigate to the hatch on top. Starcrest pounded a few more times—he might have shouted something too, judging by the faint sounds that reached Maldynado's ears, but it was impossible to see his face behind the dark faceplate. Then he swam up as well, joining Sespian on top.

"We're going in?" Maldynado yelled, hoping they would hear him. The others had to realize doing so would flood the inside, but he felt compelled to ask anyway.

Starcrest ignored him. He waved and pointed at the hatch handle. Sespian nodded and gripped it. He tried to tug it open. Starcrest shook his head and bent over the side of the hatch, fumbling with a gloved hand. Some sort of emergency access panel? His hands were shaking and he had trouble prying it open. It could have been anger, but it could have been the effects of the poison too. He had been looking worse and worse all night.

Sespian produced the black dagger and waved for Starcrest to move his hands. He pried the panel open, catching the cover before it could fall away. Starcrest pushed a switch inside, then he and Sespian returned to the hatch. They tugged on it together, clearly expecting it to open.

It didn't.

Starcrest swore loudly enough that Maldynado heard some of it. Something that sounded like, "He's sabotaged it," reached his ears.

Sespian kept trying to tug open the hatch, and Starcrest swam back toward the viewport. Maldynado wasn't sure how to help, so he chewed on his lip and gazed around them. Plant stalks waved in the current behind the rock, reminding him that they hadn't destroyed the thing yet, not completely. They were beyond the barrier, too, a barrier that had been turned off. The plant might figure that out soon and attack.

Maldynado pushed away from the submarine and headed back into the circle. When he reached the device Starcrest had pulled out of his pack, a copper box a little smaller than the gray batteries, he grabbed the cable extending from it. Starcrest had been holding it when waving for Mahliki to bring the craft closer. There were a couple of prongs on the end. He had meant to attach it to some socket on the hull. Maldynado remembered that much from their hasty briefing, but not *where* that socket might be. One thing was certain: the cable wouldn't reach. He doubted the submarine was going anywhere anytime soon—especially if Sespian and Starcrest flooded it—so he would have to move the device, and hope it could do its job from a different location. Given how precise Starcrest and Mahliki had been with their map, he wasn't certain it could, but he had to try.

He lugged the thing toward the submarine, all the while monitoring the increasingly active stalks behind the rocks and keeping an eye on his companions as well. Sespian still had the dagger and was trying to find a way in—the hull was truly designed well if it could withstand *that* blade—while Starcrest... He had swum back to the viewing port, but dropped down lower than it, his boots on the lake floor. He was leaning against the rocks, his helmet drooping to his chest. Maldynado couldn't believe the legendary admiral would give up, but if he had exerted himself aggressively, maybe the poison tainting his veins was taking advantage.

Maldynado kept dragging the device and the cable closer. What else could he do?

Mahliki lay on the deck for a moment, in part because she was truly stunned and it took her body some seconds to start responding again, and in part because she wanted to figure out what in all the Kyattese sea channels Major Rydoth was doing. Betraying them, that much was obvious, but what was his next step, and how could she recover enough to stop him? Stop him and tie him up somewhere so he wouldn't be any more trouble.

She wasn't wearing any weapons, not even her utility knife. She had left it back near the science station where she had used it last. The major, on the other hand, wore his pistol as well as a dagger, both hanging on his uniform belt, which Mahliki had a unique view of from below him, her cheek plastered against the cold metal deck. He stood over her, his hand on the rudder control. Steering them where?

He seemed to have presumed her unconscious—he must not know how much padding her braids gave her back there—and wasn't checking downward often. Mahliki put down her palm, with a notion of leaping up from behind and trying to lock her arms around his neck, but the submarine crashed first.

Rydoth had been prepared, and he braced himself against the controls, but the force flung Mahliki forward, ramming her into the base of the control panel. The most painful scrapes she had ever heard echoed through the submarine. She lay on her back, looking up at the major. His face was screwed up in a rictus of emotion that she had trouble reading. She would have expected triumph—wasn't this what he had wanted?—but regret, pain, and chagrin seemed closer to the reality.

If he felt bad about it, maybe he shouldn't have crashed it... Bastard. He had served with Father, hadn't he? Mahliki thought he had been chosen because of trust. Father so rarely read people wrong. How had he done so with this engineer?

Something to muse about later. If it was possible, Mahliki needed to get the *Explorer* off the rocks and back over to help the others. If they didn't stop the plant now, before it recovered from the shock of the batteries, everything they had fought through would have been for naught.

But launching an attack from her back wouldn't work well. And catching him by surprise would be difficult when she was lying at his feet, her head not three inches from his boot. Maybe if she bit him in the ankle...

Though she hadn't moved yet, Rydoth chose that moment to look down. He saw her eyeing his leg. That pistol came out faster than Mahliki could blink, and certainly faster than she could snap her teeth down on tender flesh. He aimed it at her eyes.

She tried to read his eyes. Did he mean to kill her? Or hadn't that been part of the plan?

"Has the hull been breached?" she asked. "We're going to need to swim to the top if water starts leaking in." She hoped saying *we* would deter him from the idea of locking her in the cabin or something of that nature. That would be a death sentence. Worse, she couldn't do anything to wrestle the sub back from him from there. Not that she had come up with a plan to do so anyway. Think, Mahliki. What wouldn't he be expecting?

"Not yet," the major said. "But I need you out of the way until—"

Something banged against the viewport. From the deck, Mahliki couldn't see what, but she assumed it was one of the men. She let her head loll back, seeking inspiration from the underside of the control panel. Or from Akahe. Or some dead Turgonian ancestor. She would happily take it from anywhere.

A memory from her childhood flashed in her mind, of playing with giant stuffed insects with her brother and sister while sitting at Father's feet. They had been passing time during one of the long voyages. To where, Mahliki couldn't remember, but she suspected that was the last time she had rolled around on the deck and experienced the submarine from this viewpoint. Agarik had gotten in trouble, she recalled, because he had found a panel down there and poked into it, then turned a little wheel. The end of a hose had fallen off a coil and sprayed water that had drenched Father's trouser leg. Mother had pointed out that perhaps four-year-old children shouldn't be allowed to play in the navigation area. Mahliki had nodded sagely at this and smiled happily as Agarik and Koanani were led into the back. As a much more mature six-year-old, she had been allowed to stay up front and help Father navigate.

While the major was distracted by the viewport thumping, Mahliki slid her hand up the bulkhead, searching by feel for that panel. She found the small thumbhole. It was meant to be easy to access, and even from her awkward position, she managed to get it open. The cover almost fell out, and she had to do a quick grab to keep it from clattering to the floor. The movement drew the major's eye back downward. She didn't think he could see the opening—the control panel hid what she was doing—but she had to shift her arm up to hide the cover.

He watched her suspiciously. "What are you—"

A thump and scrapes from the top of the *Explorer* drew his attention.

"Sounds like someone's trying to get in through the hatch," Mahliki said. She didn't like the idea of being flooded with icy lake water, especially when she didn't know how deep they were, but if it thwarted the major's plans, she would root for it.

"I disconnected the outside access override," Rydoth said.

When had he had time to do *that*?

"Been planning this for a while, have you?" Mahliki had only meant to distract him, but her voice came out bitter and accusing. That brought his attention back to her.

"Waffling is more like it." His lips twisted, some of that regret touching his eyes again, but his grip tightened on the pistol. He jerked the barrel. "Get up. You can wait in the back."

Mahliki had inched her hand into the access panel and was trying to uncoil the hose without making any noise. She didn't need a lot, just enough to point at his face for a couple of seconds. If she couldn't jump up and overpower him in that time, she wouldn't deem herself fit to carry her father's name.

"Wait for what?" she asked, needing a few more seconds.

"The hull hasn't been breached. I need a few moments to make sure the sub is inoperable."

"*Why?*" There, that ought to be enough hose. Now if she could just turn on the faucet and point her weapon all with one hand... "Why would you sabotage the mission? We might be the only hope to save the city."

"Destroy the submarine, that was the deal. And the city... there are others who can kill the plant."

Ugh, he was working with those cursed priests. "As effectively as we can from down here?" she asked. "Do those zealots even know the roots are the vulnerable part? They haven't studied it as closely as I have. They're not even *good* practitioners. That display outside of the warehouse was pathetic. You may have condemned the whole city, and for what?"

The certainty on his face faltered. Good. "My son's life," he said quietly.

"They have him? And they're bargaining with him? Do you even know if he's still alive?"

The major chewed on his lip for a moment before his expression hardened. "We're done talking. If you stay out of trouble, maybe you'll live to help those priests figure out how to save the city. Now get up."

"Fine."

Mahliki shifted onto her side, ostensibly to climb to her feet, but she used her body to block her hands, just for a second, long enough to finish. Holding the hose, she cranked on the water and pointed it at his face. It splashed him solidly in... the neck.

His finger twitched on the trigger. She had anticipated he might shoot reflexively and tried to dodge to the side as her water stream attacked him, but she wasn't fast enough. The bullet burned into her arm, and a scream of agony escaped her lips of its own accord. She dropped the hose, but managed to keep her wits. *He* hadn't dropped the pistol.

Bracing herself against the bulkhead, Mahliki lifted a leg and kicked him in the stomach, thrusting with all the strength the wall could lend her. He folded in half. She kicked out again, this time targeting his hand. The pistol flew into the air, clunking onto the far side of the navigation panel. She wanted to kick the major a few more times and knock him to the deck, but her arm was screaming with pain. All she could manage was to sprint past him, ramming her shoulder into his on the way by. She doubted her blows would down a trained soldier, however gray-haired he might be, but all she needed was to reach the pistol first.

A flashing gauge nearly distracted her. The power to the hull had gone out during the crash. That meant the running lamp was off. It also meant the energy going to the socket Father needed to power his final device was off, curse the stupid engineer.

Mahliki reached for the pistol at the same second as the major grabbed her by the collar. He tried to yank her away before she could grab the weapon, but she snatched it off the control panel first. She spun into him, pulled back the hammer to chamber another round, and fired. If she had been in less pain, she might have taken a less abrupt action, but blood was saturating the sleeve of her shirt, and she wasn't in any condition to play fisticuffs.

He pitched forward again, grabbing his stomach. Later, Mahliki might muster sympathy for him, but not now. She pushed him out of the navigation chamber. When he stumbled, trying to fall to his knees, she grabbed *him* by the collar, and hoisted him up. He was heavy, and she had to use two hands—her bloodied arm cried out in protest—but she didn't stop until she had manhandled him into the cabin. Unfortunately, the lock was on the *inside* of the hatch, but it took a wheel spinning to open it, so she found a spare piece of piping and jammed it through the wheel. That ought to keep him from getting out, at least for the moment.

Mahliki debating between running to navigation to try and signal a message to her father and running to engineering to get the exterior power flowing again. She hadn't seen him outside the viewport when she had been grabbing the pistol. Engineering it was. The device had to be the priority anyway. If the *Explorer* was destroyed but the city was saved... She would miss the craft, source of so many childhood memories, but she had to consider that a fair trade off.

CHAPTER 31

T HOUGH THE LORRY BUMPED ALONG at a rapid clip, taking corners with enough force to tilt the passengers into each other's laps, Sicarius stood on his feet near the back of the bed, his arms folded across his chest. He glared at the two rows of prisoners lining the benches as the vehicle drew closer to the city. Amaranthe had offered to ride in the back with him, but he was taking his assigned guard duty seriously and did not wish any distractions. Four soldiers were also stationed in the back, but they deferred to him.

The lorry came to a stop earlier than expected, and Sicarius peeked past the back flap. He had assumed they were going to the alternate headquarters that had been set up for the president, where they could drop off the prisoners and check on Starcrest's progress at the lake, but ramshackle tenements lined the street, the tottering brick buildings leaning against each other for support. Many had broken windows and graffiti painted on the walls. The air smelled of wood smoke, rotten food, and feces dumped outside in the alleys rather than channeled into sewers.

"Sicarius," Colonel Starcrest said from the street. "Sergeant Matic is coming in to relieve you. Come outside, please."

"Yes, sir," Sicarius said, though he didn't move until his replacement entered and he had briefed the man, letting him know which prisoners had attempted to escape or were whispering suspiciously to each other.

Once outside, he noticed the street name on an old copper sign hanging from a single nail. Windy Lane.

Amaranthe was waiting next to the lorry with the colonel.

"We detoured to pick up the child," Sicarius stated, then glanced at the back of the truck to indicate the prisoners and in the direction of the lake to indicate President Starcrest who must be in need of a cure by now. "You made this a priority."

"Was that a question?" the colonel asked Amaranthe. "It's hard to tell with him."

"That's because his questions sound like statements. I assure you, he's puzzled."

"I sent a scout up on a roof," the colonel said. "The submarine hasn't come up yet." A muscle ticked in his jaw.

Amaranthe gripped Sicarius's arm. "It won't take long. That girl has to be terrified and wondering when her mother is coming."

Sicarius took no comfort from Amaranthe's touch, not this time. He admitted that a lone child would be helpless and scared in this neighborhood, but he did not want to see this girl and explain how her mother had come to die. By his hand. He did not want to explain his feelings in front of the colonel, but he gazed into Amaranthe's eyes, willing her to understand. She would be the best choice to go in and find the child. Not him.

She smiled and took his hand. "Three-seventeen Dee-Four, isn't it?"

"Yes," Sicarius said stonily.

"Make it quick," the colonel said. "Lady Starcrest is eager to find her husband."

Sicarius followed Amaranthe to the front door of the building, which was an awkward two feet above ground level. If wooden steps had once led up to it, they were gone now. He usually led the way, but Amaranthe seemed content to go first here. He kept all of his senses alert. Though he did not expect trouble, not with the military vehicle parked out front and his knife collection on display, he would not allow his reluctance to find the child to put Amaranthe in danger. She had experienced enough danger already that night, thanks to Deret Mancrest. Admittedly, the man's associations had allowed them to find the treacherous vice president, but Sicarius would not credit Mancrest with anything other than accidental competence.

The wooden floorboards of the front hall creaked like rocking chairs and were scattered with rat droppings, some smashed by passing feet. A pile of human feces sat near the wall, the accompanying smell making Amaranthe crinkle her nose. Sicarius could not imagine allowing his child to dwell in such a degenerate environment. An assassin of any skill ought to be able to earn enough to pay for a more suitable home, however temporary.

Oh? And would you find it easy to find employment in Nuria? It was Amaranthe's voice, sounding in the back of his mind. Sicarius wasn't sure when that had started happening, but recognized it as something that came up during questions of morality. No, he would not have found it easy to find employment in Nuria, no matter how great his skills, and he would like to think he would never have been in the position to take a child with him to another nation, but what if Sespian had been born to some street doxy instead of to the princess? Sicarius did not know what he would have done.

Amaranthe stopped before the door. "This is the address. I assume the girl will have orders not to open the door to strangers." She sniffed and eyed the hallway. "Or anyone."

"You wish me to pick the lock?" Sicarius checked to see if the door *was* locked. It was. "Or go around to the window?"

"The colonel put a man on the window. He thought the child might flee when she saw... someone who wasn't her mother walk in."

Sicarius doubted that was exactly what the colonel had said, but didn't comment. He took out his lock picks.

"You are fairly intimidating when you're running around shirtless." Amaranthe smiled, clearly trying to lighten the mood.

Sicarius did not believe himself influenced by such tactics, but he appreciated that she cared enough to try. He slid a torsion wrench and pick into the lock and attempted to manipulate the pins without making noise. Morning had come during their time in the crypt, and the girl would doubtlessly be awake by now.

When he finished, he stepped back and inclined his head toward the door. It was not, he resolved, cowardly for him to defer to Amaranthe in his matter. Her face would be less likely to alarm a child.

A thought came to his mind, and he caught her by the wrist before she could open the door. "Though I deem it unlikely, it may be a trap."

Amaranthe tilted her face toward him. "Oh?"

"The assassin may have yet hoped to slay me and, in her dying breaths, given me the address of a flat she had booby-trapped."

"Why do I get the impression you would prefer that to be the case?"

Because it was... easier to deal with a trap than a child.

Sicarius released her wrist. "I am merely voicing possibilities."

"Mmhmm. You may go in first and check for trip wires, alarm systems, and booby traps if you wish."

Though he sensed she was teasing him, Sicarius listened at the door, then, when he heard nothing, eased it open. Sunlight filtered through a grimy, cracked window. A small bed, a chamber pot, and a backpack sitting on the floor were the room's only furnishings. The single blanket on the bed lay in a rumpled pile spilling onto the floor. Nobody was in sight.

Sicarius spent a thorough minute checking the entryway for traps, though he had already detected the soft inhalations of someone breathing. They were quick, fast inhalations and came from under the bed.

For a time, Amaranthe leaned against the hallway wall, but eventually she said, "The others are waiting for us."

Reminded that Starcrest was in danger, Sicarius steeled himself and strode into the room. He lifted the edge of the bed with one hand. A squeal came from underneath, and a small figure darted out. Sicarius caught the girl before she had fled two feet, holding her off the ground so she couldn't make trouble. This didn't keep her from flailing and trying to punch, bite, and claw Sicarius. Her black ponytail whipped back and forth, and her teeth gnashed at the air. He calmly held her out toward the door.

Amaranthe strode inside and gave the girl a dry smile. "Hello, my name is Amaranthe. I work for the president of Turgonia. What's your name?"

The girl thrashed and flailed. Sicarius was tempted to let her down, as he had no true reason to keep her restrained against her wishes, but if she fled, it would only be into that neighborhood, and she couldn't find a decent life there.

"Not ready to share, eh?" Amaranthe asked. "I don't blame you. Having your mothers' enemies stalk into your apartment in the morning must be alarming. You probably don't speak Turgonian, either, do you?"

As soon as she asked the question, Sicarius took it as a given, though it hadn't occurred to him. He could have spoken in Nurian, but doubted anything he said would soothe the child.

"Let's take her outside to talk to Tikaya," Amaranthe said.

The girl started screaming as soon as they stepped out of the room. Trying not to feel like a kidnapper, Sicarius walked down the hall. None of the doors opened. Sicarius knew from the sounds and smells of cooking that people were home, but those who lived in this area had learned to look the other way at screams.

Perhaps having anticipated her skills being needed, Tikaya was waiting outside the front door. She frowned at Sicarius, or maybe the way he had the girl pinned to his chest. What else was he supposed to do with her? He had no wish to be pummeled by seven-year-old fists.

"I'll take her." Tikaya held out her arms.

Sicarius was relieved to hand off the squirming burden, but at the same time felt a sense of guilt at foisting this... problem onto someone else. Odd, he had not experienced guilt often in his life. He had rarely cared what became of the families of those he was assigned to kill. It was part of the job and the job was not to be questioned. Or perhaps he had always known that in questioning it... he must question everything. Including himself. And to question himself would be to hesitate at a key moment, to invite death because of that hesitation.

With Tikaya speaking in Nurian, the child quieted down, though nothing in her wide eyes bespoke acceptance. She started shaking her head and crying out, "No, no," in her own tongue. This denial continued on, though at one point, tears wept down the girl's cheeks. The first sign of acceptance.

It seemed a strange moment for realizations, with Tikaya and Amaranthe kneeling on a grimy cobblestone street, trying to explain things to this foreign child, but one came then, nonetheless. At some point this past winter, or maybe at that very moment, he had become someone who questioned.

Sespian cut and sawed into the access panel Starcrest had opened, having no idea if he was doing any good. The hull of the sturdy craft wasn't any easier to pierce than the flesh of that plant, and if he hadn't had one of the black daggers, he doubted he would have attempted this, but he had to try.

A gun fired inside the submarine, the bang unmistakable, even underwater.

The engineer. He'd turned on them. That had to be it. Sespian didn't stop hacking and cutting, but he glanced toward the nose of the craft where he had last seen Starcrest, pounding to get the attention of those inside, or maybe just pounding in frustration.

He was nowhere to be seen. Maldynado had disappeared as well. No, there he was. Dragging the cable and Starcrest's device over to the submarine to hook it up. A good thought. Sespian was too frustrated with his inability to get inside to have thought of it himself. And no one would tear him away now, not until he had figured out a way in. Mahliki needed his help.

Sespian gave up on the switches within the panel. They weren't working, and he had cut them into unrecognizable metal shreds anyway. He grabbed the top of the hatch and leaned in as close as his helmet would let him, squinting at the seal around it. Maybe he could break *that*.

He did his best to jab the black dagger into the crease. It slipped in a fraction of an inch. He wriggled it back and forth. A normal knife would have snapped off at the tang. This one didn't... but he didn't have much luck on the seal, either. He switched from prying to sawing, trying to cut it off like the lid of a sardine can.

Something bumped his calf. Thinking it one of the plants, Sespian whirled, the blade raised.

It wasn't a plant, but another man in a diving suit. In the dim lighting, he couldn't identify who at first, but from the way the figure threw his arms up in exaggerated surrender, he took it for Maldynado.

Maldynado pointed at the ground, where he had left the device, and held something up in his hand. The end of the cable. He shrugged his shoulders.

Oh, he was trying to figure out where to plug it in. Sespian used Basilard's hand code to respond, though he didn't know how much Maldynado would make out in the poor lighting.

The socket is underneath the rudder, but if the running lamp is out, I don't think there will be power running through that point, either. Sespian grimaced. He hadn't known all of the Mangdorian signs for those words—there probably weren't any signs for some of them—and feared he had looked like a drunken mime relaying his thoughts.

Maldynado stared at him for a moment, then pointed at the rudder.

Sespian nodded. If he had managed to convey that much at least, it was a start. Another gunshot went off inside the submarine.

His heart filling his throat, Sespian forgot Maldynado and went back to his original task. He had to get in. If they were still shooting at each other, there was hope they were both still alive. Especially Mahliki.

Sweat dripped down the side of his forehead and beaded in his eyebrows as he sawed. More than once, he tried to wipe the moisture away, knocking his hand against the faceplate. His heavy breathing, or maybe he could blame the sweat, was making the inside fog up too.

"Stupid helmet," he muttered illogically. Yes, he needed it to breathe, but he wanted to rip it and the gloves off so he could more effectively see and feel.

Abruptly, the light level rose. Sespian knelt back for a moment, wondering if Maldynado had done something with the device. But it was the running lamp that was glowing, not anything on the lake floor.

"She fixed it," Sespian said. "That means she's alive."

And if she was alive, then maybe he didn't need to saw his way into the submarine. Maybe she had taken care of the engineer by herself.

Bubbles drifted past his faceplate. Sespian frowned down, afraid he might have stabbed his sleeve, and his suit was letting out air. But the bubbles were dribbling up from the seal around the hatch. He had succeeded in breaking it.

"Blasted slag heaps," he groaned. Had he just poked a hole in the craft for no reason? One that would let in water and threaten the very woman he had wanted to save? "Brilliant, Sespian. Brilliant."

He jabbed the dagger into his belt and pushed away from the hatch. He needed to find Starcrest and explain what he had done. And he needed to see if Mahliki had indeed saved herself.

Before he could head for the nose where he had last seen Starcrest, he spotted Maldynado tipped sideways in the water, his body unmoving. The device that had been an unremarkable copper box a few moments before blazed with white light so bright Sespian had to shield his eyes. Some sort of legs or prongs had descended from it, sinking it into the ground. Into the roots? He turned in a full circle, trying to decide if it had affected the stalks in the distance. With the foggy faceplate, everything out there was a blur.

As much as he wanted to find Starcrest and help Mahliki, someone needed to check on Maldynado. If he had managed to electrocute himself, Sespian would blame himself. He should have been helping, prioritizing the mission to save the city, instead of hacking away at the hatch.

As he dropped down from the submarine, he almost crashed into Starcrest, who was coming along the bottom, also heading for Maldynado. He was supporting himself by feeling his way along the hull. His face was pale and bleak behind a faceplate almost as fogged as Sespian's.

"I think Mahliki made it," Sespian yelled, not knowing if he had figured that out. Starcrest would have heard the gunshots too. Maybe he had assumed the worst.

Whether he heard or not, Sespian didn't know, but Starcrest pointed toward Maldynado. When he tried to move away from the craft, his boot snagged on a rock, and he pitched forward. Sespian caught him, new fear rising in his chest as he wondered if both men would fall unconscious, leaving him to figure out a way to bring them to the surface. Or choose which one to bring.

"Long dead ancestors, not that."

Sespian looped Starcrest's arm around his shoulders and they staggered over to Maldynado. He had yet to move.

Blinded by the light, Sespian felt his way toward the adrift diving suit, leading Starcrest every step. As they neared the device, Starcrest pulled away. Sespian let him, needing his hands to check on Maldynado. His eyes were closed, his face slack, his hair... it was hard to tell inside the helmet, but the tufts around his faceplate seemed to be sticking out in odd directions. How could one know if a man breathed or not when he was encased in these suits?

Sespian tried the obvious. He shook Maldynado.

His eyes flew open so wide the whites were visible around his brown irises. He jerked away from Sespian, then flailed a bit, as if he couldn't remember where he was. Or maybe even who he was.

"Maldynado," Sespian called, "are you all right? I think you were zapped with electricity." He tried signing the words as he spoke them, too, though again, he wasn't sure of all the gestures. How often did Mangdorian hunters need to say zapped and electricity?

Maldynado gathered himself, finding the lake bottom with his boots. That seemed to steady him. He touched his helmet and grimaced, as if he were trying to convey that he had a hangover. He probably did.

Sespian pointed upward. "Can you make it to the top?"

A hand latched onto Sespian's shoulder so hard it was painful.

Starcrest. He pointed at the top of the submarine. The hatch had opened. Sespian stared. Water had to be not just leaking but pouring in now.

A figure swam out—Mahliki. And she had the engineer with her, dragging him by his collar. He was curled into a ball and didn't resist. It might have been Sespian's fogged faceplate, but he thought he read pain on Mahliki's face. A *lot* of pain.

Starcrest pushed off, waving for them to follow, and tore the weights off his belt. He paddled so he angled toward his daughter, but Mahliki was wasting no time in arrowing to the top. Without a helmet, she probably couldn't see and had no idea where anyone was. She would have only known the submarine was leaking and she had to escape before the air disappeared. She would also be defenseless up there against the plants.

Thinking of that enzyme that could burn through clothing—and flesh—Sespian pushed off the bottom and swam after Starcrest at top speed. He shucked the diving suit's weights, but he wasn't fast enough to catch Mahliki or even her father. Poisoned or not, he was rising quickly.

Sespian reached the surface, almost coming up between Mahliki's legs. An idiotic thought flashed through his mind, that Starcrest might revoke his willingness to allow courting if he saw *that*. Sespian veered aside at the last moment, popping up a couple of feet to the side of her. Starcrest had already reached the surface and had a supportive grip under Mahliki's armpit. She sucked in deep breaths. The water streaming down Sespian's faceplate didn't keep him from determining that he had been right—her mouth was twisted in a grimace of pain. She hadn't let go of the engineer though. Even as her father held her, she kept the major's face out of the water.

"Good," Starcrest said. "Sespian. We need your help."

Sespian reached for Mahliki, thinking to grab her other armpit so they could swim her to shore, or at least try. The plants were blocking the view in every direction, although... maybe it was his imagination, but they appeared a tad wilted. Dare he hope the device had worked? It hadn't been deployed in the location Starcrest had originally chosen.

"Grab our wayward engineer," Starcrest said. "He's barely conscious."

Erg, Sespian wanted to help *Mahliki*, not the treacherous engineer. He grabbed the man from behind, though, and tipped him onto his back so he would be able to breathe. The major cried out right beside Sespian's ear—the helmet did little to muffle the scream.

"What happened?" Sespian asked.

"I shot him," Mahliki said, then, like a teenager justifying beating up a sibling, added, "He shot me first."

Maldynado popped out of the water with a splash and a grunt. He thrust the metal wand of the electricity generator into the air like an athlete holding aloft a trophy. "Made it! And also... for anyone wondering... this slagging generator is heavier than a box of bricks. Was wondering... why I didn't need... any weights to stay down there." He spun around with the weapon, as if he expected savage vines to beat down on them at any moment.

They were in the clearing above the battery ring, though, and nothing leaped out at them.

"Which way to shore?" Sespian asked.

"This way." Starcrest paddled toward a forest of stalks that didn't look much different than the stalks in the other directions.

Sespian followed him without question. The engineer was alternating gasping and whimpering. He would need medical attention soon.

"You two will need to keep the plants off us and cut a path through to the shore," Starcrest said.

Maldynado waved the metal fork in acknowledgment, though he looked to be having a hard time keeping afloat with the generator on his back. Sespian thought about telling him to tear off his air tank, but no... the air inside ought to be helping counteract the weight. Unless Maldynado had used most of it already. As a bigger man, he might consume oxygen more quickly than Sespian. Besides, Sespian had his own problem. How was he supposed to fight off a plant while dragging the engineer behind him? Nonetheless, he waved the dagger in acknowledgment of Starcrest's order. He would have to use his legs for propulsion.

"It didn't work, did it?" Maldynado asked. "The plants are still everywhere."

"We'll assess the situation when we reach the shore," Starcrest said.

Maldynado's expression was bleak when he met Sespian's eyes. Sespian also worried they had failed, or at least not done enough.

With everyone injured or exhausted, not to mention demoralized, the team swam after Starcrest without much discussion. Mahliki paddled along with one arm and had no trouble kicking. Sespian hoped that meant her injury wasn't life threatening. At times, it appeared she was supporting Starcrest as much as he was supporting her. Maybe she was.

Despite his burden, Maldynado swam ahead when they reached the barrier of tree-like stalks. He jabbed one with the fork. Before he turned on the power, it fell over like a limp noodle.

"Uhm?" he asked.

Starcrest pushed on another stalk. This one didn't fall limp, but it did tilt, and he was able to push his way past it. No vines stretched down to menace him or the rest of the team.

"I think they're dead," Mahliki panted. "Maybe your... root-frying gizmo worked... Father."

"Root-frying gizmo?" How a man dying of a poison managed the effort to sound indignant, Sespian didn't know, but Starcrest did.

"Last I heard... you hadn't named it yet," Mahliki said. "I'm simply offering... a suggestion."

Maldynado pushed aside more stalks, clearing the way for the others. Sespian tried to help, but keeping the engineer's head out of the water so he wouldn't drown was a demanding assignment all by itself. Though not vigorous, the lake waves did exist, and they lapped at the man's face, occasionally splashing over his mouth. If Major Rydoth had shot Mahliki, Sespian wondered if he was simply saving him for a court-martial and hanging later.

Wearying hours seemed to pass as they pushed through the thick stalks. The plants didn't fight back, and Sespian began to believe that Mahliki was right and they were dead, but their presence wasn't easy to get around. If they didn't decompose like the ones that had been directly treated with electricity, someone would have a very big job in cleaning up the harbor. Despite his exhaustion, that thought tickled Sespian enough that he had to comment.

"Maldynado, I think I know what job you can ask the president for next."

"What?" Maldynado asked, his tone wary.

"Aquatic weed control."

"*I'm* not cleaning up this mess."

"It can't be any more unglamorous than being called Shovel Head on a construction site all day."

"You heard that?" Maldynado groaned.

"I think *everyone* heard that foreman."

"I hope he got eaten by the plant."

"I doubt a plant would find anyone that crotchety pleasant eating," Sespian said.

The idle chatter distracted him, and he was surprised when he kicked something with his boot. The ground, he realized. They had finally reached land. He had expected to come ashore near the docks—or where the docks had once *been*—but Starcrest had brought them to a beach.

Sespian dragged the engineer out of the water and laid him on his back. Dead, wilted plant matter caked the beach like overzealous seaweed brought in by an ocean tide, and he couldn't tell whether sand or pebbles lay beneath it, but he didn't care. He flopped down in exhaustion and fiddled with his helmet. He had wanted to remove it as soon as they popped up to the surface, but it took some flexibility—or the help of a comrade—to unfasten the bindings in the back.

A heavy clunk sounded as Maldynado heaved the generator and the tank off his shoulders. "That was as hard as a Sicarius workout, maybe even harder. I want to sleep until next week. Maybe next month."

"Me too." Sespian hoisted off the helmet, then pushed himself to his knees to check on the others. Starcrest and Mahliki had made it to the beach but both had collapsed as soon as they climbed out of the water.

After hesitating over who to check on first—they both lay on their backs, faces to the sky—Sespian went to Mahliki. Starcrest might be in worse condition, but Sespian knew how to *help* someone who had been shot. Poison... he could only hope he and Maldynado could find someone who would know how to cure him. If anyone remained in the city at that point. He had no idea how long they had been underwater or what time it was now.

Sespian had no more than touched Mahliki's arm to ask how she was doing when the weird squish-crunch of dead plants being stepped on made him lift his head. He expected Maldynado, but a squad of black-uniformed soldiers was picking their way down the beach. Sespian nearly flopped over in relief, for he recognized the man leading the troops. Judging by the way his black hair stuck out in unbrushed clumps and his bloodshot eye scanned the beach, Colonel Dak Starcrest had been up all night too. He stalked straight up to the unmoving Rias Starcrest and stared down at him through the faceplate.

"This isn't the agreed upon rendezvous point."

A few silent seconds passed, the wind scraping down the beach and rustling the drying plant matter, before he got a response—Sespian had started to wonder if there *would* be a response.

"I apologize for my miscalculation," Starcrest said. "I'm not at my best. Health issues, you understand."

The banter relieved Sespian. If Starcrest could speak—and joke—he wasn't so far gone after all.

"If you want to haul your presidential carcass off the beach, we might have someone who can cure you of that," Dak said.

"Sir," a sergeant whispered from behind him. "Should you... Won't you get in trouble for talking to the president like that?"

"Dear ancestors, I hope so. I've been wanting to be fired all winter." Dak reached down to help his uncle sit up and remove the helmet. "Mahliki, are you injured?"

"Someone shot me because he wanted to destroy Father's sub." She glowered over at the unconscious engineer.

"It's a real reward being related to the president, isn't it?" Dak pointed at one of the soldiers. "Janik, you brought your medical kit, right?"

"Yes, sir."

"Well stop gaping at the pretty girl and put it to use."

"Yes, sir!"

Mahliki snorted. "Can't imagine I look pretty with blood leaking out of my shoulder and my hair plastered all over my face."

Sespian took her hand. He thought about denying her claim and complimenting her beauty but suspected that she might appreciate a chuckle more than praise of something as meaningless as physical traits. "I think he was talking about Maldynado," Sespian said.

"What?" Maldynado had managed to remove his own helmet by this point, and he shook out his headful of wavy brown curls. "I'm not a girl."

"But you don't deny being the pretty one here?" Sespian asked.

"Of course not. But in a manly way."

The silly conversation did draw a smile from Mahliki. Good. Her face was pale, and Sespian worried about whether she had lost a lot of blood. He kept holding her hand while the medic knelt on the other side of her. Meanwhile, Dak and two more soldiers helped Starcrest up the beach. Sespian hoped they had a lorry parked up there, so Starcrest wouldn't have to walk far. He also hoped Dak's claim to having someone who could cure the poison was true and hadn't simply been a comment designed to make his uncle feel better.

After cutting open part of Mahliki's shirt and examining the wound, the medic said, "The bullet is lodged in your shoulder."

"No kidding," she said, then switched to Kyattese for a short soliloquy addressed toward the sky. Judging by her tone and the handful of Kyattese words Sespian knew, it wasn't a compliment on the medic's skills.

"Now, now," Sespian murmured. "Being sarcastic toward the man poking in your shoulder isn't a good idea."

Mahliki's face crinkled up in an expression he couldn't read. "You should probably distract me then."

"Ah, yes, forgive me for not coming to that conclusion on my own. Would you like me to tell you a story? Or a joke? Or discuss my plans for adding a plant-proof layer of shielding to your father's new building?"

Sespian thought he was being rather charming, especially considering he was wearing a big uncomfortable suit coated in congealing plant grime, but Mahliki's face crinkled up further, and he had the sense that he had disappointed her.

"Emperor's warts, boy," Maldynado said, "kiss the girl already."

Sespian blushed at this interruption—shouldn't Maldynado have trudged up the beach after the others?—but something about Mahliki's raised eyebrows made him wonder if that wasn't exactly what she had been hoping for.

"Here? *Now?*" Sespian waved at the desecrated beach and his own suit and appearance. He couldn't even imagine how bedraggled he must appear after the night they'd had. What kind of reward was that for a woman? And she was injured. Surely she wouldn't appreciate such a gesture from even the tidiest and most handsome suitor right now.

"Unbelievable." Maldynado stood up and started dragging the generator and his equipment up the beach. "Not only am I the prettiest one here, but I may be the *smartest* one here as well."

"Maybe the smartest male," Mahliki murmured.

The medic lifted his brows and met Sespian's eyes. "Normally I'd take that as an insult, but I think you're the one in trouble here."

"I think so too."

Sespian looked down at Mahliki, but she wasn't looking at him any more. He had missed his opportunity. It would be stilted and awkward if he tried to kiss her now, especially with the medic right there. He would find another opportunity, he vowed, a more *appropriate* one. And she wouldn't be disappointed. Definitely not.

As the medic finished bandaging Mahliki's shoulder and helped her to her feet, Sespian wondered if it was too early to panic and hyperventilate over his vow.

"Sespian?" came Maldynado's voice from the top of the beach. Something about his tone made Sespian forget about kissing and his own stupidity. "You... might want to come up here now."

Sicarius was at the top of the beach as well. He stood off to the side of the path, his leg propped on a rock, as if he had been there for a while. Watching Sespian to make sure he was all right? Waiting and not wanting to interrupt Sespian's moment with Mahliki? Whatever he had been doing, Sespian was glad that he hadn't kissed Mahliki after all. He doubted Sicarius would judge him or say anything about it, but there was something intrinsically awkward about having one's assassin father watching for a first kiss. Er, second kiss. But Sespian had been so surprised at the other one that he hadn't responded, so it hardly counted.

Sespian gave Sicarius a wave to let him know he was fine, then headed toward Maldynado, who was chewing on his lip thoughtfully. When Sespian reached the top, he spotted a black military lorry that was covered with dust and had a couple of broken branches sticking out of the nooks. Tikaya was embracing her husband near the front. Amaranthe was standing next to Colonel Starcrest and holding the hand of a little girl who was leaning against her. She had a dusty, tear-streaked face and the almond eyes and black hair of a Nurian.

"So..." Maldynado tried to stick his hands in his pockets only to realize he was still wearing the diving suit and didn't have any pockets. "You remember that arrow with the note?"

"How could I forget it?"

"Well, it seems... *that's* your favor." Maldynado pointed at the girl.

"I... what?"

"There wasn't really time to explain it earlier. Besides I thought it should be his job to—er, that he could explain it better." Maldynado pointed his chin at Sicarius.

Sicarius was also grimy and dusty, with a rare day's worth of beard stubble adorning his chin. "Come." Sicarius put a hand on Sespian's shoulder. "We must take President Starcrest to a suitable facility for his care. I will... explain along the way."

Sespian rubbed his eyes. They were gritty from lack of sleep, but when he happened to meet the haunted eyes of the girl, he had a feeling he had nothing to complain about.

EPILOGUE

TIKAYA STROLLED INTO THE BANQUET hall in sandals and a comfortable dress that wafted around her ankles, relieved that the Turgonian spring had finally grown warm enough that she could forego the itchy wool leggings that she had worn since arriving. She was also relieved that the decor for this dinner party was more sedate than she had expected. Oh, the purple and pink ribbons and bows twirling up the columns were questionable, the sparkly waist-high candles were garish, the drummers setting up in the corner were cause for concern, and the less said about that kissing-elephants ice sculpture on the table the better. But given that Maldynado had planned the gala, Tikaya thought the room could have come out much worse.

That would have been a shame, given the architectural elegance of the hall, its clean and simple lines managing to convey light, airiness, and a sense of freedom. Sespian had done well. The wings of the new presidential residence were still under construction, but the building's core had been completed a week earlier, at which time Rias and Tikaya had moved in, along with more staff than she could name. They had hosted a couple of dinner events in the hall already, most for diplomats and city leaders who had to be schmoozed—among other things, there had been a petition to have the capital moved in the aftermath of the plant's devastation. Tonight's party was "a small gathering for a few friends, no business to be discussed, thank you very much." While Tikaya might have preferred a family dinner in their rooms, this ought to be pleasant enough, with no need to worry about warrior-caste snobs and self-important such-and-suchs judging the president's plain foreigner of a wife.

Rias had been waylaid in the hall by a couple of Dak's officers, so Tikaya decided to wait for him before hunting for her name card on the dinner table. She walked over to Basilard and his translator, who had stopped to puzzle over the elephant ice carving. What exactly those trunks were supposed to be insinuating, Tikaya didn't want to think about. She caught a blush on the woman's cheeks. Basilard shook his head, more rueful than embarrassed. He gave Maldynado, who was gesturing expansively as he delivered instructions to the musicians, a long look over his shoulder.

"Good evening, Basilard and Elwa," Tikaya said. The last time she had seen him, he had been covered with soot and grime after helping out at the fire. Now he wore clean Mangdorian buckskins with colorfully dyed fringes that brought to mind spring colors. His head was freshly shaven, though he had started growing a tidy goatee. His assistant wore a yellow-dyed buckskin dress with floral beadwork that must represent many hours of a craftsman's time. Her red hair fell about her shoulders, rather than being back in her usual braid.

My lady, Basilard signed. *Good evening.*

"I understand you've finally had a chance to address your country's concerns with Rias," Tikaya said. "I'm sorry it was so long in coming."

My grandfather used to say you cannot rush the buck hunt, when it is into his homeland you have traveled.

"Especially when his homeland has been taken over by a giant plant."

Indeed so, my lady. Basilard shifted to stand in front of the elephant carving. Blocking it from Tikaya's view? Or Elwa's? It wasn't *that* bad... Though perhaps Tikaya had not yet deciphered all of the innuendo. *Has your husband recovered from his poisoning? And your daughter from her... injury?*

From being shot, he meant. At the time, Tikaya had wanted to strangle Mahliki *and* Rias for risking their lives so out there, but these last weeks had been more peaceful, and she had relaxed a little. "Yes, they're both doing well, thank you. Amazing since they're both horrible patients. Stay in bed and rest? Impossible. Mahliki has been down in her new laboratory since dawn, utterly oblivious to the passage of time."

Basilard smiled. *I have already heard a few explosions coming out of that laboratory. It's two floors below our rooms. Directly below.*

"Ah, we may have to find her something in a more industrial part of town. Visiting diplomats probably shouldn't be woken in the middle of the night by detonations." Tikaya shook her head, wondering what Mahliki was working on now. She was certain that the biologists back home didn't blow things up on a regular basis. The chemists, yes, but that was to be expected.

I've been woken up by worse events, Basilard signed.

"Will you be needing my services tonight, Leyelchek?" the translator asked. Leyelchek? Was that Basilard's Mangdorian name? Tikaya hadn't heard it before. "It seems all of your friends can understand your hand signs already."

No, no, Basilard rushed to sign. *Maldynado invited you as well, not simply myself. He wanted you to enjoy yourself and have a good time.* He smiled, but it soon faltered. *Unless... you do not wish to be here. You are certainly not required to stay. But I...* Basilard glanced at Maldynado and then at the table. Seeking inspiration? *I know he set a name card out for you.* He winced. Perhaps he had sought *better* inspiration.

"I don't mind staying," the woman said with a smile.

Good, Basilard signed. *Why don't we get a glass of wine?* He pointed to a pair of servers who had strolled in bearing trays of appetizers and alcoholic beverages.

Though he kept his smile slight and his face calm, his blue eyes gleamed with hope. Tikaya wondered if the young woman knew Basilard had romantic interests.

"I'd love to," Elwa said. "My lady, will you join us?"

"I will later, thank you. I'm expecting Rias shortly." Tikaya wondered if she would ever stop feeling odd at being called my lady.

The pair headed off toward the servers. Across the hall, Maldynado waved to someone—ah, he was trying to catch Basilard's eye. He pointed at the translator and made a few gestures that Tikaya, with her superior foundation in deciphering languages, written, oral, and signed, interpreted as... *Put your arm around her waist. No? Well, at least touch the small of her back. Women like that!*

Basilard turned his back on Maldynado. Good.

"Good evening, Professor Komitopis," came Amaranthe's voice from behind. She also wore sandals and a dress—it seemed everyone was appreciating the warmer weather—one with a more contemporary cut than Tikaya's. It revealed a little more flesh, including well toned arms and calves, but not to a degree that would cause men to stop and ogle. Not that they would dare with Sicarius standing nearby. Although, for the moment, he wasn't lurking behind Amaranthe's shoulder.

"Good evening," Tikaya replied. "Sicarius was unwilling to attend Maldynado's dinner party?"

"He's here. Ready for the festivities." Amaranthe pointed toward the closest thing the well-lit hall had to a dark corner. Sicarius stood against the wall, wearing black clothing and boots and several knives. Admittedly, there were fewer knives than usual.

"Such as the weapons throwing competition?" Tikaya asked.

"Will there be one?"

"No, I was joking. I mean, I think I was. Are such events common at dinner parties in Turgonia?"

"Athletic competitions and exhibitions aren't unheard of," Amaranthe said, "and given Maldynado's motives tonight, I wouldn't be surprised if he had arranged a few ways for the males present to display their prowess."

"What *are* Maldynado's motives? All I heard was that he wanted to host a celebratory dinner for old and new friends who had battled the plant and the priests and survived."

"There's one set of motives." Amaranthe pointed at Basilard and his translator. "I don't see Sespian yet, but he and Mahliki are another. He promised he would arrange a dinner companion for Deret Mancrest if he came as well. He'll probably encourage you and President Starcrest to do some pressing of bodies, too, just to let everyone know there aren't any disturbed feelings about that extra wife. And that way, people can see that he's recovered from his poisoning. I hope he's doing well?"

"Yes." Tikaya digested the rest of the information thoughtfully. "This is about setting up couples?"

"Of course, though it's a shame I don't see Evrial—Sergeant Yara—anywhere. I had hoped she might have decided... well, Maldynado is a good man, even if he's not an entirely serious one. I think she'll regret letting him go. Opportunities for career advancement should come often to those who deserve them."

"Hm."

Amaranthe looked up at her. "What did *you* think the theme of the party would be?"

"Lobbying for a statue."

"Ah, I think he's decided to let that notion rest for a while. At least, he hasn't mentioned it in my hearing of late."

"My second guess was that he wished to show off his new hat."

Tikaya nodded toward the musicians, where Maldynado was using said hat as a prop as he gestured and explained. Limp golden vines stuck out of a green felt cap like noodles tangled around a fork.

Amaranthe snorted. "Most of us have already seen it. It's supposed to represent the plant and the role he played in defeating it. Apparently, he doesn't care that it doesn't quite match his silver and blue suit." She pointed toward the door. "There's your husband if you wish to discuss how you'll press bodies with drum beats reverberating from the columns. I better go tell Sicarius that *we* might be required to dance. Convincing him to come was already a challenge. I'm not sure how to break the rest to him."

Watching her try might be entertaining. "Perhaps I could... offer something that might soften his mood."

"Oh?" Amaranthe asked.

"A few weeks ago, while we were rather distracted, you were asking about doctors in Kyatt with certain specialties."

Amaranthe's brows rose. "Yes."

"I believe Haonii Kolitaarui could help you."

"I see. Thank you. Ah, would you be willing to write that down for me in the event that I can't remember how to pronounce the name?"

Tikaya smiled. "I would."

Rias strolled over to join her as Amaranthe walked away, a lively sway to her hips. He wore a black tunic and trousers, the garments trimmed with silver. The look was more reminiscent of a military uniform than cheerful spring attire, but he looked good in it, as always. Professional. Like a leader of men. Tikaya supposed she would have to wait five years—make that four years and eight months—before she could convince him to wear a loose floral shirt and sandals again. Too bad. The few months he had been in office had aged him further than the last ten years, deepening the lines at the corners of his mouth and his eyes. He was still recovering from the poisoning, she reminded herself. With luck, the next months would be less arduous.

"You haven't found the drinks yet, my lady?" Rias caught her hand and lifted it for a kiss.

She gave him a bemused smile at the "my lady." Some of the Turgonian mannerisms that had been worn away by the years out of his homeland had returned of late, making him seem once again the warrior-caste aristocrat rather than the simple scientist who had earned a modest living as they explored the seas together. She had decided to find it quaint and charming—until she could get him back home.

"Not yet." Tikaya kissed him on the cheek. "Are *you* going to imbibe? I thought you'd decided to swear off alcohol until your retirement." When Dak had interrogated Serpitivich, it had come out that a shared drink one evening had been the delivery mechanism for the poison. The vice president had consumed wine from the same carafe as Rias, after taking some prophylactic to ensure the substance didn't affect him.

"Perhaps... I will stick with water, but I thought you might like something stronger."

"Why? Do you think I'll require alcoholic fortitude to make it through the night?"

A few drumbeats drifted out of the musicians' corner. Maldynado danced a jig Tikaya hoped she wouldn't be expected to duplicate at any point.

"I don't know about the night, but I have news that may make the next few minutes memorable." Rias offered a tentative half smile.

"News?" Tikaya thought of the officers who had drawn him aside to talk in the hallway. "Nothing... that will cause us trouble, I hope."

"That depends on whether you decide to accept or not."

"Accept... what?"

"As you may have heard, Dak hasn't been the most willing chief of intelligence," Rias said. "I brought him down because I knew he was capable and because I could trust him, but he just tried to resign. Again."

Tikaya winced, thinking of her own suspicions and how little she had trusted Dak when he had turned out to be one of the few people she should have trusted completely. "You're not letting him quit, are you?"

"He wants to go back to the work he likes, being a field agent rather than sitting behind a desk and squinting at reports all day."

Tikaya didn't know exactly what a Turgonian field agent did, but she could guess. "He would rather be out there getting shot at than having a safe office position? Sounds incomprehensible to me."

"Yes, he mentioned that you have a preferences for offices and desks. Even those that aren't your own."

Tikaya tried to decide if she should be embarrassed at this point. Rias had heard about her attempt to take over Dak's files weeks ago. "Only when those I care about are at risk, and things to mitigate that risk aren't being done quickly enough."

"It's a foregone conclusion that I'll be at risk again in the coming years."

"I thought this was going to be a light celebratory dinner party, not an opportunity for you to remind me of your mortality."

"Actually, I was trying to muster your enthusiasm for a new job," Rias said.

"A what?"

"How would *you* like to head the intelligence office?"

She stared at him. Actually, she gaped at him, with her mouth hanging open and her spectacles in danger of sliding off her nose.

"You mentioned a couple of times that you haven't been sure what to do since you don't have colleagues over here researching archaeology. You've worked in an intelligence office before, and made quite a name for yourself." He wriggled his eyebrows.

Tikaya would have scoffed, but her mouth had gone dry, and she struggled to utter anything. As if her brief time spent decrypting enemy messages during a war twenty years in the past qualified her to run an intelligence office in a country she had only spent a few months in.

"I thought this might be a new, fun challenge for you." The other side of his mouth quirked up, and Rias took both of her hands in his.

Tikaya knew that smile, the I'm-sure-you-would-love-to-do-this-for-me-because-I'm-adorable-and-I-genuinely-believe-it-would-be-fulfilling-for-you smile. "Challenging, I'll believe, but *fun?* I'm certain Dak never used that adjective in describing the job."

"Yes, but Dak doesn't use that adjective to describe anything. Think about it, won't you? I won't be able to let him move on to a new position until I find a suitable replacement." He squeezed her hands, then waved down one of the passing servers for beverages.

"You probably should have plied me with the alcohol *before* you propositioned me," Tikaya said, causing the server to quirk an eyebrow.

"My adoring smile has always worked in the past," Rias said. "Is it losing its appeal?"

"I don't know. How would all those young military pups feel about working for the president's civilian wife? More than that... there are some decisions I would hate to be in charge of—such as whether a military officer should be put to death for sabotaging the president's submarine when he was in fact being blackmailed himself, not knowing that his only child had already been killed by the heartless soul doing the blackmailing."

"Major Rydoth was discharged without benefits, not put to death. I wouldn't expect you to make such decisions, regardless—we have courts-martial for that. I'd simply hope you could uncover such schemes and instances of blackmail before they became a problem, such as when the president is enacting the final stage of a plan to rescue the city from certain doom."

"Ah, is *that* all you want?"

"A small matter for a capable woman." He smiled, the adorable please-do-this-for-me one again, and added, "As for the young pups, we could have a colonel or similarly ranked officer on your team who could command the military men, and then report to you. Ideally, we will add competent civilians to the office as well, so you wouldn't only be dealing with soldiers."

"So, I might even have some women on the team?" Tikaya searched the hall until her gaze landed on Amaranthe.

"That is certainly a possibility."

"I'll have to think about this."

"I wouldn't expect a hasty decision." Rias handed her a glass. "Now, shall we enjoy the festivities?"

As Tikaya took a sip, she noticed Sicarius wasn't the only man holding up the wall. Two armed and uniformed soldiers stood near the doors, clearly on duty, protecting the president—and mentally composing reports to hand to their superiors who would in turn hand them to the chief of intelligence. Dear Akahe, was she up for that challenge? The problem-solving aspect was appealing enough, but commanding legions of analysts and operatives? On the other hand, did she want to be in a position again where she had to plead and wheedle for information? If she didn't take the job, the next chief might not be as willing to concede that the president's wife might have a bright thought or two. Besides, if she *did* take the job, she could find out whatever secrets lurked in the archives that Dak had alluded to. Tikaya took another sip of the wine. Hm.

"Shall I consider it promising that you're smiling?" Rias murmured.

Tikaya didn't want him to think that his "adoring smile" had had anything to do with her thought process. When Sespian walked into the hall, Tikaya said, "I'm merely pleased to see that the designer of this fine building has joined us."

"I see," Rias said. As usual, he saw much.

Mahliki wasn't there yet. Disappointment and relief mingled in Sespian's mind. He had been so busy supervising the building construction in the last weeks that he hadn't seen much of her. He worried that she had been avoiding him, or had turned her interests elsewhere after his unromantic fumbling on the beach. Maldynado had assured Sespian that she had accepted his dinner invitation and that tonight would be his opportunity for... everything.

Sespian had washed and scrubbed every inch of his body, shaved, gotten a hair cut, and spent no less than an hour dithering over which item in his sparse wardrobe would make him appear impressively masculine in front of a woman as tall as he was. He had been standing in his flat, nude except for a towel around his waist, when a messenger had delivered a garment bag from an expensive clothier on the Ridge. As soon as he spotted Maldynado's name scrawled on the card, he had been worried, but the sleek gray and black suit in the quasi-military style that never lost its popularity in Turgonia fit him nicely. He had left the dubiously colored scarf and kerchief in the bag, certain that Maldynado had chosen those without the help of the clothier. Though he felt dapper, Sespian worried that he was sweating far too much, and that Mahliki would fail to find him... irresistible. Dear ancestors, he would settle for vaguely appealing at this point.

Maldynado spotted him and strolled in his direction. Good, Sespian had news for him. Maybe delivering it would take his mind off worrying about Mahliki's arrival.

"Good to see you," Maldynado said, "and in such a fine ensemble, too, though I see you forgot your kerchief."

"It was floral," Sespian said.

"And the scarf."

"It had tiger stripes."

"Accents of color, dear boy. I didn't think you wanted to appear as monochromatic as..." Maldynado tilted his head toward the corner where Sicarius stood. How *had* his father found a shadow to lurk in? Sespian had specifically designed the windows, walls, angles, and lighting fixtures so there shouldn't be shadows.

"You don't think the gray trim will set me apart?"

"Enh." Maldynado rocked his hand back and forth. "Maybe you should have brought the kid. Women love cute kids. On the other hand, Mahliki might not be old enough to appreciate a child. She certainly doesn't seem the sort to be entertaining the idea of motherhood yet. No, you were smart to leave the girl at home."

"Do you think Mahliki will be... scared away by a child?" Sespian caught himself asking before he thought better of it. Maldynado was the *last* person he ought to be asking for advice on... well, anything. Still, he caught himself adding, "I'm her legal guardian, it's true, but the Starcrests said they would watch her if I ever felt the need to run off and do young person things, as Tikaya called it. I assured them I'm more mature than that. I haven't been a young person since... I don't ever remember thinking of myself as a young person."

"That's... a little sad. You should share those feelings with Mahliki. Women love somber introspective men. And brooding. Can you brood?"

"Has anyone ever told you that your mind has a singular focus, Maldynado?"

"That sounds like a compliment. I don't usually get compliments about my mind."

"How odd." Sespian had spent enough time with Maldynado at this point to know he wasn't as shallow as his mouth implied, but it was hard to remember that at times. "I actually wanted to talk to you about another matter, if you don't mind. Or has the president already spoken to you?"

"Spoken to me? I'm not certain he knows I exist."

"You were on the team that helped save the city from the plant," Sespian said dryly.

Maldynado blinked at him. "What's your point?"

"He *knows* you exist. He approved of this. Actually, he suggested it." Sespian opened the flap of his jacket and withdrew an envelope, the flap smeared with old-fashioned blood-red wax and the president's seal. "He asked if you wanted Marblecrest included, but I thought not. As it stands, they're looking at using your first and middle name. It's just as well. Crests aren't very popular with the new entrepreneurial and political classes."

"What is it?" Maldynado reached for the envelope.

Sespian waved it around as he continued to speak, evading Maldynado's reach. "Now that the Edgecrests are in jail for plotting against the president—and partaking in a rather unwholesome religion—I assume we won't have to worry about further sabotage of the building—that should please you. Can you believe my very own professor was the one who suggested sabotaging the construction site? Oh, sure, it was supposed to be one of several delaying tactics to keep the intelligence boys busy, but *his* design came in second in the competition. I bet he figured that if bad things kept happening during the construction of my building, it would be considered a sign that I was the wrong architect for the job and that his own work should be reconsidered."

"Indeed." Maldynado reached for the envelope again, his fingers twitching with curiosity.

Hiding a smile, Sespian extended his arm—and the envelope—toward the ceiling beams. "Professor Oddak was probably encouraged by his older brother, so I can't hold too much malice against him. It turns out that old Ploris and Serpitivich go way back and have been secret members of the Kriskrusian religion for decades. The vice president—*former* vice president—a cult member. I never would have suspected, would you? Well, they can remain friends until their sentences are delivered. They're in adjoining cells. They're lucky they weren't both killed outright, since they're suspected of having knowledge of the mental sciences, even if it was that practitioner friend of Serpitivich's who had the skill necessary to heal President Starcrest. Did you ever meet him? Apparently he nearly dropped a rock pile on my father's head and is the one who modified that ugly little statuette that Sauda Shadowcrest gave to the president. I hear her cell is more posh than Serpitivich's but no less barred. Did you know—"

"*Sespian.*" Maldynado finally used his longer arms to snatch the envelope from Sespian's grasp. "I don't care about those shrubs. I care about—what *is* this?" He turned his prize over a few times in his hands, as if he expected booby traps. The crazy tentacles—or maybe those were supposed to be plant vines?—on his hat flopped into his eyes as he moved his head from side to side, considering the envelope from all angles.

Done prolonging the satiation of Maldynado's curiosity, Sespian said, "Why don't you open it and see what's inside?"

"All right." Maldynado broke the seal and withdrew the single piece of stationery folded inside. He opened it and read slowly: "Maldynado, your efforts in protecting the new presidential residence from saboteurs have been noted and appreciated. We are also grateful that you came along on the underwater mission and had the presence of mind to deploy the... uh, some technical engineering doodad I can't pronounce." Sespian raised his eyebrows, but Maldynado continued on without further improvisation. "Especially when others among the team were losing their minds. We will find you employment suitable for your talents if you still wish it. We would also like to name the new presidential residence after you."

Sespian grinned as Maldynado repeated the last sentence silently, puzzlement turning to enlightenment.

"They want to name the whole building after me?" he asked. "It's signed by the president and his wife. It can't be a joke. They don't joke, do they? The Kyattese are so serious..."

Sespian didn't think that was true, but he assured Maldynado, "It's not a joke. They asked me if I minded. I said I didn't. Much."

"Much?"

"Well, I had been thinking of naming it after my cat..."

Maldynado stared at him.

"That was a joke. I'm not Kyattese."

"Oh, right." Maldynado lifted a fist to his mouth, then searched the hall until his gaze halted on the president and his wife. "I have to—I'll be right back."

He jogged over to the couple, waving the letter and calling, "My Lord Starcrest?"

Sespian didn't *think* Maldynado would do anything overly foolish, but watched with some wariness. Maldynado ran up to them, halted, opened and closed his mouth a few times, then flung his arms around the president. Judging by Starcrest's wide eyes—and those of Tikaya—it surprised both of them. The soldiers stationed along the walls surged from their posts, hands falling to their weapons as they raced across the room. Sespian dropped his face into his hand. What had he started?

"This is *wonderful*," Maldynado cried. "You don't know how much this means to me." He released the president, oblivious to the approaching soldiers, then hugged Tikaya as well.

Starcrest lifted a hand to stay the concerned—and armed—men.

"That is inappropriate behavior," Sicarius said.

Sespian managed to keep from jumping in startled surprise, though he hadn't seen his father leave his position in the shadows to come up behind him. Some things never changed. "I agree," Sespian said, "but is there any other kind when it comes to Maldynado?"

"Rarely."

Sespian faced Sicarius, suspecting his father had come over for more than idle chitchat. If he knew how to be idle—or chitchat—Sespian had not heard about it.

"The child is doing well?" Sicarius asked.

"Mu Lin is... attending school, learning Turgonian, and has stopped trying to flush Trog down the washout to spite me."

"Trog."

"My cat."

"Yes, I remember," Sicarius said. "That is also inappropriate behavior. It is good it has ceased."

"Yes." Sespian groped for something else to say. Sicarius seemed to be doing the same thing. Would there ever be a day when they could speak with each other without awkward silences? Of course, Sespian had observed silences when Sicarius and Amaranthe spoke too. She simply didn't find them awkward. Remarkable woman.

"It was honorable of you to take her in," Sicarius said. "Colonel Starcrest completed his research and learned why Ji Nah had no kin she could rely on in Nuria. Last fall, she was unsuccessful in an assassination attempt on their Great Chief. The prodigious bounty that was placed on her head would have assured her eventual death had she remained in Nuria."

Sespian digested this. Ji Nah's choice to bring her daughter along when she came to Turgonia suddenly made more sense. In Nuria, a person's honors and denunciations affected how the whole family was seen and treated in society. Ji Nah's daughter would have had a difficult childhood, if she were allowed to grow up at all. "Perhaps this is a better place for Mu Lin after all."

"Likely."

Sespian wondered if Sicarius would mention that his killing of the woman's father might have played into this as well. Whether it had been the father's choice to come to Turgonia, or Hollowcrest had kidnapped him, he—and his family—would have been disgraced because he had helped the empire train an assassin that would one day haunt Nuria. And because Sicarius had killed the man, he wouldn't have been there to help raise Ji Nah... Maybe she had joined the secretive mage hunter society because she'd had few options for honorable employment. And growing up in a disgraced family must have influenced her decision with Mu Lin too. She wouldn't have wanted the same life for her daughter.

Sicarius said nothing about it. He wouldn't deny it, most likely, but apparently saw little point in bringing it up. Sespian wondered if Sicarius had any idea that the main reason he had accepted the responsibility for the little girl was that he didn't want her growing up to hate Sicarius and seek revenge on him. There had been enough of that already, and it only led to suffering and death. Sespian hoped he could encourage Mu Lin to study the arts or some other intellectual passion that had nothing to do with swords and daggers and killing people.

"I understand you are returning to your studies at the University," Sicarius said. "Will your financial circumstances allow you to provide for the girl and yourself?"

"You mean can I afford to feed everyone?" Sespian decided to find this parental concern promising rather than intrusive—his father cared enough to make sure his new responsibilities wouldn't overwhelm him. "Yes. Designing the president's new building drew attention to my architectural style, and I already have new clients. Also—and I have Amaranthe to thank for looking into this and negotiating with that Sarevic woman on my behalf—I'm now receiving a royalty on every weed zapper being sold in Turgonia."

"Weed zapper?"

"Ah, yes. Due in no small part to that plant, there's now a market for the portable generator I helped design. The first orders have already shipped, and it seems farmers everywhere are delighted at the ability to use the technology to electrocute invasive weed species."

Sicarius considered this for a moment—perhaps imagining cackling farmers running around their fields, flinging blue streaks of electricity about—before nodding and saying. "I am pleased. You have done well."

Sespian bowed his head at this rare praise.

"Amaranthe wishes me to inform you..." Sicarius gazed across the room to where Amaranthe was chatting with Basilard and his translator.

"*We* wish to inform you that, if you need assistance with the child rearing, we are available to help you."

Dear ancestors, Sicarius as a babysitter? It was all Sespian could do not to shudder. He would probably teach the girl how to throw knives. "I'll keep it in mind, though I think you'll be too busy to offer child rearing services in the near future."

From anyone else, Sespian would have expected a puzzled, "What do you mean?" or at least an inquisitive head tilt. Sicarius merely gazed at him and waited for an explanation.

"I'll let the president enlighten you further," Sespian said. "Why don't you take Amaranthe over to talk with him? After Maldynado is done mauling him, that is."

Sicarius inclined his head. "I will do so."

When he left, Sespian went back to planning how he would approach Mahliki when she arrived. That was what he intended to do anyway. Mostly he stood by a lewd elephant ice sculpture and sweated.

Sicarius headed over to talk to Starcrest during a lull when nobody else was pestering him—more guests had filtered into the banquet hall, in spite of Maldynado's promise that this would be a small dinner among friends—but the banging of a gong made him pause. Everyone paused and faced the person with the cloth-covered mallet. Maldynado, of course.

"The caterers will begin serving momentarily," he announced. "Please find your assigned seats at the table. Then plan to eat up. You'll need your energy for the dancing afterward." Maldynado searched the crowd for a moment, spotted Sicarius, and smiled. "The *required* dancing."

Sicarius returned his flattest stare. He had no intention of swaying and bouncing about for non-training purposes, and no one would convince him that the drunken gyrations these people intended to partake in were training for anything.

Amaranthe stepped out of the crowd and took his hand. "Good to see you off the wall."

He eyed her warily, concerned she might also believe dancing should be required. She merely smiled up at him... with pleasure he sensed must be due to more than his position in the room. "I wished to speak with the president. Sespian implied he might have work for me." Or so Sicarius had interpreted Sespian's oblique comment.

"Good. We're sitting near him at dinner. I'm sure he would be delighted if you engaged him in a conversation. Before we sit down..." Amaranthe tilted her head to the side and led Sicarius away from the table instead of toward it. They weaved past the herd of people finding their seats.

Maldynado walked past, leading four women Sicarius hadn't seen before. Sicarius had no interest in who they were or why they were here, but Amaranthe stopped to watch the procession. All of the women were moderately attractive and of ages ranging from the mid-twenties to early forties. Perhaps Maldynado sought to replace Yara, though the questions coming out of his mouth didn't make sense if that were the case.

"You all like soldiers and retired soldiers, right? Warrior-caste officers of good rank and with good familial connections? And you agree that looks aren't the most important measure of a man? Scars are what give a gentleman character, after all."

Maldynado was walking as he spoke, and the group passed by Amaranthe and Sicarius, so the women's responses were lost among the other conversations in the area, but several nodded their heads.

"Goodness," Amaranthe said. "He certainly came through on my request."

"Your request?"

"Yes." Amaranthe pointed toward the main doorway, where two familiar men had walked in, their expressions similar, a mix of nervousness and wariness. Perhaps they had heard about the required dancing.

Amaranthe waved for them to come over. Sicarius watched her through slitted eyes, wondering what arrangement she was a part of. Deret Mancrest, dressed in a beige shirt and brown suede jacket walked over right away, using a new swordstick for support, this one ebony with an ivory grimbal head handle. One of the soldiers propping up the wall rushed over and pointed at it, asking some question. Sicarius had heard a few comments about weapons not being allowed at the dinner, though nobody had spoken to him about his knives. At Amaranthe's behest, he had brought fewer than usual, but he was clearly still armed.

The second man who had come in the door strode up and waved the soldier away from Mancrest. Colonel Dak Starcrest wore his black and silver dress uniform, with rows of ribbons across his breast denoting campaigns he had fought in while medals signified awards for heroic acts. For the first time since Sicarius had met him, he wore an eye patch to hide his missing orb.

Sicarius clasped his hands behind his back and attempted to appear indifferent as Mancrest stopped in front of Amaranthe.

She smiled at him. "How's your shoulder? Are you recovering well?"

"Yes. The wound to my pride was greater than the wound to my flesh."

"And the newspaper? You haven't sold it yet?"

"No, I've decided to try running it for a few years before deciding whether to give it up or not." Mancrest ignored Sicarius as he spoke. He wasn't that focused on Amaranthe, either. He glanced at Maldynado, or perhaps at the gaggle of women he was ushering to seats. "Is one of those... uhm."

"I believe so," Amaranthe said, "though I'm not certain if two are here for you and two for Colonel Starcrest or if it's one and three, or one for each of you and two for him..." She shrugged. "You'll have to ask him. Better hurry. He's seating people now."

"So I see. Thank you." Mancrest left without casting any longing backward gazes at Amaranthe. Good.

"You seek to find him a woman?" Sicarius asked.

"I?" Amaranthe touched her chest in wide-eyed innocence. "That's Maldynado's task tonight. I believe he's trying to match just about everyone here with someone."

Sicarius considered the number of people in the room. "Ambitious."

"Yes, he even promised me he would get you to dance with me."

"Very ambitious." Sicarius might have said more, but Colonel Starcrest stopped in front of them.

"Good evening, sir," Amaranthe greeted him.

He grunted. "You've spoken to Rias?" The question seemed to be for both of them.

"Not yet." Amaranthe looked at Sicarius, a question of her own in her eyes. He could not offer a hint, for he did not know what the president wanted to discuss, either.

"Better do so. He's talking of sending me off to Nuria, so he'll need... well, I don't know exactly what he'll need. Depends on what his wife decides to do, I suppose."

"Nuria?" Amaranthe asked. "What will you do in Nuria?"

The colonel's smile had a lupine aspect. "Diplomacy."

"Er, is it likely they're ready to accept a diplomat from us? Given... how poorly their plans went last winter?"

The colonel's smile widened. "No."

Sicarius read this as he was being sent over there to spy and warn the president if Nuria had any more trouble in mind for Turgonia. Just because the mage hunter hadn't been an officially sanctioned assassin didn't mean there wouldn't be others.

"When do you leave?" Amaranthe asked. "Will you have time to get to know..." She extended a hand toward the table. "I believe one of those ladies Maldynado is chattering with wants to meet you."

"If it follows the usual pattern, she'll be *done* wanting to meet me by the time dinner ends." Dak grunted a farewell and, despite his pessimism, straightened his tunic and combed his short black hair with his fingers on the way over.

"You wished to speak with me about something?" Sicarius asked. If she did not, he would like to join Starcrest at the dinner table and learn what this news was everyone except him knew about.

"Yes." Amaranthe took his hand again. "Tikaya gave me the name of a healer to visit on the Kyatt Islands. In case we should wish to... I mean, at some point. Investigate certain possibilities."

"Children," Sicarius said.

"Yes."

The news pleased Sicarius. It was not imperative that they produce offspring immediately—Amaranthe was young, and he was... still fit and virile certainly—but he should like to do so at some point. Amaranthe would make a fine mother. And he could have another chance to make a... less poor father. Perhaps with her help, he might aspire to adequacy in that area.

Sicarius nodded. "Good."

"I see you're ecstatic." Amaranthe smirked and leaned into his chest.

"I am pleased."

"Perhaps I can work you up to ecstatic by the time one is ready to be born."

"Hm."

"Or perhaps if I told you that you didn't have to dance tonight, you would be ecstatic."

"That is a possibility." Sicarius offered her his arm.

Amaranthe took it, though that smirk still played about her lips. "Too bad Maldynado is in charge of the dancing."

Amaranthe sat at the table with Sicarius at her right side. Maldynado had shown a bit of wisdom in placing Sespian on Sicarius's other side, so no one else would be intimidated by having his silent presence as a neighbor, especially since he likely wouldn't eat the catered food. He would simply stare about stonily, wondering why a seat had been reserved for him when he would have preferred to stand in a corner. The president sat at the head of the table and to Amaranthe's left. She didn't know why she had been given such a priority spot, but was pleased it would allow Sicarius to converse easily with Starcrest, insofar as he ever "conversed." Tikaya sat across from Amaranthe, and Basilard and his translator, Elwa, sat to her left. An empty seat waited beside Sespian with Mahliki's name card on it. He looked miserable, either because he had to attempt to woo his lady with his father sitting next to him, or because his lady had yet to show up for dinner.

Maldynado hadn't taken his seat—he was walking around encouraging the servers to keep the wine flowing. Deret and Dak, each with a lady on either side, were stationed farther down the table, along with a few officers and women Amaranthe hadn't been introduced to yet. Maldynado had a shoulder pat or a smile for each though, when he happened past, and she wondered how many people he had promised to set up tonight. It was unfortunate that Yara had chosen not to come, or had he actually invited her? Amaranthe hadn't seen her in a couple of weeks and wondered if she had officially transferred to the job in the country. She would have to check and send congratulations if the promotion had gone through, though it stung that Yara had disappeared without a farewell.

"Pardon me, my lady," Maldynado said, bending low next to Elwa. "There's a squeaky floorboard there, and I'm a messy eater. Let me push your seat over a couple of inches, will you?"

The woman gave him a perplexed look, but lifted her rear so Maldynado could scoot the chair closer to Basilard.

"There are *no* squeaky floorboards," Sespian said with indignation. "They were just laid a couple of weeks ago."

"Hush, now. Or I won't adjust your lady's chair when she arrives." Maldynado pointed. "I believe the same floorboard runs over to that side of the table."

Sespian narrowed his eyes, but he didn't say anything else.

"Subtle, Maldynado," Amaranthe said.

Maldynado waved without embarrassment and took his own seat.

"Ms. Lokdon," Starcrest said from the head of the table, "Sicarius. I've been meaning to talk to the two of you. Albeit, I had planned a more private setting, but I suppose we can trust all of those within earshot." He gave a nod to Basilard.

Amaranthe wondered what they had spoken about during their first official diplomatic meeting. In the beginning, Basilard's mission had been to make sure there was an end to underground slavery in Stumps, but she had heard Starcrest had sent his intelligence men out to handle that of his own accord, or perhaps because of a word from Sespian. There must be other matters their Mangdorian neighbors wished pursued, however.

"Yes, sir?" Sicarius asked.

Amaranthe turned an attentive eye toward the president.

"You both have been very helpful since you returned," Starcrest said.

"Does this mean he forgives us for wrecking his submarine?" Amaranthe whispered.

Sicarius gave her a baleful do-not-interrupt-the-words-of-my-childhood-idol stare before pointedly turning his attention back to Starcrest. She smiled and noticed that Tikaya smiled too.

"I understand neither of you is employed at the moment," Starcrest said.

Amaranthe decided Sicarius wouldn't appreciate a joke about how someone had finally noticed... and that she hoped he hadn't noticed how much presidential food she had been mooching. There was a pastry chef in the kitchen who made apple tarts to rival Curi's. Amaranthe hoped the desserts would make an appearance at this dinner.

"We are available for employment." Sicarius spoke in his usual monotone, but somehow managed to get a hopeful note in there, at least to Amaranthe's honed ear.

Before Starcrest could speak again, several servers descended on the table with small bowls of distinctively green soup. Basilard took a sniff, then raised his eyebrows at Maldynado, who folded his hands in his lap and smiled benignly.

"Bas," Amaranthe whispered. "This soup isn't based on something you foraged in a... dubious location, is it?"

I had nothing to do with it, Basilard signed. *I simply recognize it as a Mangdorian dish.*

"What dish?" Starcrest asked after Elwa had translated the signs for the rest of the table.

Loveweed soup. It's considered an aphrodisiac.

Maldynado blinked innocently. "Is it? I merely told the caterers to include dishes that would please our international guests."

"He's trying hard on other people's behalf," Amaranthe murmured. "I'll grant him that." If he had tried this hard with Yara, that might explain why she had fled. No, that wasn't fair. She was clearly one to put her career ahead of her personal life. Amaranthe had done the same once. If she hadn't been given an order to assassinate a certain criminal, she wouldn't now be sitting next to him, wondering if anyone would come over to push her chair closer to his.

Sicarius was ignoring this exchange and was probably unaware of the fond smile Amaranthe had given him. Instead, he was gazing intently at Starcrest. Fortunately, the president wasn't a man to grow unnerved by that stare. He might even sense the hope lying beneath the blank facade. Although at the moment he was poking at the green soup—it was truly a thick, rich green—and exchanging glances with his wife.

"You were saying, My Lord President?" Amaranthe prompted, sensing Sicarius never would do more than stare.

Starcrest lowered his spoon—with relief, perhaps. "Yes, I was saying that it would be foolish of me to let such talented people wander away to be snatched up by some opportunist."

Amaranthe decided not to mention how few opportunists there had been. Although two more young enforcers had stopped her in the streets and asked for her autograph. Aside from her newfound fame, she didn't quite know what else she was qualified to do. And Sicarius... she hoped he no longer wished to do what he was qualified for.

"Given your unique skills and your proven ability to accomplish missions with little or no direction," Starcrest said, "I would like to offer you jobs working with the chief of intelligence. You would essentially be civilian field agents, working in and out of the nation, often with little input and guidance from above. We've been busy managing internal affairs this past winter, to our detriment, I fear, and it's time to put some good men—and women—out there to keep an eye on the world for us. Is this something you would be interested in?"

"Yes," Sicarius said.

Amaranthe lifted a finger. "One moment please." She tapped on Sicarius's arm. "Shouldn't we take our little trip to Kyatt first?"

"Kyatt?" Starcrest asked, looking to his wife.

"They didn't get an opportunity to visit our islands on their previous travels," Tikaya said.

"Ah," Starcrest said, though the drawn down eyebrows suggested he wasn't entirely enlightened. "Perhaps an early mission could take them through there."

"So long as said mission is truly *through* the islands and not *to* them for field agent work," Tikaya said dryly.

"This would be acceptable?" Sicarius asked Amaranthe, the words in his eyes more earnest than the ones that came out of his mouth.

Amaranthe leaned back in her chair. She knew he wanted nothing more than to work for Starcrest, but this past winter had started her thinking of children. Odd since she had so rarely thought of them before, but then she had never been with someone whose children she could imagine having. If they were to receive good news on Kyatt... she couldn't imagine a female government field agent birthing babies in between missions. Of course, she was still young; she could do this for a while and then move on to motherhood. So long as she and Sicarius both survived the work. She couldn't imagine it would be anything but challenging. A challenge *he* longed for. Did she still long for such challenges? The previous year had brought her so many, and laid so much death in her hands, that she didn't know if she craved such adventure any more. On the other hand, could she see herself waiting back at home for months on end? She would worry for his life and also about what kinds of choices he might make without her there. Of course, if he wanted to go off on his own, she would let him. She might inflict her morality on him from time to time, but he was certainly his own man, and he had pointed out more than once that he was faster and more efficient by himself.

"Do you... *want* to do this with me?" Amaranthe whispered.

"Yes."

His prompt response warmed her heart, though she felt compelled to say, "Don't you think you should take some time to contemplate these life-changing decisions before blurting out these responses?"

"I have contemplated this possibility all winter," Sicarius said. "Do you... not want to do this with *me*?"

"*You're* not the part I'm hesitating over. But... I think it could be interesting."

"I see you are ecstatic."

Amaranthe snorted. "I'll be ecstatic when you dance with me."

Tikaya was watching this exchange silently, her fingers to her lips. Maybe she was just looking for an excuse to avoid the green soup. Basilard and his translator had slurped theirs down. Sespian kept watching the door with a morose expression and seemed unaware of his father's new job opportunity. Just as well. Sicarius never cared for an audience to his personal conversations—or personal anything.

He was still watching for her, waiting for more of an affirmation. Amaranthe nodded and wiggled her fingers toward the president.

Sicarius faced Starcrest again. "We accept the position."

Even dead, the cells were fascinating. They reminded Mahliki more of interlocking crystals than—

"Mahliki?"

At her mother's voice, Mahliki straightened and turned toward the laboratory door. A twinge of pain came from her upper arm, a lingering reminder of the bullet that had spent a couple of hours lodged there. The wound had healed well, especially given the lack of a true healer—stitches, how primitive—but it still made itself known first thing in the morning and any other time when she didn't move the arm for a while.

"Yes?" Mahliki asked, frowning at her mother. Why was she already dressed in pearls and her favorite goat leather sandals? "Are you on your way to dinner? It's still early, isn't it?"

"Early? It's two hours to midnight. All seven courses, all of them starring aphrodisiacs from around the world, have been served, and Maldynado has hustled everyone onto the dance floor."

Mahliki stared, certain her mother was joking. The basement lab lacked a window and a clock. "I... I'm sorry. I only meant to stop in for a half hour. An hour at the most. I was intrigued by Agarik's letter. Did I show it to you? He wanted to know if the incredibly regenerative plant tissues might teach us some new medical applications, such as for healing burns or even creating new human flesh."

"I'm sure it's fascinating, love. You know I've missed any number of meals, social and otherwise, because of being caught up in my work, so I imagine you get that from me, but... well, poor Sespian had to sit next to an empty chair all night at dinner, and I... just wanted to make sure you weren't snubbing him for some reason. He's a fine young man, and if he made a mistake, I'm certain he regrets it."

"Snubbing? No, that wasn't it at all." Mahliki pushed away from the table and grabbed her shoes. The heated floors Sespian had designed for the basement were wonderful and kept the laboratory perfectly warm. She kept meaning to compliment him on it. "I just lost the time. Is he still there?" Mahliki pitched over while stuffing her foot into one of the shoes. "Do I have time to change?"

"He was there when I left, but he was mumbling about going to check on Mu Lin and his cat. I gather the cat might be in some peril, even with an attentive babysitter on hand. It's possible that child needs a larger pet to tussle with."

Mahliki would have cursed if her mother hadn't been standing five feet away. "I can't go to a fancy dinner like *this*." She pointed at her baggy coveralls—how *had* the front gotten smeared with plant guts again?—and waved at her hair, which was falling out of the loose braid she had hastily made to keep it from tumbling onto the microscope lenses. There had been a small explosion earlier as well—a lab mate's fault this time, not hers—that left her cheek smeared with soot.

"Perhaps you could simply pop your head in and see if he's still there," Mother said. "Then invite him for a walk in the gardens if he is. It'll be... dark out there."

"Meaning the soot on my cheek won't be that visible?" Mahliki finally managed to tug both shoes on and stand upright.

"Yes. Oh, and Mahliki...? It's not just the cheek that's covered in soot."

"What?" Mahliki looked herself up and down. The laboratory lacked a mirror more than two inches long.

Mother stepped into the room, turned Mahliki around, and swatted black dust off her bum.

"Dear Akahe," Mahliki groaned. "I *can't* show up like this."

"Just go. He'll be disappointed if you don't come. At this point, you could show up wearing a grimbal suit, and he'd be tickled."

Mahliki snorted and headed for the door. "Sometime I'd like to see one of these grimbals the Turgonians are always talking about."

"I believe there's one in the zoo," Mother called after her. "Perhaps you can ask Sespian to take you one day."

Mahliki ran down the basement hallway without replying, disappointed that she had missed a chance to sit next to Sespian at dinner. And eat aphrodisiac courses. She snorted. Maybe that would have put him in the mood to finally give her a kiss. Or more likely imbibing a few glasses of wine would do it. She had never seen him drink and wasn't sure if he did. Too bad. He could use loosening up.

"You're talking?" she asked herself, taking the stairs two at a time. "How long did it take you to find the courage to kiss him?" And that had not been more than a peck. Of course in her present attire, he would probably be repelled rather than attracted. At least she was wearing plant guts instead of frog guts or something truly disgusting. She seemed to remember that happening at a childhood dinner, much to her grandmother's chagrin.

Mahliki turned into the broad open hall of the main level and almost crashed into the backs of two servers heading from the kitchen to the banquet room with trays of a steaming amber liquid that smelled apple-y—and alcoholic.

"Sorry," she called, racing past them. Fortunately they were agile enough not to lose their glasses when she jostled their elbows.

One started to curse, but the other hushed him. "President's daughter."

The privileges of being related to someone of rank... instead of cursing her out loud, they had to do it in their heads. At least those drinks meant the festivities were still going on.

She slowed down minutely as she approached the double doors leading to the banquet hall, but not quite enough. Two more servers were stepping out with trays of empty glasses. She swerved, but the doorframe boxed her in, and she ended up knocking a man's arm. His tray tilted and glasses slid off the side.

Cursing herself—this night was *not* going well—Mahliki caught two of them. The server righted his tray before the whole pile tilted to the floor, but one more empty glass wobbled and fell off the edge. Mahliki lunged for it, but with her hands already full, she only ticked the stem with a pinky finger. It hit the marble floor and shattered.

"So close," she muttered.

"Sorry, ma'am," the server said. "I'll take those and take care of this mess."

"No, I'm sorry." Mahliki let him take the glasses, but bent to pick up the shards on the floor. That crash had been her fault. She had only plucked up one piece before he foisted the tray on his comrade and knelt, holding up a hand.

"Please, my lady. Do not concern yourself with this."

Mahliki might have protested, but she happened to look up and notice all the sets of eyes staring at her. Father was sitting at the table with Dak and two other officers, but most of the people were out in the cleared area, in the middle of some dance that involved couples with hands on waists—and other places. All except one of the drummers in the corner had faltered to a stop, and even the one was only tapping a faint background beat.

"Sorry," Mahliki said again, feeling more sheepish than ever. Were they staring because she had crashed in and broken glasses? Or because she looked scruffier than a chimney sweep? "Go back to your dancing, please." And public fondling. She kept that thought to herself, though Maldynado's special dishes had clearly worked. Or perhaps people were simply relaxing and expressing their relief at having survived the plant invasion.

Even after the server had picked up the glass shards, Mahliki lingered near the doorway, not certain whether she should go in. She searched for Sespian among the dancers. For whatever reason, there were more women than men, so some ladies were waiting out, clapping in rhythm with the drummers. Would he have chosen someone else when she didn't show up? Or maybe he would have chosen someone else even if she *had* shown up. She sighed in irritation at her own insecurity, which she surely had no cause for, glass breaking habits or not, but the fact that she had kissed him on the submarine, and he had never said anything about it or returned the gesture... that was disheartening.

"You're here," a soft voice came from the side.

Sespian was standing against the wall a few feet from the door, holding a sketchpad and a pencil. If he had been there the whole time, he had noticed her ungainly crash. Oh, well. At least he was there. And not dancing with one of the numerous women in the hall. Though they would be foolish not to do so if he asked... He looked quite handsome tonight in his black and gray, the shirt and jacket tidy and trim, accenting his lean form. He had the figure of a warrior, even if there was a pencil stub tucked behind his ear.

"Yes, sorry I'm late." Mahliki winced, knowing she had said she was sorry at least three times since she crashed into the hall. "Was the dinner good?"

"Lonely. I had to sit next to my father. And he was more interested in talking with *your* father."

Mahliki kept herself from apologizing again. Barely. Sespian's smile was wry, and there wasn't any hint of anger about him. His eyes were more... intent than usual as he gazed at her. "I, uhm, got distracted by... well, it doesn't matter. I meant to come. And I meant to be clean."

"You're beautiful," Sespian said, then glanced at the guards standing on either side of the door. They were doing good statue impersonations, but he blushed, nonetheless. "Would you like to go for a walk?" he blurted.

"Yes."

He took her hand and led her into the hall.

"Thank you," Mahliki said.

"For helping you escape the room full of old people groping each other in the president's banquet hall?"

Mahliki giggled, then rolled her eyes at herself. She *never* giggled. Ugh. "The word that came to my mind was fondling," she said, trying to sound mature, or at least not vacuous, "but actually I meant for the compliment."

"You're welcome." Sespian turned up a wide set of stairs.

"Are we going anywhere in particular?"

"Is there somewhere in particular you would like to go?"

Mahliki's mind went blank. A library? A closet? Somewhere they wouldn't be interrupted and where they could... do what? Sespian hadn't indicated that he had anything... touchy in mind. And she was hardly dressed to seduce him. "My mother suggested the zoo," she said, then rolled her eyes again. The zoo? Really?

Sespian paused on the landing. "In the middle of the night?"

"No, just in general. She said you have a grimbal there. I've never seen one. Maybe we could go for a walk there sometime. When it's light."

"That would be nice." Sespian tilted his head toward the next set of stairs, then led her up to the third floor.

He must have had some destination in mind. As far as Mahliki knew, there were mostly meeting rooms and spaces up there for further expansion. All of the offices and common areas were on the first floor and the personal quarters on the second.

Only every third gas lamp was lit in the hallway, and Mahliki found herself thinking that there was no reason they had to travel farther. They hadn't passed anyone on the floor, and there were more shadows than light, perfect for two people to have... private time together.

Sespian took her into a large unlit room. Enough moonlight filtered in through glass double doors on the far side that Mahliki could make out a conference table and walls full of maps.

"This is the war room, isn't it?" Mahliki had received the tour when the family had moved in.

"Yes, though I would like to think it'll be used more for signing treaties and negotiating with diplomats than for convening about war."

Not the place she would have expected Sespian to lead her, but they *were* alone. If someone kindled a fire in the hearth and dragged over a couple of chairs, it might be cozy.

Sespian continued through the room, though, not stopping until he reached the doors. "This balcony happens to have the best view in the house. Technically, it's so any president standing in here can see enemy ships entering the harbor, but I thought we might appreciate the lake for other reasons. Especially now that it's mostly free of dead plant matter." He pushed open one of the doors and stepped aside, inviting her out with a gesture.

A large balcony overlooked the newly planted rose garden below, and they were high enough up to see past lower buildings to the lake beyond. They walked to the railing. Gentle floral scents wafted up from the garden—the roses would take a while to grow to maturity, but someone had planted nasturtiums and marigolds to enjoy this year. A three-quarters moon laid a silvery path across the water. The air was cooler than it would be on a Kyattese night, but Mahliki wore enough clothing that she wasn't chilled. She stepped closer to Sespian anyway, in case he had any notions about putting an arm around her.

He turned toward her, an elbow on the railing, his face lit by the moon. "I vowed that when you came to dinner, I would sweep you into my arms and kiss you."

Mahliki bit her lip, delighted by the admission. For so long he had seemed either oblivious or disinterested. That he had such things on his mind meant... everything. "And then I didn't come." She caught herself before she could apologize again, but was certainly regretting that she had missed this experience.

"I took up a strategic position by the door in case you wandered in late," Sespian said. "And then you did, and I was ready to act... only you knocked the server's glasses on the floor, and I was afraid kissing while standing amongst shards of crystal wouldn't be romantic."

"I wouldn't have minded."

"No?" Sespian leaned closer and took her hands.

A flutter of nervous delight ran through her at his warm touch. "No. Though... I'd like to clarify that I only knocked *one* glass to the floor. The others I caught. Quite deftly, you might have noticed." Mahliki inched closer as she voiced her protest, until little separated their bodies except their hands, fingers now entwined.

"I did notice that. Most impressive." He was kind enough not to point out that her deft catches wouldn't have been necessary if she hadn't crashed into the server to start with.

Mahliki meant to thank him for the compliment, but she found herself watching his lips instead. She scarcely remembered them from their last kiss—the one he had been too startled to respond to—and vowed to savor the moment this time. When his lips touched, warm and sensual, with a hint of whatever minty last course had been served, she closed her eyes, her own lips parting in invitation. He was gentle but intent, and she allowed herself to believe he had been thinking about this for some time. The notion filled her with warmth, or maybe his kisses were doing that. His hands slipped free of hers to ease around her waist, inspiring delicious goosebumps wherever they touched. She slid her hand up his arm to his shoulder, feeling the lean muscle beneath his shirt.

Warrior and artist... an unlikely combination, but she liked it. She also liked what he was doing with his hand and wriggled closer.

Something clinked. Oops, she had forgotten about the vials and tools tucked inside her coveralls.

Sespian's lips left hers, though he didn't draw back far, just enough for her to see the arched eyebrows. "Your chest is poking me," he said.

"Yes. It's a sign of my... keen interest." Mahliki fished in her coveralls for the tongs she had stuck in there earlier, moving them down to a lower pocket. She also dug out a test tube and a couple of other items—dear Akahe, when had she jabbed all those things into her coveralls? She didn't even remember.

"Was that a magnifying glass?" Sespian asked.

"Yes, and a graduated cylinder."

"You're an intriguing woman, Mahliki Starcrest."

"I'm glad you think so. Can we go back to kissing now?"

"Love to," he murmured, and pulled her close. If anything else clinked, neither of them noticed it.

Maldynado took a break from dancing with... he wasn't sure what her name was, Fee-something—to pluck a glass of wine from a tray and lean against a wall. Most of his dinner guests were still wiggling their hips and twirling about with their partners, so he considered the evening a success, even if Rias and Dak Starcrest and a couple of other officers had bowed out on the dancing in favor of discussing who knew what at the table. Politics or military issues probably. How dreadfully drab. At least Deret Mancrest was still out attempting to dance with one of the available women—the swordstick did make things awkward, alas. Basilard and his lady had found a quiet dim corner—Maldynado had ordered the lighting softened to provide such spots—and were swaying together. He had caught a little more than swaying during an earlier glance. Good for Basilard. The soup must have worked. Amaranthe and Sicarius were... holding up the opposite wall together. He had an arm around her, while she leaned against his chest, but it all looked rather boring. Despite Maldynado's suggestions, Sicarius wouldn't be drawn out to dance—probably because he had refused to sample any of the dinner courses. Maldynado wasn't all that certain he wanted to see Sicarius gyrating to drumbeats anyway. Fortunately, Amaranthe didn't seem to miss seeing it, either. She seemed content standing against the wall with him and watching the others. Presumably they would sway to their own beat later in private. It wasn't their fault they weren't very fun people and wouldn't sway in front of others.

Maldynado glanced toward the front door. Sespian had slipped out with Mahliki. Also good. Maldynado had been quite put out with the young woman for not showing up. He had even attempted to set Sespian up with one of the other younger ladies, but he had fled at this notion, grabbing a sketchpad and suggesting his talents would be most useful in creating drawings to commemorate the evening. He hoped Mahliki was out in the hallway showing him a different way to commemorate things.

A satisfying evening overall, Maldynado decided, at least for those he had helped set up. For himself... he lamented that he didn't have a lady to go home with. Oh, Fee-something and one of the others he had brought to introduce to Mancrest had offered, but he wasn't ready to wander off with random women. Though he didn't know why not. It wasn't as if Evrial were even in the city anymore. Though she *had* written a couple of times, asking how he was doing and telling him about her promotion ceremony. Maybe if he were to go to her, she would still be... amenable to it?

Colonel Starcrest walked up to Maldynado. "What is this, Marblecrest?" He held up a business card.

"That's for your uncle. I left it at the table, so he could pick it up after he and his wife were done dancing." The pair had swayed through two songs, but had both lifted their hands at further entreaties to partake in the festivities. Maldynado hoped he could handle more than two dances when he reached their venerable ages.

"A sculptor?" the colonel asked. "Having a building named after you isn't enough?"

"I simply wished to make the president aware of the fine craftsmen in the city. Don't you think that the entryway with the fountain would look fine with a statue of a handsome and noble warrior gazing benevolently upon visitors?" Sure, Sespian had said he had deliberately departed from old traditions by making a fountain that featured branches and leaves instead of hulking war heroes, but that spacious foyer had room for a statue or two in the alcoves.

"You're incorrigible," the colonel said.

"Yes, now shouldn't you be dancing?" Maldynado pointed to one of the young ladies sitting this round out. "Even Mancrest is wobbling his hips, and he can barely walk without that stick."

"Yes, he's wobbling them so effectively that all four of the women you brought have been doting on him. And you. The one who deigned to dance with me kept looking over my shoulder at you and wondering, 'Why does he look so sad?'" The colonel used an alarming falsetto for repeating the woman's words.

"Ah," Maldynado said. "I didn't realize my... mood of lament would make me appear so alluring."

"I ought to punch you for saying something as idiotic as that, but I'm going to give you the news I came to deliver anyway."

"Which is?"

"One of my men reported that an enforcer woman who isn't on the guest list seeks entrance to the residence—and your party."

"An... enforcer woman?" Maldynado gulped. Was it...? Who else could it be? But here in the city? How? Why?

"You have no one but yourself to blame for your laments if you didn't invite the girl to your shindig." The colonel didn't roll his eye—he was probably too fierce and military to exercise such theatrics, but he sounded like he wanted to. "I assume you don't want her kept out?"

"No! I mean of course not. I—is she here now?" Maldynado kept from grabbing the colonel's arm—barely. "Or are they keeping her outside in the cold?"

"It's not that cold." The colonel waved to a soldier by the door.

He stepped into the hall. Maldynado leaned forward on his toes, tempted to spring across the room. If Evrial had come, what did it mean? That she missed him? That she wanted to give him another chance to join her in the country? That she... wanted to arrest him for something? He did a quick search through his brain, trying to remember if he had partaken in any misdemeanors in the past weeks. He didn't think so, but he suddenly felt guilty.

When Evrial Yara stepped into the banquet hall, his feeling of guilt, a certainty that he had done something wrong, intensified. Not only was she wearing her enforcer grays, the uniform pressed so crisply that the seams on her trousers stood to attention, but her baton, short sword, and handcuffs hung on her belt. All business, that uniform said. His gaze lingered on the lieutenant's baton-and-dagger rank pins on her collar flaps, then lifted to her face.

Evrial spotted Maldynado then and strode toward him, not sparing more than a glance for the president and his officers at the table. She did cast a brief withering gaze toward the dance floor—and the women in dresses wiggling their hips out there. Maldynado wondered if he could have talked Evrial into dancing if they had still been together and if she had deigned to come to his event. She preferred to unleash her emotions in private.

Maldynado caught Amaranthe and Sicarius watching Evrial's approach, and wondered if Sicarius would step in if Yara tried to arrest Maldynado. Probably not. He would probably hold open the door for her to drag Maldynado out.

"Good evening, Lieutenant Yara," Maldynado said warily.

"Good evening, Maldynado."

She wore a determined expression, and he waited for more, but she didn't seem to have her next line worked out.

"Are you here to arrest me?" he asked.

Evrial blinked. "Have you done something illegal?"

"Not that I know of, but that doesn't mean much. I don't always pay that much attention to the legalities of the world. It's a flaw. I'm a creative and unrestrained spirit."

She glanced up at his hat, the golden vines dangled to either side of his eyes. "Yes."

"If you're not here to arrest me, what brings you all the way into the city?" Maldynado noticed Basilard and his lady dancing by, their ears turned toward him. Had he just become the gossip for the evening? He thought about taking Evrial into the hall, but didn't know if she wanted privacy for... whatever she had come to say.

"My new promotion. In the NoDoc District." A small smile found its way onto her stern face. "I just got off my first day's duty."

It dawned on him slowly that yes, that *was* a city enforcer uniform, not one from rural district whatever number she lived in. "I... How? I thought..."

"I told Captain Brinst that I had an offer for a promotion back in my home district and that if he wanted to keep me on his team, he would have to offer me a promotion here."

"When was this?"

"A few weeks ago. After we... chatted that night at the building site." Evrial lifted her eyes toward the ceiling and nodded, maybe impressed that this was the same site.

Mahliki and Sespian danced past, much as Basilard and his lady had a moment earlier. Maldynado noticed it because they were obviously spying and also because they had left the room earlier—quite a bit earlier. Mahliki was still wearing her plant-smeared coveralls, but Sespian didn't seem to mind. Indeed, they were both wearing large grins. Well, one mission accomplished.

"He was slow in making up his mind," Evrial said. "I'd already been working back at home for two weeks when he made his offer. Are you still..." She glanced at the extra women on the dance floor again. "Unattached?"

A grin stretched across Maldynado's mouth. "I'm still *attached* actually, to this strong, brave enforcer woman, who must have a lot of courage to come back to the city and seek out the man her father and brother so dearly loathe."

Some of the rigid enforcer-ness melted out of Evrial's body. She rested a hand on his arm, her eyes crinkling. "They loathe you less now."

"Oh?"

"They heard someone was naming a building after you."

"*They* heard? Way out in the country?" Maldynado realized his jaw was dangling open, so he shut it. "Did everyone know about this except for me?"

"You didn't know? There was an article in the *Gazette*."

Mancrest shambled by with a young lady supporting him. He winked at Maldynado as they headed for the beverage station.

Maldynado sniffed and made sure Mancrest heard his comment. "I don't read that droll periodical."

"Regardless," Evrial said, "I've... missed you."

"You must have. You haven't called me a dolt or a dunderhead once tonight."

"I've only been here five minutes. The night is young."

"Oh? Will we be spending it together?" Maldynado wiggled his eyebrows.

Evrial draped her arms over his shoulders and gave him an inspired kiss, though all she said was, "Why don't we start with a dance?"

"I would love to, my lady. So long as you don't prong me overmuch with that baton."

"No promises."

THE END

Printed in Germany
by Amazon Distribution
GmbH, Leipzig